797,885 Books

are available to read at

www.ForgottenBooks.com

Forgotten Books' App
Available for mobile, tablet & eReader

ISBN 978-1-330-71236-8
PIBN 10095694

This book is a reproduction of an important historical work. Forgotten Books uses state-of-the-art technology to digitally reconstruct the work, preserving the original format whilst repairing imperfections present in the aged copy. In rare cases, an imperfection in the original, such as a blemish or missing page, may be replicated in our edition. We do, however, repair the vast majority of imperfections successfully; any imperfections that remain are intentionally left to preserve the state of such historical works.

Forgotten Books is a registered trademark of FB &c Ltd.
Copyright © 2015 FB &c Ltd.
FB &c Ltd, Dalton House, 60 Windsor Avenue, London, SW19 2RR.
Company number 08720141. Registered in England and Wales.

For support please visit www.forgottenbooks.com

1 MONTH OF FREE READING

at

www.ForgottenBooks.com

By purchasing this book you are eligible for one month membership to ForgottenBooks.com, giving you unlimited access to our entire collection of over 700,000 titles via our web site and mobile apps.

To claim your free month visit:
www.forgottenbooks.com/free95694

* Offer is valid for 45 days from date of purchase. Terms and conditions apply.

Similar Books Are Available from
www.forgottenbooks.com

The Black Pearl of Peihoo
A Tale of the Malay Seas, by Stanley Portal Hyatt

Adventures of Sherlock Holmes
by Arthur Conan Doyle

Stories of Strange Women
by J. Y. F. Cooke

Adventures of Don Quixote de la Mancha
by Miguel de Cervantes Saavedra

A Princess of Mars
by Edgar Rice Burroughs

A Resident's Wife in Nigeria
by Constance Belcher Larymore

The Story of a Pilgrimage to Hijaz
by Sultan Jahan Begam

The Adventures of Hajji Baba, of Ispahan, in England
by James Justinian Morier

The Adventures of John Smith in Malaya
1600-1605, by A. Hale

Among Malay Pirates
A Tale of Adventure and Peril, by G. A. Henty

Andree at the North Pole
With Details of His Fate, by Leon Lewis

Kidnapped
Being Memoirs of the Adventures of David Balfour in the Year 1751, by Robert Louis Stevenson

The Arabian Nights
by Andrew Lang

Captain Calamity
by Rolf Bennett

The Charm of Kashmir
by V. C. Scott O'Connor

The Voyages and Adventures of Captain Hatteras
by Jules Verne

Commodore Bainbridge
From the Gunroom to the Quarter-Deck, by James Barnes

Confession of the Hills
by Austin Walford

The Conquest
The True Story of Lewis and Clark, by Eva Emery Dye

A Daughter of the Sea
by Amy le Feuvre

Edward Plummer Alsbury

GUY RAYMOND

A STORY OF
THE TEXAS REVOLUTION

BY
EDWARD PLUMMER ALSBURY

HOUSTON, TEXAS:
STATE PRINTING CO., PRINTERS
1908

Entered according to Act of Congress in the year 1908, by
EDWARD PLUMMER ALSBURY,
in the office of the Librarian of Congress,
at Washington, D. C.

*THIS WORK
IS AFFECTIONATELY DEDICATED
TO THE
DAUGHTERS OF THE REPUBLIC
OF TEXAS*

PREFATORY REMARKS.

In placing before the public a story of the revolution which gave to Texas a position among the nations of the earth, the author has not presented incidents that necessarily call for particular mention of leaders, but has tried to delineate the characters of the men in the rank and file, whose spirit of adventure, whose hardihood and endurance, made possible the ultimate independence of the republic. Criticism is expected; for the bounds thrown around the latter-day novelist have been ruthlessly disregarded in many particulars. But as no favors have been asked at the hands of publishers, the story has been launched upon the sea of literature on its merits, in the hope that an indulgent reading public will be more charitable than exacting critics and professional reviewers.

GUY RAYMOND

A STORY OF THE TEXAS REVOLUTION

CHAPTER I.

A lovely grove. Tall, stately trees with commingling branches forming light and darker shadows on the half sodded, half leafy carpet made brilliant by tiny patches formed by the trembling sunlight, that struggled through the verdant canopy, as the stirring leaves yielded to the morning breeze. A gentle slope stretched to denser shades and formed the margin of a running brook, whose gurgles mingled with the music of the wood. The cliff-like bank, which marked its further edge, rose boldly, studded with pointed rock, with here and there a boulder overhanging the limpid current. A winding path, but dimly marked, traced its way to the stream where, on the further edge, a miniature cataract fell, with pattering noise, into a basin cut by human hands from the level surface of the limestone ledge. From the basin, lashed to bubbles by the fall, the transparent water escaped, through artificial conduits, to the brook. A fitting scene for artist's pencil or for poet's pen to add to the wealth of art or legendary lore. A handsome youth, reclining easily on the ground, watched the little waterfall. There was no mistaking the admiration which so plainly marked his expressive features as he gazed upon the pretty picture. The rude mallet and the chisel, still white with lime from the soft rock and lying near, were the tell-tale instruments of his recent work; and he noted, in full enjoyment, the effect of the new direction his hands had given to the volume of the cascade, through the bubbling basin and the converging ditches that poured a single stream into the eddying waters at his feet. A bright smile lighted up his handsome, boyish face as he turned from the contemplation to look up the pathway, and he said audibly:

"I'll bring mother down to see it this afternoon."

He rose from the ground and took from its position a cocked rifle which had been leaning against a tree close at hand. In stature he looked to be six feet; his age about eighteen, and as he bent his head and lowered the hammer of the piece, light, wavy locks fell across a cheek and temple fair but rosy and brown from health and exposure. Resting his rifle on the ground he looked inquiringly around as if in search of some object that was missing, then gave a loud whistle, which brought a dog bounding from the upper end of the grove.

"What have you been hunting, Rolla? I've finished my work, except some extra touches which I will put off 'til another day. Come, old boy! Let's see if we can find a squirrel to take home. Hie on, sir!"

Rolla darted off in the direction taken by the youth, fully comprehending the command he had received. His master followed, taking the way up stream. Soon the sharp barking of the dog indicated that he had discovered something. He was making demonstrations around the root of a gigantic pecan, now gazing intently into its branches, now looking towards the approaching youth as if in mute appeal for him to hasten his steps.

"You are making a terrible fuss, Rolla! One would imagine you had treed an elephant from your noise."

The dog whined in answer; then bristling his back, growled and barked furiously. The youth now began to look in earnest to find out the real cause of this unusual display of Rolla's anger. He walked around the tree and peered through the branches overhead. Suddenly he caught sight of two glaring balls, fully six inches apart, that looked savagely down upon him from a fork of the tree, high up, and concealed almost entirely by the foliage of a lateral limb.

"You have treed something bigger than a squirrel, my good Rolla. Just keep still until I find out what owns those shining yellow balls."

The report of the rifle rang through the grove, followed by a commotion among the branches and, an instant later, the unmistakable form of a grown panther struck the ground with a thud.

A few struggles and the beast was dead. Rolla, frightened at first by the sudden descent of so formidable an antagonist, resumed his courage when assured that his master's shot had been effective. The youth, having reloaded the rifle, bent over his game to examine it or to determine the precision of his aim.

"Pretty good shot, Rolla! Right between the eyes."

The high, rocky bank on the further side of the brook had scarcely echoed the rifle shot when the undergrowth, which crowned its summit, was parted and the dark, stolid face of an Indian looked cautiously down into the grove and took in the last act of the scene just described. With a grunt of surprise he drew back and was concealed from view.

"Now, Rolla, we will leave this fellow here until I can get my sharp hunting knife to take off his hide. You, my boy, shall have a choice piece of meat for your dinner."

Rolla seemed delighted to be thus addressed, for he cut unnumbered capers around the dead animal. His master turned to leave, possibly with the intention to fetch his knife, when a shot from the high bank again broke the quiet of the wood and the youth staggered and fell across the body of the panther.

Poor, distressed Rolla, we leave you to whine in sorrow over your fallen master, while we use the privilege of an author to take a survey of a house, about four hundred yards from the waterfall, along the winding path that led from the grove. Three cabin-like houses, connected by passageways, built of upright poles secured in the ground, the intervals plastered or daubed with mortar, and roofed with long reed-like grass, called "tule," stood in an opening bounded by a mesquite chaparral on the west and south and the timber of the Salado creek on the east. The buildings were of the Mexican type, called by the natives "jacals," and were constructed from materials abounding in the country, and in a manner that necessitated the smallest amount of labor in their preparation. The appearance of the houses and the general surroundings, the new clearing, the absence of fences and outhouses, the wagon and old-style carriage, depending upon the shade of an adjacent oak for protection, all bespoke the newness of the settlement, and the mountain of work yet to be done to constitute the plant of a successful farm or ranch.

On the morning mentioned in the opening of the chapter, a woman sat in one of the rooms of the jacal, engaged in sewing. At her feet, on a bearskin rug, sat a girl about twelve years of age, her attention occupied by a book, the leaves of which she was slowly turning. The child bore a marked resemblance to the youth whom we found in the adjacent grove, engrossed in admiration of the waterfall, beautified by his own artistic touches. The room was rather comfortably furnished for a frontier abode, although there was a lack of newness in its appointments that indicated quite a long service, and an appearance that bespoke an origin less remote from Anglo-Saxon civilization than the banks of the Salado. The woman, intent upon her work, bore evident traces of sorrow, the calm expression of her countenance indicating that with grief, or perhaps disappointment, had also come resignation. The face, though wan, was handsome; the brown hair showing a few threads of white, as she bent low over her work, now and then casting a glance at the little girl. A heavy sigh escaped her occasionally. One of these attracted the attention of the child, who, looking up from her book, asked:

"Mamma, what makes you sigh so?"

"Did I sigh, Stella?"

"You have sighed so often this morning."

"I suppose it is because I am here. I shall never become contented in this wild country, and cannot see what could have possessed your father to banish himself and us from friends and acquaintances to undergo the dangers and hardships that seem to beset us on every hand."

"But papa says that others are coming and we, being the first, can choose the best land, and after a year or two we will be nicely fixed."

"Of course you will side with your father."

"But Guy says so, too."

"Your brother Guy is a perfect sage, I suppose. He should be at school, but he will have no schooling now, after this move.'

"Guy studies, mamma. Papa says Guy knew more at fifteen than he did at twenty. I see him studying every night. He talks to me about what he reads and I learn lots of things that way."

"What, pray, have you learned lately?"

"Oh, plenty! The distance to the sun, and how many satellites Jupiter has, and that Mercury and Venus are nearer to the sun than the earth, and how to find the north star, and who invented the first telescope and ——"

"He has been only instructing you in astronomy, then."

"No; he told me plenty more, about the air being made up of oxygen and hydrogen, and that oxygen keeps us alive, and—and—I can't remember all he told me. He is reading a book that he said you would object to, but papa told him he could, as it was about the best book in our house."

"If your father said that I am certain it is not the Bible."

"No, it isn't. Guy called it the 'Age of Reason.'"

"Where is your brother?"

"Don't you remember? He went down to the spring that he found coming out of the high bank. He says he is going to make it the prettiest thing in Texas."

"Poor boy; I suppose he must have some diversion."

"He says he has plenty to amuse him. He likes to go out in the woods by himself, with just Rolla along. Sometimes he goes without his gun, and papa told him he ought not to; but he thinks there isn't a bit of danger. He says that you and I must go down to see the spring when he gets through fixing it. We must go, mamma, just to please him."

"There is your father coming, and you do not know your lesson."

"I almost know it, and have yet until twelve to study."

Paul Raymond had moved to the Salado, from San Felipe de Austin, where he had first settled in the colony of the Empresario, having sought an asylum from disappointment, caused by the dissipation of a large property in Mississippi, in the wilds of Texas, whose territory was now attracting the notice of the more adventurous spirits, in the Southern States, and offering a field for speculation to men of ruined fortunes and blasted hopes. On an extended scout, a year before, he had seen the spot on the Salado, where he was now located, and determined to move from the malarial banks of the Brazos to the high and healthy plateaus of Bexar. It was a bold step, by a bold spirit. For in those days it was hazardous for an American to live in a place so isolated as was his new home. Indian hostility and Mexican jealousy were alike to be feared; but despite the advice and warning from friends, and Austin himself, he made the movement. In the State he had left, he had been an influential citizen, a lawyer, and a man of education. He had represented the Southern counties in the Senate, and the laws of the State bore the impress of his legislative ability.

A wife, son and daughter composed his family, and these, with an Irishman, employed to be jack of all trades, were the only beings in the settlement. The children, Guy and Stella, had been taught by a private tutor, but since coming to Texas the father and mother had assumed the duties of the teacher. They were far advanced for their ages, both having apt minds and inclinations to study. This was especially true of Guy Raymond, who was well read and conversant with literary subjects that are familiar to few minds not possessing the advantage of maturity. His mother often called him a dreamer, but his father, whose skepticism he inherited, pronounced him already a thinker.

"Where is Guy?" asked the father, as he entered the house.

"He is off with Rolla, engaged in some project about the new spring he said he had found," replied his wife.

"He worked on it some yesterday; but as it was Sunday, he would not tell you of it. He will make a nice job of it, I'll bet. Guy does everything well."

"Working on Sunday is one result of your infidelity."

"Such employment is not work. It's the purest amusement to the boy. Know your lesson, Stell'?"

"Very nearly, papa."

"That's a good girl. I want you to study well and it will take one argument from your mother against our move to Texas."

"There is a shot! Did Guy take his rifle?"

"Yes, papa. I saw him get it."

"He has shot a squirrel, I suppose. I heard Rolla's bark a minute before."

"Did your Irishman come with you?" asked his wife.

"No, he is splitting out the boards for the barn. He proposed to stay and let me take him his dinner."

"There is another shot, papa. I expect Guy has killed another squirrel."

"Doubtless, if he aimed at one, for he is a fine shot with a rifle."

"He beat the Mexican shooting, the other day, and he told brother he had never been beaten so badly before."

"How did Guy make out with his Spanish?"

"Very well, although brother said that the Mexican's pronunciation was so unlike the real Spanish he had to guess at some of his words."

"It is not to be wondered at; these Mexican half-breeds have a dialect of their own."

"It is nearly noon," said Mrs. Raymond. "I wish Guy would come in so that he will be ready for dinner. Stella, take the small bucket and get some drinking water. I presume your brother will be here presently."

Stella took the bucket and having donned her bonnet went for the water. Her destination was a little spring under the bank of the creek, near at hand, to which a path led through the bushes of mesquite. She tripped along with her bucket, casting side glances toward the grove to see if she could catch a glimpse of her brother. Arriving at the spring she scooped it out with her hands, and then waited for it to clear itself. This she repeated again and again, b way of amusement, taking no account of the flight of time. Finall a strange shout, which seemed to come from the plateau above, cause her to realize how long she had remained playing in the spring, an that perhaps they were waiting for her return with the water. Sh filled her bucket and started to ascend the steep bank, when sh heard the report of fire arms, followed by demoniac yells from th direction of the house. Her first thought was "Indians!" Her next— concealment. With a heart full of terror and apprehension for he parents' safety, the child crept cautiously through the thicket, to the left of the path, and setting down her bucket, stealthily proceeded to a position whence she could view the open ground. The scene completely overpowered her, and she fell moaning and sobbing, and calling piteously for her father and mother.

CHAPTER II.

Guy, who had fallen across the body of the panther, was wounded in the scalp by a shot from the opposite height. He was just regaining consciousness when he heard the same yells from the house, which had so terrified his sister. He had not sufficiently regained his senses to comprehend the full meaning of the sounds, but he struggled to a sitting posture, when he was caught from behind and his arms securely pinioned. Two dirty-looking Indians confronted him. One of them had secured his rifle, and both were making signs and, apparently, talking about the slain animal. The youth now began to realize his own danger, and that of his family. He remembered the shouts which greeted his ears, on the return to consciousness, and his fears multiplied when he saw smoke and flames in a direction which told him, as plainly as language could express, that the Indians had done their fiendish work in the home which contained his all in life.

Oh! for freedom and his rifle. He would sell his life dearly and avenge to some extent the cruel work of the savages. Dread suspense! His mother! His little sister! What was their fate? Poor Rolla! Even he was gone. Perhaps the poor dog had considered him to be dead and had gone to mutely convey the news.

It would be difficult to depict in words the emotions that crowded the breast of the prisoner in the space of the few moments succeeding his recognition of the character of his captors. The latter now motioned him to move on, and before he had time to obey, one of them seized his arm and pushed him along. They took him in the direction of what was once his home. On passing the scene of his morning's work he cast a sad look at the waterfall still pouring its ceaseless stream into the basin. How different it sounded now! Then, its music seemed like an harbinger of joy—something to soothe him when he would seek the fairy spot, to muse and speculate, to commune with nature. Now, it was the sad requiem of his hopes.

The grove once cleared the opening disclosed the smoking remains of the house, while to one side stood a dozen Indians, around a pile of plunder. If there had been any victims, they were not to be seen, and a hope succeeded that his people had escaped. Thus encouraged, he recovered his composure, and was now satisfied that Rolla had gone with the family. The Indians had already secured the horses belonging to his father, and proceeded to pack them with sundry articles from the pile. After he had been inspected by the whole party he was placed in the custody of a tall, raw-boned Indian, who ordered him, by signs and several unintelligible sounds, to go with him. Guy obeyed, but found it to be difficult to keep up with his guard. They soon crossed the little brook, near where it emptied in the Salado, and ascended the bank on the further side to the high ground constituting the forks of the two runs. About a half-mile further on they reached the camp of the Indians, which had been left in charge of two warriors and two squaws. Near a small fire sat the two latter, one old and wrinkled, the other young and just about grown. To this point the tall Indian directed his steps with his prisoner. The two women arose from their squatting positions and began, in their gutteral monotones, an evident discussion of the events of the morning. They devoured Guy with their eyes, pulling at his coat and going through his pockets. The old one appropriated his knife and two small keys on a ring. One of the latter belonged to his trunk, the other to the little box in which were kept those treasures, odds and ends, valuable to a boy, and little mementoes of the happier days spent in the place of his nativity The younger squaw claimed his handkerchief, which she held up before her for inspection, and then amused herself by picking at the red embroidered letters in one corner, which spelled his name. He thought of the little hands which had worked those letters—her first attempt—and wondered where they then were. The response was the scene of desolation across the creek—the smouldering ruin, the yelling savages and the most agonizing feature of the cruel tragedy—the cloud of uncertainty that veiled the fate of his dear ones. Dejected, crushed by the weight of his reflections, he sank in tears at the foot of a tree under which he had been halted, and bowed his head upon his knees. The wound in his scalp pained him exceedingly; the clotted blood had hardened in his hair and produced irritation. His bowed head disclosed the cruel wound much exaggerated by the mass of coagulated blood, and the crimson stains that marked his neck and discolored his clothing.

A hand upon his head interrupted his reflections, and, starting from his painful reverie, he beheld the young squaw bending over him. She had brought a horn full of water from the creek, and wetting the handkerchief she indicated that she desired to wash his wound. He could only submit, and the girl proceeded to wet his head, while he bent forward to allow her treatment without incurring a wetting. By degrees she removed the traces of blood and, closing the wound, tied the handkerchief over it. He made signs to her to loosen his bound arms, but she replied with impatient motions in the negative. The older woman and the men had disappeared during the time while Guy had his head bowed upon his knees. He had only a squaw to contend with, but his arms were securely tied, and the squaw had weapons at hand and knew how to use them. The noise of approaching Indians indicated the coming of the fiends with their plunder, and perhaps with the cruelest of intentions towards their prisoner.

Guy's active mind had already been involved in speculation as to his fate, and it was not without apprehension that his ear caught the sounds. The squaw suddenly changed her position and demeanor. She sprang from a seat and, resuming her rifle, stood facing her charge, as if she were closely guarding him. Guy thought he read in this a fear lest her recent ministrations might be discovered by her people. To avoid suspicion that she had betrayed the weakness of sympathy, she had assumed a vigilant attitude. The party filed into camp, passing near their captive. one of them rudely snatching the handkerchief from his head and dashing it in his face. A discussion then followed, apparently about something of great importance. The tall Indian was especially demonstrative in his gestures, and loud in his talk, appearing to wholly dissent from the views of the others. Finally the council came to an end. With grunts and yells they separated to seek their ponies which, securely hoppled, were grazing near. The animals were brought in, the packs adjusted, and the band moved off one after another, except the two squaws, the tall Indian and another of low stature, who appeared to be a half-breed, as his skin was brighter, resembling the lower type of Mexicans. These were also making preparations to leave. A pony was produced for the prisoner; his arms were unbound and he was directed to mount. After securing his feet with a hopple, passed under the horse, the party started off, the tall Indian taking the lead, the others following, leading the prisoner's animal, the two stolen horses packed with the booty bringing up the rear. The wild country grew wilder as the party moved on their pathless way, along the timber of the creek, pointing to the distant hills whose blue summits piled up, tier upon tier, blended in one dark belt beneath the bright horizon. The young prisoner's arms were sore, his wound was throbbing, but the greatest pain was in his heart, which was crushed under the weight of the uncertainty hanging over the fate of father, mother and sister.

The morning had been so happily spent at the waterfall in an occupation so congenial to his nature; in the maturing of an artistic conception, planned weeks before to give a pleasant surprise to his family. There could be no overruling Providence in the wreck of so many hopes.

The Indian ponies were travelers, and good progress was made by a uniform, ambling gait, which they were not allowed to break. The timber of the creek had long been left to the right and the sun was nearly touching the western hills when the party entered the outskirts of a dense cedar brake, which extended up a canon, formed by the first well-determined hills of the chain they had been approaching. The dry bed of a run that drained the canon and its tributaries furnished the passway through the dense growth. The sure-footed ponies, accustomed to the rough courses of Indian travel, made good headway over the rocky, broken surface; but the pack horses frequently stumbled and had to be urged forward At length a small canon, to the left, disclosed a miniature lake with rocky margin and enclosed by a wall of cedars. To this the guide directed his course and, in a few moments, halted the sad procession at its edge. The savages at once dismounted and began preparations to camp. Guy was released from his pony, stiff and sore from his long ride without a saddle, and was forced to gather fuel under the surveillance of one of the Indians. Before dark the horses had been placed to graze and the packs disposed upon the ground. By the aid of punk and steel a fire had been started, and was crackling its flames through the dry twigs and branches, lavishly supplied from the adjacent thicket. The picture was wild and interesting. The placid surface of the water reflected the light green of the cedars, whose pointed tops surmounted each other in regular gradations, as their positions marked an increasing altitude on the side of the gorge. The column of smoke rose thick and blue, settling lazily overhead, then floating slowly back, enveloped the treetops in long, thin stretches, then assumed fantastic shapes as it cleared the foliage. Below, along the narrow space, where the water encroached upon the timber, on either side, grew a species of rank mountain grass, and here the Indians disposed themselves to the abandon of the camp. Rations of jerked beef had supplied the necessities of the evening meal, to which the prisoner had been invited, but of which he had no inclination to partake. Fortunately for him, he was allowed to possess himself of a blanket, one stolen from his own home, and upon this he stretched his tired limbs. Darkness had settled over the hills a long time before he was wooed by the wiles of slumber. His rest was fitful and he relapsed into a dreamy stupor, while contemplating the grim form of the tall Indian as he squatted by the fire, with perfect immobility of features, except when casting a glance, from time to time, to become reassured of his prisoner's presence. It was nearly daylight when he awoke, and his first realization was the contact of a warm body with his back and shoulders. Feeling of the object he discovered it to be a dog, and the low, familiar whine, responsive to his touch, proved it to be Rolla. Guy's satisfaction was intense. He hugged and caressed the faithful dog, while his heart was full of emotions He whispered:

"Dear Rolla! Oh Rolla! Where is father and mother and little sister? Oh! If you could only talk. You must have been with them since you left me in the grove. How can I be glad to see you, dear old dog, since your coming causes me to doubt, still more, their safety?"

The dog nestled closer to his master and expressed, in his mute way, his unfeigned sympathy.

The captive boy no longer felt that complete desertion he experienced the evening before. One sympathetic heart in the camp beat for him, and although it pulsated in the body of a dog, it possessed the merit of fidelity.

The bright July sun had mounted well up above the hilltops before the Indians bestirred themselves and, from their slow movements, it was apparent that no speedy departure from their camp was contemplated. The appearance of Rolla excited their surprise, and they had much to say in their unintelligible talk concerning the new arrival. Their close inspection of Rolla elicited a deep growl and a movement to a position still nearer his master who, fearing that such defiance might lead to his cruel usage, commanded him to be silent. No violence, however, was offered to the faithful brute, and Guy experienced a feeling of relief as he saw the larger savage disappear down the canon, followed by the two squaws. The short Indian remained on guard and Guy was wishing that he could speak their language in order that he might sound the fellow, to learn his probable fate. While still in this train of thought he was much surprised at being accosted by the Indian in rather imperfect Mexican.

"Hablas Mejicana?" he inquired.

"Yes, I speak it pretty well," Guy replied in the same language, at the same time eagerly assuming a sitting, from a recumbent, position.

"What your name?"

"Guy," was the ready answer.

"My name Pedro."

"Pedro is a Mexican name."

"Me Mexican—not Indian."

"What are you doing with the Indians then?"

"Me so big when Indian kill my people. Me same as Indian, but my people Mexican."

This to Guy was encouraging information. Might not this fellow have yet a little of the milk of human kindness left, despite his long absence from civilization? Then he remembered that Mexican treachery was but one degree removed from savage barbarity, and the new-born hope fell under the reflection.

"Pedro, do you kill people for nothing, just like the Indians?"

"Indian make me kill plenty. Me same as Indian."

"Do the others speak any Mexican?"

"Muy poco, few words."

"Will these people kill me?"

"Maybe so, if you not be Indian, like me."

"Pedro, will you be my friend and tell me what to do?"

"Me be friend, if you be Indian. You no want be killed and if Indian want, he kill you. He not kill you when you be same as Indian. All Indian want kill you, but Walumpta say no. He say, maybe so, you be same as Indian. He say you pretty and shoot gun well. Walumpta shoot you in head."

"Who is Walumpta?"

"Walumpta chief."

"Is he the Indian who has just left here with the squaws?"

"Yes, he Walumpta. He gone to make smoke on the mountain."

"He shot me, then saved my life," mused Guy.

"What tribe do you belong to, Pedro?"

"Lipan—all Lipans."

"And where are those who left the camp yesterday before we did?"

"Gone; steal horse on El Cibolo. Walumpta gone to big mountain. He make smoke so other Indian come here, when they steal plenty horse. Squaws go find plums. Plenty plums in big canon."

Guy looked in the direction of the mountain and recognized it as one he had often seen from the new home on the Salado. It was the highest point for miles around and he had been told that it was called "Indian Lookout."

"Well, Pedro, if I turn Indian, will you be my friend and see that my good dog is well treated?"

"Pedro be your friend; all Indian and squaw be friend too."

Guy would have asked him concerning the fate of his family, and the question rose to his lips, but it merely trembled there for a moment, while the great lump in his throat choked down all possibility of its utterance. The tears fell from his eyes and dropped upon the upturned face of Rolla, who looked, as if in wonder, at his master's familiar talk with the barbarian. Guy began to discern the bare possibility of escape in the assumption of a new nationality, and resolved to feign an earnestness of purpose to that end that would deceive even the cunning of an Indian. He reclined again on his blanket, while he gave his new intention his profoundest thought.

While thus engaged he suddenly saw a smoke rise from the top of Indian Lookout, and called Pedro's attention to it.

"Walumpta up there," said Pedro.

"And here comes the squaws," said Guy, as the objects of his remark came in sight down the canon. Then, as if he thought it best to make the announcement before the return of any of the absentees of the party, he said to his guard·

"Pedro, I want to be an Indian."

The words cost him an effort, but he had made a resolution.

Pedro manifested some satisfaction at the announcement, and gave Guy to understand that when Walumpta returned he would make known his determination, but that some test would be required to prove his sincerity of purpose.

"Chicha be glad," he added.

"Who is Chicha?"

"Chicha my squaw; look, she come."

The two squaws now approached, each carrying the plums they had been gathering. Pedro communicated with them, at which the younger one seemed to become interested, while the elder remained silent, merely casting an indifferent look in the direction of the prisoner.

The former, to still further prove her satisfaction, suddenly crossed over to Guy and stooping down opened the cloth containing her plums, and motioned to him to help himself from its contents. Instead of complying he fell back as if he had received an electric shock, and covered his face with his hands. Rolla, not comprehending, bristled his back and growled in anger. Poor Guy! The cloth which held the plums was an apron, worn by his mother the day before.

CHAPTER III.

Summer had ripened into Autumn. On the hills and in the valleys, chaparral and forest had put off the green and assumed their gaudy foliage. Winter had come again and melted into Spring. The birds sang as sweetly and the flowers bloomed as profusely as in preceding seasons. The mellow sunlight cast pleasant shades and picturesque shadows. Cooling waters laved the bold banks of rivers and the mossy margins of rivulets. Nature—transcendantly beautiful—smiled through every feature of her creation. The little fall, on the Salado, still poured its crystal water into the bubbling basin to find its way, in ceaseless current, to the stream below. The grove, still beautiful in its garb of verdure, still stately in its giant trunks, still resounding with the music of the woods, had not, perhaps, been trodden by human feet since the day when the young dreamer had rested in admiration of his work—planning future hours of happiness beneath its umbrage; for was not there the rude mallet, and there the rusty chisel, with blade just visible from out the matted leaves? The winding path, scarce worn to plainness by the unfortunate settlers, was now hidden by the fallen foliage. Here and there a bleaching bone, and further on a grinning skull, bespoke the feast of the wolves as they scattered the severed remains of the dead panther in their fight over the prey. Out in the bright sunshine —in the opening where stood the home—the grass was struggling from out of the cinders, now only discernable by the black remains of charred substances lying loosely above the weatherbeaten mass.

Is there nothing further to indicate the tragedy of the year before?

Let us approach the old oak, whose shadow once fell across the doorway of the apartment where Stella and her mother sat on that fatal day. Yes, those two mounds speak eloquently, and we, who know of the sad occurrence, would be at no loss to guess who lay beneath, even if those rough stakes did not bear the initials of the dead. Down there, leading to the little spring, is still the path along which Stella tripped for water, while she looked in vain for the appearance of her brother, who lay, all unconscious, across the carcass of his victim. Perchance we could find the cup and bucket which the frightened child had abandoned, ere she surveyed the opening filled with howling savages.

But why linger in this devoted spot, and court the melancholy which its reminiscences engender? Other scenes demand our attention, through which we will follow the fortunes of Guy Raymond, and leave to the future to unravel the fate of his sister.

Picture a range of hills, shaggy with alternate growth and crag, timbered or bald as the chances of flood or eruption had denuded of soil the rising steppes, or left it to support the stunted thicket in its precarious tenure above the mass of limestone. Extending west by south for an hundred and fifty miles or more, this range was flanked by pretentious spurs thrown off diagonally to the northeast with intervals of miles of level or undulating surface of open country, through which coursed, ever and anon, a stream or run, seeking its way to the Colorado or to reinforce one of that river's tributaries. These runs were fringed with the inevitable lines of timber, giving variety to the prospect and shelter to the timid herds, descending from the hills to graze, or slack their thirst at some favorite waterhole. Through these wild valleys roamed the buffalo, the mustang, the deer and the antelope, hunted by the Indians, not wantonly, but to satisfy the necessities for food and raiment.

It was to one of the most southern of these spurs that Walumpta had guided the party which held Guy a prisoner; it was here we left them encamped while the signal smoke was rising from Indian Lookout to attract the attention of the raiding band.

The two parties having formed a junction on the afternoon of that day, they took the trail leading east by north, along the range, to the headquarters of their tribe on the distant San Saba. Across the projecting spurs and through intervening lowlands the party pursued its course without incident save an occasional dash after a herd of buffalo, the shooting of a deer, or the stampede of a drove of mustangs. Despite his load of sorrow, the bold riding of the Indians, the excitement of the chase, the grand, wild scenery and the novelty of the situation in which, by a most sudden transition, he found himself, so engrossed the mind of the prisoner as to detract much from his mental depression.

* * * *

It was one of those days when the temperature attains that equipoise, between the extremes, which is to be found in the altitudes of the highlands, and which makes this world seem a paradise by reason of the invigorating effect of the atmosphere when inhaled by healthy lungs and expanding chest. From the top of the ridge, constituting the northern extremity of the range, hitherto described, could be seen the timber of the Colorado joining that of the Red Fork. To the west was a small chain of hills extending so far north as to touch the picturesque groves of Lipan and Kickapoo springs, while to the southwest a vast plane stretched away in the direction of Devil's River and the Pecos. Below, nestled in a mountain valley, through which coursed the San Saba, was an Indian village, built upon the pricipitous banks of that stream. To the casual observer it would have been difficult to locate any approach from the outer world to this nest of the Indians, so completely was it hedged in by its abrupt and rugged surroundings. Few individuals could be seen about the village, other than an occasional passer from one lodge to another, or a group of youngsters practicing with bow and arrow at a target on the opposite bank of the river. A peep into the gorge-like bed of the latter would have disclosed several of the Indian women engaged in washing—pounding with sticks articles of clothing lying on the smooth flags that abounded in the bed proper. At the upper end of the valley a herd of ponies was slowly moving towards the foot of the hills, the animals cropping grass as they went. Over the hills to the east was a narrow trail pursuing a devious course towards the settlement. It was little better than a cattle track, for the lazy bucks of the tribe were too indolent to fell a tree, clear a thicket or remove a stone to secure the conveniences of a direct path. Along this trail two horsemen were approaching the valley and both were, apparently, Indians. The one in the rear bore behind him the carcass of a deer, from which the warm blood still dripped, and which seemed to demand his attention, between the snatches of a nasal monotone that might have been intended for an air, to keep it from slipping to one side or the other. The first horseman, upon a closer scrutiny, would have disclosed features decidedly non-Indian and his complexion, though exceedingly browned, looked most suspiciously Saxon. He was dressed in Indian costume even to moccasins. A jaunty cap, made of some pretty fur, protected his head. Unlike his companion, he rode upon a handsome Mexican saddle. The two had reached nearly the highest point in the hills when he who carried the deer exclaimed, in Mexican:

"Caramba!"

"What is the matter, Pedro?" asked the other in the same language.

"Can't you see? Deer fall off again."

"I'll help you put it up again."

"Next time you kill deer, you pack him. You 'fraid dirty your fine saddle."

"Come! Pedro, cease your growling. You know you offered to pack it, and now you are complaining. It is just like you Indians. When I used to play with little white children, we called the one 'Indian giver' who would give a thing and be sorry for it afterwards."

"Pedro is no Indian, but Indian steal me and make me Lipan. Chicha my squaw now and Pedro always be Indian."

"If you made one change to Indian, you certainly can make another back to Mexican."

"Peuede ser—but Pedro 'fraid to try. Lipan and Mexican fight so much—fight all the time."

"The more reason you should side with your people. You were as savage as the rest the last fight we had with the Mexicans."

"Es verdad—but you, you killed six—more than Indian kill. You get fine saddle and fine name; Indian call you 'el bravo.'"

"True, too, but I had to prove my Indianship, and besides I wanted a good saddle. More than that I was not fighting my own people, but a merciless race who never spare an American prisoner."

"Then, Senor Bravo, Mexican is worse than Indian and Pedro better stay with Chicha."

"Take her with you."

"Will Laoni go with you?"

"Talk not of her, Pedro. She is not my squaw, and can never be. True, I owe her my life; yet——"

"Walumpta say Laoni must be squaw for El Bravo, and Laoni has eyes only for you."

"She will forget me. She only feels an interest in me from the fact that she kept me from being burnt alive."

"If ten squaw keep Pedro from burning, Pedro take all ten. Pedro no like fire."

"If that were the penalty, in my case, for living, I'd take fire, first, last and all the time," thought Guy.

"Come, Senor Bravo, this squaw talk make us forget about deer."

"Take hold then; now, up with it. I think it will stay this time."

The deer secured, the horsemen commenced the descent into the valley. Pedro took up his monotonous refrain, while his campanion rode in silence. Reaching the edge of the village, they turned to the right and directed their way to the upper portion, where, in the door of a lodge, stood the slight figure of an Indian girl. She was fondling a dog, who would stand on his hind legs and place his paws on her shoulders, while his head was being stroked. At sight of the horsemen the dog ran quickly to meet them and almost leaped to the saddle of the first, in his demonstrations of delight.

"Ah, ha, Mr. Rolla! I stole a march on you this morning. Where were you straying, sir?"

"What is El Bravo saying to the dog?" asked the girl, in the Lipan dialect.

"Laoni is not jealous of the dog," said Guy.

"Not jealous, but Laoni does not like the words."

"They are the words of my mother-tongue."

"You speak the Lipan—why speak any other?"

"I spoke them to Rolla; they are the words I spoke to him like to a friend, before I ever saw Laoni."

"You have known him longer and like him better."

"Have you nothing better to be jealous of than a dog? Laoni knows that since the day she saved me from the fire I would risk my life for her. Because of her I slew the enemies of her people and earned the name of Bravo. Her good act saved these strong arms for service, and I have used them to repay the debt I owe her. If a buffalo falls or a deer drops at the sound of my rifle, straightway it is hers. Here, Pedro, undo the buck. See, Laoni, here is my offering of today. It is another grain of sand to make up the mountain I owe you."

"Laoni wants not a deer, nor a buffalo, nor a prairie full of them, as pay for what came from her heart. Your living body is her reward, and she asks no more than to see her Bravo happy in the strength of his manhood, and to receive his kind words."

"Walumpta has treated me like a son, and Laoni is my sister."

"If Walumpta make you his son, it was for Laoni's sake. Laoni's love is not the love of a sister. A sister's love can fail, but Laoni's, never!"

"Pedro has hung the buck to the tree without help," said Guy, impatiently.

"And will skin it without help, if you and Laoni stand there jowering and making long faces," said Pedro, using the language of his adoption more fluently than the Mexican.

"Call Chicha, or the Muja, to help. It is enough to kill a deer, without having to skin it."

"I'll call both and make them finish it, for it is more work to pack one deer a mile than to kill many."

Laoni retired into the lodge, while Guy walked away in a moody state of mind. The latter's domicile was unlike any other in the village. With Pedro's help, he had constructed it more on the plan of a Mexican jacal, except the roof, which, in lieu of tule, was covered with buffalo skins tightly stretched and well secured. The Indians had fully intended to sacrifice their young prisoner, on their arrival at the San Saba. His acquaintance with the Spanish language, as it happened, was the remote cause of his preservation from a painful death. It interested Pedro, who yet had a tender place in his heart for the old tongue, and through him the chief became prepared to yield to the pressure of potent influences. Walumpta was the chief of one faction of his tribe, which was divided on some questions, reaching, however, merely local considerations, as in all extra tribal policy and diplomacy the Lipans were united. The chief had saved the prisoner's life when captured, but promised to deliver him up to the torch on their return to the village. While half regretting his promise, Walumpta did not like to disappoint his followers, but deferred the execution, from time to time, until weeks had passed. Pedro had made good use of this time by contriving to throw the young white man frequently into the company of the prepossessing daughter of the chief. The latter became interested in the story of the prisoner, in his desire to be adopted by the tribe, and in Pedro's praises of his prowess and marksmanship, which he held up to his attentive auditor as fitting accomplishments of one who was the impersonation of manly grace and beauty. Laoni's desire to listen generated into a wish to visit and speak with the unfortunate. The Indian girl had a woman's heart, which either prompted her to a noble resolve or caused her to succumb to the attractions of the ideal created by Pedro's recitals.

Pedro had posted Guy as to the murderous intentions of the Indians, and outlined his policy to defeat their purpose. The terrible extremity in which he found himself must be an extenuating circumstance, if Guy Raymond encouraged the rising interest which Laoni manifested, by repeating to her in their interviews certain telling sentences in the dialect learned from Pedro.

Finally, by the advice of Laoni, Guy sent a formal request to the chief that he be permitted to become a member of the tribe, promising, if his request were granted, to faithfully defend the people of his adoption against all enemies and to conform with the rules and customs established by and common to the Lipans. Laoni lent her influence to the petition, and Walumpta called a council of the Indians to consider the matter. The meeting was a stormy one, for the burning of the white man was to be a jollification extraordinary, and the majority were opposed to entertaining the petition.

At this juncture the daughter of the chief, roused to the extreme of interest, entered the circle of the squatting warriors and held out her hand for silence. Her mien was majestic; her manner pregnant with simple enthusiasm. The wondering council, made mute by the movement, interchanged expressive grunts and then silently awaited her speech. With heaving chest, expanding nostril and eyes dilated, she thus addressed them:

"My fathers: Laoni is the daughter of the tribe; the good of her people has been to her as dear as her own life. She would give her life for her people. It is said the white men were coming to take the country of the Lipans. You know, my fathers, that our land had been seized by the Mexicans who came from beyond the long river, before the coming of the white man. Our warriors who have been to the lower country tell us the Mexicans are fighting the white men. Shall we help our enemies? Every white scalp you take, every drop of white blood you spill, is good work for our enemies. Our fathers, long ago, had their hunting grounds from the Colorado to the great water, when the strangers came from beyond the long river and made their homes on the San Antonio.. They told our people of a Great Spirit who was a friend to the Mexican and who would be a friend to the Indian. The Indians who listened and went to worship their Great Spirit were made the slaves of the black gowns. From sun to sun the Indian bent under the heavy stones to build houses for their Great Spirit. To pay us they have robbed us of our hunting grounds. The prisoner that you would burn has never fought the Indians, and his people are the enemies of the Mexican. Shall it be said that the Lipan is worse than the Mexican? The young white man is brave; the Mexican is a coward. The prisoner is wise, for he already speaks the words of the Lipan; he is good, for after all the harm you have done him he asks to be one of our tribe. My fathers, Laoni asks for his life. She asks you to make him a brother; and when the moon will throw the long shadows from the mountain, let him fight with our warriors. The daughter of the tribe, the child of Walumpta, will answer for his bravery."

Laoni's words produced the desired effect, and Guy was saved. A few of the warriors shook their heads depreciatingly and some of the squaws howled in their disappointment.

The test was made on the first foray, when the Lipans, accompanied by Guy, attacked a train of Mexican carts under escort. His fearless conduct and exquisite marksmanship, in the fight, gained him the sobriquet of "El Bravo," and confirmed him in the confidence of his dusky comrades. It was a severe ordeal, but he was young, and his ambition, with a conscious capability, made him impatient to penetrate the future as it advanced to meet him on the rapid wheels of time. Among his troubles there arose a crowning perplexity. He was beloved by the young Laoni who, in the simplicity of her nature, did not hesitate to make it known to him, or to keep him in remembrance of it. He discovered that in her attributes, which raised her far above the level of the Indians, and he endeavored, as he progressed in the mastery of her dialect, to instill in her mind the ideas and obligations of civilization.

How could she help loving him? The knowledge of her attachment was a solace in his banishment, but he feared that when it would reach its full fruition it must eventuate in her disappointment, if not in more serious consequences. While consorting together frequently he was cautious to not evoke allusion to her love, and so shaped his words and planned his acts, as to fill, to the full, the measure of her happiness, by his companionship, without raising the reflection as to what it might all be tending.

CHAPTER IV.

A little distance, perhaps a quarter of a mile, above the Lipan village, the water of the San Saba poured over a fall of several feet. Its perpendicular descent was made with even, glass-like surface until it reached a mass of broken rock at the base, through which, roaring and leaping in foamy masses and whitened spray, it escaped to the level bed below. A mile or so further on was the river's source where, welling up from solid ledge rock, more than a dozen springs of surpassing beauty united their waters to form the limpid stream. The topography of the country indicated that these springs were fed through one of nature's syphons, being merely a subterranean current crossing through the rocky labyrinths underlying the plateaus beyond. To the west, and close at hand, was the most elevated peak in the contiguous hills, from whose side approached a canon, in a winding direction, and ending at the gorge through which the river coursed. Its entrance had a weird, wild appearance to Guy, who had often passed it, and had cast curious looks up the narrow opening. One of the few prohibitory rules which he was directed to obey, when he gave his fealty to the tribe, was, on no account, to visit that canon, or to ascend the elevation beyond. This was not special as to the new recruit, but bore equally on the Indians, except the chiefs and certain older warriors, who were named as exceptions, and who constituted their advisers. This prohibition naturally aroused the curiosity of our hero; but as he attributed the regulation to some preposterous Indian superstition, he did not think it worth while to run the risk of its gratification.

But he was destined to learn, from other lips, enough to seriously tempt him to venture on the exploration of the forbidden ground.

One afternoon, shortly after the day when he and Pedro had brought the deer into the village, Guy, accompanied by Rolla, was returning down the river bank from a hunt in the hills, his rifle swung carelessly on his shoulders, his mind so absorbed by some train of thought that he did not see Laoni, who was sitting on a rocky projection just above the falls.

She called to him.

"Why, Laoni! I did not see you."

"Your eyes are for everything but Laoni."

"My thoughts were far away."

"And El Bravo would like to be with his thoughts."

"You are right, Laoni. I was thinking of my little sister, about whom I have often spoken to you. She may be living, and I often hope she is. But it is almost foolish to hope. The day I was captured she, with my father and mother, must have been killed by your people."

"If they were killed, the warriors know it; they will tell El Bravo."

"I could not ask; the words would die on my lips."

"They will tell Laoni."

"I do not want to know it; for if the slayers of my family were to make themselves known to me——"

"Would El Bravo fight?"

"I might do worse."

"If El Bravo's people were dead, the warriors would have scalped them. They brought no scalps to the village."

A shudder ran through Guy's frame at the thought and he grew moody and silent.

"Is El Bravo sorry, that he will not speak?"

"I am sorry that you saved me from the fire. It would have been better to let me burn."

"Has Laoni made El Bravo sorry?"

"You are not to blame, poor girl, for my captivity, or for any sorrow that I may have. You have a good heart and I believe that it strives to do right. If I had my way, you would not be long in this valley."

"Where would Laoni go?"

"To my countrymen. There you could learn our language and be taught the peaceful way of living. After you would learn our customs, you could return to your people and lead them from the bloody paths they now follow, into the broad road of peace and plenty. Then would you have large villages, surrounded by fields of corn and grain, with sheep and cattle and horses of your own raising; with schools to teach the children how to read and write."

"The warriors do not like to work; the prairie is full of buffalo and deer, and the hills with turkeys. The prairie chicken and the partridge in the valleys, the squirrel and the rabbit in the woods are only waiting the coming of the huntsman. The water at our feet gives them fish when they tire of the meat from the prairie and the valley. Here they are free as the mountain breeze; and before the coming of the strangers who have pushed the Indians back from the south they were like the leaves of the trees, and the scalps of twelve moons could be counted on the fingers."

"My poor Laoni cannot know the pleasures of a different life. This little valley is your world. The scalping knife and the tomahawk seem to you more useful than the hoe and the plow."

"Laoni believes the words of El Bravo. Laoni has not seen the white people, and she cannot know if they are better than the Indians. The Mexicans say the white men are bad, but the Mexicans come with lies. They made our fathers work to build big houses for their Great Spirit. They came to this valley before the village was here, when Walumpta was in his mother's arms. They made a great hole in the side of the hill in the canon at the foot of the mountain, and our fathers worked for them. They took out loads of metal. They brought their fighting men at last and tried to take our land. The Lipans were strong and many. They told the Mexicans to go back to their country. The Mexicans laughed at the Lipans, and before the next sun went down their scalps were hanging from the belts of our warriors."

"What metal were the Mexicans taking from the hole in the canon?" asked Guy.

She told him the Indian name, but he, not knowing the word in her language for any metal except the one for iron, was in doubt as to which of the precious ores had excited the cupidity of the unfortunates.

She, seeing his perplexity at not comprehending her meaning, drew from her bosom a medal, and holding it up, said:

"This is the metal. This came out of the hole in the canon and was made by one of the Mexicans. Walumpta's father got it from the neck of the man when he took his scalp."

"Guy took the medal in his hand and mentally pronounced it pure silver. On one side was engraved the figure of the Virgin; on the other the monogram for "Ave Maria." He knew there must be a silver mine where the medal came from. If Laoni's words were true, the Mexicans had probably discovered it and had worked it to some extent. In their greed they had, doubtless, attempted to occupy the country in force; had antagonized the Indians and got the worst of it. The slaughter of so many in the canon had invested the place with a species of dread for the superstitious Indians, and they had made a law forbidding anyone to visit it. He concluded he would ask the chief to suspend the rule in his case.

The girl watched him closely while these thoughts were rapidly passing through his mind.

"Is the killing of so many Mexicans the reason that Walumpta does not want any one to go to the canon?" he asked.

"No, my Bravo. I listened while Walumpta and the old men were speaking. I learned the secret of the canon. I will tell it to El Bravo, but he must not let it fall from his lips. If he tells it many Laonis could not save him from the fire or the rifle."

It cannot be a very great secret, for the Indians do not dig for silver."

"When the Mexicans were killed, the chiefs said no one should go to the canon, so that in time the silver would be forgotten, and strangers would not want the land of the Lipans. The Mexicans love silver more than they do their Great Spirit. Walumpta says the marks on this piece of silver keeps away the bad Spirits."

Guy was doubly interested now, and resolved to visit the canon at any risk. He explained to her that the image on the medal represented the Mother of the Christian God, and that the monogram on the reverse was calling on her name.

Laoni was much pleased at the explanation, and cast an unmistakable glance of admiration at her "Bravo" for this display of erudition.

As night was approaching Guy gave a whistle for Rolla, who had gone in pursuit of a rabbit. He came bounding from the bushes, and the two arose for a return to the village.

"Do white men wear the mother of their God on their breasts?" asked Laoni.

"Few white men have any love for her."

"Why not love her?"

"Some are too wicked; and a great many do not believe she was the mother of God."

"Because she was a spirit, and they could not see her?"

"No, she was a woman, just like you; and God was born, a little baby, just like the little one of Chicha's. The Christians say the Great Spirit was his father."

"I thought the little baby was the Great Spirit, and now El Bravo says the Great Spirit was the father of the baby. Could the Great

Spirit be the father of himself? Could he live before he was born?"

"Laoni does not understand. There are said to be three Great Spirits, and all three make one God. One is the father; one is the son, and the other is— is——"

"The uncle?" suggested the girl.

"No, you simple one. The other is a spirit related in some way to the other two."

"That is funny," said Laoni. "And did the baby God grow to be a man?"

"Yes, he lived to be a man. He was a workman, and helped his father build houses."

"His father! The Great Spirit came down from Heaven to build houses? Could the people see his father?"

"Laoni does not understand. It was not the Great Spirit; but the husband of Mary, the mother of God, who was only a man whom she took for a husband, after the baby God was born."

"Why did the Great Spirit make his son do work?"

"I suppose because he thought it was right, as he went about teaching people to do right and be good. The people would not listen to his wise words and only a few followed him. After three years of teaching the people of his nation killed him by nailing his hands and his feet to a tree."

"That is worse than Indians! Lipans would not kill the son of their Great Spirit."

"But the son of Mary had to die," explained Guy. "The Great Spirit sent him to this world to be killed, just like he was, and somebody had to do it."

"Then his father was glad of it, and the men who killed his son were not bad for doing what they had to do."

"No, Laoni, God was angry; and he made darkness and lightning come; the earth trembled, and all the people who had anything to do with his death are said to be in torment, burning in a fire that never dies out."

"Laoni does not want a Great Spirit like that. The Great Spirit of the Indians will not burn his people for what he makes them do."

"It would not be easy to make you a Christian."

"Does El Bravo want Laoni to love a bad Great Spirit?"

"No, Laoni. He wants you to love and believe in one who is good and just; in one who is above our weak human nature; who directs by unchanging laws this great and mysterious creation, and who, if he takes note of actions here, wants all his people, Indians and whites, to be good to each other. If he is a person, like Christians believe, this would please him. He would like to have the white men love gold and silver less, and see the Indians throw away the scalping knife and learn the ways of peace. In place of the shouts of the raiders, you would hear the songs from the cornfield. You would forget, in the bustle of the harvest, the revelry of the war dance."

"El Bravo speaks well. The heart of Laoni has panted for such words, and they fall like honey from his lips. If our warriors could learn your ways, happy days would come to our tribe, and this valley would be fit for the lodge of the Great Spirit himself."

CHAPTER V.

Guy, after leaving Laoni, turned towards his lodge. He passed along the hovels of the braves, many of whom were squatting around their doors, some smoking and others chatting, while the squaws were here and there visibly engaged in several occupations. He heard his sobriquet pronounced more than once as he went, and several times he gave grunts of recognition in exchange for similar salutations. The Indians looked upon him with a kind of awe. He had escaped from the jaws of death, by little less than a miracle, and had stood all tests to prove his bravery and loyalty. For a long time his steps had been followed by spies when he would leave the valley, and his actions noted to glean the first intimation of any attempt to escape. In no instance had the Indians been able to find fault with his allegiance. Satisfied with his loyalty, he had captivated his captors by his mild dignity, his bravery and his fine presence.

The discovery that a silver mine was near at hand, and that it had been the scene of a massacre years before, occupied Guy's thoughts so completely that it was long in vain that he courted slumber. When he finally slept, dream visions of molten silver pouring from glowing furnace would be dissipated by the warwhoop of the Lipan, as the Indian brave closed in the death struggle with the avaricious Spaniard. Then he dreamed that he was exploring the mine with a torch whose light was reflected back by polished slabs of silver, leaning against the sides of the excavation. He attempted to carry one of these away and was bending under the weight of the treasure when he encountered Walumpta at the opening. He hung his head before the chiding presence of the chief, but raised his eyes on hearing the voice of Laoni bewailing the fate that had taken El Bravo to the mine. It was a positive relief on awakening, to find himself in his bed, and that he had been dreaming.

The rays of morning were struggling through the chinks in his cabin wall as he arose, unrefreshed, from his bed of robes. The next lodge to Guy's was Pedro's, and here he took his meals, which never varied from some kind of meat and the Mexican tortilla. Few of the Indians ever enjoyed the luxury of the latter article of food, but Pedro, having inherited a fondness for the national cake, had made sure that a knowledge of its preparation was one of the accomplishments of the squaw of his choice.

When Guy made his appearance, Chicha was busy preparing the morning meal, while the old woman they called the "Muja" was tending the infant half-breed and grumbling at Chicha's slothfulness.

"What makes Chicha cook so many tortillas?" asked Guy, as he noticed an unusual quantity of the cakes.

"Pedro goes with Walumpta and the others," responded Chicha.

"Where are they going?" he asked her, with apparent interest.

"Far away on the Colorado, so Pedro says."

Guy became thoughtful for a moment.

He was about to question Chicha further, when Pedro made his appearance, armed as for a raid. To his inquiring glance Pedro made no reply, but beckoned him aside.

The two remained in conversation for some time, until interrupted by the impatient calls of Chicha, who declared that the grumbling of the Muja would run her out of the village. Rather than be thus deserted Pedro repaired to the feast of venison and tortillas, followed by Guy.

In discussing the merits of Chicha's cookery none of the adjuncts of the board, nor the board itself, were available, and first principles asserted themselves in handling and preparing the food for mastication. Guy was very silent during the meal and, so soon as it was over, he lost no time in seeking Laoni. The girl was in her father's lodge, attending to the simple duties claiming her daily attention. The abode of the chief was constructed partly of rock, procured from the river bed, where it was to be found in large supply, and in every shape and size. The apartment of Laoni was luxuriously furnished, in Indian style, and boasted a carpet of skins ingenuously joined together. In lieu of seats, bearskin rugs were disposed around the sides, while the virgin couch consisted of hair encased in soft and finely dressed buffalo robe.

As Guy was an unceremonious visitor, he entered at once, and greeted the mistress of the room, whose countenance brightened, as it usually did, whenever El Bravo appeared. Laoni was, by no means, an ordinary girl, even when contrasted with the average of her sex representing races advanced in civilization. She appeared to rise above her surroundings and seemed conscious of her superiority. The springs of her mind needed but the magic touch of demonstration to cause them to send it bounding to complete appreciation. This was true in all questions which appealed to heart and conscience, and not involving principles based merely on the usages or culture of civilization, or the dogmas of religion. Her features intelligent, her head shapely and well poised, her figure rather slender, made up a combination which lacked only advantages to bring her to the standard of refinement. Guy's magnetism and teaching had attracted and instructed her until she had developed, in no inconsiderable degree, a natural superiority to her surroundings.

She noted the cloud upon the brow of the youth and the earnest glances which she cast rapidly and inquiringly to his countenance were sufficiently intelligible to elicit an explanation. Guy remained mute and thoughtful.

"Has El Bravo lost his voice? Has he no word for Laoni?"

"Call me no more El Bravo; I am a coward, a renegade, anything but brave. I have lost the friendship of Walumpta. He has forgotten the arm which did him service, and he goes today to raid my people, and would leave me to skulk in the village while the firebrand and scalping knife are at work on the Colorado. Laoni, are my words not true?"

"El Bravo speaks the truth. Walumpta goes to the Colorado. He must listen to his braves. His voice is but little more than one in the council. He would not harm your people, but the warriors do not look upon them or upon you with the eyes of their chief and his daughter. They are jealous of the white man, and many are not pleased that El Bravo has not only won his name, but the love of Laoni."

"I expected the truth from your lips, and am not disappointed. Honor forbids me to stay longer in this village, which is now become the spring from which will pour out the waters of destruction on my unhappy countrymen. Duty commands me to go, if not to assist, at least to warn them of danger."

"Would El Bravo leave the village when his people have not been harmed? Is the raid of the few warriors enough to part him from Laoni, who will be forgotten when the life of the Indian is put aside?"

"I have not used false words to Laoni. I have been as open as she has been truthful. My duty is plain. If I am to be betrayed, you know my resolution. The warriors are yet here, and if the blood of my people must be spilled, let my scalp be the first from the victims of the coming butchery."

"Did Laoni save a life to betray it? When you were a prisoner I pitied you. For pity I braved the anger of the council and took you from the fire whose smoke had already risen above the lodges. You taught me to love you by your words which became to my ears as honey to my taste. For you I have found myself hating the acts of the Indian. My body and my spirit have seemed only to move and act and think for you. If only pity saved your life, by what white man's rule do you look for the mad love of the Indian girl to betray it?"

"Forgive me, Laoni. I did not mean to doubt you. I wished to show you how determined I am that the end of this raid shall not find me here."

"El Bravo has said it. The words of Laoni cannot change him."

"I am glad you know me so well, and I honor you for this calmness. Laoni, why cannot you fly with me? With my people you will be more content than in the savage life of these hills. In me you will always find a friend who will toil for you so long as life lasts."

"Is Walumpta dead? Must my father lose his child, that El Bravo may have a poor Indian girl to work for? Leave Laoni with her people. If her heart only goes with the one she loved, he will be the freer for it. If Laoni is not forgotten, if she is worth El Bravo's love, he will again seek her in these hills, where first she pitied and then learned to love him."

Guy was much affected by the words of the girl. He turned aside with moistened eyes, and looked out upon the hills rising in tiers to the east.

"Oh!" he thought. "What a bitter cup is mine. I would now prefer this girl's treachery to her love. Yet, true hearts are so rare, the very thought seems monstrous. I admire and am attached to her, but how can I yield her the love for which she craves. It would blight my future by chaining me to an Indian life, or weighting me with the odium which the conventionalities of my race would place upon such a union."

His thoughts were interrupted by the girl.

"Have Laoni's words made El Bravo sad?"

"Not your words alone. I, too, have a heart which must beat for those who love me; and the thought of leaving her who saved my life must make unhappy the hour which will separate us."

"Think not of my words then, and let us laugh at parting. Laoni would have her Bravo go away happy. He will sometimes think of the village and of the Indian girl, who waits his coming. When the sun will sink behind the hills Laoni will sit on the rock above the falls and think of El Bravo, who used to sit beside her."

"Let us talk of something else," said Guy, "or you will make me sad again. See, there go the raiders! Laoni, the time is near when I must leave the village."

As Guy spoke a long file of Indians was winding up the pathway leading east over the hills. It was the party which Pedro had joined, and whose destination was the cause of the sudden resolution to escape from his enforced residence among the Lipans. Walumpta had opposed a raid upon the white settlers on the lower Colorado, as he had often assured Guy he would do, but he had been overruled by a nearly unanimous vote of the council and had to yield to established custom. He did not intend that the true destination of the party should be made known to his young friend, and had directed Laoni to deceive him. Guy's sudden appearance at her lodge and direct charge as to the true purposes of the expedition had changed her already wavering intention to mislead him.

Her devotion to El Bravo was supreme and her resolution was taken not only to shield him in his plan to escape, but to assist him in preparations. Unselfish in her love, she was willing to lose his presence to advance his happiness. The last raider had disappeared in the hills, when Guy, turning to the girl, informed her that he must go to prepare for his departure.

"When the sun casts no shadow, come to the springs," he said. "I will be there with my pony and Rolla, and go west around the big mountain."

"Loani will come," was her laconic reply.

Guy took his way to his cabin full of the interest inspired by the prospect of his trip, which he was impressed must be attended with more or less danger. On reaching Pedro's lodge. Chicha and the old squaw were in a wrangle which had lasted since the morning meal.

"Have Chicha and the Muja nothing but cross words?" he asked.

"Old squaw like to fuss," said Chicha. "She mad because Pedro took all the dried meat."

This was a disappointment to Guy, who had depended on getting a supply of cured venison from Chicha to serve for two or three days' rations. He determined, however, not to let this deter him, but to start at once and trust to chance for the wherewith to appease his hunger.

"El Bravo must kill a deer today," said Chicha, "or we will have nothing to eat."

"I will go this very morning," said Guy. "Have you any tortillas to give me? I may be gone until the sun is low."

The squaw procured several of the desired cakes and Guy, taking them from her, went to his own abode. Here he gathered together what articles were necessary for his trip, including his rifle and ammunition, and then went out on the green for his pony. A half hour later he was in his saddle and, saying to Chicha that it might be night before he returned, he galloped off up the valley, followed by his faithful Rolla. Just before reaching the falls he descended the river bank and, crossing the stream, continued towards its source. Arriving at the canon leading to the commanding peak he turned into it and was soon lost in its turns. He experienced a species of awe as the clatter of his pony's hoofs awoke the silence of the forbidden ground. His rapid pace brought him to the expanding area of the terminus of the gorge, whose irregular lines were bounded by the mountain side as a base, with abrupt, rocky acclivities on the north and south. At the latter point, tunneling a spur of the peak, was the mine, the entrance looking darkly forbidding, half concealed by the bushes and weeds, while the debris and refuse of the excavation reached in a long line from its vicinity to a huge pile, occupying the center of the space.

Dismounting, Guy was not long in gaining the entrance, and found himself in a tunneled excavation, extending until the shadows concealed its furthest recesses. To the right was a shaft, into which he peered, without being able to calculate its depth. Stooping to pick up something to toss into the vortex, he raised a human skull, which he threw from him in disgust. The hideous relic of humanity served his purpose as it rolled into the shaft and went thumping its sides to the bottom. His eyes becoming accustomed to the gloom, he had a better view of the uneven bottom and jagged sides of the cave-like apartment. In a search for specimens of ore he was not to realize the visions of his dream, but contented himself with a few fragments of rock, containing small particles of glistening metal, apparently silver.

While in contemplation of his samples a slight noise caused him to raise his head, when he beheld Laoni within a few feet of him.

"El Bravo is not at the springs, and eyes, that are not Laoni's, saw him come into the canon."

"Nor is the sun overhead. What brings Laoni here?"

"Does El Bravo ask? The metal so dear to the Mexican, so loved by the white man has won even El Bravo's heart, since it has made him forget his hurry to leave these hills and brave the spies of the council. What brings Laoni here? More than the silver, that he loves. Come, we must leave the canon, for it is known that you are here."

"Your story of the Spaniards that were killed at this mine made me wish to see it. We will go to the springs and then——"

"El Bravo will go. But we must not go to the springs now. Spies will see us, and the council will know that we have been here."

Guy, submitting to her guidance, followed until they reached the spot where he had left his pony. Here Laoni produced a buckskin pouch filled with dried meat, and gave it to him, saying that she had learned from Chicha that he had none. Much affected by this additional kindness, he could not refrain from embracing his little less than guardian angel, while conflicting emotions filled his breast and his eyes brimmed with tears of honest regret that he could not snatch this faithful heart from her environment and place it on the very pinnacle of earthly content. Guided by the girl, he followed to the southeast angle of the level, where was disclosed a narrow trail, barely visible, that wound up the rocky steep among tall bushes, concealing them effectually as they made the ascent. The sure-footed Indian pony clambered after them, and ere many minutes they gained the brow of the elevation, and looked down upon the lower hills and the stretch of valley beyond. The September temperature had not changed the vernal appearance of the view. Not a leaf had assumed a single tinge prophetic of the autumn that was so near. To the left a silver thread, lost here and there in the mass of emerald, marked the course of the river as it wound round the valley where the smoke of the village could be seen as it rose above the quaint habitations. Here they rested while Guy took a survey of the distant prospect, towards which he must bend his course, when he once quit his present locality and parted with the faithful girl at his side. The rugged chain of hills was lost in the smoky horizon to the southwest and would separate him, in his flight, from the raiding Lipans who would journey along its eastern foot for some distance before they turned their course to the Colorado.

"Does El Bravo know the trail that will take him to his people?"

"Trails will not bother me. I have the mountains and the sun for guides. My course will touch the foot of the range for three or four days."

"See!" said the girl, pointing to the opposite side of the canon. "Laoni did well to follow and lead you here."

Guy looked through an opening in the bushes and beheld the well-known form of Ponseca, an old Indian who belonged to the council of the tribe, and who possessed great influence in its deliberations. He had voted for Guy's execution with the minority, and had never manifested any real good-will for the white convert. His object was quite plainly indicated by his actions, which appeared to be directed to the discovery of some object in the vicinity of the mine.

"You are a brave girl, Laoni. Ponseca wants to catch me in the mine. Your coming has saved my life—or his."

"Where is Rolla? If he sees the dog, he will know the master is near."

Guy gave a low whistle, then a little louder call, and Rolla came rushing from a direction opposite to the canon.

"Good Rolla! I might have known you had not remained to betray me."

To avoid observation they moved further down the slope. Guy busied himself with tightening the girth of his saddle and securing to the latter the few traps necessary for his journey.

"Now, Laoni, we must part," he said, in a voice tremulous with emotion. "Your Indian tongue, or even the language of my own people, cannot give me words to tell you how much I suffer to leave you here, in this wild place, among these Indians, who are so different from you. You saved my life; you gave me your friendship and your love. You have been the bright star whose light has shone in the black sky of my captivity. My life is yours. You have returned it to me that I may go back to my people, learn the fate of my family, and perform the tender duties of a son and brother."

"Laoni is an Indian; El Bravo is a white man. My people are taught to brave trouble and even death, without a tear in the eye or a quiver on the lip. Laoni's love for El Bravo is more than her life. She can give up her life, but as long as it lasts her love must remain. El Bravo will go to his people, but the Indian girl would not keep him. Laoni will wait until the leaves will fall and come again, and longer; and if he comes no more, her heart will be sad, but it will always be with El Bravo."

"If your heart will be sad, my own will be full of sorrow at leaving one who is so true and so good; who, while she loves me, is brave enough to sacrifice her feelings for my interests"

Guy took her in his arms as he said this, and gave her one long embrace.. She clung to him with the energy of despair; then releasing him, she threw herself upon the ground, uttering a long, plaintive cry that could only come from a heart almost broken with grief. With a bound he was in his saddle, and the next moment he was making the descent of the broken hillside at a pace that would have been dangerous for an ordinary rider. He did not look back until he had cleared the hills and turned his pony's head to the course he was to pursue. The rough descent looked smooth enough above the green foliage of the mountain growth. The grand old peak above the mine reared its commanding head in majestic superiority above its fellows. But the center of interest with our hero was a lone figure beneath its shadows, that was waving him the last sad adieux of a brave and faithful heart. Oh, strange world! Oh, stranger humanity! If, on the dialplate of time, the last eighteen months could be turned back from the past with their terrible record, what a load it would lift from more than one suffering heart! Wiser then to yield to the inevitable without sigh or lamentation. The wheel of destiny must revolve. Who would clutch its spokes must be maimed for the temerity.

CHAPTER VI.

"This is an excellent place to camp for the night, senor. We will have fine water, plenty of wood for a fire and grass for the animals."

"Then we had better stop here, by all means; and, as you say, it is only eighteen miles to town, we will be able to make the distance by noon tomorrow."

"Easily. Jose, undo the packs. We will make camp over there, under that fine tree; let a fire be made at once, for a cup of coffee will be most acceptable after our day's ride."

The speakers were of a party of five mounted travelers, who had arrived at a picturesque spot on the banks of a clear, running watercourse. It was late in the afternoon, and the fatigued party was lured, by the attractions of the locality, to decide on resting for the night where the wants of man and beast could be so readily supplied. The language in which they conversed was the pure Spanish, which fact, coupled with an ease of bearing and a polish of manner, bespoke education and gentle breeding. The first speaker was a man of middle age and ruddy complexion, with clearly cut and rather handsome features. The expression of his face was remarkably benignant and cheerful. His voice was musical and, when addressing Jose, was mellowed by the kindliness of his tone. His dress and the peculiar shovel hat he wore indicated his priestly character. The other, habited in the garb of a Mexican civilian of means, was a favorable representative of the type. Like the priest, he was somewhat above the medium stature, while his complexion was darker and features less regular. The latter, in expression, contrasted singularly with those of his companion, indicating a superciliousness in their possessor that would join to the indifference of the man of the world a stimulating self-esteem calculated to chill and repel.

Jose and the two others of the party were typical Mexicans of the lower order. Jose was perhaps somewhat superior in his get-up, from the mule he bestrode to the general toilet of his slight person, including the enormous spurs that decked his heels. His two peers had each a pack mule loaded with the baggage and effects of the travelers.

The entire party dismounted after the order to Jose, who came forward and took charge of the horses of the priest and his companion. The packs were removed by the muleteers, and soon the crackling blaze of a fire sprang from the dry brush and wood collected by the men, and gave an appearance of animation to the camp. Jose, after spreading blankets on which the priest and his companion might repose their weary limbs, busied himself to put the camp in order and to prepare the coffee as directed. His actions indicated that he was quite an adept in his occupation, for his celerity of movement was remarkable, taking into consideration the facts, first, of his nationality, and then the spurs on his heels.

While the men were busy, the two central figures were taking their ease, reclining on the outspread blankets, conversing in easy tones of the camp, of the country, of the pretty prospect on the further side of the San Geronimo, where lay an open, undulating plane of several miles. Through the latter wound the road they were pursuing, showing itself plainly at intervals, and again looking like a mere thread, as it marked the side of a distant rise.

"The Americans would, doubtless, like to possess this fair country. Their immigration here and naturalization is a mere pretext to gain a foothold with an ultimate design to sever it from Mexico," said the civilian.

"The truth of what you say is only too apparent from recent events," replied the priest. "The next few months, I hope, will settle this colonizing business and see a policy inaugurated that will effectually dampen the rebellious temperament of these Texans."

"When once His Excellency puts foot on Texas soil he will make short work of them. He has been wise to conceal his real intentions towards this people. That policy of his was adopted through my advice after my official visit here to estimate the population and resources of the country. I discovered one fact at that time; that it would never do to give them warning of the advance of our troops. Before many days there will be national troops enough in Texas to crush the enemies of Mexico."

The report of a gun interrupted the conversation; and while they were still speculating as to who it could be so near, a deer came bounding from the thicket and, leaping over the brook, fell struggling a few feet below them. Anticipating that the shot might have come from Indians of a hostile tribe, the whole party at once stood to their arms.

'An Indian must have shot that deer," said the priest.

"Most probably, and the best thing for us to do is to take a tree," the other suggested.

"Jose, you and the others get to cover. We will soon see the slayer of that buck."

Jose and the two men did not stop to argue the matter, but sought the nearest available protection, in accordance with the good father's suggestion.

Their eyes were actively scanning the direction whence the shot had come, when the cracking of the brush attracted their attention, and the next moment an Indian, mounted and followed by a dog, came into view, within gunshot of the fallen tree behind which Jose was lying. The intruder was evidently surprised at the appearance of a camp, for he reined up his pony and glanced quickly from side to side, as if in search of the human occupants to whom belonged the grazing animals and the bright fire that was shooting its flames up to the very branches of the tree. He caught sight of Jose's sombrero, just as that individual raised his musket and fired deliberately at him. Understanding now the situation, the supposed Indian called out in good Spanish

"Do not fire! I am a friend!"

Then reversing his gun to show his peaceable intentions, he rode to the campfire and dismounted. He was quickly surrounded by the campers, curious to inspect the hunter whose habiliments were Mexico-Indian, but whose features contradicted the inferential nationalities, while his accent and correct Spanish confirmed the contradiction.

The priest first questioned him:

"Who are you, and which way are you traveling?"

"I have been a captive, and have just effected my escape from the Indians."

"What is your name, my young friend?"

"Guy Raymond, sir; whom have I the honor to address?"

"I am Father Ignacio of the parish of San Fernando, in Bexar. This is—is—Senor— Gonzales, and these are our servants. Jose is a bad marksman or you would be the worst for his impetuous disposition."

"I thought he was a sure enough Indian," remarked Jose, apologetically.

"By the way, young man, you killed your deer. He is lying just over the brook," said Senor Gonzales.

That's good news," said Guy. "We had better skin him before it grows dark. Jose, can I have your help?"

"Give yourself no trouble about it, Senor Raymond," said the priest. "Those two Mozos will dress the deer, while Jose will serve the coffee. It seems like he has taken longer than usual to get it ready. Jose, you used to get around faster, muchacho mio."

"I was about to serve it when Senor Raymond gave us the scare."

"I call that most ill-mannered and ungenerous, to lay your shortcomings on our guest, who, at the same time, is our benefactor, having brought us a deer."

Jose took the priest's words half in earnest until he caught the smile on his jovial face, which soon terminated in laughter, as he motioned Guy to the inspection of his game.

Over the coffee which Jose brought steaming, to them, Guy related to Senor Gonzales and the priest the story of his capture, his life among the Indians and his escape four days before. He was delighted with his new company, especially with the priest, whose kind manner won his heart. The coffee and crackers were a great treat, not having partaken of the beverage, nor of any kind of bread for nearly two years. Surfeited with meat, he scarcely tasted of the venison that Jose had cooked for their supper. Rolla, however, not so dainty as his master, did not refuse a huge cut from the rejected shoulders of the buck.

Guy, much fatigued by his long and lonesome ride, was glad to stretch his limbs on the pallet he made under the same tree where he had enjoyed his supper. His new friends had also lain down quite near, and quiet rested over the camp. He tried for a long time to go to sleep, but he was conscious of the least sounds, such as the low nasal whines of Rolla as he skirmished with the fleas, or the tramping of a horse, as he broke the twigs in the undergrowth while browsing on its leaves. His restless mind had all to do with his wakefulness. The Indian village, with its huts and lodges, nestled in the hills he had so lately left, was plainly pictured. His own apartment, with its rawhide roof, most familiar, presented itself in all its details, within and without, now done with him forever. The chief's abode, with the bower of his friend, the passionate and faithful Laoni, with its orderly arrangement of handsome furs and robes, passed in mental review. He thought over their last long interview in her apartment, her touching words and her devotion to Walumpta. His mind wandered to the rock above the falls, where they used to sit and where he knew she would often go again to think and wait for El Bravo. It was very late, and still the Goddess of Slumber he would fain woo to his arms, held herself aloof and pointed remorselessly to recollections of his late wild life. From the rock above the falls he dreamily wandered to the canon, and up its rocky steep. Its jagged sides and impending boulders projected threateningly above him, while he approached the mine. He felt that some one followed stealthily behind, but he could not turn to look. Some geni of the mountain had fixed his view to the front and he was powerless to cast over his shoulder the glance which it seemed he would have given worlds to make. Courageously he pushed on to the opening, on the further side of which was the mine. He gained the excavation in the mountain side and peered within. The yawning shaft was dark as ever, and when he looked yet closer, human skulls with eyeless sockets and grinning jaws floated round its margin. Terrified, he turned to fly, when he was caught in some one's arms, and carried to the heights which overlooked the village. His captor placed him gently on the ground, and looking up he saw it was Laoni. He tried to speak to her, but she signed him to silence, and pointed meaningly down the line of the mountains which lost itself in the far southwest. He rose to his feet and held out his arms to embrace her, but she withdrew and pointed him to his pony, grazing near. He hesitated; then turning resolutely he caught the girl, but she broke away from his grasp, leaving in his clutched hand something that emitted a soft, silver glow like that reflected by the evening star. He regarded it closely. It was the medal hanging from its snowy beadwork. He raised his head to look for Laoni. As he looked she seemed to rise from the ground, still pointing down the mountain range, and her form grew fainter and fainter and larger and larger, until it only became identified from the mountain mists by a deeper shade of outline. Guy awoke, half oppressed by his dream, to find the glow of the morning and the camp astir.

The rising sun found the travelers ready to mount to renew their journey. The priest and Senor Gonzales were the first to leave. Guy rode by the side of Jose. The two mozos brought up the rear with their pack-mules. The leading couple of the travelers rode for a time without speaking. The priest was evidently thinking of the young American who had so unexpectedly joined them the evening previous, for he broke the silence with the remark:

"Our young recruit appears to be a most intelligent fellow. His brightness and manners have greatly prepossessed me in his favor."

"He is doubtless intelligent. His Spanish, though wanting in practice, shows the remarkable tact he possesses in acquiring it almost entirely from books. Intelligence is with him a race characteristic. You know my love for Americans. Their push and impudence but augments my hatred for them."

"But one may dislike a race and yet admire one of its individuals for a particular virtue or accomplishment."

"An aversion for everything American has become inherent in my nature. Perhaps before another twelve months the name of Almonte will be equally hated by all American Texans."

* * * *

"Jose! What distance is it from here to San Antonio?" asked Guy, as they stopped on the brow of the first hill and awaited the approach of the two mozos, who had been detained by the slipping of a pack.

"Father Ignacio said it was about six leagues from the San Geronimo."

"Is that the name of the creek where we camped last night?" asked Guy.

"Si, senor."

* * * *

"That American looks like a true Indian, with his back to us," said one mozo to the other.

"He is no better than one if he did stretch himself on a fresada and drink coffee with the padre," was the reply.

"Jose took my moral to feed his Indian scrub, and this morning I could not find it."

"It was a bad fortune that misdirected Jose's shot."

"It would have saved him some trouble and me my moral. He is riding bravely by him now and tonight he will be fetching his supper and water for his bath."

"Maybe—if he stops with the padre."

"That he will certainly do, or it will not be the fault of Father Ignacio. I wonder if he will pay me for my moral. If he don't I'll keep this medal of Our Lady, which he dropped in camp. It is pure silver and will buy many morals."

By noon the travelers had reached the Alezan and were on the eve of entering the quaint old town of Bexar. The sudden sound of a bell rang clearly in the distance, striking slowly three distinct peals. The sounds conveyed an admonition. The travelers reined their animals to a halt, while the priest and the uncovered Mexicans made the sign of the cross and, with bowed heads, muttered the prayers of the Angelus. Twice three more peals of the bell and the chime succeeded, when the parties replaced their hats and again moved forward. The dark walls of San Fernando rose stately above the low buildings in its vicinity, while further east the ornate front of the Alamo was plainly distinct. The willows of the San Pedro fringed the view with a line of pale green, skirting the entire western limits of the place; and away beyond, on the further side of the swift-running San Antonio, were the majestic rows of the cottonwoods that lined either side of the Alameda. The grim walls of "El Campo Santo," around which wound the road they were pursuing, were finally reached, the San Pedro was forded, the military plaza was crossed, and Father Ignacio found himself at the door of his quarters opposite the south side of the venerable old church.

"Welcome, Senor Raymond, to San Fernando. There, in that old church, is where I belong. Here is where I stay when I am not attending to my spiritual duties. Alight, Senors. Jose, take the animals in the yard and see that they are attended to."

The good father seemed elated with his arrival home and wore his most pleasant smile as he addressed Guy and Senor Gonzales and gave his order to Jose.

As he rode into the town Guy began to be impressed with the fact that his dress was most uncivilized and he could not restrain a feeling of annoyance which the reflection caused. Yet he observed that the garb of the Mexicans was of a diversity that seemed to require no particular style, and that buckskin entered more or less into the makeup of every article of the outer garments of the general populace. In fact, diversity of apparel was so common from the ingress of Spaniards, Mexicans, Indians and Americans, that no notice whatever was usually taken of an oddity in the way of dress. Guy, therefore, passed without comment to the priest's home, and instead of proving an object for the curiosity of the San Antonians, he, himself, was greatly amused at some queer sights that greeted his eyes. A procession of donkeys loaded with wood, a bundle of which was balanced on either side, moved along the south of the plaza. Behind these came three moving piles of hay, completely enveloping the motor that propelled them along. A nearer approach, however, disclosed the mininutive hoofs of the same patient animals, upon whose backs the grass was ingenuously packed, covering their bodies and heads and trailing to the ground.

He gladly accepted Father Ignacio's hospitality. The room into which he was ushered fronted on the narrow alley that separated the building from the church and opened on the sidewalk. It was apparently the priest's sitting room, being plainly furnished, like all Mexican houses of the better class, a table and a half dozen chairs constituted the furniture. The floor was of flagstones, laid with all their natural irregularities, but quite ingenuously matched so as to leave no very wide spaces to be filled with mortar. A plain crucifix and a thermometer hung over the opening of the fireplace. No mantel piece graced the latter. The cold, bare walls were unbroken, save by the doors, front and rear, and the high, narrow, grated window that overlooked the alley.

Senor Gonzales paced the apartment in a restless manner, apparently paying little attention to the young American, or to the apartment and its appointments. He did, indeed, stop several times in his turns and cast glances through the grated window to the main plaza on which fronted the church of San Fernando. This plaza, smaller than the one in the rear of the edifice, was the mart of the town, where were the tiendas and vinoterias; the resting place of the hay and fuel-loaded burros in the interim of display and sale of the commodities they carried. Father Ignacio soon returned and invited his guests to follow him to the court in the rear of the apartment, where they would find water and towels with which to remove the dust of travel. This invitation, with the announcement that later they could enjoy a bath in the river or a full-length wash in the tub, was agreeable news to Guy, who coupled the intelligence with visions of a wardrobe more consonant with his nationality, and which would be, he thought, most acceptable, if obtainable, when he should cast off his Indian toggery for the luxury of a bath. The court was a square space paved with flags, surrounded on all sides by the walls of apartments belonging to the residence. The portions on the south and east boasted of a second story with piazzas overlooking the pavement below. In the center grew a tall banana tree, its broad leaves over-reaching half the circumscribed limits of the place.

Beneath the eastern piazza was a stone shelf, upon which were the basins, and near by a huge jug of pottery filled with water from the swift-running Acequia that coursed along the western side of the plaza. Jose, who appeared to be the priest's right-hand man, approached with towels, and the guests proceeded to test the virtues of limestone water and soap as antidotes for the more visible evidences of a dusty journey. It was not a great while after their ablutions before the comida, or dinner, was announced by the ubiquitous Jose, who seemed to be everywhere and engaged in all work, obedient to whose summons the party repaired to the apartment across the hall from the sitting-room, and found a table moderately supplied with dishes of Mexican cookery. Two huge platters, one containing "chile con carne," red with its peppery infusion, and the other filled with frijoles, the Mexican national bean, occupied the prominent positions while a half dozen entrees, unnameable preperations, and a plate of smoking tortillas were ranged in the center.

"Take that seat, Senor," said Father Ignacio, pointing to the end of the table. You, Senor Raymond, occupy this one by me."

"Your cook, Father, must have anticipated you arrival, since he has gotten this dinner so quickly," said Senor Gonzales.

"Ah! There is where you are mistaken. My cook did not expect me at all this week. These dishes are from Senora Candelario's, who always has something good ready cooked for her customers. Senor Raymond, let me help you to some of this chile con carne, and frijoles."

Guy passed his plate, which was amply supplied with the savory compound, and the trio were soon discussing the excellence of the Candelario's dishes. The entrees were duly tested, but found little favor with the American guest, who, nevertheless, swallowed the quota each time the test was made, being determined to satisfy his curiosity on the subject of the Mexican menu. The chile con carne was a little hot, and indeed, several other dishes he had tasted contained more or less strong infusions of the favorite pepper. This caused a longing for water to cool the burning effect on his gums and throat, and as there was none in sight he signified to his host that a drink would be most acceptable. The services of Jose were again brought into requisition and the water produced, supplemented by wine and glasses Guy eagerly swallowed a couple of glasses of water and felt much relieved. With the subsidence of the burning he felt renewed courage to taste the contents of a very small saucer, which was the only dish of whose merits he had not become fully cognizant. He therefore reached for it and took a small quantity on his plate. The substance was minced to a fineness that defied any attempts at ocular analysis but its inviting green color evidently relegated it to the category of relishes. Being Mexican it would have been preposterous to doubt the presence of pepper; color green, it must therefore be green pepper and, thought Guy, "Anybody can eat it green, as the fiery property culminates at maturity and then it is essentially red."

Emboldened by this assumption, he carried the entire quantity on his plate to his mouth, feeling, while it was in transit, a relief that this was the last gout that the demands of an acquaintance with the menu Mexican would require of him for the present.

The effect was terrible. Color green? If he was not color-blind then the taste was red. For it seemed to him as he gulped down the *relish* that all the concentrated fires of an inferno had become incorporated in that saucer of verdant deception. Water streamed from his eyes. Strangulation, hiccough, prevented his frantic attempts to drink for a time. He made his exit from the room and to Jose out into the court. Senor Gonzales was nonplussed as to what had happened to the young man, but the priest was wiser as he had witnessed the act which had caused the trouble, and notwithstanding his sympathy for the sufferer he could not refrain from laughing heartily.

"What makes you laugh? I think it disgusting that a person should so gorge himself as to choke at table," said Senor Gonzales.

"Why, the poor fellow has not eaten so much," said the priest. "He simply tried to eat these minced chiltipines like he would any simple vegetable and that is what even Mexican throats could not stand. I'll go and fetch him back; a glass of wine will relieve him."

Guy, in a very little while, had regained his breath and suppressed the hiccoughs. He laved his face in the basin, and was about to accompany Father Ignacio back to the dining table, when he perceived a letter under the shelf on the pavement. Supposing it to be one of several that he saw Senor Gonzales drop before dinner, and which he inferred had been overlooked, he picked it up. It was addressed: "Senor Edourdo Gritton, San Antonio de Bexar."

On entering the room he found the senor sipping his wine and looking abstractedly across the table. That worthy did not appear to notice the entrance of the others, until Guy addressed him.

"Were you not, Senor, the bearer of this letter? I found it just now, near where you dropped the papers from your pocket."

Senor Gonzales reached for the letter and, on noting the superscription, scowled darkly, casting a look at Guy in which were blended inquiry and suspicion.

CHAPTER VII.

The month of September, 1836, found Texas ablaze with excitement over the relentless policy which the Mexican general government, impersonated in Santa Anna, manifested towards the American Texans who had settled as colonists under guarantees, by the Federal power, of all the rights and immunities incident to citizenship. San Antonio was at that time the headquarters of the military department with Colonel Ugartachea in command. The spirit of resistance to exactions, and resentment for the unreasonable withholding of those privileges of free government, which naturally accrue, and should keep pace with the progress and population of a free people, had become general throughout the State. The notes of preparation for the coming struggle filled the political atmosphere. The appointment of committees of safety, the secret accumulation of arms, the dispatch of messages to friends across the Sabine for assistance in any shape, constituted initial steps of the Texans. The Mexican commandant and his superiors were not slow to realize the brewing of a storm and, while they used all the arts of pacification to allay the suspicions of the turbulent colonists, the Mexican army was en route, in three divisions, with Texas the destination and coercion the object. Through spies they had singled out and demanded the surrender of the leaders of the war party, that they might be subject to the justice of a court-martial, and the tender mercies of a Mexican military official.

Already Captain Castonado with a troop of cavalry had attempted to remove a cannon from Bastrop to Bexar, but had been repulsed by the vigilant Texans, and the gun retained. Other collisions between the soldiery and the people had occurred at Goliad and on the coast, all of which tended to draw the lines between the military authority, which in fact had absorbed the civil, and the American colonists. San Antonio was therefore almost entirely deserted by the latter, the remaining few being kept under the most rigid surveillance. When Guy, therefore, later in the afternoon informed Father Ignacio of his intention to go out in the town for the purpose of disposing of his horse, saddle and bridle, to enable him to purchase the clothing he needed, he was advised by the friendly priest to allow Jose to perform that office for him.

"Perhaps he will prove a better trader than I am."

"It is not that supposition which prompted my suggestion, although Jose, from his wide acquaintance, doubtless would be more successful in making a good bargain. But, my son, the times are growing troublesome. Your people are at outs with the government, and are looked upon with suspicion by the authorities. So you see, amigo mio, I do not want you to run any risk by going out by yourself; a stranger you know, just come in town, will have to produce vouchers. Remain indoors today and I will see that, after, you can go where you please; of course, on your parole."

"What! Have I escaped from the Indians, only to find myself a prisoner? But tell me, good father, what you have heard from my people. Are they in arms against the government?"

"I cannot speak plainly. All I can tell you is, there is trouble coming, and my interest in you makes me anxious to have you do nothing that could compromise your safety."

"As you will then. Let Jose make the trade."

On the eastern side of Main plaza, about midway of the row of shops and apartments, was an establishment common to every Mexican town of even limited size, and deemed by the population as essential as the church, the tienda, or even the cock pit. The letters over the door spelled the words "Monte Pio," the Spanish for pawnbroker. The average Mexican would have a much greater idea of Heaven if he believed it contained a peculiarity of this nature. To the Monte Pio he hies for his stake to test his fortune at the game of monte. If the gnawings of hunger are about to goad him to desperation, the Monte Pio is often his saviour, by making an advance, however small, on almost any article of jewelry, dress or property, be it the very shoes from his feet or the snaked sombrero which surmounts his cranium. The Mexican Monte Pio is different from his foreign brother. He will accept the most apparently valueless things in the world, which may, by any conceivable chance, be made applicable, not only to personal necessities, but to the most inconceivable eccentricities of taste. He is therefore a benefactor; and to the Aztec race, a positive necessity. Imagine, for a moment, a town in the sister republic, boasting a few thousands or a few hundreds of people, and no Monte Pio. Preposterous! It may have no church, nor a regular Piccadilla stand, nor even a cock pit. But the Monte Pio, with his dark apocento, his jumble of stock, his odds and ends, his indiscriminate display of toggery, arms, jewelry, spurs, bedding, blankets, sombreros and what not, with his suave manners and patronizing style, is an indispensable requisite.

Jose, on being informed of the duty which would be required of him, readily signified his willingness to render the service to the young American. As major domo of the popular priest of San Fernando, he was known to every man, woman and child in Bexar, thereby possessing an influence among the ordinary people that was often potent, where failure would have attended efforts from more pretentious sources. He held intimate connection with the father, who ministered to their spiritual necessities, who entered into all their sports, encouraged the parades on holidays, their furious riding on "El dia de San Juan," the ante-Christmas lanterns, the ludicro-dramatic performance of the pastores, and various and sundry celebrations of fiestas without number. Hence his weight in the community. He was envied by the class from whose ranks he was drafted, but the feeling was dwarfed by an awe for the importance of his office. With the Monte Pio he was solid, and to be solid in this direction was the ultimathule of the ordinary Mexican. There was, however, a purpose in this solidity, as there are purposes in all strong manifestations without the pale of the affections. The purpose, of course, was with the Monte Pio. His business, in spite of the role we granted it as a benefaction, possessed features not in harmony with ethics prescribed by holy church. Therefore, to avoid the anathemas of that institution for possible and probably lapses, for deviations from the perpendicular of rectitude, for sundry grinding exactions, amounting to positive oppression, Jose was propitiated at all times and on all occasions. Jose was near the padre. He could stifle complaint. He could smooth over reports and restrain persistence by timely compromise.

Jose, therefore, when he found that he had a bargain to make, immediately thought of the Monte Pio, his refuge in all difficulties pecuniary.

On the afternoon in question, a knot of ciudadanos were grouped in front of the tienda del Monte Pio. The characteristic grave expressions of the silent, apathetic race of which they were individuals, were worn by the faces of the party, as they conversed almost in monosyllables, and ejected from lips or nostrils the curling, white smoke of their ciragetas. The plaza and streets were nearly deserted by the populace, most of whom were still indoors, indulging in the conventional siesta or not yet fully aroused from its lethargic influence.

"I hear that Father Ignacio returned this morning," said one of the group, to his nearest companion, as he completed the artistic rolling of a fresh cigareta and motioned for a light.

"I saw him crossing the Military plaza coming in. He was accompanied by another gentlemanly-looking man, and a curiously dressed fellow, a decidedly Indian dress and a fair skin. I wonder who it could have been?"

"Where were you, Manuel?" queried another. "I saw the party myself. They passed very close to where I was, and, if I mistake not, I know the gentlemanly fellow. If it was not General Almonte it was his ghost in citizen's dress."

"Why should he or his ghost want to dress like a citizen? These officers are never guilty of being out of uniform. They are as vain of gold lace as a peacock is of his tail."

"Sometimes it is policy to travel without being known. Besides, El Presedente may have sent him on some secret service. I saw the same man, that was with Father Ignacio, walking with Captain Castonado, going to headquarters. I am almost certain it is Almonte."

"I wonder if Castonado informed him how the Americans bluffed him at Bastrop. He ought to have his gold lace pulled off, after such an expedition."

"You never tire of scoffing at our officers and soldiers. You should go and join these Texan-Americans. Do you know, Manuel, that you are suspected of having sympathy for the other side?"

"Let them suspect. I have done nothing except to condemn mismanagement and cowardice. I have received and expect no favors from the powers that be. They persecuted Juan Seguin with suspicions until he was driven to the other side. Let them look to it that Manuel Ruiz is not forced to follow his example."

"This is but the braggadocio of a would-be traitor. Would you help the gringos in an attempt to destroy our government?"

"Call it what you please, Sancho, but the Mexican who would prefer the unscrupulous rule of military satraps to the blessings of a popular government sinks so far below the traitor that he is not fit to have a country to betray."

"Have you no pride of race?"

"Pride of race can never exist in a race of peons. And this is what we are coming to, under His Excellenza El Presedente."

"Here comes Jose. He will tell us if it was Almonte."

The major domo here rode up mounted on Guy's pony, with the bridle and saddle that the latter had captured in the fight with the Mexicans. He saluted the bystanders, all of whom he doubtless knew by name. They indolently returned his salutation of "Buenas tardes." Sancho having propounded the question to elicit the desired information as to the identity of Senor Gonzales, Jose, dismounting, merely repeated the latter name, looked wise, and placed his finger on his lips, as if to enjoin a discontinuance of such inquiries.

Sancho was satisfied with the pantomime, and turning to Ruiz, said:

"You see I was right."

The Monte Pio was just rising from a siesta on the floor of his shop, when Jose entered, having converted a pile of blankets into a pallet for the purpose of taking his daily nap. He greeted his visitor pleasantly, made particular inquiry after the health of the padre, about the cause of their delayed return from the Rio Grande, and concerning many other topics suggested by their intimate relations and interests.

"I see you have a new horse and outfit," said the Monte Pio.

"That is not mine. It is about that same horse and outfit that I have come to see you this afternoon, amigo mio," said Jose, putting his hand lightly on the other's shoulder and looking quizzingly in his face.

"It is a pony of good appearance, and the saddle has been a fine one."

"I am glad to hear you say that," said Jose, "for I have come to trade you the horse and outfit."

"Well, in that case, I will have to look closer. It occurs to me the pony is pretty well along in years, but I must admit the silver mounting of the saddle."

"What will you give for all?"

"For the pony, saddle and bridle; let me see—diez, quinze, diez, y sies——"

"Come, compadre, what are you talking about. I don't want to pawn them; I want to sell them."

"You don't think I would pay that much on them in pawn. It's what they are worth, that I was calculating."

"We can't trade then. I know Father Ignacio will be disappointed when I tell him the miserable price you offered."

"Is it for the padre you are making the trade?"

"For Father Ignacio himself."

"De veras?"

"De veras."

"Bueno. What say you to twenty pesos?"

"You are getting stingy, as you grow richer. You had better keep on the good side of the padre."

"Better say on your good side, for Father Ignacio is not the one to be bribed by the price of a horse. If I have escaped censure for certain piccadillos, it is because you stood between me and him for a price. Come, Jose, name your amount."

Jose, after a moment's deliberation, took the Monte Pio aside and engaged him in an inaudible conversation. After some gesticulation and seeming difference, they arrived at some understanding. The pony was stripped of his saddle and bridle, which were brought into the shop and deposited, while the horse was led away around the corner of the street next to the river. The major domo, having concluded the trade to his satisfaction, left the shop of the Monte Pio and, after bandying a few words with the men assembled around the door, departed in the direction of the priest's house.

CHAPTER VIII.

About midway between the plaza and the bridge, on the north side of Main street, stood a house retired a little from the thoroughfare, and almost touching the bank of the stream in its rear. In its front marched, with measured stride, a barefoot soldier with a tattered uniform. His long musket rested upon his shoulders, its bright bayonet flashing in the sunlight, as he turned at the end of his beat. A veranda extended the full length of the building facing the river and separated from it by a parterre of shrubbery and fig trees. The afternoon sun was casting shadows from walls and foliage over the grounds, and upon the blue and deep current that passed in graceful eddies under the steep embankment. In a rude and capacious cage of native workmanship, swinging from a limb of a tree almost touching the house, a mocking-bird was caroling his wildest notes, to which one of his untamed species made answer from a willow on the further bank, under which a lot of Mexican women, washing clothes and chattering ever and anon, formed a picturesque group.

The veranda was occupied by three men, who were seated in apparent consultation around a table upon which were papers and writing material. One, a thin-visaged, dark-complexioned man, dressed in the uniform of a Colonel of the Mexican Army, occupied the central position. He sat stiff and upright in his chair, while his features wore a worried expression that gathered the deep wrinkles to his forehead. On his left, in the uniform of a captain, was a young officer of quite a careless mein, indicated by his expression and the easy, lounging attitude. The third would have been easily recognized by the reader as the Senor Gonzales, introduced in a former chapter, while the traveling companion of Father Ignacio. He still wore the garb of a civilian, and had lost none of that immobility of countenance which seemed to repel all approaches of familiarity. The latter was the first to speak.

"This letter from Senor Gritton does not place you in a very favorable light, as commander of a responsible expedition, Captain Castonado."

"The opinion of a mere citizen amounts to little in the case since he was ignorant of the instructions I had to guide me. The Colonel, here, gave me my orders, which were to avoid all hostile collisions with the people, and if I could not succeed in getting possession of the cannon by a show of force, to retire and await further orders."

"The Captain is correct," said the Colonel. "It has always been my opinion that a pacific and liberal policy towards these colonists would accomplish what harsh measures could never effect. They have emigrated from a country where every concession is made to individual liberty that is consistent with the ends of mild and popular government. This should be patent to you, General Almonte, who received your education in the United States."

"With your policy in force these Americans would not only root out every vestige of Mexican customs and interest, but would soon grow strong enough to threaten the States on the other side of the Rio Grande. Force must be used, and that soon, to check their audacity. General Cos will soon be here, and he will be followed by two divisions, the last and larger under the command of Santa Anna himself. The President is determined on subjugation and, if need be, annihilation, deeming it necessary for the security of this territory to the Republic. Your policy, Colonel Ugartachea, is a wrong one in dealing with the kind of stuff the colonists are made of."

"If my theory is wrong in practice, it is right from a liberal or republican standpoint."

"How many names of ringleaders does Gritton's list contain?" asked Almonte.

"It is here among these papers. You can examine it yourself."

While Almonte—for Senor Gonzales was no other than the noted staff officer of the Mexican dictator—was looking over the lists handed him, a soldier appeared and delivered a document to the commanding officer. Directing the messenger to retire and await orders, the latter opened the papers which, having read, he passed to Almonte.

"That means war, and no mistake," said the latter. "I know this Henry Smith."

"The President should be advised of this move without delay, and a courier should be dispatched at once, with your endorsement."

"No need of that, Colonel," said Almonte. "I am to return to Mexico myself within twenty-four hours, and will see Santa Anna as soon as a courier could reach him."

"Your stay is brief."

"Necessarily so. The object of my mission here has been more than realized by what I have learned. Here is a communication for Edward Gritton. A reliable courier disguised in the clothes of an ordinary citizen must place it in his hands. I will rely on your judgment in the execution of the matter."

Ugartachea took the letter, promising to have it safely in the hands of the party whose address it bore.

We will leave the officers to discuss the situation, which appeared to be growing critical for Mexican supremacy in Texas. The courier had brought the news of the action of the council in its issue of a circular, designed to conciliate the Texas tribes of Indians, of the return of Stephen F. Austin from Mexico, and the warlike resolutions at Brazoria.

When Jose returned home he found Guy just emerging from the luxury of a bath, and the clothing which the former brought came in good time for him to try on. The major domo had indeed been lavish in his selection, not only in quality and style, but in proportions. The first suit he got hold of was sufficiently ample for an individual of exaggerated corporosity, and the second and third gained on the first in length, to compensate for shrinkage in amplitude. He began to despair of a fit as Jose re-entered. The latter gave his assistance and by their joint efforts, a suit cap-a-pie, was found that, by dint of a little tightening here and a little altering there, could be made to serve the purpose of our hero until something better could be accomplished in the matter of attire.

"You don't look like a Lipan any more, senor. Your hat is just the thing and sets off your handsome face."

"Jose, you are a flatterer."

"De veras; you are handsome in your new clothes."

"It is the clothes that makes the man," said Guy. "My father often said that dress had much to do with our destiny."

"Your father was a fine looking man?"

"He was the type of perfect manhood," said Guy, with a sigh, as memory recalled the last time he had seen the subject of their conversation.

"Was he smart?" continued Jose.

"Aye, he was a philosopher. A man whose life was a period of study."

"Like el padre, Ignacio. He always has his nose in a book, when he is not attending to his church duties."

"There, Jose, I think I have put the finishing touch to my dress. The clothes are so decidedly Mexican that I could be taken for one of your countrymen. I wonder if Senor Gonzales would know me if he met me on the street."

"Certainly. That face of yours, and those locks of wavy golden hair that any senorita might envy, would tell on you."

"Well, as I have no cause to disguise myself, there is little desire to conceal my identity. I am, therefore, Senor Jose, transformed, through the medium of clothes, from El Bravo, the Lipan, to Guy

Raymond, the American, Mexicanized by appearances. I have neglected to thank you for thus advancing me several degrees nearer to civilization, or to ask you about the success you met with in trading off my pony and saddle."

"These clothes you have on are a part of the trade. In addition I got twenty-five dollars, which will be at your service in the morning."

"You are a pretty good trader, Jose. Count on five dollars of that amount as your own in payment for your trouble."

"Senor Raymond is too good. I did not charge anything."

"But you will accept."

"If you will not tell Father Ignacio that you paid me."

"Never fear, we will keep our own secrets. While I think of it, Jose, I have lost something which I highly prize. It is a medal of the Virgin, attached to a string of fine beads, and belonged to an Indian girl who saved my life. When I left the Lipan village, this girl gave me that buckskin pouch, full of dried venison and in it I found this medal I spoke of. She evidently intended it for me, and that I should discover it after our parting."

"The girl loved you, then."

"She loved me too well, Jose; better than I deserved."

"Most girls would love Senor Raymond."

"Let us talk about the medal. You have not seen it?"

"No, Senor. When did you see it last?"

"Not since the night before I reached your camp."

"You may have lost it then before you joined us."

"Perhaps."

Guy and the major domo, continuing their conversation, moved to the sidewalk and took seats looking out on the plaza, over which the shades of evening were falling. The population had moved from indoors, and there were a goodly lot of passers and groups scattered here and there. Occasionally one or more female figures, almost enveloped in capacious rebosas, would pass out of the church and take their way in different directions, conversing in their musical language. Jose explained to his companion many points about the actions and customs of his people, that proved interesting to the listener. In reply to the question if church was going on at that hour in San Fernando, he explained that the women he had seen issuing from its portals had been confessing, and that Father Ignacio had been there all the afternoon hearing confessions.

"Do any of the men confess their sins?" asked Guy. "I did not see one among the number that came out of the church."

"The men do not care much for their souls. Once a year is about as often as most of them attend to their duties."

"As with all nations, the goodness is all in the women."

"The men of our country like fast living, fine horses, and to bet at monte; they have not much time to pray."

"So much the worse for them, I fear," said Guy. "For the sake of morals the uneducated should have some sort of religion. I should like to see a game of monte, as I have read of the passion your countrymen possess for betting at it."

"If Senor Raymond will allow me, I will take him to see a game tonight."

"I will accept your offer, Jose. Here comes Father Ignacio from the church. Jose, the father is a good man."

"He is a living saint."

CHAPTER IX.

Late on an October afternoon, along a prairie pathway that led eastwardly to where a line of scattered timber fringed the nearer side of a watercourse, rode a solitary horseman. Miles of valley, in unbroken level, disclosed naught beside the golden waving grass glinting in the sunlight and clumps of mesquite here and there, lending variety to the vista. Opposite, the bold hills impinged upon the stream and marked its course by the red border which periodical torrents had worn to precipitous banks. The ambling gait of the pony swayed the rider in easy motion from side to side, keeping perfect time to a monotonous nasal sound of a Mexican song that issued in low notes from his lips:

"Yo no soy de aqui, soy de Carecel
Solo me devierto, con mi pito, real.
Este pito, real, Yo me lo halle
Si yo no lo gusto, yo lo vendere."

Furtive glances, to the left and rear, were cast occasionally by his dark eyes, from under the broad brim of his sombrero. The jogging pace of the animal at length brought him to a deep gully, that dived below the surface and coursed away towards the run, deepening and widening, until lost in the level forming the wide, dry bed of the stream. Suddenly, quickening his pace, he urged his animal into the depression, and soon horse and rider became lost to view.

"See, Ducio! There is a horseman beyond, and he's coming from a suspicious direction."

"Where?"

"Across the creek. Have ye no eyes, man?"

"I see him now. He is a greaser, too."

"As if that was so hard to make out! Step back here and don't let him see us, until he gets closer. Do ye mind?"

"I don't see him now. He must be in one of those big washes. He disappeared just as you spoke."

"He got a sight of you; that's what's the matter. You'd be a bother on any scout. You are too slow, man. When I told ye to come back out of sight, ye should ha' moved."

"What's the difference, Mr. Trigg? If you want to get to close quarters with him, we can do so, whether he sees us or not."

"What do ye know about close quarters? If it was an open sea and ship and ship the lightest heels would win. Close quarters if it was wanted. But in these gulleys and hiding places ye might have a race horse and it wouldn't do no good in overhauling a greaser that's out of sight. Ye should obey orders, man."

"If you will remain here I'll bet you the best league of land in Texas I will bring you that fellow in thirty minutes."

"You've got so many leagues of land to bet away and it's been a bare month or six weeks that ye came to Texas, and wid more brass in yer face than money in yer pocket."

'Brass is sometimes the very best kind of capital, and often succeeds where money and modesty would go to the dogs."

"Well, well! Maybe you are right, but let us ride for that Mexican, and see what he's after doing, coming from the course he did."

One of the speakers was a man of middle age, and powerful build, the other younger and of light figure, but athletic mould. The former had a light ruddy complexion, suited to the nationality which his brogue betrayed. The latter was dark almost to swarthiness which, with his physiognomy, indicated a genealogy that had touched upon the dubious bounds of some race darker than Caucasion. The two men had been resting under a tree on the opposite bank of the creek towards which the Mexican was approaching, while their saddled horses grazed near at hand. They were scouts sent out from the force of Texans, encamped on the Cibolo creek, under the command of Stephen F. Austin. The younger had seen the Mexican disappear in the gully, as has been learned from their conversation. The two were not long in filling their saddles and setting out at a rapid pace for the creek, distant a hundred yards or so. The elder took a course to intercept the Mexican below the gully, while he who was called Ducio by his companion, went towards a point above.

At a distance not exceeding four miles above the spot where Mr. Trigg and his companion had observed the strange horseman, across the arroyo, and situated on the margin of the same run, was a mott of timber skirting the crescent bank of a waterhole, made by the sudden deepening of the bed of the creek and the consequent retention of its waters, which, in dryer seasons, sought the rocky strata lying beneath its sands. Opposite the grove, the banks rose to the proportions of a bluff, contrasting with the easy slope that ascended through the timber and terminated in the open prairie, where the bright silver of the horizon shone cheerily through the foliage. A more picturesque location could not have been chosen for an encampment, for here was cooling shade and water, fuel for light and cooking, protection by the circling bluffs and stately pecans, from wind and storm, while out upon the plain the tall, rich grass made a wealth of pasturage. It was not then strange that here, on this October afternoon, we should find groups of men, wagons and grazing animals. The first were scattered here and there in every conceivable occupation, or in no occupation whatever. The wagons, two in number, stood where the timber touched the opening, while the horses were beyond on the prairie, secured by rope or hopple. A single wall tent occupied a central position, facing the opposite highland, and gave additional shelter to numerous and indiscriminate articles which were disclosed by the raised sides of the canvas. Several fires through the wood, each of which formed a nucleus for a group of men, sent up columns of smoke, denser where the green fuel resisted the struggling flame, and light and blue where the blazes rose and crackled through dryer twigs. The absence of almost all appliances for camping, save those essentials which, however rude and improvised, must follow the frontiersman and constitute his paraphernalia, for all occasions and uses, would have been noticeable to an observer studying the personnel of the camp and endeavoring, from their surroundings and equipments, to pronounce their intent, or unravel any mystery their presence might suggest. The men were Americans, in the sense of a Saxon origin, and were evidently Texan colonists, in the verbiage of the Mexican federal statutes, which defined their rights as well as their duties to the central government. They were a hardy, careless-looking set, embracing all ages, from beardless youth up to the years when the furrowed brow and sprinkled gray above the temples tell that the vigor of manhood but resists the encroachment of time. The pioneers of civilization, they descended a step or two below its plane, from sheer gravitation towards the wilder influences of a novel situation, devoid of many restraints imposed by social order.

The nearest fire, as the camp would be approached from the south, was surrounded by a party whose hilarity and occupations did not suggest any great degree of gravity in the expedition that had called them afield, or that apprehensions of a serious movement was in contemplation calculated to termination in disaster or dearly earned success. Over the coals, all aglow beside a fallen tree, hung two quarters and a saddle of venison, which two men were tending, while a third, watching their operations, sat upon the unignited portion of the trunk. Near by, on the spread surface of a highly colored Mexican blanket, four others were engaged at cards. From these came frequent ejaculations, with occasional bursts of laughter.

"Don't you see that meat is burning on this side? Two cooks for that little quantity of meat ought to keep it from charring like that."

"Why didn't you say it was burning sooner? You have been sitting there on that log looking straight at it, and kept your mouth shut," said one of the men who was tending the meat.

"It is something new to charge Jones with keeping his mouth shut," said the other cook.

"He hasn't talked much since the elephant story," replied his comrade.

"What elephant story?"

"That is a fact, Perry, you were on the scout the day Jones gave us the elephant story."

"The last one I heard him tell was that one about fleas. He took a big thing to lie about this time," said he who was addressed as Perry.

"Oh! Jones believes in jumping from one extreme to the other. It tends to diversify his romancing."

"What in thunder could he have to say about elephants?"

"Why, he related that while he was in the service of the East India Company, he was walking out one day in the jungles at the foot of the Hymalayas, when he came to a bridge crossing a river, and while he was seated there, eight hundred elephants ran across it at full speed."

"What a whopper!"

"Couldn't a man see elephants crossing a bridge?" asked Jones. "I don't see anything very strange in that. I have heard you tell worse yarns than that, Perry."

"Must have been a powerful bridge," said Perry. "Why, you numskull! Don't you know that eight hundred soldiers crossing a bridge without breaking step would shake it up. Of course you stood there and counted the elephants. Why didn't you tell something more probable? Fir instance, that you saw that cow of yours, which used to give two gallons of milk out of each teat, jump over the moon."

"Oh, give him a rest. The boys rode him on a rail for telling that elephant story."

"I don't ask you to plead for me, Mr. Tip Hamilton, and may be you will be sorry yet for the part you took in that same rail-riding."

"Oh, Oh! He is threatening me, boys. You simpleton, 'twas Ducio who led the lynchers. I did the laughing; it excited my risibility."

"And Mr. Ducio Halfen will have to settle for it," continued Jones, doggedly.

"The Jones is growing dangerous," said Hamilton. "He will constitute a phalanx when we join issue with the Mexicans. Here comes Ducio and the noble Trigg. As I live! They lead a scion of the Aztecs."

"They've got a Greaser," exclaimed several voices, as the party rode into camp, the Mexican between them. A crowd soon gathered about the prisoner, who sat stolidly returning the glances of his captors while they indulged in a multitude of expressions and badinage, in regard to himself and the cause he was presumed to represent.

"Gents! Perhaps he is envoy extraordinary and minister plenipotentiary from the veritable Santy himself, offering us the olive branch, conditioned by our return to our homes," said Tip Hamilton.

"If he is a spy, the only branch we will have any use for is the one right over his head," said another.

Mr. Trigg here interposed and directed the prisoner who had dismounted, to follow him.

The capture of a plain Mexican was no very important affair, especially as in the present instance, the object of such sudden interest was apparently a ranchero of the type and dress of an ordinary herder. His appearance would have caused but little notice, had not a rumor gone the rounds, traceable to Ducio Halfen as authority, that important documents had been found on the person of the fellow. The men, grouped about, discussed the capture, a few following Mr. Trigg and his charge towards the wall tent, where sat several men who had been partaking of the evening meal. Tip Hamilton, in his grandiloquent way, was entertaining quite a crowd and, by intimation of a grave importance attached to the documents taken from the Mexican, lent tenfold interest to the affair in the minds of his hearers. The truth was Tip knew no more than the reader of the prisoner or of anything taken from his possession. He was a character that stood boldly out in the individuality of the camp. He was large in person, quite good looking, and seemed to be well informed on any subject that would arise in conversation with his fellows; and was inclined to so amplify as to exceed all reasonable bounds and draw in matter far from germane to the original discussion, but so blended by grandal and insensible shades of differences, as to render his digressions pardonable if noticed at all. His pedantry, so manifest in his language, would have elicited a contempt from the more intelligent of his comrades, had it been severed from his inimitable manner and facial expression.

To auditors not blessed beyond the rudiments which constitute an avoidance of illiteracy, Hamilton was so far a conundrum, as his language would veil his meaning in mysteryy. He was an adventurer, like many who had left their State behind, to seek in the new field the something that persistently refused to turn up, notwithstanding long, patient days of waiting in the old haunts. His education was due to a remarkable memory, more than to express application in his school days, and he retained what had been acquired despite an indolence only half overcome by parental injunction.

The world has many such. The Southern States had many examples of superficial acquirement, as was exemplified in Tipton Hamilton. Perry, whom Jones had taunted with a possession of his own infirmity, was not wholly guiltless. The advantage rested with the former, inasmuch as he kept more or less within the bounds of probability, while Jones, in his drafts upon the imagination, had no thought of the result, which even a lax application of reason to his statements would produce. Perry was a stripling, nearly of age, brave when led. He was of a good Kentucky family which had several sons in the colony all, like Perry, venturesome and marked by characteristic generosity which this, the youngest scion, carried to extremes. He would not have hesitated to bestow upon another the only article or the last cent he possessed.

He of the vivid imagination was in citizenship cosmopolitan, by his own testimony, but saw the light first under the cross of St. George and by the comity of nations would be entitled to British protection. No known portions of the globe that he had not visited or could not relate some story about. His penchant for invention had become a byword in the camp. Jones was held in special aversion by Ducio Halfen on account of a yarn spun at the expense of the dark creoles, of whom the latter was a true type, in which the inference to be drawn was that African blood was responsible for the hue of their complexion.

Ducio doubtless owed his color to the source indicated, as there is an unnameable something which tells of the admixture in every real instance. But that the blood of Ham courses in the veins of all dark-skinned natives of French or Spanish colonies cannot be granted, inasmuch as European contact with other dark races has left behind a progeny who claim the appellation "Creole." Ducio may have been ignorant of the facts of his birth or family antecedents, or he may have chosen to deny a lineage, when to admit it would have placed him under the social ban. At any rate, he fiercely resented the implication and vented his spleen by actively assisting to ride his traducer on a rail.

Ducio Halfen was a rascal, and his character was as wanting in the elements of honor and honesty as his name was devoid of euphony. He had made his appearance in Texas in company with Hamilton and together they had joined the volunteers previous to their coming to the present camp on the Cibolo.

The momentary excitement caused by Mr. Trigg's arrival with his prisoner subsided when the latter was dismissed from the headquarters under charge of the guard. Evening closed into darkness broken here and there through the camp by the failing glow of the fires. As the night grew apace, the sounds became fewer; the low laugh and voices in conversational tones soon gave place to the sentry's tramp, the neigh of a horse, or the march of a guard relief, and the Texans slept.

CHAPTER X.

When Mr. Trigg brought his prisoner to that portion of the camp where stood the tent, he found himself in the presence of the party which had just finished their repast, and whose attention became directed to him as he approached with his charge.

"Who have we here, Mr. Trigg?" asked one of the party who sat with his hands clasped in front of him, while the thumbs made nervous revolutions around each other.

"We caught this Mexican about three miles below, on the creek, and as he failed to satisfy me that he was on right business, I brought him to camp. These letters were in a pocket sewed on the inside of his shirt."

"A suspicious circumstance," said the other.

."That's what I thought, General," replied Mr. Trigg, handing the letters to him he called General. The latter took the documents and, after looking at the address and the seals on the opposite sides, turned one carelessly over to the man by his side, who read deliberately:

"Senor Edward Gritten, San Antonio de Bexar."

"What do you think of it, Fannin?"

"The name adds to the suspicion, but the contents will doubtless explain everything."

"We will examine the contents after a while. I will interrogate the fellow and hear what he has to say for himself."

"Mr. Trigg, bring your prisoner nearer, General Austin wants to question him," said Fannin.

The Mexican approached when ordered and the general, after a few moment's consultation with Fannin, addressed him in Spanish.

'Where are you from?"

"Casa Blanca."

"Where is Casa Blanca?"

"It is the rancho of Don Juan Seguin."

"How far is that from here?"

"About six leagues."

"Where did you get this letter?"

"Don Juan gave it to me."

"For what purpose?"

"To give to some American who might be passing east, to take to the man to whom it is written.

"Did you have any particular business out here other than the delivery of this letter?"

"Si, senor."

"What was it?"

"Hunting two horses that have been missing."

"Why, Mr. Trigg, that's pretty straight. Did he tell you the same story?"

"Yes, General, but this man is fixed up for the occasion. He is no ranchero."

"Open the letters, General, and there will be no need of more questioning," said Captain Fannin. "This fellow knows that Juan Seguin is a friend of our cause and his idea is that the seal of a private letter from him to that address will be sacred to us. Gritton is a suspected man and even if there existed a strong probability that Seguin is the sender of this letter, the gravity of the present aspect of affairs would warrant us to make ourselves acquainted with its contents."

"You are right. My idea was the same, but I preferred to have your expressed opinion, before acting in the matter."

So saying, General Austin broke the seal of one and then of the other, and glancing along the lines, his expression scarcely changed until every word had been scanned, when a light smile played over his features, as he passed the papers to the other officer.

"Mr. Trigg, you will please see that this man is closely guarded."

Trigg was about to turn away with his Mexican, when the General called.

"Hold! Did you find nothing else on the prisoner?"

"I did; this silver medal and beads were in his pocket."

"Just keep it, Mr. Trigg. It is of no importance."

Mr. Trigg placed the trinket in his pockets and conducting the Mexican to another part of the camp, turned him over to the guard.

When the two officers were left alone they entered the tent, where the General carefully read over the letters; then, folding and placing them in his pocket, he remarked:

"This places Gritton where he properly belongs—among our enemies—and his position emphasized by a stigma; for he is really the spy of the Mexicans."

"He must not be allowed to escape, but I fear it is too late to apprehend him, as he was to have set out for the coast some time this week. I will write to San Filipe and if you will be good enough to select a reliable man from your command as messenger, I will be obliged."

"I have the very man in my mind, who will fill the bill," said Captain Fannin, leaving the tent.

Stephen F. Austin had been encamped but a day or two on the Cibolo with his band of a few hundred Texans, when the capture of the Mexican by Mr. Trigg occurred. His presence with such a force constitutes a page of Texas history and was a forerunner of tragic scenes and deeds which, culminating at San Jacinto, made the name of Texan soldier the synonym of valor and the realization of reckless daring. The reader will have recognized one of the letters whose contents decided the detention of the Mexican, as the same which Guy Raymond found at the priest's house and returned to Senor Gonzales, who had dropped it. The presence of the silver medal, taken from the prisoner, will perhaps be made clear in the progress of our story.

Austin was waiting in his present position for reinforcements and supplies before making further movements toward the investment of San Antonio, where General Cos had arrived and was preparing for a vigorous defense.

After Mr. Trigg had been relieved of the custody of the Mexican, he repaired to his mess with the intention to rest his limbs, made weary by a long day's scout. Trigg was a hale and hearty Irishman, not more than fifty, and consequently in the prime of a sound manhood. He had seen service, however. What particular adventures he had met with were not known to many, and perhaps to none of his present comrades. He was rather reticent when the boys were spinning yarns, although he had related some few tales of the sea, which he seemed to have followed. In these stories, however, he would not place himself as the hero, nor even as a witness, evading all questions of his listeners as to his connection with the incidents related. His mess had great respect for him, and always spoke of him as Mr. Trigg.

The first three characters introduced to the reader as engaged in conversation over the roasting venison belonged to his mess, as did also Ducio Halfen. The latter was no favorite with him, although he expressed his feelings no further than to repel any familiarity on his part. For Jones he entertained a good-humored contempt, while he was amused at Hamilton and liked Perry. The latter was awake when Mr. Trigg sought his blanket, and tried to draw his friend out on the subject of the capture; but his curiosity was good-naturedly resisted, with an injunction to go to sleep and he would tell him the whole story on the morrow.

"Don't be so curious, my boy; it's tired I am now, and talking will disturb our neighbors."

"I just wanted to know something about the silver medal you found on him," pleaded Perry.

"Who was telling you?"

"Tip Hamilton saw you show it to General Austin."

"Tip is the devil's own; he is always knowing too much."

"He only said that he saw it."

"Well, it's only a medal of the Blessed Virgin hung to a string of beads."

"Which virgin is that, Mr. Trigg?"

"You young heathen! Not to know who the Blessed Virgin is. Sure, she's the holy mother of the Saviour, and it's her picture that's on the medal."

"What's the good of it, Mr. Trigg?"

"It's a keepsake, and if it is blessed by a priest, it is fine to wear around your neck to keep harm away from a man."

"I never heard of that before," said Perry, wonderingly.

"Because it's a heathen you are."

At this point of the conversation the tall, dark figure of a man appeared in front of the dying embers close at hand, and the voice of Captain Fannin called to the senior of the two, in an undertone:

"Is that you, Captain?"

"Mr. Trigg," responded the Captain, "I want young Perry to go on courier duty at once. Where is he?"

"Right here, sir," replied Perry, rising as he spoke. "Where am I to be sent?"

"You will get your instructions at headquarters. Come immediately."

"All right, Captain," said Perry, "just as soon as I get my shoes on."

"I wonder what they want me for?" he asked of Mr. Trigg, when the Captain had disappeared.

"You will know soon enough, my boy."

When Perry was about to leave the other said to him:

"Perry, come back here before you leave camp. If it is going where I think you are, I want to send a message by you."

Perry, stating that the nature of the duty awaiting him necessitated his return to get his saddle, blanket and bridle, left to get his orders. When he entered the tent, the general and his subordinate were sitting by a rough box, on which lay a package which the former was sealing with a piece of wax, ignited from a dim tallow candle whose feeble light threw flitting shadows on the canvas. When he had completed the operation he turned to the youth and asked:

"Are you well acquainted with the country between here and San Filipe?"

"Every mile of it, sir."

"Got a pretty good horse?"

"He is a pony, but fat and well winded."

"When can you be in San Filipe?"

"It is one hundred and eighty miles."

"About——well?"

"By changing horses once, in three days."

"Can you get a change?"

"I can at Beason's, on Peach Creek."

"Take this package and deliver it to Governor Smith as soon as you can. Be discreet; tell nobody your business or destination."

"Can't I tell Mr. Trigg to what place I am going?"

"Tell no one.'

"But——"

"No buts, sir! Captain, we have got hold of the wrong man."

"No! general," rejoined Perry, swelling up at the reflection. "If it's orders not to tell, torture won't wring it from me."

"Ah! that sounds more like it," General Austin said. "Now, sir, show what metal you are made of. Stay—the countersign is 'Velasco'."

Perry was rather mortified that he could not reveal to Mr. Trigg his destination, as he understood that his friend wanted to send a message by him, provided he was going to the right place. He was rather moody, therefore, when he returned, and Mr. Trigg asked him if he was to go to San Felipe.

"You must not be angry with me, Mr. Trigg. The general said I could not even tell you."

"He is particular! Well, my boy, obey orders if it costs you friends, and true friends won't be out with you long, when it is found that you have done your duty."

"If you have anything to say to me I can listen to you, and if by any chance it comes in my power to serve you while I am gone, I can do so, no matter where I have been ordered to."

"Go fetch your horse, my boy, if it's to be quick you are, and I'll study the matter over while you're gone."

While Perry was gone for his pony, Mr. Trigg rose and chunked the fire, adding a few twigs to make it blaze. Then unrolling an extra blanket, which had been serving him for a pillow, he took from the inside fold a small wallet fastened with strap and buckle. This he undid and drew forth some papers, which he inspected by the dim firelight. Selecting one and laying it aside, he replaced the others, and from another pocket took something, and holding it up for a moment's scrutiny, put it with the paper.

"I'll send it to the child and the good mother whose image it bears will take her under her protection while I am away."

He spoke the words in an undertone, as the medal with its string of snowy beads was deposited with the letter, for such was the paper he had taken from the wallet. By a better light the heavy handwriting of the address would have disclosed the name of

"Stella Raymond."

Mr. Trigg, having replaced his roll of blanket, seated himself and leaned his head forward on his hands above the glowing coals, which seemed to invite him to rumination.

The consuming element at his feet, so typical of life in its mutations, set him to musing. Perhaps he had, in youthful anticipation, felt the little flame of hope that began to grow in size and brightness as the kindling of ambition had been supplied to feed it still higher. How it had increased to a vivid light, and then become suddenly checked by the green, incombustible fuel of mistaken judgment or misplaced confidence, and had shrunk away beneath the fumes of disappointment, or the blinding smoke of despair. Often by unremitting efforts the blaze is re-established at the expense of humid eyes and bitter experience, resulting in the cheery glow, enduring for a time, perhaps for a long period, then failing slowly, imperceptibly, until the ruddy coals have paled, and we think and wonder, and while yet we wonder the dying embers become cold, dead ashes.

Whatever may have been his reflections, Mr. Trigg gave vent to an occasional sigh, as his gaze was riveted to the fire, and he repeatedly muttered to himself. He finally arose and peering through the darkness, rendered more impenetrable from his long gaze at the bright coals, he said, half audibly:

"What can the youngster be after doing—staying this long?"

Perry had been absent nearly an hour, and his friend had become really anxious to know the cause of his delay, when the sounds of horse's hoofs were followed by the appearance of the subject of his thoughts, mounted bare-back.

"I thought you would stay the night out."

"I began to think that way myself," said Perry. "My pony pulled his stake, and I had to hunt for him among all the other horses. In this darkness it was no easy matter, and he was a mile, nearly, from where I left him."

"Get ready, my boy, and be off. There is a bit of bread and some meat in the can, left over, which will keep you from hunger until you can do better."

Perry, naturally active, stood ready for departure in a very few minutes. He was examining the priming of his rifle, when the attention of both was attracted by the sound of footfalls, as if some one was cautiously moving towards them. After a hail from the elder, in a low tone of voice, the same sounds were heard, as if some one was retreating, and Perry was quite certain he distinguished the form of a person moving off in the direction whence he had just come.

"Mr. Trigg, I believe that was Ducio Halfen."

"Not from the looks of him, in this darkness."

"No, sir, but when I passed the lines, going for my pony, there was no sentinel on post, at which I thought very strange. When I came back Ducio challenged me and I gave him the countersign. He pretended that I did not have the right one, and kept me several minutes, and while detaining me, he did his best to find out what I was up to. Of course, I could not tell him, and I believe he followed me here to find out what I refused to tell."

"Was it him, that was off post?"

"Yes, for the relief went 'round just before I left here, and the next round has not been made yet."

"I'll speak privately to the Captain and have the fellow watched. It's little use I have for him."

"Now, my boy," continued Mr. Trigg, "I don't ask where it is you're going, and if I knew it, it would be safe in my breast, but I more than suspect what you're going for, and want you to take this note and this medal, and if San Felipe is the place, you can deliver them to my little girl. It is only tonight that I thought about sending it, and I said nothing about it in the note. Tell her to wear it around her neck for the sake of her old friend, and the Blessed Mother will be good to her, even if she don't belong to the Holy Church, which is all the worse for her. I want her to send me an answer by you, Perry, and, my boy, I want you to see her all you can, and tell me all about her when you're back; do you mind?"

"Certainly, Mr. Trigg—that is, if I go to San Filipe."

"Before you come back we will be after moving out of this to the Salado or the San Antonio; and it is quite likely we will tackle the Greasers thereabouts."

"Good-bye, Mr. Trigg."

"Good luck to you, my boy."

"He's a brave lad," mused Mr. Trigg, as Perry disappeared. "If he was of a more careful way and knew how to manage better for himself, I'd like to see her take a fancy to the youngster. But Perry would squander a million in a month, and give away his soul for the asking."

CHAPTER XI.

"Look, Stella! What a sunset!"

"Oh! Isn't it lovely?"

"Those blending of shades and colors are too artistic to appear natural. It is a wonder we did not notice it in its earlier stages."

"For a very good reason. We were facing the east while sitting under that tree, and I was so taken up arranging those grasses that I thought of nothing else."

The sunset was indeed beautiful. A broken cloud of chocolate hue stretched along the western horizon, touching the earth, in denser shades, while on its summit, in long-reaching fragments, diverging from a common center, lines of vapor reached the very zenith on either side in strange regularity. The pencilings of the deeper shade were lost insensibly as they mounted the blue empyrean and mingled in the fanciful shapes which lined the outer edges and reflected the golden background. Amber shreds, unravelled from the texture of floating cloudlets, crossed blue patches, here and there disclosed, then gave place insensibly to crimson tints interspersed with threads of gold. From below, in one grand blaze of beauty, shaming the radiance of Aurora, the great orb poured a flood of golden splendor that lent magnificence indescribable to the shifting foreground. The western prairie glowed with the reflected hues from its patches of gray and lingering green, interspersed with clusters of tall, rank grasses, whose yellow tufts nodded gracefully before the evening breeze. Mottes of timber, some verdant in their perpetual evergreen, some half denuded, half clad, in autumnal garb, filled the eastern view. One of these half concealed a house, built of logs and boards rived with froe and maul from the native growth, and the remainder of a fence whose zig-zag course stretched a half mile or so until again lost in the chaparral.

The speakers, whose conversation commenced the present chapter, were two females. One apparently in that indeterminate age that defies conjecture, and the other, who was addressed as "Stella," a girl, perhaps fourteen, of light build and of lithe and graceful form. Her bare head disclosed a wealth of golden hair. In her arms she carried a collection of dry grasses, their fuzzy yellow and brown heads arranged in bunches.

"Aunt Ida, there comes someone on horseback," said Stella, pointing a little to the right of the direction they had been facing.

"I see him," responded the other. "Now he is hid by that bunch of small growth."

"There he is again," said Stella. "He is loping his pony."

"Suppose we go back towards the house. It may be a prowling Mexican. If he is a friend he will doubtless stop at San Felipe over night."

"I am quite certain it is not a Mexican; but we will not wait here if you think it better not to do so."

The horseman overtook them before the house was reached, and, reining up his jaded pony, touched his hat respectfully.

"If I am not mistaken, the very lady I want to see," he said looking directly at Stella.

"Want to see me? Has anything hap——? Do you come from Mr. Trigg?"

"I am not his messenger, Miss Stella, for I now recognize you; but I have a letter I promised to deliver."

"No bad news, I hope. Is it from him?"

"Not a bit of bad news had he to write, that I know of. He was well when I left him in camp, twelve miles this side of San Antonio. Here's the letter. I must see the Governor at once, and——"

"Haven't I seen you before sir?"

"You have," answered Perry, blushing under the coat of dust that covered his face, "but I didn't expect you to recognize me in this fix."

"But I can't remember your name."

"Asbury—'Perry,' as you heard Mr. Trigg call me. I was with him when he last parted from you."

"I remember you now," Stella said, coloring slightly at the recollection of a little pleasantry of her guardian on that occasion, enjoining Perry to not fall in love with her.

"This is my Aunt Ida."

Perry's bowed acknowledgment of the honor of the introduction over, he touched his hat rather awkwardly and turned his pony's head down an open lane which their present location disclosed and on which fronted three or four houses, similar in appearance to the one heretofore described, constituting the remainder of the settlement of San Felipe. To one of these Perry made his way to deliver the dispatches entrusted to him on leaving the Cibolo.

Stella did not wait until she gained the house before opening her letter, and soon after the messenger had left, was deep in its contents. Her Aunt Ida, as she had just denominated her companion, quietly seated herself on one of the blocks composing the steps of the stile in front of the dwelling and awaited the conclusion of her reading.

"Well, what news, Stella?" she asked, as the letter was dropped from before the girl's face, disclosing a troubled look.

"Mr. Trigg says I am to go to New Orleans to school."

"That is not such bad news."

"No."

"Then why your serious look?"

"He wants me to go to a convent."

"I suppose he hopes to convert you to his religion."

"No, I think not. At least, he does not want to influence me, although he would like me to become a Catholic."

"In a convent you would be sure to have influence enough."

"I would not mind any influence they could bring to bear on me. I am strong enough in my father's opinions to be proof against anything that would not be for my good."

"I know very little of them, but have always heard that the nuns were very pious and good women. When are you to start?"

"Here is the letter. See what you think of it all."

Mr. Trigg, who had constituted himself the guardian of Stella Raymond ever since the massacre on the Salado, had written to his ward quite a lengthy letter, for him, in which he detailed his plans for her future. He wrote that he intended to prove a guardian worth having; that he was possessed of ample means to give her an education worthy of her superior and lamented father, and being determined to remain with the volunteers until the approaching conflict with Mexico would terminate, as he hoped, in success to the colonists, he had decided that she should accompany her aunt on her return to Mississippi. The latter was to leave her in a convent in New Orleans, where it was his wish for her to remain until the completion of her education. He had forwarded a letter of credit to New Orleans for her benefit; also a communication to the Mother Superior of the Convent of the Sacred Heart, with whom he was personally acquainted. Stella had become very fond of the man who had protected her ever since that fearful day when she had fallen, terror-stricken at the sight of the Indians surrounding her burning home.

The letter, sent by Perry, contained the first intimation that her benefactor was the possessor of means sufficient to educate her at a boarding school, and while disappointed in the location of the latter, she was prepared to obey him in every particular. Her father had taken a liking to the rough Irishman, whom he had first met at the headquarters of the colony, and who had accompanied him to the beautiful, but ill-fated spot on the Salado. She had heard it stated that Mr. Trigg had invested in land to an extent that had rendered him impecunious and had necessitated a resort to manual labor to secure the means for a livelihood. Hence the reader found him at work for Paul Raymond at the opening of this story.

When her aunt had finished reading the letter she remarked to Stella that she deemed her to be most forunate to be able to escape from a country so rough and go to a metropolis celebrated for its wealth, refinement and gaiety.

"But I shall carry with me the heaviest of hearts, for then all hope of ever seeing poor dear Guy again will be shut out forever."

"You are wrong there, my dear child. If your brother is living he will know your whereabouts from friends here and will not fail to join you."

"Mr. Trigg has always said that he was positive of his having been taken captive, and was equally sure that he would, some day, escape. But I have suspected that his words were intended to calm my fears for my brother's safety."

Stella's trembling voice and brimming eyes brought silence to the two. A few moments sufficed to bring, crowding in masses, the incidents of years, as her busy mind and sorrowing heart actively took in the past, now that distance threatened to postpone the hope of meeting with her brother.

Her averted face concealed the emotion from her aunt, who sat humming a low air, as was her custom when occupied with the solution of a question. She was thinking of Stella's destination and of what a splendid opportunity her neice would have in the great city of making a fine matrimonial match; not only on account of her beauty, which it was apparent would become greatly enhanced as she would approach maturity and blossom into perfect womanhood. Then, the letter in her hand certainly stated that the self-constituted guardian had means which, if not sufficient to make his ward an heiress of importance, would place her in an enviable position of independence. She somewhat impatiently remembered that Mr. Trigg had decided on a convent. Of all places a convent was the least calculated to produce a "showy" girl, one calculated to take in society at the moment of her debut.

Stella's aunt was a woman of the world; had blossomed from a fashionable boarding school and remembered well the contrast between her own powers of attraction and the quiet demeanor and subdued manners of one of her contemporaries who had emerged from the precincts of a convent. She could not account for the stupidity of people who failed to profit by experience in such matters.

The lady's reverie was arrested by the reappearance of Perry, who had almost joined them in the fading twilight, without having been perceived. He was afoot and without a coat.

"Why, Mr. Asbury! You performed your mission in a hurry. Have you gotten through with the Governor already?" asked the lady.

"He was not at home. He went with a party across the river and has not yet returned. I hastened back to bring this, which I forgot to deliver with the letter."

Perry held up the medal as he spoke and placed the trinket in the hands of Stella.

The latter examined it in surprise and gave Perry a look of inquiry.

"He said for you to wear it, Miss Stella. It is something that belongs to his religion, and he believes it will keep one from harm."

"Such superstition!" exclaimed the lady.

"I wore it inside my coat until I gave it away, and then I placed it in the pocket of my waistcoat. I had the medal convenient and in case of danger would have tried what virtue there was in it."

"It is a medal of the Virgin," said Stella, examining it closely in the dim light.

"And I suppose you are quite ready to accept all the twaddle about the efficiency of these medals as a prelude to you conversion at the Sacred Heart," said her aunt.

"Let us go in to the light and examine it, Auntie. Mr. Trigg can believe what he pleases. I will preserve it as a curiosity."

The party ascended the steps to the hall, turned to the left and enterd a room in the middle of which stood a table, spread for a meal. Plain, rawhide-bottomed chairs composed the rest of its furniture, while a bright light shone from the tall chimney-piece at the further end. Stella, after examining the medal and its string of beadwork, expressed her satisfaction by putting the latter over her head with the former pendant on her breast.

The appearance of the hostess called their attention to the supper table, on which she was placing dishes, their tempting odors filling the apartment and whetting the appetite of Perry, whose ride had prepared him to do justice to his next meal. Recognizing the latter when she entered, the landlady invited him to remain to supper.

"I did not expect to stay to supper, Mrs. Morgan," said Perry. "I returned to bring Miss Stella this medal, and am without a coat. Going to table without a coat will make no difference at the tavern, but here——"

"Oh, that will make no difference with us either. You are a soldier-boy now, and they are not always expected to have coats."

"I believe Mr. Asbury did say that he had given his coat away, before we came indoors," said Stella, giving him a side look of inquiry.

"Perhaps that involves a story. Come, Mr. Perry, have you been playing good Samaritan?" asked the aunt.

'I met a poor fellow who was sick and shirtless, except a tattered rag over his shoulders, and I gave him my coat. A sudden norther, in his fix, would have settled him."

"Such an act entitled you to dine with princes in your shirt sleeves, my good boy, and always be sure of your welcome here," said the hostess.

CHAPTER XII.

The next morning's sun had peeped above the landscape and sent his beams stealthily through the crevices of Stella's apartment, resting on the coverlet of her bed or dancing on the opposite wall, as the mellow light was swayed by the movements of the window curtain, fluttering in the breeze that poured through under the slightly raised sash. A golden beam kissed her cheek and forehead, then stealing to her eyelids, woke her suddenly. Half rising, she looked around with a startled expression, then sinking again to her pillow, she said:

"Oh! I was dreaming."

"What dreaming about, Stella?" asked her aunt, whose bed she shared.

"About my brother Guy. I dreamed the Indians had him bound, ready to burn. I saw the lighted pile on which he was to suffer. Suddenly a girl, with wings like angels are pictured to wear, came and hung about his neck the medal that Perry brought. Instantly his hands became free and he defied his persecutors, and while the Indians stood around dismayed, the girl took him under her protection and the two seemed to rise gradually in the air, until their distant forms became blended with the clouds."

"The medal was filling your mind when you went to sleep; hence your dream."

"It was my brother rather, of whom I was thinking. I always think of him when I lie down at night."

Stella's aunt was such by affinity only. She had married the brother of Paul Raymond, a wealthy speculator of Mississippi, who had died and left his widow, Ida Raymond, the possessor of ample means. She was a woman of gay disposition and mourned her husband but a short time. Handsome, childless and wealthy, she had received much attention in a society upon which she was unsparing of her smiles and means. News of Paul Raymond's fate had reached her and anxious for the safety of the sole surviving daughter of her husband's brother, she had accompanied her own brother, Clarence Lambert, to Texas a short time previous to her introduction to the reader.

"When will Uncle Clarence return, Auntie?" asked Stella, as she, already dressed, sat watching her aunt doing up her toilet at the ten-by-twelve looking-glass suspended to the wall.

"The Lord only knows, child. He is perfectly infatuated with this wild country and will never stop until he has traversed every foot of its soil. It's terrible to have to make one's toilet in such a hovel! Just contrast this wretched little glass with my full-length mirror!"

"I do wish Uncle Clarance would come back. If I have to go it is better to have it over with."

"We won't wait for him if he is not here to return by the schooner that brought the volunteers—bless me! What a glass to dress by."

"If you go by the schooner, Auntie, it will be well to get ready, for I heard she will sail right soon."

"The Governor is to let me know, child. He will send a special messenger to New Orleans on her——there! I've got those eyebrows smoothed to suit me at last. What a relief it will be to get back to the comforts of civilization."

"And a good mirror," suggested Stella, laughing.

"Yes, a good mirror," returned her aunt, with a half reproachful tone and look, which betrayed a suspicion that Stella's remark and manner contained a reflection upon her excessive primping.

"Would Uncle Clarance like it if we were to go without him?"

"I could not help his likes. He has no business to be gone so long He came to invest in land, and it seems he is so hard to please that he must ride over half a continent to suit himself in a few thousand acres. The Governor told the simpleton that the Brazos lands were the finest in the country."

"I do hope the Indians won't hurt Uncle Clarance."

"It would serve him half right to meet with some misadventure— I declare! Your collar is all awry, my child. Fix it and let us go out to breakfast."

"So it is," said Stella, going over to the little glass. "You know, Auntie, you monopolized the mirror, and I had to primp without one."

"That's a great mirror! Don't forget to write your letter to Mr. Trigg this morning so that man can take it back with him. And you had better ask him to change his mind about putting you in a convent, if you ever want to have any accomplishments. They do not know how to teach music, and a girl is so cut off from the world that she does not know how to act or make a good appearance in society. If you want to be a religieuse, why a convent is the place for you, for religion enters into two-thirds of their curriculum. Have I too much powder on my face?"

Stella replied to her aunt's question in the negative, without taking pains to examine for any superfluity of powder and, opening the door leading out of the bedroom the two proceeded to join the hostess.

The morning had progressed apace when Stella had procured paper, pen and ink to write a letter to Mr. Trigg. She repaired to the bedroom occupied by herself and aunt and closed the door for privacy.

Seated by a little table at a window she heaved a deep sigh as a prelude to the reflection that her contemplated communication would be a difficult one to compose, if she desired to especially please her guardian. She had never written many letters, and she tapped her penholder on the windowsill for many minutes while she gazed abstractedly out upon the open prairie before she turned finally to her task.

Stella wrote for a long time, frequently correcting and interlining, until she had covered a good deal of paper. Looking up with a sigh of relief, she said, just audibly:

"I'll read it over and then copy it in a nicer hand."

While Stella is reading over her production, we will glance over her shoulder and glean the contents.

"My Dear My Trigg:—

"Mr. Perry brought me your letter and I was so glad to hear that you were well. The roads were so terribly dusty and Mr. Perry was so covered with dust, that at first I did not know him. He knew me right away. When we met him Aunt Ida and I were out walking and saw him coming a long way off. We gathered some beautiful long grasses which Auntie will take home with her and put in her parlor vases. I am ever so much obliged for your kind intentions towards me. I have heard a great deal about convents—much against them and much in their favor. You know my father was what they call an infidel. He did not believe that God had ever established any of the religions of the world. He always claimed that his religion 'duty to his fellowman,' was all sufficient. But my father always had great respect for the Catholic sisters in and out of convents, and gave them great credit for devotion to their ideas of duty.

Between you and me, Aunt Ida has not much idea of convent education. She thinks that girls are kept too much in seclusion while being prepared to take a part in the affairs of life, and are little more than mummies when they leave school. But Auntie is all for society and dress, and is as particular in her toilet out here as she would be in a city. My own opinion is that of my poor, dear mother—that girls soon enough learn the arts of society after they finish their studies. I then have no objection, and feel that I have no right to express one, to do just as you desire me to do.

As Auntie has tired of this place, she has made up her mind to go home right away, by the schooner that landed the New Orleans volunteers at Velasco. So I will soon be off to school and leave you in this wild country with a cloud of war hanging over it. Oh! You have no idea how my heart aches when I think of turning my back on the graves of my dear parents. And my dear Guy! Where is he? He, too, may be dead. If not, his life may be wretched as a captive. Do try, my dear Mr. Trigg, to learn something of his fate. News came to us today that a company of settlers had pursued a band of the same Indians who destroyed our family, on a late raid on the Colorado, and that the Texans had killed their chief and burned their villages on the San Saba. It may be that the men who were in this expedition learned something of my brother. I believe if it is in your power you will find out whether he is dead or alive.

"Mr. Perry will take this to you. The poor fellow has no coat, having given his away to one in need. My aunt brought a suit for poor, dear Guy and I mean to give it to Mr. Perry. Take good care of yourself, Mr. Trigg. If you should get killed by those terrible Mexicans, what would become of poor me? I hope you will write to me whenever you have a chance. Good-bye. Your little friend,

Stella Raymond.

P. S.—I knitted you two pairs of socks which Mr. P. will give you.

When Stella had copied her letter nicely and had added the postscript, it was nearly noon and she could hear the preparations being made to serve the midday meal. Mrs. Raymond had been over to see the Governor, in regard to the day set for the sailing of the schooner, and had remained to chat with the family, as was her custom whenever she visited the executive mansion.

Mrs. Morgan came in to call Stella to dinner and to ask if her aunt had expected to return in time for the meal.

It was an hour or two after noon before Mrs. Raymond returned, and with her came Perry, leading his pony, prepared for his return trip to the Cibolo.

Stella had her letter in readiness, and in a neat bundle she had placed the suit of clothes, which were intended for her brother, together with the socks she had so thoughtfully made for Mr. Trigg. Perry entered with the lady to tell those in the house good-bye and receive whatever messages Stella might wish to send.

"You did not make a very long stay, Perry," said Mrs. Morgan.

"I hadn't the say-so, ma'am. When we get orders we have to go, night or day, rain or shine."

"Won't you sit down awhile?"

"No, I thank you, Mrs. Morgan. My orders are to lose no time and my dispatches are, no doubt, very important."

"Well, here's a little lunch for you, Perry. I thought you would not get much to eat on the road."

"And here," said Stella, "is my letter to Mr. Trigg. Tell him all about us and give him my love. Mr. Perry, it is said that he who casts his bread upon the waters will find it after many days. This is said to mean that whoever helps those in need will himself be helped in turn. Here is a suit of clothes intended for my dear, lost brother, which I ask you to accept. You have earned it by your kind act in parting with perhaps your only coat."

"Have you forgotten Mr. Trigg's socks?" asked her aunt.

"I came near forgetting to mention them. They are in the bundle Mr. Perry."

Perry, who had experienced a choking sensation at the kindness showered upon him, had a little difficulty in enunciating words of thanks. He had really parted with his only coat, and felt more gratitude than he expressed.

"You all are kinder to me than I deserve, Miss Stella. I can never forget you."

After the good-byes had been spoken the young man bowed his way out and was soon upon his pony, and with the ladies' donations secured behind his siddle, he galloped down the road, turning occasionally to give an answering salute to the handkerchiefs waving the ladies' adieux.

"Stella! Do you know we have to get ready this afternoon to leave for Velasco in the morning?" said her aunt, leading the way to their room.

"How should I have known it, Auntie? This is the first I have heard of it."

"Mr. Trigg should have known it," said her aunt, "and I ought to have told Perry. I wanted to see your letter. Those ladies would make me stay to dinner. What did you write about?"

"I wrote so many things, I cannot remember all. I mentioned we were to start very soon to take the schooner for New Orleans."

"That will be notice enough. Now, child, let us get our things ready and have it over with. I do hate to be rushed at the last minute. Your Uncle Clarence should be here. He has run crazy over Texas lands. I will leave a letter for him with Mrs. Morgan."

"What are we going in, Auntie, from here to the coast?"

"Oh! The Governor has put his ambulance at our disposal," she said gaily. Then, going to the wretched little glass and scanning her face for a moment, she enquired of her neice·

"Stella, does my complexion look as well as when I first came here?"

"It looks the same to me, Auntie."

The next morning the Governor's ambulance was at Mrs. Morgan's betimes, and found the travelers ready for the trip. The strong, fat mules and commodious vehicle promised them a safe and speedy transit to their destination. With a Godspeed, we will cast an old shoe after them and drop the curtain, for the present, on that part of our narrative connected with their after movements.

CHAPTER XIII.

The morning that Mrs. Raymond and Stella left for Velasco, the camp of the Texans on the Cibola was astir with preparations to march. The large tent was struck and rolled, ready for deposit in one of the wagons. The men were variously engaged. Some were saddling horses, while others who had already arranged their trappings were securing blankets and clothing to their saddles, preparatory to mounting.

The dismounted troops were busy placing their light traps in the wagons, and examining their guns and ammunition.

The contemplated movement must have been welcomed by the army, for the air resounded with the men's merriment as jest and repartee were exchanged, or a snatch of song rang out in a well-turned voice, or some adept at whistling imitated the sharp notes of a fife. In the midst of it all, grouped in deliberation, were noted men whose names were to go into history, as the redeemers of an empire or martyrs to its liberation. The well known person of Austin and the commanding form of Houston were conspicuous near the trunk of a majestic pecan whose branches covered the party, while near, paying respectful attention to their conversation, were members of the consultation and officers of the command. Here Fannin stood with folded arms and nervous look, little dreaming of the martyrdom he was so soon to suffer for the cause he had espoused. There, near him, reclined Bowie, silent, save when addressed, to make some laconic answer, with the veiled future pregnant with the fame of the fallen Alamo.

It was Austin who spoke:

"I am perplexed with this delay of the promised reinforcements. The blame may lie at my door, through my lack of military experience and those powers to organize and conduct a campaign so essential to a soldier in command."

"You have left nothing undone to arouse the country and concentrate your force," replied General Houston.

"But I feel my lack of experience in the field, and would much prefer position in the council, or a mission for assistance to the States. In either capacity I would be useful. As commander in chief, one mistake may work irreparable injury to our cause. General Houston, you should command here."

"No, Austin! The army I found here had chosen you for their

leader; any change now, may tend to dissatisfaction that would be more fatal than the grossest error of a commander."

"But fully one-half of these troops are from the East, and came here under your recognized authority. You have had experience as a volunter commander and possess great influence over men. These two facts point to you, of all men here, as best fitted to lead us."

"No arguments you can make, General Austin, will change my determination. I will only take command by your orders," replied Houston, firmly.

Austin, after a moment's reflection, in which his face wore a troubled expression, turned to the several officers and gave orders for the immediate marching of the command. He designated Fannin's company to lead the movement, the direction of the march to be taken from the guide who would ride with its commander.

The orders of the chief were obeyed with alacrity. The head of the column crossed the stream, and the Texans were on their way for the Salado creek. The mounted men, who comprised about one-sixth of the troops, were divided into three divisions, one to act as advance guard, another to bring up the rear, and the third were thrown out to the right, as flankers, to examine the country towards San Antonio. Among these latter it was the fortune of Mr. Trigg and his mess to be numbered. Captain Bowie, who was in command of the flankers, was instructed to cross the Salado within four miles of the town, and to scout the country thence to the San Antonio river, with the view of detecting the presence of any force which the enemy might have pushed forward to anticipate the pending movement of the Texans.

After a trot of some five or six miles the crossing indicated was reached, and the party filed down the steep embankment to the gravelly stream that ran swift and shallow where it crossed the road they were pursuing.

"Halt, men! You may dismount here for a little while. I will go to that hill yonder and take a survey of the country towards town. Henry Karnes, I want you to go with me."

So saying, Captain Bowie rode off at a brisk pace towards the elevation he had indicated, followed by Karnes, who was one of his most trusted and faithful men.

"We might as well act on the Captain's suggestion, Mr. Trigg, and get down and rest our nags," said Tip Hamilton. "This is a pretty little stream here. If I had a little more time and a propitious muse, I believe I could indite a little verse on its beauties."

"You won't have any use for verses and such like, I'm thinking.

We are pretty near the Greasers now, and no telling what hot work is waiting for us. You call this a pretty stream! You should see it above here, at the forks, where those Indian devils destroyed the home of Mr. Raymond, who I was telling ye about."

"The father of the little girl to whom you wrote the other day?" asked Tip.

"The very same. But she's not so little. She's over fifteen. It makes me sad to think of the work of those murderin' Indians."

"Did you not say that she had a brother of whose fate you were uncertain?"

"I did. Poor Guy! He was as fine a lad as ever lived. I wonder what ever came of him," said Mr. Trigg, in a sad tone.

"Guy R-a-y-m-o-n-d!" pronounced Hamilton, musingly. "It is a pretty name and sounds more musical than Tipton Hamilton."

"It is a wonder that you would acknowledge it! You are so blastedly conceited," said Jones, who had come near and heard the last of the conversation between Mr. Trigg and Hamilton.

"Conceited, say you? You knight of commonplace romance! You champion prevaricator! You brazen narrator of the impossible, the impracticable, the incredible! You hero of the wonderful bridge and the eight hundred elephants! You——"

"What in the d——l are you up to, Tip?" asked Ducio Halfen, approaching.

"Apostrophizing Jones.'

"Apostrophizing him?"

"Yes, he belongs to the supernatural."

"He is good natured, that's sure," said Ducio.

"If I wasn't, you'd both been dead men before now. My patience won't always last, however."

"Well, Jones," said Hamilton, "with all your faults you have but one serious one, and if you don't want to be the butt of the camp, just take my advice on one point."

"And what is that?" asked the victim.

"Stop lying."

"Here comes the Captain back. I wonder if he has spied the Greasers," said one of the men.

"They can't be coming this way, if he did, the slow way he's riding," said another.

"I don't b'lieve Jim Bowie would run from fifty Mexicans," said the first speaker.

"Neither would Karnes. He's an ole Indjun fighter. Up to ther head of the Trinity once, me and Karnes and two other fellers kept forty or more Injuns off untell night come, and we 'scaped down the river in a dug-out. He's all grit, he is."

This was said in a drawling tone, by a tall, lank individual, who seemed to be all bones and muscle, whose attenuated form would have furnished an uncertain mark for shaft or bullet. His appearance afforded an opportunity for the exercise of Hamilton's wit.

"I can understand the risk run by Mr. Karnes, and perhaps by the other two on the critical occasion you mention, but, my dear sir, you certainly could have entertained slight apprehensions of any contact by your attenuated anatomy with the missiles of the dusky lords of the prairie."

Hamilton's sally, not comprehended by the backwoods man, caused a laugh among some of the bystanders, among whom was Ducio.

The lean individual looked from one to another for a moment, then, comprehending that something had been said at his expense, he clubbed his gun in a menacing manner and addressed himself to the Mississippi man:

"See here, my frien,' I don't know nuthin' about you, and still less about yer talk, but if yer got anything ag'in Nathan Roach—why, jes' sail in an' I'll show yer that you ain't no more'n nuthin'—you game makin,' stuck-up counter-hopper—w-h-o-o-p!"

Mr. Roach, as he gave a regular Indian warwhoop, circled his clubbed gun and cleared a ring in a second.

The presence of the Capain and Karnes at this moment put a stop to further demonstrations.

"What's the matter, Nathe?" asked his companion of the Trinity fight.

"A little trifle, Karnes; not enough to make a feller rale mad. I was jes' a-showin' a counter-hopper a flourish or two. It takes a man to rile Nathan Roach."

Hamilton was amused at the fellow's language and capers, and half put out at his offensive estimation of himself. But he concluded he had got hold of a bad subject for ridicule, and that the best way would be to smoothe over what had occurred.

"Here's my hand, Mr. Roach. I did not mean anything by my incomprehensible jargon. You are true grit, and I want you to save it all for use right along side of me when we jump the Mexicans. My name is Hamilton."

"All right, Mr. Hamilton; you know how to talk sensible like when yer wants to. Ef yer know me long ye'll find it heap safer to have Nathan Roach's good-will than to make a enemy out'en him."

The Captain's voice, calling the men to mount, cut short the discussion, and the saddles were soon filled.

Bowie directed Karnes to select six men and to proceed at once on the duty to which he had assigned him. As the latter rode along the line, several signified a willingness to volunteer, but Karnes stated that he wanted good horses as well as good men. He told them he knew all the riders were fearless, but that some of the horses were poor. The detail was at length complete. Among those selected, five are already known to the reader. Mr. Trigg was taken first, as his animal was the best in the command. Then came Tip Hamilton, Nathan Roach, Jones and Ducio Halfen, in the order named. The sixth and last man belonged to that large family whose name is cosmopolitan. His name was John Smith. Jones was a little miffed at not being selected first, on the score of horseflesh, as he had the pedigree of his charger in a memorandum book and had regaled his messmates on his merits over many a campfire.

Karnes drew his men aside and ordered them to dismount, while the main body, under the lead of their commander, filed away and proceeded down the right bank of the stream. When the last trooper had disappeared over a rise in the rolling country Karnes said to his men:

"Boys, we've got to scout right into San Antone, almost. We've got to go to the powder house, anyhow, unless we meet a force. After we get there, I will be guided by circumstances."

"Hurrah!" cried Hamilton, "we'll have a little excitement, if nothing else."

"How many of you have ever been in San Antone?" asked Karnes.

No one responded in the affirmative. Mr. Trigg had not answered. Finally he said:

"I was there once, but it was a long time ago."

Karnes then had an inspection of the ammunition and the pieces of the men. Finding everything in good order and condition, he gave the word to move, and his little squad were soon on the road leading to the city of the Alamo. As they reached the summit of the first rise, at a distance of about a thousand yards from the creek, the white top of the powder house revealed itself just peeping over the mesquite growth, which crowned the brows of the intervening hills. Away to the right was the line of timber bordering the San Antonio and its tributary, the Olmos, a beautiful stream whose pellucid waters largely supplied the former's volume. This fringe of wood, seeming to skirt the blue hills that were in fact many miles beyond, lost itself behind the rising foreground that alone shut out a view of the white walls of Bexar.

Karnes rode off a few yards and placed himself on a knoll some what more elevated than the road, and slowly swept the country wit a small glass which he drew from his pocket. His view was take to the southwest and south, then, passing the latter point, he turne the glass slowly eastward, and remarked to the men who had gathere around him·

"There is the main command. You can see the dust with th naked eye. They are making for the mouth of the Salado."

"Can you see the Captain and our other boys?" asked Hamiltor

"It don't take a glass to see them," said Mr. Trigg. "Look there way to the southwest—no—they couldn't a-got that far."

Karnes turned his glass in the direction indicated.

"They are Mexican cavalry, Mr. Trigg! They are a long way off but may see us, if they are using a glass. Get back to the road boys, and we'll keep on to the powder house."

A half mile, and the latter showed more than half its white lime stone masonry to the scouters, now grown more cautious in thei movements. Karnes halted them and ordered all to leave the roac and dismount in the chaparral.

This disposition made, he nodded to Nathan Roach:

"Nathe," he said, "I want you to come with me afoot until we can see every inch of that powder house. I don't want any shooting unless we're obliged to. Maybe there's nobody there."

"All right, Karnes. I'd like to draw a bead today on a Greaser,' said Nathan, following the other.

They moved off through the mesquite bushes, watched by thei comrades until lost in the foliage.

Up over a hill or two, with here and there an open glade tc pass, the frontiersmen pushed stealthily along until they reachec the brow of the tableland on which stood the object of their approach. The powder house was built of white limestone and rose with nearly perpendicular walls slightly converging at the top, tc a height of about forty feet from its foundation. It was built probably for the purpose disclosed by its name, and partly to answer for a lookout to detect the presence of Indians or enemies of any description. A door on the northern face of the building was the sole entrance and each side, near the top, was pierced by a smal window.

Our adventurers found themselves in a dense growth, which made an oblong circuit of the opening where towered the structure.· They crawled to its edge and peered through into the open space. The door of the house was open and before it stood a stack of muskets.

Just within could be seen several Mexicans seated and apparently playing cards. Another came lazily around the northwest corner, rolling a cigarette. He stopped at the door, said something to the others which caused a laugh, took punk and steel from his pocket and procuring a light, began to smoke.

"Golly! What a shot I could make," said Nathan Roach.

The Mexican looked suddenly in their direction.

"Hush talking so loud, Nathe. Looked as if that fellow heard you," said Karnes.

The smoker entered the house, and could be seen to mount the stairs, the foot of which was immediately at the right of the door.

"One, two, three, four, five, six, seven, eight," counted Karnes. "Eight muskets in that stack. Reckon that's their number.

"Look, Karnes, that fellow is spying the country."

The Mexican was at the east window and, leaning out, looked earnestly to the eastward; then gradually swept the horizon to the southeast.

"Golly! Couldn't I fetch him from that hole," said Roach, drawing a bead.

"Behave, Nathe! You're acting the plum fool. I want to bag them Greasers. Go back and bring up the boys. Let 'em draw straws so as to see who will have to stay and hold the horses. Let 'em come mounted 'round that first hill and leave the nags in that ravine we crossed. It is too far to leave 'em at the place where they are now."

"All right, Karnes. Won't be gone long," said the other, moving off with his long back in a horizontal position.

Karnes amused himself watching the unsuspecting enemy. The Mexican had quit the window and reappeared below. The bells in town announced the hour. It was noon.

CHAPTER XIV.

Quite opposite the cathedral of San Fernando, running as nearly east as a conformance with the winding river would permit, a short street opened, ending at the extremity of the peninsula through which ran the parallel and principal avenue of the town. The latter was known as "Calle Principal." The short street was named "Calle de Carcel."

As a pedestrian would leisurely turn into the Calle de Carcel from the main plaza, he would see a very narrow street, wide enough to allow two vehicles to pass each other, provided the drivers would be careful and in full sympathy with the universal custom which governs the choice of sides to take. On either side of the narrow way, abutting on the sidewalks, extended the low, thick walls of the Mexican houses, relieved alone by the deep portals and grated windows. Here and there, on the river side, jacals were interspersed, lending contrast to the view by their tule roofs and mud-bedaubed sides. The river, encroaching upon the street, caused an interval that terminated at a rude footbridge spanning the stream where an old mill stood, with its huge wheel conspicuous, and turned in ceaseless revolution by the rapid current. Below the bridge, the waters, seething and foaming as they escaped the narrow passway that caused the power, changed to deep, cool eddies, then to a thousand ripples and streaming lines of white above the blue as the translucent flood poured over the stones and pebbles of the broad shallows where passed a ford. Above a low stone wall comprised the dam. Through this rude work the searching waters found exit by many a moss-lined crevice and came in rills and spurts to half inundate a cress-covered island that held the center of the bridge. Beyond the dam the blue river formed a pretty picture with its receding banks lined by willows, whose half weeping branches fell pendant until their graceful foliage kissed the tranquil surface.

Two doors from where the Calle de Carcel left the plaza, as one would turn into it to the right, was a tienda containing several tables, spread with snowy cotton cloths, occupying the sides of its small front room. A back door, half open, disclosed a rear apartment and allowed a glimpse of a large iron pot swinging from a tripod. A little further on a small sign was faintly scrawled over a door and spelled out, on a closer inspection, v-i-n-o-t-e-r-i-a. Opposite the vinoteria, the structure not differing materially from its neighbor's, was the carcel or jail, whence the street had derived its name. At a stone's throw from the carcel, with the market intervening, and slightly retired from the paved walk, was another sign, swung so as to be visible up and down the street. This bore the rough draft of a bull's head while, partly above and partly below, were the words "Cabeza de Toro."

Next to the shop of the Monte Pio, the resort of the Cabeza de Toro was the most popular. Here was dealt the game so fascinating to the average Mexican. The Bull's head was open, at all hours, to the votaries of monte; but night was the favorite time for the crowd, which would then assemble at the rooms in goodly numbers, and should the occasion be the evening of a fiesta, would fill them to their utmost capacity. The monte room equalized all distinctions. Here the patrician and the plebean met and puffed the fumes of the cigareta in each other's faces. The high official and the ladron, the owner of the hacienda and the mendicant rubbed against each other, the interest in the all-absorbing game suppressing every feeling that elsewhere would have been engendered by offensive contact.

To add to the attractions of the place, the proprietor had appropriated two apartments for other purposes. One of these, fronting on the street, was devoted to nightly fandangos, free to all the patrons of the monte rooms. The other, to the rear, was the wine room, where a villainous native beverage, called mescal, was served for a quartilla a drink. In this latter room were tables or stands, where Mexican dishes were sold by women who paid a rental for the privilege. Each stand had its own furnace and coals, over which were placed the pots containing the edibles, and from which they were dished out, hot and steaming on demand.

Such was the most notorious resort in Bexar, at the time of our writing. The presence of the army of the Mexican General Cos, consisting of about two thousand troops, gave unusual life to the town and trebled the usual attendance at the Cabeza de Toro.

After Jose had finished the duties which devolved upon him as the mozo to the Father Ignacio, he reported to Guy his readiness to accompany him to witness a game of monte. He cautioned him to not mention the fact of the proposed visit to the priest, as the latter had very curious ideas about going to such places.

"But I have been told," said Guy, "that priests often bet at the game, considering it no harm to gamble."

"What you say, senor, admits of much qualification. In Mexico I have seen some of the padres, who are not any better than they should be, gamble in just such a place as the Cabeza de Toro, but they would not tell their bishop of it. Again, I have known good and holy priests bet a real or more and sometimes win quite a pile of silver. And what would they do with such winnings? The next day would see the last quartilla distributed among the poor and sick. As a rule the padres are lucky, and when they give it to the hungry and needy, where is the harm?"

"If you could take away the bad influences of the example, Jose, there is much philosophy in your remarks," said Guy.

"The example is good enough, senor. Suppose everybody would follow it and give their winnings to the poor?"

"Your remark is ingenious," said Guy, laughing. "The example I alluded to lay in the act of gambling and frequenting a place where the associations are usually fatal to good morals."

"But, on the other hand," contended Jose, "when a padre is present the gamblers are quiet and well behaved, and an oath is seldom uttered. The Mexican people have a great respect for the fathers."

"Would Father Ignacio bet at a game of monte."

"Not he!" said Jose, emphatically.

"Does he approve of it in other priests?"

"No, senor; neither in priests nor people. Just confess the sin to him, if you want to be amazed at the penance you will get."

"I think Father Ignacio is right," said Guy, musingly.

They had just turned into the Calle de Carcel, when Jose, pointing into the tienda, remarked.

"There is the tienda of Senora Candelario."

"I'll never forget her minced peppers," said Guy, glancing into the place.

Operations at the place of their destination seemed to be in full blast as they approached. The hum of many voices from the crowd around the door, where hung the sign, was mingled with the lively strains of music from the room devoted to the dance. Jose looked into the monte room, but, discovering that dealing had not begun, suggested to his companion that they take in the fandango first. Guy submitted to the other's leadership and followed into the next room. Four musicians were playing in one corner, producing very creditable music from two violins, a harp and a flute. Seated on benches lining the walls were a score of senoritas looking as immobile as statuary, save an occasional turn of the head towards the entrance, as some fresh arrival attracted attention. Guy, at Jose's suggestion, took a seat near the door, while the latter prepared to interview the proprietor or other authority, to ascertain how soon the game would begin.

Left to himself Guy took in the movements of the arrivals and of the men who sauntered in and out of the room. Many of the latter scrutinized him very closely and with more or less expressions of surprise, on account of his nationality.

Jose presently looked in to see how his young American friend was getting along, and brought with him a tall, graceful Mexican, whom he introduced to Guy as Manuel Ruiz.

"I am happy to know you, Senor Ruiz," he said.

"Consider me your friend and servant, Senor Raymond. But how well you speak our language!"

"I believe I speak it pretty well for an American. I had an excellent teacher."

"Jose tells me you arrived with Father Ignacio. It is a good recommendation to have been in such excellent company, notwithstanding, I presume you have given your parole and are all right at headquarters."

"On the contrary, senor, I have not given any parole, not deeming such a step——. Now I remember, the padre did say I must not venture out in town before I gave my parole. He does not know I have left the house. Jose proposed to satisfy my desire to witness a game of monte and here we are."

"It may be all right tonight, but must not be repeated for your own sake. There are eight hundred Texans encamped on the Cibolo. The capture of Goliad has opened the ball and war has certainly begun. You will see why it will be necessary for a man of your complexion to carry a pass to escape arrest."

"What you have communicated is news to me. I have been a captive among the Indians for two years, without a word from my own people."

At the request of his new acquaintance Guy related much of the story of his captivity, which enhanced the interest first awakened in the mind of the former, and led to a promise to remain near him until he desired to return to the priest's house.

The dancing here begun and couples filled the floor, turning in the easy measure of the Spanish waltz. Ruiz, excusing himself, soon joined the throng with a little woman, who had been sitting near, for his partner.

Guy knew how to dance. The music and the scene before him seemed to electrify him. All at once he caught sight of a neglected senorita in the opposite corner, and, without hesitation, hastened to her side and asked her to waltz.

When the music ceased, Ruiz, who was looking for his American friend, caught sight of him leading his partner to a seat. Jose was also waiting at the door to show Guy to the monte room. The Mexican is a natural gambler. The passion for gaming seems to have become ingrained through heredity. The chance upon which he will stake his last article of property may be determined by the turn of a card or the cutting of a watermelon. Losses, great or small, are endured with perfect stoicism, while success induces no expression indicative of exultation in the Aztec physiognomy.

Crossing an unlighted passage dividing it from the scene of the fandango, Guy and his two companions entered a square apartment with flagged floor, high ceiling and the inevitable deep, grated windows. On the side opposite the street, three small tables were ranged near the wall, over each of which an individual presided. Above the middle table, begrimed with dust and smoke, hung the picture of a saint, which the rude letters below it indicated to be that of Saint Anthony. Several persons were gathered around this table watching the dealer as he dexterously manipulated a pack of cards. The men seated at the other tables were carelessly disengaged, while before them lay the cards, ready for use, with their representatives painted upon the board. The game had fairly begun at the middle table, and silver coins from a real up to the Mexican dollar, or peso, were placed upon the favorite cards of the bettors, while the dealer mechanically drew the gaudy pieces of pasteboard from the deck. As the bank would win, the dealer would rake in the winnings and deposit them in a drawer. When it sustained a loss, he would pay from the drawer or from moneys won by the bank on another card. The bets were all very light. After watching these operations for a half hour or more, Guy expressed his disappointment to Jose and Manuel as to the character of the game he had expected to see, and wondered how it could be so attractive to the Mexicans.

"You would be much interested if you would bet at the game," said Jose.

"Suppose you try your luck, Senor Raymond," suggested Manuel Ruiz.

"I am not supplied with funds tonight," said Guy, laughing, as he remembered his empty pocket. "But tomorrow Jose is to get me the money for my pony and I will risk a real or two."

"No need of waiting until tomorrow, senor," said Jose, "for here is a peso at your disposal."

"I feel as if I could break the bank tonight, Jose, and if I should have such luck it would make the dealer my enemy. You bet four reals, and if you lose, lend me the other four and I will be pretty sure to win."

"That does not follow, but here goes. Quatro reales on the seven."

Jose put down his half dollar and—lost.

Manuel followed his example and won.

"The seven was always my lucky card," said Jose, "but tonight it seems as if it is not. Now, Senor Raymond, let us see if my loss will be your gain."

Guy waited for a new deal and chose his card without hesitation. He won.

He handed Jose back his loan, and bet again.

Jose and Ruiz both followed his example and lost.

"Que mala fortuna!" exclaimed Ruiz. "There, Senor Raymond has won."

"El no es indio por nada," said Jose. "Indians are always lucky gamblers."

Guy had no particular confidence in his further success. He had repaid Jose and was careless, if he won or lost. Each time he won he placed the entire amount on some card, and invariably he would win. His companions had lost all their change, besides several small amounts he had prevailed upon them to accept. They were amazed and amused at his success which, as one of them had predicted, now caused him to become highly interested, and not a little excited. A dense crowd had gathered around the table, and many voices were heard expressing more or less surprise at the luck of the American.

Guy counted down fifty pesos and staked them on Jose's lucky seven.

He won again.

He now had one hundred pesos. Ruiz was delighted. He suggested to Guy to put aside ninety pesos and to bet small amounts, until he should lose the ten—or win another hundred.

Guy handed him the ninety pesos and again put his trust in the seven. Success did not desert him. He was highly elated, and, for the first time, looked around at the faces whose eyes were regarding him with wonder. One pair of eyes, however, met his glance with a vindictiveness of expression that arrested his attention, and caused him to look up again several times, only to meet the same sinister look. The fellow's expression annoyed him to such an extent that he lost interest in the game and was not aware of a change in his luck, until he saw the dealer rake his stake into the drawer.

He looked up and encountered the gaze that had so perturbed him, and this time the owner of the eyes were close at hand. As he encountered the other's look with one of defiance, and was about to demand what was meant by his offensive glances, they were partially explained by the following words from the individual himself, who pointed directly at him:

"Companeros! This Gringo is a murderer and a thief, and I can prove it."

The words were scarcely uttered before the fellow went sprawling to the floor from the force of a blow dealt by Guy's muscular arm. The confusion which ensued would be difficult to describe. The crowd surged back and forward, having completely closed in upon the combatants. Jose and Ruiz tried to get to their friend, being much alarmed for his safety on hearing on all sides cries of "Mueron los Gringos."

Their efforts were unavailing.

Jose beat his breast in very agony at the thought of what Father Ignacio would say to him if anything happened to Senor Raymond. He would be blamed for having brought him to the Cabeza de Toro. He looked wildly up and caught sight of the saint's picture. As a last resort he uttered a fervent prayer to Saint Anthony to get him out of the scrape. Just at this moment the crowd parted and revealed Guy overpowered by a half dozen men, while Manuel Ruiz was in the custody of as many more.

"You cowardly dogs! You are none of you a match for that American boy. If it had not been for me and this good knife, you would have killed him for resenting an insult from that dog of a Vasquez."

The words from Ruiz infuriated the crowd, who would have offered him violence, had not a short, thick-set, military man interfered and brandished his sword to keep them back.

"Release Senor Ruiz," he said, in a firm tone.

The command was obeyed.

Guy had ceased to struggle with his captors and now stood passive. His bare head and disheveled hair, his torn jacket and a bloody mark on his cheek were evidences of the rough handling he had sustained. He had left his mark on many of his antagonists, whose bloody physiognomies proved that his blows had not fallen lightly, while his first assailant was completely hors du combat.

So soon as qiuet was restored, the officer demanded of Ruiz the cause of the broil.

"This young man was called a murderer and a thief by a fellow named Vasquez and, like a man of courage, he knocked down his insulter. He was then set upon by these cowards, who would have killed him but for my efforts to prevent them and his own bravery in defending himself."

"Why did Vasquez use such language to the young man?"

"Quien sabe, senor. The fellow never saw him before."

"No es verdad!" said a voice, as the owner of it limped forward.

"Who are you?" demanded the officer.

"Yo? Yo soy Vasquez," making a salute.

"What is it that you say is not true?"

"That I never saw this Gringo before," he replied, looking towards Guy.

"Was that any reason that you should call him bad names?"

"Oyez, senor. Let me tell you the whole story, and Your Honor will say that I am in the right, and that this Americano, Tejano or Gringo, or whatever he is, ought to be punished.

"Buen; proceed with your story."

"Senor, it is more than a year that I and my brother were coming to Bexar from Paso del Norte, with some caretas of Don Pedro Sandoval, when we were attacked by a band of Indians near el Rio Pecos. We gave them the best fight we could make, but they captured our train and killed all of our men but four, including myself. Strange to say, among these Indians, and they were Lipans, senor, was a young Gringo who fought like a devil. He killed my brother with his rifle and took his horse, saddle and bridle. The man who did this is before Your Honor, and is the one I called a murderer and a thief."

"You may be mistaken, Vasquez."

"No es possible, Your Honor. This fellow came in town only today, dressed as an Indian, and he has sold my brother's saddle to the Monte Pio."

"What have you to say to this, senor?" asked the officer, turning to Guy.

The latter made no reply.

"Perhaps he cannot speak Mexican."

"You are wrong there, senor," said Vasquez, "you should have heard him talk when he was winning all that money. El habla puro Mexicano, senor."

"Es un diablo para pelear," said a bystander, with a closed eye.

"Es la verdad," chimed in Vasquez, "for my poor nose is broken."

"Do you speak Spanish?" asked the officer.

"Si, senor," Guy replied, stiffly.

"Are these charges of Vasquez true?"

"I will answer at the proper time."

"Are you an American?"

"I am, sir."

"Tejano?"

"Yes, a colonist."

"What are you doing in San Antonio?"

"Only passing through."

"Have you a pass?"

"I was a captive among the Indians. I made my escape only five days ago and this is the first settlement I have reached. I came in today with your priest."

"Every word that he says is true," José ventured to suggest. I came in with Father Ignacio and Senor Raymond came with us, from the San Geronimo. Oh! Dios," he continued, aside, "what will the padre say to me about this scrape I have got Senor Raymond into?"

"You will have to account well for being inside of our lines, or it will go hard with you. Besides you will have to answer to the charge made by Vasquez," said the officer, sternly.

"Senor," replied Ruiz, "the young man has informed you of his escape from the Indians, and if he was long a captive, he could not know that we are in a state of war with his countrymen.

"I do not want any explanations from you, Senor Ruiz. You are not free from suspicion yourself."

The officer here gave a signal and a file of soldiers entered, in charge of a sergeant. Giving the latter some instructions in a low tone, he left the monte room.

Guy understood at a glance that he was in the custody of a military patrol, and had no doubt that he was to go to prison. When the sergeant ordered him to fall in, in front of the soldiers, he did so at once and was marched out into the street.

CHAPTER XV.

Guy's surmise as to his destination was correct. The patrol had very few steps to make before they reached the entrance of the carcel. They entered the corridor connecting the street and the court within, and the prisoner found himself in a paved yard, not unlike the one at Father Ignacio's, where he had performed his ablutions in company with Senor Gonzales. A dreary light from a lantern, which swung from the rear wall and barely made objects discernable, disclosed a sentinel walking beneath it. Small, grated windows looked in upon the court from high places in the masonry in the southern wall, indicating the positions of the prison cells they were intended to ventilate. The sergeant brought the patrol to a halt, then spoke to the sentinel, who immediaely knocked at a door in the wall opposite the cells. After repeating the summons, the door slowly opened and sufficiently to admit the passage of a round, fat head, which protruded itself and in an effiminate voice, demanded:

"Que cosa es?"

"Abra la puerta, viejo; we have a nice young Gringo for you. If you know what is good for yourself you had better put him in your safest cage, for he is a strong bird."

"Where did you catch this pajorro, tan fuerte? Have you had a battle, and is this one of the prisoners?"

"No, tonto. The fight was only a fisticuff, and this young savage, who is a kind of Lipan, broke half a dozen noses, and closed up as many more eyes before they secured him."

"Wait until I get my keys," said the owner of the fat head, as he drew it in again.

He soon reappeared muttering:

"Pajarro muy fuerte, pajarro muy fuerte."

The rotund form of the jailer was in keeping with his head.

He strode along the paved court with a shuffling pace to retain possession of his buckskin slippers, into which his feet were thrust, without regard to the exposure of his bare yellow heels, just visible under the bottoms of his loose trousers, that depended in remarkable fullness from a waist past the medium of corpulency. He thrust a heavy iron key into the lock of a door to the left on the corridor and, while doing so, he scanned the features of the prisoner from under his elevated left hand. The door yielded to his pressure and motioning to the sergeant to bring on his man, he enterd, repeating to himself:

"Pajarro fuerte."

Guy, obeying the order to follow the jailer, found himself in a narrow passage and could dimly distinguish another doorway, just as he heard a movement of a rusty bolt, followed by the deeper darkness of a cell that became apparent as the door opened.

"Entre," commanded the fine voice of the jailer.

Guy half hesitated, when the sergeant assisted him by a slight push. The door was quickly closed, the rusty bolt grated harshly as it shot into place, and the cell was filled with inky darkness.

Left alone to his reflections, Guy stood for a while motionless, half dazed by the change which a few minutes had made in his fortunes. The monte room pictured itself before him; the dealer with the cards, slowly manipulating them, the crowd, interested, wondering at his strange luck, the sinister expression of those eyes in which he had divined mischief to himself, his subsequent collision with their owner and his struggle with the mob, all passed rapidly through his mind. And his winnings? His hand sought his pocket, but he remembered that he had entrusted every cent to Ruiz, the gallant fellow who came to his assistance. The latter had proven a better comrade than the timid Jose, whom he had seen looking wild and irresolute while Manuel was uttering the tirade against his assailants. Even the little senorita, with whom he had waltzed, looked at him with her soft eyes from the mental panorama that passed before him. What would Father Ignacio say when his erring mozo, Jose, would communicate the news of his mishap, brought about by his well intended chaperoning?"

As the subject matter of his thoughts terminated in the rapid digestion of all the incidents of the evening, a feeling akin to despair weighed upon him for a moment. It was only for a moment, for, raising his head, he caught the lighter shade of the heavens in a space scarcely larger than a hand, in the midst of which glimmered the soft, silver light of a star. As trivial as was this circumstance, his heart sent back a greeting to the celestial monitor that, of all the universe, was peeping at him through that little space of the window of his cell. He groped about, feeling to discover what objects, animate or inanimate, might be his co-occupants. Nothing more than the bare, damp walls. Not a seat to rest upon. He did not expect to find a bed. He walked slowly up and down the narrow limits, pausing at every turn to look at the star, the only object he could see in the whole universe. He began to feel very weary, when the noise of the sliding bolt arrested his attention. The next moment the door of the cell opened and the peculiar voice of the jailer sang out:

"Aqui esta su cama."

A rustling noise on the floor indicated that something had been tossed in. The door closed the bolt shot forward to its place, and all again was quiet.

Guy, on examining his acquisition, discovered it to be a tick of cornshucks, amply filled, but too short for a comfortable bed. He stretched it out to its full length, however, and improvising his coat for a pillow, laid himself down for a rest, without any hope of being able to sleep. He was exceedingly weary, having had little repose since the early morning, to which was added the effects of his struggle with the crowd after he had disabled his denouncer, Vasquez. He had escaped with little injury, sundry bruises about his head being the extent of the damage to his person. He continued awake for a long time, nursing his thoughts and speculating as to the outcome of his present predicament, when he gradually lapsed into a dreamy slumber.

Jose had kept in sight of his unfortunate American friend until the darkness of the prison corridor shut him out from view. He heaved a sigh and uttered a Spanish imprecation as he turned towards the plaza. He was about to pass the tienda of the Senora Candelario, when he observed Manuel Ruiz, seated at one of the tables in her establishment, with his head leaning on his hand, as if absorbed in deep reflection. Anxious to find sympathy in his dilemma, Jose immediately entered the shop, seated himself opposite to his friend, and placing both elbows on the table aped, without intending it, the position of the other.

"You are not playing monkey, are you?" asked Ruiz, rather indignantly. "I feel too mad to stand any foolishness, and the business we have just been through is too serious for aping."

"Not so serious with you, amigo, as it is with me. If you had to tell Father Ignacio what I will have to tell in the morning, and then to confess it besides—Oh, Dios! That my mother never had borne me!"

"It is for yourself that you feel then. If I could have rescued that gallant boy, I would be willing to face a thousand priests, and confess every sin in the calendar. It is his imprisonment in that infernal jail that I regret."

"I am as sorry as you, Manuel; but was it not lucky that he gave you the ninety pesos."

"D——n the money! It is of him I am thinking."

"But if he had kept the money, those soldiers or old Bonito would have got it. Now, you can keep it for Senor Raymond until he gets out."

"If he ever gets out!"

"Don't say that, Manuel."

"I tell you, these are serious times, and he may be shot as a spy, even if he gets clear of the Vasquez matter."

"Get him free from that, and I am certain he will never be shot, with Father Ignacio here to account for him."

"But how to shut Vasquez's mouth?"

"It was his brother's saddle and Senor Raymond got me to sell it to the Monte Pio. That proof would fail, but he recognizes in him the slayer of his brother."

"Has the fellow anything."

"Vasques?"

"Vasquez."

"No, not a quartilla, but what he picks up here and there at odd times. He lives around the Cabeza de Toro and owes the women for tortillas. He is lower than a peon."

"Then I have an idea how to shut his mouth," said Ruiz, striking the table with his hand.

"Como?" asked Jose, electrified by the hopeful suggestion.

"I will do it with Senor Raymond's money."

"Con todo? With every cent? The idea is capital! But, amigo, not all those ninety pesos! Why, a third of that amount would appear, to that wretch's eyes, like a great fortune. No, Manuel, it would be a shame to bestow such an amount on such an object."

"Well, if he takes a part, all right; but what are ninety pesos compared with that young fellow's freedom?"

"Es verdad; but, Manuel, not the whole ninety."

"Your mind dwells on small matters, Jose, when great ones are at stake. I feel better, now that I can see some hope for our friend, and with hope returns my vagrant appetite. Oyez, Senora! Dos platas de chile con carne, con tortillas y frejoles."

The summons and order were heard by the senora, who had peeped in from time to time, and had caught snatches of the conversation. feeling confident that their order would follow shortly. Soon two smoking dishes of the savory preparation ordered were placed in front of the men, with a third plate of tortillas.

"I was to bring Senor Raymond here tonight, after we had taken in the Cabeza de Toro," said Jose, with a half sigh, cut short by his first mouthful of supper. "Instead of supping here, he is now in prison, and the money he won so beautifully on deposit for the beast who caused his misfortune. Manuel, did it ever occur to you what kind of a world this is?"

"The old padre, who taught me, impressed me with the idea that it was round."

"I don't mean its shape. I mean the circumstances of life, the events which shape destinies, the influences which affect our fortunes."

"You didn't find that in Father Ignacio's books. He accounts, no doubt, for good and bad fortunes as special acts of Providence. Take care, Jose! Any drifting into a different philosophy will add to the already heavy penances in store for you."

"Que bruto! To call me back to that dreaded subject, when I had just got it out of my head."

"Very well, I will relieve you of my presence and you can find your way to bed, while I search for Vasquez and——"

"Don't, Manuel, pay him all—not the whole ninety—to such a——"

Before Jose could finish what he was going to say, Ruiz had hurriedly left the place and was out of sight. The deserted major domo called to Senora Candelario, who promptly appeared.

"What will Don Jose have?" she inquired.

"Call me not Don Jose! Call me a burro—bruto—or anything. Here is the money for our suppers.

"Gracias, senor, but what is the matter that you are so worried?"

"Enough is the matter," said Jose, approaching the street door.

"Has the fight over the way anything to do with your trouble?"

"Everything. A young friend—an American—has been put in the carcel for breaking the noses of a dozen peons who set upon him."

"Is it the young man who came with el padre Ignacio?"
"The same."
"Is he a friend of the padre?"
"He has taken a great fancy to him."
"Then why bother about it. Surely the friend of el padre Ignacio will come to no harm. Go at once and tell him."
"There's the trouble. If I had not taken him there he would not now be a prisoner. The blame will rest on me, and telling it may cost me my place. My young friend was to take supper here with me."
"You are a good customer, Jose. Poor young fellow! Perhaps he has had no supper."
"Not he! Old Bonito would not take the trouble to hand him a cold tortilla."
"He shall have his breakfast then, for Bonito will be glad to let me furnish it."
"Good Candelario!"
"Where did Senor Ruiz go in such a hurry?"
"He is half out of his wits. To think of giving ninety pesos to a peon, to whom five would look like a fortune. He has gone in search of the fellow who caused all the trouble. For ninety pesos I would take myself off. Buenas noches, Candelario," and Jose went out into the street.

"Una cosa muy triste," sighed the senora, as she turned back into her shop.

Instead of going towards home, Jose proceeded slowly down the street until he came to the vinoteria. He looked in and saw three or four soldiers at a table in the further end. After a moment's hesitation he entered and, taking a seat, called for something to drink. A pottery jug with a mug was placed before him by the shop tender.

When Ruiz left Jose so unceremoniously he made his way directly to the Cabeza de Toro. He there looked in every nook and corner, but the object of his search could not be seen. Gambling was still in progress in the monte room, whose atmosphere was almost stifling from tobacco smoke. The chink of silver and the even, musical voices of the crowd went on as if no undue excitement had lately disturbed the quiet of the place. In the danceroom the baile was at its height, and Ruiz was scarcely noticed as he elbowed his way, scrutinizing the faces of the men. He sat down, rather impatiently, and concluded to wait until the dansa, then playing, was over. The music ceased and a young girl seated herself near to him. She was the same with whom Guy had waltzed. A sudden impulse, probably induced by a desire for some kind of sympathy, caused him to communicate with her the misfortune of her late partner.

"Que mala gente!" she exclaimed. "To put such a pretty fellow in that dirty carcel."

"He was brave. You should have seen him easily handle a half dozen men."

"And what a skin he has! I would bet he has a pretty sister."

"The Americans are all brave."

"And so handsome."

"Well, I am off to see what I can do for your pretty partner."

"Oh, Manuel! Can I help you?"

"You, little one! What could you do?" and Ruiz strode away, glancing back with a half smile at the girl.

Out in the fresh air once more Ruiz walked on mechanically until he found himself in the plaza. He turned to the right, down the sidewalk leading to where, half a block ahead, the light from the Monte Pio's streamed into the open square. When near the door he could hear voices and when opposite, he paused and saw, to his satisfaction, Vasquez, the object of his search.

He quickly entered. High words were passing between that individual and another worthy, but little more respectable in appearance. Vasquez, who was in his shirt sleeves and hatless, had his swollen eye bandaged and was in the act of pulling off his shoes.

"Pull them off, you rascal!" the other was saying. "You lied to me to get the money, and now you must pawn those shoes to pay me or I will give you a worse beating than did that young Gringo."

Ruiz made inquiry of Vasquez concerning the trouble between him and the other and having fully posted himself, prepared to carry out his scheme.

"Look here, fellow! You have the heart of a dog to force a poor, wounded devil to give up his shoes for a trifle of four reals. Here is your money. You, Vasquez, keep on your shoes. Where is your hat?"

"Senor, the Monte Pio gave me three reals on it, to pay that same fellow. I borrowed the money, hoping to win, but I had bad luck tonight."

"Here is your hat. You owe me seven reals now."

"Mil gracias, senor. I am your servant."

"Come, Vasquez, I have something to say to you for your own good," said Ruiz, leading the way out to the plaza.

"For my good? You have been so good to me already."

"Yes, but you are in great danger, and I found it out merely by chance."

"What is it, senor?"

"The young man, the American you had arrested."

"What about him?"

"You were mistaken about him—about his being with the Indians."

"But——"

"Hush, and I will show that you are honestly mistaken. You noticed how well he speaks our language?"

"Si, senor, like a Mexican."

"Well, he is American born, but he is an adopted son of el presedente, Don Antonio Lopez de Santa Anna, and came only this morning with the president's chief of staff."

'Por Dios! Lo que dice V., es la verdad?"

"As true as there stands San Fernando."

"Oh, senor, what will I do?"

"Remain here and get shot, or get out of the way and join the colonists, or—or, do something."

"If I had a horse I would leave tonight, right now, but, senor, I have not a quartilla."

Ruiz reflected a moment.

"I have it!" he said. "I am glad I thought of it. The Texans are not far from here and I have something to send to the commander, General Austin. You can take it for me. It is a package of money. Will you do this for me?"

"Senor! Would you trust me?"

"Why not? You would not be fool enough to stay here and get shot. Besides, I will give you some money for yourself. You know, with money, a man can go most anywhere. The quicker you get out of this, the safer will be your head."

"I will do just what you tell me, senor."

"Follow me, then."

Ruiz turned into the Calle de Carcel and directed his steps towards the tienda where he had left Jose so unceremoniously. Senora Candelario had closed for the night, but a faint light came from the vinoteria, a little farther on. Keeping an eye on his protege, Ruiz continued down the narrow pavement and entered the latter place. It was apparently deserted by all but the shop boy, who was dozing in a corner. The noise made by the comers awakened him.

"How can I serve you, senor?" he inquired, rousing up as he spoke.

"My good boy, it is nearly time you were closing for the night and I will take the liberty to shut your street door for a few moments, and will pay you well if you should imagine that it has cost you anything. Here are four reals as a pledge for what I say. I have a little private business with this honorable gentleman and do not wish to be interrupted."

The boy took the money, while Ruiz closed the entrance from the street.

"Now, my little friend, you step into the back room and allow no one to bother us for a while."

After the boy had retired, Ruiz turned to Vasquez.

"Now, what is your full name?"

"Enrique Jose Maria."

"You have name enough, at all events, if you are a pauper," thought Ruiz, as he took a lot of silver from his pockets and counted it on the table.

"Ten, twenty, thirty, forty," he called, as he shoved four stacks of pesos to one side.

A voice in a corner repeated the enumeration and caused Ruiz to look in the direction whence came the sound; but seeing nothing, he concluded it was an echo. He rolled up this money in his handkerchief and then counted and stacked ten more pesos.

"Well, Senor Don Enrique Jose Maria Vasquez, here is a package containing forty pesos, which you are to deliver to General Austin, the commander of the Texans, now in camp on el rio Cibolo. He is a friend of mine and will take care of you. Here are ten pesos for yourself. You know the country well. Do not get caught or your life will be forfeited."

"Mil gracias, senor. All shall be done as you command."

"Can you read?"

"No, senor."

"I thought of sending a letter by you, but it is best that you carry nothing indicating your destination. Now be off and do not let tomorrow's sun see you in Bexar."

"Adios, senor," and Vasquez was disposed of.

"Al diablo," said Ruiz, as he went to the door and looked after the fellow as he disappeared in the darkness.

"Fifty pesos did the work," muttered Ruiz, turning towards the back door.

"Is it you, Manuel?" asked an unsteady voice in the shadow of the opposite corner.

Ruiz saw, with surprise, the half recumbant form of Jose gazing stupidly at him, with his hand shading his eyes.

"You here! And I thought I was alone."

"Hic! Did you give the fellow the ninety pesos?"
"Buarachon! I did not know you ever got drunk."
"Por via de mi madre! Manuel el padre se anoho con migo."
"Come, you poor devil. I will see you home."

Ruiz helped the inebriate to his feet, and led him out of the vinoteria.

CHAPTER XVI.

When Guy awoke, after having fallen alseep on his rude prison bed, the light of morning had penetrated through the high, deep window into the recesses of his apartment. As his eyes grew accustomed to the varying shades that hung about the rough and mildewed walls, they wandered inquisitively over every foot of surface, as his thoughts mingled the quaint appearance of his surroundings with the strange mischance which had consigned him to a cell. Deep fissures and jagged points everywhere appeared in the masonry, predominating in number in the arched ceiling. From these his glance was directed to the opening, as he remembered the little star, that had peeped into his solitude and cheered his faltering courage. He thought over his case.

Its most serious aspect was doubtless involved in the charge of the fellow who called himself Vasquez. The saddle, which had betrayed him, must have belonged to the man's brother, else the true story of the fight and the recognition of the property could not have followed, so quickly, his arrival in the town. Indeed, he himself had been recognized, unless the presence of Jose had betrayed his identity, as the party who had authorized the sale of the saddle to the Monte Pio. He rose from his bed not very much rested, his limbs stiff, and a dull, heavy ache about his temples. A basin of cold water to lave his head would have been worth more money than all that his strange luck had brought him but a few hours before.

What had become of that array of silver dollars which had made the eyes of Jose glisten with eagerness? Ruiz would probably keep it for him or entrust it to the major domo. It might possibly help him some in his difficulty. But the termination of every speculation as to his liberation would be the hope he had in the friendship and influence of the good priest of San Fernando. He, of all persons, was incorruptible. He had been pronounced by his most intimate underling to be a living saint and appeared to be the terror of that worthy whenever he suspected the pious father had discovered any of his lapses from a prescribed rectitude either in religious or secular matters.

Guy's reflections were interrupted by the sounds of the jailor's voice, the tones indicating displeasure. Old Bonito, as the sergeant had called him, appeared to be in altercation with someone whom he would not allow to enter from the corridor. Although the young prisoner was possessed equally of resignation and resolution, still the sound of the voice was pleasant and welcome. His father had inculcated in his son's disposition much of his own self-reliant philosophy. At fifteen his thoughts had expanded from the chrysalis of traditionary channels to the transcendant realms of speculative inquiry. His Indian life had been a study of nature. The instincts of the savage, which placed him beyond the pale of a civilization that lowered him by its arbitrary standard of morality, were offset and even overbalanced by the gilded vices and insatiate rapacity of his white brother. The stoic fortitude of the Lipans had impressed their young prsoner with a feeling of admiration for a racial characteristic that held in contempt a display of fear or weakness in any vicissitude.

The voices outside had ceased for many minutes, when he heard the shuffling step of the jailer approaching. A rap followed.

"Senor Pajarro! Are you awake?"

Guy remained silent.

"Oyez, senor!"

"The bird cannot be flown," muttered Bonito. "I'll just open the door and see if he is dead, deaf or asleep."

He unlocked the door and cautiously opened it. Guy stood before him, erect, with a stern expression in his eyes as they encountered those of the jailer.

"Por Dios! Senor Pajarro has bad eyes."

"My name is Raymond, Senor Bonito, and if you wish to keep on the good side of me you had better drop your nicknames."

"Senor Raymond, your servant! You cannot be half so vicious as the sergeant would have one believe. Ciertamente, siempre, Senor Raymond. No more nicknames. The sergeant introduced you as Senor Pajarro; Pajarro, fuerte; but now Senor Raymond. Stupid sergeant! Bonito is a nickname for me, but I have long ceased to mind it, for honestly, senor, my true name is something wonderful for length, the fault of my parents, however. Strangers, and even some intimate acquaintances, could never remember it, and therefore I submitted to my nickname. I always answer to Bonito. I hope you slept well last night, although your bed was none of the best. They don't furnish me with beds for prisoners and this bag of shucks was all that could be found among my own effects. I will never get pay for this act of my charity; but Bonito manages to keep even from certain tricks of his own. For instance, I will charge for your breakfast this morning when it is not my intention to furnish you with a morsel. Not that I could have a heart to starve my prisoner, but I have my permission asked, by a senora who makes the best dishes in the town, that she may have the honor of providing you with a breakfast. Of course, my permission was given, for I will make a real. I am fortunate in getting hold of a prisoner who is so popular with the senoras. I hope, senor—senor—your name has gone from me already. I was going to say that I hope you will remain with me just as long as Senora Candelario will supply you with meals."

The loquacity of the jailer seemed interminable and would have continued to an indefinite length had not Guy interrupted.

"See here, Senor Bonito! Your tongue would have been better employed by making inquiry as to the wants of your prisoner than in discussing yourself and your trickery. I want a basin of water and something to sit on. If you do not attend to me properly I shall apply for a release at once and you will lose your real for my meals. Furthermore, if you treat me well I have money to pay you."

"The sergeant did not search you then! If he did not, it is more wonderful than a miracle. Under the rules it becomes my duty to carry out what the patrol failed to do."

As he said this, Bonito advanced as if to execute the asserted duty. The statement of his prisoner that he was possessed of means to pay was taken in the sense that he had the money on his person. The idea roused his cupidity and the first thought was to dispossess his victim in advance and make the manner of treatment a subsequent consideration. Guy at once perceived his intention and thwarted him by a display of determination, coupled with a warning signal from his half extended arm and open palm.

"It is plain, Bonito, that you do not know with whom you have to deal. You cannot search me single-handed, but I will relieve you of the torture of believing that I have money with me, by informing you that I have not a cent here. My money is with my friends. It will be to your interest to get me what I require and to do so at once."

"You are a bold pajarro, sure enough. You shall have the water and the seat."

Bonito made a motion to close the door of the cell, then remarked:

"No! I will be gone but a second, and you could not get out of the court if you tried."

He left the cell door half open and shuffled away across the court.

Guy rolled his bed into a corner, made a round or two of his cell, then waited at the door. Before Bonito's return someone was pounding on the closed door leading into the corridor. He heard the summons from the opposite apartment, whence he had stuck out his head on Guy's arrival with the patrol, went through the same performance on this occasion, and shouted to the caller to have patience.

"There ought to be a half dozen Bonitos," he said. "Here I have to be run to death serving this one, and answering that one, and a peon is better paid. I half believe that pretty bird has the money on him. (Santa Maria! That fellow will batter down the door.) He would have had his basin of water ten minutes ago if it had not been for Linda's tongue. Even she knows him, and Candelario knows him, and that Manuel Ruiz was here this morning trying to force his way in, without a permit, to see him. Este pajarro es una vera aguila."

Bonito finally supplied the coveted water, and depositing the basin and a three-legged stool inside the cell door, he made all the haste he could to answer the loud knocking at the corridor.

It proved to be Guy's breakfast which had been sent as promised. The fat old fellow was puffing from his unusual celerity of movement as he deposited on the doorsill of the cell a basket covered by a snowy cloth.

"If you have many more wants, Senor Pa——your pardon, senor, but your name is ——?"

"Raymond," answered Guy, amused.

"I fear I will be poorly paid, Senor Raymond, for to attend to you one will have to run himself to death."

"Give me the liberty of the enclosure and I will give you my word that I will make no attempt to escape."

"That is exactly what that little tonta, Linda, said when I went for the basin and the stool."

"Who is Linda?"

"She said she knows you. If true, it seems to me you should know her. Linda is my rattle-brained daughter."

"She must be mistaken," said Guy, wonderingly.

"She is mistaken in nothing. She has said it, and means it. She knew of your arrest and asked me to let you walk about the court in the day time. Like all women, she is soft-hearted. If she were jailer all the prisoners would get away, for she would parole them all to walk where they pleased."

"Not all, Bonito. An honorable man is safer kept by his parole than by the strongest walls. Perhaps your Mexican race does not understand this sentiment as its men are unusually treacherous."

"I am no Mexican, senor. My father was Portugese and my mother Italian. My wife was Mexican. Mexicans are a pretty bad set—that is, the men. The women are all right and would turn anybody loose. You had better look into your basket, now that you are washed. Your breakfast will get cold."

Guy was not loth to comply with Bonito's suggestion, for he had tasted nothing since the dinner at Father Ignacio's. Seating himself on the doorsill he converted the stool into a table and took the edibles out of the basket. Everything was steaming. At the very bottom he found a mug of chocolate covered by a plate containing tortillas.

"This is better than prison fare," said Bonito, his appetite sharpened by the smell of the dishes.

"Ruiz must have had a hand in this," thought Guy.

"Do you know Manuel Ruiz," he asked, turning to the other.

"Si, senor. He was here this morning to see you, but had no permit; and my orders are strict."

"And Jose, he who stays with the padre. Do you know him?"

"Everybody knows Jose."

"Has he been here?"

"No, senor."

"And Linda, your daughter, was she here?"

"She is here all the time, except when she goes to a baile, or to mass, or to walk in the Alameda. She lives with her father; where else?"

Guy knew that the last girl he had spoken to, since he left Laoni on the mountain side, was she with whom he had waltzed the evening before.

"She asked you to let me walk about on parole?"

"As I told you."

"And you refused?"

"I made her no answer. That fellow with your breakfast was about to break down the door, and I had to run with your basin full of water in one hand and the stool in the other. You saw how out of breath I was, and senor, my pay is beggarly."

"Well, Bonito, I will allow you two reals each day that you permit me to enjoy the freedom of the court."

"That is a small pay for the risk, senor."

"No risk at all. Every morning I will renew my parole."

"I will think about it, senor."

Bonito gathered up the dishes, and promising to return shortly, closed and locked the door.

He halted for reflection as he crossed the yard:

"Two reals for the liberty of the court; two for the meals that I don't furnish—four reals. If he stays a month, that will be fifteen pesos. I believe the fellow has the money in his pocket. He won't let me search him, and if I tell the patrol he has it, where will Bonito be? Better close the bargain. He can't get out except through the corridor door, and that is locked all day."

"I thought you were going to stay the rest of the day, papa."

These words greeted Bonito as he returned to the apartment from which he had emerged with basin and stool.

"Your American is hard to please. He wants everything. I have a notion to put him in irons."

"Dear papa! Do not do that. He waltzed with me at the baile and was so polite and agreeable. He would have stayed with me longer, but another came and took him away. After a long time the same one returned and told me of his bad fortune."

"Bad fortune! I think he is doing well. He has money and friends; everybody is trying to get a peep at him; the Candelario is feeding him like a king; you are begging for his liberty in the court; besides, I am making a real for every meal sent to him. Linda, between you and me, I believe the fellow has plenty of money in his pocket. He admits the patrol did not search him and says that I shall not. He is impudent."

"He is brave," said Linda.

"You are a fool."

"And he is handsome."

"Caya te la boca!"

"Papa, do not keep him in the cell all day."

"We will see; we will see."

When his cell door was again opened Guy had a long chat with his jailer who tried, in every conceivable way, to draw from him an admission that he had means on his person to defray the promised outlay for the daily privilege to walk about on parole. After finally consenting to the arrangement, he exacted a promise that Guy should not inform his daughter, if by chance he should meet her in the court, that he had exacted any pay for his release from close confinement. There was no sentinel in the yard, which fact was explained by Bonito, who stated that his post during the day was in front of the prison, but at night the corridor was left open and the sentinel walked in the court.

Noon came and passed. The Candelario did not forget his dinner, but he was disappointed that no one had called to look after his interests. Ruiz had been denied admittance, but what had become of Jose? What of Father Ignacio? Guy thought he should be arraigned on the charge against him, but then he reflected the accusers, judges and jurisprudence, were Mexican, even if he were not to be dealt with by summary military measures. The thought rather discouraged him, and he began to lose confidence in his powers. He seated himself on a bench under his high cell window and lowered his head into his hands. How friendless he was! True, he had no claims on the new acquaintances of the last few hours, other than those of common humanity and that chivalrous generosity whose mutual possession draws persons together through the magnetism of a noble similarity.

The valley of the San Saba rose to his mental vision. The rock above the falls supported the form of his truest friend, who was waiting, and would wait until the leaves would fall and come again, waiting for El Bravo. A touch upon his shoulder awakened him from his reverie and starting up, he beheld his little partner in the waltz.

CHAPTER XVII.

The morning after the termination of Jose's visit to the Cabeza de Toro, Father Ignacio was astir betimes. He had duties to perform about his premises before repairing to the church to say early mass. His absence had not tended to improve the domestic arrangement of his household, and he was too thorough and methodical to trust important matters to irresponsible servants. Jose was usually faithful, but was sometimes derelict in depending too implicitly on others, not actuated by motives so disinterested as was the major domo in the affairs of his patron. On the morning in question he waited, rather impatiently, for the appearance of his trusted steward. The cook had reported that Jose had not been seen, and consequently he had no orders. All about the premises were ignorant of his whereabouts. He was not in his room. Finally, at his wit's end, the priest directed a servant to go to Senor Raymond's apartment and inquire if he knew anything of the major domo.

The servant returned in a moment and reported that the reputed occupant was not there, but that he found Jose fast asleep on the bed and that several vigorous shakes had failed to arouse him.

Lost in amazement at such news, Father Ignacio hastened to investigate for himself. Sure enough, he discovered Jose in the condition reported, and after several efforts, succeeded in getting him to a sitting position on the bed. The smell of mescal at once apprised the priest of the cause of the major domo's stupidity. Why his trusted man had imbibed the execrable stuff to the extent of beastly intoxication, where he had been, what occasion had tempted him, and how he came to be in Guy's room and bed, and the latter gone, were mysteries to be solved.

Jose, after sitting up a while, became sufficiently conscious to respond to inquiries.

"Jose! Where is Senor Raymond?"

"I know not, mi padre. Is he not in his room?"

"Why, this is his room. You are in his bed, and he is not to be seen. How came you here?"

"I know not, mi padre, unless I walked in my sleep."

"Jose, you have been drunk, and only now are getting over the effects.

"I may have taken a drink, but not drunk, mi padre. I am sick—so sick."

"If you are sick, it is from the effects of mescal. Have you no shame? I had need of your assistance at the church, for this is the eve of the Feast of the Holy Rosary, and you well know that I wanted you to do the heavy work in arranging and decorating the grand altar. Now, upon whom am I to depend? Where is this young American? You say you do not know; but since I find you in this wretched, disgraceful condition, I cannot believe you. Confine yourself to this room until I give you permission to leave. Disobey me, and you will forfeit my friendship."

Jose became rapidly sobered during the priest's lecture. Indeed, his debauch had been slept off, but had been succeeded by a stupor that rquired a little time after awakening to admit of a full return of the senses. He had not dared to admit to a knowledge of Guy's misfortune. The denial, once made, rendered it all the more difficult to tell the truth. He was full of remorse, but dared not acknowledge sua culpa, sua maxima culpa to the priest whose life was so pure.

Poor Jose! He fell over on the bed and wept bitter tears on account of the father's displeasure. His fault had not been so great, after all. If the arrest of his friend could have been avoided, he would have been home in time, perfectly sober, with bright pesos which his unfortunate companion had so beautifully won, and which now, alas, had all gone most probably to the vile Vasquez, who was the cause of all the trouble. Jose came to the conclusion that the worst feature of the whole affair was the discovery of his wrong doing. He pondered on his case and concluded the safest defense would be a general denial as to his knowledge of Guy's imprisonment. The first use he would make of a release from the restriction to his present quarters would be to institute a pretended search for the missing guest and report the discovery of his arrest under the charges of Vasquez. The fact of his inebriation must be accounted for in some manner, but how, the present state of his muddled brain rendered him powerless to decide.

It was quite noon before Father Ignacio relented towards his crestfallen major domo, and consented for him to return to his accustomed duties. The latter had effaced all traces of his late condition and appeared fresh, but serious, when his master's dinner was served. The father's manner was austere and reserved during the meal. He scarcely noticed Jose, and refrained from interrogating him on the subject uppermost in his mind, for the reason that he believed his steward had lied in answer to the questions asked him in the morning. When he had concluded his repast he leaned over the table in a thoughtful mood, mechanically using his goblet in making circles on the cloth, until he had ringed the surface in front of him into a score of interlaced figures.

Jose watched the proceedings with many misgivings, for he knew he was on the eve of receiving either a lecture or reprimand or some order, that was to be the outcome of this deliberation. Finally the priest broke the silence:

"Jose, I will not ask you to say if you know aught of the cause of Senor Raymond's disappearance, or why he did not occupy his room last night. Still more will I refrain from pressing you to an explanation of your own conduct and its resulting debauch. I will say this, however, that you have incurred my serious displeasure, and if you would make some atonement for the sin you have committed, as well as for your attempt to conceal it, you will employ this afternoon in making searching inquiry for this young American who, I fear, has been foully dealt with."

As Father Ignacio left the dining room, his auditor stood speechless, mentally relieved by the modified rebuke expressed in tones which, while moderate, conveyed to the major domo the full measure of a distrust, which he hoped the events of the afternoon and his own ingenuity would remove.

As soon as Jose had disposed of a hasty repast, he set out for the Calle de Carcel.

When Vasquez left the vinoteria with his treasure he had not the remotest idea of his destination. He had listened to the words of Ruiz in all credulity and mentally resolved to let alone the adopted son of el presidente and to rely on concealment to escape any penalty for his mistake. Refuge with the Texans was the furthest from his thoughts. The astonishment which first seized him when Ruiz proposed to entrust him with a sum of money was supplanted by eagerness to possess it. His first precaution, on leaving the vinoteria, was to watch for the exit of his benefactor, from a safe position in a doorway. He soon saw him come out, supporting the unsteady form of Jose, and turn up towards the plaza. He followed them until the latter had been duly deposited in the hallway of the priest's house, and he had seen the other walk briskly away and enter the Calle Solidad at the northeast corner of the square. Satisfied that Ruiz had disappeared for the night, he hastened back to the Cabeza de Toro. Before entering he sought the shadow of the carcel wall, where an alley separated the two buildings, and taking the handkerchief from his bosom, he undid the roll and deposited the silver in the several pockets about his person. The coins chinked in spite of his precautions and he dropped a piece, for which he groped about for several minutes, raking the ground with his fingers. He uttered an oath at his want of success, then hurriedly left and entered the gambling den, without having noticed two forms, which turned the corner in time to hear a tell-tale clink of the silver to betray his presence.

"Who was it?" asked a voice.

"I saw his face as he went in the door and think it was Vasquez."

"He! With money?"

"Perhaps he has been winning."

"Let us go in and watch him."

Vasquez's face wore the expression of supreme content as he stood over the gaming table and made his first bet. He became deeply interested as the game continued and fortune favored him. His first varying success now changed to one continuous flow of luck and so absorbed him that he did not notice anything but the cards and the dealer. Finally he lost. Another bet, and he lost again. He hesitated as if uncertain what to do, watched the game a while, then turned and left the place.

"Which way did he go?"

"To the left, down the street."

"You cross over. I will follow him on this side."

The two, who had heard the clink of silver in the alley, followed Vasquez as he hurried in the direction of the old mill.

When Jose arrived at the Calle de Carcel he apparently changed his mind, for he continued down the east side of the plaza until he reached the door of the Monte Pio. He found the proprietor busy bargaining with some woman over several articles of jewelry, and while waiting until he would be disengaged, he peered into the showcase at the various articles of silver and gold ornaments, jewelry, spurs, silk sashes, medals and other things of more or less value. His attention was attracted by a silver medal of the virgin attached to a string of pure, white beads, ingenously interwoven. He remembered Guy's description of his lost trinket, and concluded that this new addition to the monte pio's stock must be the medal lost in the camp on the San Geronimo.

The Monte Pio saluted Jose gaily as he turned from his departing customers.

"The very man I wanted to see."

"That accounts for my coming here instead of keeping on to the carcel."

"My thoughts attracted you."

"And why did you want to see me?"

"I have a letter—a message—and some money for you. The money is to be in trust for—— but I will give you the letter and that will explain."

Jose took the letter and opening it, read as follows:

"My Friend:—I would have called to see you, but events have happened which compel me to leave the city very suddenly. On account of my defense of the young American, the authorities, who already distrusted me, have resolved on my arrest. I go from here the enemy of despotism, which is personated in Santa Anna, and am resolved to never submit to it. I leave in the hands of the Monte Pio thirty-eight and a half pesos, which is the balance of Senor Raymond's winnings, after using what was required to get the fellow Vasquez out of the way. I used a little artifice and fifty-one and a half pesos to induce him to leave. It is pretty certain he will not be seen around town again shortly. You will doubtless be glad I did not give him the whole ninety. I hope you have told Father Ignacio all, and that he has taken steps for the release of that brave young fellow. The only charge against him will be his nationality, and the good father can account for his presence in town.

"Your friend,   Manuel Ruiz."

Jose was so glad that Ruiz had saved a portion of the money, and had disposed of Vasquez, that he forgot all about the medal in the showcase. He directed the Monte Pio to retain the amount mentioned in Ruiz's letter and add it to the proceeds from the pony and saddle, for the credit of Guy Raymond.

The major domo had scarcely left the Monte Pio's when a Mexican, dressed as a ranchero, rode up to the door, dismounted and entered. The proprietor, who had just commenced to cast up the amount of Senor Raymond's credit, looked up and asked the newcomer what was wanted.

"I want to redeem my spurs," he replied, showing a ticket.

After glancing at the bit of pasteboard, the other took down a pair of spurs, whose huge rowells were out of all proportion.

"So, Pedro, you have made a raise."

"Si, senor, I won twenty pesos at the cock fight."

"Better get that handsome sash, now you have the money."

"What is the price of this medal, with the white beads?" asked Pedro.

"That? Let me see; you can have it at a bargain. I bought it from one of the mozos who came with Father Ignacio from the Rio Grande. Take it for four pesos."

"Es demasiado," remonstrated Pedro.

"Too much! It is worth seven."

"I will give you twenty reals for it."

"You are a good customer, Pedro. Take the medal, if I lose by it. But where are you going, dressed like a ranchero? On more business for the Colonel?"

"I have a pretty dangerous errand before me. This disguise is furnished by the Colonel. The sight of that medal made me think it well to go under the protection of our good mother. I will get it blessed and wear it on my trip."

"You are right, Pedro. The Blessed Virgin never deserts those who appeal to her for protection. The times are getting dangerous, and it is well to be prudent."

"Adios, senor."

"Adios, Pedro."

"Only twelve reals profit on that medal," mused the Monte Pio, as he watched Pedro secure his lariat to his saddle, mount his pony and ride away.

* * * *

When Guy was startled from his reverie by Linda's touch he was pleased. but not surprised, to find that the jailer's daughter and the girl he had danced with the night before were one and the same person. She was not at all abashed when she encountered the look of the young prisoner. Her face wore an engaging expression, illumined by a quiet smile, characteristic of the sisterhood of her race, that meant half to encourage, half to pity a misfortune which she would fain remove.

"Does the senor remember me?"

"I could not fail to remember the only woman I have spoken to in Bexar."

She answered him with a smile.

"So, you are Linda."

"My father has been telling you my name," she said, looking into his eyes. "I am afraid you found him very rude."

"No, he amused me. He has been quite good to me. You see, he has allowed me the liberty of this court. Perhaps I owe this favor partly to you?"

She only smiled.

"My father worships money. You must not let him impose on you, for he will want you to pay for everything he does for you. If you have much money do not let him know it."

"You are very kind, Linda, to take this interest in a stranger."

"It is a part of our religion, senor. The men of our people are so cruel, but God has made our women with tender hearts."

"Do you live here, inside this carcel?"

"Si, senor."

"Are you not lonely here?"

"Sometimes; but when I am I can go to the Alameda in the evening. I go to mass every morning, and now and then I enjoy a dance at the Cabeza de Toro."

What a difference there is in ideas of the proprieties when viewed from the standpoint of race custom, thought Guy. Here is a pretty, sympathetic, religious girl who could attend festivities without impairing her good name, which the Puritan mind would condemn as a debauch, and which even the license of a more liberal social code of his people would pronounce immoral, held, as they were, under the shadow of a place devoted to the demoralizing vice of gaming. But here race characteristics intervene to extenuate practices whose evil tendencies are merely co-extensive with actual effects produced on race morals, and to point to the difference between customs ingrained in a peculiar civilization and habits confined to the more vicious and disreputable haunts of a more enlightened and progressive population. Gambling among Mexicans is only a degree less natural than is dancing, and with them dancing is one of the necessities of a contented existence.

"And does not the padre object to your going to the Cabeza de Toro one day, and to mass the next?"

"Why should he? One must dance."

"You think, then, that dancing is as necessary as praying?"

"I go to San Fernando in the morning for mass, and you know, senor, the bailes and fandangos are at night."

"Are you going to dance tonight, Linda?"

"No, senor. Tomorrow is the Feast of the Holy Rosary."

"Then it is not right to dance on the eve of this feast?"

"It is not if I go to confession; and I must confess this afternoon. After confession I must be very quiet and think of nothing but my communion in the morning."

"You are a good girl, Linda; I can hardly believe that you are Bonito's daughter."

"He says I am; but sometimes I doubt it, especially when he tries to make me promise to marry the monte pio."

"The monte pio?"

"Si, senor. He lives on the plaza, and he is very rich."

"And why won't you marry him?"

"He is old enough to be my father."

"But he is so rich."

"I could not love him, senor; and with all his riches, he made his first wife work like a peon, and he is ugly and——"

"Then I would not marry him, Linda."

A loud knocking at the door interrupted them and Linda went for her father, who had already retired for his siesta. When, after a lapse of a few moments, that worthy appeared, the knocking had been repeated several times. He was terribly cross at having been disturbed and jowered and grumbled as he crossed the court:

"A poor devil can't take a siesta."

"Tonto!" he continued, on a fresh recurrence of the summons, "can't you wait until a fellow can get to the door? It is a dog's life at best; run my legs off, and after all it will be some one to ask after that pajarro."

"Quien es?" he shouted, as he half introduced the key in the lock.

"Yo, Jose."

"Jose! Jose!" and Bonito contemptuously made his voice still more effiminate. Then he replied to the candidate for admittance:

"No conozco, yo, Jose—Jose—diablo?"

"Jose, el major domo," suggested Linda.

"Who told you to answer?" asked Bonito between his teeth. "You are putting on airs before this pajarro Americano."

"What do you want here?" he shouted, with the key still unturned in the lock.

"El padre Ignacio sent me to see you."

"See me?"

"Si, senor; on business."

The key shot back the bolt, the heavy door slowly swung, and Jose was in the court. Without noticing the jailer, he passed quickly over to Guy and saluted him warmly.

"That is fine business with me," said Bonito, locking the door and casting a savage look at the two.

"It seems like a whole week since last night," said Jose.

He soon posted Guy on all that had transpired outside the carcel as a sequel to their misadventure.

Bonito interrupted them so often with his growling and demands to know Jose's business that Guy used a little artifice to silence him. He said to Jose:

"I want you to go to the monte pio and get me some money. I owe my friend, the jailer, a small sum and must pay him."

The change in Bonito's face was instantaneous and he subsided at once when Jose signified his willingness to comply.

Guy regained his elasticity of spirits when he became informed of the service which Ruiz had rendered him, and regretted the necessity that forced his benefactor to leave the city. When Jose had exhausted every other topic, he remembered the medal he had seen in the show-case.

"I am certain I saw the medal which your Indian girl gave you, senor. It was lying snugly in the show-case at the monte pio's, but I was so full of joy to know that all of your winnings did not go to the villian Vasquez that I forgot to ask who had pawned it, or sold it, rather, for the monte pio has it for sale."

"Be sure, Jose, to tell him to keep it for me at any price."

"That shows you are a poor trader. I will not let him know that you, or any one, places any value on it. I will price it with much indifference, beat him down afterwards on the amount he will ask, and then take it very reluctantly. Senor, you don't know the monte pio."

"Well, at all events, secure it."

Jose promised to see after the medal at once, to execute Guy's directions about the money, and then hasten to inform his master that he had discovered the young American. Guy added a request that he procure for him, from the monte pio, one or more books, provided he had any, as reading or study would help pass away the time.

"If Linda would go with me, she could bring you the money and the book, while I go to inform Father Ignacio."

Linda was quite willing to act on Jose's suggestion, and going for her rebosa, accompanied him out into the street.

"You are the worst prisoner I ever had."

"How so, Bonito?"

"It is lock and unlock, open and shut, run here and run there. A person can't be still a minute. If this keeps up I will get so thin that I won't be able to keep my clothes on, and I will wear out a pair of slippers a week. The two reals for your meals that I don't furnish and the three you are to pay me (that makes five) will not make up for the damages outside of my loss of flesh. Do you think the monte pio will send the money?"

"No doubt of it. But see here, Mr. Bonito, you are raising on me. The price I was to pay for walking out here was to be two reals, instead of three. But we won't quarrel about one real. My talk with Linda is worth the extra one."

"I will bet she said nonsense enough. Senor Pajarro—your name will slip my memory——"

"Raymond."

"Raymondo?"

"That is good enough. Perhaps you will remember that better."

"Bueno; but what was I going to say? Was it about the four reals you are to pay me?"

"Come now, Bonito. You raised it to three a while ago; now you've got it to four. It was about Linda you were going to speak. You were saying she spoke nonsense."

"Ah, si, me acuerdo. It was not about the five reals. It was about Linda. Si, senor, about Linda—L-i-n-d-a. She was to return with the money—f-i-v-e reals—yes, five; it was not six, was it, senor? You very properly corrected me when I said six; I will not forget again."

"Your memory is so treacherous, old fellow, that I fear for your sanity."

"My memory sometimes fails me, Senor Raymondo; but never about money. You remember I said it was only six. Linda stays long. Old and fat as I am, I could have been back before this. If the monte pio was twenty years younger and better looking, I would be suspicious that she was dilly-dallying in his shop. But no such good luck. The tonta has not sense enough to marry him, when he is c-r-a-z-y for her—and r-i-c-h."

When Bonito pronounced the word "rich" he shut one eye tightly and ran out his great tongue in the most comical manner, to better convey his conception of the plethoric state of the monte pio's exchecquer. A light tap at the door was sufficient to rouse the activities of the grasping old jailer who, on the qui vive for the sounds of Linda's coming, lost no time in admitting her. She handed to Guy a few pieces of silver, which act was closely watched by her father.

"Bonito, I had better settle with you before you raise the figures much higher. Shall I pay you those seven reals?"

"Seven, senor! Was it seven? Not eight—although it might have been; but, senor, you are a man of honor; I leave it to you."

Guy tossed him a peso.

"It was eight, sure enough! I said, senor, that my memory was always good about money."

He dropped the piece into his pocket and shuffled off to his room, doubtless to deposit it with his hoarded treasure.

"Here is a notebook and pencil which Senor Jose sent you," said Linda.

"Had the monte pio no books?"

"Here are two old ones he bought long ago, and as they are old and damaged he said the charge for them would be very small."

As she spoke she took from beneath her rebosa two delapidated volumes and handed them to her companion. The back of the first was gone. He turned the fly leaf and read, in his own handwriting:

"Guy Raymond."

It was his Virgil! A film passed over his pupils, as he read the name and recognized his book, until the letters faded and left the page—a blank. His knees grew weak; he sank down upon the bench and leaned against the prison wall. The other volume was clutched in his fingers, still unnoticed when his sight grew clear and the letters grew plain again:

"Guy Raymond."

He laid down the book.

Before he raised the lid of the other, his eye caught the title upon the back:

"AGE OF REASON."

Upon the flyleaf of this he read the name:

"Paul Raymond'

written in the bold hand of his father. How strange! These two volumes had found their way to him, to use all their mute eloquence, to rouse from the recesses of his bosom the memories of a happy past, and to paint, in vivid colors, its terrible finale. The whole panorama passed before him: the spring, the grove, the murmuring current, the dead panther and the nearly fatal shot, the smoking ruin and his captivity. These silent witnesses of the tragedy, these sad reminders of a thousand tender recollections, that linked successively the records of his young life, had escaped destruction to be rescued in mutilated form by alien hands. "Oh, Stella! Stella! Can it be that you survive? If I had but Rolla with me now to give a whine of sympathy!" He laid the second book down by its companion, and realized that Linda was watching him with great solicitude depicted in her countenance.

CHAPTER XVIII.

It was late in the afternoon before Father Ignacio returned from the cathedral. Without the assistance of Jose he had to devote more of his time to the arrangements and changes he had contemplated making in the decorations of the grand altar; and when the duties in this direction had been discharged he had to attend to the spiritual wants of those of his people who claimed him for confessor. These were not a few, and by the time the row of kneeling figures who, enveloped in their flowing rebosas, lined his side of the church had told their faults and the last shriven penitent had issued from the great front portals the sun was looking red and dull from the tops of the western hills.

The good man had often thought of his young American friend during his varied occupation of the day and wondered what his wayward major domo was doing to discover him. His own time was so nearly filled that he could not often carry out his own wishes, because to do so would encroach upon some duty he owed to his sacred office. But for this he would have sallied forth in quest of Guy when he discovered he had not slept in the room assigned to him. He was met by his major domo as he was about to issue from the enclosure of the church.

"Well, Jose, what news?"

"Good news, and bad news, Father."

"You found him——?"

"In the carcel."

"Arrested by the patrol?"

"By the patrol. It appears that a fellow accused him of killing his brother and taking the horse his brother was riding; but Senor Raymond was arrested for fighting and whipping his accuser. His being an American is also, perhaps, against him."

"I will write a note to the Colonel and maybe we can get him out tonight," said Father Ignacio, in a half meditative tone, as he walked away towards his house.

* * * *

"Were you unwell just now, senor?" asked Linda, when Guy had laid down the volume, in which was written the name of his father.

"Not unwell, Linda. Those books you brought me were mine, years ago. My name is written in this, my father's name in that. See, look for yourself."

She looked as requested.

"That is my name. I wrote it there, myself. It is my Virgil, a book I studied when I was learning a language from which your own beautiful tongue has been largely drawn. These books made me remember happy days—days that never can return."

"Jose spoke of your Indian girl, who gave you a medal. Was she with you in those happy days?"

"No, Linda. The great sorrow of my life, the time which ended those happy days, was the cause of my meeting the Indian girl of whom Jose spoke. Her tribe took me captive and but for Laoni this body of mine would have been burned to cinders on a fire already lighted for my destruction."

"Laoni. Was that her name?"

"Yes, the daughter of the Lipan chief."

"She saved your life?"

"She did."

"She must have loved you. Was she good and pretty? All Indian women I have seen were anything but good looking."

"Laoni was an exception. She had none of the savage in her nature. No truer heart ever beat than hers. Her form was perfect, her features intelligent and regular and her step elastic. Unfortunately, she loved me too well; but she would not leave her father to escape with me."

Bonito here called for Linda, in a half angry tone, and she left her companion to himself.

Guy examined the notebook which Jose had sent him and discovered it to be a very plain affair, containing about twenty leaves of blank paper. His object in sending for it was to amuse himself by writing, in the event that he should be kept in confinement for a number of days. He turned to the first page to record the date of his arrival in the city, when he discovered that his pencil was a new one and had never been sharpened. Having no knife, he approached Bonito's door and called:

"Bonito!"

That individual was fussing with Linda, who appeared at the door, with her rebosa thrown over her head and shoulders, her father following. The daughter had requested him to let her out that she might go to confession, and he was complaining at being disturbed.

"If this Raymondo would keep in his cell I could leave the corridor open and you could confess fifty times a day and not disturb me once."

"Well then, Bonito," said Guy, who had been hitherto unobserved by the grumbler, "I will remain in my cell tomorrow and perhaps you will miss the money which I would have to pay if I used the privilege of the court."

The jailor was so well caught that he made his way doggedly and silent to dismiss his daughter. On returning from the door, he approached close to Guy and, in an apologetic undertone, assured him that no one could comprehend how vexatious was Linda at times and that he must not mind the hasty words used by him when out of humor.

"I'll not mention it again, Bonito, if you will lend me your knife to sharpen this pencil."

"Prisoners have no business with knives. After sharpening the pencil, you could cut my throat," said the old fellow, drawing from his pocket and opening a long-bladed knife.

"You are a cunning pajarro. I will cut your pencil for you." So saying Bonito took the pencil and surprised the other by the dexterity he used in fashioning a point.

"Thank you," said Guy, as the pencil was handed to him. "You have sharpened pencils before. But you forget that I am on parole to not attempt to escape; and therefore, your throat would be safe if I had a dozen knives."

"Ah! Paroles are good enough to talk about; but they are continually broken."

"By Mexicans, perhaps."

"By all nations. I have seen pirates keep their paroles, in intercourse with pirates. Lafitte had honor, but it was the honor to be found among thieves. Paroles are binding as long as it is less dangerous to observe than to break them. Senor Raymondo is young yet."

"Were you acquainted with Lafitte?"

"It would not help you to know it. Sometimes people ask too many questions."

The jailer shuffled off to his den as he said this and Guy, turning to his bench, seated himself to try his pencil. The means of writing had not been within his reach since the distruction of his home. He began to write on the first page:

"Arrived in San Antonio October, 1835. Escaped from the

Lipan village, on the San Saba, four days before. The night before entering the town I camped with a party on the San Geronimo creek. The party consisted of Father Ignacio of the Cathedral of San Fernando, his major domo and two mozos leading pack-mules. Also with the party was a Senor Gonzales, who was evidently a man of some rank. The latter probably used an assumed name. On this creek I must have lost my medal. From Jose's description of a medal in the pawn broker's it must be the one I lost. Owing to a difficulty I had at the Bull's Head (Cabeza de Toro) I was put in this prison the night of the same day of my arrival in the town. The night of my arrest I was betting at monte and had singular luck, coming out winner ninety Mexican dollars (pesos). Notwithstanding my success it may be my last indulgence in gambling. 'Bonito' is the name of my jailer. He is an oddity. Gross, flabby and rotund, he is a mere animal. His memory is very elastic where particular amounts of change are involved. The old villain went from one real to seven, as the charge for my remaining in the court of the prison during the day. When I tossed him eight, he took the entire amount. Linda bears no resemblance to him. One would never suspect the close relationship of father and daughter. The old man has not given her many advantages; yet how well she speaks! Bonito uses very good language, however. I must tell Jose to bring Rolla, if I stay here. He must miss me! Poor dog! He has been faithful through all our adventures. Adventures! We had a plenty the last two years. The first opportunity I intend to write the story of my captivity. It would be interesting reading. But I will not be content to do anything until I can know of Stella's fate. I wonder what ever become of Mr. Tr——''

As Guy reached this far with his scribbling, Bonito passed to the corridor and admitted his daughter, who had returned from her duty at the church. She hastened over to the young American and, with one of her pleasant smiles, informed him that she had just left Father Ignacio and Jose in consultation in front of San Fernando and that she was quite sure they were talking about him and the chances for his release. Her father cut short their interview by reminding her that duties unperformed awaited her indoors, and if she gossiped much longer he would have to go without supper. It had grown so late that Guy did not return to his writing, but walked up and down the court for exercise, thinking about a thousand and one things bearing on his past, present and future. A strange fate seemed to be in pursuit of him ever since the eventful Sunday on the Salado. Yet, when the heavy hand of wrong had crowded him to the verge of disaster, the genius of pity had waved back the oppressor and developed saving influences to shield and protect him. When bloody and disfigured from his wounded scalp the savage heart of Chicha softened. The renegade Pedro had counselled him to turn Lipan for safety. Laoni's was the crowning favor, and her subsequent devotion to his interests was second only to the love she bore her father. The good priest and Jose were now his friends of a few hours, while the chivalry of Ruiz had made him an ally simultaneous with an introduction.

Old Bonito broke up his meditations.

"Senor Raymondo must go to his cell. It is time for the sentinel to take his post in the court. Here is a blanket and a pillow that rattle-brained girl said I must bring for you. I furnish this and not a quartilla of pay do I get for it—not a quartilla, senor."

Guy followed him, not heeding his gabble. Once in his cell, he prepared his bed and had just laid himself down, when the door was opened, disclosing Bonito with a lighted candle.

"Here is a piece of candle that will last you for an hour or so and here are the books you left on the bench."

"Thanks, Bonito."

"Don't thank Bonito. If she had her way a prison would be a palace, and prisoners would be treated like princes. Good night, senor."

"Good night, Bonito."

The tramp of the relief was heard in the corridor as the jailer gained the court and, a minute more, a sentinel was walking the usual post. Bonito hung the lantern over his door, then disappeared within, muttering his satisfaction that the day's duties were over.

The sentinel crossed to the bench that Guy had occupied, picked up something, examined it for a moment, then slipped it in his pocket.

It was the notebook in which Guy had been writing.

The light in the cell, struggling through the high, narrow window until a late hour told that the prisoner was making the most of his piece of candle. Its flame, though feeble to illumine, possessed giant power to dispel the oppressiveness of solitude in confinement. With light, books are appreciable companions; they speak to our reason; they supply the motive power to thought to bear us away on the wings of speculation to the transcendant fields of the conceptual or the ideal world. Guy's library was limited, but his two books were old friends. With these we will leave him to commune, until the flickering light will have warned him that he must seek solace from a slumber now easier to woo through Linda's thoughtfulness.

CHAPTER XIX.

The Feast of the Holy Rosary was destined to be bright and sunny. The chime of San Fernando pealed a merry melody as the hour arrived to summons the faithful to the grand high mass, which was to be offered in honor of the day. The crowd at the entrance to the cathedral grounds presented a conglomerate of the population. The scarlet sash of the young swell and the gaudy uniform of the military mingled with the plainer dress of the average citizen, these contrasting with the dirt and rags of the proletariat and the slouchy garment of the barefooted common soldiery. A redeeming feature of the scene was the presence of a moving line of female passers who, half enveloped in rebosas of every hue, moved gracefully through the crowd to the grand portal of the edifice. These latter disclosed features varying from those bordering on the pure Indian to the more delicate types which approached nearer to the Castillian. The throng had parted to let them pass and many a rebosa was more tightly drawn, to evade the rude inspection of the crowd, or the brazen stare of a group of young bloods who, standing near the gateway, indulged in a review of those who entered.

"Here comes the princess," said one of the party.

"She moves like one," said another.

"Don Juan spoiled her by an American education," said the first speaker.

"How so, Sancho?"

"She has little use for Mexicans and has, doubtless, lost her heart in the United States," replied Sancho.

As Sancho spoke, the lady, who had been the subject of their remarks, swept by them with a nod of recognition, and passed on into the church.

"A beauty, and no mistake! She has a proud look and a foreign air that tells plainly she has not passed all her days in Bexar. What is her name, Sancho?"

"Senorita Beatrice Navarro. The younger daughter of Don Juan Navarro, a man of prominence here. His elder daughter was the widow of Perez, now the wife of an American."

"Your princess been back from school long?"

"But a twelvemonth, and she already has broken the hearts of two suitors."

"Say you so? Who, pray, are the unfortunates?"

"Captain Castanado, the first; Manuel Ruiz, the second victim."

"Ruiz! He is the one who so recently disappeared?"

"The same. He is a traitor to Mexico, and I trace his treason to this girl's American proclivities. I tell you, she is *puro Gringo*. Her sister's husband is a Gringo and poor Don Juan, their father, is greatly under their influence."

As Sancho ceased speaking, a confusion in the crowd attracted the attention of the group around him. The approach of four men, bearing a litter, proved to be the cause of the commotion, while a closer inspection disclosed that they bore a human form, covered with a coarse cloth from the head to the waist. The bearers set their burden down near the edge of the acequia, as if to rest.

"What have you here, friends?" asked Sancho.

"We do not know, senor. We are taking the body to the office of the Alcalde.

Sancho lifted the cloth from the face of the dead, and was startled to discover the rigid features of Vasquez, his hair and clothing wet and dripping, while a ghastly cut laid open his throat from ear to ear.

"Por Dios!" he exclaimed. "It is Vasquez, the fellow who used to hang around the Cabeza de Toro."

"The very fellow," said one of the litter bearers. "I recognize him now since you have named him. The last time I saw him he was with Manuel Ruiz, coming out of the monte pio's."

"That is important to remember," said Sancho. "But where did you find the body?"

"By the old mill, senor, in the eddy between the rapids."

The presence of the ghastly spectacle added to the motley throng which now blocked the walk and prevented ingress to the cathedral, whence issued the loud tones of the organ, indicating the commencement of the service. A way was finally made for the litter bearers, who resumed their burden and proceeded on thir way. The crowd receded from the gateway and perceptibly thinned as the complement of proletarians furnished an escort for the murdered Vasquez, while the most respectable element either entered the church or lingered a while before following their inclinations as to immediate points of destination.

"Are you going in to mass, Sancho?" asked one of his companions, who, alone of the late group, still lingered near him.

"No, Carlos, I believe I will follow that corpse. I feel a singular interest in this murder; yet, to tell the truth, I cannot tell why."

"Well then, adios. You may turn detective; but as for me, I am going in to see how the princess looks at prayers."

"Like other women, doubtless, unless it be to eyes whose owner is deeply enamored, like poor Castanado, or the traitor, Ruiz."

"Bueno! Amigo, mio. Adios, hasta la tarde."

The two friends parted. The one followed the litter, now well up the street; the other entered the church, now crowded by the kneeling or seated figures of the congregation. The old church would have presented a scene at once novel and weird, to the eye of a stranger. The high, dark walls reflected none of the struggling light from the narrow openings, and the moon-like glow which fell in mellow waves from the ample dome lent a ghostly appearance to objects below, while deep shades rested in the angles of the transcept. The tall tapers upon the grand altar illuminated the western extension with an unsteady light that caused shadows to dance across the surface of a mammoth painting of the crucifixion, which extended from wall to wall, and from the tabernacle to the high triple window overlooking it. The solemn chant of the Kyre Elison lent its influence to weave a magic charm in an already impressive scene, as the choir responded to the celebrant who, with outstretched arms, was invoking the descent of the man-God to the terrestial altar. The congregation did not appear in sympathy with the sublime conception involved in the august sacrifice, for there was a calmness and notable absence of devotion in their facial expressions which indicated mechanical performance of exercises, ingrained into their natures by the accidents of birth and training. The entrance of two persons at the conclusion of the Kyre Elison caused the turning of many heads to get a look at the late comers, who, seemingly not satisfied with remote positions, were pushing their way nearer to the altar. One of them, a youth just entered into manhood, rather hesitated to obey the girl companion, but her significant motions decided him to follow her through the crowd of kneeling worshipers. The girl, a brunette, seemed perfectly at ease as she led the way to a position which she evidently had aimed to occupy. She knelt at once and, crossing herself, arranged her rebosa, then looked complacently around the church. Her companion, taking a place close at hand, leaned gracefully against the northern wall. He took in the situation with a look of blended interest and curiosity. His eye kindled with intelligence as he comprehended, first, the words of the Gloria, then the Credo, from the choir, followed, in the progress of the mass, by the chanting of the Pater Noster by the celebrant. Guy—for it was he—owed his power to master languages from his proficiency in the Latin. The first time he had ever witnessed a celebration of the mass, yet he found he was able to comprehend the drift of its cermonies. In this fact he recognized the splendid tact of the Church of Rome in adopting a universal and unchanging language as a fundamental requisite for the establishment of a universal faith. He was pursuing this train of thought in oblivion to the personnel of the congregation, feeling his own superiority to these unread and credulous votaries of a traditional religion, when a lady, who had been kneeling near, arose and turned to leave the church. As her face became revealed, it appeared to Guy to be very beautiful, and when she passed close by him, their eyes met for an instant. It was but for an instant; yet both received a shock from the encountering glances. In the lady's case it might have been from surprise; with the gentleman it was doubtless surprise, reinforced by ill-concealed admiration. The latter had not imagined that within the bounds of Bexar there dwelt so fair a woman. It is to be presumed that, next to an apparition, the unexpected presence of the handsome youth, with blonde complexion and unmistakeable Anglo-Saxon lineage, would most surprise the lady. Carlos had signified his curiosity to witness her at prayers, while Sancho might turn detective. She was the "princess" of their conversation and now he had seen her at her devotions. Carlos was on the opposite side of the church when Beatrice Navarro rose to leave. He had been closely watching her and had observed the exchanged glances between Guy and the beauty. The eyes of the two men met. Those of Carlos expressed defiance. Guy turned to follow with a last look the retreating form, then sought the eyes across the way, which had so plainly indicated disapprobation. They were still fixed upon him and the menace of their expression was unmistakable. He thought perhaps he had aroused the ire of a jealous lover, and simply smiled in answer to all the look might mean. The remainder of the mass apparently claimed his attention, as had done the earlier exercises, but a lovely face was pictured in conjunction with every object mirrored in his vision. His thoughts recurred but once to the jealous lover, and coincident with the thought he glanced in his direction, but Carlos had disappeared. He concluded to whisper to Linda, whom he had accompanied to church, and make inquiry about the lady whose beauty had so impressed him, but on turning to carry out his intention, he found that she, too, was missing. He felt like taking himself off at this discovery. The appearance of Father Ignacio, however, as he left the chancel to ascend to the pulpit, altered his mind, and he resigned himself to the hearing of a Spanish sermon.

The good father took for his text, "He that will not hear the church, let him be to you a heathen and a publican."

From the consideration of this command he drifted to the special injunction of the church to practice the devotions peculiar to the uses of the Rosary, and reminded the faithful of the special indulgences which had been from time to time granted by the sovereign pontiff to those who had frequent recourse to means so potent for salvation. The father was a fluent speaker, but his audience was evidently apathetic. Guy himself, interested from the sheer novelty of the points of faith discussed, observed the listlessness of the congregation and concluded it was due to the frequency of these feast-day discourses about a religion rendered too familiar by an unchanging routine which offered no room for animal excitement or emotional display. He sauntered out of the place when the congregation had been dismissed, intending to wait at the gate for the priest, who must pass out at the front on his way home. He made his way through the crowd of women, of whose sex four-fifths of the attendants were composed, and reached the open air in time to see Jose just leaving the gate. He was about to call to him, when a touch upon his shoulder caused him to turn, and he saw Linda by his side.

"Ah, runaway!" he exclaimed, "why did you leave me among all these people?"

"I thought senor could take care of himself anywhere, and surely, in our holy church you needed no protection."

"But you missed a good sermon, Linda. Father Ignacio told us all about the Holy Rosary, and of all the indulgences to be obtained by bead praying."

"It was good for you to hear, because you are no Catholic. We hear it so often. You are a Protestant, senor?"

"I am no Protestant, Linda."

"No? You have no religion?"

"Yes—duty."

"I never heard of more than two; Catholics and Protestants. Ours is the true faith, senor, for Father Ignacio says so."

"Well, Linda, you continue to do and believe as the father tells you. He will never give you bad advice."

"I will, senor."

"Tell me, Linda, why you left the church before mass was over."

"Why do you ask?"

"Curiosity."

"Do you imagine my leaving concerned you?" she asked, looking up at him archly.

"Not especially. But you were my companion and it seems to me if you had not wished to conceal your going you would have let me know about it."

"But the padre would have been displeased, had he seen me speak with you at mass."

"You could have given me a sign. Tell me the truth, and say that your leaving did concern me."

"If you will not urge me, perhaps I will tell you the next time I see you."

"Now I am sure it concerned me.'

"And I am sure I will see you very soon."

"Adios, senor," and Linda left him with a smile and a look that accused him of possessing an abundant share of curiosity.

Guy mused as follows:

"Perhaps her leaving the church just after *she* left it, are incidents between which there may exist some privity. And if this be true, how can I be concerned with either incident? I never will forget those eyes of hers."

Father Ignacio overtook him a few steps further on and slapping him familiarly on the shoulder, greeted him cordially.

"I was glad to see you at mass. From the carcel to the cathedral. If you were only a good Catholic I would have thought that your purpose was to give thanks for your liberation."

"My thanks are due to a more definite benefactor. But for you I would be a prisoner still.'

"The Colonel was not very willing to trust you, but I had no trouble with my friend, General Cos."

'He arrived after my arrest?"

"Yesterday."

"Are there any charges against me?"

"There were some, but your accuser has disappeared."

"My parole then will be good until my accuser shows himself?"

"That I cannot answer. What you have to do is to keep quiet and get into no more scrapes. Your nationality is against you. Senor Maverick and two other Americans were sent out of the lines yesterday. Had it not been for these charges you would have been sent out with them."

"That would have suited me, for I long to join my countrymen."

"You will be safer by remaining with me, provided always you follow my advice."

"But Father, my inaction here is chafing me while the country is in arms. And then if I were at liberty I could begin the search for my dear little sister."

"True, senor, but remember always, that the truly brave are patient and self-commanding."

Jose met them at the door and announced that dinner was ready to be served.

CHAPTER XX.

Guy also attended vespers on the Feast of the Holy Rosary, going to the cathedral with his reverend host. The sparse congregation surprised him as he glanced around after the singing had commenced. The afternoon service had several rival attractions in this typical Mexican town, chief among which were the cockfights, a sport dear to Mexican hearts, not alone for the excitement produced by the battles in the pit, but as a gambling device. The cockpits were always well attended Sunday afternoons by votaries who had performed their religious duties by mass attendance in the morning.

Among the faces, half concealed by the draperies of the national wrap, he vainly searched for that of the beautiful lady whose momentary glance had so electrified him. That face had haunted him ever since and turn his thoughts into never so remote a channel, the fair apparition would form a part of the mental picture wrought by his reflections. After vespers, which he enjoyed as a diversion from the prospective dullness of the afternoon, he rejoined Father Ignacio in the sitting room of the priest's house, where the latter repaired to enjoy a smoke and a rest after the good work of the day.

Guy, as has been already hinted, professed no religion as taught by orthodox creeds, but had been raised a free thinker. He had been taught to rise above mysticism in his inquiries after the truths of existence, to view nature and her laws from the standpoints of reason and experience, aided by actual discovery and scientific development. He found himself now in the very atmosphere of orthodoxy with a priestly host and benefactor whose honest work and pure life seemed to combat the negations of infidelity and demonstrate a heaven-born inspiration. He could not resist such reflections as he watched the placid expression of the handsome features of the priest. He finally opened the conversation.

'Father Ignacio, I would like to ask you if, in pure reason, you actually believe that the use of rosaries are necessary for salvation."

"Yes and no," the priest replied. "It is not necessary for salvation that you use beads to pray, but if you reject the use of the rosary, through rebellion to the authority of the Holy Church, which has decided that it is a help to devotion, or if you bring ridicule on customs adopted by her authority, you will be guilty of mortal sin, and through mortal sin one will surely be lost, without contrition and penance."

"All this which you say is predicated on the divine mission of the church which, having such origin, is infallible, making her decrees the commands of the Creator."

"Senor Raymond is quite right."

"Then your position is absolutely unassailable, granting your premises which affirm the incarnation of God in Christ."

"And Senor Raymond does not believe in the incarnation?"

"Not more than in the incarnations of Vishnu."

"Those were extravagant superstitions."

"I admit that."

"The incarnation of our God was a long-looked for event by a chosen people who were for many generations under the immediate protection of heaven, and in constant communication with the Creator, who appeared often to the prophets. Besides, the miracles of Christ and the works of his followers fully substantiate his claims to divinity."

"These are all potent arguments, my good Father, and I presume neither of us could convince the other. I merely want to learn something of your views about rosaries and those indulgences you preached about this morning."

"Indulgences are those bugbears which make the Protestants rave so much. They construe them into licenses to commit sin. An indulgence can be gained only through earnest prayers and good works, and instead of being pardons for sins to be committed, they are remissions of temporal punishment for sin already committed; are conditioned on valid performances of good works and sincerity of prayers. Rosaries were doubtless first introduced for the illiterate, but they became endeared to the faithful and, when blessed, are without doubt great incentives to devotion."

"You have many such helps to holiness. The scapulars, medals and pictures are also regarded as very necessary auxiliaries in the attainment of heaven, are they not?"

"They are certainly reminders of the sacrifices which a loving God has made for us directly and through His saints and are no more objectionable than the prized mementoes and portraits of our loved ones who have preceded us into eternity."

"That is a very reasonable view, but I have heard that some Catholics attach undue virtue to articles that have been blessed, such as beads, medals, candles and water, and imagine that their mere possession will ward off evil. We once had an Irishman in our employ, a Mr. Trigg, who owned a blessed candle and a bottle of holy water. To these he attached the greatest importance. I remember one night, there was a terrible blow which threatened to increase to a hurricane. We were all very much alarmed, when Mr. Trigg produced his piece of candle and, lighting it, assured us that as long as it continued to burn we need not feel uneasy. On asking an explanation he stated it had been blessed by a holy priest who was since dead and who, he knew, went straight to heaven without having to pass through purgatory."

"There is no doubt, senor, that blessed articles like medals, candles, scapulars and holy water often protect their possessor from harm, through the intervention of God; for He is pleased always at the devotion which incites the faithful to wear these badges of His service and to use what is consecrated by the church. If you, senor, were a powerful lord and should see one in trouble who wore your livery, would you not protect him? You would be a craven not to do so. How much quicker would the good God, the source of mercy and justice, protect those who wear these evidences of their faith?"

"That is quite true, Father, if you endow the great Creator, or the first cause, with a personality like ours, and measure Him by our standards. But take care that you do not disclose a most vulnerable point in your defenses, by such an assumption, for I would have only to extend the simile to show that there is no eternal hell, a location which some of your saints claim to have explored and have described minutely, even to the degrees of suffering, its dungeons, gates and modes of torture."

"'Tis true. St. Teresa saw it all by special permission of God. The sight nearly froze her blood! But how, senor, can the non-existence of hell be shown from any assumption of God's personality?"

"By attributing to Him a personality and emotions like those which control humanity, as you a did moment ago. You, my good Father, would not burn the worst wretch in Bexar for ten minutes, and if you saw one thus tortured, your tender heart would be touched by his anguish and you would use all your power to arrest the holocaust. How much less probable then it is, that the great Creator of this magnificent universe who, you claim, is the source of mercy and justice, would mar the beauty of his work by decreeing the establishment of that terrible hell, which your church proclaims, and where she has centered all the terrors and horrors that the wealth of human language can describe. If your God is the source of mercy and justice, He could not thus torture poor, frail humanity, even for a short time, much less would he gloat over their punishment for an eternity."

"Ah! my son, I am sorry for you. It is plain you have had no religious training. You are not even a good heretic. What a pity! What a pity!"

"The good man rose as he uttered the last words and walked up and down the apartment. Stopping before his companion he continued:

"You have a fine intellect; your head, your eye, your singular proficiency in my mother-tongue, all indicate a rare genius, that could have been utilized, oh! how well, in our glorious priesthood. Could you feel the sublimity of our faith; could you realize the grand destiny of our immortal being, if we but keep the commands of God and His church; if you could look back, as I do, upon the concatenation of eminent saints and martyrs, reaching back to Calvary, sanctifying and strengthening an infallible church, you would beg for holy orders and devote your talents to saving precious souls from that very hell about which you are so skeptical."

To this prediction Guy mentally demurred, coincidentally calling up the recollection of the beautiful face he had seen at mass.

"No, my good Fathtr, I do not think such a retrospect would so influence me. I have read of some of those saints who used to wear pebbles in their shoes as a self-inflicted punishment for some supposed sin. While I admire your enthusiasm and your sincerity in a vocation you so well fill, I fear the hard lives and penances of the saints shall ever deter me from taking orders, lest I might, like them, be influenced either to asceticism or to go limping around the world on pebbles"

"You are perhaps right to turn our little tilt into pleasantry, for there is little use to argue, unless we could agree upon premises involving an admission of the incarnation."

"With that conceded your deductions would be irresistible."

It had grown quite dark at this point of the discussion and simultaneously with Jose's appearance with a light a tall young man, in priestly attire, entered the apartment from the hall.

"Father Nicolas, this is Senor Raymond of whom I spoke to you," said Father Ignacio.

Guy advanced to meet the newcomer and gave him a cordial shake of the hand. The other winced under the pressure, for his hands were as soft and flexible as those of a delicate woman. The elder priest noticed the effect of his guest's hearty grasp and laughed good-naturedly.

"Father Nicolas is not rough like me, senor. I do not suppose he ever did any hard work. My hand is hard, and fingers strong; but as for my deputy, he is frail as a girl."

Guy said apologetically

"I hope Father Nicolas will pardon me. I have a habit of giving a grip when I shake hands, and do not realize how hard I squeeze———"

"Do not think of it any more, senor. I am not very strong when I am well; but I have been sick and everything seems to hurt me."

The young priest spoke this in not very excellent Spanish, and Father Ignacio explained that his assistant was an Italian and had not been learning the language but a few months.

"You were well enough to say mass this morning."

"Oh, yes, senor. I say mass every morning."

"Father Nicolas has been down to the lower missions," said Father Ignacio. "I sent him on a hunt for health; but he returns as puny as before. He is a good disciple of St. Francis, however, and never shirks a duty."

"Father Ignacio is a flatterer, Senor Raymond."

Jose here brought in a tray of chocolate and a few edibles, and at the host's suggestion the trio were soon discussing the merits of a drink whose aroma had already filled the apartment.

"Have you seen Don Juan today?" inquired Father Ignacio of his subordinate.

"He was at dinner today with General Cos, and I met him there," replied Father Nicolas.

"Did he say anything about his daughter?"

"Not that I remember."

"She left church this morning right after the Pater Noster and I imagined she might have been unwell."

"I saw a lady leave at that time," said Guy, feigning indifference.

"She was sitting in front of you. You should know her, Senor Raymond. She speaks your language, having been educated in Baltimore."

"I should like to know her very much. It has been long since I have spoken with any of my people, and if she has been educated in the United States and speaks my language, she will appear like a countrywoman."

"Don Juan Navarro is very popular with your countrymen, senor. He has sympathized with the colonists in all their collisions with the central government. His house has been a resort for them and his elder daughter is the wife of Doctor A———, an American of education, physically tall and powerful and, like yourself, an adept in speaking the Castillian tongue. Through the influence of his

American friends his other daughter, whom I had occasion to mention a moment ago, was sent to an American school. She has but recently returned to San Antonio and has evidently made good use of her time at school. Don Juan is very fond of his handsome daughter. Her friends find her considerably Americanized which, with some Mexicans, is more than an objection—something to be condemned."

"Race prejudices will crop out and I know of no occasion more calculated to bring them to the front than when invading manners and customs threaten to obliterate those which are time-honored and cherished by a people. We Americans are less sensitive on this score than your more exclusive race. With us the rapid influx of foreign elements and the change of the home sphere by each succeeding generation makes us in a manner cosmopolitan. Then, in religion we have represented, in more or less force, every Christian sect, while in Mexico the one faith has stamped its impress upon the population."

"There! If Father Nicolas is not asleep," said Father Ignacio, as he saw the priest's head fall over on his chest and heard his deeper breathing. "He is a weakling, Senor Raymond. His mass and vespers have worn him out. When I was his age I had already established two missions and never knew what it was to have more than five hours' sleep out of the twenty-four, year in and year out. It was a mass every morning and confessions at any hour necessary. I never missed my evening office or neglected my breviary, and when my last mission was being built, I often helped to carry mortar and tried my muscle in turning over large rocks, that the under sides might be dressed. Although I look so well my imprudence has told against me. I have rheumatism in this hip sometimes, and when it has been aching I have often wished for my dear old mother to come and rub me. Senor Raymond, she had a hand to rub! It would make a pain leave in no time—Bless me! How Father Nicolas snores!"

When Guy had gone to bed he found it impossible to sleep. Thoughts crowded on him thick and fast. His eyes were hot and dry, and the balls, no matter how he tried to give them the natural motion which they perform just preceding sleep, refused to induct him into the land of dreams. The sudden release from prison in the morning, his going to mass with Linda, the strange ceremonies, the earnest sermon, the defiant looks of the Mexican, rosaries, indulgences, medals, holy water, and much else connected with the day's experience went crowding through his mind in strange confusion. Through it all the face of the beautiful girl, whose eye had met his own as she passed to leave the cathedral, was behind each subject, composing the medley, peeping, as it were, over its shoulder.

CHAPTER XXI.

"Will Senor Raymond go to see the monte pio this morning?"

"Do you think it will be necessary, Jose?"

"One should look sharply after his money these times, senor. The country is restless and no one can tell how long before this good town may be shook as by an earthquake."

"Perhaps you are right. But the monte pio is a solid man and a friend of yours. He would not be tricky towards a guest of the priest of San Fernando."

"Friendship is a poor stick to lean on. A full pocket will make and hold friends—but, an empty one! Oh, senor! An empty one!" and Jose shook his head.

"You are a confirmed misanthrope, Jose, I can plainly see; but then it is probably best that we go to see my banker this morning."

"I will go with you, senor, for I have unfortunately lost the paper showing the amount you have there, as well as the letter from Manuel Ruiz, informing me of the deposit. I have looked for the lost papers everywhere, but 'despair of ever seeing them again."

"That will not matter. Your friend will doubtless do us justice," said Guy, somewhat amused at the annoyed manner of the other.

"There is not much left of all that money. Ninety dollars—more than half gone—and you have not had the benefit of a quartilla," said Jose.

It was just after the breakfast hour on the morning after the Feast of the Holy Rosary that this dialogue between Guy and the major domo took place. Guy was out in the court to see Rolla eat his breakfast and was fondling him, when Jose appeared. Rolla had been kept a prisoner to prevent his straying off and getting into trouble and was quite impatient with the restraint after his long sojourn in the mountains of the San Saba. He whined a welcome as his master appeared on this morning and ceased his meal at once.

"Poor old dog! You, at least, are unselfish. Your appetite gives way to joy at my coming. See, Jose! Here is a friend to count on. None of your broken sticks here."

"But he is not a human, senor. He does not know the power and influence of money. He lacks reason, and missing that, knows nothing of avarice. He does not moralize, senor, and therefore, is no hypocrite. He has nothing but instinct. Instinct causes him to know his master and recognize his dependence on him. This dependence involves a supply of food. Even, therefore, with a dog, attachment to the master comes from a selfish desire to remain with the one who feeds him."

"But it is a known fact that between animals the strongest attachment springs from mere association. Unlike you, I believe in friendship—a pure and lofty feeling that may exist between the honorable and the good."

The monte pio was waiting on a customer when the two entered his establishment some little time after their conversation. Nodding familiarly to Jose and casting an inquiring glance at his companion, he turned again to the party who was inspecting some goods displayed on the counter. Guy, who had heard much of the place in which he now found himself, used his eyes to advantage while satiating a curiosity that had possessed him for the last three days to view the contents and arrangement of a Mexican pawn shop. The first place which attracted his attention was the show-case, which was nicely arranged with articles of jewelry, medals, crosses, rosaries, beadwork, knives and various other trinkets. These were all absolutely for sale. Guy thought of his lost medal. It was in this case that Jose had seen it, or one very similar to the parting gift of Laoni. On shelves in rear of the counter or table, were ticketed articles of clothing and other effects pertaining to almost every department of Mexican necessities or extravagance. There was plenty of time to take in the whole arrangement, examine the odds and ends of its stock, as well as to speculate on the needs of those who had to pledge their property for less than a moiety of its value. Finally the proprietor was at leisure and, with his usual bland smile, accosted the major domo.

"Amigo mio, this is Senor Raymond."

"Su Servidor de V. senor," said the monte pio, taking Guy's proffered hand.

After the salutations were over the proprietor remarked that he presumed the senor wished to get the amount to his credit, and, without waiting for a rerly, took from a drawer a lot of silver, counting it carefully on the counter.

Guy, having verified the amount, found himself the possessor of sixty-five dollars, it being the balance left from the sale of his pony and saddle, together with the amount left by Ruiz. He pressed Jose to take ten dollars, who received it under protest and the injunetion that his master be not told of the matter.

"Have you heard of the death of your accuser, Vasquez?" asked the monte pio.

"I had not," replied Guy.

"Nor I," said Jose.

"What caused his death?" asked Guy.

"Murdered. He was found in the river just below the old mill with his throat cut from ear to ear."

"Did you learn if money was found on his body?"

"No, Jose. Not a cent."

"Then it was done for robbery," said Jose. "He had a large sum of money the last time I saw him."

"Well, his death will relieve me of my parole, and perhaps now I will be allowed to join my people."

"I am not so sure of that, senor. The Americans are marching on this city and you would make too good an addition to their force."

"But Maverick and others were sent out and surely——"

'That was last week. When war has once begun, the policy of today may be the opposite of that of yesterday."

"I hope you may not be allowed to leave, senor. Remain with us. If you join those headstrong men you will certainly be shot when you all will be taken prisoners. Santa Anna himself will soon be here and he never spares a rebel against his authority. You speak our language like ourselves. Be a Mexican; marry the pretty Linda and make Bexar your home."

"You forget that Linda is promised to me," interrupted the monte pio.

"But she will not have you, even with your money," retorted Jose.

"What say you, Senor Raymond?"

"No, Jose. I played Indian for nearly two years and I don't desire to masquerade in another nationality. I have nothing to be ashamed of in my race. They are impatient of restraint, liberty-loving by nature and detest personal government. Santa Anna is an adventurer, full of bombast, and if he fools with the Texan colonists they will take some of his conceit out of him before the end of this quarrel. Sensible Mexicans detest him. The Navarros, the Seguins, Benevides and Ruiz have as good as pronounced against his government."

Before leaving the monte pio's Guy questioned him about the medal, taking down the name of the man who had purchased it. From the description he was positive the medal sold was Laoni's gift and mentally concluded that it was lost to him, probably forever.

As they were crossing the plaza Guy remembered his promise, made the day before, to visit Linda, and suggested that Jose accompany him to the carcel. The latter, nothing lothe, consented, and in a short time they found themselves at the door where paced the sentinel. The inner door was open as no prisoner was within who had the liberty of the court, and in consequence Bonito was not annoyed by knocking at the street door to gain admittance. The bench stood under the cell window as Guy had left it the afternoon before, after he had recorded his adventures. The sight of the bench recalled the fact of the writing and he felt at once for the little book. It was nowhere in his pockets. He was wondering what had become of it when he heard Bonito's voice in answer to Jose's rap on the door under the lantern. The jailer was calling:

"Linda! Linda!"

Finally a faint answer was heard, and a moment later Linda opened the door to the visitors, inviting them in. It was the first time that either of the two men had entered there. It opened into a hall, with doors on each side. Through the one to the left the girl conducted them, when they discovered a comfortable apartment, neatly kept, and boasting about the usual appointments of a Mexican sitting room. There were unmistakable evidences of womanly care in a degree somewhat above the social plane on which such a creature as Bonito should, by the law of experience, live, move and have his being. The two windows of this apartment looked into a small yard, bounded by walls of adjoining houses which, green with vegetation, disclosed here and there brilliant patches of flowers. The sight of the latter calling forth an expression of surprise from her guests, Linda explained that on this little garden she devoted those leisure moments at home that could not be more pleasantly occupied.

"I often wondered, Linda, what pleasure you could find behind the dreary wall that fronts the court, when your home duties came to an end."

"My garden and fancy work always gave to me enough to do, senor, when housework was finished. My father allows me to do whatever I please after I have attended to his wants."

"And they are many," remarked Jose.

"No; he is very fussy, but, after all, he is easy pleased. Fussing is one of his few pleasures."

"He is at it now," said Jose. "I hear him shouting at some one."

"He has some business with the notary," said Linda. "They have been going on that way for a half hour."

Presently the front door opened, when the subject of their talk thrust in his head.

"Por via de mi madre! If there is not Senor Pajarro! And the major domo! Come, Jose, I want a little help, and besides I want you for a witness. Come at once; we will be through in a few minutes."

Bonito disappeared and Jose, obedient to the summons, left the room. The exit of Jose was quite agreeable to Guy, who had half regretted the want of foresight in not coming alone as he desired for a certain reason, to see Linda without a witness.

The door had barely closed, when the girl said, mischieviously:

"I did not think that you would wait until this morning to some."

"I must confess, Linda, that I was anxious to be here last evening, but did not know how to excuse myself to Father Ignacio."

"Then you are still curious to know why I left the church?"

"No—yes—that is, I was a little surprised when I missed you."

"You must own that you were curious about *somebody's* leaving. Perhaps it was not my disappearance that interested Senor Raymond but someone else's appearance as she passed him by."

"If what you say be true, Linda, would there be any harm in the fact?'

"No, senor; no harm."

"You left the church——"

"I did."

"You promised to tell me why."

"Because the other lady did."

"You are friends?"

"Si, senor; good friends."

"You wished to see her on some particular business."

"Senor Raymond guesses well."

"Tell me what you have to tell—or—let us talk about something else."

"Now you are getting serious. I will find out your secret."

"I am not serious," insisted Guy, endeavoring to dispel a blue look that had settled on his face.

"Now, listen and I will tell you all about it," said Linda, drawing her chair closer to her visitor.

"When I went to mass I took with me a beautiful rosary to have blessed and which I intended to give to a friend. You saw me take it up at the blessing of the rosaries. Well, who should I see leave the church, but the very person I wished to give it to. Yesterday was her birthday and I did not wish the day to pass without putting the present in her hands. You know, senor, if one has a birthday present to give it destroys half the pleasure to not give it on the very day. I knew that I would have no time to see her after mass as I had to return home, having other plans for the afternoon. So what could I do but follow her from the church?"

Linda paused and looked into the other's face.

"And you gave her the beads?"

"I gave her the beads."

"Well——"

"I've told you all."

"There is something behind, else you would not have said what you did yesterday in front of San Fernando."

"I walked home with Beatrice."

"Beatrice! Is that the name of the lady?"

"Beatrice Navarro."

"I was struck with her beauty."

"She was impressed with your appearance."

"She saw me then?"

"As if you did not know it!"

"How so?"

"Did not your eyes meet?"

"She must have told you."

"And you fairly blushed under her look."

"'Twas she—whose color heightened. I'd swear it by all your saints."

"In whom you don't believe."

"Then by my honor."

"Then you both turned red. 'Tis plain to me, senor—love at first sight.'

"I am not in love with Miss Navarro. She is very beautiful and moves with exceeding grace. Possibly I am too easily impressed by a beautiful woman, seen for the first time, and may have thrown my thoughts into my looks when I encountered Miss Navarro's glance. But as for love—why, Linda, love is deep rooted. It has a germ which must be nursed to life by a glow that springs from acquaintance and association, from sympathies that flow out of congenialities of character and tastes. Real love can be no more called into existence in a moment than can an oak arrive at its giant size without being first nursed to life by heat and moisture from its acorn prison. No—no—Linda, I am not in love."

"If you deny it another time I will believe you are in love. But, senor, I am really sorry——"

Linda heaved a little sigh, took up a corner of her apron and began to twist it.

"What makes you sorry, Linda?"

"That you cannot love Beatrice."

"I said, 'I *am* not in love."

"Then there are hopes."

"Hopes?"

"That you *will* love her on better acquaintance."

"Perhaps she will not care for my love."

"But she will."

"How can Linda know?"

"You have interested her, and I believe that acquaintance will do the rest. Then, you would make such a handsome pair."

"I—have interested—her?"

"I told her of your life—as much as I had it from your lips."

"Why—Linda!"

"Did I do wrong?"

"No—but——"

"But what?"

"Tell me all she said."

"'Tis strange you are so interested, since you are not in love!"

"Interest is all—interest begets interest."

"It then needs not to be warmed into life like love?"

"By no means."

"She said you—were very handsome and—but I should not tell you all."

"Handsome! She was blinded by her interest."

"Only love is blind."

"True—interest is oftener critical."

"Then you must be handsome; for as love grows slowly like the oak, she could not love at once and therefore was not blind through love. I should hate to have my lover's love keep pace with such a growth, for we would be old and weak before our loves grew strong."

"It was but a comparison I made. A year may ripen interest into love. A few months in our maturer life may bring many changes, while in a sapling oak no great increase might be apparent after years of growth."

"You will not renounce the germ, senor?"

"No, the germ must exist."

"But, once started, you admit the growth is very fast."

"That depends on the amount of association."

"Then go to see my friend tomorrow."

Jose and Bonito here made their appearance, preceded by a dried-up, weazen-faced specimen of humanity, who had a scroll of paper under his arm and a huge quill pen behind his ear.

"Senor Raymondo has not forgotten the carcel, I see. It has been lonesome since you left. Can't you manage to get into some devilment, so that we can grant you the privilege of the court?"

"For eight reals a day? Ah, Bonito! You want to fleece me again."

"It was your liberality, senor; you forced it on me. I claimed but seven. This is the notary, senor. Talk about fleecing! He knows the art to perfection. He charged me twenty reals for poking his nose into my room and fixing up some papers for me. I would have gladly done half the work for twice the money. Think of the drudgery I do, and what miserable pay!"

"I am pleased to know you, senor," said the little man, in response to this queer introduction. "If it should please your worship to have any business done in my line, I can be found in hours at my office, Calle Soledad cerca la esquina de la plaza."

The notary obsequiously bowed himself out.

"Call on him, senor, if you want to get fleeced. Twenty reals for a half hour's time! Es un puro ladron," growled Bonito as he closed the outer door with considerable emphasis.

As Guy and Jose were about to leave, the door leading to the little garden opened and a female figure entered enveloped in a dark rebosa. She hesitated in apparent surprise as she beheld the two men, her hand still retaining its hold on the door fastening as if doubtful whether to advance or retreat. The party in the room had turned their attention to the new arrival simultaneously with her entrance.

"Buenas dias, Josefa, I thought you had given up coming. This is nine o'clock with two hours added on," said Linda, advancing to meet the lady.

"I am late, I know. I see you have company. A stranger? Jose, of course, I know."

Jose made her a respectful salutation.

"Senor Raymond, I present to you my friend, Senorita Josefa de la Torre, a neice of Father Ignacio."

"It gives me additional pleasure to meet the lady, since you tell me the relationship existing between her and the good father." said Guy.

Josefa bowed stiffly, while her countenance assumed a proud smile in recognition of the complimentary allusion to her uncle. She was tall and slender, and moved with dignity across the room to deposit her removed wrap upon a lounge. Her large, black, spiritual eyes took in Guy Raymond at a glance, while her quick perception placed an estimate on his appearance prior to debating in her mind the possible impression she was making. Josefa's eyes suited her long, narrow face and well defined features. She was not ugly. Her face could be very attractive in certain moods of mental activity, but its general expression was calculated to put one on guard. Linda's first callers soon took their departure, leaving her alone with the Senorita de la Torre.

CHAPTER XXII.

The even temperature of the first autumnal month scarcely marked a change in the sunny days and cool, refreshing nights which came and went since the buds of springtime first swelled to repletion, then burst into vernal life and clothed the river valley in soft, merging shades or handsome contrasts. Nature seemed loth to undo the work of months and the lazy weather lingered to confirm, by its enervating influence, the indolent population in the extreme of lethargy. Even the equinox had failed to lend its wonted animation to the elemental forces, and here was October still aping her summer sister. June, as if old Boreas, concealed within his northern haunts, was not merely waiting a signal to tear aside the veil and expose the masquerade. But the ides of the dissembling month were not to come and go in balmy sunshine or pass their languid course, perfumed by incense from the lap of summer.

The norther came in fitful gusts, raising clouds of lime dust and sending the light debris of the town in eccentric whirls through the narrow streets and across the plazas. The oxen of the loaded wood carts lowered their tethered heads and huddled from the wind. The donkeys brayed beneath their piles of hay, and turned their tails towards the storm of wind and dust. The teamsters and burro drivers swore many a Spanish oath, as tangled teams and carts, or tufts of hay, flying on the wings of the wind, called forth an anathema. Men hurried along the streets to the protection of house or warmer clothing. A few women, who issued from the door of San Fernando, drew their rebosas closely around them, hesitated at the gate, then made haste in different directions.

The wind storm soon reached a violence that indicated no ordinary visitation from old Boreas. A great whirlwind swept across the miliatry plaza, carrying with it a column of dust that mounted many feet above the church tower. In its course it struck a herd of cavalry horses, four hundred strong, returning from a graze, just as it entered the plaza, terrifying the animals by its force and fury and blinding dust, then sent them, in mad career, through the square to the narrow street ahead. Hastening along with enveloped head, to ward off the stifling dust, was a female figure whose position must soon be in the wake of the stampeded animals, just started on their headlong course. Unmindful of her danger, she must soon have perished beneath a hundred unpitying hoofs, had not her better fate brought rescue in quick decision and stout arms. She heard the tramp of hoofs, descried the danger, and felt a tight embrace that bore her away, with scarce an interval for thought; and ere she could recognize the agency that snatched her from her feet, the ground beneath her was trembling under the furious onset of the herd. It fell to the lot of Guy Raymond to be the rescuer of the woman. He was returning from a walk to the northern portion of the town, in quest of the source of the acequia that ran past the church, when the storm commenced. He entered the plaza from Flores street and saw a woman hastening along the eastern side. As they neared the cathedral wall the whirlwind had swept to the southwest and frightened the animals. Taking in her danger at a glance, he unhesitatingly risked his life to reach and rescue her. As has been related, he succeeded. Having no time for thought, he bore her to the corner of the wall and pushed her behind an abutment constructed to protect its sharp angle. It was done in the nick of time for the rush had passed before he could realize her safety, or his escape form serious damage occasioned by a collision with one of the horses that sent him reeling to the ground. Recovering himself, as speedily as possible, his first thoughts were of her whom he had rescued from almost certain death, and the same instant he was by her side. To his astonishment she had not fainted, nor was apparently much excited, for she stood on tiptoe looking over the wall, with both hands on the parapet.

"I trust the senora is not much unnerved by the narrowness of her escape," said Guy, brushing the dirt from his sleeve, but eyeing the woman curiously.

He had not long to wait for her reply, but judge of his astonishment when she quite calmly remarked in distinct tones, and purest English, still looking over the wall:

"I saw your hat blow into the churchyard and was peeping over to see where it had lodged."

Then turning to him, she continued·

"Doutbless sir, I am indebted to you for my life. I was so blinded by the dust I could not perceive my danger. I suppose it is in order now to learn the name of my deliverer."

"You certainly are acquainted with his nationality, or you would not have addressed him in English, unless, indeed, my awkward use of your mother-tongue announced it."

"And may I ask how know you that I am not your countrywoman for surely my English is as pure as yours."

"But I addressed you in Spanish."

"Understanding a language does not necessarily imply the speaking of it. For aught you know the purity of your Spanish made me hesitate to use the same language in reply. But do you know I am fairly freezing in this cold wind? Get your hat, which I see has lodged against the further wall, and see me home. While on the way I can shower on you my thanks. The debate on our nationality we can safely postpone to some more favorable time."

"An excellent proposal," said Guy, laughing and at the same time, placing his hands on the wall, he leaped into the enclosure. Securing his hat he went out the western gate, where his companion joined him.

The first bluster of the storm had passed with the disappearance of the whirlwind. A partial lull had followed and then the steady blow of the norther, stronger and weaker at intervals, drove the dust clouds against the heavy walls and through the streets, whistling and wailing a requiem to the memory of the verdure and sunshine and the balmy, lazy days that had lingered in the train of summer. At the gate Guy courteously offered his arm, which was accepted, and requested the lady to act as guide in view of his ignorance of the locality of her home.

During their conversation, already recorded, Guy had not been able to get a good look at the face, half concealed in the folds of a rebosa, but when the first English words fell from her lips he thought of the girl who Father Ignacio had said could speak his language, and had been educated in Baltimore.

While his admiration was excited at her excellent nerves, he remembered the glances exchanged at mass, and when she asked his escort to her home, the thought of Linda's rehearsal of some of his adventures to her, who, beyond doubt, was now vis-a-vis to him, complacently pointing him to his hat, after escaping not five minutes before from the very jaws of death.

Proceeding on their way a short distance, she broke the silence:

"Your daring act has laid me under an obligation, and my father under a much greater one, for he has an idea that I am a valuable piece of property. As you forgot to tell me your name, may I beg to know to whom we owe the debt?"

"I more than suspect that my name is as familiar to you as yours has become to me."

"Grant that your suspicions have color or substance, an exchange of names will lend a finish to our rather sudden introduction."

"Guy Raymond, then, at your service," he said, bending his head low to catch her eye, then added:

"He is proud in having been able to rescue from injury so valuable a piece of property as Beatrice Navarro."

"I see it all now. My English betrayed me. He who told you of me gave you the secret of my education. Is it not so, Mr. Raymond?"

"You are quite right; but I should have found you out by this time in spite of that rebosa."

"You were at high mass?"

"On Sunday last."

"And have seen Linda?"

"Yes."

"She is a simple, good girl. Probably I joked a little too freely with her, when she came to give me my birthday present."

"Why so?"

"I then did not expect to ever know you."

"Well?"

"But those terrible mustangs introduced us without ceremony. What did Linda say?"

"That I should go to see you the next day."

"The little goose!"

"Why a goose?"

"You could have called without advice. What else?"

"Nothing more than a little innocent badgering, that it will be better not to mention, even could I recall a portion. I remember she gave me good advice, and pleasant to follow."

"Here is our home. Come in, Mr. Raymond. My father will not be home 'til late. When he hears of my escape he will hunt you up and insist on adopting you at once. He dearly loves me because I am so like my mother."

"You will excuse me for not going in. My torn sleeve and soiled coat are but outward signs of an inward hurt. It is nothing serious, but the smarting indicates that speedy attention will prevent an extended soreness."

"How thoughtless of me! I have not inquired if you were hurt. All my anxiety was about your hat, that went sailing over into the churchyard. You must call on us, Mr. Raymond, just as soon as your wound will permit. My father and sister will be impatient until they see you."

"Then you will see me soon. Good-bye."

"Good-bye."

Beatrice left the door ajar and peeped through the opening to follow with her eyes the retreating form of her new acquaintance.

"Poor fellow! I did not even ask him if he was hurt. That detestable Josefa! She talked of nothing but 'Senor Raymond' this afternoon. I'd have bet on her getting acquainted with him first. She set her cap for him. She went to Linda's for no other purpose than to lay siege to the handsome American. Oh! Those dear old mustangs. Whew! I just begin to feel the cold."

As she said this she closed the door and turning met her sister.

"Who were you talking to, Beatrice?"

"Oh, Jane, such an adventure!"

"It is nothing for you to have adventures."

"But this particular one is not a common affair."

"Well, let us have it. But first come into the sitting room, where I have built a fire. You are shivering now."

"The warmth of the house makes me realize how cold it is outside," said Beatrice, following her sister to the fire.

"I was so excited I scarcely felt the wind. Oh, Jane! I have just missed being killed."

"Killed?"

"Trampled to death.

"Explain."

"Those miserable cavalry horses. You know they passed here the other day, going out to graze. Well, as I was nearing the cathedral on my way home from Josefa's, this herd, for some cause, became frightened and came sweeping across the plaza, right in my direction, and in another moment I would have been killed, but for the strong arms of my rescuer, who bore me from the street none too soon."

"Did you learn the name of your rescuer?"

"Yes. You heard me joking with Linda about an American who was at mass?"

"Was it he?"

"The same—Senor Raymond. But Jane—how strong! I was like a child in his grasp, and you know I am no feather."

"Had he heard of you before?"

"I believe he asked if my name was not Navarro—or said he knew it was."

"Did you see Josefa?"

"I stayed there for an hour and was about to leave when the norther came. She is an artful piece, and so conceited."

After expressing this decided opinion of Josefa, Beatrice leaned her head upon her palm and gazed into the fire reflectively. Her sister sat opposite, engaged in sewing, by a small table on which her work was spread. Now and then she would glance at Beatrice to make some remark or to scrutinize her half averted face. There was little resemblance between the Navarro sisters. Beatrice was fair, though not a blonde. Hers was the Castillian complexion, coupled with the dark hair and lustrous eyes indicating Moorish blood that had crept in after Granada had succumbed to Spanish arms and Christian antipathy had become more tolerant from absolute conquest. As she sat looking into the blaze upon the hearth, with the flush of health augmented by the excitement that gleamed from her wondrous eyes, she made a lovely picture. Unlike her sister, her features were small and regular, her rounded chin sufficiently advanced to give character and poise to her face. When at rest the latter wore a dreamy beauty that suggested thoughts of a Madonna. Her height was above the medium, her figure full and shapely, and her carriage was of that graceful, easy nature so common to her countrywomen.

Her sister Jane had been married for about two years to Doctor A——, an American surgeon from Kentucky, who had emigrated to Texas to seek his fortune. Her face was oval and handsome, her complexion dark, but her hair and eyes were lighter than her sister's. She resembled her father; Beatrice her dead mother.

"Do you know, Jane, I nearly hate Josefa?" said Beatrice, looking up from the fire.

"You two are always falling out. What is the matter now?"

"Matter! It is her conceit which disgusts me. She thinks that every man who looks at her is in love with her."

"Has Senor Raymond been looking at Josefa?"

"Did I say he had? Jane—you—are—stupid."

"Not so stupid as to be blinded by it."

CHAPTER XXIII.

After Guy left Beatrice he hurried to his room with the intention to attend to his arm, which was smarting very unpleasantly. Evening was near at hand and with the departing rays of the sun the temperature was steadily lowering, making warm quarters pleasant to contemplate. His mind was full of his adventure, or rather overflowing with thoughts of his heroine. Her beauty had attracted him. The rescue, the interchange of words, and the walk to her home had woven a charming spell around him. He was so occupied by his thoughts that he came in collision with Jose in the hall.

"Ah, senor! Is it you? Father Ignacio was fearful you had gotten in another scrape, you had been missing so long."

"Not a scrape this time, Jose; but really a dangerous, though pleasant adventure," said Guy, laughing.

"Walk in that room. There is a fire in there and the father is waiting for you."

Guy found his host sitting by a bright fire, his face cheerful and ruddy, while he vigorously used a poker to readjust the burning fagots of mesquite. He turned as he heard the door open.

"Ah, you young runaway! Here it is nearly night, with a prospective freeze, and you not to be found, high or low. We were about coming to the conclusion that you had been blown away, or had gone off in the whirl wind which swept the plaza. I never saw such confusion among the caretas and burros."

"Well, my good Father, I came very near meeting with an accident from the stampede of the herd of cavalry horses. I was knocked down and my arm considerably skinned by the fall."

"And where have you been ever since?"

"I walked home with a young lady who had been in some danger from the same source."

"And you accompanied her to afford protection from a second herd of horses?"

"Not exactly from horses, but from any danger, as she must have been somewhat frightened, and I concluded company would reassure her."

"And pray, who was the lady?"

"Miss Navarro."

"Senorita Navarro!"

"The young lady who you said spoke English."

"I know—I know—Beatrice is a fine girl."

His last words were said more aside than they were addressed to Guy, but the latter hearing them, mentally endorsed what the father assented.

The priest poked the fire a while in a meditative manner, then suddenly turning to the other, asked·

"Did you hear of the skirmish at the powder house?"

"Skirmish! Who were the skirmishers? I had not heard it."

"The guard of eight men posted at the powder house were relieved at noon today, and at four o'clock the officer of the day visited the post and discovered that a fight had occurred. Five of the soldiers lay dead at the door and the others are supposed to be prisoners, as they were not to be found."

"Is it positive who were the attacking party?"

"The American colonists. Who else?"

"I had no idea the ball would open so soon."

"Scouts report that a large force is concentrating on the river below here, near the mission of Espada."

"Then Stephen F. Austin must be in command, for Ruiz said to Vasquez that Austin was encamped on the Cibolo," said Guy, in a tone indicating that he was not addressing his companion.

"Ruiz, did you say?" asked the priest.

"Manuel Ruiz. He who befriended me just before my arrest."

"You would be in less trouble, only for his friendship. You might have been relieved from your parole, but for your connection with Ruiz."

"How?"

"Ruiz is suspected of being the murderer of Vasquez."

"And I——?"

"And you are a possible accessory."

"And in confinement?"

"Else you might have been a principal."

"Perhaps my being an American militates against me. After this collision at the powder house I shall be in bad odor here."

"No doubt you will draw more attention in public, but remain quiet and you are in no danger."

When Guy retired to his room he went to bed, but sleep was out of the question. The news of the bloodshed between the revolutionists and the Mexican guard opened up a new subject for thought. He pictured the camp of his countrymen, so near the city, preparing for attack, and dwelt upon his own position, under parole, not to attempt to escape from the town limits. He was in honor bound to observe it while he accepted his limited liberty. He could only plan and execute an escape by surrender and reincarceration, depending on his own ingenuity and the cupidity of his guard. He would consider the matter deliberately befor acting. Meantime he could get better acquainted with Beatrice and call occasionally at the carcel. It would be out of the question to even think of going back to confinement or to attempt an escape without making Beatrice his friend. His friend? Yes, his very dear friend. He even thought of Josefa, whom he had

seen but a few minutes in Linda's sitting-room. He would go to see Josefa—that strange, tall, graceful girl with the big black eyes that fairly spoke to you, and who looked so decidedly Spanish. Josefa was not at all *en regle*. She was a girl to make a lasting impression, but—Beatrice—Beatrice—was——
Guy fell into a restless slumber

CHAPTER XXIV.

When Guy awoke the next morning he did not feel that freshness which one should experience after a good night's sleep with the temperature at freezing point. His rest had been of that character which is constantly broken through by mental activities that follow into the land of dreams and, shorn of the guiding element of discriminating reason, make practicable all sorts of absurdities and impossibilities. He dreamed that he saw Beatrice drinking from the basin his hands had chiseled into the rock. She espied him approaching and beckoned him to come quickly. In her hand she held the cup from which she had been drinking, and it shone like silver. He mended his pace, but despite his efforts to reach her, the spring receded further and further. He became impatient, but this provoked only her smile. Finally she threw down the vessel, which rolled towards him, and proved to be a human skull. In dismay he looked up for explanation and saw in lieu of the gurgling fountain the mouth of the mine and the dark, deep shaft before him. Amazed at the transition he turned to retreat, when he was arrested by the appearance of Laoni, who stood with folded arm proudly and sadly regarding him.

"Laoni! Is it you!" escaped his lips.

She was silent.

'I thought it was—" he continued, hesitatingly.

"Speak her name. El Bravo is ashamed of it.?"

"Oh, Laoni!" he expostulated.

"The pretty face of the Mexican has made him forget her who waited in the mountains."

As Laoni said this she gave a signal, and several Indians sprang from concealment, and seizing him, bore him to the opening of the shaft and threw him into the dark abyss. Instead of being dashed to pieces by his fall, he found himself transported to a beautiful valley, lined with the white tents of an army. On a nearer approach this proved to be the camp of the Texans, who seemed to be greatly excited over a prisoner, whom they were preparing to burn. He asked a soldier near him why they were going to resort to a method of execution so barbarous, when he was informed that the fellow had murdered Vasquez, a bearer of funds for the army. On this he looked on the prisoner more attentively and discovered that he was Manuel Ruiz. He was about to intercede for him when a female, whom he recognized as Josefa de la Torre, ran frantically through the crowd and, throwing her arms around the condemned, begged for his life. This much of his dream Guy found himself able to unravel, as he lay in bed after awaking, and mused for some minutes on the philosophy of dreams, and the subtle influence they wielded over weak and ignorant minds.

Notwithstanding, his dream impressed him so far as to put in motion an examination of his conscience.

Did he love Beatrice? He remembered his argument with Linda to disprove a sudden kindling of the tender passion. True, there could be and doubtless were exceptions to this theory. Possibly when love is all passion, more of a superficial than a deep-rooted sentiment, it was the offspring of sudden emotion, a natural selection springing from an undefinable magnetism. Dreams were the result of mental states, impressions carried into the domain of sleep. Had his mind ever entertained the idea of Laoni's displeasure should he love the beautiful Mexican? He answered, no. But, he reflected, that the Indian girl, so pure, so brave, so unselfish, so superior to thousands of her sex who were included in a pretentious civilization, loved him with a wealth of love that could never have been purchased, that was given to him as nature bestows her offerings—without recompense, Must he give nothing in return for all this? His gratitude? She had that. He had offered to fly with her from her own people and work for her happiness. But Walumpta was not dead, and duty forbade her acceptance of that which implied no adequate requital for her affection. He could not marry a Lipan. He could not afford to transmit his blood to his posterity weighted by the odium of such a union. He consoled himself by this reflection of what he owed to the future, and cringed a little under the momentary reflection that, possibly, he might never meet again the girl who saved him from the stake, and that fact would settle the matter.

Guy was not mean; he was human. His last thought had scarcely found birth before he discarded it, and resolved, if opportunity ever offered, he would yet show his gratitude to the Indian maiden. Having comfortably disposed of this matter, his thoughts at once reverted to Beatrice, and were occupied by her during the progress of his toilet, which he arose to make.

The brush with the revolutionists at the powder house had thrown the garrison into excitement. The people of the town were in groups discussing the incident on the next morning and watching the movements of troops from one point to another. Officers were riding back and forth from headquarters to barracks and to the advanced posts looking to the east and south. A cordon of Mexican cavalry had been extended as far as it was deemed prudent to anticipate any contemplated surprise.

As Guy issued from the house on the morning in question, after enjoying a late breakfast with his host and patron, who had been delayed at San Fernando, at the conclusion of his mass, he witnessed the departure of two hundred cavalry from the plaza through Carcel street to the ford. He halted to inspect them and could not restrain an opinion of the weakness of such a troop before an equal force of the men under Austin. A knot of Mexican men of the lowest order stood near him, in dirty, tattered blankets, conversing in their nasal tones about the display. To one of these he propounded the question:

"Where are these soldiers going??"

"Not far down the river, senor, to make prisoners of some rebels."

Guy, following on the heels of the troops, walked to Carcel street, musing on the fellow's answer and mentally concluding that these rebels would probably refuse to be taken. He, 'ere long, arrived at the carcel, and encountered Bonito in the court.

"Ah, pajarro mio! The very one I was thinking about.'

"Is that true? Bonito, you must have me often in your thoughts. You gave me the same greeting the last time I was here."

"That may be, senor. But truly, I had a bad dream of you last night and it bodes you no good."

"Dreams are but dreams, Bonito, and amount to nothing."

"With some, yes; but with me they always have a meaning."

"If it bodes me ill luck, then out with it, amigo mio. Let me know my fate at once," said Guy, smiling.

"The upshot of it is, that you are to be again a prisoner, and the mischief of it is I cannot tell if I am to be your jailor. If I am not, it will be the worse for Senor Raymondo. Not all are like myself who have the care of prisoners. You remember, I once gave you liberty and many privileges. Would you want the liberty of the court again, senor? You remember you paid me a trifle, just what you pleased, and it added a little to the beggarly pay I receive for my pains."

"It will be well to await arrest before we talk of privileges and terms. I have no faith in your interpretation of your nightmare."

"It is well, but take Bonito's advice and lay aside a few pesos for prison use. It will not hurt, senor, and you have drawn all your money."

"You know too much, Bonito.'

"One has to keep posted; it pays."

"To cut the matter short, I will save enough to meet all future wants, and if it is my luck to be again a prisoner I want no better jailor than Bonito. Is Linda in the house?"

"Si, senor, in the sitting-room. But stay; you have heard about the affair at the powder house?"

"I did."

"Yours is a plucky race, senor."

"I am glad you think so."

Bonito having nodded permission, Guy directed his steps to the sitting-room, where he had before interviewed Linda. He did not find her alone. To greet his entrance the great, dark eyes of Josefa were raised in conjunction with those of Linda. She rose gracefully from a half stoop over the latter's shoulder, which position she had assumed in the inspection of some fancy work which the deft hands of the jailer's daughter were manipulating, and returned his greeting with a smile that mutely alluded to the pleasure of their previous meeting. Linda expressed her pleasure at seeing him in a manner in keeping with their now well cemented friendship, and motioned him to a seat.

"Linda, you are a capital housekeeper. Around you everything looks cheerful. I cannot decide if the open windows and view of your garden had a more pleasing effect than this bright fire and the comfortable temperature."

"Thanks, senor, for the compliment. Maybe it is Josefa's presence that lends a charm to the room."

"Certainly that helps no little to make it pleasant here," said Guy, giving an inclination to his head, as he met the glance of Linda's visitor.

"Have you seen no pleasanter room than this; none where every object was invested with interest from association with the attractions of its mistress?" asked Josefa

"I know of no such apartment," said Guy.

"We have heard of your adventure," said Linda, mischeviously.

"Adventure!"

"Did you not rescue a senorita?"

"And accompany her home afterwards?" put in Josefa.

"Oh! I begin to undertstand your drift," said Guy; "news travels fast in San Antonio."

"But we heard it from a witness."

" 'Tis all true, young ladies. I admit it. I had the good fortune to be of service in time of danger; saved the young lady; escorted her home; did not enter her house and have not seen her since."

"Your whole experience in that direction has been exceedingly romantic," said Josefa.

"How so?"

"The first impression made at mass; communication through a third party; then an adventure in which her life is saved and a tete-a-tete to the lady's home."

"I grant you are right, except in your choice of terms. The term —impression—is vague and a tete-a-tete is out of the question. A tete-a-tete here with Linda in a cozy apartment would be practicable and agreeable; but with the Senorita Navarro or the Senorita de la Torre, on a limited acquaintance and in the public street would be an unwarranted presumption."

"Mexican gentlemen are not so punctilious."

"Senor Raymond believes that love is slow to kindle into a flame," added Linda.

"A creed of the Saxon race. We Latins have more fire."

'And less endurance—you soon burn out."

"We are more impulsive."

"And perhaps more generous, but not so practical as Americans. Even in religion the Latins require something grand and mysterious with solemn rites and showy ceremonies. What success would a Quaker, or even a Protestant missionary have in Mexico? The people would never give up the pastores, beads, scapulars and holy water for a plain unattractive religion."

"Remove the load of ignorance, senor, and your argument would fall to the ground. Many educated Mexicans are infidels. My uncle is the priest of San Fernando and I am not a Catholic in belief."

"You not a Catholic!" said Guy, surprised.

"I have been cured for a long time."

"Cured?"

"I said cured, because if such credulity as faith requires springs not from ignorance or a diseased mind, it certainly arises from infatuation."

"And your uncle, with his devotion to his church; what a thorn in his side your disaffection from the faith must be. While I honor your independence of thought, I have the highest respect for his sincerity of belief."

"My uncle is so bigoted."

"Give it a softer name."

"I cannot. He believes that my father is in everlasting torment because he was once a Mason."

"Let him believe it. You who discredit the existence of so foul a blot on this fair creation know that it is not true."

"Senor Raymond, I will not let you come here if you abuse my religion. I am going to get Father Ignacio to give you a talking."

"Abuse it! I was defending those who truly believe."

"It was I, Linda. I'll bear all the blame. My uncle and myself have had many a hard fought battle. He once tried to exorcise me, thinking I was possessed."

"How did he go about it? Is there a stereotyped incantation to be used on such occasions?"

"Ha, ha!" laughed Josefa; "I'll not tell you. Linda, I must be going. Mother is afraid for me to be out long since the stampede."

'Perhaps I had better see you home for protection," said Guy.

"It is not on account of my tender years that her anxiety is aroused. She has been ill, and her nerves are weak."

Linda showed them out through the garden. Many of her plants were covered to ward off the cold, but the high walls usually afforded sufficient protection for the more hardy.

The home of Josefa and her mother was not distant from the carcel. Across the plaza and a turn up North Flores street brought them to the place.

Guy entered and was introduced to the mother. A glance at the two would have demonstrated to a less keen observer that there was a radical difference mentally as well as physically between mother and daughter. The latter showed intellect and indomitable will that gave a hard cast to her expression on occasions when she did not purposely control it

Have you heard anything lately of Manuel Ruiz?" she asked, as Guy was about to take leave.

"Not since he left the city," he replied.

"I presume he writes to the Senorita Navarro."

"To Beatrice? To Beatrice Navarro?"

"She is the only senorita here of that name. I suppose you know she is engaged to Ruiz."

"Engaged to Ruiz!"

"Si senor; to Manuel Ruiz."

"I was not aware of it."

"No, you scarcely know the senorita, only met her once, have never been in her house. It is not to be supposed you know much about her private affairs."

"True—but Manuel—did not—yet I never met him but once."

"I hope it is not having a depressing effect on Senor Raymond."

"On me! How could it?"

"True; Americans are practical, not impulsive; do not fall in love except by slow degrees. Senorita Navarro's engagement cannot affect you, yet you appeared annoyed at first."

"Not from what you said. In fact, my manner belied my feelings; it must, for I was not annoyed at all."

"You were possibly condemning Ruiz for not telling you of his love."

"No, I said I only met him once, but he befriended me and his act made him seem like a freind of years. Was it Beat—the Senorita Navarro, who told you of her engagement?"

"She will deny it. I heard it from Ruiz and saw the ring before it was given. But I am telling this to you who have no interest in the matter, seeing you are almost a stranger to the parties. I will not detain you further, except to thank you for the pleasure of your company to my home. Being both unbelievers, as the Christians call us, I trust to see you often, senor."

Guy moved abstractedly down the street, not noticing the few pedestrians he passed. One of these—a tall, young Mexican—regarded him with peculiar interest, and turned to look after him until he had reached a distant corner.

"What has he been doing in this quarter," he muttered, as Guy disappeared; "the murdering Gringo."

It was Sancho.

Guy reached the plaza and mechanically crossed towards San Fernando. He was about to pass the front entrance of the church without noticing Jose, who stood at the gate awaiting his approach.

Jose's hail brought him to himself again.

"Senor Raymond, Father Ignacio would like to see you. I went to the carcel, but Bonito was as cross as a bear and would give me no more satisfaction, save that you had been there this morning."

"All right, Jose; where will I find him?"

"In the sitting-room, senor."

Guy entered the house, but avoiding the room to which he had been directed by Jose, repaired to his own apartment. It looked to him gloomy enough without a fire in his present mood. He threw himself upon the bed without any apparent purpose, and, bolstering his head with the hard Mexican pillow, said just audibly:

"Beatrice—engaged!"

CHAPTER XXV.

We left Karnes watching the movements of the guard at the powder house, while Nathan Roach went back to pilot the rest of their party to the chaparral surrounding it.

The angelus from San Fernando had not yet ceased when a squad of soldiers marched into view from where the road lost itself in the direction of the town.

This was the relief.

The guard saw their approach, formed lazily into line and took their pieces from the stack. The relief passed before the line, bringing down their pieces in answer to its present, halted and dressed backward on the right. The sentry was then relieved, arms again stacked and a general pow-wow ensued.

"Why in thunder don't the old guard go back?" muttered Karnes.

The reason was explained to him, Karnes thought, when he saw the corporal and three others of the old guard resume an interrupted game of cards.

"The gambling yaller-bellies! They'll neglect anything for a game. If they crowd it on to me we'll just light into the layout Seven of us ought to be equal to sixteen greasers. Nathe and me could lick half of them"

The watcher began to grow impatient. He did not much like the augmented force of his enemy, although he would not admit a fear of numbers, and he vented his displeasure on Nathan for not having given some signal of his return.

"The blasted poke! He's crawling on all fours there and back, I reckon. If ever I wanted a thing done quick and well I've had to do it myself."

His muttering was interrupted by the appearance of a Mexican at the window above, who looked intenely to the eastward, then called to those below, pointing at the same time in that direction.

Karnes could not divine his words, but knew he must have seen something of interest, as instantly two others ascended to his side and scanned the country from beneath their palms.

"What can Nathe be doing?"

Impatience getting the better of him, Karnes crawled away in the direction Nathan Roach had taken. He had not proceeded many yards when he perceived his men cautiously approaching, led by the tardy messenger. After whispered consultation, a plan was decided upon, which involved an effort to capture or destroy the whole detachment of the enemy. Three of the party had pistols in addition to their guns. The men were to deploy until a distance of several feet would separate them, then move steadily to the verge of the opening, or until a further advance would endanger a disclosure of their positions. The men severally on either flank were to take delibcrate aim at an enemy opposite. The center was ordered to direct their shots at men on neither extreme, but to choose an aim to the left or right, according to position, the object being to make every bullet count, in order to ensure to the enemy the possible maximum loss at the first volley.

The signal to fire was to be a quail call from Karnes. The program having been arranged, the movement began. The commander occupied the center and was first in position. The old guard was in line, having just taken arms. The two non-commissioned officers were talking to one side. The sentry was walking his post. The other men, who had formed the relief, were inside the house.

Karnes saw at once there was no time to be lost. He anxiously peered through the undergrowth to satisfy himself that his men were in their places. He instantly covered the right-center man of the squad, waited until the sentinel had come in line, just two or three feet behind him, and gave the signal.

An almost simultaneous discharge of all the pieces followed.

Karnes, Nathan and Hamilton, who had pistols, immediately rushed forward with yells, while the others followed, loading their pieces. The terrified Mexicans became demoralized. The charge had followed so quickly after the shots, whose fatal effect was now plainly visible, that the luckless soldiers inside the building did not sally for their arms, still stacked a few feet from them.

Three shots only received the onset of the Texans. The discharge of the pistols at close quarters brought to terms those who had escaped the first fire, while the occupants of the house shut and barricaded the door.

The whole plan had so far succeeded. Six of those with arms, including the sentinel, had fallen. Two corporals and two privates surrendered. Karnes posted Ducio and Jones to pick off any of the Mexicans inside who might show themselves at the window above for the purpose of acting on the offensive. He then examined those who had been put hors du combat and found that five of them had been killed outright and one mortally wounded. His next thought was how to make prisoners of the balance.

"Fire the door," suggested Roach.

"Suggest to them the propriety of surrender. I will draw up the articles of capitulation," said Hamilton, gaily.

"Fire will never do," said Mr. Trigg; "it will signal to the balance of the town."

"Hamilton's idea is the best. Let us first ask them to surrender," said Karnes. "Mr. Smith, remove the prisoners further away to the left."

Karnes then approached the door and demanded in indifferent Mexican that those within should surrender at discretion, adding that on failure to comply, the virtue of fire would be tried as a persuader.

After a parley that extended a quarter of an hour, terms were agreed upon and the door was opened. Five men only made their appearance. Karnes demanded the whereabouts of the remaining man. They denied that any more had constituted their force.

"He must be in there," said Karnes, "for sixteen of the yaller devils were here when we woke 'em up."

"If he is in here I will find him," said Hamilton, as he entered the place.

Seeing no vestige of humanity below, he bounded up the steps.

Karnes saw that the prisoners were secured, and placing the last quota in charge of Smith, he ordered Ducio and Jones to go for the horses, and to lose no time.

"Wouldn't it be safer to go to the horses?" suggested Jones; "when I was in India——"

"D——n India, sir! Do as you are ordered; start the horses this way; we will meet you."

"All right, Mr. Karnes; I only wanted to tell you of a rule of Lord Dalrymple's."

"My rule is the one for this squad to follow—be off."

A noise on the steps here attracted the attention of all, and Hamilton appeared, dragging a Mexican after him.

"Here is your sixteenth man, captain. He was up at the top concealed like a hedgehog in his periodical retreat. He was ensconced beneath a pile of hay that these sons of Montezuma doubtless used as a bed when they should have been guarding the interests of old Santy."

"It was a job to get the devils in town after us. The feller was to break for there no sooner'd we be out of sight," said Roach, chucking the prisoner under the chin. "You're a sooner, you is."

"Mr. Roach is likely enough to be right," said Mr. Trigg.

"Nathe, search the prisoners and take from them everything in their possession and put all in a pile. I will examine the pockets of these dead fellows. Hamilton, go up and keep a lookout towards town, for this is a bad place for a squad without pickets, as these poor devils found out."

Karnes' orders were obeyed, while he bent over the dead. Nathan dexterously relieved the living of the odds and ends that he could detect about their persons and placed them, as directed, all together on the ground. The commander added the result of his search and found variety, if not value, had constituted the effects of the vanquished. A half dozen sheath knives were the most acceptable. A lot of monte cards, some silver change, buckskin strings, a clasp knife, tobacco, a few shucks ready fashioned for cigarettes, a rosary and a common memorandum book were about the sum of the articles. Nathan held up the beads with a quaint expression upon his quainter physiognomy.

"These here is what them heathens prays on."

"You had better be making light of things that you are after knowing something about, Mister Roach; for it's heathens they are that don't know about a rosary and don't say the prayers that's said on it."

"Then I want to be a heathen."

"It's glad I am that you're suited."

"Here's a book, Mr. Twig. It's got writin' in it. I can't read printin', let alone writin'. Mebby you can guess it out."

Mr. Trigg took the book and put it into his pocket.

"Return the prisoners all their property except their knives," commanded Karnes.

"If there's any papers keep them also. I thought I saw a memorandum book."

"Mr. Twig's got it, Karnes, but I lay he can't read it."

"Trigg's my name, sir."

"Your pardon, friend; I meant no 'fense."

"Come, Nathe, get along with the prisoners. You and Smith take an extra gun. I will call Hamilton and we three will bring the rest of the arms. Take the direction to the horses, so as to meet Jones and the other man."

Hamilton obeyed the summons down, reporting everything quiet in and towards town. He called attention to the hazy appearance of the northern horizon and predicted that it meant a blow.

The three men gathered up the captured arms and followed after the prisoners. Meeting the horses a little further on, they stopped to arrange for the march to rejoin the command. The muskets were distributed; the prisoners secured in pairs to a lariat, one end of which was tied to Nathan's saddle horse. He and Ducio followed after Karnes; the others brought up the rear. In this order they commenced their march, skirting the hills whose range pointed to the southwest and divided the valleys of the San Antonio and Salado.

"A right smart brush that was. Sixteen at a lick and none of our'n hurt," said Nathan to Ducio.

"I got my man, but some one missed," said the latter.

"Ef anybody missed, it must a been you or Smith."

"There were six killed and seven guns fired. Mr. Karnes, who do you think missed."

"I don't like to say, Halfen; I think I got two with my one shot."

"How could that be?"

"That shows the boy ain't up to snuff. I saw your play, Karnes; you know it's one of our tricks."

"If Mr. Karnes killed two, then two of our shots missed their mark. What was the trick, Roach?"

"Why Karnes jest waited tel the sent'nel lined his man, and then he popped them both. Can't yer see? He nor me don't miss, we don't."

The progress of the party was slow. The prisoners were sullen and made no attempt to move with celerity. Hamilton was keeping up the spirits of the rear by an occasional hit at Jones. The latter bore it with scarcely a ruffle to his temper, now and then appealing to Mr. Trigg to help him out.

"Jones, I would like to hear that rule of Lord Somebody's over in India that you attempted to quote to Mr. Karnes up at the powder house."

"What would be the use of telling it to a rattle brain like you. You would be sure to ridicule it."

"Rattle brain! You don't know my prowess. I'm naturally gay and, with my present environment, do not show the polish which exists under this rough exterior, nor the intellect imprisoned behind this massive brow, awaiting but the occasion to call it forth to benefit my race and country."

"Bosh! You got that out of some trashy book."

"One can't expect the truth from you. A recognition of my worth would be an expression of truth—ergo, as the logicans say you could not do me justice."

"You rarely say a sensible thing."

"Would you have me e'er with clouded brow, grim-visaged, uttering only sage expressions and moral truths; or worse, telling impossible adventures or palpable lies, that neither point a moral nor adorn a tale? The mess would die of ennui if I did not come to the rescue and offset your lugubrious falsifications by my flow of wit and fund of folly. Why, Mr. Trigg wouldn't have smiled in any other mess, and I have kept him healthy with laughing."

"It doesn't hurt to have a bit of fun," said Mr. Trigg.

Karnes here cut short their talk by riding to the rear and directing Hamilton, Jones and Mr. Trigg to hand over their captured guns to the others and accompany him in a detour he intended to make, so as to pass near the mission of Concepcion. Nathan was put in command of the others with instructions what point to make for, and the parties separated.

The mission was in plain view and situated two miles below the town. Karnes, like a true scout, wished to learn if any force was there, and to pick up any information that would be likely to benefit the army, from a point he knew must be in the line of march in the advance soon to be made on the Mexican stronghold. The squad went forward at a gallop, without any attempted concealment, heading first obliquely towards the river, until not more than six hundred yards intervened between the dark old structure and their position. Heading boldly in its direction, they circled it in close rifle shot, but not a foe could be seen. Two women appearing in the door of a jacal in the rear of the mission, Karnes rode near and addressed them in their language:

"Any soldiers been here today?"

"Si senor, esta manana."

"How many?"

"Yo no se, muchos."

"A great many! How many?"

"Ciento, dos cientos, mas o menos."

"One or two hundred, more or less," he repeated after her. "How far is the picket from here?"

"No se yo."

"Don't you go to town sometimes?"

"Si, senor."

"Well then, where do you pass the soldiers when you go and when you return?"

"Oh! si yo lo intiendo bien, en esta casita blanco a lado del camino."

The woman had understood and definitely located the position of the picket at a little white house near some trees by the side of the road.

If he had not been encumbered with the prisoners, Karnes would have indulged his humor to call up his full force and surprise the guard at the little white house, but he had done enough to set the hive in an uproar. He had not received a sting and would rejoin his command with a whole skin and plenty of evidence of his success.

"Well, men, let us strike out for our friends."

"In good season, too," said Hamilton. "There comes the blow I predicted. The air has cooled in the last minute."

"It's a norther, and it's time we had one," said Karnes.

"From the looks of yon sky we will have a stiff one this time," said Mr. Trigg.

"You have followed the sea, Mr. Trigg?" asked Karnes.

"I did, sir."

"Then there ought to be many a good yarn in you."

"He let us have one or two on the Cibolo," said Hamilton.

"If I had the 'magination of Mister Jones I could be after telling many a one."

"And you, too, Mr. Trigg," said Jones.

"Et tu Trigge!" corrected Hamilton; "why don't you use your Latin. I will wager you were more classical in India."

"Sure—them elephants must a knocked it out of him."

"Or that rule of Lord Dalrymple's proscribed its use," said Hamilton.

"Sure, I heard nothing about the rule."

"No, for Mr. Karnes sealed him up. The gravity of the occasion and our proximity to the enemy, encumbered as we were with the spoils of victory, rendered necessary the postponement of its promulgation. Now, Jones, is the opportune moment. Give us his lordship's rule, and I will take it down phonetically."

"You'd pronounce it a lie. Even Mr. Trigg is against me."

"Here's the norther, boys," said Karnes.

The flying hats of all except the last speakers went sailing in advance and a merry chase was given them by their owners. Even Mr. Trigg, unusually good humored during the scout, gave vent to a hearty laugh as he spurred after his truant covering. The wind increased to great violence, sending the dust flying in blinding clouds. It was the same blow that stampeded the herd whose onset endangered the lives of Beatrice Navarro and her rescuer.

Opposite the mission of San Jose, four miles further down the river, Karnes caught up with Captain Bowie, whom Nathan Roach, with the prisoners, had already joined. Bowie was very fond of Karnes and was proud of his achievement. Roach had given a spirited account of the affair, much to the entertainment of the listeners.

The detachment had picked a camp and already several huge log fires were burning brightly, giving protection to the men from the blast, which had well nigh chilled them to the bone. The rest of the command had communicated their arrival at the mission of Espada, a little further down the stream, and Bowie was ordered to keep a vigilant lookout to prevent a surprise.

From Karnes' report there was no immediate danger to be anticipated from an attack. The boldness of his conduct at the powder house, which doubtless became known in the town during the afternoon, must have confirmed the enemy in the belief that a large force of Texans were at hand. This would keep them cautious for a while, until a reconnoitre should disclose the absence of any enemy to be feared. When our squad had refreshed themselves after their day's work, they sat by a comfortable fire recounting the brush with the Mexicans, and wondering when the next affair would come off.

"By the way, Mr. Trigg," said Hamilton, "have you that memorandum book in your pocket? I'd like to see what is written in it."

"That's whar you'll get left, Mister Hamilton. You kin use jaw-breakers, but the Mexican lingo is what'll git you."

Mr. Trigg drew from his pocket the book in question, and, passing it to Hamilton, said:

"You can study it out. If I had a mind to, I couldn't, for my glasses are put away in my roll."

It was early evening and as Hamilton turned it to the firelight and bent over to examine the contents, he exclaimed:

"No Mexican—this. It is the pure vernacular and the best of English."

"What's it about?" asked several.

"Read it," said two or three voices.

Hamilton began reading, and when he finished, had imparted to his auditors the complete memorandum made by Guy Raymond of his adventures up to the time of his imprisonment in the carcel. One of the Mexicans who met his death at the powder house was the sentinel at the carcel, who secured the pocket book left by Guy on the bench under the window of his cell.

Mr. Trigg became interested at the commencement of Hamilton's reading, and was much excited when the dog Rolla was mentioned. When it came to Stella's and his own partly spelled name, he could scarcely control himself.

"Give me the book, sir. I had it all this time in my pocket and none the wiser of what it could tell me, just for the looking at it. I'll get my specs and read it over."

"Is it anyone you know?" asked several.

"It's the boy I've been wanting. I feared he was dead. He might as well be under the ground or back with the Indians as to be in the power of the dirty greasers."

Mr. Trigg would brook no more questioning, but set to work to unroll his blankets and get his glasses from a pouch where he carried his little valuables. We will leave the big-hearted Irishman to pore over the record of his boy's troubles while our squad, relieved from guard duty, got tired of story telling and lapsed into slumber.

CHAPTER XXVI.

Reveille at daybreak on the following morning roused the men of Bowie's command, who were still sleeping. The norther had greatly abated, but the air was crisp and raw, piercing the scanty blankets and light clothing of the volunteers, most of whom had left their homes hastily and unprepared for a winter campaign. The last laggard had crawled from his nest and joined his squad around the fire, when another call sounded. Very few of the men knew much about military calls, and several conjectures were indulged in by our squad as to its meaning. Mr. Trigg, who had descended the bank of a little stream running near to perform his morning ablutions, now joined them with the remark:

"What's the assembly call for, Mister Hamilton?"

"I presume it is called for us to assemble, sir," replied Hamilton. Hamilton had been the only one who had not admitted his ignorance of the purpose of the call.

"Why didn't you say what it was for when we were talking about it just now?" said Jones, addressing Hamilton.

"Do you expect me to be everlastingly lighting up your benighted mind?"

"I will bet he didn't know it was assembly call until Mr. Trigg came up," said Ducio; "did he, Roach?"

"No tellin', when it comes to knowin' things what he don't know. He must a learnt that whar he learnt them hifalutin words he's always poking at Jones."

"Where did you learn that call, Mr. Trigg? I thought you were a sailor."

"Fact is, I'm after being a little of everything. I was at Orleans, sir. The call you have heard is the same as they have in the army over there; and that chap with the bugle was in Uncle Sam's band," he says. "There'll be a second call, if he means businesss, and ye all will have to get into line. Do ye mind that fellow going around a telling of them?"

Here Karnes came up and asked what the bugle had sounded for. Hamilton informed him with an air imparting a thorough familiarity with calls of all descriptions.

"Suppose we march up in file at the second call, if one is made. The other greenies will imagine we are veterans. In India when——"

"Blast India! It is dangerous ground for you, Jones. But his suggestion is nearer wisdom than usual. Suppose we do it. I'll command the squad," said Hamilton.

The words were scarcely out of his lips when the bugle sounded.

"Fall in squad! Tallest in front! At the tail end, Smith! There! S-t-e-a-d-y—s-o."

The squad had fallen in promptly, but were rather merry at the assumed authority of their pedantic commander.

"Stop your laughing! Left face! Right dress! Back a little, Mr. Roach. Steady! Front! Squad forward, guide right—March!"

The men marched briskly along, keeping pretty fair step, except Nathan Roach, whose long body made a curve, while his head bent forward, continuing the arc of the ragged circle formed by his back.

"Straighten up, Roach. For God's sake stop bobbing up and down, and shorten your everlasting step. You are disgracing the squad. Just look at Mr. Trigg, old enough to be your grandfather, but as straight as an arrow."

Hamilton marched them in front of headquarters, halted and dressed the line, reported their presence and took his position on their right.

The movement caused a hearty laugh and did more to assemble the men than the notes of the bugle. The volunteers were a raw set, as a body. They knew nothing of discipline, and the younger ones had probably never heard a military command.

Captain Bowie finally obtained silence and thus addressed the crowd:

"Fellow soldiers: I have called you together to inform you that we have marching orders that will admit of no delay. The contemplated movement is one of importance, and every man in my command must at once set about preparing cooked rations for twenty-four hours; see that his arms and ammunition are in first-class order and make himself ready in every respect to meet our enemy. Captain Fannin's command will march with us, while the main army will follow in supporting distance. I noticed just now a germ of discipline, which I trust will be emulated by every squad in my company. I am aware that the men who displayed it were actuated by a spirit of fun, but it shows how voluntary may discipline become among men prepared to surrender a little personal liberty and ease for the sake of that civil liberty which will be the result of the triumph of our cause. Men, obey the orders I have just given you."

"Hurrah for Jim Bowie!" came from a score of throats.

The camp was soon in the bustle of preparation. It was the twenty-seventh of October. Karnes' discovery of the position of the enemy within the walls of San Antonio, with only light pickets thrown out within a mile or so from town, had been dispatched to General Austin by courier the evening before. The messenger found him at the mission of Espada, just dismissing the members of the council to return to the seat of government. After a brief consultation with his principal officers, the commander-in-chief determined on a forward movement to terminate in the investment and capture of the town and the Alamo. He therefore sent orders to Captain Bowie and Fannin to put their forces in motion; to approach San Antonio as near as prudence might determine, and await the arrival of the army. In obedience to this order Captain Bowie assembled his company as detailed in the beginning of this chapter.

"I'd like to know where the twenty-four hours' cooked rations are coming from. These two quarts of meal wont more than do for breakfast, and the dried beef in these saddle bags won't last two meals," said Karnes.

"That comes from taking Roach in our mess. He is so long it takes three rations to fill him," said Hamilton.

"But he stands starvation," put in Karnes, apologetically. "You should have seen him up on the Trinity where we were without grub for three days, and the red devils after us."

"It is a wonder that our friend from India don't see you on that and go twenty days better."

"I am glad, Mr. Hamilton, that you see fit to doubt somebody else's veracity, as well as mine."

"Never had a doubt about yours, sir; never once since the elephant story."

"Give him a rest, Hamilton, for the Lawd's sake. Ef I was Jones I'd whip you before night," said Nathan.

"Just save your fighting propensities for the greasers, as I told you once before. Jones and myself understand each other."

"Hurrah! If there is not Perry!" cried Hamilton, dropping his gun, which he was cleaning, and starting to meet the mesenger to San Filipe, who had come in sight a few yards up the road.

Mr. Trigg had been making his own preparations in silence, paying little attention to the light talk of his messmates, but when he heard Hamilton's exclamation he could not refrain from following to meet the boy.

"We thought you had deserted us, Perry. You played us a pretty trick, sneaking off at night and never a good-bye."

" 'Twas orders, Mr. Hamilton; I hadn't a minute's warning."

"You missed all the fun, Perry. Sixteen greasers succumbed to our valor and——"

"Howdy, Mr. Trigg."

"Welcome back, my boy. I hope it's good news ye have?"

"None bad, sir. A letter which I have for you will tell all about those you want to hear from. Where is General Austin?"

"It is a matter of five or six miles to his camp down the river. The captain is in command here and you had better report. Soon as you've reported, fetch the letter."

"It is right here in my pocket. Here it is."

Mr. Trigg reached eagerly for the letter and walked aside to read it.

"You had a fight, then," said Perry.

Hamilton related to him the particulars of the affair at the powder house.

"So the old man was in it."

"He's true grit," replied Hamilton; "and Jones, and Ducio, and that fellow Smith; and you remember that specimen of the genus homo who came to the camp the day before you left—that long, lean, lanksided, awkward cuss, whose hands reached below his knees when he stood as near erect as his semi-circular anatomy could attain a perpendicular, and whose thin, hungry-looking visage was emphasized by his drooping chin and high cheek bones—that fellow who rode that fine sorrel with the antedeluvian saddle and stirrups too short for him by a foot, and at whom we all laughed so?"

"Ha! ha!" laughed Perry—remember him! That's what I'll do 'til my dying day."

"Well, he was with us. But, my boy, you can risk you last cent that he is a whole team. He can crawl on his belly like a snake and hide in grass a foot high."

"What's his name?"

"He pursues his awkward way through the world under an appellation whose lack of euphony is in keeping with his tout-ensemble."

"For God's sake, Tipton Hamilton, do talk English."

"Forgive me, Perry, but Roach's appearance is, in itself, a source productive of merriment, irony and their sisters laughter and wit.

But, boy, he is touchous. In my first sally at him he raised the war whoop and circled the air with his ungainly arms until I apologized. The fellow will fight."

"But this is not reporting; where's the——"

"There's the captain at his breakfast."

Hamilton pointed to where four men were sitting on a log by a fire eating, and followed the youth in the direction indicated.

"Perry, we have got marching orders to go right into town. We will be off in an hour and are sure to have a brush with them. If you are to go to Austin's camp with your dispatches, you'll miss the fun again. If I were you, I'd beg off and let some one else take them. Ask Bowie; he'll do it."

"All right, come along and back me up; you're good on the talk."

Perry approached and accosted Captain Bowie, telling him whence he came and informing him of his possession of dispatches for army headquarters.

"Well, sir, you know your duty. General Austin is at the mission of Espada, six miles below here. What road did you travel to reach us?"

"I followed the cavalry trail that left the main body and it brought me right to you."

"Have you picked up any information that you can communicate for our benefit.?"

"No, sir; I have not met a soul on the way."

"Take the dispatches at once to General Austin; but stay—have you had your breakfast? If not, join us here."

"Can't some one else take them to General Austin?" stammered Perry; "I missed the powder house fight and now I am ordered to the rear."

"How do you know you would have been at the powder house? Picked men were sent there."

"Mr. Karnes would have picked me," replied Perry, confidently.

Here Hamilton suggested that a fresh man and a fresh horse would be better to entrust with important dispatches.

"That is true," said Bowie. "Young man you can march with us."

Mr. Trigg had finished reading Stella's letter and sat in meditative mood by the mess fire thinking over its contents.

"Pity it is she's been so long with that giddy aunt, without any religion at all. But the dear child writes sensible like, and it's straightened out she'll be when the nuns get her, of all that infidel talk about duty for a religion. What's duty and such like without the Blessed Mother and Saints and the Holy Church? The next letter she gets from me she'll be after hearing from her brother being in San Antonio. But sure it's out of the frying pan into the fire he is—from the Indians to the greasers. 'The New Orleans volunteers,' them's the fellows that's joined the general since we marched. It's a bad time to be knocking around the gulf in a schooner; but it's good luck I hope she'll have——"

"Mr. Trigg, I am not to go any further, but will march with you. Here's some socks Stella sent you."

"She spoke of them in the letter—the dear child—did she look happy, Perry?"

"She was not gay, but appeared contented."

"Were the cheeks rosy—like when I left her?"

"Just like peaches, sir."

"In good health, then. Perry, her brother is in San Antonio."

"How did you hear?"

"We got this memorandum book off a dead Mexican up yonder. It's Guy's own writin' and tells about his being in the prison and getting away from the Indians."

"That was strange," said Perry, looking over the book.

"It's what I call providential," said Mr. Trigg.

"That's not the word," said Hamilton, who had just joined them.

"It was rather one of those fortuitous circumstances that permeate human experience and pander to our inclination to attribute to the supernatural all that appears to us unaccountable. What can be easier to explain than the incident you attribute to an act of Providence? Your young friend is a prisoner in a military stronghold and consequently his guard is a soldier. He wrote in this book. The sentinel got it into his possession by some means. In the course of his duties the powder house became his temporary post. We captured him there, and the book is in your hands. See it?"

"You may have it that way, Mister Hamilton, but remember that God directs everything, even the likes of the falling of a leaf."

"Mr. Trigg, you are a born pantheist."

"It's a Roman Catholic I am, sir. Did you mane I was a Protestant?"

"By no means; I said pantheist."

"And what is that?"

"One who believes that the whole creation is God."

"Everything in the world?"

"Everything in the universe."

"He's a born fool as believes the likes of that."

The bugle sounded the assembly.

The men had made hasty preparations for the march, after having partaken of their breakfasts, and at the summons from the bugle, they commenced to mount their horses and assemble in the road. The company of Captain Fannin, which had been camped near, came in sight, with their gallant ocmmander riding at the head of the column. They numbered fifty men. As they passed, the men of Bowie's company cheered them with a will. The latter, now formed, answered to roll call, then followed in Fannin's rear with forty men in ranks.

These ninety Texans marched away with the mission of Concepcion as their objective point, where they were to await the commander in chief while reconnoitering the position of the enemy.

This mission was not unlike the others founded by the Franciscans early in the eighteenth century. The difference consisted in their dimensions and the amount of ornamentation displayed in the architectural finish bestowed on the front elevations and side openings. Concepcion ranked about third in area and importance. It was situated four hundred yards from the river in a bend made by the latter to the west. In front the northern view was open. To the east a prairie stretched a thousand yards to a chain of hills. Riverward was timber, just beyond a bluff that bordered the valley proper, and which made an angle conforming with its flow. This bluff formed the western and southern sides of the plateau that stretched indefinitely to the north and mingled on the east with the undulations of the prairie. A few Mexican jacals occupied positions near and in rear of the church. A single tower surmounted the northwest corner of the latter. The whole structure was blackened and defaced by the ravages of time, and presented all the aspects of neglect that inevitably follow a continued absence of occupation and care.

A travelled road approached from the direction of the town and passed along its eastern side and on down the river. This road branched to the right about one hundred paces before reaching Concepcion and found its way to a ford, where it crossed and led to San Jose, four miles distant.

A position on the parapet of the church afforded a good view of the plateau, whose level was unbroken for nearly a mile, save by clumps of bushes dotting it here and there. Then a series of mottes, beginning at a small white house to the right of the road, disclosed themselves in tiers, until the low walls of the houses of the city, circling the more pretentious masonry of San Fernando, filled the background. To the left, the timbered river; to the right, the rolling country, culminating in the hills, where the garita—or powder house—

showed itself above the now paling foliage of the mesquite, completed the picture.

It was in the forenoon of the twenty-seventh. The mission had its usually deserted appearance, looking dark and grim, in contrast with the flood of sunshine that poured from a cloudless sky.

The norther had spent its fury, but the sharp air still contended with the warmth of heaven, and yielded only where cover from the polar current gave vantage to the descending rays. The day had a lazy look with all its brightness. The recent fierceness of the wind, cutting and cold, had driven all animated nature to retreats, whence it emerged only to bask in sunshine where protecting leaf or limb, hillside or wall, gave inviting shelter. Behind the low wall of the mission wing two donkeys stood with lowered heads, motionless as statuary, their long ears limp and horizontal. They looked the picture of repose. Two Mexicans, with blankets thrown close around their shoulders, leaned lazily against the same projection near its eastern corner and were conversing, while apparently watching a woman near, who, in a sitting posture, was busily working her arms as if she was scrubbing. A nearer inspection, by a connoisseur, however, would have at once disclosed her true occupation to have been the preparation of paste for tortillas. A slab of stone on the ground held the softened corn, while a half rounded rock, firmly held in both hands, was used to reduce the grain to the required fineness. The doorway of an adobe hut, from which hung a fresada with looped corner, disclosed a bed and articles of its simple furniture. It was the domicil of the tortilla maker, who had moved to the shelter of the wall for protection. She frequently ceased the movement of her arms to scrape back the truant grains to the middle of the slab, and while thus engaged she rattled away in rapid talk to the men, who would reply to her loquacity in nasal tones, while a smile would occasionally relieve the apathetic expression of the Aztec features.

"It is true, or my name is not Locaria Landina."

This was said by the woman in response to some doubt about a previous assertion she had made.

"How many did you say?"

"Five. Five mounted Americans."

"At what time in the day?"

"About three hours after dinner."

"What shall we do, Juan? Here we are between two fires. If we join these fellows there is no telling what desperate fights we will be led into. If we do not join them General Cos will force us into the army and we will have to meet these devils of Americans."

"It is true, Ramon. The best thing is to steal horses from the herd and get away from these parts. I see no other way."

"A good idea of yours, but the herd will be kept close, now that the Americans are around."

"The greatest trouble will be——"

"There comes a man now," said Locaria. "If I remember right, he looks like the officer who forced my brother into his company."

The two men made a movement as if to retreat, but before they could move more than a pace or two, a horseman came up at a canter and reined his animal to a halt opposite the woman.

"Buenas Dias! amigos," he said, saluting the three.

They all returned the greeting.

"Where is your brother—Locaria?"

"My brother! Do you know him?"

"Well, that is the reason I could call your name."

"True, you did call me Locaria. I was so frightened I did not notice it."

"Still you have not answered my question."

"Oh! About my brother. They took him for a soldier. When I first saw you I thought you were the one who took him away."

"Is that the reason you were frightened?"

"Si, senor. And yesterday there were five Americans here asking about the soldiers in the town. But they were good Americans and very polite."

"F-i-v-e A-m-e-r-i-c-a-n-s! Can you tell me where they went?"

"Abajo, senor. Down that road as far as I could see them.

"The mission of Espada, doubtless," mused the new comer. "Just as I was informed."

He thought awhile, then addressed the men who had remained to listen:

"Well, my good fellows, where are you from? Perhaps dodging the military. Am I not right?"

"Si senor," they replied.

"I don't blame you for not wanting to serve with a lot of convicts brought here to destroy the liberties of the people. Why don't you help drive them out?

The men looked at each other, but were silent. The horseman regarded them with contemptuous pity, then turned his looks down the road.

"Por via de mi madre!" he exclaimed. "If that cloud of dust does not mean something I am mistaken. Here, Locaria, hold my rein until I see what it means."

So saying, he dismounted and darted into the mission. A moment later he was looking from the parapet in the direction of the dust rising in the distance. He soon descended and relieved the woman if her charge.

"What did you see, senor?"

"The army of liberty. The Americans will soon be here, Locaria. But where are those two fellows?"

"Gone. They made off as soon as you entered the mission."

"But, senor, will the Americans harm us?"

"Fear not, Locaria, they are our friends."

"Friends! They come to fight Mexicans."

"But Mexicans stole your brother from you."

"And they would not?"

"No. They will get him back for you."

"Que buena gente."

CHAPTER XXVII.

Manuel Ruiz did not remain long chatting with Locaria before his solution of the cause of the distant cloud of dust proved to be the true one. The ninety Texans, under Fannin and Bowie, were soon drawn up in line in rear of the mission, with Ruiz in conversation with the leaders. The gallant Mexican was acquainted with many of the Texans, and among them was Captain Bowie. The latter was apparently well pleased to meet him and plied him with questions in regard to the strength of the garrison in the town, and upon other matters pertinent to its coming investment. Ruiz was able to inform him on many points, but the result was anything but satisfactory to the cherished hopes of carrying the place by assault. The whole army on the ground after the arrival of the main body would not number more than eight hundred men. It had little, if any, transportation, no commissariat, insufficient ammunition, was armed with every conceivable style and caliber of guns, and no tents, even for the field hospital. It would be hazardous to attempt an assault with such appointments, while a seige, without cannon, save two light twelve pounders, and no military chest whence to draw the funds needed, even to supply the simple wants and absolute necessities of an inactive camp, whose monotony and leisure so illy accorded with the adventurous spirit of the volunteers, was out of the question.

"Ruiz, do you think we can capture the place with eight hundred boys like these?" asked Bowie.

"That number of brave men can do wonders."

"My opinion is that an assault is the thing. A seige should not be thought of for a moment, with the poor fix our men are in. Why half of them would not stay."

"Captain Bowie, let us ride around here and select a camp," suggested Fannin.

"Come with us, Ruiz."

The ground chosen was in the edge of the wood where the friendly bluff would afford ample protection against the attack of a superior force. Here the two commanders decided to await the arrival of General Austin. As there were no signs of activity among the Mexicans, a chain of sentinels extending from the mission and along the open space to the wood was supposed to constitute the requisite precaution to guard against surprise. A party of observation sent out towards the town were, ere long, seen to be slowly retiring before the enemy's pickets, exchanging shots as they retreated. A dozen men were dispatched to the relief of the retiring Texans, who, thus reinforced, drove back their assailants to the little white house where they were first discovered. After an hour's skirmishing, in which the Texans held at bay the first force largely augmented by additional numbers sent to their support from the garrison, the firing ceased as if by mutual consent, and each party retired to their respective lines. The men returned to camp elated at their success in having replused a greatly superior force.

The close proximity of the enemy in force rendered necessary the issuance of orders confining the men to the bounds of the camp, unless specially detailed for duties whose performance required them to pass beyond its limits. A squad was sent across the river to slaughter beef for the army and to scout the country between the ford and the town, to discover any movement that the enemy might attempt to make on that flank.

In the camp itself the men busied themselves in accumulating fuel for the night, which promised to be cold, despite the moderating temperature; in caring for their animals and in making ready for any emergency that might call for the use of arms and the display of desperate valor. It was a body of individual heroes. Each felt that success depended on his own action and example. By noon the camp was well established. The strict orders of the commanders had been obeyed, and it would have required a near approach of the enemy's scouts to have determined that a body of near a hundred men lay close to the mission, hidden as they were in the depression and screened by the leafy panoply of the wood. The sentries did not expose themselves unnecessarily to view, while their range of vision swept the plateau for a thousand yards. A peep over the bluff would have disclosed the camp made up of mess fires, around which the individuals were ranged in all the abandon of posture and careless ease or exceptional occupation, called forth by deferred performance of duty or by anticipated necessity. The absence of tents detracted from its military appearance. A half score of guns resting there against a tree; here a half dozen powder horns depending from a limb; water gourds, canteens, now and then a coffee pot close by a fire; saddles strewn about on the ground, or used to pillow the heads of recumbent forms stretched lazily upon blankets, made up a scene that would have rewarded the observer, who, if a student of human nature, would have had ample matter for mental dissection and with which to compare ideals of character. The excitement incident to the morning skirmish and the opening campaign formed a copious fund whence to draw topics for conversation.

Our mess had early concluded all necessary duties and the late afternoon found its members in excellent shape for passing the approaching night. Karnes had been detailed for guard duty, but in the absence of strict military regulation, the guard possessed no more autonomy than the list containing the names of the detail, and the members were summoned to their posts whenever the relief was ready to make the rounds. Ducio and Smith had gone with the party after beef and had not yet returned. Around the fire Tip Hamilton was the most conspicuous figure. He had not been in Texas long enough to spoil the handsome blue of his coat, that formed such a contrast with his light drab pants. The lustre of the black satin vest with its double row of buttons bespoke him a fresh importation from the States, unassisted by his boots, whose red tops reached far down towards the instep. He reclined upon his blanket with the upper part of his body resting on his elbow, a cheerful expression indicating that he had, as usual, accommodated himself to surounding circumstances. Mr. Trigg was seated upon a broad stump, with elbows on his knees, drawing consolation from the bowl of a short-stemmed pipe, and puffing whatever of care he felt into the realms of ether along with the whiffs of smoke that escaped his lips. Jones sat near him on the trunk of a tree, which had been felled from the stump and rested his back against a limb that forked conveniently near. He had his hat lowered, well shading his face, but not so depressed that he could not see his friend Hamilton opposite. Karnes was standing to the right of Jones, examining his gun, having just come off his post near the mission. Nathan Roach was visible in the distance approaching the group, laden with several gourds and canteens that swung by their straps and strings from his shoulders.

"Karnes, where did that Mexican spring from who is up there at headquarters?" asked Jones.

"He has been only three or four days out of town. Capt. Bowie knows him and has got considerable information from him about the strength of the garrison and the kind of troops we have got to fight."

"He is recreant to his race if his errand is not to mislead we noble Texans," said Hamilton, grandiloquently.

"Hamilton's on the spout agin', is he?" said Nathan, coming up and commencing to unload. "Here's water for a million. Ef any more's wanted, why Mister Jones or Mr. Hamilton will fetch it, ef I ain't mistaken."

"Now, Mr. Roach, you have spoiled it all. We were only just now discussing your many virtues and lauding the lamb-like resignation you displayed when it fell to your lot to fill these vessels with water. It was not I who proposed to draw lots to see upon whom should fall this duty. No, Mr. Roach, not I; but Jones—Mr. Jones—of India, who stated that such a practice obtained in that dependency of Great Britain among the veterans of the East India company. Jones is a great trickster, Mr. Roach. All characters like him, so impregnated with the basic element of romance, must necessarily be tricky, and I should not be surprised if there were much color in the charge that he tricked you into drawing the short straw."

"Ef I thought he put up a job on me, I'd smash Mr. Jones of India, as you call him," said Nathan, regarding Jones doubtingly.

"It is wrong—very wrong—to put off everything on a good natured comrade, and all through trickery," said Hamilton, with assumed gravity. "I could not stand it."

"I don't mind going for water, but I want the drawin' done fair."

"It was fair, Roach; don't mind him," interrupted Jones.

"It is the second time he has drawn the short straw and we have drawn only twice. Jones, you know you said it was a trick of Lord Dalrymple's command. Own up now and play no more tricks on Roach. Don't you know, Nathan, that he was talking of a rule of Lord Dalrymple's up at the powder house.?"

"I do, by jingo," said Nathan, springing for Jones. "That proves it, dad blast your picture; for you know you said somethin' 'bout Rimple's rule, and you was hatchin' it up then to make me tote water."

Jones rolled off the log on the side opposite Nathan as the latter darted at him, his laughter at Hamilton's introduction of an irrelevant circumstance to prove his charge of trickery, turning into veritable apprehension when he beheld the menacing action of the victim.

The others had enjoyed the joke being played on the backwoodsman, but when the latter sprang to avenge the supposed indignity praeticed upon him, they took in the necessity of interposing to protect the East Indian from serious bodily harm. Nathan had bounded over the log and planted both feet upon the prostrate Jones, who protested loudly, but in vain, that Lord Dalrymple's rule had nothing in connection with the drawing of lots. Karnes seized his old friend by one arm and Hamilton, taking hold of the other, they pulled the irate Roach back to the fire.

"Nathe, you should not fight for such little provocation," said Karnes.

"Didn't he get up Rimple's rule on me?"

"Perhaps I was mistaken," said Hamilton. "Sorry if I was wrong. But Jones did not explain, and I was misled perhaps by interest in Mr. Roach to interpret the rule to allude to drawing lots."

"I don't intend to be imposed on."

"I'll acknowledge I was wrong, Roach. Let's all make friends."

"If you was wrong, Hamilton, all right, I'll let it drop," said Nathan, cooling off.

"Yes, kiss and make up, as the children say."

"I don't like these practical jokes a bit, and I will just serve notice on Tip Hamilton that I won't stand it. My side is bruised terribly by that fellow's feet," and Jones seated himself with his hand on his ribs.

"I heard ye talking about saving your fighting qualities for the Mexicans. Now be after following your own advice and I will warrant ye ye'll have enough fighting afore forty-eight hours," said Mr. Trigg, who had remained on his stump smoking, but secretly enjoying the fun.

At this juncture the corporal, with the rlief, appeared, descending the bluff, with an old Mexican in charge, who bent under the weight of a sack, whose contents were not discernable. The squad marched up and halting, the corporal pulled forward the old man with the sack, who stood smiling and grimacing, with his doffed hat held before him and his head obsequiously bent, as he timidly returned the glances of the new batch of Tejanos.

"Who have you got now, Waters?" asked Karnes, towards whom the corporal seemed to be pulling the prisoner.

"That's what I want to know, Karnes. This old Greaser was captured on post number three, and we can't understand 'a dinged thing he says. I did think I could talk a little of their lingo, but this old fellow gets away with me."

"The old Mexican cut his eye at Karnes, as if to read his fate in that individual's expression, his own countenance further disfigured by a grin of abject submission. As Karnes addressed him in his own tongue, the grin subsided until his ugly physiognomy betrayed naught else save superlative satisfaction.

"De donde vienes, y que haces aqui en este campo?"

"Tengo una carta por el commandante, senor; y estos piloncillas con una botilla de mescal, que manda el padre," replied the prisoner.

"He says," interrupted Karnes, "that he has a letter for the commander and some piloncillas and a bottle of mescal, sent by the priest."

"An envoy extraordinary—with presents," exclaimed Hamilton. "The bottle of mescal—is good. Produce the bottle, old Montezuma."

The Mexican eyed Hamilton rather distrustfully as this was said in a dramtic manner with a swaggering step or two towards him.

"Deja me ver la carta," said Karnes.

"Vuestra Merced, es el commandante?"

"No," answered Karnes, in Spanish. "I am not the commander; but I would like to see the address, and then you can go to him."

He produced the letter, which proved to be addressed to General Austin.

"Now for the bottle," said Roach.

"None of that, Nathan. The contents of that bottle would only increase the difficulties of an individual already intoxicated by a superabundance of eccentricity."

"Don't talk no Mexican to me, Hamilton; preach to the pris'ner."

Karnes, directing the fellow to produce the bottle, he lowered his sack and, opening it, disclosed what was demanded.

The corporal here interposed, and thanking Karnes for having acted as interpreter, he marched his squad and his prisoner towards headquarters.

* * * *

"Hello, Perry! Where you been?"

The youthful member of the mess was thus addressed by Karnes, as he came in sight on the bluff above. The next moment he had descended and stood among them.

"I have been all the way back to where you camped last night."

"And for what?" asked two or three.

"To take dispatches to General Austin."

"Is the army there already?" asked Mr. Trigg.

"No, sir. Captain Bowie left a courier there this morning to wait for the papers and take them on. I suppose he wanted the general to get them as soon as possible, for we had orders not to spare horseflesh."

"Perry is yarning, for his horse is back there with mine," said Jones.

"Now, Jones," interposed Hamilton, "don't you imagine that Perry has your failing."

"The captain furnished me his own horse," Perry explained.

"Something important and urgent must' have been disclosed by that Mexican this morning, and Bowie has sent to hurry up the lagging rear."

"Do you mean the Mexican, Ruiz, Mr. Hamilton?"

"His name is a sealed mystery to me, Perry; but that he is a Greaser of the bon ton variety I am quite certain."

"I think that Ruiz caused the captain to send for General Austin sooner than he intended. I happened to be near and he made me get his horse, while he dashed off a few lines which he called the dispatches."

"Somethin's up, by hookey!" exclaimed Nathan.

Perry looked at the latter rather curiously, when Hamilton remarked:

"Mr. Roach, I do not believe you know our youngster. Perry, this is Mr. Roach, whose Christian name is Nathan—signifying a gift. Dame Fortune bestowed him upon us temporarily, but we perceived that, beneath a rough exterior, there dwelt intrinsic worth, that our diamond gift but lacked the polisher's hand to disclose priceless scintillations of character. And so we kept him with us, and henceforward, through the rigor of camp life and the vicissitudes of war, he is to be our messmate and comrade. Mr. Roach, this is Perry Asbury, the youngest soldier in the army, but for all that— a veteran."

"I saw Mr. Roach the day he joined us on the Cibolo," said Perry, shaking the other's hand.

"S'pose I seen you, too, Mister Perry, but I didn't know nobody but Karnes. But look here, my friend, how can you make out my name means a gift?"

"Nathan is a Hebrew word and means gift in our language," said Hamilton, with a pedantic air.

"You knows a power, cert'in. You don't talk 'Merican like common folks. Ef I could read I s'pose I could understand you more'n I do. But I can trot you through on a shoot, or a trail, or fightin' Greasers, and don't you forgit it—w-h-o-o-p!"

Nathan gave the whoop in Indian style and executed a revolution sidewise on his hands, and landing on his feet right in front of Hamilton, made a hideous grimace directly in the latter's face. Hamilton patted him on the back, saying:

"You'll do, Nathan. You're a diamond of the roughest water."

"I know how to pack the stuff in canteens—but lots or not lots—rimples or no rimples—you an' Jones will have to fetch it nex' time."

"Did you hear the captain say if it's here we are to fight if the Mexicans come out?" asked Mr. Trigg of Perry.

"I heard him and Captain Fannin and that fellow Ruiz talk about this bluff being a good breastwork to protect our men if they came out in force."

"It is too high, if it is to be a breastwork. If we should want to fire over it, we'd have a mighty poor footing, steep as it is."

"That puts an idea in my head," said Jones, who had got over his bruise.

So saying, he picked up the mess hatchet and going to the foot of the bluff, he began to chop into its side.

"What the nation is he a-doin'?" queried Nathan.

"There is something in Jones besides lying," said Hamilton.

"It is a good idea."

"It's steps he is cutting," said Mr. Trigg. "Every mother's son in the camp should do the same thing."

"Steps for every two," suggested Karnes. "One to fire while the other is down loading."

"I'll cut mine right now," said Perry. "This long knife is just the thing for it," and he began his work a few feet from Jones.

Before many minutes the members of the mess had steps cut in a half dozen places, sufficiently high up to look well over the bank. At Mr. Trigg's suggestion, Karnes was sent as a committee of one to give the idea to the officers, and the consequence was that before dark Jones' idea became an accomplished fact, all along the line.

The scouters from the right bank of the river returned with an ample supply of beef, reporting all quiet in that direction. A picket was placed at the ford, to prevent a surprise, and night spread her mantle over the Texan camp. The fires glowed through the timber, while the voices and laughter of the men could be heard as they cooked their rations of fresh beef and talked of the probable happenings of the morrow. The sentries walked their posts on the plateau, keeping viligant watch in the direction of the enemy, braced by the frosty air of a still and cloudless night that, despite the brilliant firmament, rendered the vision so uncertain a shadow might be turned into a prowling foe, or a bush magnified into a nocturnal spectre.

It was the same day on which the Texans encamped at Conception, that Guy witnessed the passage of the Mexican cavalry down Carcel street to the river ford. The approach of the revolutionists had become known to the authorities and this force was posted south of the town on the left bank of the river. On a peninsula formed by a circuit of the stream and opposite the southeast corner of the plaza a body of infantry was mustered on the forenoon of the day in question. A general officer with a numerous staff, gaily uniformed, all mounted on prancing ponies, dashed through the narrow streets and turning to the ford crossed to where the infantry was undergoing an inspection. The arrival of the mounted party terminated the inspection in a salute, when a consultation ensued between the newly arrived official and his officers, in which they were joined by the commander of the infantry. During a discussion pertaining to the presence of the rebels in the vicinity, a mounted man, in the ordinary garb of a civilin of the lower class, rode near and saluting, stated that he desired to speak to Colonel Ugartachia.

"Tell him to approach," said the colonel.

"Who is he?" asked General Cos.

"I am a sergeant, sir, of Captain Castinado's company, and was detailed as a spy to find out the movements of the rebels. I have gained important information and wish to communicate it to your worship."

"Por dios! Cut short your preface and give us the news, man."

"The rebels are approaching Concepcion in force and perhaps their advance is already there."

"How know you this, sir?"

"I saw them in the distance with my two eyes. Myself and the man detailed to go with me left our horses in the wood and while we were questioining a woman who lives at the mission, one Ruiz, a Mexican, rode up and while he was talking to us about joining the rebels and advising us to help drive out the national troops, we suddenly saw the dust in the road about a mile below. The dust was caused by the march of the rebels."

"Their number? Do you know it?" asked the colonel.

"About two hundred."

"And Ruiz—did he meet them?"

"We returned without delay to our horses and made haste to town."

"What else said this Ruiz?"

"He said our soldiers were convicts and were brought here to destroy the liberties of the people."

General Cos called to an aid, and after a minute's deliberation, said hastily

"Lieutenant! Order Castanado's company to reinforce the pickets on the mission road at once. This infantry battalion will be held in readiness for instant action, with cooked rations, prepared for any forward movement which developments may render necessary."

Then turning to Colonel Ugartachia, he said:

"Colonel, it will be well to have an immediate inspection of the entire garrison and the whole available cavalry force put into the best shape for service by morning. These Americans mean mischief."

The lieutenant galloped away to carry out the orders of his chief, while the latter and his staff rode in the direction of the Alamo.

"Ugartachia," said the general. "I would like to find out if Austin is with this force. If he is present, we have the whole rebel crew to fight. How can I manage it?"

"How would a flag of truce do?"

"They would only meet it by one in charge of a subaltern, and he would not give the information unless by accident"

"Let us send the old fellow, who sells piloncillas next to my headquarters, with a present to Austin of some of his stock in trade. He is so old they would never hurt him; and he is so avaricious he will undertake it to get paid for a score of his sweetmeats."

"A present from whom? They would imagine the things were poisoned."

"Send it in the name of the padre, Ignacio. He is not a belligerent, and is acquainted with the rebel chief."

"An excellent idea! Ugastachia, you put it into execution."

* * * *

Guy had not lain long on his bed, thinking of the news imparted by Josefa in regard to Beatrice Navarro's engagement, when his door opened and the voice of Father Ignacio called to him.

"What is it, Father?"

"Why have you come to this cheerless place without a fire, when the air is so raw? If the fellow is not lying here on his bed in the dark! Come to the sitting room, where there is a grand fire, and nobody to keep me company but prosy Father Nicolas. Come down and help me poke him into activity."

"All right," said Guy, rising. "I just threw myself down here for a moment, fully intending to join you after a while."

"Getting homesick, and wanting to join your people, no doubt.

You had better stay with me and study for the priesthood, than be with them, murdering our pickets and now about to lay siege to San Antonio. Come along, child, I know you are cold."

The priest preceded Guy to the sitting room, where Father Nicolas sat, looking vacantly into the fire. He rose awkwardly, greeting the young American, but not offering his hand.

"Where have you been all this afternoon?" continued Father Ignacio, and without waiting for a reply, "I concluded you had deserted after hearing that those daredevil countrymen of yours were in force at Concepcion and were firing on the national troops."

"I am yet on parole, sir. I trust the fact had escaped your memory, when you concluded that I had done an act to violate it."

"Oh! Muchacho mio, I was just joking. I have every faith in my boy's honor."

"I have heard nothing of any fighting today," said Guy, in a softer tone. "If there has been, I should like to hear the news."

"Where could you have been, sure enough. It is all over town."

"I walked home with the Senorita de la Torre and spent the afternoon there.

"Father Ignacio knitted his brows at the reply.

"So you know her! Two unbelievers. Poor, poor Josefa; pedida! perdida! But never mind about Josefa; I must tell you of the excitement. General Austin is supposed to be at Conception; at any rate there is quite a force there and most of the afternoon there has been skirmishing between the opposing armies. Two or three of our troops have been wounded—one quite seriously."

"Very seriously!" interrupted Father Nicolas. "I gave him the last sacraments an hour ago and he may not live through the night."

'War! War! It is terrible," said Father Ignacio, leaning back in his chair and looking reflectingly into the blazing logs.

"And yet your people are ever waging it among themselves, and internecine warfare is the most horrible of all; yet it is maintained by some of our philosophers that all wars are great civilizers and that their ultimate effects have been to improve mankind. Your church has sanctioned conquests where butchery succeded butchery, until race annihilation left little obstacle to Christian supremacy. Did the church consider terrible the means employed?"

"If the church has sanctioned such it was God's act. God speaks through an infallible church."

"Then I suppose it is God's will that the unbelieving Texans in this struggle be wiped up by the national troops."

"Very likely—very likely."

"But suppose, Father, that the Texans succeed in driving the national troops across the Rio Grande."

"God permits the devil to triumph occasionally; why not these rebels?"

"In the interests of liberty and civilization, it is to be hoped then, that He will be in His occasional humor."

"You may not hope for the highest civilization until you arrive at the true faith."

"If you mean that the highest civilization exists where your religion has exercised the fullest sway, then my reading has been to little purpose, if you are correct. Take your own country—Spain —for an example. With all her prestige and golden opportunities she has retrograded until she has become a third-class power. Superstition made her indifferent to progress and controlled her kings, who owed allegiance to Rome. Her greatness and achievements rested upon the mysticism, that, for every effect, found a supernatural cause and flowed from the king to the people, like the principles of a deductive system whose defects are hidden in the glow of a priori conceptions."

"What is the matter with Father Nicolas? I believe he is counting the logs in the ceiling to keep from hearing Senor Raymond's homily."

"No, Father Ignacio, I was praying for the senor."

"Well, senor, how did you find out our superstition? You are a young reasoner and I will make all allowances."

"From history. You and I differ in the definition of superstition. I term it superstition, when the people of Madrid, instead of resorting to sanitary methods to abate the ravages of a plague, had recourse to religious processions and outdoor masses; leaving the reeking filth of their streets to infect the atmosphere and render more fatal the scourge caused by their own neglect. I call it superstition when a king of Spain, instigated by episcopal dictation, forbid the introduction of Newton's beautiful philosophy into the Spanish universities, remarking that the prayerbook was good enough philosophy for the Spanish students."

"My dear child, God is all powerful, you must remember, and as he found it easy to create this universe by his mere will, how easy, if he desired, would it be to arrest a plague. In the case you alluded to he scourged the people until his anger became appeased, and the difficulty came to an end. In regard to the teaching of philosophies in the universities of Spain, the Holy Church is always careful to investigate all new theories to discover if they contain principles adverse to dogmas. She accepts the good and rejects the bad."

"Being infallible," suggested Guy, "she should readily discern the merits of a theory without subjecting it to the test of examination. Examination necessitates reasoning, and to reason is to depend upon human judgment and human experience; to depend upon human experience is to reason synthetically or by induction from particulars to generals. Inductively considered, your religion and civilization would both be condemned."

"No tienes miedo!" exclaimed Father Nicolas, half rising and leaning earnestly towards the young man. "Are you not afraid to talk in such a manner?"

"Afraid! Be quiet, good Nicolas. This boy has never had instruction. He is steeped in the ignorance of heretical education. Such training as his gives him no advantage over the aborigines, for whose conversion to the faith these missions were erected by the good fathers of our order."

"And where, good Father, are these aborigines today? The Indian of the pure type is still a savage. Those who succumbed to the power of the church are lost in the mongrel race, that possesses a questionable advantage over the wild tribes in all that pertains to true civilization."

"The lower class of Mexicans, I admit, are unlettered; but, senor, they are a pious people; they love their church and therefore occupy the most essential position to secure their happiness hereafter. A home in heaven is vastly more important than the highest literary attainments, with the danger of lapsing into infidelity like yours."

"The senor should read the lives of the saints and learn of the great miracles they have performed," said Father Nicolas.

"I have a volume he will like better," said Father Ignacio. "It is called the 'Influences of Catholicity on Civilization.'"

"That must be an ingenuous work from a Catholic standpoint," said Guy.

Here the door opened and Jose appeared, stating that a messenger had come for Father Nicolas to attend the dying soldier. The young priest lost no time in responding to the call, and left his two companions with a pleasant good night.

"Will he be gone until late?" asked Guy, as the door closed.

"Who knows? A priest must go and he must stay as long as needed. Father Nicolas is very willing, but he is no company, Senor Raymond. His mind and body are both frail. I am satisfied he will never be a cardinal."

"He said he had given this soldier the last sacraments. If I have been rightly informed, that is all that a priest can do for a dying man."

"That is all true, but the poor fellow may have thought of a sin unconfessed. It would not do to die with a fault unconfessed, with a priest at hand to give absolution. Perhaps he may want him to say prayers for the dying. This revolution is going to be a bad, bad affair, Senor Raymond."

"Did you learn if the garrison expects an immediate attack?"

"Attack! General Cos has already ordered a movement, to commence early in the morning, that will no doubt result in the capture of those fellows at Conception. He has learned their position and numbers and feels confident."

"The Texans will be hard to whip, even with great odds. They have the advantage of strong individualities that make every man a leader. It would not surprise me if you and Father Nicolas will have your hands full tomorrow, giving consolation to the wounded and dying victims of Texan bullets."

"Puede ser, puede ser. But we will not shrink from our duty, senor."

CHAPTER XXVIII.

The moderated temperature brought with it a thick fog, whose floating mists hung like a veil over mission and woodland, retarding the advancing light of early dawn, enveloping in moisture the grass-covered plateau and the sylvan foliage overhanging the Texan camp. The pattering drops from the dripping leaves, the cracking of a twig, caused by the movements of a horse browsing near, the leap of an early squirrel, in quest of his morning meal, causing a rustle among the branches of a pecan, were noises greeting the first struggling glimmers from the east, that disclosed the bivouac beyond the bluff with its blue smoke rising among the trees, scarcely distinguishable from the maze of vapor. Around the dying embers of the mess fires the recumbent forms, enveloped in blankets, began one by one to move, until the later and clearer light found the whole camp astir and busy in preparation.

"Perry, wake up that lazy Frenchman," said Hamilton, as he came up, dragging a small branch of deadwood, that an urchin might have shouldered. "Here I have been hunting wood since daylight, and he wrapped up in his blanket. Stir him up, boy."

Perry advanced to where Ducio Halfen lay, as described by Hamilton, and pulling away the blanket, shouted to him to get up.

Ducio responded with a vigorous kick that struck Perry squarely in the stomach and sent him reeling to the ground. He followed up the kick by rising and springing at the prostrate boy, with the fury of a beast; but before he could reach the object of his rage he was felled by a well aimed blow on the temple, from the brawny arm and ponderous fist of Mr. Trigg, who, having witnessed the cowardly kick, intervened to prevent a more serious sequel.

"Perry, is it much hurt ye are?" asked Mr. Trigg, as he bent over the boy.

"He had the breath kicked out of him," said Hamilton. "Don't you see he is just getting it back again?"

"The murderin' devil! He'd best keep out o' my way. Perry! Perry! My boy."

Perry looked up at the good old Irishman.

"I am a little hurt here," he gasped, placing his hand on his stomach.

"The dirty devil!" muttered Mr. Trigg, scowling at Ducio, who stood near with a blood-stained temple.

I'll get even with you—you Irish Hessian," said Halfen.

"Wait 'til I mind the boy and I'll be after teaching you a bit of manners."

"What in the name of the incomprehensible did you kick that boy for?" asked Hamilton.

"Don't you like it?"

"Now, Sir Ducio, if you are for war with the whole mess, it is best that you get out of it. I told Perry to awaken you and it was mean to assault him as you did. You should be ashamed of it."

"I don't want any of your lecturing, Tip Hamilton. I'd have kicked any one who had no better sense than to strip me and hallo in my ear."

As Ducio said this he walked sulkily away and seated himself at the further end of the fallen tree.

Perry had so far recovered that he was sitting up and breathing quite regularly, while Mr. Trigg remained by him, asking him frequently how he was feeling.

"I saw a man laid out for good from a kick no worse nor this."

"Dont' worry about me, Mr. Trigg, for I feel nearly all right again. Ducio was half asleep, I suppose, and didn't mean to hurt me."

"Didn't he, though? It's the charge he made after ye was down that ye should 'a' seen. My fist it was that saved the finishing of ye. A wild beast couldn't 'a' looked worst when he came charging after ye. Didn't mean to hurt ye!"

One—two—three—four shots; then a fusilade.

The shots came from the plateau, close at hand, just over the bluff. The magic of the reports produced activity in the camp. Through the timber, along the line, men flew to their guns; questions and replies were shouted back and forth in quick succession. The officers hurried to the bluff, hastily giving orders as they passed. Suddenly a man sprang over the embankment, his gun in one hand and his powder horn in the other.

It was Karnes. The men greeted him with a cheer and a shower of questions.

"It's the Greasers," he said, "and the damned reseals have shot the bottom out of my powder horn."

Karnes had been placed on post when the four o'clock relief went the rounds and had the honor of receiving the enemy. They fired on him just as they became visible through the fog. He returned their fire—once with his rifle, and again with his pistol, in answer to the volley. They retired after his pistol shot and he retreated to the camp. Certain that the enemy was present in force, the two commanders ranged their men under the bluff, with instructions to mount the steps they had cut in its side until their heads would appear above it and their eyes could sweep the platen beyond. The Mexican field music could be distinctly heard and an occasional sound of a voice, as a command was probably shouted preparing for an advance.

The Texans were on the alert and eager for the fray. Perhaps thirty minutes elapsed before the enemy gave any account of himself.

"Here they come!"

It was Jones who spoke.

"Where?" asked Hamilton.

"Are you blind?"

"My optics are splendid."

"Look there!"

"So! I see them."

"The dirty yaller-bellies!" exclaimed Nathan, ten yards away.

"They are not coming," said Perry, now oblivious of his hurt.

"Sure, they're not," said Mr. Trigg. "It's the fog a-lifting."

"Divide your powder, boys, quick! I've got another horn."

"Here's mine, Mr. Karnes. Leave me enough."

"All right, Perry."

"This reminds me of when we were waiting for a charge from the Sepoys," said Jones.

"What's a Sea Poys?" asked Nathan.

"I was speaking of a people in India——"

"Who in thunder wants to hear of India now?" asked Hamilton. "You had better be saying your prayers; because if those Greasers——"

'By the powers! They're on the move. It's a dirty set to be after shooting. The British at Orleans made the purtiest mark—with their red coats—and we behind the cotton bags."

"Be ready there, men!" shouted Captain Bowie. "Every other man throw up his rifle and reserve his fire until we see the effect of the first volley. Whatever they do—give them the second volley then—and aim well."

The Mexican infantry, now about three hundred yards distant, were advancing in common time in line of battle. Over their heads a force of mounted troops could be seen, making flank movements, right and left, intending, perhaps, to clear the infantry front. On their right, two pieces of field artillery were planted with the caissons in the rear, drawn by mules.

Suddenly the artillery belched forth to cover the infantry's advance, and grape and cannister went crashing through the branches of the trees in the Texan rear, doing no other damage. At one hundred yards the Mexican infantry opened fire. Like their artillery, they aimed too high, if they aimed at all, for the Texan position effectually concealed their force, save here and there, where a head would pop up, its dardevil owner inviting the aim of their marksmen. The silence of their enemy was, of itself, an ominous circumstance. The approaching line evidently felt that death lingered but a few rods in advance, only to make surer of its victims, for when only seventy-five yards intervened between it and the bluff, it wavered—then halted. Their officers expostulated—then ordered them to fire, to reassure them. After two volleys from their ranks, they again advanced at quick time, but ere a dozen paces had lessened their distance, the crack of fifty rifles sent a leaden hail into their ranks with deadly effect. A waver of the line, succeeded by desultory firing, and a curve that brought the flanks far ahead of the more stricken center, was followed by hesitation and much confusion.

Another volley from the alternate files, who had reserved their fire, decided the matter and the shattered line fled in dismay, followed by irregular shots from the Texans as they reloaded. The latter kept their position. In the absence of pursuit, the infantry halted at six hundred yards. The two field pieces were now brought in close range to sweep the Texan line. When the enemy commenced the latter movement Captains Bowie and Fannin, anticipating its purpose, marched their commands by the right flank, under the cover of the bluff, so as to bring the former's company completely around the angle of that embankment. This brought the Texan right in rifle distance of the new position assumed by the two guns, without having disclosed its proximity. The enemy's ignorance of any change in the position of their opponents was soon disclosed by the artillery fire directed against the point but a few minutes before occupied by Fannin's company. The gunners were not allowed to continue this waste of ammunition.

"Here, Karnes! Let six good shots keep those guns silent," shouted Bowie.

A moment more two gunners fell in the act of firing.

"Good shot, Nathe," said Karnes. "We both got 'em. Now Hamilton—and you—Perry."

Bang! Bang! Bang! Three shots rang out with scarcely an interval.

"It wasn't your turn, Jones!" expostulated Hamilton.

"I got mine all the same," retorted Jones.

More shots; and then others followed as fast as a gunner attempted to fire a piece, and at each discharge more victims were added to the exquisite marksmanship of the Texans. A spent shot struck a mule attached to one of the caissons and stampeded the team. The later went, at full speed, across the plateau, and meeting the infantry, again returning to the conflict, dashed through their ranks, throwing them into confusion. The cavalry bugler now sounded a charge, more perhaps, for the purpose of making a show of attack, than from any reasonable hope of dislodging a well-fortified foe. Nevertheless, on they came, while the remorseless rifles of their enemy but awaited a surer aim. Although they ventured not too closely, yet when they wheeled in retreat, several empty saddles went with them. The retreating horse disclosed the devoted infantry again in motion to attack. The diversion created by the cavalry evolution enabled the artillery to hurl a storm of grape at the Texan right and center. The missiles tore the ground and swept across the brow of the bluff and threatened serious execution, until again the avenging bullets of the right cleared the guns and abated the danger. By this the infantry had gained closer quarters and began a rapid fusilade at the Texans, whom the din of battle had rendered indifferent to the exposure of their persons, and who kept head and shoulders into view, disappearing only to reload.

"Why can't we charge?" asked Perry, with boyish enthusiasm.

"Down with ye, boy! It's below ye should load."

"All right, Mr. Trigg."

"When the first sign of confusion appears among the Mexicans, up and charge them!" shouted Bowie, and then added:

"Pass the order along the line."

"By the nation!" exclaimed Nathan. "If that Greaser didn't jump six foot when my bullet hit him!"

The Mexican line here moved suddenly forward with a yell, after having delivered a heavy fire. But the Texans were prepared. A deadly fusilade made havoc in their ranks. Confusion and dismay made easy work for the Texan onset which followed. With a wild yell, that rent the air from center to either flank, the impatient men threw themselves forward upon their enemy, who turned and fled.

"To the cannon!" shouted Hamilton.

"Here I am!" answered Roach.

These, with several of their comrades, charged the guns and soon possessed them. Just as they reached the pieces, a gallant Mexican was attempting to spike them. Nathan was about to send him to his last account, when Hamilton knocked away the clubbed rifle.

"Don't kill the poor devil! Turn the guns on the flying cowards."

Hamilton took the plucky Mexican prisoner and joined his comrades in directing the cannon after its late owners.

"Hold, men!" commanded Bowie. "How much ammunition for these pieces?"

"Only two loads," answered Hamilton, after having hastily made the inspection.

"Then reserve it in case those people should return."

The Mexicans proved to be completely routed. A few minutes had served to clear the plateau after the rout began. The victors returned from the pursuit and proceeded to collect the fruits and calculate the cost of their victory. The battlefield was strewn with dead and wounded Mexicans, where their infantry had suffered, while around the cannon lay the ghastly corpses of twenty artillerymen.

The Texan loss was trifling, one man having been killed and a few wounded. Among the latter was Mr. Trigg, who received a musket ball in his shoulder, making a painful wound. The enemy had suffered grievously through his own mistakes. His tactics were unpardonable and exhibited the grossest incompetency, rendering unavailable his superior numbers and diversity of arms. Bowie and Fannin were jubilant and proud of a victory secured before the arrival of the main body of the army.

Before the camp had again settled down from the excitement of victory, and the confusion incident to collecting the spoils of battle, Austin's little army came in sight. The newly arrived troops were greatly enthused at the heroism of their comrades and were clamorous to be led against the city. A council of the officers, however, decided against it, and the ardor of the men had to succumb to authority.

By permission, Mr. Trigg was conveyed to the jacal behind the mission, where lived Locaria, the little Mexican woman with whom Ruiz had conversed the day previous. Here Perry was detailed to attend his old friend with any of his mess for relief who might be designated. At noon a flag of truce arrived from the town, under the charge of a priest, who requested leave to bury their dead. This last rite was performed most expeditiously, by using a deep trench and laying the bodies side by side, after the fashion of war, shroudless and coffinless. General Austin, who was standing near the mission when the interment was about concluded, sent for the priest, to have a talk with him. When the latter came, the recognition which followed seemed to be mutual.

"Father Ignacio, as I live!"

"General Austin! How are you?"

"This is sad work, Father."

"Then why make such work?"

"To secure liberty."

"The Mexicans are satisfied."

"Then I pity them."

"They ask no pity—but to be let alone."

"Are we aggressors?"

"Yes, primarily, as colonists."

"We are here under contract."

"Which you have transcended."

"By Santa Anna's interpretation."

"It is Mexican territory. The sovereign authority may interpret without appeal."

"Except the appeal to arms."

"The argument of unreason."

"The resort of men who will not be enslaved."

"The resort of territorial bandits."

"An imputation that should never be raised by a Spaniard."

"The Spaniard conquered but to save. Where his banner waved the cross was planted."

"And extermination began."

"A truce to this war of words. General, you are thin in flesh."

"Is that why you sent me the mescal and the piloncillas?"

"That was a 'ruse de guerre,' as the French say. My name was used, but I knew nothing of the matter, until I was told at our headquarters of the device to ascertain your presence."

"Father, there is an Irishman, wounded and lying in yonder jacal. As he belongs to your faith, you had better visit him. He is a true revolutionist, however."

Father Ignacio stated that his time was limited, but he would see the unfortunate for a moment.

Mr. Trigg was lying on the bed in the jacal. Locaria was removing the remains of a lunch of which he had been partaking, when Father Ignacio pushed aside the fresada at the door. The little woman saluted and invited him to enter.

"Is there a wounded man within?"

"Yes, my father."

'Can he speak Spanish?"

'I think not."

As soon as the priest entered, Mr. Trigg recognized his office by his dress, and held out his hand.

"God bless you, my poor man. Are you badly wounded?" the father asked in Spanish.

"I know it's your blessing you're giving me, Father, and it's thankful I am to your reverence, if I can't understand a word you're saying."

"Not—speak—Spanish?" the priest asked, in illy articulated English.

"I could never twist my tongue to it. But it's your reverence who can speak a little of my language."

"No entiendo—not—un'stan."

"It's little use we'll be to one another, for our lingos are like oil and water. Is it from town ye are sir? But sorrow a word he knows of what I be telling him. He might know the boy too, or the priest he fell in with. If I could talk their lingo like Guy, I'd soon be knowing all about it. He might be knowing the name of the lad if I should speak it."

He looked earnestly at the priest, as if devising some means by which to make himself understood, then said slowly:

"Is your reverence acquainted with Guy—Guy Raymond?"

Despite the peculiar brogue, which augmented the Spaniard's difficulty in reconciling Mr. Trigg's pronunciation of Guy's name with the sounds given it in the more euphonious enunciation to which he had been accustomed, he caught the surname and asked in his own language:

"Did you say something of Senor Raymond?"

"Sennour Raymond! That's Mister Raymond—yes, Father, Sennour Raymond." Then pointing to his own breast, he continued:

"My boy—my boy."

See muchacho de V!" said the father, in surprise. Then he said, as if in soliloquy: "He told me his father was dead."

"Not a word! Not a word! Oh! If he could speak a decent language."

"Raymond—Guy Raymond," repeated Father Ignacio.

"That's him! That's him" said the other, excitedly.

"Como se llama V.?" asked his visitor, imitating the motion of writing.

"Sure, I couldn't write in this fix," said Mr. Trigg, mistaking his meaning. "It's my right arm and shoulder that's hurt."

Father Ignacio took from his pocket a pencil and piece of paper. Then, motioning to himself, he said:

"Father Ignacio." Then, pointing toward the town, he pronounced the name of Guy. Then, putting his hand on Mr. Trigg's breast, he said:

"Mister——?"

"Oh! It's my name! Trigg, it is, sir—Trigg, it is sir."

The brogue here again had a bad effect, while the three monosyllables which the Irishman, in his volubility, unfortunately employed, and which were not intelligible to his auditor, merged themselves into the short sobriquet and, in the mind of the priest, danced attendance as terminal parts of suffixes. He accordingly repeated, after Mr. Trigg's announcement:

"Trigatissa—Trigatissa."

"What is the creature after saying? He should learn a decent talk or take off his cassock, One little Irish priest is worth a ship's load of his kind."

Father Ignacio had written the name as he had repeated it, and held it up for its owner to recognize.

"I haven't my specs; but I can see that if my picture would look as little like myself as that looks like Trigg—then my ould mother would not know it."

He looked at Father Ignacio, and shaking his head in an emphatic negative, said emphatically:

"Trigg's my name—Trigg's my name."

The patient priest again took his pencil and wrote: "Trigsminem."

He held it up as before. Mr. Trigg scrutinized it, first to one side, then to the other; then held it off to the length of his left arm.

"Sure, it looks longer than the other thing he put down. I'm after thinking it's out of your power to understand anything about names. I said it as plain as a mortal man could, and ye've got it all wrong, which I can tell by the length of it; for it's short my name is; no more nor five letters—T-r-i-g-g—Trigg."

The good priest was, of course, lost to know what Mr. Trigg was saying, but secured the paper and put it in his pocket. Then he drew forth from the opposite breast of his cassock a pocket from which he selected a picture of the sacred heart and a small medal. These he gave to the wounded Irishman, at the same time signifying, by making the sign of the cross over them, that they had been blessed. This the other comprehended at once, and thanked the donor.

Consulting his watch, Father Ignacio gave both the inmates of the room his blessing and departed.

Mr. Trigg indulged in a short soliloquy when left alone, in which he gave vent to reflections suggested by his interview with the priest of San Fernando.

"I'm thankful for the picture and the medal. He is a good man, no doubt, but has a weakness about understanding names. If it hadn't been for that tower of Babel God's creatures would all be speaking one way."

CHAPTER XXIX.

Guy laid awake the next morning after his conversation with his host and Father Nicolas, ruminating indiscriminately on the mass of events crowded into the chapter of his life, that opened with his advent into San Antonio. His mind was in that peculiar state that fixes upon no certain circumstance, but each newborn thought yields successively to a follower, crowding its way to the attention only to be in turn discarded with scarcely a recognition, the whole train forming a mere jumble of conscious realizations not to be dignified by the name of reflection. The kindness of the good priest, who had been his fast friend, was uppermost in his mind, but gave place to a mixture of subjects, among which the face of the fair Beatrice would intrude itself constantly and dwell longer than its fellows. He was roused suddenly from this medley by the sound of artillery and the popping of small arms, whose report told that the affray had opened at about the distance of the first mission. He sprang from the bed and listened from the window. He knew his countrymen had been attacked in their position and that the artillery whose reports had been brought to him on the heavy atmosphere of the misty morning was directed at their ranks, and the thought sent the blood rapidly through his veins, while he made a mental picture of the conflict. He hurried on his clothes as if some purpose necessitated haste, but pausing as he was about to descend, he reflected:

"What can I do but remain here inactive?"

Parolel to not leave certain limits, he could not join his friends, nor could he get sympathy from any, even should he go to the sitting room or out into the town. Father Ignacio was awaiting him for breakfast.

"Have you heard the firing?" he asked of Guy.

"The sounds of the guns aroused me."

"General Cos intended a surprise just before day, but the first gun fired at seven."

"Perhaps he waited for daylight, in order to be able to see how to catch all the rebels," said Guy, ironically.

Jose having announced breakfast, the two repaired to the dining room, where they found Father Nicolas. The meal was dispatched in almost total silence. The boom of the guns caused ever and anon an expressive glance to be exchanged, while the busy mind suppressed its fullness. Guy partook only of coffee, and in mere courtesy addressed a remark or two to his companions.

Excusing himself, Guy left the room, receiving a parting injunction from his host to be seen in the streets as little as possible pending the excitement. He nevertheless sallied forth, feeling that close confinement was better than this seeming liberty, limiting him by viewless barriers, which, while inclination tempted him to disregard them, honor made stronger than the walls of adamant. He strolled along aimlessly, anxiously listening to the distant firing. The sound of artillery fire had ceased when he found himself opposite the home of Beatrice Navarro. Without pausing to debate the propriety of the action, he entered the gate and rapped at the door. The delay made in responding to his summons grew into minutes and furnished the caller with time for reflection. He disliked to repeat his knock, and was equally reluctant to withdraw without another attempt to make his presence known. He wanted to see Beatrice—Beatrice who was already engaged; Beatrice whom he had seen but twice, and spoken with but on one occasion. He had rendered her a service and had been invited to call. He had promised. He was here. Was he calling to claim more thanks? Her father's thanks had been promised. He did not care a cent for that gentleman's gratitude. This call seemed to him purposeless; but like the needle he was drawn to this magnet of a girl, who was engaged. He wished he had never seen Josefa. He hoped to never again hear of Ruiz. He rapped again. Sounds of steps were heard inside. A little flush of anticipation colored his fair cheek as the impersonation of a divinity was expected to appear and bid him welcome. The door opened and disclosed an old gentleman of quiet demeanor, with gray hair and beard who, glancing inquiringly at him, exchanged the morning salutation in Spanish and inquired:

"Who have I the pleasure to greet?"

"Guy Raymond, sir."

"Will you walk in, sir, and have a seat?"

Guy entering, glanced around the apartment and took the proffered chair. The old gentleman, seating himself quite opposite, placed his hands upon his knees and inclining his body slightly forward, cast another inquiring look at his visitor.

"You are Senor Navarro?"

"At your service, senor."

"I came around to see—to see—to see you, sir."

"I am at your disposition, senor."

"Are the ladies at home?"

"My daughters! Do you know them?"

"Assuredly he has not heard," thought Guy. "Yes—I know the Senorita Beatrice."

"The ladies are not in just now. But, senor, I understand it was I you wished to see."

"The Senorita Beatrice said that she would like to have me make your acquaintance, because you are so fond of her."

"Beatrice—said—that? De verras! That is a queer reason. If my fondness for my daughter makes it of moment that I should know you, there must be something between Beatrice and yourself that should not have existed without my previous knowledge."

The old gentleman straightened up as he said this and rising from his chair, made a couple of strides and looked for an answer. Guy colored deeply and hastened to explain:

"It is quite evident, Senor Navarro, that you do not understand my motive in calling. I——"

"Yes, senor, from your own lips. It was to make my acquaintance, and that my younger daughter desired it."

"If you will allow me I will explain why she desired it."

"Then you will reach the point I wish to understand."

"It was my good fortune to render her a service."

"A service!"

"Upon which she places too much importance, and which she thought you would appreciate highly for the love you bear her. Under these impressions, what more natural than her desire—that—at least—we be not strangers."

"Well, senor, the service. What is it?"

"Since the Senorita Beatrice has not seen fit to mention it, it is not meet that information come from my lips. What allusion I have made to the subject has been only in an attempted apology for my presence here. A stranger to you, I have nothing to say of your cool, but courteous reception of myself. The custom of your people forbids social intercourse between a comparative stranger and a daughter of the household; and I pledge you my word of honor, this call would never have been made save under the circumstances as I have partially related them."

"You speak very fairly, senor. I shall ask an explanation of Beatrice."

"Good day, senor," and Guy bowed himself out.

Once upon the street he bit his lip in vexation and hurried along towards the military plaza in a not very enviable state of mind. It was the dinner hour before Guy returned to Father Ignacio's. The absence of the priest was voluntarily made known by Jose, who came to see who it was entering the sitting room.

"Father Ignacio went with a flag of truce to get permission to bury the dead."

"So, there have been some killed on the government side."

"A few, senor; but the rebels lost more heavily."

"In that case it is a strange proceeding to get the services of a priest to beg permission of the worsted to bury the dead."

"Sometimes that may happen. Victories are often dearly won."

Guy relapsed into silence and drawing his chair closer to the window, looked abstractedly into the plaza. A careta containing wounded soldiers passed in from Carcel and continued on up Soledad street. Mounted officers were riding about and knots of people were gathered here and there.

Guy witnessed this passively, his mind full of his own defeated purpose in calling at Senor Navarro's. Where could Beatrice have been? Why had she suppressed his service from her father? Was she a flirt? Had she heartlessly laid a trap for him? If Senor Navarro had not been apprised of her rescue he could not be blamed for his courteous coolness to a stranger invading unheralded, the privacy of his home. Instead of proving the fortunate circumstance he had regarded it, providing a key of admittance to the presence of the lovely Beatrice, her rescue now placed him in a most unhappy position. Now it seemed to him all a mistake. He felt that all the world was against him. Ruiz, who had befriended him, was engaged to this enigma in woman's most beautiful shape and would doubtless resent even the suspicion of admiration for her from any other quarter. A feeling akin to desolation nearly overpowered him, as, with a deep sigh, he leaned his head forward on his arm. The rescuer is not always repaid with love by the rescued. Laoni's image rose before his closed eyes. Laoni was true and loving, but, like himself, *she was the rescuer.*

Guy was aroused by the priest.

"I am glad to see you at home, senor. Those bad countrymen of yours have killed many of our poor fellows. Such a sad sight! So sad, senor!"

"Did you go to their camp?" asked Guy, brightening up with interest.

"I saw General Austin at the mission and Bowie, also."

"Were many of our men killed, Father?"

"Some. I did not ask how many. One wounded rebel is a Catholic and him I saw by request of General Austin. He could not speak Spanish, nor I English, so we had a very poor interview. He called your name, I think. It sounded very like it."

" 'Tis a pity you did not learn his name."

"I did try. I wrote it down as near as I could understand it. The poor fellow had such a dreadful way of pronouncing his words, I thought. I have here a memorandum of his name," said Father Ignacio, fumbling in the capacious depths of his cassock pocket, but without producing what he was searching for.

"It is quite probable I have lost it," he continued, "but I can repeat it. It sounded like 'Trickomum,' or 'Trickissin,' or 'Triggitizzor.' "

"I wonder if it could have been Mr. Trigg," mused Guy.

"He accepted a picture and a medal from me and after giving the poor fellow my blessing, I came away. He has a good little woman nurse, senor; so, if he is a friend of yours, he is in good hands."

The next day after Guy's disappointment, consequent to his visit to the Navarro home, Josefa de la Torre was sitting at the grated window of her home that looked upon the narrow street, with one arm resting upon the slab which formed the sill of the opening. Her head reposed easily upon her palm as it turned towards an elder lady with whom she had apparently been conversing.

"You are a strange girl, Josefa. You are all your father's."

"It is natural that I should want revenge when it is my nature to be revengeful. Shall I contend against nature?"

"Certainly. If we have bad inclinations, reason, if not religion, should show you the necessity of controlling them."

"Nature does nothing bad. If it gave me character, marked by certain propensities, their indulgence is a natural sequence and is but the following out of natural law. Beatrice Navarro has caused me unhappiness and I hate her."

"She has not done so intentionally."

"It makes no difference. It is enough that she is the cause."

"I should think, with your pretended philosophy, that tramples under foot every principle of religion, you would rise above these petty jealousies which, to me, indicates more weakness of mind than belief in all the dogmas of the church, termed by you superstition."

"This is my existence. I know of none other. When I get through with this world; when I exhaust the knowledge of life's medium, I come to the stone wall. What is beyond, I know not. I care not. My happiness here is my all. If anyone comes between me and my happiness none shall deny me the privilege of hating."

"But, Josfa, you, yourself acknowledge she does not love Senor Ruiz."

"What difference! He loves her."

"Much. He is the fickle one; she the innocent cause."

"But still the cause. What difference is there in the effect?"

Much again. Ruiz, having no encouragement, may return to the old love."

"Let him dare—to return—on such terms! He will feel my keen resentment in such a shape that his heart's blood may answer."

"Santa Maria! Josefa, you have gone mad."

"There will be method in my madness, as may yet be seen."

The excited girl arose, before her mother's exclamation, and paced the floor.

"Beatrice loves this American," she said, "but I will try to find the means to thwart her. I have a purpose in view, and now is as good a time to execute it as any."

So saying, Josefa left the room. In a few moments she reappeared equipped for the street.

"Where now?"

'San Fernando."

"To your uncle's?"

"Yes, mother, to uncle's."

"What freak is this—that——"

Her daughter was in the street before she could complete the question.

There was a slight drizzle without, but Josefa had enveloped her form in a thick rebosa and cared little for the dampness. The streets were almost deserted, as it was the hour in the afternoon when more or less of the population indulged in the national siesta. She looked in at the church as she passed, to see if Father Ignacio was within, but the gloomy old pile was dark and vacant, without a single relief save the tiny glimmer of the light, to the right of the altar, whose constant flame never failed year in and year out. It was the first time Josefa had been even in the enclosure of the cathedral for months and it was with no little surprise that Jose encountered her at the gate as she was coming out.

"Is my uncle at home?" she asked of him.

"Si, senorita," he replied, uncovering.

Jose really feared his master's niece. He thought she must be possessed, for the reason that she was not religious, never going to confession or mass, or showing any reverence for the things or traditions which he held so sacred and regarded so essential for a happy hereafter.

"Is any one with him?"

"No, senorita, sola."

"Not even that stupid Nicolas?"

"No, senorita, nadie."

She swept by the major domo, who followed her with his eyes for a moment.

"Perhaps she wants to confess," thought Jose. "No," he continued, "if she had repented she would not have called Father Nicolas' name without putting the 'father' before it. And then she said 'stupid' Nicolas. No, she is not bent on confessing this time."

"Josefa reached the hall just as a boy entered the door, and as he stood hesitatingly, she asked him what he wanted. The little fellow was poorly clad, and she concluded he must be one of the pensioners of her charitable uncle. She pulled out a real and handed to him, telling him at the same time that the father was engaged and could not see him.

"You must come another time," she said to him.

"But I am to leave a note here."

"A note! Let me have it and I will give it to Father Ignacio."

He drew a note from under his blouse and held it towards her. Her face flushed as she read the superscription.

"Mr. Guy Raymond."

It was in a handwriting she at once recognized. Beatrice Navarro had written it.

"Who gave you this?"

"Una senora. She called me as I was passing and gave me a quartilla to bring it here."

"Well, you have a real and a quartilla and are well paid. Here are two reals more to keep your tongue. If you should be asked about this note, say that you left it here."

As Josefa spoke she threw the missive on the bench in the hall, to demonstrate where he was to say he had left it.

The delighted urchin ran off with his money and the other took up the note and placed it in her pocket.

The uncle and niece remained long in the sitting room. At least an hour passed before the latter came out to take her departure. Her eyes were red as though she had been crying, and her face plainly indicated vexation and disappointment. She took rapid steps homewards and before many minutes was in the privacy of her own room. So soon as the rebosa was laid aside she drew back the window curtain to let the light fall upon her face, as it was reflected from her mirror. The reflection was not satisfactory. With impatience she repaired to her washstand and laved her eyes in the basin; then drying them, again had recourse to her glass, where, with the aid of powder all traces of her recent emotion were removed. A more satisfied look settled on her countenance as she sank in a chair by the window and leaned forward reflectively over the sill. The afternoon was about to merge into evening and already the bats had left their crevice retreats and were flying hither and yon, fluttering by the grated opening where Josefa sat. The bats, however, were not in her mind. It was most probably the intercepted note that claimed her thoughts, for suddenly she thrust a hand in her pocket and drew it forth. Scrutinizing the address for a moment, she tore it open; then rising, bent further out towards the clearer light to glean the contents. An exclamation of disgust escaped her lips as she crumpled the paper in her hand.

"Written in English!" she said. "And I cannot know a word of its meaning."

CHAPTER XXX.

A week had passed since Josefa's visit to her uncle, and nothing of importance had occurred in military or social circles in the city. Guy, rather crestfallen from the misadventure which had attended his call at the Navarro's, and dejected still further by unremitting reflection upon the singular termination of a prospective intercourse so auspiciously begun, kept rather closely in his quarters at Father Ignacio's. He had been once to see Linda, whom he found in her usual quiet, placid mood, so glaringly in contrast with the coarse and boisterous manners of her father. Bonito was as gracious as ever in his rude way. He had vivid recollections of his former prisoner's generosity and would not have hesitated to wish for his reincarceration, since it would mean an increased revenue to his exchecquer. The old fellow was never slow to perceive the slightest pointer to a method that might work out a resulting acquisition to Bonito's possessions. Its insignificance mattered not. Once the peso, the real or the quartilla slipped Bonito's purse it there remained. The old jailer had remarked Guy's love for the books which Linda had brought from the monte pio's, and he could not comprehend how the latter had let slip an opportunity that offered so rare a chance to exact at least a fair amount for their recovery. He turned it over in his mind at the time and the following night the thought fairly kept him awake. He concluded that the monte pio was certainly ignorant of the value of books, or rather of the value placed upon them by others. He heard Guy say that his family lost other books on the same occasion when those recovered had been taken. Now, by a deductive process of his own, Bonito concluded that the monte pio might have others of the missing volumes, and would part with them on the same terms he had surrendered the two in question. If this should prove the case, a fine field for speculation would be open to Bonito, who could secure the prized volumes and then he could dictate terms. He could not sleep after the new-born thought had attained its fully developed shape as to ultimate results. Linda should never know of the scheme. The silly fool would oppose him. She would starve if left to her own resources. Bonito kept his secret and if he visited the monte pio in the interest of his contemplated speculation his daughter was none the wiser. The latter, however, in the round of her domestic occupation, explored one day the depths of Bonito's chest where he usually kept his clothes not in immediate demand, besides odds and ends of no known value to the owner or any one else. The presence in the chest of a book was more than a surprise to the daughter, as she knew her father was illiterate and the house contained no volumes outside of the little school collection all her own and the "Camino del Cielo," which she took to mass on Sundays. A mention to her father of the discovery of the volume called forth a reprimand for spying into his affairs.

On the occasion of Guy's call, mentioned at the opening of the chapter, Bonito's manner was so restless as to call forth remark from the young people who, by the old jailer's frequent leaving the apartment, only to reappear in a few moments either to take a restless seat or to give a glance into the door, were often left to themselves.

"What is the matter with your father, Linda," asked Guy, finally.

"Quien sabe, senor," the girl replied languidly and half sighing.

"It looks as if he wants to tell me something and cannot make up his mind to do it."

'Maybe so."

"Linda, does he treat you well?"

"In his way. But, senor, he does try me at times."

"He loves money."

"Better than his soul. Would you believe it, he never confesses."

"That is bad."

"You think so? But Senor Raymond does not confess."

"But I do not believe in such things. If I did I should go to confession."

"I am sorry for you, senor—and for my father."

"And for Josefa? The Senorita de la Torre has no faith."

"Ah, Josefa! Josefa is lost!"

"Has she been here lately?"

Not since you went home with her."

"No?"

"She came here then only to meet you, senor."

"I can't believe that."

"She told me so."

"She! Interested in me?"

"Curiosity, perhaps. She loves Manuel Ruiz."

"Ruiz!"

"Everybody loves Ruiz," said Guy, half sighing. "Linda, are you in love with Ruiz, too?"

"I? Not I, senor."

"But—the Senorita Navarro and the Senorita de la Torre are

in love with Ruiz, and I thought perhaps the Senorita Linda had also fallen a victim to his charms."

"Beatrice Navarro! Senor Raymond mistakes. I am certain that Manuel is no favorite with Beatrice."

"Possibly, for she may be heartless. Ruiz, however, loves her."

"That is very probable, senor. Beatrice is so beautiful."

"But so heartless."

"You have discovered it! And so soon?"

"She forced me to perceive it."

"You have been often to the Navarro's?"

"But twice. Once when I rescued her from the herd and again the day of the Mission fight."

"And in two interviews, senor, you find my friend to be heartless? Have you not been too impetuous?"

"She gave me no opportunity, Linda," replied Guy, smiling. "I was received by the old gentleman the last time I went to see her, and he politely bowed me out of the house."

"And why?"

"Quien sabe," answerd Guy, mimicking the other's manner. "The Senorita Beatrice had not only not informed her father of my timely service, but had never hinted at our chance acquaintance. She was not at home and could not be called to explain. Since she had not thought fit to mention the rescue, I of course left the house and let her father remain in ignorance of the accident that led to our meeting."

"Something is wrong here," said Linda, half aside. "What you have related, senor, is so different from what I had to expect from my friend, that I am confident there must have been a mistake whose explantion will make everything plain."

"It has been to me a serious drama. I wish it could end a comedy of errors. If Miss Navarro had wished to correct a mistake, made by her father, she has failed to profit by a week's interval to accomplish it."

"I could clear this up after a twenty minutes' walk," said Linda, half rising, as if to go.

"I will not have an arbitration in this matter. I would not have you go to her as my messenger, after what has happened, for the whole of Texas."

"What are you two young fools crowing about in here?" asked Bonito, poking his head in at the door. "I had something to say to Senor Raymond, but you, worthless pigeon, are keeping him cooing and cooing like another pigeon. A pajarro he is, de veras."

"What is it, Bonito? Can't Linda hear it?"

"Must a woman know everything? It is not much they can keep and it is little you can keep from them. You are young, senor, and have much to learn of women. They are riddles, even after you think you have learned them by heart."

"You judge them by a hard rule, Bonito," said Guy, looking at the girl. But he thought of Beatrice the next instant and mentally concluded there was some little philosophy in the jailer's remarks.

Taking leave of Linda, Guy joined the other in the hall. The old fellow shut the door carefully, put his hand softly on Guy's shoulder and with upturned head gave him a quizzical look from the corners of his eyes. This tableau was maintained only for a moment, to give impressiveness to what was probably to follow.

"Has Senor Raymondo the books that Linda brought from the monte pio's?"

"Yes; at San Fernando."

"Senor likes books?"

"I am fond of reading."

"And would like yet more books?"

"Well, Bonito, you have somthing to say. Out with it."

"Would senor pay something for a nice book?"

"Perhaps I would. It is plain to see now, that you have hatched up a job to get money out of me, Bonito. Come to the point at once, you miserly old sinner."

"If it should be—one of the books you lost that time when the Indians——"

'A truce to your preamble, you skinflint. If you have a book of mine, or any other one, show it and name your price."

"Would—three—four—reals?" said Bonito, hesitating.

"Not a cent, if you keep this up a minute longer," said Guy, determinedly.

Bonito took a step or two to a lounge against the opposite wall and turning back the blanket which served as a spread, drew forth a book and held it up.

"This must be worth four reals, senor. I had trouble and money to pay, besides, before I could get it."

Guy took the volume and recognized it as "Wealth of Nations," from his father's library. He put his hand in his pocket and drew out the four reals, which he handed to the jailer. While taking it, Bonito looked the picture of disappointment and self-reproach. He turned over the piece of money and glanced from it to Guy, who was thoughtfully regarding the recovered treasure.

"It was worth more, or he would not have paid to readily," Bonito reflected.

"Senor, did I not say five reals—or six? I can't remember which amount I said; my head is so befuddled. But the book is worth a deal. It must be; for it is larger than the two that Linda brought, if both were put together. What was it I said, senor—six, or seven reals? A poor amount for such a book."

"Bonita, where did you find this?"

"No matter, senor, since you have it. But seven reals is cheap— or eight is nothing for such a book."

"Where will you end presently? It is your old game renewed. To punish you for your greed for reals, I shall not pay you a cent more than that piece of money. I know you well enough to be sure that you saved yourself in your first demand."

"Santa Maria! Your ears are sealed with wax, or worse has happened to your hearing. By all the saints, it was six I said at first, but contended last for eight. Senor, liberty has made you a miser. As a prisoner you were over generous."

"Nature made you a miser, and practicing the arts of one has developed you into a rogue. I would not begrudge you a full peso for this book, which has doubtless cost you nothing; but I wish to cure you of your penchant for lying. You first asked but three reals. For shame! When you have bags of money hid away!"

"Valga-me-dios! Que mentira! Por dios, senior! It is little money that I have. Bags! A glove would hold more than I possess."

When his visitor had left, Bonito abused himself unmercifully for not having been shrewd enough to secure more than the trifle of four reals.

"But the monte pio has more," he muttered. "He half suspected that I wanted it for a purpose and not for waste-paper. Que mala fortuna! I missed four reals at least. A boy would have managed better. Manoel Canastadomiento—fifty years of life have but made you a fool. From now on I am willing to be called 'Bonito the Ass'!"

The addition to his stock of reading, made by the possession of Adam Smith's great work, furnished Guy with mental occupation while indoors. Father Ignacio had placed several volumes of Spanish theological works at his disposal; but, beyond the desire to improve himself in Spanish instruction, he had little taste for that kind of literature. He produced his Wealth of Nations to give Father Ignacio an insight as to its drift, but discovered that his host had procured a Spanish translation. This proved a source of gratification to Guy, for he found diversion in discussing with the priest the theories advanced by the noted Scotchman.

* * * *

The very day that Guy was discussing with Linda the discouraging termination of his intercourse with the Navarros, the young lady of that family was conversing with her sister, the Senora A—— on the identical subject that engaged the attention of the pair at the carcel Beatrice had not been herself for over a week. Her changed manner and repeated abstractions were noticed by the sister, who readily guessed the cause, although she refrained from any allusion that might post the other of her divination. On the day in question, however, the two had been sitting together for some time in the same apartment where they were first found at home by the reader, without having exchanged a word. The elder sister broke the silence.

"Batrice, did you not write that note to Senor Raymond?"

"I did."

"Has he replied?"

"No."

"What do you suppose can be the reason?"

"Too deeply offended, perhaps, at father's cool reception."

"Did you explain clearly that father had not been informed of his service to you?"

"I did."

"Nor even of his acquaintance with you?"

"Oh, Jane! I told him everything," said Beatrice, petulantly. "If he is so deeply offended that he can't get over it, why let him remain so."

"Then why take it to heart, if you can so easily discard the matter and the man?"

"Can't you say something that will not be a question?"

"My anxiety must be my excuse, sister mine. You have been blue ever since father informed us of Senor Raymond's cool dismissal."

'That everlasting Mexican custom of having to know every man first, through an introduction by the parents, has proved, in this case, how stupid it is. In Baltimore, if a man is a gentleman, he may call on a lady without having to cut a ridiculous figure in approaches and manuevres, or be froze out by excruciating politeness."

"You remember what a time the Doctor had getting acquainted with me?"

"What music is that?"

"Look, Beatrice and see."

The latter went to a front window and looked out into the street.

"Jane, it is the picadores. Two riding in front, and behind are the chulos playing. I wonder where they can come from, and the Texans around the town. Is it not pretty music?"

Jane had joined her at the window.

The music came from a curiously dressed procession of eight persons. Two, mounted on prancing ponies, were dressed in the fanciest toggery, consisting of blue vestments, glittering with numerous spangles on breasts and arms. Scarlet breeches, ending at the knees, buckled over striped stockings, while their craniums were surmounted by close-fitting skull caps, from which depended tails of some red material, ending in tassels. Underneath their right forearms each held a long lance in rest, from whose silver spearhead fluttered a miniature silken flag displaying the colors of Mexico. The six followers were habited a la zouave, four of them playing on instruments that produced the sweetest music. The remaining two brought up the rear, bearing crimson banners and armed with swords. They passed on up the street, turning the corner in the direction of Main Plaza. The horsemen were picadores, or bull fighters. The "chulos" were assistants, who take certain parts in the fight to attract the bull's attention with their red flags, or they torment him by using barbed darts or explosives. They are sometimes called "banderilleros." The matador is the one who finishes the animal by a *coup de grace*. These strollers become well known to the towns and cities of Mexico, to which they make annual visits, their stay in a place being determined by the ability and inclination of its population to make their performances remunerative. From Beatrice's remark, these must have been new arrivals in Bexar. The attraction in the street having subsided, the ladies returned to their seats and occupations, the married one to her fancy work, the single one to her reverie.

The latter, after a long silence, during which a myriad of thoughts had coursed through her mind, turned to the other and said passionately:

"Jane, I have a presentiment that Josefa has something to do with his not replying to my note. Presentiments rarely have deceived me. If she has tricked me in this instance, I will find it out."

CHAPTER XXXI.

Eight or ten days' time that had passed since the battle at Conception, produced noted changes in the Texan position as well as in their forces and the character of their operations. The little army had become reduced in numbers very perceptibly by the leaving of many who were disappointed and disgusted because an anticipated assault had settled down into a seemingly hopeless siege. The force had been divided into two camps, one above and the other below the town, and each had its scouting ground allotted to it, to prevent surprise and to bar the ingress of reinforcements as well as the egress of the besieged, in quest of supplies. The upper camp was at an old mill a mile or so from the plaza; the lower one near the mission at the scene of the recent engagment. Patrols kept vigil, night and day, to detect any movements of the enemy, while an occasional show of force within rifle shot of the fortifications was made to draw them from their cover. The cautious Mexicans, however, had too recently tested the spirit of their foe to venture without the lines, and kept behind the friendly walls, well satisfied to await the ever-impending attack.

Austin had thrown up the command and had left the field for the diplomatic arena, where his talents could be freely utilized for the benefit of the embryo nation, whose star, just struggling on the horizon, was soon to rise through bloody mists and lurid clouds of treachery and massacre, until it should attain the blue vault in the system of nations, glowing and brilliant amid a halo of victory.

Burleson succeeded to the command.

It was the third night after the battle. Blustering winds blew hither and yon; the ragged, low-flying clouds that appeared to touch the mission's tower, dimly outlined against their lighter shade or obscured by their darker shadows . The night had grown wilder in the short hour since the twilight had merged into its deeper gloom, and the increasing winds, true to no point of compass, sighed through the openings and whistled around the corners of its massive walls. Far across the opening where its western side was fringed with timber, a number of fires throwing their lights among the foliage marked the new camp where lay Bowie's detachment, composing the force that invested the lower side of the city.

A solitary figure, scarcely discernible in the obscurity, paced up and down before the great door giving entrance to the church. A rifle resting carelessly upon his shoulder, a powder horn swung by his side would, in a better light, have shown him to be a sentinel of the Texan army. He made a few more strides upon his beat, then, turning suddenly to the door, he rested his gun against the side, and seated himself upon the sill.

"I'll be d———d if I walk here any longer. There is no sense anyway keeping watch here."

The speaker said this in a grumbling tone, then making himself comfortable, he gave a yawn and lowered his head over on his knees.

"Come, Perry, you are wrong, boy. Here's the mission. It is so dark I did not discern the grand old pile. The house that contains our invilad is over here."

"I believe you are right, Mr. Hamilton."

The voices were distinctly heard by the sentinel, who, remaining perfectly still, peered through the darkness and, without catching a certain glimpse of their figures, heard the footfalls of the speakers.

"What the devil are they going to see old Trigg for?" he muttered, as taking his gun he rose and went to the corner of the building to listen. The parties attracting his attention had made for the rear of the mission, and he could hear their voices in the distance.

"I'll follow them and see what's up. Old Trigg and Hamilton have no use for me since I boxed that boy. It must be a full hour before the relief, and I will have time to get back on post."

So saying, the recreant followed the direction taken by the speakers. He gained the rear of the wing that joined the structure just in time to see the fresada raised that hung within Locaria's door and the parties enter. Moving now more cautiously along, he made a slight detour to the right and approached the jacal from the further side. He gained the wall and, crouching down, put his ear to one of several small crevices and heard quite distinctly a conversation carried on within.

Inside the jacal a tallow candle was burning on a small shelf projecting from the wall. The light afforded by its tiny flame was lost in the brighter glow proceeding from the hearth in the end of the apartment. Mr. Trigg was lying on the bed where Father Ignacio had communed with him in pantomime. Perry and Hamilton were sitting near him, while little Locaria stood in an opposite corner, looking in admiration at the handsome American with raven locks and fancy boots.

"It's glad I am to see you both looking so fine," said Mr. Trigg, after the two had greeted him and established themselves in seats.

"I am happy to be able to return the compliment," said Hamilton.

"You are not looking worse for your wound. Perry and myself would have been over yesterday if we had not been on a scout north of town."

"We came just as soon as we got your message," said Perry.

"I'm satisfied you did, my boy. I wanted to see you and Mr. Hamilton for to take you into a secret that it wouldn't do to have die with me."

"Die with you! Why, just now you said that two or three days would see you up and about," said Hamilton.

"Oh! Wait a bit. You haven't a clear idea of my meaning. It is not of this wound I'm thinking that will be killing me. Some other bullet may have a surer aim, Mr. Hamilton, and then it will be too late. It is against the danger of not being able to say what I wish to say at all, that I want to guard. In two or three days I shall be as well as ever of this, so far as moving about is concerned."

"That puts the whole situation decidedly in a more optimistic light, Mr. Trigg. We miss you sadly in the mess and I rejoice to think that in so short a time you will be with us again. So far as making me and my amiable young friend, Perry, here the depositories of your secret as a precaution against those emergencies brought about by the vicissitudes of war, I assure you we are at your service and are anxious to hear what you have to impart; not from any morbid curiosity, but from a sincere desire to serve you. What say you, Perry?"

"Mr. Trigg knows he can rely on me."

"Laconic, truly laconic, my boy," said Hamilton, slapping Perry on the shoulder, "but your words contain a world of meaning and a volume of eloquence might be deduced from them in a tribute to friendship and confidence."

"You should have been a stump speaker, Mr. Hamilton. You are so ready with words, and can say so much about nothing. You could make a fortune in Mississippi."

"I have come to Texas to make one. If this war terminates favorable to us, my voice may be heard in the councils of a young nation. In the American revolution were men who afterwards became nearly deified, but who really were commonplace and without any brilliant traits to justify the characters they have been credited with by posterity. The success of the struggle shed such a halo of glory on the army and public men that it concealed every fault and magnified every virtue. There is nothing which succeeds like success, Mr. Trigg."

"Begging your pardon for interrupting you—it is sure I am

that you're right; but let me talk about what I had a mind to tell you, and after I am up we can talk about all them things over the camp fire. Perry, did you bring the wallet?"

"Here it is, sir."

Perry drew from his breast and handed him a leather pouch, not dissimilar to the kind usually carried on stage coaches for way mail. Mr. Trigg unwound a buckskin string from the wallet and opening it, looked among its contents until he found what he wanted.

"Here is what I was looking for," he said, holding up a stained paper tied with a piece of faded red tape.

"That is the secret that you——"

"Please be quiet a bit, Mr. Hamilton, and you'll know about it, and the less you and Perry say, the sooner you will be after knowing it."

"Leave out the boy, Mr. Trigg. I'll try to keep quiet. So proceed."

"Thank ye sir. But first I want you to promise that what I will be after saying to you will not be repeated; that you are to do no more than to think about it and that you solemnly promise me never to take advantage of the knowledge of it, without I am killed before we take the town above. Do you promise this, Mr. Hamilton?"

"I do," replied Hamilton, biting his lips to suppress a flow of words.

"What say you, Perry?"

"I promise to do as you wish."

"I am beating you on laconics, Perry, but it costs an effort."

"I took a liking to you, Mr. Hamilton, since I got to know you well, for at first you talked so much and used words so uncommon that I was almost forninst you. But I have seen you in much that tries men, for honesty and fairness, and I soon saw you was all right. You seem to have to boil over like a brimming kettle once in a while, so full you are of words and information. What I have to tell you and Perry will open up a bit of my past life. It's a little ashamed I am of it, now; but that is all bygones, and with the help of the saints I'll try to do only good in time to come. When quite a lad I came to New Orleans on a clipper that sailed from New York, working my passage, for I had a sailor experience in the coasting trade in the old country. I had little money, and being a stranger in the city I knocked around for a month or so, doing odd jobs, and had a berth at a sailor's roost on the levee. After a bit I fell in with a good-looking man who came around the roost more than a dozen times, and who used to visit the shipping and talk with the idle sailors on the wharves. I was a bright and active chap then and the man took a fancy to me. One day he told me he was the captain of a fine vesel that lay in the gulf, and asked me how I would like to ship with him. I didn't give him an answer at once. Before I made up my mind I was after finding out his ship to be a privateer, and that he was cruising against Spanish commerce. This much he told me from his own lips as a secret. To cut my story short, I agreed to ship with him, as he said the prize money would pay fine, and that took my eye. The day came for us to leave the city and I shall never forget the bayous and the crooked ways we took to reach the ship. To cut short again, I found myself, at the end of forty-eight hours, on Barrataria Island an enlisted sailor under the banner of Lafitte, the pirate of the Gulf."

"Lafitte! Jean Pierre Anatole Lafitte, the pi——!"

"Please dont' bile over now, Mr. Hamilton. You see Perry is listening and not saying a word."

"Excuse me, Mr. Trigg—I——"

"You are excused, sir, without the asking. I am not going to tell you about Lafitte, or what I saw or did under him in the six years I followed his fortunes. I just wished ye to know how I came to get into such company, for getting with such is how 1 came to have the secret that you and Perry are to know.

Outside of the house a noise, as of some falling article, startled those within. A silence followed, which was ended by Mr. Trigg suggesting that the others go out to ascertain the cause. The little Mexican woman, who had been quiet in the corner, said to Perry in Spanish that the noise was similar to that which would be made by the falling of a gun. The latter and Hamilton went out, and, after some minutes, returned reporting that nothing could be seen to explain the noise which had interrupted them. When the two had re-entered the jacal, the figure of the listener emerged from the shadow of a tree and crept back to the rear wall of Locaria's abode. As he did so he muttered:

"That d——d gun like to have betrayed me. It won't do so again. One of Lafitte's men! What can that secret be? He is a fine specimen to be preaching virtue and fairness, and training up that young angel, Perry. A pirate! Ha! Ha!"

Ducio settled himself down and placed his ear close to a crevice indicated by a ray of light issuing from the room.

"Among the crew of the ship, which was a fore and aft Spanish brig and a fine sailer, was a Portugese gunner who became my friend. As he was a favorite of the commander, I had a very nice time at the start, learning the ways of the men and the duties to be performed. This man served with me off and on for the six years; for sometimes it would happen, in the changing fortunes of Lafitte, that ships would be lost or abandoned and crews separated to serve apart until we joined each other again in port. My friendship with the old gunner, for he was a purty old man, Mr. Hamilton, continued without interruption. I was a lad that always respected authority and never had a cross word. The crews of Lafitte's vessels made lots of money while at Barrataria; but it was the second year after I shipped that the navy made us leave Uncle Sam's coast, and after we went to Galveston for a rendezvous, the men were always discontented about the prize money. They were extravagant devils and saved nothing, as a rule. A few buried their treasure or otherwise put it by for worse times. After being forced away from Barrataria there was more of a watch kept upon Lafitte's rovers, and he and his chief men began to see that not many months more would be left to the business they was in. This made them more anxious to save their swag, and to be stingy in paying it over to the sailors. The old gunner was lacking just a little of being a miser. He always got a liberal allowance from Lafitte, for he was as good with a cannon as a marksman with a rifle. I have seen him in a rough sea, that would hardly leave legs on the oldest seamen, fire on the rise and cut away the mainmast of a chase. This made him a favorite, while the common men thought he was a kind of supernatural. They would not have grumbled if he had got half the prize money, after doing one of his feats with his gun."

"Can't you tell us of one of those chases, Mr. Trigg; it would be inter——"

"I asked ye to be quiet, Mr. Hamilton. What I am telling ye is to prepare for the secret, and sure it's enough to have one thing in view at a time. What I am trying to tell ye is business, and the shortest way to it is the best way. Remember, it's under your solemn promise I'm letting you know these things. It's not to be breathed."

"I'll try not to forget again, sir."

"The gunner saved his money, as I was very sure of; but it was not until long after Lafitte had broken up that I found it out from his own lips in New Orleans. The old fellow got to be a perfect miser, and lived by himself in the humblest way, in a little bit of a creole house near the French market. I was some time in the city before I found his whereabouts, but after I dropped in to see him off and on for a year or so, when one day I found him very sick. The next day the old woman he rented from sent her boy to hunt me.

When I got there my friend was speechless, but sensible. He made known by signs that he thought he was about to die, making me understand as well as he could, poor man, that he wanted me to attend to some business. I took a key from beneath his pillow and unlocked the chest that was near, in full sight of him. It held his clothes, some money in Spanish doubloons, and a packet of papers. The poor fellow made me understand that he wanted to leave me what he had in the house, likewise the papers on which he seemed to set great store. I got his landlady to care for him while I went for a doctor; but he died that night without a pain. The old gunner had worn out."

Mr. Trigg here paused for a while. The two listeners inside had paid the closest attention as the narrative progressed. Locaria, not comprehending a word, sat indifferent and motionless, save when she gave the fire a poke, or mechanically turned her head without any apparent purpose. The listener outside impatiently muttered:

"Why don't the old devil go on? It will soon be time for the relief."

"This paper," continued Mr. Trigg, "was among those in the package. There was also a will, leaving all he had to me. No doubt this piece of paper is worth a great deal. The old man went to Mexico after the break-up at Galveston. From Mexico he went to Orleans, passing through the very town we are now trying to take. He stopped in San Antonio with a countryman of his, and left with him some valuable papers that, if I had them, would tell me where a great portion of his treasure is now buried. A lawyer in Orleans thought that it was hid up here; but I know it is on the island."

"Galveston island?" interrupted Perry.

"Galveston island," answered Mr. Trigg.

"Perry, you interrupted that time."

"But he was laconic," said Mr. Trigg, smiling.

"This paper," continued the narrator, "gives the name of the man in San Antonio who has the documents that will show the bearings. I could never remember the name. Bring the light, Mr. Hamilton. and let us see if we can make it out."

Hamilton brought the tallow dip from its shelf and Mr. Trigg, rising on his elbow, opened the paper. Hamilton, advancing the light, stooped to scrutinize the name, while Perry tiptoed and peered over his shoulder. Hamilton, after spelling it through, slowly pronounced, syllable by syllable, the name indicated by Mr. Trigg's finger:

"Man-o-el—Can-as-ta-do-mi-en-to."

"All three pronounced the formidable name.

The listener outside made a mental memorandum of the ten liquid syllables.

"This paper," continued Mr. Trigg, "will be on my body if I be killed, before I can see the man with this long name. My will is here with it, and if such a mischance should happen to me, you or Perry, or both will be my executors. What I have got, and this treasure, if it, ever be found, will belong to Guy Raymond, and to Stella, his sister. The other paper is, I am thinking, of service to find what the poor old gunner buried, and is no doubt in the possession of this Manoel What-ye-May-Call-It, who is in the town beyond."

"There were sounds of footsteps outside," said Locaria, in Spanish.

Perry interpreted her words.

They all listened.

The eavesdropper had heard the approach of the relief and hastened to his post.

CHAPTER XXXII.

"By the ghost of Lord Dalrymple! I am glad to see you about again, Mr. Trigg."

"I'm blowed ef I ain't proud to see the old gent."

"Welcome, Mr. Trigg."

Such were the salutations from Jones, Nathan Roach and Karnes, as their convalescent messmate walked up to where preparations were being made for the evening meal, Jones acting as chief cook. Hamilton and Perry came with him, having gone to Locaria's jacal for the purpose of accompanying him to the camp.

"He would have been back before this, if Perry and myself had not objected to his leaving a roof too soon," said Hamilton.

"When did you and Mr. Karnes get back, Mr. Roach?" asked Perry.

"About half an hour. We tuck some Greasers and brought 'em in."

"Are they from town?" asked Hamilton.

"No. They was making for town and we naturally swooped 'em in. The head feller says he's a bull-fighter. That Mexican, Ruiz, was out with us and he kinder scraped up kin with him. There they come now, and Ruiz with 'em."

As Nathan ceased speaking, Ruiz was seen approaching with five other mounted Mexicans, one of them leading a pack mule.

They halted near the mess fire, and by direction of Ruiz, the strangers dismounted.

"The colonel says he has no objection to these men passing into town, Mr. Karnes. So with your permission, they will rest here tonight, and tomorrow I will go in with them."

"You!" said Karnes. "Old Cos would have your head on a pole before tomorrow night."

"In that case, my time will have come. But, seriously, I am going; but pretty well disguised. Gentlemen, let me introduce to you my cousin, Senor Trevino. He cannot speak English, but he knows how to fight bulls, and that is his business."

The mess saluted Senor Trevino.

"How can you disguise yourself, Ruiz?" asked Hamilton, "when you are so well known in town?"

"Easy enough. A razor will remove this beard, and a costume in that pack will transform me into a bull fighter."

"Your awkwardness may betray you."

"My cousin there cannot beat me sticking to a horse; and then I need not go too actively to performing in my new calling."

After the mess had partaken of supper, Senor Trevino caused his four attendants to produce their instruments, consisting of harp, clarionette, violin and flute, and to play for the entertainment of their captors and hosts. The music rendered was beautiful and as the sweet strains filled the air they attracted the attention of the soldiers from other parts of the camp, until quite a crowd gathered to listen. The youngsters cleared a space around the fire and indulged in a regular break-down. This was succeeded by jigs borrowed from plantation life. The fun reached its climax when Nathan sprang into the arena and began a series of gyrations that would have shamed a whirling dervish. He cut a pigeon wing as he announced it to be, and shuffled from side to side, while his awkward, lank anatomy assumed divers contortions, culminating in a spring in the air and an Indian warwhoop that would have done credit to a Lipan. The diversions had lasted some time, when, to the surprise of the crowd, two fancifully-habited men appeared and occupied the space now, vacated by Nathan. One said, in broken English:

"Gentlemen, this in Senor Trevoni, the celebrated juggler and bull-fighter. He has been so well treated by the soldiers of this camp that he proposes to give you an exhibition of his powers as a juggler. Tomorrow he will go into San Antonio, where he will remain until you take the town, when he will show you how he can conquer a bull."

The soldiers gave a cheer at the mention of the capture of San Antonio.

"Who is that fellow who introduced him?" inquired Jones.

"One of his men. There were five," replied Hamilton.

"He makes six," said Karnes. "Call Ruiz, he probably knows."

Ruiz could not be found. Meantime, Trevoni had a cloth spread upon the ground and one of his men produced swords, daggers, balls and other articles with which he was to exhibit his skill. His performances were really marvellous. It was no effort for him to keep four sharp daggers whirling around and above him without letting one drop to the ground, and finally making two of them disappear, apparently down his throat, while he caught the other two. The performer amused them for an hour by his feats, when he bowed himself away, and his pleased audience dispersed.

The person who had introduced the performer stood looking on all the time with folded arms. When the crowd had retired, he went close to Karnes, and said in his natural tone of voice:

"Karnes, don't you recognize me?"

"What! Ruiz!"

"Yes; pretty well disguised, eh?"

"Your mother would not know you, with your beard off and in that toggery. But how could you make such a change in so short a time?"

"We went up to Locaria's and Trevino took off my beard in five minutes and furnished this costume."

"You can go into town now, if you will keep your voice changed.'

"And I'm going."

The next day the sun was high up when the Mexican party, with Ruiz added to their number, rode out of the Texan camp, dressed in their costumes. Ruiz and Trevino were the most conspicuously dressed, and carried long lances with polished steel spearheads. The four others were in fancy attire, and carried their instruments. The troops gave them a parting cheer as the cavalcade passed out by the San Jose road leading to the river.

Leaving Ruiz with the bull-fighters to proceed on their destination, let us turn to other incidents of the camp before we follow him to see what adventures will befall his incognito appearance among his enemies.

After Ducio Halfen had become possessed of Mr. Trigg's secret, his mind gave him no rest for thinking of the buried treasure that lay somewhere waiting only the turning of a little earth to disclose its presence to the fortunate one who should first reach the still doubtfully located spot. He no longer messed with the men with whom his first introduction to the reader found him. His surly disposition had made him unbearable as a companion, and his disagreeable conduct had culminated in his unwarranted attack on Perry. That he was mean and treacherous has been abundantly shown by his acts, the last and most despicable of which was the desertion of his post and his eavesdropping in the rear of Locaria's jacal. He as fully possessed Mr. Trigg's secret as either of the other two to whom the old Irishman had detailed it for a purpose. Its possession had helped the more fully to develop the innate fiendishness that controlled his nature and prompted his acts. He thought and dreamed of the treasure. His imagination took in the possible career of the gulf pirates and he reveled in thoughts of the chases and the captures of rich prizes; the division of plunder, and the secreting of pots filled, to the brim with Spanish gold. He repeated the long name he had heard pronounced, going over its many syllables from time to time, until he reached the camp and a light, where he could write it in memorandum. Concocting a plan of action was the duty of the succeeding days, during which he was reticent and passed every possible moment alone. If he finally matured anything from the diabolical ramifications of his evil mind remains to be developed by subsequent acts.

It was late in the afternoon of the day that the picadores left the camp, that Captain Bowie, while returning from an observation of the enemy's lines from the battlements of the mission, found Ducio waiting for him in the path leading to his headquarters. The creole accosted him:

"Captain, I would like to say a word to you."

"Well, sir."

"I want to go into San Antonio."

"That's the wish of the whole army."

"But it is a matter of business with me."

"Something on your own private account?"

"Some news I have heard, that affects me privately makes it necessary for me to go thére."

"Have you been communicating with town?"

"It is nothing I have heard from town. It is purely my private business, or I would tell you. I thought it best to make you acquainted with my intentions, and get permission to pass from your lines into those of the enemy. Besides, I might make my presence there of service to you."

"As a spy?"

"Well—yes—as a spy."

"I am aware, Mr. Halfen, that you are not enlisted, and have only done duty thus far voluntarily. But I feel as if you and Mr. Hamilton, who has been serving the same way, through the courtesy of the officers, are as much soldiers as the rest, and as bound to obey orders as any. Yet, if you now say you wish to leave the command I shall not object. It seems to me to be of doubtful propriety to allow you to enter the enemy's lines unless it be in the service of Texas."

"The fact of my coming for permission proves I wished to do right."

"That is plausable. But are you not afraid the Mexicans will suspect you and take your scalp?"

"No, for I have not belonged to the army, and can pass myself off for a Frenchman. I speak the language, and have papers from the French consul in New Orleans."

"But you are a native of Louisiana."

"True. The papers I brought through prudence. The French consul is a relation of my father."

"When do you wish to go?"

"Before tomorrow morning."

"Come to my camp in an hour. Perhaps I may have a commission for you besides the permit you wish."

Ducio's face assumed a satisfied expression as he left the officer and took himself to his camp to make ready for a trip. His quarters were soon reached and without making any unnecessary demonstration he began to prepare for his move, with or without the consent of the military authorities. His blankets were snugly rolled and strapped and the little odds and ends, besides his clothing, were stowed in a pair of capacious saddle bags. His whole kit put in order, he placed it suspended from a limb of a tree convenient for his reach, when occasion should come for him to take it unperceived. To questions from messmates, who saw his movements, he explained that Captain Bowie had some night work for a squad, which he was to accompany.

"You are a kind of favorite with Bowie," said one.

"And not regular mustered, neither," said another.

"Him and Hamilton are too fancy fixed for soldiers," said the first.

"But they's fell out. What was it about, Halfen?"

"Nothing much," said Ducio, indifferently, wishing to humor them. "I slapped over a saucy boy, and he took it it up. I may have been in the wrong.'

Before night closed Ducio had visited headquarters and came

away with the consent of the commander, after a lengthy interview, to which two other officers were admitted. His steps were directed to a glade that nestled in a curve of the river below the camp, where were grazing several horses secured to stakes. One of these he approached, and unfastening the, rope coiled it up in his hand, secured it with a loop and led the animal to the rear of the position occupied by his mess. Darkness had now set in. The forms of men and objects of camp furniture could be seen here and there in the vicinity of the camp fires. Notwithstanding the sanction of the commander, the conscience of Ducio was guilty and his stealthy, cat-like movements were clearly indicative of the illegitimate purpose impelling him to proceed upon the errand he had conceived. He did not bring his horse more closely for fear of observation, and he succeeded in fully caparisoning him ready for departure without having attracted the attention of anyone. This done, Ducio boldly stalked into camp, joining his party as they were dividing up the supper.

"Hello, pard! Thought you was goin' to sup at headquarters," said one.

"They did not have politeness enough to ask me."

When his mess had concluded their meal Ducio was restless until he made up his mind to leave. He told the men he had to go back to see Captain Bowie and left in a direction proper to carry out such a purpose; but when out of sight he made a detour that brought him to his waiting horse. Thoroughly testing his girth, and feeling that all was right, Ducio mounted and rode away in the direction of the rear of the mission.

About the time that Ducio Halfen was taking leave of Captain Bowie, the camp fire of our mess was blazing brightly. The men had eaten supper. Jones, whose turn it was to cook, had cleaned up the mess things and the party were comfortably disposed around in different positions, engaged in conversation.

Mr. Trigg had evidently let drop a hint that he had followed the sea in company with the noted rover of the gulf, for Jones was just saying that he would never have taken a man of his modest appearance to have been a pirate.

"No telling what you did in Idnia, Jones," said Hamilton.

"Mr. Trigg could no doubt tell some interesting sea yarns," said Karnes.

"Specially ef he was with old Lerfitte," said Nathan.

"Hamilton wouldn't believe a word of it," suggested Jones.

"But Mr. Trigg would not soar into the impossible; for instance, he would never try to impose upon us anything like your elephant story," retorted Hamilton.

"I advise him to not regale you with anything the least strange. You who have never been a hundred miles from home won't admit the truth of any adventure, above a 'possum hunt or the pursuit of a runaway darky."

"Now, Jones! We are not going to be cheated out of a yarn from Mr. Trigg, just because we won't let you impose your East Indian stories upon our credulity."

"Or Rimple's rule. We never knowed what that was," put in Nathan.

"Well, my lads," interrupted Mr. Trigg. "If you will stop your cross-firing, I will tell you a short yarn. I am not over strong and I won't sit up late. I have to sleep in the house for a night or so, and by then I will likely be myself again. One morning—it was the month of October—I had been in the service at Barrataria about a twelve-month. The boys was laying 'round loose, and we was all getting a little tired of about six weeks idleness, while the old man was in Orleans. We saw his gig coming down from the mainland where a bayou emptied that connects, through other bayous, with the river. We saw him a-coming, and as the wind was fresh and quartering, his little boat was making good headway. I remember some of 'em said that the haste he was making might mean some business for the crews. But it was the wish that was father to the thought; for they was itching for some service. The most of us crowded down to the little pier to see him land and, as he stepped from the gig, he smiled in a good-natured way at the welcome we gave him and shook hands with the last one of us. Some dared to ask him if anything was up, but he just smiled. We wasn't long in suspense, however, for after he had been something like an hour shut up with the captains of the two schooners we had orders come to get ready for sea. This did not take so long, as the vessels had been provisioned within the week by a schooner from Orleans, and we had little more to do than to fill the casks with water, to be ready to weigh anchor and be off.

"The men never worked with a better will than that afternoon as the canvas fluttered to the breeze and the run of the capstan soon brought aboard and made snug the anchors. Besides the two schooners that I mentioned, Lafitte himself had his own vessel, a handsome brig-rigged ship of narrow build, that carried a cloud of canvas when he wanted to put her to her best. The smaller ships carried two light guns apiece and were pretty fast themselves, but the brig could soon make them hull down, if she felt like it, without spreading a topsail or letting fly a spanker. She had a broadside of two thirty-two pounders, but her best arm was a pivot gun amidships, that Lafitte captured from the Spaniards. Well, we stood out in fine style, the brig a-leading, and when we got into blue water orders were given to the man at the wheel to head for the mouth of the river. The sun went down red that evening and the wind freshened so that it looked like a gale would be upon us before midnight. I was in the second watch and when we turned in it was little sleep we had for thinking what we would be after doing in the morning."

"You were aboard the brig?" asked Jones.

"I was. I never left Lafitte's own ship as long as I was with him. Myself and Antone, the gunner I was telling ye about, who died in Orleans, was never separated from the old man until we quit for good. Well, as I was saying, we couldn't sleep much that night, and the next day we laid off and on, in sight of the shipping at the mouth of the Mississippi, until night, when the captain signalled the schooners and brought aboard their commanders. After some understanding the vessels all stood to the eastward and sailing abreast, with orders to increase the intervals until about three miles apart. We continued this course for two days and nights without sighting a sail. The wind had lightened so that we made hardly three knots an hour the last twenty-four hours. About three o'clock the lookout called: 'Sail, Ho!' It proved to be a sail on our starboard bow. The old man went aloft with his glass, and after a while he signalled the schooners to stand well to the southeast, while our ship was brought a point or two closer to the direction of the stranger. We could see Lafitte's idea at once. He wanted the other two to keep away out of danger, while we would speak, or look after the new sail, and if we must run we had the heels to do it. The wind stiffened and made the brig fairly split the water; but Lafitte wanted to reach the stranger in good light, and he sent hands aloft to spread the topgallant sails, while Antone and myself rigged the spanker. The cloud of canvas kept her steady as if she was in a groove, and it wasn't long before the ship was hull-up. She turned out to be a three-master under easy sail. Lafitte kept his eye on her until she couldn't be more than a couple o' miles away, when we put about and ran at right angles across her bows. His idea was to circle her and find the kind of a vessel she was. We sailed in the new direction, making two or three points on her larboard bow, when we changed to about south-southeast; then after a bit to southeast, until we had a good view of her broadside.

"Lafitte ordered the English colors to be shown.

"After the flag was up a few minutes, the stranger showed the Stars and Stripes. The old man called Antone and handed him the glass. Antone took it, and in a breath, declared it to be a vessel of war. The schooners were hull-down in the southwest, and Lafitte determined to find out what man o' war it was. The brig was now about abreast with her, when up went our helm and we came about in pretty style. It was as fine a movement as was ever made on salt water. When our sails filled again, orders came fast; away sprang our boys and in the time I'm a-telling it we were under half canvas and making equal speed with the other ship. The vessels neared each other as they went, and by the time the sun was near touching the water, they were not half a mile apart. The men were growling about fooling around a man o' war, and wanted to be off; but Lafitte had a good deal of the daredevil in him and loved a little danger often when there wasn't a cent in it. There wasn't a sound on the brig, when finally a hail came over the water:

" 'What ship is that?'

"The answer went back:

" 'His Brittanic Majesty's ship, Dauntless.'

"To this was responded:

" 'I don't believe it. Send an officer aboard with proof.'

" 'Aye, aye, sir,' replied Lafitte, and asked:

" 'What ship is that?'

" 'The United States ship, "President." Hurry up your boat.'

" 'Aye, aye, sir,' we responded.

"By this time the twilight had faded, and now the only light left was from the stars, that was out thick enough. The President showed all her lights while the hailing was passing; but aboard us all was dark, saving a light in the binnacle. Both ships had luffed, the President having shortened sail, and soon after the last words was spoke, the brig had nearly crossed the other's bows. Lafitte waited for this, and when the time came, one order of his made every rag of sail fly to its place. Our brig yielded to the helm, and before the man o' war knew what was up we were showing him our heels at the rate of fifteen knots. A broadside would have ruined us at that close quarters, but before they could ware ship with their clumsy hulk, it would have been accident to hit us with iron. The balls came, however ,just as quick as they could get 'round, and twenty guns thundered at us until we got out of reach. Several shots passed over us, one carrying away the gaff of the spanker. They sent up at least twenty rockets that showed us to them, very likely, but not long enough to make sure work. It was exciting whilst the thing lasted, and Antone was itching to bring his long pivot gun to bear, but Lafitte wouldn't hear of it. When the morning came there wasn't a sign of a——"

The narrative was here interrupted by the screams of a woman, coming from the direction of the mission. Their repetition aroused the whole party, who were at once on their feet.

"That's from Locaria's," said Hamilton, reaching for his rifle and bounding off at full speed.

"Let us all go," said Perry, following Hamilton.

The entire mess was soon making haste in the direction of the mission, although the screams had ceased.

Hamilton, the swiftest, arrived at the jacal only a little before Nathan Roach, whose far-reaching stride kept him close behind. The scene in Locaria's abode indicated the source of the screams whose utterance had put a termination to Mr. Trigg's yarn. A firelight was blazing on the hearth; a chair overturned near the door, while across the threshold lay the form of the Mexican girl. Hamilton raised her and deposited her limp form on a lounge.

"Perry, stir up the fire and let us see what is the matter with her."

"All right, Mr. Hamilton. Ain't that blood on her cheek?"

"Your are right, boy."

"Who in thunder could a-done it?" asked Nathan.

"Here, Perry, is some dry stuff, but thar's a taller dip. Light that."

The candle was lighted. An inspection disclosed a cut on the side of the head, from which a little blood had trickled down the girl's cheek. Mr. Trigg was the last one to arrive. He bent over his wounded friend, who was breathing heavily, and at once called for water to throw in her face. The water had the desired effect, causing the unfortunate to open her eyes and look wildly around at the faces bending over her. In reply to a shower of questions, she merely replied in Spanish:

"He hit me with the chair. Oh! My head! My head!"

When she finally collected herself she made known to the party the cause of the trouble.

A little after dark she suddenly beheld a man standing just inside her door. She felt no fear, bade him good evening and asked him to be seated. The intruder said he had a paper for Mr. Trigg, and had not come to be seated. She told him Mr. Trigg was in camp. To this he replied that Mr. Trigg had sent him to put the paper in a leather pouch, along with some others kept there, and asked her to get the pouch, so that he could do as directed. Having no suspicion that the man was an imposter, she went to the wallet, drew out the desired article and handed it to him. He took it deliberately to the fire and stooping down, examined several papers, one of which he selected and slipped into his pocket. Locaria's sharp eyes detected the act. She saw no paper deposited, while she knew one had been abstracted. By a little inductive reasoning of her own, she concluded the man was an imposter and that she had doubtless proven a very careless custodian of Mr. Trigg's papers. She bravely charged him with having taken out a paper, while he had put none in the pouch. To this the intruder smiled, saying she had misunderstood his words. Mr. Trigg had sent him for a paper. But Locaria was not to be so easily imposed upon a second time. She demanded the return of the paper. He made no reply, but pitched the pouch on the bed. She caught hold of his coat and told him that he could not leave with the paper. This seemed only to amuse the man, for he caught her around the waist, and chucked her under the chin. He finally attempted to leave, but she clung to him and commenced to scream. He ordered her to hush, but she screamed the louder. She remembered that he seized the chair and struck her on the head, knocking her senseless to the floor.

Mr. Trigg had proceeded to examine the pouch at the first mention of the man's confessed object in visiting the jacal, and made the unpleasant discovery that he had lost valuable papers.

After all had left the jacal except Hamilton, Perry and Mr. Trigg, the latter said:

"Do you guess what papers the fellow took?"

"I cannot imagine, unless——"

"It's the will he took, and the other papers I was showing ye."

"With the name and——

"Yes, the Portugese and the drawing."

"Who could have known?"

"None but ye both."

"What service could they be to a stranger?"

"I can't say, Mr. Hamilton, unless we had an eavesdropper that night."

"Can you suspect anyone?"

"I can't, sir."

"And you, Perry?"

"No one, unless it was Ducio."

"Prejudice, Perry."

"No, sir. Locaria described him pretty well."

CHAPTER XXXIII.

When Ducio left Locaria lying insensible from his cruel blow, he hastened to where his horse was secured, a hundred yards away. Mounting at once, he rode leisurely down to where the glade, in which his horse had been lately staked, touched the embankment, and proceeded up its grassy level until he cleared the precincts of the camp. Putting spurs to his horse he soon reached the ford and crossed to the right bank. Here he entered the plain road that led from San Jose to the town, and turned his face toward the latter. Not many minutes' ride brought him to the Mexican pickets, who challenged him.

"Quien vive?"

He replied in the same language, which he spoke after the dialect of the Spanish Creoles of Louisiana. He stated that he was a Frenchman en route to Bexar, that he was belated and had a certificate from the French consul.

The sentinel on duty took him in charge and gave him the comforting information that he must await the coming of the corporal of the guard. When at last that worthy arrived, he doubted every word that Halfen said as to his nationality and purpose in entering town. Besides, he searched his person and saddlebags and confiscated what money he could find and took his watch and pistol and among other things, the papers which had been so recently stolen from Mr. Trigg. Ducio used every argument and artifice to make him return the latter and was so very anxious in regard to them that the corporal felt sure he had captured the evidences of some infernal plot against the national government or of some deep-laid conspiracy. Ducio was conducted to town, where he was placed in the carcel, to remain until the commandante should decide if he were French and innocent, or a Texan spy, seeking martyrdom.

* * * *

Next to the padre and the monte pio, the piccadore or bull-fighter takes rank as one of the necessities of Mexican civilization. His coming is heralded with demonstrations of delight and is usually attended by the pomp and circumstance of a parade with music, fancy regalia and such exhibitions of horsemanship and peculiar dexterity, calculated to elicit manifestations of popular satisfaction. He is often admitted to the very best society, where his claim to the distinction of prominence in the category of national benefactors is freely accorded. To the rabble he is elevated beyond the ordinary plane of humanity, partaking largely of the supernatural, whence come the extraordinary powers exerted in the bull pen. The reader had divined that the party which Beatrice saw passing her father's house, with music playing and clad in fancy costumes, was that of the toreador with whom Ruiz had left the Texan camp, disguised in their dress and so transformed in appearance that he had not been recognized until he had resumed his natural voice. When the toreador's party reached the Mexican lines, they did not suffer the detention which was in waiting for Ducio, for their avocation constituted a passport not to be questioned even under the harsh rules and summary methods of Mexican military law. When the gay party entered the main plaza, a large per centage of the admiring population were on hand to greet the welcome arrival. The music was started afresh, the ponies of the lancers plunged and pranced, while the riders displayed much admirable horsemanship.

Ruiz was a splendid horseman and was equal to the emergency. He cast a curious look towards the priest's house, as he passed, and saw Guy standing in the door, taking in the scene in which his quondam friend was little suspected of being an actor. He ventured to throw a salute to the young American, but Guy gave no sign that he considered himself recognized by a toreador, supposed to be fresh from Monterey. Senor Trevino amused the populace by making a circuit of the square and announcing in loud tones his purpose to fight the fiercest bull that could be obtained on the range of Bexar.

"That's a splendid fellow, and rides well. He would make a fine looking officer. Don't you think so, Sancho?"

"Your brain is always full of fine looks and brass buttons." replied Sancho. "Perhaps a lively sense of your own failing has created a morbid longing for what nature denied you."

"Sancho's companion was a sallow, thin-visaged little man with very prominent features, and was apparaled in the uniform of a lieutenant of the staff.

"I am not envious, at all events. There is no harm in admiring in others, what we cannot ourselves possess," replied the lieutenant.

"Forgive me, Pedro. Your reply deserves an apology. There goes your handsome toreador down Main Street. Shall we follow with the other pelados?"

"No. For a wonder I have something to do. The general is thinking of sending Colonel Ugartachea to the Rio Grande for the expected reinforcements, and I have a quantity of writing to do.

Letters, you know, to the president and other matters such as reports and requisitions."

"I see; I see. Well, I give you credit for denying yourself a run after the toreador, to attend to business."

"I am an officer, Sancho; an officer all over," replied the lieutenant, stiffening himself to as full a height as five feet four would allow him.

"Yes," said Sancho, surveying him deliberately, "an officer all over. Buttons and lace from head to foot. It is a pity Mexico did not have more soldiers and fewer officers."

"Come to headquarters tomorrow morning, say at ten. I may be able to let you know all about the matter we were speaking of."

"It is well. You may look for me, Pedro."

The little officer moved away with an air that aimed to be military and suggest importance. Sancho followed him with his eyes for a moment.

"The little ass," he muttered, and moved away in the wake of the shouting populace.

The toreadors had made the length of the street, and were now returning to the plaza. Sancho leaned lazily against the corner, commanding a view of their approach. He carelessly scanned their faces until the last one was about to pass, when the pony the fellow was riding became frightened, plunged, reared and fell back. The rider escaped injury by a wonderful agility, and when the animal recovered his feet, he regained the saddle by a bound. A shout went up as he surveyed the crowd and waved his hand.

"Por via de mi madre!" exclaimed Sancho. "I know that eye. Where have I seen that eye before?"

He gazed after the active toreador, musing on the expression of his eyes as they had mutely boasted of his feat.

Sancho turned up Solidad street, muttering to himself:

"The man who owns that pair of eyes has been intimate with me some time. But he! He is a toreador. Of course, I am mistaken."

The next morning Sancho kept his appointment with the little lieutenant of the staff. Headquarters presented a lively appearance at the hour of his visit, the front grounds being filled with knots of officers and soldiers and crossed by arriving and departing orderlies. Sancho found his friend in the hallway, dismissing a soldier with instructions, that were imparted with all the importance of manner that so slight a stature could assume. At the conclusion of this duty the lieutenant led the way to the rear office, looking out upon the river.

"This is a quiet retreat," observed Sancho.

"It's the general's sanctum," replied Pedro. "Himself and staff are the only privileged ones here."

"Then I had better retire."

"By no means. You are my guest."

The two men seated themselves at a low, green-covered table occupying the center of the apartment, and on which evidences of the character of the office were placed, in the shape of military orders, reports and letters, while a handsome sword with ornamented belt lay across one end.

"By the way, Sancho, I want to show you a paper taken from a fellow last night, who claims to be a Frenchman and who entered our lines on the Matamoras road. The general thinks it may have some meaning important to us, and the fellow is from the rebel camp. What do you think about it?"

Pedro handed his friend the paper taken from Mr. Trigg's pouch the evening before and which, among other things, the guard had confiscated when Ducio was made a prisoner. Sancho smoothed the paper out upon the table and commenced to examine it.

"This is a plan of something," said Sancho. "The ship would make it appear that this is the outline of a sea coast. The letters and characters on it appear to be references to an explanation of the plan."

"What can be that double row of circles?" asked the lieutenant. "And that mark like an S, that runs nearly through the figure. And that straight mark across? It looks like a road. See! Here it crosses the stream and these are two bridges."

"I believe you are right, amigo," said Sancho. "If so, then there is no meaning in this paper that portends evil to us."

The friends scrutinized the documents under examination for some minutes longer and discussed the probable mission of the alleged Frenchman, from whom it had been taken.

The paper itself, as had been stated by Sancho, had the appearance of containing the outlines of a coast on two sides. The upper coast was bordered by two rows of circular marks running parallel, commencing on the right, from where an "S" like tracing, that might have been intended for a bayou, made its exit into a body of water. The first three of the outer row of circles were marked one, two and three, in figures. The first two of the inner row were marked one and two. Across the figures, from coast to coast, ran two parallel lines, as of a road, which intersected the S at two points. On the lower side and below the figures was the rude tracing of a ship under bare poles. Opposite the ship, and through which ran the road, were several rectangular figures that might have indicated houses. Such was about the divination of the problem by the little lieutenant and his friend, Sancho.

* * * *

"Father, what sort of a prisoner was it, who was brought last night?"

"Well, if I tell you? You women are over-curious. It was late enough for you to be asleep; but no, you are awake listening for prisoners to come, so you can be getting soft-hearted about their not having beds and so on. I'll tell you nothing."

"You are in a bad humor, father. It was the noise you made that awoke me. You were very angry and talked loud enough to awake the soundest sleeper."

"And haven't I enough to make all the saints mad, from St. Stephen down? When I peddled oranges in Lisbon I could save more money in one month than I can now in twelve; and no bother. A man can run his legs off now and no thanks for it; only blame."

"You spoke of giving this up."

"Give it up! Give it up! Yes, and starve."

"Then there is no danger of starving here? Then let us be contented until times are better."

"Better! Better! Great chance of getting better. El pajarro had money, but it was precious little I got. And now this Frenchman has been——"

"A Frenchman?"

"There! I've gone and told you that much. A Frenchman he is. He tried to get through the lines and of course the soldiers stripped him of the last cent and I got the leavings."

"Poor fellow! If he has been robbed, he better deserves our attention."

"Well, instead of prating so much about him, get him a tortilla and a cup of coffee. That's more than he is able to pay for."

In a few minutes Linda had prepared food for the prisoners and her father was shuffling across the court with it, covered by a napkin. He entered the passage and stopped before the same cell where Guy Raymond had been confined. He drew forth the ponderous key, deliberately placed it in the lock, and shot back the bolts.

As the door swung open, Bonito was greeted by a voice not at all indicative of that equanimity that results from contentment with surroundings.

"You dog of a jailer! You said you would return last night and furnish me with something to rest upon, even if it were a little straw."

"Straw, indeed! Am I made of straw?"

"You'd not ask if I had something to tip you with, you old tub of fat. You cowardly devils will pay for ill treating a subject of France."

"Ill treating? And here I am with a tortilla and a cup of steaming coffee for your breakfast."

As Bonito said this, he pulled aside the napkin, and was surprised to find that the menu exceeded the bill of fare just announced.

"Por via de mi madre!" he exclaimed. "Ill treatment, indeed! Here that foolish child of mine has sent you what is doubtless a part of her own rations. Ill treatment! With this pile of tortillas, two eggs and a chop, and not a centado do I get for it."

"I'll not complain of my breakfast, Mr. Jailer, but your lodging is contemptible. A civilized people would not put a dog in such a hole, without something to lie on."

"It will be your fault, Mr. Frenchy, if you are without a bed."

"How so, Fatty?" asked Ducio, taking the coffee and tasting it.

"A real or two will find you one."

"Must I buy a bed, you old heathen?"

"No, no. Only pay two reals a week."

"Week?"

"Seven days. Payment in advance, and on the afternoon of the seventh, the fourteenth, the twenty-first, the ——"

"That's enough, you old thief. I'll not be here the seventh day."

"No telling, senor. But three reals for one week is not too much for a good, clean shuck bed, with a blanket. But no pillow at that price—pillows are scarce, senor. The tame geese died off, from a goose epidemic, and the wild ones—the wild ones, senor——"

"Now you are hatching up a lie," said Ducio, eating his chop. "You are not even a skilled liar, Mr. Jailer. These miserable tortillas are not fit for a dog to eat. Why can't you Mexicans make bread like civilized people?"

"That's an insult to Linda! She made those tortillas, and a better cook is not in Bexar. I am not a Mexican, Senor Frenchy, any more than yourself."

"What country then, brought forth such a caricature on human shape?"

"I am a Portugese."

"A Portugese?"

"Ducio started, as a thought struck him. He repeated the words after the jailer deliberately, and remembered that the fellow with the long name, mentioned by Mr. Trigg as the depositary of the paper that Hamilton and Perry were to secure in case of his death, was a Portugese. The papers taken by the sergeant of the guard had been depended on by him, and the name had slipped his memory. He would know it if repeated. He at once determined to sound the jailer.

"Two reals for a bed!" he said, as if turning the price over in his own mind.

"Was it not three, senor? Three, I said."

"Well three, if you insist."

"I don't think it was four, but——"

"Say, Mr. Jailer. I don't know your name, but how many——"

"Bonito, senor, Bonito. A few have the impudence to call me 'old Bonito.'".

"Well, Bonito, are there many of your countrymen in Bexar?"

"Not one, senor. I am the only one who had so little brains as to come here. A man would starve if he was not careful. Not a real, except the miserable pay of jailer, has Bonito had since el pajarro left this cell. What is four reals for a bed for seven——"

"Four? Make it ten or twenty, or more, for all the good it will do you; but look, you, Senor Bonito, there must be another Portugese here besides yourself, for I have his name in my papers and would like much to find him out."

"And I tell you, Mr. Frenchy, that Bonito knows to a certainty. He has not been in Bexar for more than a dozen years, with his eyes shut and his ears stopped."

The conversation was interrupted by the appearance of a corporal and two soldiers, who halted in the court, while the non-commissioned officer called to Bonito. The latter gathered up the remnants of Ducio's breakfast and, waiter in hand, shuffled to the doorway going into the yard. The corporal had come for the French prisoner, who was wanted at the headquarters of the commanding general.

Ducio was not loth to quit his cell, and high hopes filled his breast to be able to convince the authorities of his assumed nationality and pacific mission into the city. The corporal walking along by his side and the two soldiers following in the rear, they took the way to the plaza, and turned down towards the entrance of the main street. A crowd was assembled near this point and just as they reached the corner, the toreadors rode through it, from Soledad street, passing near the soldiers, who stopped with their prisoner to see the sight. Ducio recognized the party as the same which had left the Texan camp, but was ignorant of the presence of Ruiz among their number. The latter and Trevino rode side by side and when within a step or two of where stood Ducio, the fancifully colored lasso that Ruiz carried at the horn of his saddle became disengaged and he dismounted quickly to recover it. The act brought him face to face with the Creole, whose presence so surprised him, that he involuntarily expressed it in an ejaculation in his natural tone of voice. Quickly recovering his self-possession, however, he mounted and dashed to the side of his companion.

Ducio's keen observation, assisted by the unguarded utterance of the other, caused him to recognize Ruiz.

"What can he be doing here?" he muttered. He was hand in glove with that smart mess of Hamilton, Trigg and Co's. He is doubtless here as a spy. Perhaps my recognition of him may help me out of my scrape."

*   *   *   *

Sancho and the little lieutenant were interrupted in their examination of Ducio's papers by the entrance of General Cos, who seated himself at the green table a few moments before the alleged French subject was ushered into the apartment.

The General did not raise his eyes until he had completed the signatures he was affixing to several documents spread out before him.

Meanwhile Ducio stood biting his lip in sheer vexation at the indifference to his presence, as well as on account of the impudent ogling to which he was subjected from Sancho and the lace covered lieutenant of the staff.

"Who have we here?" asked General Cos, when he finally looked up.

"This is the fellow who had the mysterious paper," explained the lieutenant.

"The Frenchman, eh?" said Cos, with a full breath and an ironical emphasis. He gave Ducio a severe look, then asked him in French:

"Vous etes Francais?"

"Oui, monsieur."

"Que faites vous ici?"

"Seulement pour voir le pays."

"He speaks French, at all events," said the general, turning to his companions.

"You speak Spanish also?"

"Tolerably well"

"Let me see his passport, lieutenant."

The man of gold lace selected a paper from a pile and handed it to the general, who looked it over carefully.

"This seems to be an official document, and you answer the description perfectly. What other evidence have you of your neutrality in this rebellion?"

Ducio thought a moment, then said:

"If I point you out a real spy in your midst, one whom you know to be a rebel, and my indication of him leads to his capture, will that prove my innocence sufficient to cause my release?"

"It will."

"Write it down that it will. Sign it and give it to me and I will disclose who is here as a spy."

"Can he be captured today?"

"In a few minutes."

The general took a pen and wrote a few lines, signed his name and handed it to Ducio. The latter scanned it curiously, then with satisfaction, folded it and placed it in his pocket.

The lieutenant whispered to the general, who interrupted Ducio as he was about to speak.

"Hold, sir! What about this paper?"

That—that—that is a little sketch of the outlines of Galveston island, where the town stands. I made those outlines the day I stayed there."

"But the letters and marks?"

Ducio answered with a ready lie:

"They are references to an explanation I sent with a letter to my sister. I forgot to put it in my letter."

"Well! Who is this spy?"

"Ruiz."

'Where is he to be found?"

"Disguised as a toreador."

"Santa Maria!" exclaimed Sancho; "I thought I knew those eyes."

CHAPTER XXXIV.

Ruiz was at a loss to account for the appearance of Ducio in the town, and in the custody of the military. He supposed that he must have been captured without the lines, either in a skirmish or by having ventured too closely to the Mexican outposts. In the many surmises which passed rapidly through his mind, he imagined that the prisoner might have been commissioned with a message for him from the camp and had been indiscreet enough to brave capture in the attempt to communicate with him. The thought bothered him exceedingly; the more so as he felt confident that the Creole had recognized him. There were not more than three men in San Antonio in whom he would have been willing to confide the secret of his presence within the hostile lines. These were Father Ignacio, Jose and Guy Raymond. Troubled with his thoughts, Ruiz found himself opposite the priest's house, and saw the major domo standing in the front entrance, looking and gaping like the rest of the populace at the show of which he formed a part. The toreadors stopped here and Trevino ordered the music to play in honor of the good priest, before whose house they had halted.

Ruiz took advantage of this to interview Jose. Under the pretence of wanting a drink of water, he dismounted, threw his reins to a piccador and approached the door.

"Senor, I want to get a drink of water." Ruiz used his natural tone of voice, which caused Jose to regard him closely.

"Enter, senor; I will bring it."

"Allow me to go back with you."

Jose was puzzled at the familiar voice, but invited the toreador to follow him. Arrived at the court, Ruiz caught him by the arm and said:

"Jose, don't you know me?"

"Senor Ruiz! A toreador?"

"Yes, Jose! but you must not give me away."

"Por nada, senor," responded Jose earnestly.

Ruiz then hurriedly communicated to his friend the fact of the presence of a young man from the Texas camp as a prisoner. He wanted Jose to find out how he came in the town and to ascertain anything else in connection with his capture and detention. Jose promised to faithfully endeavor to get all the information as speedily as possible. Ruiz returned to his masquerading while the other departed with alacrity on his errand. He had no difficulty in tracing the prisoner and the file of soldiers to headquarters. Here he was a little puzzled how to proceed. He strode up and down for a few minutes, like the sentinel who was walking his post, trying to devise some excuse to go into the building, and into the office of the general if necessary. Finally a thought seemed to strike him, and he boldly entered the hall. The first door to the right was the office of the adjutant general. It was vacant, but as Jose poked his head in he heard voices to the rear, the sounds coming through a door communicating to the back veranda overlooking the river. He quietly entered the room and noiselessly approached the back door and took a seat, ostensibly to await the coming of the occupants of the room. His new position enabled him to hear distinctly what was being said on the veranda.

There were two speakers.

"This fellow Ruiz must be shot," said one voice.

"He is a murderer," said the other.

"Murderer?"

'Yes; he killed a poor devil named Vasquez and threw the body in the river."

"What do you think of this Frenchman, Sancho?"

"He may be all right. He will deserve his liberty anyway for letting us know that the traitor Ruiz is in our lines masquerading as a toreador."

"You said this American had something to do with the murder of Vasquez."

"He did. Besides, he murdered Vasquez's brother when he was with the Lipans. The last crime, doubtless, committed to destroy all proof of the first."

"And Father Ignacio protects such a serpent?"

"He is living on the fat of the land."

"Will the general order his arrest?"

"If he don't it won't be much trouble to put him out of the way."

As this was said, Sancho and the lieutenant walked into the adjutant's office. Jose, to all appearances, was fast asleep, with his head bent over on his hand. His long, heavy respiration indicated oblivion to all perceptible things.

"Por todos los Santos!" exclaimed the lieutenant. "Whom have we here?"

"A borachon?" suggested Sancho, giving Jose a shove.

Jose jumped up, rubbing his eyes, having all the appearance of awaking from a deep sleep.

"The adjutant general has not come?" he asked, rubbing his eyes.

"Why this is the major domo."

"Si, senor," said Jose. "I have a message from Father Ignacio, and while waiting I fell asleep."

"Too much Cabeza de Toro, Jose," said Sancho, laughing.

'Late hours and mescal."

"What is your message?" asked the lieutenant. "I will deliver it."

"The Padre Ignacio heard you had taken some prisoners and he wanted to know if any of them were Catholics.'

No, no, Jose; only one who is a Frenchman; but he will be released some time today," said Sancho.

Jose excused himself after begging the officer and Sancho not to let Father Ignacio know that he had gone sound asleep at headquarters while on his business.

When Jose returned to the plaza the toreadors had disappeared, but he followed in the wake of the music and overtook them as they neared the dwelling of the Senora de la Torre, on Flores street. He attracted the attention of Ruiz by shouting above the vivas of the mob so that the former could distinguish his voice and know that he wished to communicate with him. His ruse proved successful, for the amateur bull-fighter dismounted, and leading his horse to one side, loosened the saddle girth as if something had gone wrong with it. Jose was soon at his side.

"Well?"

"You are betrayed, senor. You will be arrested. Senor Raymond is in danger also. You and he are charged with the murder of Vasquez."

"From what you heard, think you they will act before night?",

"The military act quickly, senor."

"You are right, Jose. I'll have to use my wits, and right quickly."

"Come, amigo. I have it!" said Jose, throwing the reins of the horse to one of the men who had approached to know what was the matter. "Hold the senor's horse; we'll be gone but a moment."

Jose, without further ceremony, took the arm of Ruiz, who permitted the major domo to conduct him to the sidewalk, where a narrow passage afforded entrance behind a wall that concealed a jacal, in front of which sat an ancient Aztec stooping over some basketwork.

"Alejo, we want to say something in private," said Jose, after accosting the old man with a good morning. "Can we go a moment in your room?"

"Si, si! Entre, entre," replied the old fellow with the most stoical indifference.

"What do you propose to do here, Jose?" asked Ruiz.

"Change clothes with you."

"But you will suffer if——"

"We haven't a moment to lose. Off with that rig," interrupted Jose, pulling off his jacket and following it up by rapidly divesting himself of his pants. Ruiz, without further objections, imitated his friend, and in an incredibly short time they stood, each metamorphosed in appearance.

"I believe we are the same size, Jose."

"No time for comments, senor; "I must get to my horse, and you—"

"I will take care of myself, amigo mio."

The two embraced in the most fraternal manner.

Jose returned to the street, mounted Ruiz's steed, and rejoined the toreadors.

The late toreador, habilitated in the garments of the late major domo, asked a question or two of the venerable basket-maker, who replied curtly, without raising his head from his task.

Ruiz paused a moment, watching Alejo twist in and out the rushes from which he was constructing his baskets, apparently happy and contented, at any rate indifferent to everything else.

"Occupation! Occupation!" thought Ruiz; "it constitutes nine-tenths of contentment."

With this philosophical thought, he turned away, and going to the rear of the shanty, he jumped a dilapidated wall, landing in a yard of spacious dimensions, on one side of which ran the ascequia of gurgling water, darkened by the shadows of a row of stately cottonwoods. He turned quickly to the right and followed the wall over which he had leaped for perhaps fifty steps. This brought him to a gate, which he opened without hesitation, and passed through into a narrow court that terminated where an open door and window overlooked its pavement. At the window sat a lady manipulating some white material, bending over her work as she deftly passed a pair of scissors through it. The step upon the flags attracted her attention.

"What do you wish here?" she asked quickly.

"I come to see you."

"To see me?"

"And the Senorita Josefa."

"And may I ask who so honors us with a visit through the back gate?"

"An unusual way, I admit, to gain entrance to a private house, but your brother's major domo need not be over ceremonious."

"My brother's major domo?"

"Well, well; I see the dress has not entirely transformed me. Jose and I exchanged clothes a little while ago. He is now a gallant toreador, to all appearance, while I, your old friend Manuel Ruiz, am masquerading in his garments for prudential reasons."

"Senor Ruiz!"

"Do you not recognize me?"

"Your voice, but the loss of beard takes away every means of identification. How does it happen that you have put yourself in danger?"

Ruiz thought best to dissemble.

"Anxiety to see Josefa caused me to come in disguise as a torcador. By accident I was recognized by an enemy and forced to seek this new disguise and your house as an asylum until the darkness of night can facilitate my escape."

"Josefa is not at home. However, come in the house, lest some one be on your trail and catch a glimpse of you."

Ruiz had stood opposite the window through whose grated opening the Senora de la Torre had addressed to him her remarks. When she had uttered her last words of caution she withdrew from the window, and reappearing the next moment at the door, bade her visitor to enter. She cast a searching glance at him as he did so as if half in doubt that it was really Ruiz, so changed indeed was his appearance from loss of beard and from a darker hue which some preparation had lent to his physiognomy. He noticed her expression, laughed as he explained his painstaking at disguisement, and reflected how comical he must appear in the eyes of the senora, who had always seen him in the garb of a well dressed caballero. He was almost glad that Josefa was away, yet she would return and find him there. It would perhaps be best to bring back some of the old look to his face by removing the unnatural complexion the artificial appliance had produced. A hint to this effect to the hostess was followed by directions to go into the adjoining room, where he would find soap, water and towels.

"It is Josefa's apartment," she said. "When you finish your toilet you can come into the sitting-room, where we will await her return."

Ruiz found himself in a tidy apartment that bore evidences of its mistress' taste and care. He felt half tempted to forego his intention and not disturb the exquisite order of the room, but a glance in the mirror that had so often reflected Josefa's face, caused him to renew his first determination. When he finally viewed himself in the glass and was about to turn away satisfied with the change, he caught sight of a crampled paper that the draught had carried against the iron bars of the window, where it was securely lodged. Impelled by curiosity, perhaps, or a nameless impulse, he reached for it and found on a hasty inspection that it was addressed to Guy Raymond, and signed by Beatrice.

"How came this here?" he asked mentally, at the same time placing it in his pocket. "She has suspected me of loving Beatrice and here I find a letter from Beatrice to the young American. Can she have intercepted this for a purpose? Josefa is a strange girl. A girl to be afraid of if she imagined herself wronged."

It was afternoon before Josefa returned. Ruiz had passed the time rather impatiently. The object of his coming within the hostile lines seemed about to be defeated by the merest accident, and his life was in great danger, now that his presence had been made known by Ducio Halfen. He must necessarily be a prisoner within the house of the De la Torre's until night, when the darkness would permit his exit; but where to go unless it would be back to the Texan camp, he had not the remotest idea.

Ducio was promptly released and was allowed to repossess his papers and money, although the latter was short from an assessment levied by the guard. To this he submitted without a murmur for fear that complaint might compromise his safety. The streets were almost clear of people as he issued from the grounds of the headquarters, but on reaching the main plaza he could hear the shouts of the crowd mingled with the music of the toreadors as they passed up Flores street. He thought of his treachery to Ruiz and wondered if the latter had already experienced its effects. Danger to himself might result from the betrayal of the clever Mexican; but that was in the future. And what cared Ducio for danger in no wise impending?

Selfish natures, planning and plotting immoral acts, are so absorbed in their narrow propensities that they are as dead to premonitions of disaster as they are lost to any emotions involving conscience or honor. His character was that of the grasping, greedy and unprincipled world that would trample upon any human right to secure selfish ends. He was that world individualized. As Ducio strolled along the wall separating Linda's garden from the plaza, a tall lady, whose features were concealed by her rebosa, swept by him and entered that cozy retreat by the doorway in advance of him. Just before she disappeared she cast a hurried glance at the stranger, when their eyes met for an instant, and Ducio, looking after her, caught sight of the interior before the door could be closed.

"Those were piercing eyes, and fine ones," he muttered.

While he was thus musing he found himself in front of the monte pio's, with the proprietor lolling lazily in his door.

"Will you tell me who is your neighbor, with that door in the wall that opens into the garden?" he asked of the monte pio.

"That?" asked the latter, leaning out slightly. "That is the place where Bonito, the jailor, lives. If you want to see him, however, you must go to the next street and go through the jail. That gate is the private entrance for his daughter, the Senorita Linda. Does the senor want me to show him the jail?"

"No, thanks; I can easily find it. But you may tell me who was the lady that just entered that gate. Was she Bonito's daughter?"

"No, senor; it must have been the Senorita de la Torre, who is a frequent visitor to the Senorita Linda."

"Do you know a Portuguese in Bexar, Senor Monte Pio?"

"No, senor, unless it be Bonito.."

"Has none other been here and afterwards gone away? Think well. If you put me on the right track I will reward you."

"Are you a detective, senor?"

"Not at all. I seek a man whose interest it is to see me."

"You may see Bonito and tell him the gist of the interest and perhaps the knowledge of its importance may assist his memory."

"How assist it?"

"Some little particular may recall the presence of a transient countryman."

"He so worships money, perhaps a peso would be more effective."

The monte pio gave a shrug and Ducio passed on. He reflected as he walked:

"Bonito! Bonito! There was nothing Portuguese in such a name. The jailer was stupidity personified, but he loved a real. He must return to the carcel for his effects, and he would try to win the old fellow's confidence and let time draw out what he wished to know. If fortune was to be his, it would come. He would seize opportunities as they would present themselves, not endeavor to force the decrees of fate.

The court of the carcel was vacant when the Creole entered. The door leading to the jailor's apartments stood ajar; just enough open to invite a push, or repel intrusion by one unaccustomed to cross its threshold.

Ducio hesitated, then raised his hand, perhaps to knock, but arrested the motion as the sounds of voices issued from within.

They were female voices.

To a moderate knock from Ducio there was no answer. A moment's hesitation, then the door yielded to his push, disclosed the hallway with the lounge on the right side opposite the room whence the voices still issued. Ducio had an investigating disposition. He moved quietly, taking in the apartment and noting the two other places of exit, one at the end of the hall, the other quite opposite the room he knew to be occupied. Ducio listened as the voices grew distinct.

"I certainly must have dropped a letter, which I thought was secure in my pocket. I wanted you to deliver it to the owner, Linda."

"A letter! For me to deliver?"

"Yes. I will explain. I was going down to see my uncle, I picked up a letter lying in the street in front of San Fernando. To my surprise it was addressed to Guy Raymond, and signed 'Beatrice.' The letter was in English."

"And you have lost it?"

"Perhaps. I can't find it, although I was quite positive that it was in my pocket when I left home."

"Why did you wish me to deliver it, Josefa?"

"Because, I like neither the writer nor the one addressed."

"Josefa! Jealous?"

"Yes, if you would know it—jealous."

"But you have seen so little of Senor Raymond."

"Your American friend is nothing to me. The Senorita Navarro has doubtless captured him also, as the letter I found would disclose if translated.

"She came between me and Manuel Ruiz, who also fell a victim to her American accomplishments. Now I hate Ruiz, but I will never forgive Beatrice Navarro."

"How bad it will be for me to have two friends who are enemies."

"If they were all guileless like you, Linda——

"But if Senor Ruiz had fancied me——

"I should have forgiven him and held you guiltless."

"I am not so sure of that, amiga mia."

Ducio was listening attentively up to this point of the conversation and had moved noiselessly past the lounge until he could peep into the open door, which led into the opposite room. Half turning from a hasty glance into that apartment, what was his surprise to see the blanket covered mattress of the lounge rise at one end, without any apparent agency, until it doubled back and disclosed the head, shoulders and back of Bonito, who appeared to emerge from the depths below. The jailer's face was turned from the Creole as his burly frame rose, as it were, by steps from under the lounge.

Ducio, at a loss what to make of such a proceeding, felt that he was an accidental witness of something that might involve a secret, and retired at once into the room, curious to see what had placed him in his present position. There was nothing whatever behind which he could conceal himself; no way of egress by which to escape, except through the hall, where Bonito could be heard a moment later shuffling along. Ducio listened, and the steps ceased at the further end of the passage he had just left. Feeling this to be his opportunity, he slipped quickly out, passed by the rearranged lounge and stood once more in the court. He felt repressed at what he had seen; his chest heaved and for a moment he felt non-plussed. It was momentary, however, with Ducio. He reprimanded himself and instantly knocked loudly on the door.

"Diablo! Quieres quebrar la puerta!" came in response from the effeminate voice of Bonito.

"You! And where is your guard?" he said as he confronted Ducio.

"I have dispensed with guards, amigo. I am free."

"And you want your things?"

"Those taken from my pockets? Yes—the other—no matter at this moment."

"Remain here then—no—you must be a gentleman and all right to get out of their clutches. Walk in there with Linda while I get what you ask for. She has company, but it is no one but—walk right in; but stay, Senor Frenchy, you promised me four reals, and now——"

"Anything you say, Bonito," interrupted Ducio. "Only get me what I want and you shall have it your way."

"Five reals," muttered Bonito, turning away just as Ducio stepped upon the threshold to enter Linda's room.

CHAPTER XXXV.

A taste for reading and study was a fortunate circumstance in the character of Guy Raymond. The trait was commended by the good priest of San Fernando, who wondered why a youth of habits so sedate and a mind so cultivated would not yield to the evidences that so clearly substantiated the claims of dogmatic religion. Guy's agnosticism called forth protest after protest from Father Ignacio, while Father Nicholas owned to saying a mass for the reclamation of the young unbeliever. The object of their solicitude was somewhat stocial under these attempts to convert him to a belief in miraculous intervention of a Diety who had chosen to assert his personality only in ages when the human mind was so steeped in ignorance that it was ready to accept any theory of a cosmos which pandered to the instinctive longings of the heart. This sentiment only worried his pious friends and caused them to plan new methods by which to instill into the young American a religious bent. Even Jose had related to Guy numerous experiences, among which were repeated interpositions of St. Anthony, who had brought him good luck often when he least deserved it. But the evidence of the major domo failed of effect, and Guy still remained the subject of well meant solicitude. The sudden passion with which the beautiful Beatrice had inspired him had caused a conflict between literature and love. He frequently saw from behind the printed lines of his volume the mobile features of the beauty, or read between them the remembered words which her soft tones had articulated. The severance of intercourse with the Navarro abode influenced him in remaining within doors as interest in exterior things had diminished in ratio with his ability to interview the girl who filled his thoughts. Despite his power of self control he could not avoid the inevitable depression that must follow disappointment in young love's dream. The appearance of the toreadors with their extravagant costumes and grotesque movements had elicited the first smile that had broken the melancholy of his features since Navarro pere had bowed him from the house. The bull-fighters formed a topic for conversation in the leisure hours of Father Ignacio. He explained the manner of conducting these exhibitions with all the cruel details of the torture of the animals, the risk of the toreador and the final coup de grace that ended the scene.

"Do you not think such fights an unwarranted cruelty to the animals, and unworthy of our civilization?" asked Guy.

"By no means," replied Father Ignacio. "It is a national custom which the church has never condemned. Animals were made for man's gratification and it matters not if they be killed to supply physical or mental food. When we eat them it nourishes our bodies; when we kill them in the bull-pen for recreation it is a healthy diversion."

"But cruelty even in necessary destruction of animal life should be abhorent to the refined mind. It seems to me that it is rather a strained position to assume that bull-killing is a necessary diversion."

The argument lasted for a considerable time, without resulting in the conversion of either to the other's position. It was late in the afternoon of the day when Ruiz and Jose had exchanged clothing that this debate took place. Father Ignacio had duties at the church, and

Guy sallied forth for a ramble. He took his way down the Calle de la Carcel. Senora Candelario greeted him as he passed her shop with "buenas tardes," and looked after him with ill concealed admiration, his fair complexion and handsome appearance being irresistable charms in the eyes of the senoritas, while it excited the envy of the men. He passed the carcel and the Cabeza de Toro and continued his walk until the little foot bridge above the ford was reached. The old millwheel was slowly turning, just touched by the seething current, as it shot foaming and spurting past the narrow way into the wide and shallow ford below.

Guy had been told that here his enemy, Vasquez, had been thrown after having been murdered, and as he leaned over the rail and gazed into the limpid waters, down to the soft depths, carpeted with watercress and mosses, his thoughts wandered back to the Indian fight, where by his bravery he had won the title of El Bravo, and where he had captured the saddle that Vasquez had identified as his brother's property. The murder of his accuser had probably saved his life. He thought of the Indian village, and wondered how fared Laoni, and Pedro and Chicha. If Walumpta had blamed Laoni for his escape. His reflections continued in this channel for some time when he felt suddenly the weight of two great paws, and then beheld Rolla capering about him with a piece of his rope still tied around his neck.

"How did you get loose, old fellow? Gnawed your rope, no doubt."

"No," he continued, examining the rope, "cut by a sharp knife. Who could have done it?"

He fondled the dog for awhile, then taking hold of him, he threw him into the water.

"There, take, a bath since you would come."

Rolla came to the surface at once and, swimming to the shore, shook the water from his body. He came cavorting back to his master, but manifested no disposition to have the experiment repeated.

Guy was still laughing at Rolla's ducking when the tramp of feet upon the bridge attracted his attention, and he beheld a file of four soldiers approaching under the command of a corporal. He stood to one side to make way for them on the narrow bridge, but was rather surprised when the officer laid his hands upon his shoulder and stated he had orders for his arrest.

"Are you not mistaken?" he asked.

"No, not mistaken. Is that your dog?"

"Yes—but why?"

"I went to the priest's house for you and was told that you were gone. The mozo said that this was your dog, and I cut his rope and took him to the door where you went out. He took your trail and we followed him."

"Rolla, poor fellow, you betrayed me."

The dog looked earnestly at his master, then at the soldier, whose hand still rested on his prisoner, and muttered a low growl. He seemed to comprehend that there was trouble.

Guy tried to pump his captor, but he knew nothing, and there being no recourse, he submitted to be taken back over the route by which he had just reached the bridge. He walked beside the corporal until the carcel was reached, when he was conducted through the old corridor and into the court just as the night sentinel was taking his post.

"El Pajarro!"

This exclamation burst from Bonito's lips as he issued from his door and saw his old prisoner again in the toils. The uplifted hands accompanying the exclamation retained their position for a moment, as the old jailer still regarded the prisoner with expressions first of surprise, followed by regret, then satisfaction, all struggling for the mastery.

The soldiers witnessed this demonstration at rest, while the sentry paused in his walk, and Rolla, upon his haunches close by his master, completed the momentary tableau.

"A prisoner?"

"Yes, Bonito; but for what I know not."

"The orders are to keep this man closely confined," said the corporal.

"Whose orders?"

"The adjutant general's."

"Very well, senor corporal. I know my duty."

Guy sat down upon the bench wondering what could be the charge against him. The squad left and Bonito sat down beside him.

"I will have to take the fellow out of your old cell, for it is the best one in the place."

"Am I to be confined alone?"

"You may go in with him; but he is a drunken fool of a toreador, and——"

"A toreador?"

"A toreador. He was brought here beastly drunk, and he is not quite sober yet."

"Put me in, Bonito. I want to get acquainted with him. I want to know a toreador."

Bonito made haste to prepare a bed for his old prisoner, now come back; but he refrained from telling Linda at once, as he knew it would pain her to learn that the handsome American was again in limbo.

Bonito took good care to tell Candelario that Guy was a prisoner and to hint that his supper from her cusine would be acceptable. The good senora responded by sending a savory dish with tortillas and chocolate.

When Guy entered his cell after supper he stretched his limbs upon a comfortable bed, and, notwithstanding the labored breathing of his fellow prisoner in the further corner, he dropped off to sleep.

Doubtless the rough experiences that had attended the late fortunes of Guy Raymond had hardened his sensibility to any sudden change in their forecast prophetic of evil. To a naturally philosophic turn, he had added the advantage of a knowledge of human nature, gained from a varied source, and had utilized it in the study of individuality and of race. The readiness with which he accommodated himself to his cell and the ease with which he lapsed into slumber perhaps may have been greatly due to his intimate relations with his jailor, the friendship of Linda, and the tender, good will of Candelario, whose edibles were always at his command when a prisoner. In fact, reflections embracing much of this line of thought absorbed him as the consciousness of waking reality became merged into the weird phantasms of dreamland. Here Candelario met him with a basket, hid beneath the folds of a snowy cover, and beckoned him to follow. She led him through the dark streets until they emerged into the country. Before him were mountains, craggy and steep, to which she pointed encouragingly. He followed, as it were, under a spell that deprived him of any power to object to her guidance.

Suddenly they entered an opening in the side of the highest mountain, which he recognized as the silver mine above the village of the Lipans. Candelario caused him to seat himself beside her and to partake of the viands in the basket. She gave him to understand that he would have need of all his strength and must fortify the inner man to be able to perform a task. At the conclusion of the repast she produced a pick and directed him to displace a square flagstone. He mechanically took the tool and began to pick a breach on the further edge to introduce a lever. The strokes rang through the mine and echoed from hill-girt valley. Under the rapid blows of his pick the purpose was soon accomplished· and he looked around for a fulcrum, but in vain. Finally his companion threw him a skull, with a motion indicating that the revolting remnant of humanity would suffice. Guy reluctantly pushed it into position, and then introducing the handle of his pick into the hole he had made, pried up the stone and threw it over. This disclosed the entrance to a subterrean vault with steps whose outline, barely distinguishable, were lost in the obscurity below. Candelario motioned him to descend. He hesitated. She then drew from her basket a lighted lantern, whose rays revealed the bottom of the vault but a few feet below. The two descended the steps, Guy following in wonder as to the purpose of his guide. Candelario gave him the lantern and told him to search the vault for treasure. Holding the lantern above his head he groped along the narrow way until he reached the end of the apartment where there was an enormous chest. This he opened without difficulty and there, lying in compartments, were gold coins of every denomination. He filled his pockets until they would hold no more, when he called to Candelario to bring her basket; but on looking back, she was not to be seen. Hurrying to the steps he called on her to come, but the concussion of his voice was painful to his ears. He ascended the flight but the stone had been replaced. In his dismay he dropped the lantern, and the light becoming extinguished, he was left in total darkness. He struggled at the stone, but to no purpose, his greatest strength being inadequate to make it yield. In his despair, he shouted aloud for help.

"Who are you, amigo?" were the words uttered in half inebriated tones that greeted Guy's ear, accompanied by a rough shake.

"What is the matter? Por Dios! What ails you?" was asked again.

Guy, now thoroughly awake, knew that he had been at his old trick of dreaming, and collected himself sufficiently to realize that he was in his cell and that the toreador, now somewhat sobered, had been doubtless aroused by his calls to be rescued from the closed vault.

"Are you the toreador?" asked Guy, as the other rolled back to his pallet.

"Si, senor—no senor—It is possible I am a toreador, and yet, if I know myself and could only tell where I am, I am not one."

"I can enlighten you a little then. You are in the carcel, and if you take the jailor's word for it, you are a toreador."

"The carcel! The carcel! Then if Bonito says I am a toreador the illusion is on my side, and I am not a major domo, for he knows well the major domo."

"My friend, you are drunk, as your thickness of speech indicates."

"I was at the vinoteria, it is true, but not drunk, senor."

"Bereft of your senses, then, since you cannot tell if you belong to the toreadors or not."

"Es verdad, senor. It is a question. It all happened so suddenly. It is a question."

"What is a question?"

"If I am a toreador, a major domo, or Senor Ruiz?"

"Ruiz! What of Ruiz?"

"Es muy caballero."

"Your voice is familiar to me in spite of its thickness. What is your name, senor toreador?"

"Jose—no—Ruiz, senor. Manuel Ruiz."

"Manuel Ruiz! Not he whom I know," said Guy, half to himself." You are not certain then, if you are Jose or Manuel Ruiz, or a major domo, or a toreador. My friend, you had better go to sleep, and perhaps in the morning you will be able to tell your name and occupation and completely fix in your own mind your absolute identity."

"You talk well, senor, for a Frenchman, not unlike a friend of mine; in fact, senor, your voice sounds like my friend's."

"Not much of a Frenchman, senor toreador."

"It was a Frenchman arrested. It was so said on the street."

"Wait until morning, amigo, and your ideas will have more weight. I'm going to sleep."

Guy was awakened the next morning by the movements of his fellow prisoner, who was knocking on the door and calling for Bonito. The light from the grated window made objects quite distinct around the cell, and he had a fair view of his companion in misfortune, as that worthy stood bawling for the jailer and making a noise on the door with the heel of his shoe for a knocker. The thick voice of the toreador had been discarded and Bonito's name was called in such familiar tones that Guy raised himself on his elbow and gave to the other a searching glance as he turned disgusted from his attempts to gain the attention of the jailor.

"Jose! as I live!"

"What! Senor Raymond!"

"That dress! What does it mean? And your confinement here?"

"I have not a distinct recollection of an arrest; but as for the toreador part I can easily explain. But you, senor; by what bad fortune does it come that you are in the carcel?"

"That I cannot tell, not having been informed. But Jose, how about your dress? You did not desert Father Ignacio?"

"Not I. This toggery was only put on to carry a point and to save a friend. To save Manuel Ruiz."

"Ruiz? Please explain."

Jose informed Guy of the whole affair, dwelling on the minutest points with great volubility, down to the moment he left Manuel in the jacal of the old basket-maker.

"Then you know not what become of Ruiz."

"How should I, senor, when I have not seen him since, and don't even know how I came here?"

"After you left Ruiz what happened?"

"Enough, senor, or I would not be here. We stopped, we toreadors, at every vinoteria and drank, and drank. I expected to be arrested at every step as Ruiz, but it must be that toreadors—and come to think of it, it is the custom to look upon them as above arrest while they are amusing the people. It was plain that I was followed as the one wanted, and it is plain to me now, senor, that the excitement of knowing that I was running some risk, together with the happy feeling of being so finely dressed, and ogled by the senoritas from the windows, caused me to drink too much wine and mescal, and when we parted at the vinoteria, in the Plaza de Armas, I remember nothing more until you were calling for help last night, when half dazed from my debauch I rose and shook you. Do you remember it, senor?"

"I was dreaming, Jose. It was as bad as a nightmare. What treatment do you expect when they discover that you are not Ruiz?"

"They committed the blunder. Am I to blame for not being Ruiz?"

"These questions will cut no figure. You aided an escape."

"They will have to prove that."

"How about Ruiz's dress, whose tinsel made you so happy?"

"They will have to prove it is his dress."

"How about you having warned him?"

"Let them prove it."

"They will believe you were eavesdropping at headquarters, instead of being asleep, while the arrest was discussed in the next room."

"Let them prove I was not asleep."

"Perhaps your determination to rest the *onus probandi* on the prosecution when these points arise, will not be agreed to by a Mexican military tribunal. It will be apt to take many things for granted and will supply manufactured missing links to complete the chain necessary to convict you. Your act was heroic, Jose, but you ran more risk than you imagine."

"What is the *onus probandi*, senor?"

"The burden of proof. Under Mexican martial law, no proof is necessary. The will of the military despot decides the case."

"There is old Bonito's voice in the court. He heard me call and knock this morning and paid no attention to it. The crusty old miser."

"He does not know one of his prisoners, at all events."

"That's myself."

"He does not dream you are other than what that dress declares you."

"He will awake from his dream today."

"Not as much surprised as when I awoke from mine last night and found that I was not buried alive."

"Was it a bad dream, senor?"

"Worse than bad."

"You should pray to St. Anthony, senor. When I have bad dreams I never fail to pray to St. Anthony, and then they never come true."

"Perhaps they would not come true if you did not pray to the saint."

"Don't you believe it, senor. St. Anthony is good. The night when you were fighting Vasquez and the whole crowd in the Cabeza de Torro I was in despair for your safety, when I looked up and saw the picture of the blessed St. Anthony on the wall. I immediately asked his protection for you and he saved you."

"I thought it was Ruiz; and all this time I have been bestowing on him the gratitude that belongs to St. Anthony."

"It is true, senor. The good saint used Ruiz in answer to my little prayer."

"I see it all now, Jose. You should have told me this before."

CHAPTER XXXVI.

When Bonito saw Ducio well into Linda's apartment he proceeded across the court into the street and took his way towards the plaza. He muttered to himself as he shuffled along, now casting his eyes this way and that, in a nervous manner, or turning completely around as if he wanted nothing to escape his observation.

"That Frenchy came none too late," he muttered. "I had not been a minute out of the vault. Bonito must be more careful."

The jailor turned north when the plaza was reached and hurried by the monte pio's, who had quite a number of customers engaging his attention.

"The monte pio is always in luck," growled Bonito, casting into the establishment an envious glance. "Everybody making money and the jailor at his wits end. But the notary may give me some consolation."

Not more than two minutes' walk from the monte pio's, and situated on the west side of the Calle Soledad, detached from buildings on either side, stood a house of the conventional build. A single arched doorway constituted the street entrance, while two grated windows set low in the massive masonry, furnished ventilation and light. On a homely piece of board fastened over the door and in letters executed unmistakably by an amateur, was the word "Notario." A peep inside the apartment nearer the plaza, through the deep window would have disclosed the presence of a lean, little man sitting by a table, on which were books and papers placed without regard to order, his attention apparently engaged by a scrutiny of some of the documents before him. A desk, with numerous pigeon holes surmounting it, occupied a place at the rear wall and near a half dozen shelves amply filled with volumes of every conceivable size. A heavy oaken chest was just visible in the shadow of a corner, while a single chair, other than the one occupied, completed the furniture of the room. If the busy occupant had glanced but a moment from his papers out of the window, he would have seen through an opening in the row of opposite buildings a pretty bend of the river, where its blue waters were eddying and boiling above its bed of grasses, to be lost again a few feet further on in the continuation of a graceful arc. The occupant of the room, however, appeared too much engrossed to be conscious of the outer world. For a long time on the morning that Bonito had been observed by Ducio to issue from the unaccountable place under the lounge, the swarthy little notary had been busy with some papers, in which he seemed to be extremely interested. The commanding general had sent for him in great haste, and immediately upon his return from headquarters, he had been examining papers. His first act on returning was to seat himself and spread out before him on the table a paper he had taken from his wallet. He looked at it long and curiously, and occasionally would give vent to some expression of impatience or doubt."

"So the general thinks this paper is important and may yet furnish evidence against a prisoner," he said, as he leaned back and looked thoughtfully at the ceiling. Then bending forward again over the table, he scrutinized the paper and began to speculate:

"This is certainly a memorandum sketch of an island or sea coast. Here is a rude outline of a ship; here a bayou, a road, two bridges;

these small rings mean something. Two rows of these rings, and here to the right they are numbered; the outer ones one, two, three; the inner ones, one and two. One, two, three; one and two. Santa Maria! What can they be numbered for?"

Such were the notary's reflections as he peered over the paper which had been taken from Ducio by the military. The little man was considered by everyone to be an expert in all that pertained to papers, and headquarters had called on him to pass his opinion before the document should be returned to the Frenchman. But he was puzzled for once to divine the object of the draught before him. He leaned upon his elbow with an expression indicating an unwillingness to acknowledge himself baffled, and repeating mechanically the numbers "one, two, three; one and two. One, two, three; one and two."

Suddenly he sprang to his feet and exclaimed:

"Por todos los Santos!"

Hastening to the chest, he opened it quickly and took from it a package of papers, which he brought to the table with trembling hands that indicated a sudden excitement. From the package he produced a small paper, much discolored, and smoothing it out as he had done the first under investigation, he read from it in an undertone. What he read was as follows:

> Along the outer coast you'll see
> Little circles—one, two, three,
> While other circles in plain view
> Are numbered only one and two.
> The bayou makes a sudden bend
> Directly where these circles end.
> These circles are but hills of sand,
> That border on the island's strand.
> Two crossings, spanned by bridges each
> In plainest road lead to the beach;
> The first that you will have to do
> Is to draw a line from two to two;
> And if thro' a riddle you would see,
> Draw a line from one to three.
> At intersection of these lines
> Is something that one seldom finds:
> An iron pot with an iron lid
> Beneath the cross securely hid
> Holds the treasure and the gold
> Taken by a seaman bold
> From the Spaniards' ample store
> And buried here on Galvez's shore.

"Bonito's rhyme is explained at last," exclaimed the notary, after satisfactorily examining the two papers. He even drew the sand hills, numbered them like on the original, and crossed the lines as directed in the rhyme. He placed his pen on the intersection and thought of the probable treasure that lay there, known, perhaps, only to himself. In the hands of Bonito and the Frenchman separated they would remain an enigma. He must return the sketch, but Bonito would probably never think much of the rhyme if told it was meaningless. He proceeded at once, however, to make a true copy of each, which he carefully enveloped, endorsed and placed in the chest.

The notary had resumed his seat and was thinking of his discovery of the secret contained in the two papers which had reached him from such opposite quarters, when he beheld the jailor pass close by the grated window with a glance that said unmistakably that he was to be a visitor.

Bonito was greeted with the notary's characteristic politeness, and motioned to the chair on the opposite side of the table.

"This is a dark hole, Senor Notario, with little more light than one of my cells," said Bonito, glancing around, as he seated himself and thrust out his short fat legs while his hands joined before his corporosity. "Always in papers!" he continued as he ducked his head and leered at the other from under his shaggy eyebrows.

"My business requires it, senor."

"No answer from New Orleans?"

"None."

"Antonio must be dead."

"Dead or living elsewhere."

"He was old—old, senor. I am positive Antonio is dead."

"And the secret of his wealth has died with him?"

"Unless that paper and its lines mean something. Did you ever try to make the puzzle out?"

"I was looking at it only this morning, Don Manoel, and I could get no light from it. It will ever be a mystery, I fear."

"The other papers throw no light upon it?"

"No senor. Merely letters; letters of little importance."

"Es mala fortuna, ma-la-for-tuna, senor. There is only bad luck for Bonito. The monte pio would have got a fortune out of that paper. Senor, some men are born lucky; some unlucky."

"It is true, but are you not stretching a little your imagination when you place so much importance on a few jingling lines, found on a piece of soiled paper? It may be a mere doggerel written in an idle moment by a buccaneer who was weaving a web of pure fancy."

"But old Antonio set great store upon the papers he left, and you have them all here. The paper that speaks of gold and treasure is the only one that hints at value, as you say; the others are all old letters of little importance. The thing is truly a riddle and one that will never be guessed, since it baffles your cunning."

"Is there a Frenchman, a prisoner, at the carcel? Something was said about such a prisoner at headquarters this morning."

"He is free enough now. An impudent fellow, Notario; an impudent fellow, with a bad treacherous eye."

'He is from New Orleans?"

'I think he said so."

"And knew Antonio?"

'Perhaps he did. Stupid! I should have asked him."

"Well, make inquiry, Don Manoel, and let me know. It may be that this Frenchman will be of service. But hint nothing about Antonio's papers."

"Not a word. You well know, Senor Notario, that I am discreet, if anything."

"A most excellent trait, Don Manoel."

"But you are not going?" continued the notary, as Bonito rose as if to leave.

"Yes, amigo mio; I would see this Frenchman at once, and then the carcel may need me, for the town is in an uproar from the toreadors, and one of the outcomes of it all may be some lodgers for Bonito."

The jailer shuffled away down the street, after returning a polite salutation from the obsequious little official.

The latter, left alone, seated himself at his table and leaned forward in deep thought, knitting his brow and moving his head to and fro, his lean, long fingers running through his scanty locks with each forward motion. The notary was in a deep study, yet no special emotion was indexed by his immobile features.

* * *

When Ducio entered Linda's apartment he found that the parties, from whom had come the voices, had vacated it. It was certainly unoccupied, and Ducio began to wonder how they had effected an egress, when he beheld the opening leading into the garden. To this he directed his steps, and looking out, discovered the door in the wall shutting out the view to the plaza. He remembered the garden from the chance look accorded him a little earlier when he saw Josefa De la Torre enter it from the street. Ducio's curiosity was now thoroughly aroused. His natural disposition was to do something not altogether proper when he felt himself to be unwatched with the belongings of others at his mercy. He had heard the jailer make his exit and the ladies were not visible. He scrutinized everything in the apartment, then returned to the hall.

The latter was vacant with the mysterious lounge its only furniture. He explored the rooms on the other side, but the usual scantiness of effects of the Mexican household made a glance sufficient to satisfy his taste for exploration. The lounge now claimed his attention. He turned back the gaudily colored blanket and discovered an ordinary mattress. A pull at the latter failed to move it. The end of a fine hair cord, decorated with a tassel, protruded from the bed. This Ducio seized, and drawing it towards him the end of the mattress sprang up on a hinge and disclosed a narrow opening, down whose dark depths the first two or three steps of a flight that lost itself in the obscurity, were visible. Ducio shuddered involuntarily at the forbidding look of this gloomy descent, yet he fairly chafed to solve its mystery. Hurriedly casting a glance into the court, where no one was to be seen, he returned and looked once more down the dark passage. A light—a light was necessary. He remembered that Bonito held an extinguished candle in his hand when he had emerged from the place only a short time before. A short search put him in possession of perhaps the same candle used by the jailer. This Ducio lighted and with a just perceptible exhibition of reluctance, placed his foot upon the first step and, holding forward the light, endeavored to see further down the stairway. But the feeble rays from the dip lent no apparent aid to the daylight and the venturesome Creole had placed his foot on the third and fourth steps with very little satisfaction obtained from occular perception of the situation beneath him.

His head had sunk below the floor level in his downward progress when he remembered that he should close the lounge in order to defeat detection should the jailer return before his exploration would be finished. Reaching back under this sudden reflection, he pulled down the mattress, which shut with a click. The sound startled him, but urged by desperation, he began his descent step by step. On either hand the masonry was solid and the passage narrow and plainly distinct. A few more steps and he had gained the floor of the vault. The arch was low, almost within reach, and rested on rough walls not more than two strides apart. With cautious tread he moved along its length, when his leg struck against something sharp that reached nearly to his knee. Lowering his candle he discovered a chest of medium size and near it a stool, upon the top of which were those evident marks of tallow that indicate where a candle has been made to stick. Ducio comprehending, melted a fraction of the grease, and soon his candle was standing on the stool. He tried the lid. It was locked. Retaking the candle, he directed its rays into the keyhole and peered after them. It was a spring lock. He replaced the candle, produced a heavy knife from his pocket and, holding it close to the light, opened two or three curious blades. One of these, long and slim, having a turn at the end, was selected and introduced into the keyhole. After considerable manipulation the lock yielded and Ducio raised the lid with his left hand. His eyes were dazzled with the view of the contents. He seized the candle and, holding it close to the interior, its rays were reflected by yellow gold and bright silver in coins of different sizes. Several bags disclosed their precious contents by the sharp round edges of the coins that marked their sides. Excited, Ducio opened a blade of his knife and cut into the largest bag, from which fell several Mexican doubloons. A trance-like expression fell upon his features as his eyes became riveted upon the treasure, and his look was absolutely wild when he glanced from the fortune of coins, to the right and to the left, in nervous alarm as if in dread lest the genius of retribution were upon his track to bring punishment for his temerity. His features transferred to canvas as the crowding emotions of satisfaction, of dread, of vexation played with the muscles and nerves of his swarthy physiognomy, would have ranked with the chefs d'oeuvres of the masters. Here was gold, precious gold; but weighty and burdensome, and in a subterranean apartment with a single place of exit, to pass which, even without such a precious burden would be to run a dangerous gauntlet. The crime of knowledge would be scarcely less than the crime of appropriation. But did not the strange fortune which had led to this discovery intend that the eventuation of the adventure should be as successful in his favor as had been the fortuity which had directed his steps to the vault?

Such were Ducio's thoughts as the treasure filled his vision with a maze of dazzling beauty that alternated between a crowd of sparkling coins and a blended mass of wealth embodying all the possibilities of ease, of pleasure, of dissipation and gratified desire. With hand trembling from his excitement, he stuck the candle to the edge of the chest and leaned forward to handle and inspect the fallen pieces, but the nervous hand had failed to securely place the light upon its narrow footing and it fell extinguished among the coins. The lid fell forward with a bang, and candle and knife were securely locked in the chest. Darkness, unspeakably dark, followed. Ducio, bewildered, stood still for a moment to collect his ideas, but for the life of him he could not remember the direction to the stairs. He would feel his way. Slowly he felt along the wall, and after many more steps than those which it seemed he had taken before coming in contact with the chest, he found a flight of steps. Ascending these his head came in contact with a hard substance, and putting up his hand he found it to be smooth rock.

What could it mean? Ducio pushed against it with all his might; but it would not yield. In terror he called aloud, but the dull echo of his voice in the narrow confine but mocked his appeal, and finally he sat down to meditate.

* * * *

When Bonito returned from his visit to the notario, he brought away the rhyming paper, which that official had pronounced mere doggerel, not being willing to part with it as worthless, even on the opinion of a person so respected for his powers of divination and interpretation. When he reached the carcel he found that no one was at home and the Frenchman was nowhere visible. He noticed the disarrangemnt of the blanket on the lounge, but the mattress was intact and he smoothed back the cover. He pulled from his pocket the puzzling paper and hesitated as he glanced at it, as if in doubt about some course he was to pursue.

"I must be more careful," he muttered. "The Frenchman came near seeing me come from the vault. I will wait until after supper and when things are quiet I will slip down and put this jingling paper in the chest. It may be of value yet. 'An iron pot with an iron lid holds the treasure and the gold.' It sounds valuable if it does jingle. But gold jingles, it does. Bonito will keep the paper."

Bonito's face was a study while thus soliloquizing. He put the document back into his pocket and giving the blanket an extra smoothing, he went about his duties.

It was about dark before he found it convenient to make a descent to the vault. He had regretfully welcomed back his old prisoner, Guy, and concluded his attentions for the day to his prisoners, when he entered the hall, fastened the door, assured himself that all was quiet and went to get a candle to light him below. He searched in vain for the new dip he had used that same day and was forced to procure another from Linda.

"Strange! Very strange! A new candle, not a·quarter of an inch burned! There is not a rat in Bexar, or I would swear a rat had taken it off. A rat with no more than two legs, no doubt, and a candle costs a quartilla. There is no luck for Bonito. A quartilla is not a fortune but quartillas make pesos."

Such were Bonito's half uttered thoughts as he prepared his light and went through the necessary motions to gain admission to the stairs down which Ducio had preceded him some hours before. His slippers, down at the heel, made a clatter on the steps, where shuffling could not be the antidote for looseness, and so annoyed the now more than usually careful jailer that he discarded them and proceeded in stocking feet.

Ducio's meditations were anything but pleasant after he had essayed to raise the unaccountable flagstone that had so mysteriously closed up the place of exit to the hall. He was buried alive with untold treasure that was as valueless as so much clay unless he could escape with it, or a portion of it, in some way. He could not tell how soon, or how long deferred would be Bonito's next visit to the vault. The chances were that he would certainly appear before hunger and thirst would have time to claim a victim. Ducio determined to remain at the stairs, in order to take advantage of the first opening of the trap to spring forth to liberty. The seductive charm of the contents of the chest, which had at first so completely woven a spell over his mind and so unnerved his physical being, had now become lost in the yearning desire to escape from the subterranean trap. The whole marshalled resources of his ingenuity could not materialize a plan of escape, so he settled down to a waiting, which, if not altogether patient, was not without some grounds for hope of a speedy release. More than once, while seated upon the steps, he heard the sound of feet, and several times a voice in a high key penetrated from above as if struggling through the minutest crevice. The darkness was oppressive and his patience began to wear away so that he had a half mind to call aloud, when the inky blackness of the vault retreated before a faint glimmer that revealed the outlines of the walls, the rugged arch and an opening at the further end of the apartment. The latter revelation caused the truth to dawn upon Ducio's mind that, in the darkness and his own confusion, he had been trying to escape by a different flight of steps than that by which he had descended from the hall. He half rose from his seat, but crouched back again, in excited expectancy, as the light became stronger and a noise made by its bearer greeted his ears. Bonito soon waddled into sight with a candle elevated about the height of his forehead, and with that expression of conscious certainty of being alone and unseen that leaves utterly unguarded the indices of purpose that mark characteristic faces. A long breath escaped him as he entered, caused doubtless by the exertion of his descent. Three or four of his short strides brought him to where stood the chest. Cocking his eye down at the stool he gave it a momentary inspection, then reaching down he stuck the candle on it, as Ducio had done, but with much more deliberation. Assuming an erect position he put his hand in his jacket pocket, pulled it out, felt again, then running it down in his trousers pocket he drew forth a paper and bending over to the light, squinted at it.

"This is it," he muttered. "The notario thinks it only a jingle. If it jingles, so does gold and silver. Old Antonio set store on it, and Bonito will keep it. Keep it here, in this secret place that holds what little he has. This is a convenient place. The padres who built the mission made it for a different use, but it serves Bonito well to hold his little change safe from prestimos and other thieveries."

What an explosion there would have been, if the miser had been conscious of the Creole's curious gaze and his mingled thoughts, indicisive of a course, in which murder, flight, confession and deception came up for consideration.

Bonito, however, being ignorant of Ducio's supervision, deliberately produced his keys and seating himself on the part of the stool opposite to the candle, he opened the chest, folded the paper concerning which he had begun his soliloquy and was about to place it in among his treasure, when he let it fall to the floor, and seizing the candle, held it so that its rays fell full upon the shining pesos and disordered doubloons.

"Que diablo es esso!" he exclaimed, as he reached for the strange knife. "Por via de mi madre! A knife! The sack of doubloons cut! Ah! My missing candle! But a little more used," he said, holding it up for inspection. "Could Linda have ventured down here? No. This knife is strange. Santa Maria! How came it to be locked in the chest?"

"Ah! The other stairs! Christo! Could anyone have found the secret of that slab in the floor of the cell? Perhaps the toreador! Dios! The toreador!"

With this Bonito hastily arose and made his way to the stairs where Ducio had been sitting. The latter had debated the best course to pursue, and while Bonito was making his last excited remarks, he had pulled off his heavy boots with the intention of stealing past Bonito and making his exit ahead of the jailer, and if attacked the steel-clad heels of his boots would constitute a weapon of defense. Bonito's movements, however, disarranged his plans, and he crouched in the corner at the foot of the steps, to avoid being discovered. The old jailer was so intent upon his one purpose, and so blinded by the deepening darkness as he moved from the light, that he failed to observe the Creole and slowly mounted the stair, until he could feel of the stone overhead, against which Ducio had pushed so hard when he first tried to escape. Satisfied, but still more deeply mystified by the result of his investigation, Bonito had reached the last step in his descent, when Ducio dealt him a score of blows on the head with his ponderous bootheel, causing him to fall insensible to the floor.

Ducio hurriedly examined his victim with the aid of the light, and then proceeding to the chest, he rapidly transferred to his pockets as many doubloons as he could carry in them, and seizing a bag of gold he was turning to leave when he espied the paper which he had observed to fall from the jailer's hand. He picked it up and thrust it in his pocket. With rapid strides he soon gained the top of the stair leading to the hall. Here he was at a loss for a moment what to do, as the trap refused to yield to his push; but the discovery of a hair cord, similar to the one he had observed on the lounge, solved the problem, for, pulling it, the trap lifted, and Ducio was soon in the hall.

CHAPTER XXXVII.

The morning wore on after Jose's fruitlessly made efforts to get the attention of the jailer, by repeated raps and loud calls, and he began to wonder why Bonito had not made some provision for their morning meal. Guy, who had not been much exercised by the circumstance, had also remarked the unusual neglect on the part of the fussy master of the carcel. He had beguiled the time in invoking the superstition of his fellow prisoner, by commenting on his dream and leading the Aztec into involuntary interpretations of its several features. Jose placed everything, not momentarily accountable, in the category of the supernatural and attributed to some saint the responsibility for the mental or physical status quo that seemed to defy solution.

"I wish that I could dream of gold, senor. It brings luck to dream of money."

"Not in my case, Jose. Am I not in prison?"

"For the moment, yes; but your luck will turn. See how easily you won the money at the Cabeza de Toro. You will be a rich man, senor. The good St. Anthony will bring you many blessings."

"To a heretic? Jose, I am not even a Christian."

"All the more proof of your luck, for any of the saints could bring evil to you for your unbelief, and yet you live on, win money as easily as drawing your breath, and everybody likes you."

"Is it not unlucky to dream of human skulls and of such disagreeable places as caverns, where the damp air is heavy with the noisome odors that are quite as deadly to human life as the venom of the reptiles which infest the crevices and fissures of their jagged walls? My dream is so impressed upon my memory that all the horrid details of the grim picture which fancy drew, with hand unsteadied by the rest of reason, is as plain to me as if in truth I had walked the cavern and felt the mould yielding beneath my feet, the webs of ages assail my cheek, while hissing serpents, darting tongues of hate retreated to inner recesses of their dens."

"That was a vision of hell,' senor. Saint Teresa saw as much when the good God permitted her to go in person to the horrid place. Father Ignacio read about it at spiritual reading in the camp before the one in which you joined us on the San Geronimo."

"Did Saint Teresa have to raise a stone, as I did in my dream, to effect an entrance?"

"Indeed, no. She was transported to the entrance, and read the sign over the gate. Everything opened before her approach."

"Your saint then must have been able to settle a disputed question; to locate the place of future torment."

"She was, senor. The good father read from the same book that hell is in the center of the earth."

"That theory, Jose, would have intensely amused Laplace."

"Was he a friend of Senor Raymond?"

"Not even an acquaintance. He was a great man, Jose, who did not believe in the creation, as the Bible details it. He was the originator of the Nebular Hypothesis."

"And what is that, senor?"

"That the earth grew through untold millions of years from little atoms, which formed first around the minutest nucleus, until it has reached its present proportions. That it was long a heated body, but gradually cooled, until it was capable of producing vegetation and living creatures."

"It must have cooled first on the outside, senor."

"Quite correct, Jose."

"Then Saint Teresa was right. The center is still a place of fire where the good God sends all heretics."

"You are a reasoner; at least on the question of location, but why should not bad Catholics be sent to the same place?"

"All Catholics have a chance, senor, but heretics burn forever."

"A charitable view, certainly."

"Senor, your dream has set me to thinking. There is a legend that the padres once used this carcel for religious purposes and, while so using it, caused a vault to be dug that communciated from the cells to the rooms across the court. I was pretty drunk, senor, when they brought me here, quite drunk, for which my confessor will give me a charity pennance, with a dozen or two Aves and Confiteors, no doubt; but I was not too drunk to hear words and voices. Between my confused mass of visions and ideas and the real surroundings it was hard to discriminate, which is doubtless owing to the villainous quality of the mescal, senor, which has become worse and worse since those Gringo-Tejanos have kept out a fresh supply. These vinoteria men have had to make the stuff stretch, and have been most unfortunate in selecting their material for adulteration. But I remember that I heard a voice, fine and small, that seemed to penetrate from the rocky floor; and then a tapping, as if the owner of the voice was tapping for my attention. But with my willingness to answer came curious shapes and grinning spectres, whose shadowy preesnce clouded my reason and made me powerless to separate the real from the unreal. Such villainous mescal!"

"It was your delirium, Jose. You were too drunk to dream and evidently no voice could come from beneath these rocks."

"But one's wits are sharpened by mescal and a drunken man is more apt to speak his true thoughts. Delirium leaves no impression upon the memory."

"You are a born philosopher."

"Puede ser, senor; but el padre Ignacio has failed to discover it. As I was going to say, the voice and the noise might not have come from below, but I certainly heard them. Your dream of a vault and the stone you removed to get admittance, put together with my experience, caused me to think of the place beneath this prison. That square stone, senor, may be the cover which conceals the entrance. You see it is different and larger than all the rest."

"True, but was there an entrance from this cell?"

"More than probable. This is the first to open on the court, and as the object must have been to connect the cells with the rooms across it, less digging would be necessary to reach the first cell."

"A practical conclusion, I must confess; but what puzzles me is to divine the utility of this underground passageway."

"It is one of the mysteries that are buried with the first fathers. who came to convert the Indians. They were a tough set to manage, according to the records, and the padres had to use many methods to bring them to the faith. They put the vault to good use, senor, or they would not have made it."

'Jose, you have excited my curiosity. We must lift this stone and see if there is anything under it besides solid earth."

'That is not possible senor, with our fingers alone to work with; and then I have a dread that tells me no good will be coming to us for trying to pry into the secrets of the holy dead."

"Having none of your dread or superstitions to deter me, I will while away the dulls hours of this confinement by picking around this stone, even at the risk of ruining this pretty knife," said Guy, rising from his recumbent position and drawing forth a handsome dagger from the inner side of his jacket.

"From the monte pio's," said Jose, eyeing the weapon.

"Yes, from the monte pio's, and he charged me a pretty price for it."

Guy with his usual determination knelt at once upon the damp stone floor and introducing the knife into the dirt-filled spaces parting the square flag from the irregular and smaller fellows that surrounded it, he began to clean them out, in order to ascertain the thickness of the stone, and to enable him to get if possible a purchase to force it from position. He worked away steadily and patiently, watched by the major domo with a good deal of interest. The latter would occasionally utter an admonition in regard to the temerity of the young American in endeavoring to probe mysteries which must evoke the indignation of the sacred shades that linger amid the haunts, once the scenes of their labors in the flesh.

The work was necessarily slow and but for the gratification supplied by occupation that is ever a boon to a prisoner, he would have ceased the almost hopeless attempt before the lapse of an hour. Noon had come and no jailer had made his appearance. Guy philosophized and worked on, while his more animal companion had several times dozed off into a restless slumber, with occasional awakenings and maledictions upon the head of the tardy Bonito.

At length the worker was rewarded by the discovery that he could raise a stone, next to the flag, under which was supposed to lie the mystery. Its displacement gave the required purchase on one side of the flag, and by diligent work, he soon had a place in which to insert each hand under the lower face of the latter. He looked at the Mexican, with the idea to ask his assistance, but that worthy was breathing heavily in slumber; then summoning all his resolution he stooped, and placing his hands under its edge, the heavy stone moved under his muscular grasp and in another moment it was edge up, disclosing to the startled Guy an aperture about twenty four inches square, down which nothing greeted his eye but two or three steps emerging from the inky darkness of the lower depth.

Guy's first thought was to awaken Jose; but he reconsidered the intention the next moment. Balancing the stone in its position, he lighted the bit of candle left from the night before and cautiously commenced the descent of the stairs. A slight tremor passed through his frame as the damp air very sensibly asserted itself, and suggested a long deserted apartment, perhaps unused by any then living beings and, from the major domo's standpoint, a resort for the ghosts of the good padres who had constructed it. The miserable light but faintly revealed the outlines of the grimy walls as the adventurer moved slowly over the flags. His foot encountered something soft, when, stooping down, he beheld the fat form of a man stretched upon the floor. The light was placed close to the face and Guy was not mistaken in recognizing the features of Bonito. The prostrate man was breathing heavily, but made no movement upon being touched or pinched.

"What mystery can this be?" thought Guy. "This accounts for Bonito's absence."

His eyes becoming more accustomed to the darkness he beheld the chest a little further on, and being curious to know where the other entrance could be, he proceeded towards the further end. But the chest did not fail to arrest him. Its open lid disclosed the precious contents, and Guy stood amazed, as he bent forward and realized the magnitude of the find. But he was not so entranced as was Ducio in his discovery as to lose the idea, paramount but a moment before, of solving the mystery of Bonito's presence and present condition. He mechanically closed the chest and passed to the further end of the vault. Here the discovery of the steps was scarcely made before he began to ascend, after placing his light on the floor, and was in a moment within reach of the obstruction that barred his exit. A hard push, however, caused the barrier to move, and the astonished Guy found himself in the well known hall of the jailer's domicil. He took in the ingenuous disposition of the lounge, arranged to evade suspicion of what existed beneath, but expended only a moment in inspecting the trap. Familiar with the rooms, he hastened to the apartment where Bonito slept and where were gathered the odds and ends peculiarly his own. Here he opened a cupboard and taking a small earthen jug from the shelf he hastily returned to the hall and disappeared down the vault steps, closing the trap behind him. The little flame of the candle nearly went out in his haste to raise it and hurry on to where Bonito lay. A groan from the latter indicated to Guy that the old jailer was on the way to consciousness. But the next movements of Guy indicated he had matured within the short time a methodical mode of procedure, calculated to cause his discovery to include, with rescue of the jailer, a preservation of the secret of the hiding place of his pesos and doubloons, doubtless accumulated by steadfast saving of reals throughout years of self-denial. Placing the jug and candle on the stool, which he moved from near the chest to the side of Bonito, Guy hastened back to the cell. Jose was still snoring as when he had left him. Seizing the edges of the heavy stone he slowly lowered it until, resting it on his shoulders, it came down at last into the exact place from which he had so lately raised it. His efforts were now made to resuscitate the jailer.

"This mescal will revive him," thought Guy, pouring some of the contents of the jug into Bonito's mouth, which he forced open with his thumb and finger.

Bonito strangled so from the liquor that his restorer began to fear he had administered a fatal dose; but the exertion which it caused created a reaction highly favorable, for the patient was soon in a sitting position, glaring wildly at the other.

"Why did you hit me so hard on my head?" were the first words succeeding consciousness.

"You are wrong, Bonito. I found you as you were, and only for this mescal you would not now be able to talk."

"Is it you, senor? I thought it was the other, the toreador, who had found the passage from the cell, who robbed and beat me on the head until I was like one dead. Oh, how could you do it?"

"It was not I, Bonito. The fellow you call toreador is safe in his cell. I discovered this place by accident and just in time to serve you. I have found my way to your room, procured this jug from your own cupboard and brought it here to bring you back to your senses."

"And my secret! Oh, Dios! Dios!"

Safe with me, amigo. I have discovered all, but the passage to the cell is closed and none shares my discovery."

"But he who struck me? What of him? He has robbed me and escaped. Oh! Oh! Oh!"

"No, Bonito. All seems safe. The chest is there, if that be what you mean. It is there and closed."

"And empty. Dios! Dios!"

"Come let me help you up. You can inspect your chest and——"

"Know my ruin. Dios! Dios!"

The old fellow was still dazed from the effects of the blows, but staggered to the chest, assisted by the strong arm of the other. He stooped to raise the lid, and hesitated, looking at Guy with no uncertain look, expressive of his reluctance to let another eye glance upon the contents. Guy interpreted its meaning and made an excuse to go to the steps to see if he had properly replaced the stone.

The miser raised the lid and throwing up his hands, muttered in subdued anguish:

"The bag that held the brightest doubloons—gone! Oh, Dios! Fifteen hundred and one! Fifteen hundred and one! Gone—gone!"

The lid went down with a bang. Bonito drew the key and placed it in his pocket.

The time had now arrived to leave the vault, as both were impatient to be out of it. Bonito was highly exercised to think that some one else was with him in his hiding place, while Guy was anxious to get out for no very definite reasons, unless it was that he had fasted since the evening previous. The jailer had so far recovered his strength as to crawl up unassisted in advance of Guy and to open the trap, which he was gratified to think the other did not know how to do.

CHAPTER XXXVIII.

The enthusiasm prevailing in the city, by reason of the presence of the toreadors, was not confined to the masses, but found a lodgement in breasts of the notables, civic and military, as well as the religious. The mere procession through the streets of the favorites, who were to give them diversion of a character second to none to be obtained from a whole calendar of fiestas, aroused the joys of anticipation that found stimulation in the contemplation of the actors, their fantastic dress and peculiar antics. The grated windows of the residences framed faces of senoritas, fair or dusky as the Caucasian or aboriginal blood predominated, while in one quarter the balcony of a more pretentious dwelling held a bevy of ladies, all intent upon the one common purpose, animating the population.

To this latter desirable position had repaired several persons who were friends of the family of Don Fermin Casiano, the occupants and owners of the property, and among them was Beatrice Navarro. The latter's education had, to a degree, eradicated Mexican tastes, and caused her ideas of the proprieties to assimilate to the American standard. But on this particular day Beatrice felt the need of some diversion that would chase away an oppression more unendurable than positive pain, and more unwelcome than any shock the most delicate sense of propriety could sustain. Her communication to Guy had remained unanswered, although she had assurances of its delivery, and she found herself feverish from an excitement incident to disappointment and doubt which, like portentous clouds, had suddenly risen to obscure the horizon of a new found happiness. She tried to console herself by the reflection that he was not worthy of her love, if he were incapable of appreciating her explanation of the unfortunate interview with her father; but excuses for him would assert themselves at every turn as the subject was again and again revolved in her mind. She felt that an outing would do her good and resolved to repair to Don Fermin's to see the crowd and the toreadors, a diversion that would perhaps lead her from her mental depression. And so it proved; for even before the gay horsemen made their appearance, the simple remarks of the senoritas, chatting and tittering like so many magpies, amused her to a degree and banished the last vestige of the feeling which had brought her from home. The toreadors paid special attention to the balcony with its throng of beauties, and Beatrice looked with increased interest as one of the riders gave her an earnest salutation that seemed strangely familiar. She gazed after the graceful cavalier far up the street until she saw him dismount and enter a house, accompanied by another familiar form, she could not be mistaken, by Jose, the major domo.

Across the street two familiar female figures, escorted by an officer, next attracted her attention. A smile of recognition from Linda was followed by a signal to ascend. The latter drew Josefa's attention to the invitation. The Senorita De la Torre flushed a little on beholding Beatrice and gave a look of inquiry to the little officer, who was no other than Pedro, the lieutenant of the staff.

"Our house is near at hand," said Josefa. "Why join that tittering crowd?"

"The more the merrier, senorita," suggested the lieutenant. "And see! Don Fermin is calling to us."

Josefa reluctantly allowed herself to be conducted to the balcony. The greeting between herself and Beatrice accorded with the strained relations which had so recently intervened to further mark their dissimilarity in character.

Linda, warm and true in her nature, embraced her friend and nestled close by her side.

"I heard you were here, Beatrice. But the toreadors have passed."

"But will return this way."

"Do you know the lieutenant?"

"Yes." Beatrice turned, and accorded him a recognition.

The officer doffed his cap and extended his hand in a salute.

"The Senorita Navarro had an excellent view of the toreadors from this portico," he said, by way of prefacing a conversation.

"Don Fermin very thoughtfully invited me. You know he is very enthusiastic over such exhibitions, and these toreadors are said to be acquaintances of his."

"Say you so? Ah! Yes. One of them, the masquerader, he doubtless knows."

"But all are masqueraders, are they not, in their assumed characters."

"The senorita is correct, but one of the toreadors is a San Antonian, and wears his present garb to conceal his identity. He will be a military prisoner before he will have finished his ride."

Beatrice at once recalled the salutation she had received from the graceful rider and strove vainly to place him among her acquaintances of the city. Forewarned of the intention to arrest, she gave no indication of the thoughts which entered her mind. Her next words were intended to draw the name of the masquerader from the lieutenant's lips.

"Is it a crime to play toreador?"

"If the play be made to conceal the presence of a spy."

The officer's words left no doubt in Beatrice's mind that the spy was Ruiz, for she now recalled the form and bearing of the cavalier who had saluted her, and was satisfied that he was no other than her impulsive friend, who had gone over to the Texans. Josefa, who had heard the conversation, entertained the same suspicion, but, not having seen the toreadors, it remained a suspicion, while she wavered between two sensations, one a vengeful hope that he be captured, the other a tender recollection of their past intercourse.

"There will be one other arrest made today which may surprise you ladies, if indeed it does not cause you much regret," continued the lieutenant, in a tone of voice indicating the satisfaction that such a proceeding would afford him.

"Cause me regret?" asked Josefa.

"And me?" queried Beatrice as the officer gave her a meaning look.

"Both of you," he replied.

"Don't keep them wondering, senor," said Linda. "Who is it?"

"It is no secret, senorita mia. It is the young American who is staying with Father Ignacio."

"Is he, too, a spy?" demanded Josefa, in a sarcastic tone.

"He may be; but his arrest will be for murder."

Beatrice had heard, but could command no voice for questions nor an expression to conceal interest and anxiety. She therefore remained silent with averted face but with eager ears to catch every word. Josefa noticed her manner and divined her solicitude. It afforded an opportunity to avenge herself on her rival and a demoniacal feeling at once possessed her.

"Is his name Raymond?" she asked, glancing her black, fiery eyes alternately from the officer to Beatrice.

"Raymond. You are quite correct, senorita. He has been a frequent caller at your house."

"And mine, too," said Linda. "He is a noble fellow and as innocent of murder as myself."

"Can you tell us, senor, who was his victim?"

"One Vasquez; a low fellow who was a witness against this American for the murder of another Vasquez, the witness' brother."

"A regular murderer!" exclaimed Josefa.

"Josefa!" remonstrated Linda. "It can only be suspicion. A thousand witnesses could not change my faith in Senor Raymond's honor."

"De veras!" exclaimed the lieutenant. "You are an eloquent champion of this enemy of Mexicans."

"Then his arrest is to be made on the score of enmity to Mexico, and the charge of murder is but a convenient subterfuge to get him into custody," said Beatrice, who had in a measure regained her equanimity.

"I thought the Senorita Navarro would soon come to the defense of this American paragon. In fact, it was my belief that he had made the greater impression on her, for rumor has been busy——"

"Rumor that deals in unmanly twaddle would never have had an origin were it not for tongues that wag obedient to brainless heads," interrupted Beatrice. "Have a care, senor, that this rumor is not traceable to yourself."

"Mil gracias, senorita, for the compliment," said the officer with a confused giggle.

"Will Senor Raymond be sent to the carcel," asked Linda.

"Doubtless. But with such a friend in the person of the jailer's daughter it would, perhaps, be best to confine him elsewhere."

"No fear of me, senor. My father is a faithful jailer and the only way in which I could show friendship for a prisoner would be in supplying some little things to relieve the discomforts of a prison cell."

"A murderer should have no comforts. The proofs against this American are positive, and beyond every doubt he will be shot before many days for the murder of the Vasquez brothers."

"The court has evidently prejudged the case in accordance with Mexican justice," said Beatrice.

"Then it is true, senorita, that your American schooling has blotted out all love for your own race."

"On the contrary, my education has caused a revelation of the deficiencies which exist in Mexican ethics, and I would lift our people from a depth of ignorance and superstition that is a barrier to advancement. Mexican justice is at best a farce and its jurisprudence an anomaly."

"This is rank treason. I hope, senorita, that these are not the sentiments of your father."

"If you would be posted, senor, I refer you to Don Juan," said Beatrice angrily. Then turning away, she indicated by her manner that their conversation must end.

Josefa's eyes sparkled with excitement and her whole expression evinced a morbid satisfaction at the perturbation of Beatrice. She engaged the lieutenant in conversation on subjects of town news and scandals, knowing that such topics were the more acceptable to his shallow mind. She flattered him by commenting on the brilliancy of his new uniform and impressing him with the idea of the high importance she attached to his position on the staff. By her arts she soon controlled the will of her companion and ended by drawing from him the information that Manuel Ruiz was the name of the toreador to be arrested.

When the sightseers left Don Fermin's balcony Linda accompanied Beatrice to her home, while Josefa secured the escort of the lieutenant, who had been completely ensnared by her wiles. He left her at her door, with assurances of his lasting allegiance.

Josefa's expression was one of contempt as she closed the door and muttered:

"The vain little monkey! There is more of the man in Ruiz's little finger than in his whole shrivelled anatomy.

She proceeded at once to her own room, full of the thought of the danger attending Ruiz's presence in the city and wavering between impressions, the one of gratified revenge, the other of apprehension lest the fate of the spy once consummated would cause a reaction productive of ceaseless remorse that she had done nothing to avert the catastrophe.

With these reflections she descended to the sitting room, where, to her astonishment, she beheld the object of her thoughts standing ready to receive her. Ruiz smiled broadly at her startled manner, in which were represented a variety of emotions.

"What! You here?"

"And at your mercy.

"My mercy?"

"Yours. I am hunted by the military and if captured will be convicted as a spy."

"Why did you seek this house as an asylum? Has your treatment of at least one of its inmates laid us under contribution for gratitude?"

"You do me injustice, Josefa, in alluding to our——"

"Return not to that subject, Senor Ruiz. Your perfidity in that instance has a fit sequel in your treason to your country."

"I am not a traitor, but a revolutionist."

"A distinction very questionable in your case."

"A truce to politics, Josefa. This badinage will lead to a quarrel, and quarrelling is now out of the question. I am here, in some danger, and ask your tolerance if not your hospitality until the darkness will permit my exit unobserved by the military hounds on my trail. You can accord this much to one who has loved you, who loves you now, despite the barrier which you yourself raised between us. But for your own act there would not be——"

"I command you by the hope you have of escape from the vengeance of your betrayed country, to make no allusion to the past. Let me not be compelled to again repeat this injunction."

"As you will, Josefa. I would not arouse in you remorse."

"You mean indignation."

"I would not disturb you by any unwelcome emotion. On the contrary, I am ready to renew that allegiance once so happily borne, if its renewal could restore intact in your bosom the passion which was half my existence."

"A traitor to talk of allegiance!"

"Nay, Josefa, I disclaim——"

"A recreant, appealing to a passion he killed, that its revival may save his worthless life!"

"Josefa! By all the saints! You are passing the bounds of your own convictions. You will regret your words."

"Could a woman of spirit say less? In these veins courses different blood from that which pulsates in a Navarro. You have mistaken your asylum, or have yet to learn the character of Josefa De la Torre."

"This is my asylum from necessity. It was the nearest at hand after becoming aware of my danger. I will say no more, as it but tends to irritate you. So soon as night comes I will relieve you of my presence. My enemies may recognize me, but before they effect my capture some of them will precede me to purgatory. You have called me traitor and recreant, but I shall never believe that you doubt my courage."

Ruiz seated himself by the grated window and leaned his head forward in deliberation. Josefa watched him for a moment, then left the apartment to find her mother. The latter noted her daughter's excitement, and had heard the tones of the conversation in the sitting room, but was not prepared for the reversion of feeling indicated by Josefas' next words addressed to her.

"How long has he been here?"
"Since one o'clock."
"Without dinner?"
"Without dinner."
"Then, mother, prepare him something to eat and take it to him. He will leave at dark." Then aside she said: "The miscreant! He should be made to suffer more than the pangs of hunger."

CHAPTER XXXIX.

Ruiz's first precaution after leaving the house of the De la Torre's was to hunt up his cousin, the chief of the toreadors, and to invoke his aid in a further disguise to enable him to escape detection from the Argus-eyed military. Senor Trevino had pitched his tent on the Alameda and himself and attendants were discussing the merits of the savory contents of a pot that swung above a small fire burning close to the base of one of the tall cottonwoods that lined the northern edge of the avenue.

"Ruiz as I live!" he exclaimed, as Manuel, emerging from the darkness, laid his hand softly on his cousin's shoulder.

"No, cousin mine. I am Jose, until more propitious times will allow me to change my identity and my clothes. Ruiz is doubtless languishing in the carcel, having been detected in his masquerading as a toreador."

"Es verdad. They took him on the Plaza de Armas, but he was

so beastly drunk that it is a question if he comprehended their action."

"He was not then discovered to be the major domo?"

"No. They thought they had their man."

"Then I will have little trouble to escape arrest, but to make surer, you must use your skill to further disguise my features."

"With all my heart; but join us in our supper. The night is before us in which to fully transform you into any shape you desire."

"Thanks for your invitation, but the Senora De la Torre has forestalled you by giving me a regular feast, not a half hour ago."

"Who was that youth who came up just behind you?" asked Trevino. "He paused as if he wished to speak."

"I did not notice him," replied Manuel.

"Then he did not come with you?"

"No. I was alone."

"He certainly followed you. His eyes were upon you sharply and while I was expecting him to speak he turned down the Alameda."

"Perhaps a spy.'

"A neatly dressed one."

We will leave Ruiz to be metamorphosed into a shape satisfactory to himself by the deft hands and skilled art of his cousin, and relate the proceedings of the almost demoralized Ducio, after his exit from the vault where he had left the jailer for dead.

He remained in the hall long enough to transfer the treasure from the bag to the several pockets of his clothing. He found difficulty in arranging the coins so that they would not disclose their bulky presence, and after some hesitation he repaired to the jailer's apartment, as if in quest of some means to better conceal his booty. Seizing something hanging above the bed, and which proved to be one of Bonito's shirts, he transferred a portion of the gold back to the sack and enveloped it in the ample folds of the garment, fashioning it into as neat a bundle as the necessity for haste would permit. The exit from the place effected, Ducio found that his apprehensions were not abated. The consciousness of guilt, weighted by the possession of gold of yet unestimated value, increased his trepidation when, finding himself in the street, be imagined the encountering eyes of people were reading his secret. He would have given half his gold for the friendly shield of darkness, which was fully an hour and a half distant. Candelario's door was the first refuge that offered. He entered the place and finding it vacant, seated himself, placing his bundle on the bench next to the wall. Being hungry, he called for a supper, and during the course of the meal his mind

MISSION CONCEPTION, NEAR SAN ANTONIO, TEXAS

was full of his recent adventure. Fortune seemed to be favoring him; yet he was not satisfied with his luck. It brought fears with its gold. The hidden treasure alluded to in Mr. Trigg's revelation, and of which the mysterious paper was supposed to be the index, was now a secondary consideration, if not wholly surrendered as an attraction in the glowing magnificence of the fortune in the vault. But he was villain enough to understand the necessity of acting naturally in the pending emergency to avoid furnishing grounds for suspicion. Therefore he tarried in the restaurant only a few moments after his deliberate consumption of the repast. On his exit the plaza stretched before him with but few pedestrians other than several rebosaed forms on their way to, and entering the side portal of San Fernando. Ducio, quick to conceive, bent his steps to the church and entered, with several females, the ever open door of the edifice. With a purpose now well defined his countenance assumed a calm, if not sanctimonious, expression as he approached the fount and dipped his finger in the holy water. He reverently crossed himself, made the genuflection, and knelt upon the flags. His head bent forward in mock devotion as mental visions of gold, the vault and Bonito's fallen form presented themselves in silent panorama. Here he resolved to wait his turn for confession, despite the pain endured from the contact of the hard stone floor with knees so unaccustomed to such experience.

Night fell over the city before Ducio was seen to leave the church. The darkness was sufficient to gratify the cravings for concealment of even greater villainy than his. The gloom that overhung the plaza was relieved by but few glimmers from the houses; the monte pio's shop showing the most pretentious illumination. Down the Calle de la Carcel the light from the doors of the Cabeza de Toro spanned the street and was reflected from the opposite walls, disclosing passersby and a knot of men, near the door, the latter assemblage varying in size as fresh arrivals came up or individuals by twos and threes entered the place.

An hour later the crowd of frequenters had become large and continued to increase as the night wore on. The quiet Mexican character of the assemblage was apparent from the absence of hoisterousness or hilarity, save an instance of drunkenness, where the inebriate would give vent to an occasional shout, followed by the cry of "Mueron los Tejanos."

"Mescal has made that fellow patriotic," said a bystander.

"Wonder it is that there are not more patriots of his sort tonight.

for the vinoterias have been well patronized during the day," said another.

"One of the toreadors was dead drunk, when for some reason he was arrested and put in jail."

"He was only playing toreador," said a third. "He was no other than Ruiz, who went over to the Texans."

"Then he is a spy," said a youth, whose slight figure was moulded in a neat suit, set off by a scarlet sash.

"And will be shot," said the first.

The latter was apparently a man of advanced middle age, and wore a long beard and mustache. His clothes were ill-fitting and he had a slight stoop that he occasionally tried to correct by carrying back his shoulders.

"You are quite right. Death is the fate of spies," said another, who joined the party just in time to learn the drift of the conversation. His Spanish was indifferent, and as he moved closer to the door the light revealed the features of Ducio Halfen.

The individual with the long beard gazed intently at the Creole as he made the remark, and slightly started as he got a view of his face.

"You spoke feelingly, senor," he said to Ducio. "Perhaps you have a grudge against this fellow—this spy—this—what's his name?"

"Ruiz—Manuel Ruiz," replied Ducio.

"An enemy of yours, perhaps."

"No, not an enemy. I know little of him."

"Then how did you know so much of his arrest?"

"I heard it at headquarters."

"Then Jose was correct," said the fellow with the long beard and the stoop, in an undertone.

The two entered the place where monte was being dealt to a crowd of bettors. The youth with the scarlet sash followed, and as he came under the rays of the stronger light the fellow with the long beard caught his eye, then took in his whole person in one searching glance.

"Por Dios!" he thought. "Is this the fellow who followed me in the Alameda?"

Ducio had come for no fixed purpose, and nearing a table he loked on with much interest at the progress of the game. The other kept near to him, but less interested in monte, he scanned the faces of the crowd without indulging in speech. Several of the bettors were military men, and among them, seated at one end of the table, was the little lieutenant of the staff. Behind the dealer was the well known face of the notary, who was a rare visitor to the locality. He was quietly watching the varying luck of the players, while he plied his cigarette with an evident air of enjoyment.

"You look like you wanted to bet, senor," said a voice close to Ducio's ear. He turned and saw that his companion with the long beard had addressed him.

"I would like to bet and have been watching the run of the cards to get a hang of the game.'

"Bet on the seven and every time you lose, double your bet on the same card," said the other.

"I will try your method, amigo. The seven, you say?"

"The seven. Quick, before he draws a card."

Ducio placed a doubloon on the seven.

The second play he lost. He put down two doubloons. Again he lost.

Four doubloons were now placed on the seven.

This time the cards did not fail him. Ducio won. He raked in the gold, the winner of one doubloon.

"I think I'll change the method, amigo. I won't confine myself to one card. It is too slow."

Ducio took the game haphazard; now betting on this or that card, with some success at first, but later his luck was bad and he lost heavily. He became the observed of all, which added to his plainly apparent agitation. He nervously placed his hand in another pocket and drew forth a handful of gold, laid it on the table and counted it aside with a finger. Unobserved to himself, he had pulled forth the paper rhyme which Bonito had dropped in the vault in his astonishment at the condition of his chest of treasure, and which Ducio had secured.

The sight of this paper caused an exclamation from the notary, who recognized it as the one Bonito had brought to him that very day to interpret. As Ducio seemed to pay little attention to the document, the notary leaned forward to place a real on a card, and before withdrawing his hand surreptitiously secured the paper. The man with the long beard noticed the whole proceeding and divined that the notary's object in betting was to get an opportunity to secure the paper dropped by Ducio. The latter's losses had become so great that he decided to bet no more, and withdrew from the monte table. A touch on the shoulder caused him to face his unknown adviser at the beginning of the play.

"You had better stuck to the seven."

"It looks that way now."

"Your losses are heavy."

"No matter. I have enough."

"Didn't you lose a paper?"

"A paper?"

"Yes, when you pulled out the last money."

"I remember—it must have been—perhaps it is yet on the table."

"No, I saw a man steal it. You were so engrossed in your game you did not notice him when he secured it."

"What could he have wanted with that paper?"

"Who knows? He seemed to know what it was the moment you dropped it, for he gave a grunt of surprise and a look clearly indicating that he coveted its possession."

"Show me the man."

"The little fellow back of the dealer. Not the slight fellow with the red sash, the other. He is a notary and an expert in papers."

"I'll see this notary," said Ducio, moving in the direction of the subject of their conversation.

In order to reach the position behind the monte dealer it was necssary for Ducio to go to his right or left around the crowd that encircled the table. He accordingly elbowed his way, with the best haste he could make, to the right and in a moment found himself in the position lately occupied by the notary. But that worthy was nowhere to be seen. Ducio was at a loss to account for the disappearance and, in his dilemma as to how to proceed, naturally turned in quest of his quondam acquaintance with the long beard, who had witnessed the surreptitious appropriation of the paper. Here again he was disappointed, for the latter also had vanished or was indistinguishable in the crowd. Finding a further search for both parties fruitless he left the Cabeza de Toro and crossed the street to the vinoteria.

The witness to the abstraction of the paper was also an observer of the movemnts of the abstractor and of Ducio as he hastened to get to the rear of the table. The former having risked detection to possess the paper was on the qui vive to detect whatever of demonstration might be made by the party despoiled, while he, ostensibly, was deeply interested in the game. Ducio's look, after having been apprised of the theft and his subsequent movement were duly observed and were the signals for prompt action to secure an escape. The diminutive form of the decipherer of enigmas found less difficulty in moving through a crowd than did the well developed figure of the creole. He glided away with the ease of a snake, and by the time his pursuer was wondering at his disappearance he stood without the door contiguous to the spot where Vasquez dropped a portion of the money, the possession of which caused his murder. Here he drew himself up close behind one of the projections in the wall of the carcel, where he could command a view of the door whence he had just issued. The fellow with the long beard followed the course of the notary and gained the street just as the latter stepped into the shadow of the abutment.

Feigning indifference he passed around the corner of the carcel, but glided back stealthily and took a position unobserved behind a corresponding projection a few feet from the other's position. A moment later Ducio sallied forth as already stated, and as he slowly passed the two concealed men he said aloud in English:

"The fellow must have known the value of the paper. Who knows? He might be the Portuguese that old Trigg talked about. Ha! Mr. Guy Raymond, who ever you are, the hidden gold to which this paper is a key will be known to a score at this rate."

The notary watched Ducio until he was well into the vinoteria, when he emerged from his hiding place and stood for a while as if uncertain of his next movement.

"This must be the Frenchman. How came he with both papers? The rhyme and the diagram. Bonito must have dropped it. But how strange that it should have come into his possession! A chance in a million! That strange fellow with the long beard told him I had secured the paper and he is after me. He talked as he passed out, but not in French. If Bonito has lost it I will draw it out of him."

Keeping an eye on the vinoteria the notary passed on to the plaza and to his home.

"I am getting into a secret," said the man with the long beard, as he left his hiding place. "This rascally Creole who is playing Frenchman has been up to some devilment. Where could he have gotten all that gold? He mentioned old Mr. Trigg's name and Senor Raymond's. He said that the paper was a key to gold. And this little slippery notary. He spoke of Bonito as having been in possession of this paper. What can it all mean? Perhaps my cousin, the toreador can help me unravel the mystery. I am as sure there is crime at the bottom of it, as I am that my name is Manuel Ruiz."

As Ruiz moved away the young man with the red sash moved out of the opposite shadow.

"Here is a pretty business," he said. "Crime and gold! A secret! Bonito's name; Guy Raymond's. The notary, too, is mixed in this strange plot that promises to develop rascality if nothing more. In what I've heard there is yet nothing to condemn in Ruiz. He, it seems, is not arrested yet in spite of reports to the contrary. This tall, dark fellow whom the notary called a Frenchman is the same I saw yesterday when I was about to enter Linda's gate. What devils are men! They use darkness to practice their villainy. The Frenchman certainly had a supply of gold, and Ruiz thinks he stole it."

CHAPTER XL.

When Guy and Bonito were out of the vault the latter began to feel how unwelcome was the thought, that another, in fact two other persons, knew of the hiding place of his treasure. He looked at his rescuer, mentally hoping that he would soon be shot by the authorities. Yet even that eventuation would not wipe out the difficulty, for his unknown assailant had escaped and was at large with a portion of his gold and was doubtless premeditating a second raid for a new supply or a total sweep of the savings of a lifetime.

"Senor, you must go back to your cell," he said with a sigh. "I only wish they would try you shortly and shoot you."

"Shoot me! Bonito."

"Shoot you, senor. You know too much."

"But with me, Bonito, your secret is safe. My honor——"

"Honor! Honor is like smoke, with such knowledge. A little puff of temptation will blow it out of sight."

"In your experience perhaps you are correct. Bonito, in the young nation to which I belong there are those who deem honor a duty, and who place duty above gold or any of the temptations instigated by human desires."

"They are angels, not men."

"Angels are myths; mere types of human perfection."

"I wouldn't trust a saint."

"A saint is above temptation."

"I mean before they are made saints."

"Then they don't deserve canonization."

"They don't deserve it, senor, and that's why the church waits a hundred years to let their backslidings while in the flesh grow dim or become entirely forgotten. They all love money, laymen, priests and bishops; even the pope has comfort in his Peter's pence. Jesus, the founder of the faith, cared not for money, and was content with no place to lay his head. The fashion is changed now, senor; the fathers have wealth and the bishops are princes with palaces, and——"

"Come, Bonito. I'll report you and have you excommunicated."

"I am as plain with el padre Ignacio, and he is half inclined to side with me. If they were all like el padre, Ignacio, senor; he is an exception. But come, senor, you must go back to your cell, which I hope you locked when you came out to my rescue."

"You never asked me how I got out."

"God willed it, senor, and that is enough for Bonito."

As Guy was proceeding to his cell under escort of his crestfallen jailer, a mozo, bearing a basket, entered the court and announced that he brought a dinner for Senor Raymond and the other prisoner.

"If I only had your luck, senor! It is well the dinner comes this way, for I have no idea of what has happened in my kitchen since I was struck by the beastly robber. My head is turned by the blows that the cowardly rascal rained on me from behind. Take the basket, senor, and divide with the toreador, who is perhaps sober by this time."

When Guy found himself once more in the cell he discovered that his fellow prisoner was still asleep. He first removed the cloth to examine the contents of the basket, and was surprised to find a note bearing his name. He eagerly unfolded it and reading by the dim light of the apartment, gleaned the following·

"Dear Sir and Friend:

"He who befriended you at the Cabeza de Toro is in the city and is the writer of this. Your companion in the carcel has been arrested as a spy disguised as a toreador. Let him conceal his true identity, which will assist me to escape the Argus eyes of the military. Your interests are mine. Use your influence with —— to carry out my wishes.   Your servant,

"M. R."

Guy at once divined who was his correspondent and comprehended, from all he had heard from Jose, the seriousness of the situation in which Ruiz was placed. It required but a moment to formulate a mode of procedure that would consummate the wishes of his friend, as expressed in the note.

The effects of dissipation would have prolonged Jose's sleep had he not been roused by his fellow prisoner, who calculated that the appetite of the ex-toreador must be as keen as his own. Jose's first glance, after rubbing his eyes, was at the stone at which Guy was picking when he dropped off to sleep.

"So you gave it up, senor?"

"Not exactly, Jose. Another time I'll try again."

"You must be hungry," Guy added, wishing to divert the conversation into a different channel.

"Yes, hungry I am senor. Let us rap for Bonito and see——"

"Our dinner is here, and no thanks to our jailer. It comes from a friend and is Candelario's best cooking."

The two were soon discussing the contents of the basket.

"I have news from Ruiz," said Guy. "He is still in town and desires you to play the part of the arrested toreador, until he is safe from the clutches of the military."

"But Bonito will discover——"

"Not necessarily. Keep back well in the cell whenever he comes and I will manage Bonito. The authorities must still suppose that Ruiz is in their power."

Guy's thoughts crowded fast upon his mind as the confinement of his cell brought the inevitable reaction that must follow the exciting incidents through which he had passed since he first peered down the dark descent discovered by the raising of the stone. He listened patiently and answered abstractedly to the remarks of the major domo, which were rambling and speculative as to Ruiz's intentions in town, the stay of the toreadors, and other minor topics, while his own earnest reflections were connected with his future and the necessity of his deliverance from the carcel and escape from the Mexican lines. The deliverance seemed now the less difficult since his knowledge of the subterranean passage assured him of a mode of exit, a secret that Bonito had little dreamed had passed into his possession. If he could communicate with Ruiz the probability was that an escape could be successfully planned. He turned the matter over in his mind until he became nervous from the intensity of the thought, and he paced his cell for relief. In all human aims successful attainment must have for a precursor a fixity of purpose, to steel the nerves of action.

Ducio's determination was to interview the notary at once and demand the paper he had abstracted from the monte table. He had read it while dissembling in the church, and was convinced that it was the key to the diagram in the possession of the authorities, and which he had stolen from Mr. Trigg's papers. He cursed himself for his carelessness, and resolved to repossess himself of it at all hazards. He knew the treasure it alluded to was on Galveston Island, as the rhyme confirmed the statement of Mr. Trigg, while in consultation with Perry and Hamilton. He indulged in liberal potations at the vinoteria. It was customary with the Creole when in his cups to talk to himself, and on this occasion he indulged in the habit to some extent, employing at times the English and again the French to express his dissatisfaction with his losses and his intention to make the notary pay for his theft of the paper. Ruiz, who watched his entrance to the vinoteria, had also resolved to keep an eye and ear open to ascertain the destination and intentions of the man whose enmity he had somehow incurred. To facilitate this intention he gained a position outside the door of the vinoteria, whence he could hear anything that might be said within. He had to remain some time before Ducio had reached a state of talkativeness; but at length he was rewarded by learning that the notary was to be brought to account that very night. This important fact gleaned, the listener left his post and proceeded hastily down the street.

The notary's modest establishment was lost in the obscurity which hung like a sable mantle over the Calle Soledad on the night of the incidents just related and was scarcely distinguishable, even on very close inspection, from the monotonous line of wall that constituted the peculiar architecture of the city. The passing patrol on its night rounds, or some belated frequenters of the Cabeza de Toro, might have discerned the faint gleam of a light struggling through the crevice of the notary's window shutter, indicating a late devotion to some branch or department of that worthy's calling.

Within, the little dusty office presented about the same appearance that it did on the occasion of Bonito's visit. The glimmer of a low-burned candle revealed the occupant in apparent study, leaning back in his chair with right arm resting on the table, while the hand slowly, and perhaps unconsciously, turned a pencil. Before him lay the paper which Ducio had lost at the monte table, and which, on inspection, proved to be the identical original so long deposited with him by the jailer, and withdrawn by its owner that very afternoon. The notary's reflections were rapid, intense and sinister. How had Bonito parted with the paper? How was it that the Frenchman so lately from the home of old Antonio, the possessor of the diagram the rhyme explained so well, had now become the custodian of the rhyme? Was it a fortuitous circumstance? Had the jailer made a trade for a consideration, to one who knew well the value of the diagram? Had violence been used to obtain it? Were any of these hypotheses true, the indications were plain that Bonito had not overestimated the value of the documents, and that a hidden treasure awaited the coming of their possessor. That the Frenchman had missed the paper was apparent from his expression and movements. The unknown with the long beard had pointed him out as the abstractor. Could they trace him or even identify him? His copies, carefully filed away in his chest, were as serviceable as the originals. Had the Frenchman fully gleaned the import of the rhyme? If not, he was sole master of the situation. If he had— what then? Would he incur risk for its repossession? The quantum of courage and character in his makeup would perhaps determine his action. If he could only have this Frenchman assassinated, there would be no obstacle to his eventual possession of old Antonio's gold. No necessity for haste then. On the other hand, with the Frenchman living, there would have to be active movements, to say nothing of the menace to himself entailed by a mutual knowledge of the buried treasure. The notary was startled by his own sinister thoughts, for he had never plotted against a life. But here gold, or the secret of its locality, was the tempter to inveigle him from the even tenor of his life to enter the arena of crime or of criminal intent. He watched the flickering light now struggling from the socket, its motion casting grim shadows along the walls and bethought him of the necessity of a new candle before the expiring flame should be dissipated in darkness as black as his own bad thoughts. The new dip was ignited just in time, and he held it until the hot socket of the stick would be cold enough for its reception.

"If this Frenchman could only be put out of the way," he muttered. "It would be as easy as snuffing out the flame of a candle, if I could only get the authorities to believe that he is a spy, and that diagram he had is a plan of defenses for Galveston Island. A good idea! In the morning I will go to headquarters and I will put a flea into the lieutenant's ear."

The notary's reflections were interrupted at this point by a rap at the door. Snatching the paper from the table and concealing it on his person, he demanded:

"Quien es?"

The reply came:

"The sergeant of the patrol."

On receiving this reply he did not hesitate to enter the dark hall and open the street door. The caller entered and pushed his way in as far as the door of the little office, without replying to the second inquiry of the notary as to what was wanted.

The light of the candle revealed to the astonished official, not the military visitor he expected to see, but the Frenchman who had occupied his thoughts during the time which had intervened since he had quitted the Cabeza de Toro.

"You are not a sergeant," he exclaimed, as he recognized Ducio.

"But you are the notary."

"I am."

"Well, I have some business with you, and claimed to be the sergeant to ensure admittance."

"It is very late to call on business. I will see you in the morning."

"Excuse me, senor notary, but I prefer to at least arrange the preliminaries tonight."

"Your business, senor; but cut it short."

"You were at the Cabeza de Toro tonight."

"A mistake, senor. It has been six months since I paid a visit to the place."

"A liar as well as a thief," said Ducio aside.

"I saw you there myself. You took a paper I dropped on the dealer's table, and I have come to get it."

"Santa Maria! How can you say it, senor, when I have not been out of my office?"

"Did you not skulk out of the place when you saw me move in your direction?"

"Hold, senor! Did not the individual you took for me wear a white hat a little set back from his face?"

"True; but nevertheless it was you, the notary."

"I have it. It was my twin brother. A case of mistaken identity, senor. My brother often visits the Cabeza de Toro, and we are veritable Dromios."

Ducio was silenced, but assumed a doubtful expression.

"See, senor! Here is the hat I have worn for a month. The person you saw wore a white one."

"Well, senor notary, if you have any regard for your twin counterpart, you had better help me get this paper I spoke of. I will give him until tomorrow evening to produce it, and then—and then——"

"Enough, senor. No need of stating any consequences. If you will call tomorrow evening I will give you my brother's reply, or bring you both face to face."

Ducio, only half convinced, did not know how to contradict further the solemn asseverations of the other, who might be one of triplets, so resembling in features as to reproduce all the ludicrous mistakes which filled the experience of the Shakespearean twins. He therefore bade the notary good night with an injunction to be faithful to his promise, to avoid unpleasant consequences.

"The scoundrel!" said the notary as he closed his door. "He

shall account for his possession of that paper. Brother! Ha! Ha! I never had a brother. It was well that I put away that white hat."

"I'll make inquiries about this fellow's brother," said Ducio, as he turned towards the plaza.

"The notary played his part well," said Ruiz, emerging from the rear of the notarial office. "I'll be on hand tomorrow at the meeting of these worthies, an invisible witness of the finale of this affair."

The next morning the notary visited the carcel and on inquiry was told that Bonito had not been seen and that his whereabouts were unknown. Disappointed in not seeing the jailer, he turned his steps towards headquarters. On his way to the latter place he began to think that it would be better to not question Bonito about the loss of the rhyme as it would attach to that paper an importance that might defeat his own plans. He had it in his possession and would keep it.

At headquarters he was received by the pompous little lieutenant, who listened to his alleged suspicions relative to Ducio; but again he was disappointed as the commander in chief had decided that the paper was a harmless diagram, and there could be no importance attached to any contemplated defenses for Galveston Island, as it stood in no danger of an attack from Mexico in its present condition, and the Texans could have no pretext to spend money where it would be of so little service to their rebellion.

The notary therefore became uneasy as the day advanced and he had discovered no loophole through which to escape from the ire of the Frenchman, who would doubtless ascertain that he had no twin brother in Bexar. He thought of assassination, but failed in nerve to perpetrate the villainy or the chic to employ an agent for its consummation.

When the hour arrived for the meeting between the baffled notary and the scheming Creole, the former awaited the interview with a nervous feeling that sprang from the uncertainty of the policy he was to pursue in order to fend off the demands if not the attack of the other.

The door was left ajar for the latter's entrance, and upon his arrival he stalked into the room where sat the proprietor, apparently engrossed with a pile of papers. The greeting was upon the verge of frigid. Ducio seated himself and the eyes of each, as they encountered, expressed the sparring which was to follow.

"*Your brother,* not being present, I trust, senor notary, that you are ready to produce the paper which he appropriated."

"I am convinced, monsieur, from the tone of your remark, that you have serious doubts of the existence of my brother."

"Your notaryship is very correct. I have discovered that you are no Dromio. You were at the Cabeza de Toro and you are the identical party who took the paper I dropped from the monte table."

"Well, monsieur, I admit every word that you say. But, monsieur, there is a checkmate. You play chess, monsieur; you know what a checkmate means. I have found out your game and have made a discovery that effectually blocks any further move without my consent. Does the monsieur comprehend?"

"Explain yourself," said Ducio, rather impatiently.

"Compose yourself," replied his opponent.

"Proceed. I will grant you a few minutes to explain this checkmate, and then——"

"Monsieur is very gracious to grant me time, but I will assure monsieur that it is entirely gratuitous."

"You are insolent, and my patience is exhausted."

"Will monsieur explain how he came in possession of the pretty rhyme?" replied the notary, in a patronizing manner.

"That is no affair of yours."

"But it is one affecting law and practice."

"What mean you?" asked Ducio, starting to his feet.

"Be calm, monsieur. When villains confer they should not allow themselves to be ruffled like ordinary people. You, monsieur, are a villain by nature; I, by accident, a distinction without a difference as to results when the officers of the law bring us to the bar of justice. The jailer, Don Manoel, better known as Bonito, was the holder of the paper you are so exercised about. I recognized it the moment you dropped it and therefore secured it. I have discovered how you obtained this paper, monsieur, and the sooner you drop the heroic and come down to common sense, the sooner will we understand each other."

Ducio was checkmated, but not satisfied.

"What do you propose?" he asked.

"What do you know?"

"That the rhyme is a key to the discovery of something hidden."

"An iron pot with an iron lid," quoted the notary, humorously.

"That this Manoel is a Portuguese friend of one Antonio who died in New Orleans."

"'Beneath the cross securely hid,'" continued the notary.

"That one Guy Raymond, supposed to be in this city, is to be the heir of the man who has another paper showing position of the treasure."

"'Holds the treasure and the gold taken by a seaman bold,'" continued the quoter. "But how came you in possession of this information?"

"By accident; but through a natural propensity for eavesdropping."

"Accident assisted you in securing the rhyme also, but your evil nature prompted you to the crime," said the notary, narrowly watching for a clue upon which to build the true mode of the other's procedure in getting the paper out of Bonito's possession.

"Senor Notary, this must end; you know too much," said Ducio, rising threateningly.

"Hold, monsieur! If you should harm or murder me it would do you no good. We both know the secret, but I have the advantage. The papers are secure from your reach. I alone can produce them. Between us we can share this buried fortune, and we can save time and trouble by coming to an understanding."

"Go on," said Ducio, seating himself.

"We can work our way to the island and divide the spoils."

"When do you propose to go?"

"We can decide that during the coming week. It can be reported that our destination is Mexico."

Ducio hesitated a moment, then said:

"Enough! I agree. 'Tis said that there is honor among thieves, and upon this I must predicate my trust in your performance of your part of the obligation."

"There is no thievery in taking possession of treasure trove. Therefore we cannot be classed as thieves," reasoned the notary.

When Ducio left his confederate it was in a frame of mind in which it was not difficult to persuade himself that he had been baffled by an adversary for whose powers he entertained a contempt. He had made a bold play for success and through his own carelessness had exposed his possession of the secret. Necessity for action was most apparent. What kind of action must it be? His villainous disposition pointed to the death of the notary and regaining the lost paper. He would put this in execution that very night but for one thing. A murder would necessitate immediate flight, and there in the vault of old Bonito was wealth that need not be hunted among the drifting sands of a distant island. The trouble was to secure the jailer's gold and secrete it without detection. The miser, if not killed by his assault, had missed the doubloons he had appropriated and would be, doubtless, vigilant to protect his hoard, as well as to discover his mysterious assailant. He would run no risks of arrest, however, and endanger the better chances which seemed to offer easy discovery of the buried gold. Such were Ducio's reflections as he leisurely moved along under cover of the darkness, little suspecting that his interview with the notary had had a witness.

CHAPTER XLI.

The morning following the conference between Ducio and the notary, Manuel Ruiz wrote the following note to Guy Raymond:

"My friend:—As the time is pressing for the accomplishment of my errand to this place, I write to post you in order that you may profit by an opportunity to escape from the enemy's lines to the ranks of the Texans. An officer of the Mexican army of high rank is here and in correspondence with a spy in the councils of our friends. It is proposed to kidnap this officer and to convey him by the river outside the town limits. I have laid all plans necessary for the success of the undertaking. In disguise I have visited the nest and have found out the very bed on which this person sleeps. This information gained, I have asked the cooperation of a party from the Texans, who will descend the river in a boat on ——night. You will please inform me of the best plan in your judgment to be pursued to effect your escape from the carcel. I do not think Bonito can be bribed, miser though he may be. I have an idea, but would like to hear from you before I give expression to it. You should be out in time to help us in our undertaking. Reply to me through the basket returned to the Candelario's.
Your servant,
M. R."

The note came with the evening meal and Bonito, in person, was the bearer of the basket, covered as usual by one of Candelario's napkins. The jailer was reticent. His late experience had unnerved him to a degree that evidenced a marked change, not merely from a characteristic loquacity to a sententious expression, but in a physical manner, his jolly, half hopeful look having given place to a woebegone appearance emphasized by a frequent twitching of the facial nerves.

"I hope you feel in better spirits, Bonito," said Guy, as the other handed in the basket.

"There is your supper, senor," he replied, evasively.

"What news, Bonito?"

"I am not a newsdealer. And then, where's the heart to gather news and talk gossip when one's head is the target for bad luck?

But there is some news for you. The orders are to keep you and the toreador under a strict watch. There can be no privileges of court, senor, as before."

"Thanks, Bonito, for the information."

When Guy read the note from Ruiz, which he found in the basket, he began to ruminate on the necessity of escape now more apparent since the nature of Bonito's last orders became known to him. There was evidently some influence working against him more potent than the prejudice of race, or the suspicion of his implication in the murder of Vasquez. The authorities were under the impression that Ruiz was his fellow prisoner, and upon the latter and himself had converged a suspicion of complicity in that tragedy. Hence the strictness of Bonito's orders. Jose's masquerade would be lifted in the event of a trial or investigation requiring identification and a search for Manuel be instituted.

On the return of the jailer to fetch water and to take away the basket and dishes, Guy slipped in a paper among the latter upon which was written the following words:

"Whenever my services will be required give me at least three hours notice of the time and place to meet you and I will be there."

The moodiness which had possessed Bonito still asserted itself when he came for the things, but he lingered after having possessed himself of the basket as if he were inclined to say something. Guy, observing this, put his hand familiarly on his shoulder and said in an undertone:

"Bonito, amigo, make me your confident and perhaps I may help you to regain your cheerful manner. You have been a good jailer and kind to me. Unburden your heart to one who would not be ungrateful for ten times the gold you ever possessed."

Bonito's finger went to his lips as he glanced cautiously towards Jose, who was making his pallet, and then gave Guy a look full of admonition.

"Your parole, senor; not to attempt to escape," and he drew his prisoner into the passageway and out of hearing of the other inmate of the cell.

"I think I know who assaulted me in the—in the——"

"Down there," said Guy. "Well?"

"The Frenchman."

"The Frenchman?"

"He was a prisoner but was released."

"Ah! I see. The same who denounced Manuel—but the proof?"

"It could only be he."

Guy thought a moment; then facing the other he put a hand on each of his shoulders and in that attitude of confidence that is calculated to enlist the interest and win over resistance.

"Bonito," he said, slowly; "I have an idea which, if carried out, will put this Frenchman out of your way and silence a witness to—to—you understand."

"Yes senor. Yes—yes."

"Let me have tonight to think it over."

"I will, senor; think and think well, and I will be your servant. It is strange I have this confidence in you, senor. You know all, and yet I find myself arguing with myself that you would not touch one centado. But this dark-faced Frenchman, senor; he has such cunning in his eyes that when I look in them I see the treachery of an Indian without his courage; the venom of a rattlesnake without its warning. He is a favorite at headquarters and I have just learned that to him are due the orders for your stricter confinement."

"We will attend to this subject of France, Bonito. Fetch me a light after you deliver this basket."

"I will, senor, but have it put out when the relief comes at ten."

The morning after Guy's rearrest, Linda went to the monte pio's to make some trifling purchase. The proprietor, who had always had a soft spot in his heart for the pretty daughter of the jailer, received her in his usually gracious manner. Linda was really his choice for a wife, but the girl was refractory and resisted the attempts of her father who, in his blundering way, had endeavored to make her comprehend the importance of an alliance with a man possessed of untold articles of value, with no knowing how many sacks of doubloons.

"What will Linda have this morning?" asked her suitor.

"A little ring I saw here. Tomorrow is my god-child's birthday and he must have a present. But the ring is gone. How unlucky I am."

"Certainly among all these you will find one to suit."

"I had set my heart on the one sold."

"You should have engaged it; but perhaps you are opposed to all kinds of engagements."

Linda turned away as if annoyed.

"How is the American taking his arrest?" he contineud. "He, perhaps, has not heard of the rumor that he and Manuel Ruiz are to be shot, and that without a trial. It is said that their guilt is so plain that not even the decision of a military court will be needed."

"How heard you this report?" asked Linda, excitedly.

"Now you are interested, my little one. This fellow has turned the heads of the women."

"Tell me, senor, if what you said is true?"

"Sancho and the lieutenant of the staff say it is so decided. A Frenchman is the principal witness against them on one count, that of being spies within the lines, while as murderers of Vasquez, the evidence is quite plain."

Linda did not return home when she left the monte pio's, but going diagonally across the plaza she left San Fernando to her right and turned down South Flores street until she arrived before the home of the Navarros.

Beatrice admitted her in answer to her summons.

"What, Linda! In tears!"

"Oh, Beatrice! Beatrice! I hate to tell you."

The sobbing girl threw herself into a chair and was a moment or two recovering herself sufficiently to proceed.

"Do speak, Linda. Is your father sick?"

"Worse, Beatrice, worse."

"What! Dying?"

"Oh no—no—Senor Raymond! Oh, Beatrice! Senor Raymond!"

Beatrice's cheek blanched, and she held the table against which she was leaning with a firmer clutch. She spoke not, but awaited with fixed features the ability of her friend to proceed.

Linda, with averted look, continued:

"It is said that Senor Raymond and Manuel Ruiz will certainly be shot."

"Certainly?" demanded Beatrice. "Certainly, said you?"

Her lips were pale and compressed. Her handsomely chiseled nostrils expanded to a measured respiration, indicating strong feeling and a stronger purpose.

"I had it from the monte pio, and he said it came from those in authority—from Sancho and the lieutenant of the staff."

"I will see my father. I will see Father Ignacio. I will face the general himself. I will—Oh, Guy! Guy! To be a victim to such a rabble. Linda, it shall not be. As I love him I will save him. I may be absolutely nothing to him, but I am determined he shall not be shot like a dog by this cowardly mob which calls itself an army. Linda, you will help me. I may need your assistance if the fiends prove deaf to the appeal of justice or to the force of influence. There is no time to lose. This may require prompt action and moments may be precious. Do you glean everything in the shape of facts and sift each rumor that you hear to discover the grain of truth it may contain."

Beatrice paced the room excitedly, while Linda, half rising to go, watched her.

"Yes, Linda, go. Through your solicitude I detect your love for him. All the better. Your passion will spur you to his assistance. As for myself, I swear that he shall be released, and with God's help and my deep love the strongest walls of Bexar cannot hold him."

"Beatrice, I will go and learn all I can. Perhaps my father will know something. I will love him for your sake, Beatrice, and for you I will help to liberate him."

Linda stole softly out and when the door closed behind her Beatrice left the room and, proceeding through a back hall, opened a door that led into a yard. She called:

"Miguel! Miguel!"

An answer came in the strong accents of a man, and presently the owner of the voice appeared. He was of large proportions and tall, with a slight stoop of the shoulders. His whole physique indicated great strength and his dress classed him as a mozo of all work.

"Miguel, come in; I want to talk to you."

The giant followed her into the hall, and at her sign, took a seat. She drew a chair close to him.

"Miguel, I am in trouble and want you to help me."

"I am your servant, senorita."

"But this is something difficult and dangerous."

"All the same—your servant."

"Miguel, you have been with our family since years before my birth; you have been faithful and Don Juan would risk his life for you, as I know you would for him. Promise me now that what I will say to you will not be repeated without my permission."

"Your servant promises."

"Miguel, you are familiar with the carcel. I have heard you tell stories of the place, and once you said that there was a secret passage from a part of the prison leading to the jailer's quarters."

"There is a passage known only to a few. I once helped to repair the cell into which it opens, and although it has been so long ago I beleive that in the dark I could find the stone covering the opening."

"Oh! Miguel! Would you go with me to find that opening in the quarters, and when found, would you help undo the way to the cell if I, Beatrice Navarro, were with you—by your very side?"

"I am your servant, senorita. It will be only necessary to command me."

"Here, then, Miguel—good Miguel—here on this paper I will draw the plan of the carcel. Here is the court; here the hall of the cells; here the jailer's quarters; here is the plan. Now, in which cell is the opening to this secret passage?"

Miguel took the pencil and marked the cell. Then he traced the course of the passageway under the court to the hall in Bonito's quarters, where, he informed Beatrice, the other place of exit was to be found. The eyes of Beatrice glistened with satisfaction as she dismissed the mozo, and her nervous excitement rose and fell as her active mind was swayed by the passion which completely possessed her. She had not known her love until an appalling danger seemed about to intervene to shut out forever the light whose brilliant elucidation but awaited the test that was to fan the already glowing germ. The realization of imminent danger to him who had for days filled her heart with those emotions peculiar to first love, emotions which enter and abide with one, unquestioned and inexplicable, had now brought out the finer elements of character whose possession marked Beatrice as a girl superior to her environments. The warm Castillian blood, the conveyancer of so many charms in both mental and physical development, had been tempered by American education. The contact with northern character had blended self dependence with the indescribable graces and soft manners of an extraction that engendered reminiscences of the chivalry of Castile and Aragon. Beatrice was now sure of her position. She loved the youth who was all but a stranger, who had appeared upon the horizon of her affections to shed the radiance that an uncongenial environment had failed to produce. It seemed to her that a great waste, replete with barrenness, stretching out into a dim vista of stunted growth and arid temperature, had suddenly assumed a garb of verdure, while the prespect changed to cool retreats, where limipd waters laved the shaded borders of eddying brooks. What wonder, then, that she should be be aroused by a sense of danger threatening the existence of this talismanic change with the prospect of a reversion rendered more distasteful from the contrast.

He whom she loved had averted a danger to which she had been exposed, which, but for his heroism, would have resulted in death. Yet it was not for this she loved him. The obligation, perhaps, rendered her passion more comprehensive. Now that he was in danger she had the twofold purpose of love and gratitude to give impetus to her efforts to save him from a pitiless enemy. The fortunate knowledge possessed by Miguel of the secret passage that existed in the carcel gave her the power to effect his escape without the sympathy of the jailor, provided he could be circumvented during his repose or while off duty. Linda could be relied upon to give valuable assistance in this part of the programme. Linda loved him. The sharp perception of a woman made this apparent, and her estimation of the man she loved would have made her wonder that any woman should fail to love him. Full of these thoughts and brimming with the renewed interest which Guy's danger had awakened, Beatrice sought her room that she might uninterruptedly plot and plan and dream.

CHAPTER XLII

So soon as Josefa was left alone on the evening that Ruiz waited for the mantle of darkness to allow him to leave the De la Torre's house without detection, she began to reproach herself for not detaining him longer. She felt that Ruiz had wronged her and she blamed herself for not having indulged still more extensively in reproaches before allowing him to depart. She was in a mood for fussing and realized to the fullest extent a mania in which desperation points to the most unwarranted actions. The unrest which seized her with an increasing power finally culminated. A set purpose seemed to possess her. She procured pencil and paper and dashed off several lines which she hurriedly read, then folded the note. Looking through the rodded window, she called to a boy who stood in the yard below: "Juan! Juan!"

In answer he approached close to the wall.

"Take this to the monte pio" she said, throwing the paper to him, "and when you return I will give you a real."

Josefa busied herself around her apartment as if in preparation for something. She stood before the mirror, and combed her short hair over her face, then parting it on the side, she arranged it after the fashion of a cavalier.

"My features will be masculine enough, with the aid of dress, to conceal my true sex, even from him."

These words were said just audibly as she turned her head from side to side, studying the effect. When she thought it to be about time for the return of her messenger, she kept on the lookout for him, and before long was rewarded by his appearance with a bundle. She motioned to him to bring it to the front door, and, going down to meet him, was soon back with the package inspecting the contents.

"Que tonto!" she exclaimed, as she held up a pair of trousers that were literally strung with glittering ornaments.

"I would not wear such as these, for I would be a center of attraction," she decided.

Then on further inspection she selected several articles of masculine apparel which seemed to suit better.

"These are more modest and I—believe—will—fit my slight figure to perfection."

An hour later Josefa stood before her glass, looking to be a comely Mexican youth. Her hat sat jauntily upon her head. Her hair, short for a woman, was but little longer than the prescription of the Mexican custom for the sterner sex. The well fitting round-a-bout fell a little below the waist, far enough to well conceal a wide scarlet sash whose ends fell from a knot over the left hip. The pants, close fitting at the belt, fell loosely from the lower limbs and extended far over the neat instep, making the narrow foot look only two-thirds its length. Thus attired Josefa stole noiselessly down the steps and out of the front door into the street. She bent her steps to the principal thoroughfare and before she had well entered it, her gait became steadier from reassurance. She passed boldly on to the bridge that led to the Alameda. Nothing occurred to more than disturb Josefa's equanimity until she reached the bridge where the lights of several eating stands illuminated the sidewalk and were reflected from the walls of the houses. As she paused here to think about her further movements, the figure of a man passed by and as he turned his face to the lights, she recognized the features of Manuel Ruiz. Gratified at the discovery she followed him over the bridge and up the steep embankment on the further side.

* * *

The day after Ducio's interview with the notary he had an appointment at headquarters, and to meet it found himself entering the capacious yard in front of the little building on the river. He found the lieutenant of the staff and his friend Sancho in consultation on the back veranda.

"Welcome!" said the lieutenant, as Ducio entered.

"Buenas dias," said Sancho.

"Senors, I greet you," said Ducio, with a smile.

"Be seated, senor. We wanted to hear from you in regard to this man Raymond, whether you know if he has been communicating with the enemy."

"I have every cause to think so," replied Ducio.

"Explain, senor."

"He has friends, if not relatives, in the Texas camp and must be in communication with them. He knows of their presence there and, judging from the fact that he has made no attempt to escape, I believe that he remains here for the purpose of communicating information to your enemies."

"That would constitute him a spy."

"Most assuredly."

"Then he should be shot," said Sancho.

"Along with Ruiz, whose case is plain," said the lieutenant.

"A sharp fellow; he is *au fait* with the Texan commanders and took active part at Concepcion."

"The dastardly traitor," said the lieutenant.

"The murderer of Vasquez," chimed in Sancho.

"Is it certain that they will be shot?" asked Ducio.

"You mean Ruiz and Raymond?"

"Those two."

"Unlucky R's," said Sancho.

"Their fate is sealed. The order for their execution will be issued this week," said the lieutenant, with a pompous air that little accorded with his sqeaking voice.

"The general then has decided."

"Yes, and the decision is final. Besides General Almonte, who represents El Presidente, has approved it and will not leave the city until after the execution. Almonte says that this Raymond is a splendid actor. He joined his party on the San Geronimo and represented that he had just escaped from the Indians. Almonte was suspicious of him from the first."

"Has Almonte heard from Edward Gritton?"

"No. Doubtless the messenger was intercepted."

"And Gritton?"

"Will fare badly if the dispatches fell into the hands of the rebels But Gritton's action has served the purpose of the government in fur nishing the names of the leaders to be punished, and I suppose there is little more use for him. Spies run great risks."

"And should be well paid."

"A precept fulfilled in Gritton's case. But there are spies and spies. Some men risk their lives in the business for love of country."

"In which case they must be to the manor born. Gritton is an Englishman."

"An Englishman. You could not get one of those infernal Texan-Americans to give the government any information. Sancho, they fill my ideal of the Spartan character."

"They are *puro diablos*. I will never forget their obstinacy at Concepcion. They have a desperate courage which I class with that of pirates. There is no virtue in it."

"It serves the purpose at all events and it will require the presence of El Presidente and his legions to secure to Mexico this empire of territory This lost to us will be but the entering wedge to the dismemberment of our country."

"Is there news from the rebel camp later than that brought you by this gentleman?" referring to Ducio.

"Yes. Their investment of the place is complete. They are in considerable force at the old mill just above on the river. A foraging party from the garrison had a brush with them on the lower road to Matamoras."

"Then Almonte will have some trouble in eluding their pickets. If he be captured on the heels of the execution of the two prisoners those devils would resort to lex telionis measures."

While the lieutenant and Sancho were thus discussing the military situation Ducio remained silent, the words of the pair having just interest enough to make their import comprehended, while he mentally evolved the adaptability of what he heard to the furtherance of the schemes matriculated by his late experience. Ducio reflected with no small degree of satisfaction on the decision of the military authority to put to death one of the beneficiaries named by Mr. Trigg in the disposition of the hidden treasure. Not that the execution of Guy Raymond would have any direct bearing on his own fortunes, but it seemed to him that his removal would be an obstacle less to his acquisition of the contents of the iron pot. He had not seen the subject of his thoughts, but had heard the story of his capture, his escape and of his prowess from the lips of Ruiz before he left the Texan camp. The mere existence of an honorable and fearless opponent, no matter how passive he may be through ignorance of contemplated wrongs or the imminence of danger, is a power whose force is magnified in the consciences of the depraved. So Ducio mentally argued that Guy's removal would by some means accelerate his chances to fortune. Mr. Trigg's life depended from a thread which a stray bullet from a Mexican musket might snap. Without the papers neither Hamilton nor Perry could solve the riddle of the sand hills. The notary was the custodian of the secret, surreptitiously obtained and with himself alone knew of the existence of the gold which "beneath the cross securely hid" awaited his coming to enrich him. The notary must be removed by some means. He could not afford to divide the treasure which luck had brought him; yes, brought him, for it was already within his reach and it now required but his own consummate ability to devise the means to be used and the time to act. Ducio began to wonder that other men of apparent intelligence found it so hard to win fortune. A few hours had not only put him on the road to wealth, but had disclosed before his greedy gaze a mass of yellow coins that of itself constituted the prize for which millionaires struggle and toil, and to acquire it, use every device known to monopolistic tactics and legalized depredations. The execution of Guy Raymond was favorable. The capture of General Almonte by the Texans through information furnished by him would give him perfect freedom within the Texan lines with no cloud upon him for having been a brief sojourner within the lines of the beseiged city. If he should do up the notary he must, through prudence, take himself outside of Mexican jurisdiction and drum-head decisions. While the swift justice of the authorities excited his admiration in the cases of the two prisoners, its rigor was clear and alarming when it proposed to be the adjudicator of his own transgressions. Ducio's traits and tendencies were only the world's emphasized. Inductively examined, their germs will be discovered where duty and patriotism have been rendered comatose by infusions of false ideas in the problems of social life, to the destruction of its true aims, to the subversion of human happiness, to the communism of class. To Ducio the modern social drift was apparent. The science of government had been prostituted by the complete ascendency of the property idea over individual rights. Acquisitiveness had so completely developed in the cranium of the genius of civilization that the well being of humanity had shrivelled into comparative vacuity. In Ducio's conception he had accentuated the social tendency by taking shorter cuts to fortune. Robbery is robbery under any guise. It may be qualified by prefixes to save the qualms of a pharisaical conscience, or it may masquerade in fictions of legislation, yet the essence is there. Land illegally held in Mortmain became to grasping churchman legal and lucrative in trust. Men often grow rich through murder; it may be of an individual, or it may be of the masses. In the latter case it is always legal and, therefore, respectable with perhaps only a score of economists protesting against doing by wholesale what is infamous by retail. Elastic minds reconcile the brigandage of class with honesty and plead custom to refute the logic of nature and humanitarianism. Ducio, rascal as he was, had a supreme contempt for those lights of civilization who upheld the depredations of class and in the same breath denounced the individual robber. He deemed it to be many degrees braver to incur the risk of a direct appropriation of the goods, chattels and money of an individual without the cloak of a legislative act or the pursuance of an arbitrary and unnatural custom. He believed that the wrong which would crush thousands was proportionately greater than that which would injure an individual. Ducio, however, was a character who stood not upon the distinctions when the opportunity presented itself to transfer the shekels of another to the pockets of Ducio. With a little training he would have made a star in Wall street. In the lobby or in the halls of legislation he would have left the imprint of his peculiar talent on the class legislation of a political system intended to be a model for the imitation of mankind in the construction of governments looking primarily to the freedom of rights and equality of the people. Ducio recognized the truths enunciated by political economists, but it was like the knowledge which the traditional Satan has of the beneficence and power of the Ruler of the universe. Satan prefers the unrest of Hades and grim satisfaction of the exercise of an evil power to the joys of Heaven or the peace of Nirvana. Ducio thought his selfishness would be better subserved with the economies safe in the custody of the colleges and universities. Like Christian ethics, social and political economy were things to be preached and read about but too antagonistic to the present civilization to be practiced. Therefore Ducio scoffed at the teachings of moralists and economists, and in a species of *suave qui peut* rush for the smiles of fortune, he determined to take the short cuts and trust to secrecy of movement to save him from the clutches of the law.

CHAPTER XLIII.

Ruiz, who had kept upon Ducio Halfen's trail since the latter quitted the Cabeza de Toro in pursuit of the notary, followed him the same night to the house of that functionary. Concealed behind the apartment he witnessed the interview between the two worthies from the rear window and heard most of their conversation. He gleaned the fact that a compromise had been effected between them regarding the paper dropped on the gambling table. He inferred that they had a key to the treasure to which Guy had some claim, but he could not make it clear to himself what it could be. It appeared evident that Ducio had had access to some treasure from the number of doubloons he had displayed at the monte table. He could see in Ducio's manner and read in his looks a danger to the notary which the latter did not appear to realize. When the two separated Ruiz resolved to keep watch on the movements of the wily Creole. When he quitted his post as eaves-dropper, he climbed a low wall and found himself in a short alley connecting Acequia and Soledad streets. As he made his way to the former, so as to enter the plaza at a different point from Ducio, the figure of a man appeared and looked over the wall at the other's retreating form. He sprang lightly over and followed Ruiz to the plaza. Here the unknown stopped and leaned lightly against the massive masonry of the corner until the retreating figure was lost in the direction of the Candelario's.

"Well, senor Don Manuel Ruiz, you are a puzzle. What your purpose here is I am not able to say. Gambling and eaves-dropping are no clear pointers to your mission."

Such was the exclamation made in an undertone by the young man with the scarlet sash who had been following Ruiz as he left his position at the corner of the plaza and turned up towards Flores street.

"That was a handsome Frenchman," he mused, "and Ruiz was watching him. He had a deal of money. Is perhaps rich. What can Manuel have to do with him? I saw him once before while I was entering Linda's gate. Such piercing eyes! They say mine are that way. Dios! What a pair we'd make!"

And Josefa entered her door.

Josefa's escapade of the night before could not have produced any remorse of conscience in the bosom of that erratic damsel on a review of her violation of the proprieties, if indeed she took the trouble to reflect on the subject or to estimate the consequences, if any there might have been, in the event of detection. One thing is certain, that when she first recognized Ruiz at the bridge, she took care to keep him in sight or hailing distance until she turned her steps homeward. Whatever might have been her doubts of her old lover, she had that confidence in his manhood to be sure that no one could have insulted her with impunity while in the radius of his protection. This reflection may have upheld the girl in any misgivings that chanced to well up unbidden, to deter her from a successful prosecution of her espoinage. She had accomplished nothing towards the solution of Ruiz's mission, if that was her object, for an honest inquiry into her own intentions would have disclosed a mental state in which jealousy and a discontent with her present humdrum existence were kept astir by a nature full of high-strung ambition. Ruiz was not a necessity to her, yet she felt the influence of the old tie, while she half hated him because he had failed to prove the instrument which was to dispel the cloud hanging over her life. Her facile heart was ready to acknowledge any helpmeet who would promise to guide her in the life-paths, free from the restraint of certain influences repugnant to her nature. The piercing eyes of the Frenchman whom she knew not had made an impression on her waxen heart, and their owner would have only to follow up the advantage by a show of dash and means, to win for himself the ambitious daughter of the De la Torres. Josefa's thoughts pursued this very channel from the time of her awaking until an hour later she arose to make her toilet. This she did with all the indolence of leisure, until her tardiness invoked a call to the morning meal. A little later a note from the lieutenant, requesting permission to bring a friend to see her, was handed her. Josefa's eyebrows arched, as she read, in wonder as to who the unknown caller was to be. She knew all the gentlemen of the city who would likely be friends of the writer. It could not be Almonte, who was married. It suddenly flashed upon her mind that it might be the stranger with those piercing eyes. She had been told he was a Frenchman. What matter? Nationality is nothing. Push, impudence and means. They were sufficient for the attainment of the ne plus ultra of modern ambition. They were the triune elements whence were formed the materials of fortune to be acquired without the efforts and the humiliations of labor. The Frenchman was apparently in antagonism with Ruiz. He was welcome at headquarters, which had set a price on Manuel's head. The favorite had been watched by the fugitive at the gambling resort where the former had lost, with apparently small regret, so much money. Ruiz was not rich, and his treason to his country would impoverish him. The sharp Frenchman must be well off, and besides——

Josefa did not conclude her thought definitely, but allowed her imagination to revel in conclusions, enveloping the dark stranger in a mysticism of character whose blending lights and shadows reflected the varying bents of her own ephemeral purposes.

She was not disappointed, when her two callers were announced, to find that one of them was Ducio Halfen. The latter had been no less stricken by the appearance of Josefa than she was by the easy carriage and flashing eyes of the Creole. A report of the lady's prospects, exaggerated if not untrue, caused him to construe them as worthy of the aspirations of an unprincipled adventurer like himself and with the idea uppermost in his mind he sought an acquaintance with her through the instrumentality of his military friend of the staff. The meeting between the two, from its inception, lacked the stiffness that frequently characterizes the first encounters of the sexes where a suspicion of interest or design has either mutually or singly existed in the minds of the parties. On the part of Josefa this arose from her natural self-command and art in acting. With Ducio it was from an innate impudence and lack of any touches of refinement calculated to rebuke evil purposes or excite trepidation. Conscience—he had none. The call extended longer than interviews of such a preliminary nature usually last, and when Ducio left he had promised to return again in the afternoon for a walk. The lieutenant was ignored in the arrangement.

In the afternoon the engagement for the walk was fulfilled. Josefa's knowledge of the city and its environs constituted her the guide for the occasion. They followed the banks of the river until the line of pickets intercepted their further progress towards its source then crossing a rude footbridge, they traversed the fields until the Alamo, with its weather-beaten walls, rose boldly into view.

"Would you like to take a look at the country from the top of the Alamo?" she asked of Ducio.

"I should like it extremely well," he replied. "And we may catch a sight of the Texans, who are said to be much nearer town, at an old mill just above on the river."

"You said you were in their company for a while, before entering here. Are they the terrible characters that we hear described?"

"They are devils to fight. As to character, they represent every phase of life, the farmer, the doctor, the lawyer, the mechanic, the merchant, the clerk and the adventurer, and of course are made up of good, bad and indifferent men like one will find among all such gatherings of humanity."

They reached the church in a short time and by a rather difficult ascent found themselves upon the walls of the edifice which was destined so soon to become famous throughout the world as the Thermopolae of America, reserving for itself a distinction which in later years a patriotic Texan expressed in the memorable words:

"Thermopolae had her messenger of defeat—the Alamo had none."

To the north the course of the river was marked by a line of timber. Chaparral, denuded of foliage, stood in clusters or extended in stretches with alternations of openings in which the grass still showed spots of green among the gray and taller growth. There was a sleepy look in the prospect. The background of hills raised their blue summits in successive ranges until the whole was capped by the rocky elevation whose tree-clad summit marked the spot where the swift running Olmus burst suddenly from its limestone prison, to run its short course through glassy lakes and eddying pools, rippling rapids and winding currents, until its crystal waters were lost in those of the San Antonio. The old mill which the Texans were reported to have occupied was just visible on the right bank of the river. A horse or two just beyond, a faint indication of smoke a shade heavier than the hazy atmosphere, were the sole indications presenting themselves to the vision, to show that the rebel Texans were in the vicinity. To the left and west lay the town a materialized monotony of low walls, with occasional reliefs of adobe and tule where stood the jacals of the poorer class. Ducio asked half inquiringly:

"In your Monterey home you had finer scenery than this?"

"Oh, there it is grand; the city is in the very lap of the mountains. All around they lift their great heads towering far above the valley, while their sides are a picture of perpetual green."

"You would like to return to a place doubtless filled with memories as pleasant as the scenery is grand—would you not?"

"Yes, but——"

"But?"

"I would not return alone. My relatives are few, confined in fact, to a mother and uncle, and they are not congenial."

"Not congenial?"

"Both are good to me—both are bigots, and move in the narrow sphere circumscribed by the rigor and rules of the church. I crave liberty at any cost. I would rise above all restraint, all rules, all conventionalities, and live the life best suited to the happiness of beings who know no future existence and believe that they are here with the full right to employ all the traits, which distinguish them from the lower animals, for their gratification and pleasure."

"You then stand in need of a friend. My ideas run in the same grooves. Could we be friends?"

"Why not?"

"There may be barriers. For instance, my stay here is limited. Two more suns may not see me in Bexar."

"So soon?"

"Yes, business calls me away. To linger here might cost me a fortune, although I might win the prize of your friendship."

"You have been left some property?"

"Yes—no—not by will or legacy, but my presence elsewhere will bring me to a fortune, that I could not realize or secure by a delay of many more days in this queer city."

"You would be unwise to delay your going in that case—but, senor—you may return and then—and then——"

"And then?"

"We could be friends."

"And go to Monterey?"

Josefa looked away as if at a loss to answer.

"To Monterey or elsewhere if——"

"Well?"

"If I were free to go and you desired to go with me."

Ducio would have replied if a noise had not claimed their attention. It was the step of Father Ignacio, who seeing Josefa in company with a stranger, while he was passing, mounted to the top of the building.

"It is my uncle," said Josefa in an undertone.

"The priest!" exclaimed Ducio.

"The priest," said Father Ignacio in a tone of reply.

And he continued:

"You are sight-seeing, Josefa? And who is this gentleman, your escort?"

"I am rather his escort, uncle. This is Senor Halfen, a stranger whose acquaintance I have made. Senor Halfen, this is Father Ignacio."

The men bowed.

"I have heard of you Father."

"And I of you, sir. You are the Frenchman."

"I have a French passport."

"It is all the same, senor, but tell, me how is it that you make Senor Raymond a spy?"

"Those are my suspicions."

"But, my dear senor, he is not. He entered San Antonio with me, just escaped from Indian captivity, and did not even know that there was trouble between Mexico and the colonists. I am afraid, senor, that you have done a great injury to a young man whom I have found to be the soul of honor. Even my influence cannot change the attitude of the authorities towards him, and your evidence is counted strongly against him."

Father Ignacio spoke with feeling, for being a true type of honorable manhood, he despised the malignity that prompted persecution of innocence.

Ducio replied:

"I gave my views in his case not voluntarily. I merely replied to questions and what I stated was my consciencious opinion. I do not care to be lectured upon the subject and trust your reverence will take the hint."

"Your impudence does not match your nationality. French gentlemen are usually respectful to priests."

"Let us go, Senorita De la Torre. I would not let this grow into a quarrel," said Ducio.

"It will not be a quarrel, senor, for I am going myself. Josefa, you have congenial company I perceive. I congratulate you."

"Thank you, uncle," she replied ironically. Then in a kinder tone, as if to bridge over the situation, she continued:

"But where have you been out this way? You positively look fatigued."

"Oh! My major domo, Jose, has disappeared and is not to be found inside of the lines. It is certainly a mystery. Between his disappearance and Senor Raymond's trouble, I have had no peace of mind. I have exhausted my fund of influence and now I have but one recourse, and that is to my God. If prayers and masses will avail, not a hair of this gentle youth shall be harmed. I feel sure that God's power will avert the danger which menaces him. He is a noble youth, Josefa."

Josefa's reflections were multitudinous when she found herself at home again alone. Her companion of the walk was sympathetic and her uncle had dubbed him a congenial one. There was much truth in his remark and it eminently fitted her previous declaration to Ducio that she desired a congenial friend. This Halfen had an external respectability that would meet the requirements of society. His principles might be anything, all the better if they were anti-religious, so far as she was concerned. The cloud over his possesssion of gold which Manuel's musings had raised had not been cleared away by his explanation that he must leave Bexar to secure his expectancy. If wealth was to be his or if he had it already secured, by fair means or foul, *que importa,* society would not stop to inquire before extending its hand. If her uncle had not interrupted their quiet tete-a-tete on the top of the old mission, much of the uncertainty as to their future might have been dissipated by the utterance of a few more words. How much better was Guy Raymond than Ducio Halfen? His honor had landed him in jail. Ducio was free, and fortune was extending to him her arms. She did not begrudge him a tithe of the help to be expected from the mumblings of the mass or the telling of beads. She would not utter an Ave, even if it could save him, save him to Beatrice Navarro.

CHAPTER XLIV.

Ruiz had kept upon the trail of Ducio Halfen with such persistency that he was perfectly posted as to his movements. He had detected the sudden acquaintance and growing intimacy between him and Josefa, but of course he was at a loss to know what transpired at their interviews. In forty-eight hours they were together four times, and he believed that no good result would follow in the steps of his old fiancee. He had been disappointed in his calculations for assistance from the Texan camp to carry out his part of the programme that had brought him to the city. He had communicated his readiness twice through paid messengers, to co-operate with the promised aid, yet the assurance of its coming had failed to reach him. He was at great risk of detection, which was only deferred by reason of the mistaken identity which was costing Jose his liberty. One night, it was the third after Ducio's interview with the notary, Ruiz discovered the Creole passing along the east side of the plaza, and supposing that his destination was the house of the De la Torres he followed him. The so-called Frenchman moved with an apparent caution that had not been characteristic of his manner on any previous occasion, while under the surveillance of Ruiz. His entrance into Soledad street banished the first idea in Ruiz's mind that Ducio contemplated a visit to Josefa, but he felt sure now that the notary was to be honored by an interview with his confederate in the mystery of the paper. A minute later this was verified by Ducio's light rap at the door of the notary, who presently atmitted him. Ruiz began to deliberate on the advisability of playing eavesdropper, feeling half ashamed of the role. But it was evident that the villains were bent on some mischief, and as Guy Raymond appeared interested in some manner, he finally concluded to prosecute the espionage in the hope to serve his friend. Accordingly he gained, by easy steps, his old position at the rear window, and through a small aperture left by the fold of an improvised curtain he had a pretty good survey of the room. Halfen's face was fully visible as he sat opposite the notary, who only disclosed a side view as he occasionally moved his head. Their tones were low at first and, from the catches that reached the listener's ears, were on commonplace topics, foreign to the undoubted purpose of the interview. Once he caught the name of Josefa accompanied by a rascally expressive smile on Ducio's physiognomy. Finally the conversation became more earnest and serious, and erstwhile a whole sentence would reward Manuel's patience. This came from Ducio:

"But as to the division, my friend, that must depend upon the amount of trouble and risk * * * *"

This from the notary:

"But the papers must remain in my possession" * * * * "They are my security." * * * *

Ducio demanded the papers of the notary for inspection, but the latter was positive in his declination to accede to it.

"You should be satisfied," he insisted.

Finally Ducio agreed to all the notary insisted upon, and he assumed an accommodating air until he rose to depart. He held out his hand, which the notary took, and things appeared to be smoothed over between the confederates. At his caller's request the notary proceeded to let him out in the street. In doing so he turned his back to Ducio, who, seizing the opportunity, struck him on the head with something that felled him to the floor. The assassin lost no time in repeating his deadly blows upon the prostrate form of his victim. The execution of the deed required but an instant. The wretch stood over his fallen partner in crime a moment, then stooping, went through his pockets. The contents he examined by the light on the table, casting now and then furtive glances at the windows. Finally he gave vent to an exclamation of satisfaction as he finished the examination of a paper.

"This is the document," he said. "And now I will be gone."

Hastily extinguishing the light, he made his way out of the front door and stole cautiously down the street.

Ruiz was amazed at what he had witnessed and half regretted that he did not rush to the notary's assistance. But he was in the city incognito and it would have been folly to have so acted. Besides, both parties were conspirators, and he felt that retributive justice would yet overtake the murderer. Dangerous as it was, he could not refrain from entering the office to view the body and see if life was extinct. So noiseless had been the whole proceeding that no cry was uttered and save the thud which came from the fall of the light form of the victim, nothing had been heard to indicate an altercation in the interview so amicably begun. The real danger then, which Manuel could apprehend, would be from a chance discovery of his presence in a compromising position and the circumstance used as potential evidence of his complicity. An arrest would also lead to his identification, which should have really constituted his cause for alarm. At any rate, he did not allow himself time for reflection on these subjects, but soon found himself in the room and darkness. This was a dilemma. He however felt around for the body, which he carefully manipulated to discover any signs of life. No respiration—no pulse. The repose of the limp form was the repose of death. The head had received the fatal blow. Through the crushed skull the life blood still flowed upon the floor, forming a pool into which Manuel accidentally placed the fingers of his hand. He withdrew them with a shudder and was careful to avoid getting upon his shoes or clothing the red evidence of crime. This Ducio Halfen was a criminal of the worst type, he thought, as he wended his way along the street. What terrible company was such a man for a female of gentle birth, or with any claims to virtuous womanhood. He thought of Josefa and her intimacy with the fiend who had just taken human life for the possession of a piece of paper. Bonito's name had been thrice mentioned in connection with this business, as was also Guy Raymond's. Would it not be well to apprise the jailer? Full of this last idea Ruiz turned towards the carcel. No—there was the sentinel pacing his post, an obstacle in the way. He would enter by Linda's garden. It was late, but the business was urgent. Before he realized it he was at the door in the wall. It was locked. The wall was high, but he would try it. Placing his hand upon the extension of the low arch, he gave one vigorous spring and caught the top of the wall with the other. A few scrambles and he bestrided it almost out of breath with the exertion. He let himself down into the garden and approaching the door of the apartment he hesitated. The thinly curtained window disclosed a light within. Linda had not retired—so much the better. His light knock sounded strangely distinct in the quiet of the night. The footsteps he heard just before his summons at once ceased. Was Linda frightened? He would not knock again. He called:

"Linda! Linda!"

"Quien es?"

"Yo—Manuel—Manuel Ruiz."

"Surely the voice of Manuel," she replied, "but Manuel is in his cell."

"Escaped, however. Deja, me entrar."

"What would you here this time of night? A fugitive from my father would find a poor asylum with his daughter."

"You should know, Linda, that I mean well. Your father's interests, perhaps his life, may depend upon my seeing you this night. Abra la puerta."

The door just cracked a little and when Linda had ocular proof of Ruiz's identity it opened and the caller crossed the threshold

"What, Manuel! Blood on your hands!"

"True, the stains are there yet. A little water, Linda, and I will remove the traces."

As Ruiz cleaned his hands in Linda's basin he exacted of her a promise of secrecy as to his visit and in regard to whatever he might impart. He then seated himself and recounted what he had witnessed at the notary's office, together with all that he knew of the existence and character of the document causing the homicide.

Linda knew nothing definite of Bonito's business. He was often with the notary, who attended to all papers requiring attestation, besides giving her father the benefit of his legal attainments. While the two were imparting to each other all they knew in regard to Bonito's danger on the one hand and his habits on the other, Manuel had several times heard a shuffling noise in the hall, not unlike the jailer's steps, but more labored, as if he were experiencing some difficulty in his movements.

This finally aroused Ruiz's curiosity.

"Is that your father in the hall?"

Linda looked troubled, and it was a moment before she replied:

"Father has locked me in here to conceal his work. He has been busy, repeatedly passing back and forth, as you have heard, since dark."

"What can it mean?"

"I cannot say. Oh, Manuel! He is a strange man. He loves money and saves every centado. That he has money hid away I am certain, but he has hinted that he has been robbed, and I believe right now he is making some disposition of his treasure, to better conceal it."

"Robbed lately?"

"Just four days ago."

"Por Dios! The Frenchman."

"He who murdered——?"

"Lo mismo."

"That accounts for the gold lost at the Cabeza de Toro."

"You'd make a nice little detective, Linda."

"But you spoke of Senor Raymond, Manuel."

"They intimated that he must be put out of the way, but expect the authorities to attend to that."

"But, Manuel——"

Linda's voice was strong in protest, her eyes suffused with tears, and her head sank forward as her extended hand touched the shoulder of her friend.

"I know what you would say, Linda. We all love him and if there be any virtue in human effort after every available influence has been exhausted without effect, he shall not meet the death sentence of these miserable tyrants. Linda, we may ask your passive assistance."

"My assistance? I would do much to save him. I am a frail woman, it is true, but I have the will to serve him that would match the strength of giants. Oh! Manuel, I am not ashamed to say I love him—that I love him without one act of his to encourage the affection."

"He is a lucky fellow. Yet again unlucky, for it is little less than murder to blight the love of a woman."

"It is no fault of his, Manuel, to know him is to love him."

"Then tomorrow night, if I and others seek your aid to free Guy Raymond, you will freely give it?"

"Trust me, Manuel. Only be sure of yourself."

"Now, Linda, I will go, but you must warn your father of this Frenchman, and if you repeat to him what you have heard from me, perhaps he will know more of the danger to be expected than I could tell him.'

As Manuel left the room to make his exit from the garden, the heavy shuffle in the hall again attracted his attention. He nodded knowingly to Linda, while he motioned his hand in the direction of the noise. Linda followed him to let him into the street.

Ducio, like criminals generally, was too much wrought up by his act to have any very definite idea of what his next step was to be. He turned the corner to the right when he reached the plaza and drew himself close into the recess of the first door he came to. Here he endeavored to muster some degree of that coolness which was peculiarly his on all but extraordinary occasions, in order that he might determine between the comparative conditions of safety promised by flight on the one hand, and by an assumption of innocence and a longer sojourn in the city on the other.

Whatever might have been the nature of the decision that was to result from Ducio's perturbed cogitations, he was destined to be cut short in them by the sound of footsteps, followed by the passing of the owner of the feet, who almost brushed the facings of the doorway which concealed him.

"It is my evil genius," thought Ducio. "It is that fellow with the long beard. It is strange how I always encounter him."

Without definitely deciding to do so, he followed Ruiz with his eyes through the darkness, and then stealthily in person with cat-like steps.

"I'll watch what this fellow is up to, anyway," he said to himself.

As has been already related, Ruiz turned his steps finally to the jailer's home to interview Linda. Ducio witnessed the scaling of the wall and concluded it must be an affair of the heart that impelled the act.

"This fellow must be a suitor of Linda's," was the Creole's conclusion. He thought of the doubloons in Bonito's vault. These were brighter to him than Linda's eyes. He envied the chance of the fellow who had just disappeared over the wall, and thought how he could turn it to advantage if he could play the suitor and get another grip on the gold. Bonito must have recovered from the blows on the head. He had kept it dark. Wise Bonito! The story of the assault would have been the story of possession. The old miser! The fellow with the long beard had been received perhaps with open arms, for he had heard voices and then all was quiet. He put his hand on the arch. One spring and he missed the top. The other fellow did it. Another trial and the adventurer gained the wall. He surveyed the garden for a moment and then dropped over. Everything was quiet in the little enclosure. Linda's shrubs and flowers were the sole occupants. In the further corner was a tall banana plant whose broad blades cast a dense shadow. As Ducio took in the scene his first idea was to conceal himself here and await events. His patience was equal to the occasion. The long interview between Linda and her visitor at length terminated, and he drew himself closer under his shelter as he saw the two emerge from the house and move slowly, while they conversed, towards the exit to the plaza.

"Oh, Manuel!" he heard the girl say. "Do all you can for Senor Raymond."

"Rest assured Linda, on that point. Before tomorrow's sun will have set you will hear from me."

Linda stood in the doorway while she talked in lower tones to her departing visitor, and Ducio, who had been looking with longing eyes into the now vacant apartment, thought the opportunity an excellent one in which to slip into it unseen and be that much nearer the depository of Bonito's wealth. He had formed no plan, no definite course to pursue, but seemed to have abandoned himself to the successive impulses that grew out of the opportunities of the hour. Therefore, under the direction of the genius of evil, Ducio found himself gliding into Linda's room with the noiseless movements of a cat. The pure atmosphere of the virgin apartment was defiled by the villain's respiration. It was as the mixing of the noisome vapor of the marsh with the perfume of the flower-clad valley; the invasion of Satan into an Eden of purity. With a hasty glance about him he tried the door which Linda had stated to Ruiz had been locked by her father, to keep her from interrupting his operations. The door was fastened. There was no time to lose. He must conceal himself or the screams of Linda on her return would recall the visitor from whom she was parting, back to her assistance. He had but two retreats in which to hide. One, under the bed; the other behind a curtain at one end of the room, which depended before a recess in which were hung some articles of female attire. He chose the latter as the one best calculated to afford him a view of the senorita's movements. He had scarcely concealed himself behind the curtain before Linda entered and closed and fastened her door. Womanlike, her first act on turning from the door was to take a look at herself in the little mirror which overlooked her modest dressing table. She gave a little sigh as she turned away from the glass, but instead of Ruiz, the form of Guy was in her mental vision. As it was late, Linda made preparations to retire and was soon attired in her snowy nightdress, little suspecting that her movements had been subjected to the vile scrutiny of the wretch who had betrayed Guy Raymond. She walked restlessly for a moment to and from the door leading to the hall and would stop and listen a while as if to hear the noise of Bonito's movements. No sounds came from the hall. Finally she drew near the bedside and falling upon her knees she made the sign of the cross and began saying her prayers. As her petition rose silently to the God of her religion, was it a halo that shone about her temples, or was it only the light from the lamp that glistened as it was reflected from her smooth black tresses? Her position kneeling above the soft folds of her couch, with a proper comprehension of the faith implied by the act of prayer, and the air of purity that pervaded the virgin sanctum lent an inspiration to the scene that impressed even the callous heart of the rascal whose scrutiny was little less than the rape of virtue. As she was rising from her knees, the hall door suddenly opened and Bonito poked in his head.

"Linda, I have finished what I was doing. I am tired, Linda—very tired, and if I sleep too soundly to hear a call—listen Linda; if I am hard to wake, call me. Como estoy fatigado!"

The jailer slammed the door, but did not lock it. Linda fixed her light for a taper and went to bed.

Ducio poked his head out from behind the curtain several times before he ventured to leave his concealment. He watched the reposing figure of the girl and listened to her breathing for some time before he concluded that nature had yielded to the claims of slumber and that Linda was in the land of dreams. When thus convinced, he glided from the recess and taking the dim light from the table, he approached the bed and held it close to the face of the sleeper. She was in deep sleep. The long, black lashes rested far upon the rounded cheek. One arm lay in naked beauty half circling her dainty head, while the other crossed the fair bosom that rose and fell with her respiration. The eyes of the intruder feasted upon the scene as, with left arm uplifted to hold the light, he bent forward in contemplation of the Hebe-like tableau. The twitchings of his features as his eyes wandered from the couch around the room with a glare that depicted fierce conflicting passions, indicated the battle raging within between evil purposes, alike criminal, but disproportionate in the enormity of their commission. Beauty or booty. The weak side of Ducio's nature necessarily succumbed to a combination of purposes which controlled, if it did not smother the more brutal instinct. Discovery in such a place would be ignominious defeat, and would perhaps lead to detection of his latest crime. The hope of escape and the passion for plunder proved indirectly the protectors of sleeping beauty. Ducio replaced the light and opened the hall door. It made a noise, but not enough to disturb the sleeper. The hall was dark. He remembered where Bonito kept the candles. He relied upon his memory and the chance that the jailer had made no changes in the disposition of his room. He had a mind to take Linda's lamp, but feared if she awoke and found no light she would become suspicious that all was not right, and if he should take it into Bonito's room that worthy might be awakened by it and be curious to know the nature of the intrusion. Ducio's decision was wise, at least he so concluded when, after gaining Bonito's room, he heard him say

"The monte pio is not robbed—never robbed—no mas Bonito—que m-a-la fortuna!"

It was evident to the intruder that these words were uttered in sleep and the regrets of the poor old miser were merged into dreams of his losses.

"I will give him more cause to dream if I can just find a candle," thought the villain.

At length Ducio found the desired candle and lost no time in returning to get a light from Linda's taper. He shut the door after him as he came out, and then proceeded to detect the open sesame to the vault below. The lounge was there. He lifted the blanket and after a search discovered the hair cord. One pull and the end of the mattress folded back and disclosed the descent. Down the steps the adventurer proceeded slowly. What was it on the steps? He stooped and picked up a handful of sand and dirt. On inspection he found that the same substances were scattered all the way down. He wondered what it could mean. On reaching the floor below he found that sand and dirt were scattered here and there mixed with bits of stone. He looked for the chest. It stood a little further on. The sight of it caused his heart to beat faster. He pulled from his pocket the knife he had used on the other occasion and stooping over to unlock the spring he found that there would be no necessity for the knife, as the chest was not locked. The discovery weakened him. Not locked! He hesitated—then raised the lid. The chest was empty.

CHAPTER XLV.

From the day that Bonito was resuscitated from the effects of the blow inflicted by Ducio Halfen in the vault, he had not been, to all appearances, the same man. He mechanically went through the routine of his prison duties, but all vestige of his humor or his crabbedness had given place to a settled melancholy that depicted itself in expression and action. He had said more to Guy than to anyone else. To Linda he merely hinted at a loss and she, accustomed to his freaks, did not press him for an explanation. He tired of trying to solve the enigma of the discovery of the entrance to the vault, and thought constantly of what he should do with the treasure in the chest. He would repair to the vault and sit for an hour contemplating the great burden to his peace of mind and trying to devise some means for its better security. It was on one of these occasions that after much torturing deliberation Bonito hit upon a plan. At any rate he rose from his stool suddenly, and said in a tone, much more cheerful than he had of late employed in his solitary talks:

"I will do it—and this very day."

It was the same day that Ducio dealt the fatal blow that sent the notary to his long account.

Bonito began to carry out his purpose at once. He conveyed to the vault the necessary tools for his work and timed his operations so as not to be missed from his post. He carefully marked out a space in the side wall, and began to cut deeply around the line. From the way he handled his hatchet and pick and chisel and mallet he was no novice in the matter. By the early afternoon he had effected an excavation which seemed to satisfy him as to dimensions, but he had all around him a quantity of debris whose presence would indicate to those aware of his possessions the place of their concealment. Bonito was equal to the occasion. Under the stimulus of his ruling passion the flabby anatomy became strong and muscular. He decided to carry the last vestige of the signs of his work to the region above, after he had securely walled up the opening and the doubloons in it. When the hoard was secured behind the replaced masonry he painted the mortar-filled cracks so as to resemble the undisturbed mass around it. Now began the tired miser's real work. Up the steep steps he had to carry, box full at a time, the sand, dirt and crumbled rock, and it was on these trips from the vault, bending under the loads of dirt, that Bonito made the shuffling, labored steps that excited Ruiz's attention while he was interviewing Linda. The miser was worn with fatigue when he fetched his last boxfull, and he deferred until the morrow a final sweeping of steps and floor. He felt sure that he had not been observed, and Linda, locked in her room, could have been the only one who had heard the little noise he had made. The strain removed from the miser's mind by the fancied safety of his gold ensured him a rest, which he had not experienced since his robbery. Now he could dream of griefs, which erstwhile had prevented his slumber. He envied the monte pio, who was never robbed, and the beggar at the church door, who had nothing to lose. He had formed something of an attachment for the young American who was his prisoner for the second time, but a stern fact had intervened to wipe from the tablet the record of the feeling. The miser's heart knew no lasting love save for his gold. Guy had rescued him—perhaps saved him—but with him rested the knowledge of his hoard. For this crime, El Pajarro might be shot for all he cared. Since his late concealment of the treasure he had softened, but so little that he still felt callous as to Guy's fate. Poor Bonito! Of such how many are there in the world who make pretensions to Christian virtue and moral worth? Callous to human woe, indifferent to human rights, forgetful of moral aims, ready to sacrifice friendship, love and truth on the altar of Mammon, they are more to be loathed than the Bonito of our story, whose ignorance and obscurity debarred him from all conception of the feelings incident to the refinement of culture and a true philanthropy.

* * * * * * * * * *

Father Ignacio had become so worried at the continued absence of Jose that it was deemed best to make known to the good priest the true state of affairs. Jose himself became so apprehensive about the trouble and annoyance of his master in regard to himself that he added by his entreaties to the determination of Guy Raymond to divulge the secret to his reverend friend. He felt sure of the good father's fidelity to his professed friendship, and that Ruiz upon his request would not be betrayed to his enemies. Accordingly the news was communicated and the same day the good father visited the cell and had a long interview with the two prisoners. The visit was one of great consolation to the major domo, who had no peace of mind under the pre-existing conditions of his confinement. To Guy the presence of the priest was cheering inasmuch as it proved a continued interest for his welfare and besides afforded him a respite from the monotony of confinement and the narrow channel of discussion through which, perforce, flowed the stream of conversation with the simple Jose. The reverend visitor left him in a more cheerful state of mind, notwithstanding the former's assurances that his fate was sealed so far as the military were concerned. While thus destroying whatever hope that may have lingered with the prisoner, the father gave him to understand that he must prepare to effect, by some means, an escape from the carcel. While imparting the latter advice his tone and manner were plainly indicative that a powerful, and no doubt successful, attempt would be made to wrest him from the hands of his would-be executioners. On his way to the plaza Father Ignacio stopped at Candelario's. The latter was engrossed in her avocation as concocter of peppery viands for the general public, and failed to note the presence of the other, until he said in his cheery voice:

'Candelario—siempre trabajando!"

She turned quickly and with an obesiance asked the priest's blessing, which he gave her with a smile and a gentle tap on her cheek.

"Si, senor," she replied. "Always at work. I have only Carlo to help me and my custom has become over large."

"You would grow rich, senora, if it were not for your charitable heart."

"It is true that I make money, your worship, but I do not care to save it. If I put it to good use it will be treasure laid up in heaven. The church has need of money and I never refuse my little mite. Besides, poor Candelario, who is now suffering the pains of purgatory, has need of assistance in the way of monthly masses for his soul and in the good deeds which God permits me to perform."

"Your husband was not worthy of you, but you are to be honored for your noble efforts to shorten his term of punishment in the flames of purgatory."

"There can be no doubt he is in purgatory, mi padre?"

"It is not for us to judge. He received the last sacraments?"

"Todos."

Then, if truly repentant, he is now atoning for his sins in the flames of purgation."

"And the masses will shorten his sufferings by many years?"

"Hija mia, we cannot tell. It may be that your husband's soul is now with God. An hour in purgatory may seem like a year. The pains are quite equal to those of hell and a moment of torture appears to the poor soul like an age. The sufferings from the flames are not all; but are only second to those which arise from an acute consciousness of the enormity of sins which have been committed in the flesh, and the displeasure they have caused the Heavenly Father."

"Then my husband may be released," said the woman with a brightening countenance. "But," she continued, "I will not run any risk by stopping the masses, or my prayers for his soul."

"A proper spirit, nina, for if his soul has been released, the masses will not be said in vain, but will be credited to other poor souls whose friends on earth are not so fortunate as yourself."

"A wise arrangement of the church," she said, with a grateful look at the priest.

"Rather a beneficent provision of God through the church militant," explained the father. "God is not willing that any good act should be lost. Every act of faith or charity is like the good seed which springs up in good soil and is fostered throughout its growth by an environment absolutely congenial to its perfect development."

Candelario was gratified by the explanation and realized a feeling of moral excellence, in his approval of her good deeds, that brought with it resignation to her husband's supermundane fortunes and to her own widowed state.

To his inquiry she informed him that she ministered to the wants of the young American prisoner as well as to those of the major domo, and was being satisfactorily remunerated for what she did. After bestowing his parting blessing on the charitable widow, Father Ignacio returned to his residence full of meditations about the disparities existing in human dispositions. He had not far to travel from the saint to the sinner. Crime stalked by the side of virtue. From identical mental structures issued perfect faith and agnosticism, clear religious perception and contradictory scientific deduction, traditionary proofs and the contrarieties of inductive conclusions. He contrasted the agnosticism of the young American who was virtuous and honorable, from the ideas he drew from a sense of duty, with the implicit faith of the widow whose surplus funds were donated for the benefit of the dead and the glory of the church.

The good father's meditations were cut short on entering his hall by the presence of the giant form of the mozo of the Navarro's, who stood respectfully, hat in hand, as if desirous of an interview with him.

"What, Miguel! This is a rare place for you. Except to be at early mass I thought you had condemned yourself to be a recluse on the premises of Don Juan.".

"I have little business away from home, your worship. One must go to holy mass; but it is true I am very little out, and it is only now and then that I go to a cockfight."

"You are a good mozo, Miguel, and that is not saying a little, seeing how very large you are."

"I wish I were good, your worship," said Miguel, with eyes cast down and awkwardly turning his sombrero in his hand.

"I came to see your worship—about—about——"

"Well, what about?"

"It must be under the seal of confession, your worship."

"Well, proceed."

"About a secret passage."

"A secret passage!"

"Yes, your worship. You know there is a secret vault which is under the carcel and——"

"What do you know of this vault? What interest is it to you who attend to your own affairs so strictly that you have almost quit going to cockfights?"

"I have no interest that is mine alone—but the Senorita Navarro, who is my mistress and who has the right to have my service, wants me to lead the way to this vault and——"

"The Senorita Navarro! Lead *her* there?"

"Yes, your worship; but for what purpose I know not, unless it be to let a prisoner escape."

"Ah! I see. I see," said Father Ignacio, reflectively. "Well—well—after all it is nature. A kind of natural selection, assimilation of worth and character. Beatrice is a splendid woman—Senor Raymond a splendid man—I see; I see."

The priest directed the giant to follow him, and the two repaired to a private room.

"Why did you wish to see me about this affair?"

"The secret of the vault is a church secret."

"Why so?"

"Because Father Francis, the priest before you, told me so. I would not have known of the place only from the fact that I was hired to make some repairs and was ordered not to speak of it outside of the confessional. When my mistress asked me to show her the vault I promised, but since then I thought it best to get your consent."

"And if I refuse consent?"

"Then—then—I must serve my mistress, mi padre."

"You are a queer fellow, Miguel. Suppose I should refuse to absolve you for the sin of disobedience?"

"I would be unhappy, mi padre—but can my mistress be wrong in this? If you could see her pretty face look so troubled, and the tears dancing in her eyes."

"Did that affect you?"

"It went to my heart."

"You have a big heart, Miguel, even for such a big body, and I give my consent."

"Gracias, mil gracias."

"And tell the senorita if I can serve her without being known in the matter, to send me word at once. I know of this vault, Miguel, but have never seen it. It was used for some purpose by the founders of San Fernando, but for years it has been closed with nothing on record as to its contents. Some day I will inspect it through curiosity."

Miguel left Father Ignacio to ruminate on a new subject—the connection between Guy Raymond and the beautiful Beatrice Navarro. How had she come to know of this subterranean passage? What plan had been hit upon to release the prisoner was to him unknown, and he could not realize how an escape past the guards could be effected even after Guy was safely out of prison walls.

CHAPTER XLVI.

"Bravo, Perry! That's a fine fellow."

"Not a whit bigger than the last, Mr. Hamilton."

"Boy, you are a born Nimrod. Why can't I catch a fish like that?"

"It's because you are not used to it. You have got to make your bait attractive. See how I hook this lively minnow through the tail so as not to hurt him bad. He will kick and wriggle in the water and soon get the attention of a trout. The trout is curious to know what's the mater with the minnow and swims around him. When he gets near he seems to get mad because the little fellow don't try to escape and snaps him up whether he is hungry or not. And then it's owing to the depth you give your bait. It should be half the depth of the water for game fish like the trout."

"You would grace a professorship in the art piscatorial, my boy. I will see that you are not overlooked when the future university of the coming republic will have been founded. I will observe your directions and try my luck. See! Is that right? The hook does not touch a vital part. But don't the little scamp wriggle. I reckon it hurts him. Now, there seems to be a good place in that cluster of lillies where the water is eddying in the blue open space, and a sunken log just shows its moss-covered bark as it slants towards the bottom. I know there must be a monster trout lurking in the shadow of that covering of watercress, ready to spring upon any prey that will promise a breakfast. What, Perry! Another?"

"That's what, Mr. Hamilton. I got him while you were spouting."

"You are entirely too practical to be a professor. Perry, I retract my promise about the university."

"Throw in your line, Mr. Hamilton. They're commencing to bite."

"I could fish in the Yazoo, but hang me if I've any luck in the San Antonio. Well, here goes."

Hamilton threw his line carefully into the inviting looking place near the sunken log. He had not long to wait before the float bobbed under a little and reappeared, reinforced by a bubble, then it was slowly drawn under until it disappeared beneath a broad leaf of a lily. Perry looked on, amused at his companion, whose manner indicated that he was expecting a splendid catch. Hamilton gave a vigorous pull, only to find his line fastened. Patient attempts to disengage it were made, until finally a small turtle showed himself on the log, with the line protruding from his mouth, distinctly visible in the clear water. The line was foul above the hook and the turtle, securely fastened, had taken his position in full view.

"Perry, I'm disgusted," said Hamilton. "We have plenty fish for two messes."

"You want to go to camp?"

"Yes, just as soon as I rout that devilish turtle."

So saying, Hamilton armed himself with several stones, and began a vigorous assault on the object of his wrath, whom he soon caused to leave his position.

"If I had my rifle here!" he exclaimed, half out of breath.

"You couldn't have hit him."

"Why not?"

"The distance from the top of the water to the turtle was deceiving. If you had run a straight stick down to him from the surface to his back on the line of your sight, the stick would have looked bent or broken right where it went into the water. This would have been a difficulty in your aiming and your ball would have gone above the turtle."

"From the crude way you have expressed this truth is proof that your knowledge is practical, and comes from the book of nature. You are an observer, Perry. That noddle of yours is brim full of undeveloped genius. I'll carry the fish. You rescue the remnants of my tackle and bring the poles. The boys will open their eyes at our success."

The reader will doubtless welcome to the front again some of the characters who have been left aside during the narration of other events. The scene was above the city, just beyond the old mill seen by Ducio and Josefa from the walls of the Alamo, at the time they were interrupted in their tete-a-tete by Father Ignacio.

The greater portion of the Texan forces, now reduced by the departure of discontented volunteers for their homes to about six hundred men, were encamped in the vicinity. Scouts were ever on the alert, led by such leaders as Deaf Smith, Karnes and others, and repeated demonstrations in force were made to draw the Mexicans from their stronghold. A number of horses started by the garrison for the Rio Grande had been captured, and a bloody affair known as the grass fight had occurred, in which a severe loss was inflicted upon the besieged. In all of these forays and collisions with the enemy, our mess had had liberal representation, and all had commanded by their conduct the respect of their fellow soldiers. The mess was comfortably situated on the right bank of the beautiful river within a stone's throw of the old mill, where they had improvised a hut which held whatever effects they boasted in the way of bedding and camp utensils. The supply of all kinds was meager, and the hut was merely utilized in rainy weather, or as a night repository for certain articles. The mildness of the climate had made outdoor sleeping under the branches of the trees preferable to piling into the narrow precincts of a hut.

The sun was only just above the eastern hills when the two fishermen returned to display the trophies of their morning's sport. The kettle was steaming above the fire that, burned to glowing coals, was being replenished with small brushwood by a well-known figure, who, turning in their direction as he heard the familiar voices of the approaching messmates, disclosed the features of Mr. Trigg.

"What! All alone?" said Hamilton, as he looked about for the others.

"Yes, for the present. Roach has gone for a bit of wood."

"And Jones?"

"He's down the bank for water."

"I wish Karnes were back from the scout. He'll miss a treat with these fish for breakfast," said Hamilton.

"Don't let that bother you, Mr. Hamilton. I've got the hooks and as long as they last I'll get plenty fish," replied Perry.

"Not if I go along and lose a hook every time."

"Hello, boys! What luck?" cried Nathan Roach, throwing down a huge turn of brush and small wood.

"See!" replied Perry, holding up a half dozen fine specimens of black bass.

"As big as I ever seed," said Nathan, admiringly.

"I'll bet Jones has seen specimens a dozen times the size."

"Now, Mr. Hamilton, do please give Jones a rest; ye were near fightin' last night."

"Here he is now. Jones, did you ever see anything to beat this catch in an hour's time?" asked the Mississippian.

"Well—yes. Those are large enough for this country, but the bass in the east go as high as twelve pounds "

"And I will wager that six pounds and a half is the heaviest bass ever known east, west, north, or south."

"You have not traveled or seen much, friend Tipton, or you would not make the wager."

"We all said you would quote India and insist that these noble fish are minnows. These are about the size of the bait you used to catch the eastern bass."

"Come; give in boys, for here's Karnes and his crowd. It's a good thing we was just off of duty last night, or we'd 'a' been ordered out with him."

Nathan was right. A little knot of horsemen appeared over the rise from the west and in a few moments their gallant leader, Karnes, was in their midst.

"Here is a letter that I should have got sooner, I think," said Karnes. "Hamilton, will you please read it? It is doubtless of great importance to your friend, Mr. Trigg, as a report reached me, through a deserter, that he had been sentenced to be shot."

"God forbid that it is too late, sir," said Mr. Trigg, now all attention to what was to follow.

Hamilton took the communication, which was still sealed, and having opened it, read from it as follows:

Sir:—The plans made for the capture of General A. are perfected, and nothing remains now but to carry out what we have determined upon in our last interview. It is most important that there be no delay whatever in the time agreed upon, as it will be impossible to rescue the prisoner from the power of his would-be murderers if there should be any postponement of the start down the river. You will find me ready at the place of meeting to join you and to post you of any change which the nature of the undertaking and succeeding circumstances may yet suggest. You know my challenge and answer, and I hereby communicate to you the countersign for tonight, which I had to pay well for. Yours for Texas and liberty, M. P.

Saturday, 5 A. M.

"That means tonight, men," said Karnes. "I will explain to the rest of you later. Mr. Trigg is already posted. Manual Ruiz has been in town for some days as a spy, to plan the capture of General Almonte, who has been in correspondence with Edward Gritton. Gritton is a spy on our people. The result is that Ruiz has planned an expedition to go into the town and capture Almonte. He has marked out more work for the boys who are to go, and that will be to rescue a young American prisoner under sentence to be shot, and who is no other than the young friend of our comrade, Trigg—Guy Raymond. No man will be allowed to go unless he volunteers for the service, and it will require just about the number in our mess. If Mr. Trigg will remain to keep the camp, I will get a Mexican in his place who knows every inch of the town, and who is reliable and plucky."

"No, sir, I want to be along," said Mr. Trigg.

"But, Mr. Trigg," interposed Hamilton, "remember you should not run a risk of your life in this instance, for I want you and Guy Raymond to meet and settle some matters. Think; if we should rescue him and you should be killed. Then you are the oldest and should have charge of the camp, and let us younger fry take the chances. Besides, it is very important that this Mexican should be along in case we wanted to play greasers on them."

"I see I am to be put upon the shelf. Sorra the day when I should be too old to do my duty. Fix it to suit ye, but I'll put myself against the likes of you for any work that's up. An' who's to row the boat?"

"Why, Jones and myself," replied Hamilton. "He used to row Lord Dalrymple's boat, I will wager, and as for myself, I belonged to the best rowing club in Mississippi. Trust us for rowing."

"What'n thunder does we want with a boat?" asked Nathan, stretching his long anatomy and poking his head over Hamilton's shoulder.

"Never mind, Roach; we are only going to sail into the enemy's lines. They have no idea that we possess a navy, but we're going to show them a gringo trick."

"You'll have to muffle your oars; but I'll fix them for ye," said Mr. Trigg.

"The boat needs caulking," said Jones. "I'll attend to that."

"That's right, boys; divide up the work and all go at it so soon as we discuss these savory smelling fish that Perry has already in the frying pan. Let me see: Mr. Trigg will fix the oars; Jones will bail the boat; Nathan will clean the guns and see to the ammunition; Perry will put a meal's grub in our haversacks——"

"And you will play the gentleman, Mr. Hamilton," said Jones.

"No, Jones. I'll overlook the whole preparations and see that no part will be neglected."

"That's Karnes' business," suggested Nathan. "'Pears to me you're to be the lazy drone of the crowd, as usual. You needn't talk about Jones lying; you offset him by your 'tarnel laziness."

"Never mind, Roach. You'll say after the thing is over that I was no drone."

CHAPTER XLVII.

The activity among the members of the mess was unabated until a late hour in the afternoon, when Inspector Hamilton reported to Karnes that every detail had been attended to and there was nothing left undone that would be necessary for the successful outcome of the expedition, so far as the entry by the river into the heart of the enemy's lines was concerned. It remained for Ruiz's part of the programme to stand the test of practicability. The hours stole slowly by, testing sorely the patience of the bold men who were to take their very lives in their hands purely for the love of adventure, granting a possible modicum of patriotism or a touch of humane anxiety for the fate of a countryman under sentence of death. At last the landscape grew dim under the deepening shades of evening, which soon merged in the gloom of a moonless night, veiling the forms of nature and giving spectre shapes to objects within the easy radius of the camp fires. As the night advanced apace the silver host which studded the autumnal sky developed a maturer beauty and forced the deeper shadows to own their luster. The quiet of the night made audible the low murmurs of the current, which washed the base of the steep river bank, where floated the frail craft destined to bear to the brink of danger human lives, dear to themselves and yet more precious to distant hearts. Are such and kindred adventures correctly in the category of heroism? Yes; when they are born of resistance to wrong—to oppression. But war begets the lowest types of character, as does its antithesis, the laissez faire indifferentism of a lasting public inertia which awakes to no appeal for a return to purer social and political methods. The heroic in character could be so easily turned to the channels of human duty; to swell the current of human brotherhood. But a questionable civilization bars the way to lasting peace, to an attainable culture that would bring to a close, not only the reign of personal despotism and personal tyranny, but would immolate on the altar of universal liberty the tyranny and despotism of class. To what heights would that civilization ascend which would accord all natural rights to natural opportunities; which would practice the grand theories, pure and simple, which fell in burning words from the lips of the founder of Christianity, and which yet form the texts of sermons from a million pulpits. There is heroism and heorism, but the greatest hero is he who had duty for his guide and justice for his mentor, and who follows the directions of the one and the admonitions of the other.

The waiting men stood around the camp fire, Hamilton's jests eliciting characteristic replies from Jones or Roach, while Mr. Trigg appeared meditative and Perry quiescent. The old man was not well satisfied with the position assigned to him; yet he mentally admitted that Hamilton's arguments were to the point and that he would perhaps better subserve the interests of Guy Raymond by avoiding the risks of the expedition. Karnes had gone just before dark to fetch his Mexican guide, and it was with no little satisfaction that his men beheld him appear with that individual, ready to depart. As there was nothing to delay them, the men filed down the bank, responding to Mr. Trigg's "good luck to ye,' boys," by hearty good-byes.

Now that serious work was before them, Karnes impressed each one with the necessity for silence and prompt obedience to all commands. He assigned the duty of rowing the boat to Hamilton and Jones, while he took position in the stern to guide the craft with a wide paddle in lieu of a rudder. Perry, Roach and the Mexican guide were assigned places, with directions to keep a sharp lookout, as the boat proceeded, to detect the signals of friends or the presence of foes. All being ready, the little craft was pushed into the stream, the oarsmen dipped their oars, then with easy strokes, gave her headway, while Karnes directed her bow down the river. There was little noise, the muffled rowlocks worked to perfection and the light plash of the oarblades were not distinguishable from the noise of the rapid current.

"Just give her motion, boys," commanded Karnes. "Only a little swifter than the current, so I can keep her head right."

Now and then the boat shot into a pool where the river deepened, and the rowers would bend to their work, while the steerer peered forward through the darkness, to avoid overhanging branches of the trees lining either bank, that here and there bent low above the surface of the water, or to discover whatever obstructions might exist, where a sudden incline of the river bed produced a rapid or the stream turned abruptly from its course. Navigation, however, was to be a minor danger in the perilous expedition upon which the boat's crew had embarked. The river had been selected as the safest avenue through which to enter, without detection, the enemy's lines, strongly guarded at all points against the invasion of every character of force, that should menace them by field or road or footpath. Mexican shrewdness did not suspect the presence of a boat, where no such contrivance had been known to exist in all the archives of Bexar from the time the first Franciscan had planted his foot upon the banks of the picturesque San Antonio, down to the present administration. And perhaps a chapter quite diverse in its details from the present record would have added more tragedy to the story of Guy Raymond if among the rebel Texans there had not been numbered a clever boat maker, who employed some of his spare hours in his favorite occupation. The result was the production of a very sightly boat, superior in its excellence to the results promised by the materials obtainable for its construction. The idea of using the boat was conceived by Ruiz, while he was maturing a plan to carry out the mission entrusted to him by the Texan commander. The rescue of the young American prisoner was but an incident, falling in as a parallel, a necessity presenting itself and appealing to whatever of human feeling lay within the hearts of the adventurous spirits who were to constitute the media for the prosecution of the original purpose. Ruiz's idea at once commended itself to the commander, and as Guy's fate had become blended with the outcome of the project, the former had urged the selection of Karnes and the members of the mess who had, through Mr. Trigg, become more than interested in the fortunes of the youthful prisoner. Predilections of such a nature, Ruiz philosophically contended, would be additional force towards a successful accomplishment of the dual purpose, and in the estimation of the generous Mexican, the minor and incidental aim of the expedition had absorbed in importance its previous object.

The little boat sped onward. The injunction to keep silent had been heeded by the men, even by Hamilton, who more than once was tempted to say something at the expense of his comrade's oarsmanship. Indeed, he did whisper once or twice to Jones, when the latter awkwardly nudged him with his elbow, while bringing his oar handle too low on the breast: "Come, Jones, remember the East Indian stroke—deeper blade and higher handle. My ribs won't stand two more pokes."

"Silence there, Mr. Hamilton! Raise your oar, sir—quick, and duck your heads—there. A little more and that limb would have raked the boat."

Karnes' warning came just in time to prevent an accident. Indeed, the darkness hanging over the river was almost impenetrable. The starlight could not counteract the shadows from the banks and foliage, only a silver glow showed itself above, the contemplation of which but augmented the difficulty of seeing surrounding objects.

"I heerd a voice, Karnes," said Nathan, from the bow of the boat.

"Hark! Men, lay upon your oars," commanded Karnes, in a firm undertone.

All was silent. The boat, which had just entered a wide waterhole, deep and almost still, was left to spend its momentum, until it hardly moved. Karnes controlled the course with his paddle, but so noiselessly that the breaking of a twig on the bank was clear and distinct to the ear. Still further cautions for silence were whispered from the stern to the bow. Roach had the Indian ears of the party. He alone had heard the voice. All but Karnes doubted his correctness. He had served with Nathan and had learned to respect his ears. After a few minutes' suspense, the Mexican guide leaned over to the commander and whispered:

"The picket is camped upon the bank. Better keep quiet a while longer."

The moments dragged.

Finally the party were startled by the sound of voices in the Mexican tongue.

"What was it?"

"I was sure I heard something."

"What was it like?"

"Like a paddle or oar against a boat, and it seemed to me I saw something a little lighter than the shadows pass along."

"Que tonto! Don't you know these people up here never had a boat? If there is a boat in Bexar I have yet to see it. It is one of your visions, Santos. You are always seeing things."

"There is no mistaking the noise made in a boat on the water. A fellow's eyes and imagination may deceive him, but his ears are apt to be correct."

"That comes of you being once a sailor. Sailors are superstitious. Come, let us pack the water up the bank, for it is nearly time for us to go on guard."

Nathan had correct ears after all, and it was well that silence reigned in the boat, as the speakers on the bank had maintained a death-like quiet, in order to confirm Santo's first impression. No other sounds having succeeded, Santos' companion disclosed their presence by his question. The water carriers indicated their progress up the bank by their lessening voices, which finally died out in the distance.

Karnes, having waited for this moment, now slowed the boat along until it had made a headway of a hundred yards or more.

"Now, boys, pull steadily and quietly."

Hamilton answered in a whispered "Aye, aye, sir."

"No need of answering, sir. We are past the pickets, and now, Nathan, keep your ears and eyes open for anything that may turn up."

"Mr. Guide, are we near the place?" inquired Karnes of the Mexican.

"Another bend in the river."

"Put your hand on my knee when we get to the right place."

The bend was rounded. A swift current swept them past a rapid, the boat's bottom grazed the rocky bed, and they glided into a body of water whose smooth surface reflected the sparkling firmament.

The guide's hand was placed upon the commander's knee. Karnes put two fingers in his mouth and gave a shrill whistle.

A voice from the right bank called:

"Karnes."

The answer given was:

"Ruiz."

"Hold up, Mr. Jones; Mr. Hamilton, pull away."

The boat swung around to the right.

"Now, both together."

The bow grated upon the sand and pebbles. Nathan stepped ashore and grasped Ruiz by the hand.

"Hold her to the bank, boys. I must have a talk with our man before we go further. Keep quiet and you'll soon know the road we've got to follow."

So saying, Karnes left the boat, greeted Ruiz cordially, and took him aside for consultation.

CHAPTER XLVIII.

The day on which Father Ignacio called at the carcel he remained sufficiently long to encroach upon the dinner hour of that institution, much to the annoyance of the irascible jailer, who upon this particular time was anxious to have the hour go by speedily, and had actually anticipated noon by twenty minutes of the sun dial.

"These padres are like old women; they never know how long they stay to gossip, senor," Bonito said to Guy, as he placed Candelario's basket in the cell.

"What can it matter to you, Bonito? You have time, and to spare. You should not begrudge me the good Father's visit."

"Time, senor! I have much to do; much to do today, senor, and I would be thankful if you will hurry up, you and the other, and eat your dinner so that this afternoon a poor devil may attend to his business."

"Perhaps I can help you, Bonito. Let me assist you if it be anything around the carcel or your quarters. You know that if put on my parole I will make no attempt to escape."

"I would not be bothered with help; you are too wise now, too wise about my business. Besides, senor, I have orders to allow no liberty to you whatever; none whatever, senor, and to disobey and be discovered would be to lose my place, which would be no loss as to pay, but then at my age one hates to change, senor."

"I see, Bonito. As a condemned person, condemned to death, strict vigil must be kept over me. It seems to me they might wait until time for the death watch. Bonito, is there no chance to escape? Would you hold me here until these tyrants get ready to murder me for no crime, for no offense against the law?"

"How can I help you, senor? If you were to escape, what would happen? Bonito would not only lose his place, but his life. The bullets intended for you would enter my vitals. There is no help for it; no help for it, senor."

"Not if you should get a hundred doubloons?"

"Said you a hundred, senor, or two hundred?"

"Well, two; say two hundred."

"If it were two and fifty; or say three hundred good bright doubloons—but no—senor—no—there is no use to talk of it. A thousand, with no chance to fly from the devils who would sit in judgment. A thousand—nor two—nor three—Oh, senor! it cannot be. I pity you; yes, pity, but who pities Bonito? Robbed of what he has toiled for and almost murdered by the devil who robbed him."

"You are right, Bonito, to refuse a bribe. I was but trying you. If you have a post of duty, fill it well, be it never so repugnant to your tastes and feelings. A test of virtue lies in filling a post at all whose duties outrage the finer feelings of human nature. If a trust displeased me because of the involvement of my ideas of honor and moral duty, I would resign it. The discovery of my false position would terminate my connection with and make it impossible to betray it."

"You are a brave pajarro, as I said at first. Bonito is a coward. I hate my work, but must do it or be shot. And yet, I have not the courage to give it up no more than I have to let you escape for twenty pesos. But, senor, are you not alarmed at the idea of being shot? You look as contented as if you would be free tomorrow, and the fellow over there is always sleeping as if he were not going to be food for the worms in a day or two. You are a queer pair, senor; a queer pair of birds."

"There is no use fretting over it, Bonito."

"I am glad you are through eating. Scrape his dinner on that plate. It looks as if he would never get sober. Ruiz was once a caballero, senor, puro caballero. Now, senor, I am off. If you will want anything tell it now, for you will not see me until the night comes."

With assurances that nothing would be needed, the jailer shuffled off after securing the cell door. Jose, who was impatiently awaiting this event, came out of his corner and did ample justice to the contents of the dish upon which Guy had placed his meal. The latter drew from his pocket a piece of paper that he had found in the basket and, standing close to the grated door, read a message from Ruiz. He wrote to the prisoner that everything had been arranged for his escape outside of the city and that he must be out of his cell, either in the jailer's house or near it, so as to be within call, by eleven o'clock on Sunday night. If he should discover that he had not the power to release himself, his absence from the rendezvous would be taken as proof of the fact, and the jail would be raided to free him; to provide himself with whatever arms he would find available; to communicate with Linda, if possible, and secure whatever assistance, direct or indirect, she could offer through influence with or deception of her father. The rescuers would be in need of every favorable circumstance that could be raised towards facilitating their venture or lessening its peril.

Guy grew meditative over the contents of the paper. He was entirely in the dark as to the means to be used for his release, or the method of gaining an entrance into the heart of a garrisoned town ever on the qui vive as the besieged of an active and fearless enemy. He concluded that it was about time to make sure that an escape through the vault was open to him. He had not entered it since the day he had found the jailer there in an insensible state and concluded to let Jose into the secret, and that afternoon, especially, as Bonito was to be out of the way, he would explore the subterranean chamber and fix his triggers for an easy passage from the cell to the hall. As some time had elapsed since Jose had completed his repast and Guy had mentally digested a plan of escape and its possible success or failure, he concluded to draw out Jose's opinion of the vault as a means of egress from their cell.

"It will, of course, depend upon our getting into it, and then after we get into it, upon our getting out again," said Jose.

"We certainly will be able to get back here, Jose, if we don't find another way out."

"It is forbidden ground, and I have heard it hinted that the spirits of numbers who have been led from there to be shot make their visits to the vault."

"Afraid of spirits, Jose?"

"I am afraid to meet them."

"If there be such they are harmless. It is from the living that we receive injury, and they are the ones to be dreaded."

"Everyone has his notions, Senor Raymond. I have the greatest dread of meeting a ghost."

"Well, Jose, I am going to get into that vault this very day, and will go alone if you do not go with me. I am going to see if there is not a way to get out at the other end. You remember having told me that it extends from Bonito's house towards this cell and I think I can find the entrance in this floor."

"I only told you how run the legend. I have no other proofs that the vault runs underneath us. I would advise you to think well before going into this place if you should find the way to it. It may bring upon you the curse of the saints, which will be the worse for you, seeing that you are already in bad odor with them as a heretic. Senor, take the advice of a friend."

"I fully appreciate your anxiety for myself if I do not feel the force of your logic. I will invoke the aid of Saint An——what the deuce is that noise, Jose?"

This question was put to the major domo on account of a pounding noise which arose from the depths below. It came in dull thuds, which struggled up through the masonry with singular regularity, making the floor vibrate very sensibly to one standing upon it.

"It is a true warning to you, senor," said Jose, looking grave and listening intently.

"The spirits signifying their disapprobation?"

"No mas—no menos."

The noise proceeded—pick—pick—pick—while the prisoners ceased talking, the one in actual dread of supernatural displeasure, the other from sheer curiosity to solve the cause of the noise. Guy was not very long in coming to a conclusion. The statement of the jailer that he would be busy during the afternoon, with the knowledge that he had a deal of treasure in the vault which he was anxious to conceal still more securely, since the raid made upon it, and the knowledge of the secret lay at least with two outsiders, had doubtless put Bonito to work to furnish better concealment for his gold.

Guy, of course, did not tell his suspicions to his fellow prisoner, but continued to draw Jose out on the probably supernatural source of the noise until he grew tired of the amusement.

When, after a long time, the thumping ceased, he concluded to take in a view of the mysterious operations of Jose's alleged spirits. Acting upon this intention, he secured his former tool and after awhile had cleared the great square flag of all contact with its neighbor stones. Jose looked on with an expression of unqualified disapprobation during the progress of the work. All being ready, Guy invoked his assistance to raise the flag, but was persistently refused by the superstitious counterfeit of the gallant Ruiz. Seeing no other recourse he concluded to proceed as on the former occasion and, after a rather difficult lift, he had the satisfaction of seeing the weighty cover of the trap in a vertical position. It was done so noiselessly that it could have disturbed none of the supernatural inhabitants of the dark apartment that was now disclosed to the eyes of the astonished Jose.

"May the all powerful Saint Anthony protect us!" he exclaimed, as he retreated to the other end of the cell.

"S——h!" cautioned Guy, as he arose from a peep into the place.

The other relapsed at once into silence and covered his eyes.

The look below with a subsequent scrutiny of affairs solved the mystery to Guy's practical mind, while his companion was in absolute dread lest some supernatural expression of displeasure was about to occur.

The first glance disclosed a glimmer of a light just making its appearance, followed by Bonito holding up a candle. Guy looked up and silenced Jose, then returned to his surveillance of his unbribable turnkey. Bonito was at the work of concealing his treasure, and not knowing that the opening in the cell had been discovered, he felt perfectly safe from espionage from that direction. When Guy witnessed the transfer of the contents of the chest to the hole in the wall, he deemed the superstition, which confined the number of witnesses to himself, a fortunate circumstance for Bonito. When the latter had concluded his operations it was, as the reader knows, quite well into the night. The intermission in his work was confined to the duty of attending to the prisoners' supper. This Guy received at the door with an immediate return of the basket and assurances that nothing more was needed of him.

CHAPTER XLIX.

Despite Jose's fears, he was fast asleep when Bonito had carried his last load of dirt to the hall and bade Linda good night. Guy, less material, witnessed the disappearance of the light and, hearing no return of the tired worker, resolved to explore the scene of his operations. To this end he lit his candle and cautiously descended through the opening and found himself on the flagged floor below. He experienced a tremor through his frame as the damp air of the chamber penetrated to his skin. Before him the empty chest lay closed. Directing the light against the wall where he had seen the miser place his money, he was much astonished to find no apparent traces of the closing up of the hole that must have received it. A very close scrutiny, however, revealed the careful work, whose perfection had been doubtless inspired by the superlative earnestness of the money worshipper to conceal the evidences of his secret. Guy turned from the inspection to view the opposite steps leading to the jailer's abode. He ascended to the top, but could not discover the lever that would lift the trap which barred the exit. Concluding to not investigate further until the morrow, he returned to his cell and to his pallet, not to sleep, however, for the prospect of escape on the morrow, coupled with the manoeuvres of Bonito in the vault, caused his mind to wander from the probabilities of success in plans of Ruiz to the miser whose soul was so engrossed with the safety of his treasure. In the hope of better wooing sleep he put out his light. Still, as the minutes grew to an hour, he realized no nearer approach to a disposition to sleep. How he envied Jose, whose pronounced respiration was ever and anon broken by the catches of a snore. The idea struck him to renew his light and try the plan to read himself sleepy. To carry out this purpose, he rose to a sitting position, when he was startled by the appearance of a light shining faintly at first, then growing more distinct, from the opening leading into the vault. Bonito, he concluded, had been also lying awake and, to occupy himself, had returned to become satisfied on some doubted point which had raised itself in his speculations as to the complete removal of the evidences of his new place of concealment for his money bags. At any rate, he would take a peep at the jailer and amuse himself by watching him. The cell was dark and there was little chance of the miser's inspection of the cell opening.

So Guy peeped below.

He was not a little startled to see instead of the rotund figure of Bonito, a tall, spare form with sharp well defined features and dark complexion, all made plainly distinct by the light of the uplifted candle, as its holder contemplated the empty chest at his feet. From the description given of Ducio Halfen by Jose, Guy was satisfied that the intruder was the Creole, and that he it was who had made the assault on the miser and had despoiled him of his doubloons. Doubtless he had returned to make another inroad on the savings of his victim, but the latter had forestalled him in the nick of time. The intruder might extend his exploration to the stairs leading to the cell. At this thought, Guy reached for the knife that had served him in cleaning around the flag still standing upon its edge above him. The swarthy face below wore an expression of disappointment. The look of baffled intent mingled with the scowl of some evil purpose which might mean mischief worse than robbery. The floor and walls were scanned with the earnestness of intense desire; then seizing the stool Ducio struck the floor flags all around him, as if sounding to discover a hollow place whence had issued the evidences of the sand and debris on the unswept floor and stairway. It did not seem to occur to him that the walls could be excavated. Ducio sat down to think.

Thought, however, afforded neither a clue to the whereabouts of the treasure nor any panacea for the acuteness of the disappointment which racked his mind.

Ideas suggestive of revenge crowded upon him. Revenge for depriving him of his anticipated booty. What use was all that hoard which the chest, now serving him for a seat, had once contained. Fool! Why had he not packed it all away to a place of concealment when the opportunity was not wanting? His thoughts flew for an instant to the island treasure, and he started suddenly from his seat. "I'll stick around here until that, too, will be gone."

But the impatience of his present predicament reseized him with still more potent force and raged within him, expending itself in a rapid pacing of the chamber, followed by vigorous blows on the floor. Perhaps there was a latent influence in the vast sum which a thin crust of rock concealed, and which now and then, as he moved about, was in less than reaching distance; an influence undefined and mysterious that held him just without the bounds of prescience and goaded him to the verge of desperation.

Guy viewed the whole scene with varying emotions.

Amusement at the other's dilemma, which a word from himself could dissipate as to the locality of the former contents of Bonito's chest, first succeeded the surprise of the intruder's identity. Indignation followed when he thought of the rascality that made him take advantage of the jailer's hospitality. Then he became alarmed when on reflecting as to the means used to enter the vault, he began to speculate as to whether the robber had used intimidation or violence, or both. How had he got into the jailer's apartments? Not through the court, for there was the sentinel. He knew of no other entrance to the place except that through Linda's garden and her apartment. The latter thought aroused him to almost the pitch of excitement. The scoundrel may have committed the crime of murder as a necessary step to gain access to the hall. Guy grasped his knife still tighter. Ducio, after having paused for some minutes in deep study, seemed to have suddenly fastened upon a purpose. He took the candle from the chest and made directly for the steps down which he had descended.

So soon as Guy became satisfied of the other's purpose, he lighted his candle and, shaking Jose roughly, caused him to spring up and glance wildly about.

"Por Dios! senor; my arm is but flesh and bone."

"Pardon me, Jose, but I wanted to awake you and do it quickly. Clear your eyes and open your ears and listen to what I tell you."

Whatever may have been the purpose of Ducio, as interpreted by the watcher, his actions will probably be the best indicators of the conclusion which terminated his few moments' reflection.

He gained the hall and placing his light on one end of the lounge, he cautiously approached the door of the jailer's room. Here he listened. The regular breathing of the inmate denoted slumber and Ducio, returning for his light, entered the chamber. The light he placed upon the table so as not to shine upon the sleeper's eyes. He then made a search of the entire room and feeling stealthily under a pillow of the bed, he drew forth a long dagger.

"As I expected," thought Ducio. "Now we will see if the old rascal will tell."

He caught the jailer by the great toe and gave it a vigorous twist.

"Carrajo!" swore Bonito, jumping to a sitting position. "Can a dream be so true?"

Ducio had dodged below the foot of the bed.

"Santa Maria! But that rock did not fall on my foot, dream or no dream. I thought I put out the light, but I—was—so tired," he continued, yawning, "that I forgot it. But the more I get awake the more I wonder. I dreamed that a piece of that rock from the wall fell upon my toe as I was closing up the last open place, and the dream was so clear that I felt the pain in this toe."

As Bonito said this in an audible tone, he raised his foot on the table close to the candle and examined the wrenched member.

"Por mi vida! There is no mash, but the pain was there, and I feel it yet. And yet that tonta Linda will not believe in dreams. I only wish she could have such a dream and such a toe mashing, or toe paining, for really there is no mash. How hard I must have been dreaming!"

Bonito, after sundry other looks at the toe which Ducio had twisted, took the candle from the table and placing it in a small alcove near the head of his bed, blew it out and retired again to rest, but not to sleep for wondering about his dream and how mistaken he had been in supposing that he had blown out his candle when he first went to bed.

Ducio had not counted on the dream nor on the extinguishment of the light, nor had he anticipated the voluntary acknowledgment from Bonito in his own self communion that he had hid his money in the wall and not the floor of the vault. He had calculated on a forced confession and an indication of the place from Bonito. Still he dreaded the consequences of force and what it might lead to, and concluded that he would return to the vault and sound the walls. The work was fresh and a careful inspection must disclose the place. He must have a light, but the candle was out of the question. It was too near the head of the occupant of the bed. He concluded to go to Linda's room and get her light. It was a risk, but the less of the two. He glided, like a snake, from the room on all fours. As suming an erect position on entering the hall, he groped his way to Linda's room, which he was about to enter when he perceived a light emerging from the open trap in the end of the lounge. Sure that he had left the vault in darkness, he was mystified at the sight.

Ducio listened.

Confident that he heard whispered voices, he was also certain that the light was getting stronger, indicating that some one holding it was approaching nearer.

Goaded by the sense of danger and irritated by the intervention of an additional obstacle to the success of his contemplated dispoliation of the miser, Ducio retreated within the room. His first precaution was to provide for an escape. To this end he unfastened and placed ajar the garden exit from the apartment, after he had similarly adjusted the gate entrance from the plaza. This effected, he breathed easier, while he took his post at the hall door which he had already secured. The villain's movements had been so noiseless that the sleeping girl had not been disturbed.

The listener had not long to wait for indications that there were others in the house besides himself, the jailer and his daughter.

Guy related in hurried tones to Jose that there was a robber in the vault and that he wanted his assistance to prevent him from dispoiling the jailer, and to see that no harm would befall Bonito or Linda.

"Robber, senor! There is nothing in the vault to steal. Besides how do you judge? If it is by the noise it is only some poor restless spirit that——"

"Come, Jose! No foolishness, or I will go without you. True, he does not know. Jose, I've found the way into the vault. See! Here's the stone uplifted—come if you are my friend—if you love the memory of your mother—if you love Father Ignacio—come follow me and assist me to protect life and innocence."

"Saint Anthony help us!" said Jose, rising. "The stone is up and the vault shows itself. Senor, you are not going down there!"

"Follow me, Jose," said Guy, descending with the light; "I've been down here before."

"He has seen a ghost!" said Jose, shuddering. "He has been down among the spirits and they have upset his reason. Now he wants to drag me down to meet the same fate. Senor! Senor Raymond!"

"Come on, Jose, or I will believe you are a coward."

"He said by the memory of my mother," said Jose, peering down after Guy. "I like Father Ignacio, too, but my mother! He knew my soft spot—Senor Raymond. For the love of the memory of my mother I will brave even a ghost, Senor; I am coming."

Guy awaited Jose, who appeared after a short time bearing a heavy bar which had been discarded from some former use around the jail and had been appropriated by the present inmates of the cell as a clothes rack, placed laterally, the ends resting in crevices of the walls.

"You took a time to make up your mind," said Guy, in an impatient undertone. "It took an age to get you fairly awake, and then another to explain to you about the vault and what I wanted, and it seemed as if I never would get the candle lighted. The fellow has had time to get not only out of the house, but out of the town also."

"If it was a ghost it could be now out of the world, senor; ghosts take no account of distance and I've been told——"

"No time for ghost stories, Senor Jose; the party I saw was flesh and blood and far more dangerous than a thousand ghosts. Keep silent and follow me if you are worthy the name of man."

The major domo eyed the chest and stool curiously as he passed them and gave timid glances around the narrow passway as if he were in dread of beholdng some supernatural demonstration. He reluctantly obeyed the mandate to remain at the foot of the steps while his commander went up cautiously to listen. No sounds having reached him after some minutes, he signalled the other to follow, while he brought the light forward to throw its rays into the hall.

The trap had been left open so that there was no trouble or delay in gaining the floor above. Guy waited for his companion to join him, then posting him in the hall with instructions how to act in case the party hunted should make his appearance, he drew his knife and advanced upon Bonito's room. As he passed Linda's door he thought he caught a slight sound like the click of a lock, but after pausing a moment, he held the light well up and entered the old jailer's sanctum. The stillness was deathlike. Guy's form was shaded by the shadow of his left hand while the light was reflected from the long keen blade of the knife held in the right. The room, almost bare of furniture, was quickly taken in by the eager eye of the youth, who saw only the burly form of his jailer lying beneath the light covering of his bed. He still stood in the doorway, the candle illuminating the room and dimly showing in the hall the expectant attitude of Jose with his bar held at a ready, his own position completing a tableau that portended the imminence of a tragical event. Bonito, who had only been lying with closed eyes, ruminating on the strange realism that sometimes characterized dreams, suddenly opened his eyes to see the light of Guy's candle on the opposite wall. With an ejaculation as to the astounding persistency of his candle to be lighted, he turned over towards the door to take in the alarming situation of a man blocking the exit from his room with an uplifted candle and gleaming dagger.

Was it a dream?

Bonito rubbed his eyes the second time.

Despite the gravity of the situation, Guy could scarcely repress a smile.

The shadow across Guy's features, even had Bonito's vision been free from the confusing influences of a sudden awakening, would have concealed his identity from his jailer, who supposed him safely secured in his cell.

"Por Dios! What a night is this! My toe is twisted off or mashed in a dream, and here is a ghost that stands like a statue, burning up my candle. He has even taken my dagger, for it is gone from under my head. Between my night's work and nightmare, I will be dead on my feet for the next week. Senor ghost, what do you want with Bonito?"

If Guy had had any of the superstitious in his composition he would have begun to doubt his own sense of sight, and would have attributed the fact of Ducio's visit to the vault to be supernatural. The house was quiet, and with Linda's apartment unexplored, there appeared to be no intruder upon the privacy of the household. His well meant act of intervention between its inmates and harm was about to be turned into a ghostly visitation, or worse. If Bonito recognized him, what degree of pursuasion would it require to make him believe that he, who so well knew of his treasure, had not come to murder him in his sleep that he might secure it. The miser had not forgiven him for the knowledge, and his discovery in an attitude so apparently compromising would confirm his hostility despite the truthful story of Ducio's visit to the vault. Guy reflected that he would be but a few more hours in the carcel and it would not facilitate his departure to heighten the antagonism of his jailer. All this flashed through his quick mind with the rapidity of a lightning stroke, and he determined to make use of the other's superstition.

"You are the jailer?"

"Did I not say I am Bonito?"

"As a spirit I knew it; but reply to my questions."

"Well, Senor Ghost, if you will it; I am the jailer."

"You have a prisoner—one Guy Raymond?"

"You are right. I nicknamed him el pajarro."

"He is your friend. He saved your life in the vault."

"Truly you know it—but then you are a spirit."

"He did what you think is a greater service; he saved your gold."

"My gold! Yes, you are a spirit and a spirit knows."

"If you doubt it I will tell you where you have now hid your money. It is no longer in the chest, but with pick and mallet and chisel you made a place in the left wall, the height of your breast, and in this hole you put your bags, and when you had them all in you took trowel and mortar and cement and closed the hole, pointing off the cracks with great skill and hiding the freshness of the work."

"Oh, you know—you know!"

"Listen until I finish. And then to hide your work you brought up all the sand and rock that composed the debris of the excavation. But, Bonito, you neglected to sweep the floor. It was an oversight."

"I was so tired, Mr. Ghost—so tired."

An enemy has been in the vault. He who robbed you before and left you for dead has discovered that your gold has been moved, but it is yet safe. Take the advice of a spirit and send it to a safe place of deposit, when you should make over a good amount to Linda—your daughter."

"Oh, senor spirit, I could not trust it to human hands. I will move it again, and when I am dead Linda shall know and——"

"It is but advice; do with the money as you like, for it is the dross of earth. Your soul is everything. Bonito you are a wayward man. It has been ten years since you went to confession."

"You are a spirit; it was ten last Easter. Oh, Senor Ghost, if you will tell me a safe place for my doubloons I will go to my duties often."

"I cannot. Money is of earth and spirits would go out of their mission if they should pander to human greed for riches. They deal only with the soul, with character and mind. Money is of the flesh, and is condemned by the saintly who love God."

"But the church manages to get its share and——"

"Silence! Criticize not the church, or the loss of both your doubloons and soul will leave you the sport of men and devils."

"I am dumb, Senor Spirit; but I would ask you a question about my prisoner."

"You shall be answered."

"Will Senor Raymond betray my secret?"

"It is safe with him as with me."

"He would not rob me?"

"You might as well suspect me of intending to rob you."

"Es un buen pajarro."

"You should show him your gratitude."

"I could not spare a doubloon, seeing I was robbed."

"He despises your money. His honor weighs a thousand fold more than all your hoarded gold. Give him his liberty."

"I would be shot."

"Allow him to break jail."

"I cannot."

"I will make it easy for you."

"How?"

"Have your guard doubled and get permission to be absent this Sunday night from ten until two. If he escapes while you are away there is no law or precedent for your accountability. I tell you as an immortal spirit that you will never suffer for it."

"Then I will do it; but, senor spirit, would it not be right I should be paid something if but a few pesos for such a——"

"Miserable mortal! Would you ask pesos from your savior who does not own centados where you have bright doubloons. I know the contents of each of your strong bags, which are fairly bursting with their load of coin—for shame, Bonito!"

"I am ashamed, Senor Spirit, but it would not hurt any one condemned to die to pay a few reals—at least—for liberty."

"He is generous, this young American, and will doubtless help you hereafter."

"He shall have the chance; but it will be no use."

"Then you promise."

"I promise."

"Then I give you my blessing, frail mortal, and in leaving I charge you to remain in your room here until the time for rising, and to never tell to mortal of my visit. Upon these conditions will I guard your treasure and warn you should I ever know that you will be in danger of loss."

"Good spirit, Bonito will obey."

"Good-night—and—remember."

"Good-night, good ghost."

Guy backed out of the door with a slow and ghostly step until he got beyond the sight of the victimized jailer. He rejoined Jose, who was rather impatiently awaiting his return or the showing up of some object upon which to test the efficiency of his weapon. The adventure had had results so different from the anticipated outcome that Guy was at a loss to know what to do. He had certainly seen the fellow in the vault, but he had left no traces behind, and there was nothing to indicate that he had made his exit from the house. His practical mind conceived the necessity, under the circumstances, of keeping a watch until morning in order to prevent any harm coming to Linda or her father from the would be robber who, defeated in the discovery of the gold, might resort to force to compel a disclosure from the household. He had no use for the superstitious Jose and determined to see him back to the cell before he took a position to watch. He accordingly carried out the first part of this intention with difficulty, putting off replies to a score of questions from Jose until a more timely season for explanations.

Guy, after cautioning the other to remain quietly in the cell until his return, went back to the hall and took a reclining position on the lounge.

When Ducio entered Linda's garden to arrange the gate for a rapid exit in retreat, he did not notice a crouching figure in the corner he had so lately occupied when Ruiz was passing out with the fair owner. The figure arose into plain view the moment he re-entered the room and, creeping close to the door, bent forward as if peeping through the crack.

It had the slight form of a youth, and as he leaned over the drooping ends of a sash touched the tops of the plants which covered the bed ending at the door.

"The miscreant! What can be his business here at this time of night? This simpering innocent has strange company at stranger hours. We'll see if their spooning is not made notorious, even if it costs the fair name of a De la Torre."

These muttered words greeted no ear, but they came from determined lips, and voiced the emotions of a fiercely beating heart. Ducio had been watched and the watcher had noted his disappearance over the wall of the garden. Ruiz had gone before the appearance on the scene of this youth, who had been impatiently waiting for Ducio to show himself. The latter's egress to fix the gate and subsequent return was not understood and only served to irritate the watcher.

Ducio at last felt satisfied that whoever had been talking in the hall had retired out of hearing, but this gave him no confidence in the safety to himself of a further search in the vault. Who the parties could be was to him a mystery. This alone deterred him. He had little fear where things were plain of solution, but he dreaded the mysterious enough to avoid risking his life where it cast its shadow of doubt. He felt inclined to knife Bonito or to commit some diabolical act to balance the disappointment. He had brought chloroform with him to administer to the jailer. He cursed himself for not having used it instead of wrenching his great toe. The miser's monologue had saved him from assault. He turned towards the bed where Linda reposed in healthful sleep.

An idea struck him.

"Why not chloroform her?"

A sinister expression possessed his face for a moment. He drew the phial from his pocket and held it to the light. He tried the door leading to the hall. It was fastened securely. He took the phial again from the little stand where he had placed it, and as he did so, he glanced in the mirror. He could not help noting his own hard look that answered back "You are a demon." He was about to look away when an exclamation partly escaped him. A strangely familiar face was stamped upon the mirror and seemed to glare at him from fiery eyes. It was a face which had haunted his mental vision for the last few days, and the sight transfixed him for an instant. It appeared to be framed in the opening of the garden door, and he turned nervously to confront it. But there was nothing at the door to confirm the reality of the apparition. Consulting the mirror again, the face was gone. "It had Josefa's eyes and expression," he thought. He went to the door and closed it tighter.

Linda turned in her bed and uttered a sigh, followed by a few words that were not intelligible. The villain crouched. But it was evident that Linda slept a deep, dreamy sleep, all unconscious of the polluting presence. The phial was again produced and a quantity was dropped upon a handkerchief taken from the dressing table. With a catlike movement the fiend approached the couch and held the saturated cloth forward preparatory to its application. The sleeper moved slightly and talked again:

"Oh! Manuel, save him——"

The drug was applied, the nostrils inhaled the subtle narcotic and the girl was soon past the power of rousing to her defense. The Creole sat upon the side of the bed, and, taking a hand, drew the poised arm from above her head. In her dreams she pressed the villain's palm and said in quite intelligible words:

"Beatrice loves him."

Ducio leaned forward and pressed a passionate kiss upon the unconscious brow, unconscious himself of the presence of a third party to the scene. When he grasped Linda's hand the door leading to the garden had moved noiselessly upon its hinges and first the head of the listener, whose face had been reflected from the mirror, made its appearance, then followed the form of the youth. With easy tread he slowly approached the unsuspecting Ducio, and, seizing him by the collar before he had half raised from the unholy kiss, he hissed between his compressed teeth:

"What does this mean, Mr. Ducio Halfen?"

If a thunder bolt had struck him, Ducio could not have been more amazed than he was at the voice which uttered the words, and he was puzzled on turning to find they had come from a youth of slender build, who would be but a pigmy in his grasp.

"Unhand me, simpleton!" cried Ducio, drawing the dagger he had taken from beneath the jailer's pillow. "What do you mean by your interference here?"

"Use your weapon, coward, if you dare!" cried the intruder, drawing a glittering blade. "An explanation you shall make."

"I would prefer to know your authority to ask an explanation," he replied.

"This dress is to conceal me from the recognition of the street not from your's, Mr. Halfen. If Josefa de la Torre has no right to ask, then you are indeed a perjurer."

"Josefa! In this dress? I might ask how came you here? It is not a seemly hour for ladies to be out, even if disguised as men."

"Nevertheless, sir, I am here and will have an explanation."

"Josefa, put away the knife. An explanation will take too long. Let us defer it. You have spoiled all by this intrusion. A successful ending of this venture would have transferred a fortune from miserly hands to yours and mine, who know how to use it—but now—"

"From your actions, when I chanced to come upon you, I interrupted a villainous plot against this girl in place of a plan to secure a fortune. What, sir, have you done here? What ails this woman?"

"A little chloroform—a matter of a few moments unconsciousness."

"During which you would have perpetrated a crime."

"The crime of appropriating Bonito's doubloons."

"If not a worse. The winning of a mine of gold would not excuse the deviltry which I believe you would have perpetrated but for my *interference,* as you call it."

During this passage at arms between the strange pair, their voices had reached a key in sympathy with the excitement of the rencounter. Ducio was about to reply to Josefa's last insinuating charge when an evident attempt to force the door from the hall changed the complexion of the dramatic scene. Ducio was electrified for the moment, but with a characteristically quick decision, he seized Josefa by the arm and, pushing her towards the garden entrance, he said in strong undertones:

"We must never be caught here. Fly, Josefa! I will keep up with you until you get safely home. I did not count on this interruption."

"It is Bonito who overheard our voices," suggested Josefa, as she hastened out.

"Not alone, however, for I heard voices sometime before I administered the chloroform."

The two were soon far on their way across the plaza, going in the direction of Josefa's home.

The first intimation that Guy had that someone was astir in Linda's apartment was a noise so slight that he was much in doubt of the correctness of his hearing. A moment later he noted the movement of the faint line of light that struggled out from under the door. He continued on the alert for further evidences of the correctness of his first suspicion. The high words which followed Josefa's entrance, being confirmatory in the last degree, he tried the door, but finding it fastened, looked around for something wherewith to force it. Jose's bar, which had been left behind by that worthy, was the first thing he noticed. With this Guy hoped to force the lock. His vigorous strokes finally caused the fastenings to yield, but not until the game had fled. With one glance about him as he entered, he passed quickly into the garden through the already open door and found the way into the plaza unguarded by any fastening. Without, the darkness was made blacker by his sudden transition from the lighted room. No sounds could be heard. Returning to the apartment he had just quitted, he diffidently approached the bed where Linda lay, to discover if anything had befallen her. She was breathing heavily. No reply came to his repeated calls. He finally became sensible of the presence of the narcotic, whose fumes pervaded the air of the apartment. This satisfied him of Linda's condition. Taking the light from the dresser he held it closely to the face of the sleeper. She moved slightly and he called her name. He took her hand, which was resting limp beside her. The contact seemed to influence the recognition of a presence, for she murmured:

"Manuel, save him; save Senor Raymond."

Guy, fully comprehending her words, was affected. Satisfied, after witnessing the change in her respiration and an increasing restlessness that no serious consequences would follow the inhalation of the drug, he resolved to close the room securely and to stand watch until the return of day. The superstitious jailer kept his bed in obedience to the injunction of his spiritual visitor, and the morning was well broken before he rose from his slumbers with a confused recollection of the night's experience. Indeed, he lay awake for many minutes in the endeavor to disengage the tangled threads of memory; to distinguish between fact and fancy; to separate what he conceived had actually transpired from the mass of incoherence that could only have been compiled in the realms of dreamland.

So Guy was not troubled by any vigilance of his jailer, and when the first gray of morning showed itself he descended to the vault, carefully closing the trap behind him, and made his way back to his cell and to Jose. The latter was asleep. He threw himself upon his pallet and sought rest in the repose which an all night watching rendered necessary. When he again awoke it was to find Jose shaking him.

"Senor, it is time to get up; and here you are sleeping like a log. Besides, it is time for breakfast, and that lazy jailer should have come, before this, to bring it."

"He has probably not recovered from his last night's scare," said Guy, more to himself than to the other.

"Do you know, senor, that I am getting tired of this staying in jail for another."

"Well, Jose, a little more patience; and I think, after we get the contents of Candelario's basket stowed away, you may go out and return to your duties with Father Ignacio."

"And who will play Ruiz?"

"I will attend to that."

"There is the shuffling old fellow now," said Jose, as he heard the jailer's voice and step.

The bolt shot back in the lock and Bonito, looking rather the worse for his night's work, handed in the morning meal. Jose of course, had promptly retired to the far corner.

"Is be asleep yet?" asked Bonito, nodding over to where Jose had retreated.

Guy simply shrugged his shoulder in reply.

"How I envy his long naps!" continued the jailer, with a yawn.

"Amigo, you look terribly. One would judge from appearances that you had not slept for a week."

"Senor, I had frightful dreams in the night. I had a dream about you—let me see—was it a dream or a vision—or—it was a something about you, senor."

"A dream, Bonito?"

"A—something, senor."

"A waking dream, perhaps."

"Senor, did you ever see a ghost—a spirit?"

"They confine their visits to Christians, Bonito, and to the superstitious who believe in them."

"I see; I see—only Christians—good or bad Christians. Ghosts are not particular—so they be Christians."

"They are myths, Bonito. Ghosts have no existence, having no substance they cannot be seen."

"Oh, senor! You are ignorant to say so. Bonito has eyes—and if eyes can see—Bonito's eyes have seen a ghost, and heard a ghost."

"An illusion. You dreamed."

"Dreamed! It told me my thoughts—my secrets—my—my—it knew what no mortal but Bonito could know."

"You but dreamed, amigo. If you were awake, some one possessed of your secrets played the ghost."

"The ghost was a friend to you," said Bonito, under his breath, remembering his promise to his supernatural visitor. "Never tell it, senor," he continued in a low tone, "but I am sure your friend, the ghost, would not mind my telling you that much. It charged me to silence; but, senor, you must know that you are not to be shot, that Bonito must be out of the way this night that you may escape by no fault of his. It must be the will of heaven, senor, if escape you do, for how you will get out of this cell with or without force, and a double guard in the court, is a puzzle Bonito can't make out. You are lucky to have a ghost doing so much for you, seeing you are not a Christian, with no faith in its sort, and no claims on its assistance. Here is Ruiz, the sleeper, whose fate is sealed, was never mentioned and is left to his doom, although he is a good Christian. Lucky pajarro! But it puzzles me to know how you are to escape through no assistance of mine, except by my absence. If my absence will do it, senor, even that is worth much to one whose life will be saved by it. Yet I ask not for pay—such a thing as pay should be left to the one who knows the value of his life. You have a sister, senor—a young thing who needs you. She has no father, no mother, none save you to care for her. If she had a fortune she would lay it down at the feet of one who would save your life. You would do nearly so much to keep alive her protector. But Bonito asks nothing, although he has been robbed. You, senor, although you believe not in ghosts, and have no faith in the religion of the saints, have a well-balanced head and know your duty. The

duty which you have said was your religion will decide your action—
it will decide your action, senor."

Bonito said this in the low tone of confidence; and as he concluded, a deep sigh escaped him and his flabby cheek fell upon his left palm, as he assumed a disconsolate pose for his auditor's edification.

"Bonito, you combine the arts of special pleading and acting," said Guy, amused.

"I would not take a real, senor, unless you give it with a good will," replied the other, not comprehending Guy's remark.

"Nor a peso?"

"No; nor a doubloon."

"Virtuous Bonito! Have no further care, for I shall see that you are well rewarded for carrying out the commands of my friend, the ghost."

"Que buen pajarro!"

"Say, Bonito, how fares Linda this morning?"

"The child looks bad, senor. She passed a miserable night, and shows it by her drawn face and red eyes."

"Did she, also, see the ghost?"

"Not she; it would have frightened her out of her wits; but her bad feeling comes of the ghost being in the house. There—she is calling me. I promised to go back in a minute, and here I have been babbling and keeping you from your breakfast."

When Bonito had retired, Guy opened his basket and called Jose to join him. In the usual place he found a note from Ruiz. This, after reading carefully, he destroyed, and turned to Jose, with the remark:

"Well, Jose, you are to go to Father Ignacio this morning."

"And you?"

"I will remain here a few hours longer."

"I hate to leave you alone, senor."

"You can better serve me outside."

"Then I will go. Does Bonito know?"

"Bonito is in the dark, but he will be managed. Brush up a little and be ready to leave here in thirty minutes."

Jose was ready to depart when the appointed time had arrived, and escorted by Guy he made his exit through the vault. The hall was clear, and a rap at Linda's door caused her to open it and admit him. Greeting him with a smile, half sad, and as if in expectation of his coming and destination, she indicated the way out through the garden into the plaza.

CHAPTER L.

Vespers were over at San Fernando. A slim congregation had dispersed, leaving a few straggling worshippers, who quitted at intervals the grand front portal, singly or by twos and threes. The popular priest was with the last to leave. At the door he joined two female figures, from under whose rebosas peered two well-known faces. In company they turned towards the priestly residence.

"How fares the young prisoner, Linda?" asked Father Ignacio.

"My father says he is in good spirits," she replied.

"In spite of the fact that his execution is the day after tomorrow?"

"That is, if the day after tomorrow will find him a prisoner," said Beatrice, who was the third party of the group.

"Ah! Then he has hopes of a pardon."

"Perhaps—or something that will equally prove a preventive."

"Guard your secret, my child, if one you have."

"My secret?"

"I've seen Miguel."

"The simpleton! What could he have told?"

"Nothing. Yes, a hint. Miguel is conscientious, and if I know or suspect anything from what he hinted, it has my blessing."

"Thanks, good Father."

"From me—the same," said Linda. "Did Manuel see you today?"

"He saw me just before I said mass this morning."

"He told you?"

"Yes; the plan is bold. It may succeed, but it is a most perilous undertaking. I will have to do penance for engaging, even by consent, in this plot against the authorities. But, my dear children, I have a heart. To my mind it would be murder to take the life of this young American on the insufficient evidence against him, without a shadow of opportunity to defend himself. To me he has proved himself to be the soul of honor, and, talented beyond his years, it would be a wanton crime to destroy a life so full of brilliant promise. Besides, he has not yet experienced the touch of faith. The grand truths of our holy religion have not yet dawned upon his exquisite intelligence. I have prayed for it with all the ardor of which I am master, for I believe his innate purity, allied to a faith in revealed religion, would make him a wearer of the cassock."

"He would make a noble priest," thought Linda, with a half suppressed sigh.

"As if a man of honor and intellect could not believe in religious dogma without taking orders," thought Beatrice, with a slight flush, that might have meant indignation.

"But the world is full of scholars who accept the religions of our civilization, yet they have no inclination to take orders. Many of these are doubtless pure men and honorable," said Beatrice, in unconscious deprecation of Father Ignacio's idea as applied to the subject of her thoughts.

"Pardon me, Beatrice. Child, let us free him first from the impending danger, before we differ as to his career. Whatever his calling may be, Guy Raymond will fill it honorably and well. What says Linda? Shall we make a padre out of Senor Raymond?"

"As God wills it, Father. He would make a good priest, but he is too—just a little too handsome."

"You are very well content with my sacred calling which, in view of your opinion, is a thrust at my personal appearance," said the priest good humoredly.

"But you were a priest before we saw you, and of course Linda and myself have to yield to what we had no opportunity to protest against."

"Well, God bless you, my children; I must leave you here. May all our hopes be realized."

So saying the good father left them, to enter his house, while the girls soon after separated to go to their respective homes.

The parting between the two girl friends was to be of short duration, for before the dew had dampened the plants in Linda's garden, Beatrice had raised the latch of its gate and passed over the neat walk to the former's door, which was open in expectancy of her coming. Bonito, who had fussed around the whole afternoon in a state of perturbation which precluded the indulgence of his customary siesta, hailed the approach of evening with satisfaction; not that it would end the nervousness entailed by a combination of matters which pressed upon his susceptibility, but that it hastened the climax of a portion of the events whose consummation preyed upon his mind. He dreaded the responsibility for an escape made by one of his prisoners. His grasping nature had weighed, since early morning, the size of the remuneration to be expected from Guy, who had hinted at a reward for the bare absence of four hours from his post of duty. He had not removed the remaining traces of the debris in the vault, as Sunday had succeeded his night work. His superstition came to his relief in the remembrance that the ghost had directed his passive connivance in the escape of the American. It was none of his affair if the wall should prove too thick or the bolts too strong and the doubled guard too wary to permit the ghostly programme to succeed. True, he thought, ghosts cared little for fastenings, but how could his mere absence so facilitate matters? If el pajarro should fail and be executed, the secret of the chest would again be only his—if he should escape—well—*que importa,* the doubloons were gone—no one knew where—except the ghost—and then he would get some reward for which he had not asked, however, as his supernatural visitor had forbidden him. He would clean up the vault on the morrow and the most prying could pass through it without a suspicion of a secret treasure, and then, the ghost had guaranteed its safety.

Bonito had early notified the proper authority that he would be temporarily absent in the night, and was promised the double guard, with a special commendation for his vigilance. He had some business with the notary and concluded that he would make that a pretext for a visit to that functionary, at or a little before he hour he had promised to be absent. He accordingly notified Linda, at the time decided upon, and took his way northwards along the east side of the plaza. When the jailer had been fairly gone, the outer gate was fastened with its inside latch by his daughter, who then attached to it a cord with a small stone tied on the other end. The latter she threw over the wall, just above, so that it depended from the outer edge. This done, she, with Beatrice, who was an anxious witness to her act, entered her room and closed the door.

"Miguel! Come forth," said Beatrice.

In response, the giant mozo of the Navarro's issued from the identical place where Ducio had concealed himself on the night before. He having arrived before her father's departure, Linda had placed him in concealment. The huge frame seemed to expand more and more as he rose from his constrained position, and finally took a respectful stand near his mistress.

"Linda, shall we go now or wait?"

"There is little use of waiting. No one is here to interrupt us, and the time will seem too short to you, who must have much to say to him."

Beatrice blushed.

"I—I—will not know what to say. His deliverance here is easy—but the peril of the passage without the lines? This troubles me. Recapture means death—instant death, and then the chances of an armed encounter. Have you his rifle?"

"Here," said the other, producing the trusty weapon of Guy's

Indian experience, "and here his pistols, all clean and in good order. The monte pio had it done for me."

"The monte pio!" said Beatrice meaningly.

But Linda shook her head.

"Come then, Linda, lead the way. Come, Miguel!"

They gained the hall.

The giant was looked to with appealing eyes. He regarded the lounge for a moment, then pointed to it.

"The opening must be under that," he said.

"Do your duty," commanded Beatrice. "Miguel, it is all with you now."

The mozo examined the lounge curiously. He pulled away at it, but the resistance proved it to be stationary. His whole strength was put in requisition. The effect was a cracking noise, then a giving away of the end containing the trapdoor, disclosing the first step, without affording space for the passage of a body. Another effort of the muscular arms and Bonito's contrivance was a wreck. The huge frame of the mozo nearly filled the space as he began to descend to the vault.

"Are you going, Linda?" asked Beatrice.

'No. I will wait here. You go, Beatrice; go with Miguel. To you belongs the credit of this deliverance."

"Now that the moment has come, I am losing the nerve which has sustained me. If there was not still a doubt, still a fear that this effort may miscarry I should stop here from the very lack of force to proceed. This doubt—this fear will sustain me until—until——"

Linda kissed her.

Miguel reminded them that a candle was needed. This Linda supplied, and again embracing her friend, she saw them disappear into the vault.

A shudder crept over Beatrice as she viewed the rough interior of the subterranean chamber, but conscious of the presence of her powerful servant and the sacredness of her mission, she crowded down the emotions natural to delicate and refined womanhood.

Miguel was not long in reaching the ascent to the cell. This he pointed out to Beatrice and told her that the stone covering to the trap must be lifted, and inquired her pleasure. She waved him to proceed.

He drew-forth from his side a heavy blade, and going within reach of the stone to be removed, he held up the light and introduced the point of the knife around its edges. The experiment over he coolly looked down and remarked:

."The stone is loose. Shall I lift it?"

"Lift it," was the reply.

The sinewy frame of the giant was bent double, and with back placed against the ponderous flag, he made one effort and the impediment was shoved to one side. He turned quickly to grasp its edge and the next moment the hole was clear.

"Amigos! Senor—Amigos!" said Miguel, as his big body rose through the opening into the cell.

"Stand back, amigos—I'll test your friendship. Who are you, and what do you want?" said Guy, who had been lying down reading, and viewed with no little surprise the lifting of the stone and the intrusion of the strange head. His first act was to seize the stool and hold it menacingly aloft, while he felt for his dagger. These demonstrations called forth the protestations of friendly intent from the lips of Miguel.

To Guy's inquiry the mozo demonstrated considerable tact by replying:

"The Senorita Beatrice Navarro is here and will answer your worship, if you will let me get off the steps."

"The Senorita Navarro!" exclaimed Guy, moving forward and peering down the steps. He could not be deceived; there, with candle held aloft, anxiety depicted in her face, was the veritable form and features of her whose influence had swayed him like a second nature. As he looked the picture became graven upon his heart. The light and shadow playing upon her features, expressive of changeful emotions lent a singular charm to her beauty. The upturned look, the pallid color induced by the venture and enhanced by the damp and chill of the vault, the contour of the face framed by the dark rebosa, suggested a Madonna.

With a bound he was in the vault.

"Senorita! This is no place for you. Even now you look unwell."

"Senor, I came for a purpose which must be accomplished. Tuesday you are condemned to—to—die. Tonight you must escape. I knew of this secret passage—my mozo knew how to reach your cell—I claimed his services—and we are here."

"This for me! Oh! Beatrice!"

"For you—you who rescued me from a terrible death. To cancel that debt I am here. You must hasten from this foul place, as a first step. It will take some hours to decide, if the plan made by your friends will end in failure or success."

"I knew of a plan to be carried out tonight, but there was no hint of your connection with it."

"That was my secret; shared alone by my faithful Miguel."

"Senorita! I——"

"You called me Beatrice. Oh! Guy, what is the cloud between us?"

"Have I raised it—Beatrice?"

"You did not answer my letter."

"I never received one."

"Then have I misjudged you—but this is no fit place for explanations. Let us go to Linda's room. Her father is out of the way and time is flying. There remains much to be done in a plan of which I must confess my ignorance."

Guy took a farewell look at his surroundings and mentally wondered what would finally become of the miser's wealth.

Linda was waiting in the hall for the liberating party with their charge. She embraced and congratulated Beatrice on her success, and turning to greet Guy, the latter imprinted a brotherly kiss upon her forehead. He caught Beatrice's look as he raised from its bestowal, and before she was well aware of his intention he stooped and kissed her lips.

"That was right," said Linda, "but it should have been given in the vault."

"I wished to acknowledge my gratitude to both at the same time," said Guy.

"Now," he continued, "if you will allow me, I wish to rearrange the stone in the cell so that no blame may attach to my good jailer."

"Let Miguel do that. Miguel, go replace the stone, and, as far as you can, repair the damage to the lounge."

Miguel at once hastened to obey the orders of his mistress.

In Linda's room a council was held. The hour was found to be near ten o'clock when the relief would be around and supply a double guard in the court of the carcel.

"Do you know anything of Manuel Ruiz's movements tonight?" asked Beatrice.

"He was to be here at ten, or thereabouts, to see if I would be in readiness to join him then, or at some hour, which he was to name," said Guy.

"I am expecting him every minute," said Linda.

"How would you have contrived to meet him if we had not found you a way out of the cell?"

Beatrice's question was one which Guy feared she would ask.

Since she had asked it, he answered evasively, for he did not wish her to become aware of his previous knowledge of the secret passage, especially of his purpose to use it that night, as an exit through which to effect a meeting with Ruiz. To so inform her would sweep away the credit she enjoyed as his deliverer, and deprive her of the sole stimulant of the adventure.

So he replied:

"But for the vault I would have been sorely puzzled, and should have been compelled to rely upon the ingenuity of Ruiz to accomplish what you have so easily done through the knowledge of your faithful mozo."

If Linda had a thorn in her heart, she concealed it under a calm exterior. Her devotion to Guy was the outgrowth of her contact with a personality strange to her experience with men of her race. His gentleness, the purity which every act reflected, won her simple admiration, and if she loved him as she would a lover, her peculiar disposition made it possible for her to love him as a friend. She was as much interested in Beatrice as a woman, as she was in Guy as a man. As a child of nature she was a perfect type; as the issue of Bonito, a wonderful product. Under pretense of attention to affairs in and out of her room, she left Guy and Beatrice to mutual explanations and interchange of sentiment on the eve of a probable separation. The pair were engrossed with each other, when the door was unceremoniously opened and Ruiz entered in his disguise.

"No time for ceremony—so I came right in. Ha! Mr. Guy Raymond, happy to see you—and so pleasantly engaged."

"Ruiz! As I live. Your own mother would foreswear you."

"Good evening, Linda!"

"You found the string on the gate?"

"Or I would have had to jump the wall. You are out of the cell, I see," he said to Guy. "Bonito came to terms?"

Bonito? No, he was stubborn to the last. The jailer is off duty for a time. The Senorita Navarro pointed out an exit through a secret passage from the cell."

"A secret passage? But I can't stay for explanations, as time is pressing. Senor, a word with you in the hall."

Ruiz drew Guy aside, just without the hall door, and disclosed to him some new details of the plan to deceive the authorities. While so engaged a rap was given at the garden door and Linda, who answered the call, was surprised to admit the priest of San Fernando.

"You are surprised to see me here—but where is your liberated prisoner?" he asked, looking towards Beatrice.

"Here he is," replied Guy, entering with Ruiz. "Father, I am proud of this honor."

"You did not suppose I was going to let you escape, or run the risk of your life in attempting to do so, without an adios."

"Not he," said Ruiz. "Remember, if we are all caught in this affair, that Father Ignacio is chief conspirator."

"You would be thoughtless to criminate me, for as an innocent I would have influence in your behalf."

"No mercy can be expected from tyrants. But there is no time for debate. I must be off to meet—bold men and true. The fact is, I am late now, and will have to hurry."

As he said this, Ruiz waved an adios and hastened out to the plaza and darkness.

"A bold fellow, is Ruiz," said the priest, as he seated himself near Guy for a chat.

"Bold and true. I tried to induce him to let me go with him, but it seems that I am not to be an actor in the first part of the programme."

CHAPTER LI.

As Ruiz gained the plaza from the garden, he came in contact with someone moving in the opposite direction, his left arm striking the other's right. With an apologetic ejaculation, he moved briskly on to meet his appointment with his confederates.

"That fellow has been there again tonight! It was his voice certainly. There must be somthing—some plot; perhaps the release of that fellow Raymond. The fellow's actions have been strange and suspicious, and he has certainly dogged me. The gate he has left ajar, possibly with a view of returning at once. I will just take a peep in there and may learn something that will confirm my already strong position with the authorities. The dead body of the notary has not yet been discovered. Why not lay the deed on this fellow with the long beard. I can swear that I saw him prowling near the dead man's house last night. Well, here goes to see what I can see."

With these last words, half thought, half said, Ducio crept into the garden and close to the window nearest his former place of concealment. Through a small aperture he was able to take in a view of a large portion of the apartment. The sound of voices were plainly distinct, enabling him to catch here and there a sentence. To his astonishment he saw Guy, the condemned prisoner, sitting quite at ease by the side of the beauty of Bexar, by Beatrice Navarro. Linda, apparently no worse from her experience of the night before, was talking to the priest of San Fernando. Ducio understood at once that the prisoner was under no surveillance; that no restraint was present to prevent his further progress from the vicinity of his cell. Navarro pere was marked by the authorities as a rebel, and here was his daughter giving aid and comfort to a condemned spy, and doubtless intriguing for his escape from the city. But the priest was considered loyal, as was also the jailer. Ducio was resolving to make a report of this scene to the authorities, when his attention was riveted by the plainly heard words of the parties whom he was watching.

"There is a double guard in the court. My father had business in town and thought it best to double the sentinels until his return."

"It seems he did not count on Senor Raymond's power of self transmutation," said Father Ignacio, laughing.

"You have not heard of my playing ghost?"

"No! I had not heard. I merely conjectured that a change of substance had been necessary to enable you to pass the bolts and bars of prison."

"I wondered that Manuel was not more inquisitive about the manner of your getting out of the cell," said Beatrice.

"Ruiz had no time for talking or for explanations, as he had to meet our friends from the outside."

"The one thing I do not like about this plan of Ruiz," said Father Ignacio, "is the introduction of a rebel force to take a part. Senor Raymond's escape could have been insured by secretly passing the lines under escort of a guide, and as for a guide, none in Bexar could have been secured more expert in the business than Ruiz himself."

The words of the priest threw new light on the affair, and Ducio determined that he had sufficient clues to implicate the whole party. The individual who had haunted his steps was undoubtedly the bogus toreador, who, apprehended as Ruiz, was presumably in prison. Prompt action on the part of the authaorities would solve the mystery and explode any alleged powers of transmutation in possession of the prisoners. Filled with this intention, Ducio hastened from the place.

The hour was eleven when Karnes and Ruiz grasped hands, after the bow of the boat had grated upon the pebbly margin of the river. Nathan sat upon her bow as the boat's stern swung around with the stream, and with his feet planted upon the bank, he held her firmly in position. The others were silent in their places, partly from the injunction of the commander, partly from a desire to catch something that would pass between the conferees, whose councils were to detain the expedition for a time.

"Well?" was Karnes laconic inquiry.

"Everything is ready, so far as it is possible to regulate the position of things. A thorough acquaintance with the place and what we are likely to encounter has been looked after. There are risks which no one can anticipate, and whatever obstacles may arise must be met by determination and dash."

"What about the prisoner Raymond?"

"He awaits us free of his cell. I refused to let him accompany us to headquarters, as he will be of more service with our reserve should we need the assistance. Too large a show of force would defeat our aims."

"In your hands, then, Senor Ruiz, must remain the direction of this expedition. We will furnish the pluck, and if mortal courage will carry us through, you may count on success."

"Then we'll to business," said Ruiz, giving a low whistle.

In response a tall form came out of the darkness and placed a bundle which he carried on the ground before them.

"How many, Jose?"

"Seven, senor."

"Counting the sergeants?"

"Si, senor; counting the sergeants."

"But yours? You should have one also."

"I have mine on, senor."

"That will do; it is so dark I could not see the change."

"What are these—the uniforms?" inquired Karnes.

"Yes," replied Ruiz, "and we had work to get enough. Have the men put them on."

"Come, boys, tumble out," commanded Karnes, "size up this toggery and make your toilets without delay."

The men, with more noise than was agreeable to the cautious Karnes, jumped speedily out of the boat and surrounded the pile of Mexican uniforms which Ruiz had procured for their disguise. The next few minutes were consumed in sizing up the candidates for investiture.

"What'll we do with our duds?" asked Hamilton.

"There's only blouses and caps," said Karnes. "You can put them on over your coats."

"Which—the blouses or the caps?"

"The blouses, you fool."

"And our hats?"

"Leave 'em in the boat."

"This blouse will never hide my frock tail," said Hamilton.

"Cut off the tail, then," said Perry.

"That's what," said Nathan, "for the showin' of your tail mout cost you yer head."

"Bravo, Nathan! Your coat tail will never give you away."

"I reckon not," said Karnes, "for it is a question if Nathe ever owned a coat."

"They're useless things, Karnes. The old man once't made me wear one to meetin', but it cut me under the arms and I gin it to my little brother. They're the peskiest things to cut a feller under the arms. Now, I don't mind one of these blouses, altho' this un falls terrible short."

"Come, men, be ready. Ruiz, who is this man? Does he go with us?"

"This is Jose," said Ruiz, in an undertone, "the major domo of the priest. He will be with us, but now I have other work for him. He will return to give notice to others interested in our plot, and announce your coming and our approach down the river. You have the muskets with bayonets?"

"Yes; we supplied ourselves from the lot captured at the powder house."

"All right, then, we had better be off."

By direction of their commander the men resumed their positions in the boat, making a place for Ruiz by the side of the former. The command to push off was given. The little vessel floated free; the oars dipped; the paddle righted its course and it shot away into the darkness ahead. By the road which Jose had to travel to return, the town was but a few hundred yards below, but the torturous course of the river turned here and there until it nearly boxed the compass every quarter of its way. While the craft is doubling its turns, plowing the glassy surfaces of its pools or just grazing the rocky bottom of its rapids, bearing its adventurous crew to the dangers of a hostile environment, a return to the city, now quiet in the embrace of night, will disclose in some degree the difficulties which new moves of counterplotters were erecting in their path. Few lights were to be seen from the quiet streets. The Cabeza de Toro showed its usual activity with answering lights from the Candelario's and the vinoteria, while from the entrance of the court of the carcel the light from the lamp over Bonito's door struggled faintly to the sidewalk. Along Main street, headquarters alone were illuminated. Here the windows of the guard room showed the lazy sentinel as he paced before them up and down his beat. Linda's light was concealed by the high garden wall, but the plaza escaped total darkness through the faint rays of Father Ignacio's candle which, like Beatrice's taper, still burned for the return of the absent.

At headquarters a convocation of deep interest to this narrative was in progress. The room to which the reader has already paid one or more visits, was the scene. The little lieutenant of the staff was apparently the controlling spirit. He was at one end of the green table, while on the side and to his right, his friend Sancho was seated, leaning forward, his elbow supporting his hand upraised to his forehead. Between them was a chess board with a few standing pieces, showing an unfinished game. The lieutenant and his companion were both regarding a third party, who having just been admitted to the apartment, had interrupted a closely contested game of chess by the communication of some intelligence possessing more than ordinary interest. The lieutenant was interrogating him on the subject:

"You say, Senor Halfen, that this prisoner, Raymond, was out of his cell, in the jailer's apartments, and that his companions were—were—I would like to hear it again from your own lips without putting a leading question."

"The Senorita Navarro, the jailer's daughter and the priest who has charge of San Fernando," repeated Ducio, emphatically.

"Good company! And the jailer—was he about?"

'I overheard that the jailer was out in town, but had taken the precaution to double the guard during his absence."

"True, I remember now; he asked and received permission to be absent for a time tonight."

The lieutenant drummed on the table with one of the captured castles of his adversary.

"You seem to take the news coolly," suggested Ducio.

"It is best, Senor Halfen. We military men must ever be cool. The Father Ignacio!"

"The Senorita Beatrice!" chimed in Sancho.

"And the pretty Linda! She, too, in a plot to free this handsome American!" said the lieutenant.

"This nearly upsets all remembrance I had of our game, Sancho; whose move was it?" .

"Your's, lieutenant, otherwise it would be a checkmate."

"Lieutenant," interrupted Ducio, chafed at the indifference paid to the news he had imparted, "you appear so cool over the matter I had better speedily inform you of something additional that will convince you of the necessity for immediate action."

"The report you make, senor, shall have due consideration. This man may be out of his cell, but as for escape, the admirable discipline and the perfection of every arrangement for the defense of this post renders it impossible for him to pass our lines. If you have further matter to communicate we will listen."

"Then, senor, I have to inform you that Manuel Ruiz, the spy who was arrested at my instigation, is free, and has been free for days."

"Impossible! We get daily reports."

"Very well, senor. But what will you say if he, Ruiz, will this night meet a force of the Texans, of what size I know not, and guide them into town?"

"Stuff! They would but come to their death."

"Let him say on what he bases his information," suggested Sancho.

"I heard the priest say that he objected not to the prisoner's escape, but to the fact that Ruiz intended to introduce a rebel force to take a part."

"He is only a half traitor, then," said the officer.

"This needs action," said Sancho.

"It does. I am thinking about the best means to pursue to bag the game."

"It is very simple, senor."

"Yours is not a military mind, Sancho. We of the army know our power, the disposition of our surroundings and at the proper time we make a move."

"You should certainly get this American back to his cell or shoot him at once, and the traitor, Ruiz, should have no mercy."

"What say you to the Reverend Ignacio; to the recreant jailer; to Beatrice, the Navarro beauty with an American education?"

"They should be arrested."

"They shall be arrested!"

"All?"

"All."

"And punished?"

"And shot."

"Don Juan has influence."

"Not an ounce. The general has done with him and he should answer for the treason of his daughter."

"And overlook her act? It would be a pity to immolate so much beauty."

"Her beauty is of little moment to you or me or any other Mexican. There is but one punishment for treason, and that is instant death. If the general, el presidente, were here they would all be shot tomorrow. Excuse me, Sancho, until I send for the officer of the guard. There is no use disturbing the general and I will show you how to block the game of these traitors."

As he said this the little officer stepped to the further door and rapped three times, then resumed his seat. It was only a moment before an orderly appeared at the other door and saluted.

"The presence of the officer of the guard is required here at once; quick, sir, and let him know it."

The soldier saluted, backed out of the door and was gone."

"Now, Sancho; you say it is my move."

"Your move."

"I'll just take this knight that has troubled me so long, and now you are in check from my queen."

"If your military moves are no better than your chess plays, your enemies will outwit you," said Sancho, as he moved his remaining knight into a position checkmating his adversary.

"It's all owing to my mind being absorbed in the news brought by Senor Halfen," said the lieutenant.

Here the orderly returned, announcing the sergeant of the guard, who immediately put in an appearanc.

"Well, sir, where is the lieutenant of the guard?"

"He left with the patrol, your worship."

"For what?"

"A report came from post No. 10 that a boat was heard to pass down the river. It was first taken for a log, but a picket said he heard a voice that could only have come from the thing he saw pass, be it boat, or log, or what else."

"The tonto! There is not a boat in Bexar, and he is on a fool's errand. I have work for you, sergeant. Take six men of the patrol force and go at once to the carcel. You will enter the jailer's house and arrest everybody in it, be it the jailer himself, or priest, or bishop, woman or child. I suspect the prisoners are out of their cells, one an American, the other the traitor Ruiz, whom you know. Arrest them and, as I said, every soul to be found there, except the sentinels on duty, and march them to these headquarters. Go at once."

The sergeant saluted and retired.

"I will show you, Sancho, who will beat in this game."

"Ruiz is against you, and a schemer. This gentleman says he has been out of jail for days."

"Why did you not inform us, Senor Halfen?"

"I am not a professional informer, sir; besides he is so well disguised in his long beard that I would never have recognized him. I learned only tonight that it was he."

"A long beard, you said?"

"Yes, reaching to the waist."

The two friends interchanged significant looks.

It was a few minutes to midnight by the lieutenant's watch when the sergeant had received his orders to arrest the inmates of Bonito's establishment. To impress upon Sancho and the Creole his admirable self-command, he chose other topics for discussion so soon as the subordinate had disappeared. Military matters, his own bravery in several engagements in which he had taken a part, the dispicable character of the American Texans, were subjects briefly considered in the course of a desultory conversation. Meanwhile the time seemed to drag to the occupants of the office. Without, the blackness had given way to the even shadowless light of the after night as the eastern constellations, mounting from the horizon, added their glow to the silver luster of the meridian. A singular stillness, broken solely by the notes of nature, rested over the city. The caged bird on the back veranda whistled a lively answer to his free challenger in the top of an adjacent cottonwood, while the hooting of a distant owl, the yelping of a cur, or the crow of an ambitious cock served to break the monotony of the night-watch. Below the veranda the cool eddies of the river broke into ripples where they touched the shallows of the opposite bank and sent the music of the contact on the bosom of the fresh November wind.

What? Hist! Was it a splash in the water? It might have been a dead limb, long decayed, which finally parting from the parent tree, had fallen to the stream to be borne on and on, perhaps to be the sport of salt waves and ocean currents, until its texture would be pregnant with a diversity of sea life. Deception so enters into human experience. The senses are often at fault and the imagination, with the least touch of the superstitious in the mental makeup, will lend its aid to mislead and mystify and perplex.

What? A splash again! A night hawk flew from its low perch on a limb that reached above the water as if scared away.

Another splash, a low word of command, a dark object shot under the bank opposite the shallows, and a grating sound followed, not unlike the scraping of a boat's bottom upon the rocky shore.

No imagination here. The sentinel, if he had been posted below the veranda, could have been considerably enlightened by the sounds of the landing and also by the words which followed, if he understood the English tongue.

"Nathan, secure the boat. Ruiz, out in front and direct the movement. Guide, put youreslf under the instructions of Ruiz. All secure your arms and see that everything is right." Karnes gave the instructions in a quick undertone, and nimbly jumped to the bank.

While the men were being formed and the arms inspected, Ruiz, at his suggestion, went forward to reconnoiter. He was dressed as a sergeant of the Mexican army.

Ruiz found no impediment to his progress until he reached the sentinel. The latter was walking from him, and as he was not perceived, he made a detour and approached as if coming from Main street. The sentinel challenged him.

Ruiz promptly replied:

"Sergeant from the outer guard."

"Approach, sergeant, and give the countersign."

Ruiz approached a few steps, halted and answered correctly·

"Monterey."

"What is your business, sergeant?"

"I wish to see the adjutant."

"Pass on; the orderly is in the rear."

Seeing but three or four men lying in the guard room, Ruiz asked the sentinel where his sergeant was, with the balance of the force.

The sentinel merely knew that the sergeant had orders to proceed to the carcel and arrest everybody there and in the jailer's house.

"Is that the truth?" asked Ruiz, rather dismayed.

"The truth, sergeant; the lieutenant ordered him to arrest even a bishop if he found one there. But go, sergeant, lest I be seen talking on post."

Ruiz left as if to go to interview the adjutant, but after gaining the rear of the house, he darted down the bank to communicate with Karnes.

"We have no time to lose, senor."

"What's up?"

"A squad has gone to the jail to arrest everybody, the jailer included. Let me have command for awhile, and let no word be spoken but in Spanish.

"Fall in, men, in single rank! There! File up the bank and Senor Karnes will form you and hold you at the edge of the veranda."

Ruiz led the way, and when the force was aligned as he had intimated, he directed the guide to follow him. They went around the end of the building and Ruiz, approaching the sentinel, stated that the adjutant desired to see him on some important matter, and sent him orders to surrender his post to the soldier with him for a few moments

The sentinel hesitated, but concluding that the adjutant's orders had to be obeyed, he finally allowed himself to be relieved. He accompanied Ruiz to the rear, where he was promptly made prisoner and cautioned that a failure to be quiet would cost him his life. Ruiz next step was to interview the orderly, whom he discovered nodding on a bench in the room adjoining the office. He shook the sleepy fellow, who bounced up and demanded what was wanted.

"Tell the lieutenant that I am back from the carcel and that I require more force to arrest the persons there."

"Are you the sergeant? You are not Sergeant Ramirez."

"Do as I command you or I will make a hole in that sleepy head. Man, you are dreaming."

The orderly obeyed, but gave a dubious look at the sergeant as he rapped at the door of the office.

When the rap was given the lieutenant was in the midst of a description of a charge in which he participated once upon a time during one of the numerous revolutions which had torn his country. He allowed the rap to be repeated before he gave the permission:

"Entre."

The orderly opened the door and announced:

"Your worship—the sergeant—he says he is the sergeant—"

Ruiz pulled the fellow's blouse.

"Say what I told you!" he whispered.

"What is the matter with you, tonto—are you sleep?" asked the lieutenant.

"May be I am, your worship; he said I was dreaming."

"Who?"

"The sergeant."

"Oh! The sergeant; let him in. Perhaps he has the prisoners."

Ruiz pulled his cap over his face and, standing in the door, saluted.

"Senor lieutenant, the sergeant whom you sent to the carcel requests you to send him assistance, or to come in person yourself."

"Who are you, sir?"

"Sergeant of patrol No. 2; off duty until four o'clock."

"You are a volunteer, then."

"Si, senor."

"Can't seven men make prisoners of one Gringo, two women and a padre?"

"There is no time to lose," said Ruiz, thinking of his own expedition.

"I grant you that, sergeant, but——"

Ruiz gave a shrill whistle, much to the astonishment of the three occupants of the office. Before an explanation could be demanded, six armed soldiers entered the door, Ruiz having stepped aside to clear the way.

"What means this, you dogs?" demanded the lieutenant, excitedly.

"It means that you are prisoners and that five hundred men are inside of your lines, brought in by the traitor to the tyrant of Mexico, by me—Manuel Ruiz. One word from your cowardly throats will settle it with you for all time. Men, seize this upstart and bind and gag him. One will do."

"Try your hand, Perry," said Hamilton.

"You do not include me in this arrest," said Ducio.

"The French gentleman is included," said Ruiz. "I have a crow to pick with you."

It did not take long to secure the prisoners.

"Now, sir lieutenant, upon the truthfulness of your answers will depend your worthless life. If you lie in any particular you shall never more strut in gold lace and brass buttons."

The little lieutenant, already bound, was completely cowed. He gave a trembling promise to state the truth.

"Where does Almonte sleep?" was Ruiz's first interrogatory.

"He slept in the next room south while here."

"While here? Is he not here now?"

"He left this afternoon for Matamoras."

"Are you lying?"

"Upon my honor."

"Honor! As if it ever dwelt in your carcass."

Ruiz now drew Karnes aside for consultation. It was evident that they must proceed at once to the carcel to secure the safety of Guy Ramond and to keep from harm those who were guilty of having assisted him in the incipient step towards escape. The safety of the adventurers now rested upon clerity of movement. It was decided to not divide the force, but to take the prisoners, gagged and bound, with them to the carcel. The dispositions all being made, the sentinel whom Ruiz had substituted for the one on post, was instructed to allow no one to enter the house during their absence at the carcel. Manuel was well posted as to the character of the low type of the Mexican soldier, and finding that the orderly and the sentinel he had relieved were enlisted convicts, he had no trouble in persuading them to join him, under promise of good rations and pay, besides short service. This inducement, coupled with the assurance that the Texans were virtually in possession of the town, settled their cases, and they fell into line with their muskets. The expedition moved off as the regular patrol No. 1, with Bonito's house as their destination.

CHAPTER LII.

The time did not drag with Guy after Ruiz left him to meet Karnes and the boat. The moments glided by on the fleet wings of congenial intercourse. The beautiful woman whose face had haunted his dreams, whose being seemed to have become unaccountably interwoven with his own through the mysterious operations of love, was his companion. For the first time, in close communion, they read in each other's eyes the decree of fate which assigned to them a common pathway through the fields which mortals tread. It was the intuition of natural selection, the magnetism of an assimilation which never fails to become active when subjected to the blended forces of circumstance and opportunity that converged the paths of these two beings until they blended, to point the way through a future, tinted with the hues of anticipated joys and roseate with the hopes born of youth and health and virtuous lives. They improved the opportunity and were barely conscious of a call made for Father Ignacio to attend to some spiritual duty. Linda was a witness to a devotion which inspired in her a nameless content, that while it soothed yet pained, which brought a joy mingled with a dropping tear. The cooing of the doves afforded an interesting picture, but it failed to arrest a burning desire to witness the departure of the one in danger. Linda, in fact, was awed by a conscious superiority of the lovers to herself. Her sphere was more humble. The peculiarities of her father debased him to the plane of monomania, if it fell short of an alienation. The quiet which reigned without was the counterpart of the peace which prevailed where love held his sway. The moments sped until the first hour of morning began to grow, when the stillness of the plaza was broken by the hum of voices in seeming altercation. The disturbance was followed a little later by the return of Father Ignacio, who appeared worried and excited. To looks of earnest inquiry, he remarked:

"A spy has witnessed your presence here, Senor Raymond, and a squad of the patrol has been sent to arrest you and all who are to be found in this place."

"And Ruiz? Has he been heard from?"

"I know not, senor. I met the patrol at the gate and through my influence kept them out until I could get time to notify you."

"We will defend the house," said Guy.

"But you are one; they are many."

"Miguel is here," said Beatrice.

"We will hold out until overpowered, at all events. It would be base to surrender to the cut-throats and be led like sheep to execution. Father, you had better retire."

"No, my son; I will remain to absolve you, for resistance will be certain death. I believe that with your last breath you will see the light of faith."

Strong blows on the graden gate now were heard, showing the determination of the sergeant to carry his orders into execution. At this juncture Linda pleaded that they all should repair to the hall, which, while it could be taken by the attacking party, was a stronger position, with only two communications, one leading into her apartment, the other opening into the court. Both were furnished with stout oaken doors, capable of great resistance. Father Ignacio seconded the suggestion of Linda; Beatrice urged its adoption and Guy yielded to their persuasion. The party was only well behind the barricaded door of the hall when the attacking party burst into the room just vacated. With a yell of disappointment they dealt blows upon the stout door, which alone remained between them and their prey. Guy stood calmly by, armed with his rifle and a heavy naval cutlass, the property of Bonito, which Linda had procured from her father's room. Miguel, towering above the others, stood close to his mistress, with determination in his eye and Jose's discarded bar in his hand, ready to do execution in her service. Guy's object was to keep the patrol at bay until the arrival of Ruiz, which he felt sure could not be long delayed. His only trouble was his ignorance of the exact status of affairs, the size of the attacking party and the support they would have within the next hour. These and a hundred other thoughts passed through his mind while he watched the door and replied mechanically to remarks of the ladies, who were wonderfully self possessed, despite the danger which menaced them. Guy prevailed upon them to enter Bonito's room, but they filled its doorway watching the defenders. Father Ignacio walked the floor, saying his rosary with a depth of earnestness that indicated his belief in the great danger which menaced his friend.

Finally the blows on the door ceased, while a hubbub of voices, mixed with oaths, came from the assailants. Guy was listening to catch the import of their words, when suddenly the court door rattled and a voice not to be mistaken called excitedly:

"Linda! Linda! Abra la puerta!"

"It is my father," said Linda.

"Go, Linda, and ask who is with him," said Guy.

Linda obeyed.

"He is alone, but there is a sentinel in the court," she reported.

"Admit him, Miguel, but close the door quick."

The mozo did as he was ordered.

Bonito entered.

"In the name of all the saints, what is this? El pajarro with my old cutlass. Y—este—gigante—gigante—Miguel—with a club—el padre saying his beads—and—por Dios—the Senorita Navarro? This is the night of nights. Linda you have roused the hornets. The drunken patrol are sacking my house, while the notary lies dead in his blood upon the floor of his office."

"Be quiet, Bonito! This is a serious moment. I wish to hear every sound from that room," said Guy.

"Serious! I should say, but serious to me. How came you out of the cell without passing the sentinel? You are as supple as a spirit. Has Ruiz also turned to vapor and floated out through the gratings? Come, senor, although it is useless, you must go back to your cell. I have sent my surplus sentinel to report this drunken mob to headquarters. With you in the cell and the mob in the guard house I—"

"They are no mob, Bonito. They have orders to arrest me, who have escaped from my cell. I will not surrender. At present I command here. Go to your room and be quiet or it may be the worse for you."

Bonito regarded his prisoner for a moment. Guy's determined expression had its effect and Bonito shuffled off to his room. As he passed the priest, he gave him a look of significance, as he nodded his head towards Guy and muttered:

"Pajarro tan fuerte y bravo!"

The blows again began to rain upon the door, but this time with regularity and a concussion which indicated force sufficient enough to effect its demolition. The crash came sooner than anticipated. Half the splintered door fell in and a soldier jumped into the hall, only to be felled by the giant Miguel. A shout from the priest, screams from the ladies, an anathema from Bonito, the report of Guy's rifle were mingled with the yells of the Mexicans as they worked on the remaining panel to enlarge the passage. Guy threw aside his gun and brandished the cutlass for work at close quarters, when amid the din he caught familiar shouts that could come alone from American throats.

"Texas and liberty! Clean out the greasers!"

The words electrified him. He sprang through the breach, and circling the deadly blade, he dealt telling blows right and left. Guy's leap anticipated the giant's, who followed the courageous youth and protected him from more than one bayonet thrust. The melee was at its height, when Beatrice fell almost fainting at the side of her lover, who was closely pressed by three or four soldiers with clubbed muskets. Guy ordered Miguel to carry her back, while having recovered some of his wind, he dealt still more vigorous blows at his adversaries, whom he was pressing back, when welcome cries again rent the air.

"Clean 'em up, boys! Old Nathan's in the lead."

The entrance pell mell from the garden of eight or ten Mexicans followed this characteristic cry. The long anatomy of Nathan Roach followed, while he gave rapid blows with his clubbed musket. The appearance in quick succession of Hamilton, Perry, Karnes and Jones, cheering at the top of their voices, indicated a victory. The Mexicans in the room threw down their arms and begged for quarter on their knees. The rescuers sprang forward and grasped the hand of Guy, who stood panting for breath, his cutlass red with blood and his own arm bleeding.

The scene in the room at this moment verged upon the chaotic. Karnes and Ruiz shook hands with Guy, and then began their hurried preparations for the retreat, which, in all the programme, was to be the most difficult as to its safe accomplishment, and was to be the all important act to crown the expedition with success. Linda was comforting Beatrice, just without in the hall. Father Ignacio was not a moment after Guy in entering the scene of conflict, but from the fury of the fight, his pacific efforts were futile, and his offices were effective only when the din had given place to low moans and cries of suffering.

His first act was to congratulate Guy and request Ruiz to tie up the wound in the hero's arm.

Bonito stood in the hall door, apparently speechless, surveying the general wreck in the apartment and contemplating the damage to his domicile. He was roused from his reverie by a loud knocking at the court door.

"Por mi vida!" he exclaimed. "What is next?"

"Open that door!" commanded Ruiz.

"You have waked up with a vengenace," said the jailer, as he moved to obey the order, remembering in all the excitement how Ruiz had always been asleep in the far corner of the cell whenever he had gone to minister to the prisoner's wants.

Bonito turnd the bolt in the lock with some misgiving as what was to appear. The creaking of the bolt was followed by an impatient push from the outside that in no little degree disturbed his center of gravity, and which under the more favorable circumstances of his wonted authority, would have called forth an interminable jower on his part. The first person who appeared was the sentinel, whose enforced entrance was apparent from the rope around his body which seemed to have pinioned his arms together with his musket in one embrace. Two soldiers, neither having guns, had the luckless sentry in charge, and brushing the fat jailer aside, they conducted their prisoner into the room just as Ruiz had finished binding up Guy's wound.

The latter, looking with surprise at the new comers, Manuel whispered to him that his cousin Trevino and Jose had captured the sentinel by lassoing him from the top of the wall, thus securing the last of the force who was at liberty to spread the news of the raid.

When Bonito was forced aside by Trevino and Jose, he was thrown over towards the other side of the hall, the impetus of the movement carrying him to and seating him upon the lounge. To his further dismay the concealment to his trap gave way, Miguel's temporary repairs having proven unequal to the task of supporting his weight.

"Otra mala fortuna!" he exclaimed, as the opening to the regions below was plainly visible.

As the attention of everyone was fixed upon more exciting details, neither the jailer's fall nor the derangement of the trap were noticed. This becoming apparent to him, Bonito easily let himself down the opening and disappeared into the vault. A hasty council of war was now inaugurated to consider some points of embarrassment which the unforseen incidents of the night had raised to confuse the plan of procedure. It would not be prudent to take the dozen or so prisoners through the streets to attract attention, or to cumber their movements in case of an attack, when defensive energies could not brook the restraint which their surveillance would impose. Ruiz and Karnes admitted Guy to the conference, and the three moved to one side for an exchange of opinions, while to Hamilton was entrusted the duty to get the prisoners together in line and to see that they retained no description of weapon.

The elegant Mississippian felt his importance at once.

"Mr. Roach! Marshal the prisoners already in the house.

"Mr. Jones! Go out and get that bundle of buttons and gold lace and his two companions and let them fall in with the inside greasers.

"Perry! Excuse me—Mr. Asbury! When the line is formed, go through their pockets and examine their blouses for weapons, offensive or defensive, everything, from a jack knife to an Arkansas tooth-pick."

Hamilton gave vent to these orders in rapid words and with an air of authority.

Nathan was rather mystified as to the bounds of his instructions as embodied in the term "marshal." He was quite sure he was to dispose of the captured greasers, but whether it was meant that he should employ the summary measures of Mexican custom or Indian practice, or the more humane mode of his own civilization, he was somewhat at a loss.

"'Pears to me, Mister Hamilton, that Perry's orders orter been given fust, as I'se got to dispose of 'em. I 'spose you want me to choose the way, seein' you didn't say ef I was to do it injun fashion, or greaser fashion, or how."

"Get them together, you elongated specimen of the genus homo. Put the prisoners into line, everyone that's able to stand."

"Now you're talkin' 'Merican, or, at least, part was. Come, you yaller-bellies, get into line."

The prisoners not comprehending, Nathan seized one by the collar and put him in position, and kept repeating the act until he had eight of the captured men in the required positions. Perry, who had been waiting the movements of Roach, deftly searched the men, capturing two sheath knives.

Jones, who had been sent for the outsiders, returned after a few moments with the lieutenant and Sancho, reporting Ducio could not be found. This item of intelligence at once adjourned the council of war, as the escape of the Creole meant mischief to them.

"How came he to escape?" questioned Ruiz of the man who had been placed in charge of the three captured at headquarters.

"He did not escape, senor. A man, whom I supposed had been sent by you, came up only a moment ago and said that you wanted the Frenchman, and I allowed him to leave. He and your supposed messenger, I thought, entered this house."

"Describe the messenger."

"He was a youth of slender build, and by the light of my cigarette I saw he wore a red sash."

"Fool! How could you turn over a prisoner to a stranger? Search the garden."

The garden was quickly beat up, but no sign of the missing Dueio could be seen.

When Jones was entering the house to report the news of Ducio's escape, two figures, one tall and muscular, the other slender and of medium height, stole quietly from beneath the banana tree in the dark corner and hurried, unobserved, out into the plaza.

Inside the excitement bordered on confusion.

Under the escort of Guy, all the prisoners, except the lieutenant and Sancho were marched quickly to the court and thence to the cells, a demand for the keys having been promptly met by Linda, who procured them from her father's room. Every captured man able to be moved was thus safely jailed.

Preparations for departure were now at once begun. The men were formed in the court to resemble the regular patrol, the two remaining prisoners being placed in the center of the column, and here they awaited the order to move.

In Bonito's room Beatrice and Linda, each with an arm encircling the other's waist, stood in tearful anxiety. The scenes they had witnessed, trying as they were, were as naught compared with the dread which would creep into their hearts lest the termination of the adventure should prove more tragical still. The danger was yet ahead.

When Guy entered to say good-bye the priest and Linda considerately left the apartment.

"Oh, Guy! The danger which surrounds you emboldens me to cast aside reserve," said Beatrice, throwing herself into her lover's arms.

Guy held her to his breast for a moment, then pushing her to arm's length, he looked yearningly into the depths of her eyes.

"Beatrice, it is hard to part at the very moment when the light of your love first dawns upon me. It is hard to think that the dangers which await me this night may be the arbiter of our fates; that two lives seemingly destined to flow in unison throughout a hopeful future, may be this day separated by the destruction of one. I go to meet whatever exigency may be in waiting with that calm and cool philosophy which alone is worthy of the dignity of true manhood. You will be sustained by the comforting assurances of your subtle faith. Therefore in this, our parting moment, let us rise above human weakness, and resting our cause with human virtue and human courage, we will rely upon our own inherent powers to survive all casualities and overcome all obstacles which may intervene to prevent a happy reunion."

"Oh, noble Guy! I pray that I may be worthy of a love so true as yours. My heart goes with you and if—and if—oh, Guy!"

"Darling, I must be going. Every moment builds up more danger in my path, and for your dear sake I would live."

He embraced her tenderly, then tore himself away. As he passed through the court he took leave of the priest and Linda. From the latter he claimed and received a sister's kiss, bestowed in a manner denoting affection, but with a fervor that caused the recipient to recall the circumstance more than once in the next few hours.

In the court Ruiz, as sergeant, took charge, and giving his commands in Spanish, put the squad in motion.

As they filed out into the street, Father Ignacio looked after them from the narrow entrance and, making the sign of the cross, he muttered the blessing:

"Dominus vobiscum."

The light shone from the Cabeza de Toro, where a knot of men stood in the doorway. The captive, Sancho, deeming this a good opportunity to give notice of his detention and the true character of the party, yelled at the top of his voice:

"These are rebels! Help! Help!"

"Take that for your pains," said Hamilton, clubbing him with his musket.

"Another cry and you are a dead man," said Ruiz in Spanish.

Sturdily they moved along the broken streets, the walls echoing their measured tread, with no other sounds save the commands of Ruiz, uttered in mimicry of the regular sergeant greeting whatever ears were on the qui vive. The hostile city was sleeping in fancied security, strong in its appointments for defense in its guards and outposts, little dreaming that a daring band of "Gringos" had by strategy penetrated its very heart and seized the military headquarters.

The party safely gained the vicinity of headquarters into which they turned, and receiving the challenge from the sentinel still on duty, Ruiz announced his party as the patrol, and givng the countersign, passed on back of the building to the veranda. Much depended now upon time. Ruiz had a duty to perform, which he had to postpone on account of the information given by Ducio, and the consequent descent of the patrol on the carcel. Now the same slippery Frenchman was at large ready to bring down the whole garrison upon them.

He concluded that it was necessary to dare in order to accomplish. He had the convicts on his hands and numbers were a disadvantage, unless they were large numbers. Ruiz was equal to the emergency, and he speedily gave his orders:

"Mr. Hamilton, you will have the prisoner, Sancho, here; no, not that bundle of lace; this fellow; have him and those two volunteer convicts bound and gagged. Also similarly secure those fellows in the guard-room. Lieutenant, you will follow me into your office and get me out some papers. If you are quick and obedient it will be well for you, but hesitate a moment and your dead carcass will be food for the river fish."

"I'd like his coat," said Nathan. "Tarnation! with that a' coat I'd git a ferlo and turn half the gals crazy on the Sabine."

"Silence!" said Karnes. "Every mother's son keep quiet."

Hamlton carried out the orders to bind and gag the prisoners, while Ruiz was in the office with the lieutenant.

In a few minutes the two latter returned, Ruiz tapping his breast pocket in reply to an inquiry from Karnes, signifying that he had the papers.

"Who was that one wanting this pretty coat?" asked Ruiz.

"Me!" answered Nathan.

"Well, Mr. Me, you can have it. This fellow told me a lie while in that office, and to punish him I am going to make him give up his coat. I know he would almost as soon die as to lose it. Mr. Lieutenant, pull off that coat."

The officer reluctantly complied.

Ruiz took the garment, and pitching it to Nathan, the latter caught it on his bayonet.

"A hole in it to start on—and nary a needlefull of darnin' cotton left!"

Nathan's remark, uttered in a doleful tone, inspired a laugh, which, in spite of the danger of discovery, was indulged in by the whole party.

The lieutenant was gagged and sent to keep company with the other captives. Karnes ordered the men to the river to begin the retreat at once.

At the suggestion of Trevino, himself, Jose and the three men whom he had brought from his camp were ferried across the river, so that they could make a detour to the Alameda. After this was successfully effected, the sentinel was called off and the old crew embarked, with Guy along to augment their number.

CHAPTER LIII.

Sunday night had been appointed by Ducio Halfen as an occasion for a long interview with his new friend, the Senorita de la Torre; but the impulsive Creole could not resist the temptation to impart to the authorities his discovery of the suspicious appearances of affairs at the carcel. His capture by the raiding band under Karnes and Ruiz prevented him from a later fulfillment of the engagement. The no less impulsive Josefa was wroth at the non-appearance of Ducio, and in doubt as to what should have made him a truant to the tryst, she finally determined to ascertain, if possible, the cause of his absence. No better mode suggesting itself than a resort to the disguise which she had employed on a former occasion, she leisurely donned her male attire, hoping that eré her toilet would be completed, Ducio might make his appearance. When she finally sallied forth it was in time to reach the plaza as the fight between the raiders and the entrapped patrol was at its height. A strong presentiment led her to believe that the truant Ducio was in some way mixed up in the affair, and the magnetism of the idea drew her closer and closer to Linda's gate. The compromising position in which she had discovered him on the very night before, in the apartment of the pretty daughter of the jailer, might have had something to do with her suspicion that Ducio was again haunting the same locality. At all events Josefa found herself close to the wall door as the combat ceased, and was very little surprised when, of three voices heard near the gate, she recognized one as belonging to him whom she was seeking.

"What will this end in?" said one voice.

"The town will surely find out that something is wrong, and the news will reach the officers on duty," said another voice.

"Lieutenant, this does not look much like the well-appointed military government of which you were boasting a while ago." This last was Ducio's voice.

"Keep silent!" ordered the guard, who had charge of them.

Josefa edged up close to them, and when the guard lighted a cigarette she plainly saw the features of Ducio.

A whispered inquiry made her presence known to the latter, and at the same time drew from him enough to apprise her of the situation.

She rapidly conceived and boldly carried out the ruse which, as already related, set Ducio free. The latter's first idea was revenge for his capture. He prevailed upon his liberator to allow him to accompany her home, before he hurried to alarm the garrison.

"Have you arranged for our departure?" she asked.

"Tomorrow, or at furthest, Tuesday, if nothing will prevent."

"Then come early tomorrow and we will discuss those plans you spoke of. There must be an understanding, you know."

'Expect me early. I will be in a better mood tomorrow to

thank you for this night's work. Good night, Josefa."

"Adios—until tomorrow."

Ducio hurried away and made all haste to apprise the officer of the day of the rebel invasion of the place. To do this he was compelled to seek that officer either at the Alamo, or at the camp on the small peninsula just below the mill ford. At both of these places was stationed a distinct section of the guard, with prescribed limits of duty similar to the section which had been captured at headquarters. Fearful of recapture, he avoided the Main street route, and turned his steps to the Alamo.

"Pull away, right oar! There—now together—so. Attend to your muffle, Mr. Jones; your oar is striking the bare rowlock. Ruiz, you will have to say when we reach those points you spoke of."

"All right, Mr. Karnes. There will be two places to bother us—the mill above the ford and the getting around that peninsula, where a section of the guard is camped."

"I wish we could return the way we came."

"That the current won't allow; while down stream it will assist us to escape," explained Ruiz. "We left in good time," continued Manuel, "for the hounds are upon our trail. Do you hear those yells? That French scoundrel has put in his work."

"There is a racket about something, and I suppose it's us they are yelling about."

"The boat will mystify them," suggested Ruiz.

"I don't know about that," said Guy, as the boat turned a sharp bend and brought to view a light over the river. "If I mistake not, that is held from the Main street bridge to disclose our presence."

"I believe Senor Raymond is right," said Ruiz, "and a fellow is holding the torch."

"It will never do to run into that light," said Karnes. "Slow up, men!"

The boat slackened her pace. The tiller brought her under the deep shadows of a line of willows which extended along the left bank to within a hundred yards or so from the bridge.

"Pull slow and steady," was the next command.

"Allow me to suggest something," said Guy.

"That's what I'd like," replied Karnes.

"It is this. Pull easily until Ruiz here thinks we are in rifle distance. Then I will guarantee to make that fellow drop, and perhaps drop that light into the river."

"If you feel confidence enough in your marksmanship, it is a bargain; but Mr. Raymond, there are two or three of the finest shots in Texas in this boat."

"I will give way to any one, Mr. Karnes, for the work, but not in point of marksmanship. I had no equal among the Lipans."

"The horse thievin' critters," put in Nathan.

"I vote that Mr. Raymond be the one to plug that son of —— Mexico," said Hamilton.

"Well, sir, he shall have the honor, as he spoke of it first," said the commander. "The only thing to consider is: will it be the best to shoot him, and show our position?"

"We have no time to lose," said Ruiz. "We can draw up close to the bank, and they will never be the wiser of our position. If the torch is put out we can pass under the bridge before they can renew it, if indeed anyone will dare to hold another torch, to be shot at."

"Your argument is good," said the commander.

'Mr. Raymond, get ready for the work. Mr. Ruiz will inform you about the distance, as he is familiar with these parts."

The boat had been slowly feeling its way under the branches of the willows and had probably reached the proper distance, for Karnes had scarcely finished speaking when Ruiz said to Guy:

"Are you well loaded?"

"Good for one hundred and fifty yards," replied Guy.

"Get ready, then."

"I'll bring her closer to the bank," said Karnes, sweeping the water astern with his broad paddle. "Then Perry, get hold of that willow branch and let her swing with the current to give Mr. Raymond a steady aim, for he's got a hard shot to make."

"No matter about that," said Guy, bringing to his shoulder the rifle that had made many a deer and buffalo drop, up on the San Saba. A hanging branch interfered for a moment. Silence prevailed while the marksman awaited his opportunity. All eyes were turned upon the light, which moved a little up and down with the unsteady hands of the holder, whose face was at the moment visible as he leaned upon the rail, apparently watching the river.

The report of Guy's rifle, sharp and clear, was followed instantly by the falling of the torch into the swift current under the bridge.

"Pull away with a will!" instantly came from the commander's lips. "All keep silent!"

The boat was brought about and headed down stream. Under the vigorous strokes of the rowers the craft fairly leaped through the water, and in another moment had swiftly shot under and past the bridge. A confusion of voices overhead, the tramp of feet, a few discharges of firearms, the latter perhaps in random reply to Guy's telling shot, were evidences that the mystified enemy was on the alert, but had failed to catch a glimpse of the boat, and if any sounds, unavoidably produced in its management, had greeted hostile ears, they but served to further confuse and mystify them. The rapidity of the current soon brought the boat well into the pool above the dam, where stood the old mill, and where the foot-bridge crossed just below it, spanning the swift and narrow race, and overlooking the little island whose cress-covered surface was half submerged by the escaping waters pouring through the fissures in the low rock wall. It was here that Guy was arrested, while engaged in the diversion of throwing Rolla into the water. Upon this foot-bridge Ruiz had informed Karnes a sentinel would be encountered, and as it would be necessary to lift the boat from the water and to carry it over the dam, the post would have to be captured, or the risk of detection incurred, in which latter event an alarm would be communicated to the guard on the peninsula a few hundred yards below. It having been decided to take the smaller risk, the boat was landed at the eastern end of the low wall, composing the dam where it joined the bank. Ruiz volunteered to take four men, with whom he proposed to accomplish the capture of the sentinel, who was supposed to be posted at the usual place on the bridge near the mill.

Hamilton, Jones, Roach and the Mexican guide, having been assigned to the duty of acting with Ruiz, the latter formed them in line with fixed bayonets. After imparting to them the proposed mode of procedure, he enjoined perfect silence, and marched them by twos to the bridge. Once upon the boards they imitated the regular tramp of the Mexican patrol. As they neared the mill the sentinel's clear challenge was heard:

"Quien es?"

The men were promptly halted and Ruiz replied that he was a sergeant of a portion of the patrol in search of some parties who were disturbing the town.

"Advance, sergeant, and give the countersign."

"Monterey," returned the sham sergeant.

The unsuspecting sentinel made room for the passage of the supposed patrol, who were put in motion when the former affirmed the correctness of the pass-word. When they arrived to within almost reach of the sentinel, the latter, in spite of the assent which he had given to their purpose to pass, gave a yell of alarm and discharged his piece. In response, Nathan, who was nearest to him, clubbed him with his musket, felling him to the bridge floor, whence he rolled into the river. Ruiz at once comprehended the danger of their discovery by a detachment which the report of the gun would inevitably bring down upon them from the peninsula. A retreat to the boat could not be made without encountering the expected contingent. All this flashed through his mind, and in an instant he formed his decision.

"Compadre!" he said to the Mexican guide. "Swap coats with me. I wish to get rid of these sergeant's stripes."

The exchange of uniforms was quickly made.

"Now," continued Ruiz, addressing the men, "Go right back to where the other end of the bridge touches the island, and get under it near the steps. Remain there as still as death, until we can know what effect that shot will have on the guard over there. I will stay here and play sentinel. Quick! Men, I can hear the storm coming."

The men obeyed the order promptly, and were the next moment stowed away beneath the steps which rose from the little island to the level of the foot-bridge.

Ruiz walked his post.

He was not deceived as to the character of noises he heard when he urged his little squad to make haste to conceal themselves. They were the premonitions of a danger that he must somehow avert

Before he had time to mature a plan the tramp of men at a run was heard upon the bridge connecting the further bank with the island. An instant more and they were upon him. His challenge halted them.

Ruiz took care to mimic the voice of the sentinel whom they had put hors du combat.

The party announced its character, and the officer in charge demanded the cause of the firing.

The bogus sentinel replied:

"Some men tried to force a passage over the bridge. When I fired they ran."

"Citizens or soldiers?"

"I could not tell in this darkness, but I could see one who came nearest to me was very tall, and sergeant, I suspect that they were rebels, for when I came on post, a Frenchman met the relief and asked for direction to the General's, saying that a force of rebels had taken the office at headquarters, and had captured the carcel and turned loose the prisoners."

"Which way did these fellows run who tried to pass here?"

"Back towards the carcel."

"Then I'll follow them. Come, men, to the carcel!"

The squad took the double-quick step and were soon out of hearing.

Ruiz called up his men.

"To the boat! No time to lose now!"

The party made all haste to where Karnes was preparing the boat for transportation overland for a distance of forty or fifty yards, across the neck of the peninsula. This work was performed by the entire party, who, four on each side, lifted their brave little craft, and in a few minutes had the satisfaction to see it safely launched below the point they had most dreaded to pass.

At the command of Karnes all of the men, including the captured sentinel, were soon in their places ready to shove off, except Ruiz and Guy, who still lingered.

The latter, with one foot upon the bow, seemed ready to enter, but Ruiz detained him.

"You must come with us," Guy was saying.

"No, Senor Raymond. I have a duty yet unperformed, and it will require my presence in town a few more hours to give it my attention. If I have good luck I will join you in camp tomorrow night. These papers I would like to have delivered to General B——. You will be prepared to give him much information in regard to the garrison here."

Saying this, Ruiz wrung Guy's hand and turned abruptly away into the darkness.

As soon as Guy had taken his place aboard Nathan pushed the boat from the shore and once more it was headed down the stream.

Before them the darkness was too great to detect the sharp turns of the river and cautious rowing and a rapid current were depended upon for guidance, rather than to the dexterity of Karnes and his broad paddle. Behind them the score of lights and the increasing hub-bub of an excited garrison was soon lost to eye and ear.

The torturous course of the river and the difficulties of navigation were impediments preventing a speedy termination of the boat's passage to the destination of its adventurous crew. The gray dawn was visible in the east, when Karnes gave the order to haul the craft on the bank preparatory to a resort to camps, by way of the Mission of Concepcion, whose venerable walls rose darkly above the tree tops, about a quarter of a mile distant. The party were in high spirits on account of the success of the expedition, and they gave full vent to their hilarity as they struggled along over ground so suggestive of incidents of the late battle, allusions to which were indiscriminately made with other remarks on their later and more thrilling experience. Nathan's long stride kept him well in advance, necessitating now and then a turn and halt, to guarantee an audience for an occasional sally or a rejoinder to some half comprehended thrust from Hamilton. Every act and word of the backwoodsman was eminently characteristic, and the comedy of shape and movement were illy disguised beneath the hostile uniform, scant and ill fitting, which covered his own slick homespun. At each turn he made, the flashy lace of the Mexican lieutenant's coat, which depended from his left arm, shone in conspicuous contrast with his rough attire.

At the jacal, in the rear of the mission, Locaria still presided, and here, awaiting the returning party, was Mr. Trigg, anxious to greet the boy he had lost on the banks of the Salado.

"Guy, me boy!"

"Mr. Trigg!"

The two indulged in a hearty embrace.

Guy's look eloquently conveyed the intelligence of the strong desire burning within him. The scene on the Salado on that eventful Sunday morning rose vividly before him, and he felt the full weight of the impression that, in his presence, were lips that could unfold what to him had been so long a sealed uncertainty.

Mr. Trigg comprehended the mute appeal.

"Wait a spell, me boy. In the camp beyond I will have ye to myself, and I will tell ye the whole sad story. Meantime, be comforted in the knowledge that the girl is safe and happy as a girl can be, who only hopes she will see her dear brother."

Guy pressed the hand of his friend, and was about to express thanks, when the wail of a woman claimed every one's attention.

The cry came from Locaria, as she threw herself upon the Mexican prisoner, who stood with bound hands in the rear, unnoticed except by Perry, who had been placed over him as guard.

When explanations of her strange conduct followed, the captured sentinel proved to be her brother, who had been impressed into the service of Mexico. On learning this, the prisoner was promptly released, his sister guaranteeing that he would henceforward be true to Texas.

CHAPTER LIV.

After Guy sufficiently recovered from the shock which the story of the fate of his family, as detailed from the lips of his Irish friend, had given him, he began to turn his attention to the situation of affairs among the forces arrayed against the city he had just left. The small expedition which had penetrated the lines, captured the headquarters of the enemy, released him from prison and extricated itself by a bold push through his entire position, set him to thinking of the feasibility of capturing the place by a proper utilization of American pluck. Behind him, in their power, remained Beatrice, who had more or less compromised herself by aiding in his escape. This impression, perhaps the master influence in support of his idea, gave earnestness to his manner and eloquence to his tongue when, in seeking headquarters to deliver Ruiz's commission to General B——, he urged the policy of an immediate attack on the town. He became more determined than ever to rouse the men of the several commands to the necessity of the movement, when, on the following day, he received news of the arrest of both Beatrice and Linda. The latter intelligence was brought by Ruiz, who suddenly appeared in camp on Wednesday morning, having successfully passed the lines the night before. The mess were at breakfast when Manuel arrived, and having made a place for him at the log table, they invited him to impart his news from the city.

"Do you want to hear it all?"

"All!" cried several voices.

"Begin where you left us at the boat," suggested Jones.

"Give us the plain, unvarnished, Ruiz; no elephantine embellishments," said Hamilton, cutting his eye at Jones.

"Well," said Ruiz, "after leaving you all at the boat, I boldly struck out for the Alameda, to see if my cousin, Trevino, had arrived safely back to his tent. By skirting the east side of the Alamo ditch, I did not meet any one, and found Trevino looking as fresh and innocent as an angel. A special patrol had just left his camp, after poking their noses into everything to see if they could get at a sign of a rebel having been that way. After a short stay, I went to Main street, passing over the bridge where you made that fine shot, Senor Raymond. A company of infantry was just passing over it at the time, going, I suppose, to help catch the rebel force, so I fell in behind them and passed unchallenged to the plaza. Headquarters was like a beehive into which you had poked a stick. The yard was swarming with soldiers, and officers were hurrying about. I imitated everybody else and moved about, noticing and listening. I caught parts of the talk about the rebels, who had come and disappeared so suddenly, and was much amused. Some thought spirits had done the work as men in the flesh could not have disappeared. My name was mentioned several times as having led the party, and I found that this came from the lieutenant of the staff, the loss of whose uniform seemed to be generally known. Having heard it mentioned that Linda and the Senorita Navarro had been aiders in the escape of the prisoners at the carcel, I went to Bonito to try to hear from the ladies. Bonito was fussing about, directing two mozos, whom he had employed to set to rights the desecrated apartment of his daughter. The old fellow was viewing the wreck of his inner door, one panel of which he was holding up to its place in an aimless attempt to make it stay there.

"'No mas mala fortuna!' he was saying to himself.

"With my cap pulled down over my face, I disguised my voice and spoke to him:

"'Senor, are you the jailer?'

"'I am, amigo, but not for long. I am going to quit. A jailer has only misfortunes. You see, amigo——'

"'I have not time, Mr. Jailer, fo hear your troubles. I have orders to arrest the Senorita Navarro. She was here tonight.'

"'Es verdad, but she is not here now. Is this a fit place for women—for ladies? This blood, these broken doors—this——'

"'You forget, Mr. Jailer. I'm on business. Where is the senorita?'

"'Quien sabe. At home, no doubt. Linda, poor child, is with her. Arrest her! Must the government make war on women? She is as innocent as Linda of crime, and arrests are made for crimes, Senor Sergeant. Better arrest the devils who have turned my house topsy turvey and let out my prisoners.'

"'Prisoners? Who were they?'

"'You are getting over your hurry, sergeant. You could not spare a moment to hear of my misfortune; but these prisoners were brave fellows—half devils, half men—yet gentle and real caballeros. It was nothing for them to pass through the bars of the cell, or perhaps the keyyhole, and yet their flesh and blood were as yours and mine. You should see him fight—el pajarro—as I called him. He cut and slashed the mob with my old cutlass as if he were a man o' war's boarder of twenty years' service. He sent me below as if I had been—the cook—or steward—or ——'

"'What about the other prisoner?'

"'Oh! The sleeper—Ruiz—Manuel Ruiz—he is a good fellow, but he got into a habit of sleeping in the cell, until he dreamed himself out of it—and I hear he has been getting revenge on his enemies by leading a number of rebels into town.'"

"I left Bonito still aimlessly working at his broken door, satisfied that the ladies had not been arrested, and sought the repose I needed. The next day I kept close at my cousin's, sending him out to get information. In the afternoon Trevino returned and informed me that the Senorita Navarro and Linda, the jailer's daughter, had been placed under arrest for assisting prisoners to escape. After dark I went to the priest's house to see Jose about an affair between us. He was at home, as was also Father Ignacio. From the priest I learned that his niece, Josefa de la Torre, had left the city in company with the fellow Ducio Halfen. She had gone against the wishes of her mother and uncle, both of whom were much troubled at the event. Having nothing further to detain me in town, I succeeded in passing the lines last night, and here I am."

The news brought by Ruiz had a marked effect upon Guy Raymond. He laid before Mr. Trigg a plan upon which to make a move for the capture of the town.

"It is a bold one, me boy," he said. "But pluck will do it."

"That's my idea, Mr. Trigg, and Ruiz thinks it will be easy of accomplishment under the right leaders."

"There's many of the officers here as is not fit to lead. The meeting they had last night ended in the postponement of an attack, and it is reported now that orders will be coming soon to raise the seige and go home."

"If such orders are issued it will be a sorry day for some of the officers."

"They say it's all because one of the guides is absent."

"A mere excuse. I can get a dozen guides to fill the absent one's place."

"Our squad's in favor of going, and they're talkin' the men of the other companies into it. I'm tired of this do-nothing business, which is weakening us every day."

"The victory at Concepcion should have been followed by the capture of San Antonio. Father Ignacio almost admitted to me that it could have been done, and said the Mexicans dreaded an assault."

"Is he the praste that came to see me after the fight?"

"He is the same."

"I remember he couldn't get me name right, and although I told him the five letters, he pronounced it as long as if it had twenty. They are not as sharp as our Irish prastes, who take to all languages, even if they can't spake them. This Father Ignaçio is a very dacent man and has been kind to ye, which will cover up a deal of shortcomings."

The next morning the whole camp was astir with excitement. Around General B——'s tent a crowd was assembled, talking over the situation. Among the officers generally the idea of an assault on the town was unpopular, but the feeling among the troops showed the effect of the agitation inaugurated by Guy and the squad which had so recently shown what a few determined men may accomplish. A little removed from the crowd was another gathering of men, chiefly private soldiers, surrounding the well-known figure of a popular officer. The latter was listening to arguments in favor of an immediate attack, to all of which he assented. To every such indication of his approval, a cheer would go up from the men. The favorable temperament of the rank and file, whetted by the enthusiasm of the moment, suggested to Guy Raymond a plan to make it bear good fruit. Acting upon the impulse of the moment, he stepped close to the officer's ear and suggested that he step to one side and call out loudly for volunteers to follow him into town. The suggestion was most opportune, for the officer, who was Colonel Ben Milam, took at once a central position between the two assemblages, and cried out the now historic words:

"Who will go with old Ben Milam into San Antonio?"

The air was immediately rent with shouts of approval, and before many minutes three hundred volunteers were in line, ready to follow Milam to victory. During the enthusiasm of the moment Colonel Milam introduced Lieutenant V—— of the Mexican army, who had deserted from the enemy and reported the city ripe for capture. This put more confidence into some of those who had been only half hearted in the enterprise. When the lieutenant was introduced, to the surprise of Ruiz, he identified him as the officer of the staff whom he had forced to part with his coat on the night of the raid. The next morning the 5th of December was fixed for the movement, and the camp was busy with preparation.

The whole of our mess had volunteered. Their number was now augmented by Guy and the brother of Locaria, the latter having begged the mess to adopt him.

The members were just through supper, and had been discussing the organization of the two attacking divisions, under Colonels Milam and Johnson, which had been effected that evening at a meeting held at the old mill. Jones was busy cooking rations for three days, while the others were seated or standing watching him, or conversing of the event of the morrow.

Mr. Trigg had lighted his pipe and was giving some instructions to Guy, relative to the latter's future, in case the casualities of the coming conflict should include him among the victims.

"You see, I might be killed; and then there's no one but ye to look after Stella. There'll be plenty for both o' ye, and if anything comes of the paper I was telling about, ye might be rich enough."

"I trust we both will get through safe, Mr. Trigg; but why is it necessary for you to go? Let the young men do this."

"I wouldn't be caught loitering, me boy. I volunteered, and there's an end of it."

"What about the possession of this paper? If I had only known that this Creole was the thief, I could have gotten Ruiz to attend to him. You say the paper explains everything?"

"The two together. The one stole at the mission is the draft of an island and has marks upon it which the other paper explains. The other paper was in a verse like, and was left in the charge of a Portugese who's in San Antonio, or was there not a great while back."

"A Portugese—a Portugese," thought Guy. "Can it be Bonito? It must be Bonito. Hidden treasure! Can it be that the treasure the paper will disclose is the same that he has hid in the vault?"

Guy mused a while, then asked:

"Could this island treasure have been moved recently, or at all, without the paper and its key?"

"No; the old gunner said it was not possible to discover it without the sheerest chance."

At this moment Ruiz came up in company with the deserter from the Mexicans.

"Allow me to introduce Lieutenant V——, late of the Mexican army," he said, in Spanish first, and afterwards in English.

Hamilton, seeing his opportunity, said:

"Hello, Nathan! What you going to do about it?"

" 'Bout what?"

"This officer wants his pretty coat. He is the gentleman we gagged and left minus his gold lace."

"He ain't got no claim to that 'ar coat; besides, ef he's deserted, he can't wear it."

"Personal apparel in actual use is not a legitimate prize in civilized warfare, Mr. Roach," contended Hamilton.

"You keep your dictionary rubbish, Mr. Hamilton, and I'll keep the coat. See here, boss," he continued, addressing Lieutenant V——. "You'll have to fight for that coat, for I'm goin' to take it to the Sabine, and the fust time I go to Orleans I'm goin' to trade it to an organ grinder for his monkey to wear."

Ruiz interpreted this to the lieutenant as an inquiry to ascertain if he wanted his coat.

In reply he begged its present possessor to keep it as he had no further use for it. Hamilton having insisted that this answer meant just the reverse, Nathan reasserted his intention to hold fast to his prize.

There were few who slept in the Texan camp on the night succeeding the determination of the volunteers to follow the lead of Milam into the hostile city. The old mill was the scene of a hasty organization, which resulted in the formation of two divisions; one to be under the immediate command of Milam, the other with Frank W. Johnson as its leader. With the latter division Karnes and our mess were assigned to duty. As the night wore on the sounds of preparation continued and there were few laggards when the word went round from camp fire to camp fire to proceed to the rendezvous. The men fell into position under the supervision of their leaders, and there was a marked absence of levity as greetings and words were exchanged with each new arrival. The coming event, while it filled the minds and shaped the remarks which voiced the sentiments of comradeship, promised to be a collision fraught with danger and prophetic of defeat, to be averted only by a sublime heroism which inspired the movement.

The attack was deemed to be ill advised by the highest authority of the investing forces, and was therefore to be made in violation of the rules of scientific warfare. It was a movement of the men and a following of the officers. The rank and file developed a nearer tie—the tie of mutual dependence in the individual courage which augured victory against the dicta of principles.

Nathan Roach was a typical volunteer.

He would not waste time in a debate as to the advisability of attacking an overwhelming force of Indians or Mexicans where there was an apparent necessity for fighting.

His prompt decision would be to fight, and if defeat succeeded, to consider the causes at his leisure. With Nathan it was the animal; with Hamilton it was pride which overbalanced the dread of consequences.

Perry, yet under tutelage, was an apt pupil who would go down to his death under orders.

So, all through, up or down the list of the three hundred, heroism was the development of characteristic energies having their inceptions in higher or lower promptings. With Guy Raymond courage was a normal concomitant of a cultured mind, trained to a high conception of duty and imbued with a hereditary instinct of honor. His participation in the attack would not wholly parallel in motives with that of any who would follow Milam or Johnson. He was impatient with the semi-barbarism of Mexican supremacy and regarded its overthrow in Texas as a part of the mission of his race. Therefore, he was not actuated by prospective booty, or by any of the material gains of conquest. But the moral side of the advantages of victory was, for the time, but a secondary consideration with the lover of the fair Beatrice Navarro. His arder to act at once, in her behalf, was no small part of the moral force that matured the spirit to attack. It was then not strange that among the restless camp, his mind was the most active, his hopes the most earnest, and his resolution the most determined.

The news brought by Ruiz regarding the arrest of Beatrice and Linda was confirmed by the deserter Lieutenant V———, who also advanced the comforting suggestion that an attack on the city would divert the attention of the authorities from the prosecution of the prisoners. Guy, in his reflections, thought not of defeat, but of his purpose. He would fight his way to the side of her whom he loved, if it were only to lay his life down at her feet in fruitless effort.

It was not yet day when the command to move was given. The starlit night had given way to damp and fog—a curtain of mist hung around every object and concealed forms but a few feet distant. The courses of the two divisions were to be divergent. Johnson's was to enter the city at the head of Soledad street with the Veremendi house as its objective point, while Milam's was to march down Acequia street and occupy the residence of Senor Garza. Under direction of experienced guides each column moved along its appointed course in single file, the low hum of conversation dying away to silence as the light of dawn struggled through the veil of mist and disclosed the straggling outskirts of the town. The picket had been eluded by a detour to the right, the too confident outpost having become careless from the past inactivity of the besiegers.

Johnson threw his men into platoon front, when considerable progress had been made down the street, and it was only when in view of the Veremendi house that an intimation of their discovery was given by the discharge of his musket by a sentinel. Deaf Smith, the chief guide of the division, returned the fire, wounding the retreating soldier. This firing was the signal for the general alarm of the garrison. Promiscuous firing began from several points, all of which was more or less harmless until the enemy more definitely located the Texans. The latter turned their attention to securing cover and opening communication between the two columns of attack, which resulted in the occupation of the Veremendi and Garza houses. Johnson ordered Karnes to select a squad of men and proceed to pick loopholes in the walls, wherever practicable, and to open a passage to the roof of the building, for the purpose of driving the enemy from the tops of the adjacent houses. Karnes marshalled the members of his mess for the purpose, and they were soon at work with a will. Milam's division was similarly engaged a short block away, and thus the first day passed. The next day was spent in skirmish firing from the tops of buildings, through holes cut in the parapets, while the force under Milam succeeded in extending the line about fifty yards to the westward, by occupying a house in advance of Garza's. The morning of the third day, the seventh of December, found the assailants in strong position, but fatigued from ceaseless activity. The object was to gain possession of the houses fronting the north side of Main plaza, and about noon Karnes volunteered to effect an entrance into the only intervening building, which stood alone across the street and some yards further down. For this work he selected the men who had accompanied him on the late raid, with Mr. Trigg and Guy as recruits. Armed with a crowbar, Karnes advanced at the head of his party. A fusilade greeted them from the wall, while a battery of the enemy sent a storm of shot up the narrow street. Two of the daring party were cut down, while their leader was dealing fierce blows upon the oaken door. The stout timber creaked and groaned—then yielded and swung upon its hinges. The men rushed in, but behind them lay the prostrate forms of Mr. Trigg and Jones. Guy gave one glance, then bounding to the street, he lifted his friend and bore him into the house. Nathan Roach followed Guy's example, and wrapping his long arms about the body of the East Indian, rescued him from the leaden storm that raged around him. Over the door, through which an entrance had been effected at such cost, was a dim sign, upon which was written "Notario." A company of about thirty men followed Karnes to hold possession. With these came Ruiz, who had helped to guide Milam's column. He saw with much regret Guy's grief at the fall of his old friend, and suggested that the wounded men be taken into the next room, away from the crowd, to have their wounds examined and dressed. The door was fastened, but yielded to the crowbar. Inside was a scene which startled them. On the floor, in a state of semi-decomposition, was a human form. Ruiz ejaculated:

"The notary!"

"You knew him?" asked Guy.

"I saw him killed—and by that scoundrel Halfen, who betrayed us."

"He must be removed before we can occupy the room," suggested Hamilton.

"Here, men, take this body out; there is a rear apartment back of this. Lay it there for the present."

Ruiz's order was obeyed.

Mr. Trigg and Jones were tenderly moved into the office and made as comfortable as possible. No surgeon was present, but willing hands bared, then bandaged their wounds. Guy sat by his old friend, who seemed to be in great pain and manifested a disinclination to be talked to, after he had once announced that he must be fatally hurt. Jones was more communicative, and also claimed to be mortally wounded.

"Mr. Trigg is suffering so much I would give a great deal for a little chloroform to ease him," said Guy sorrowfully.

"That reminds me that the notary was a sort of doctor," said Ruiz. "Let us see what he's got in this chest."

So saying Manuel tried the chest, but finding it locked, went out and in a very short time returned with the key, having found it in the pocket of the dead owner. The contents of the chest were in good order, everything being methodically arranged. Papers, plainly endorsed, were tied in packages in the deep tray, separated by divisions forming compartments. Lifting the tray, Ruiz gave an exclamation of satisfaction as a number of phials showed themselves in a miniature chest extending across one end of the larger box. Guy assisted his friend in examining the labels of the phials and discovered one with chloroform legibly traced on its paper. After the anesthetic was administered to both of the sufferers, Ruiz recounted to Guy the scenes he witnessed on two occasions between the Creole and the late notary, the last one culminating in the murder. Guy became interested at the mention of the mysterious paper which appeared to have been the bone of contention between the murderer and his victim, and proposed to Manuel to jointly inspect the contents of the tray in the hopes of discovering it. A cessation in the firing having inaugurated an involuntary truce, the moment appeared propitious for the search.

Karnes had been summoned to the rear to participate in a hastily called council of war, and the men, save a detail, engaged in picking loop holes in the walls, were at ease in the adjoining apartment. Among the first packages glanced over was one endorsed "Papers of Manoel Canastadomiento." Guy read the name of many letters and remarked that it was Portuguese. The collection appeared to be documents pertaining to the notarial office, or the property of parties for whom the deceased had acted as attorney or agent. Finally Ruiz read an endorsement "Private papers" on a package which he handed to Guy. The latter loosed the tape which secured it, and found perhaps a dozen papers of questionable meaning, and appearing to be memorandums. The last one consisted of two separate papers fastened together. One was a diagram, which at once absorbed the searcher's attention. From this he glanced at its attached companion. His interest increased as his eye ran down the liquid lines, which began:

> Along the outer coast you'll see
> Little circles—one—two—three,
> While other circles in plain view
> Are numbered only one and two.

As the riddle unfolded itself in the progress of the rhyme, Guy's interest heightened, and at its conclusion, he mentally concluded that the paper which caused the murder of the notary was in his hands. He signified as much to Manuel, as he replaced the memorandums in the package and deposited the rhyme and diagram in the breast pocket of his coat.

During the afternoon the Texans gained two or more advanced positions on their right, and during the night succeeded in occupying the Navarro house, which commanded the northwestern corner of Main plaza and the northeastern exit of the plaza de Armas. The new position was calculated to harass the enemy's force stationed at the foot of Soledad street, and to lessen the effectiveness of his fire on the Texan left in the Veremendi house and the notary's office. Guy's attention in the meantime was given almost exclusively to his stricken friend, who before the nightfall, was resting as easy as his wound and circumstances would permit. With darkness, besiegers and besieged turned their efforts to the strengthening of their respective positions for the morrow's work. Yet the occasional discharge of a musket indicated the activity of the garrison or the spirit of some individual soldier who, despite the reverses of his side, wished to manifest his unabated defiance.

In Guy's musings, induced by his watching, he never once doubted the victorious outcome of the attack, but he could not banish a certain dread, that danger menaced the persons of Beatrice and Linda. The certainty of defeat in the last moment when it should be apparent that the city must fall before Texan valor, might be seized as the opportunity for vengeance to be wreaked upon the heads of the women who had plotted for his escape. The thought wrought upon him until the picture of Mexican revenge rose before his mind and seemed to materialize into a positive realization.

He was relieved when Ruiz entered in his brisk, earnest way and said:

"What are you dreaming about? Is there any change?"

"Very nearly dreaming, Manuel. Both are sleeping. The power of the narcotic is still unbroken."

"I came to suggest that we go on the roof. The boys have cut a hole big enough to pass through and tomorrow we can pop those fellows who man that infernal battery from the parapet."

"I'll go with you. I need something to drive away a horrid thought."

"A horrid thought!"

"Yes, a mental picture of Mexican vengeance—vengeance upon Beatrice—upon Linda."

"A possibility in case of——"

"A probability in the imminence of defeat."

"Come away and banish the thought. Tomorrow will settle it."

"Settle it! Yes, settle it; upon the way it will be settled much depends. Manuel lead the way. I'll go with you to the roof."

In the apartment to the rear a scaffold had been erected sufficiently high to enable a worker to reach the flat roof above. Between the ponderous timbers which supported the stone roof, a hole had been made sufficient for the passage of a large man. In the gloom the aperture could not have been discovered, but a tallow dip stuck upon the highest point of the approach disclosed the space that marked a patch of the black empyrean. Ruiz mounted first and Guy following, the two soon trod the slightly inclined flags above.

The chill of the night air sent a tremor through their frames. Along the southern parapet the shadowy forms of a half dozen of the Texans were visible, their whispered words greeting the ear in guarded undertones, typical of the caution necessitated by the presence of danger.

"Let us sit here for a moment," said Ruiz. "Here above the window through which I witnessed the assassination of the notary."

"That Halfen must be a villain of the first water."

"Undoubtedly," replied Ruiz.

The friends relapsed into silence during the next few moments. The ragged clouds scudded before the north wind, veiling ever and anon the silver horn of the young moon low sinking in the west and converting the heavens into ever changing patches of siderial beauty. Guy, full of his last trouble, wondered where away in the dark city were the fair prisoners, and chafed at the thought that he could not go at once to their rescue.

"Ruiz, where can they be confined?"

"The ladies?"

"Who else?"

"I know not, amigo. I wish I did. Perhaps at the home of Beatrice, a guard keeping them in durance."

"I fear not," said Guy, dejectedly.

"Who calls?" asked Ruiz, looking over the wall into the back enclosure. "I thought I heard someone call my name."

"I, myself, heard a voice," said Guy.

"Who's there?" demanded Ruiz, in a louder tone.

"Yo, amigo; Miguel."

"Miguel?"

"Si, senor; mozo de Don Juan."

"That's lucky," said Ruiz. "We'll hear from the ladies."

"How knew you that Ruiz was here?" asked Guy, puzzled that the giant should have discovered his companion's presence.

"I heard his voice and knew it; the same as I know that you are Senor Raymond."

"A wonderful ear—your's," said Guy, bending over the wall, "but what of your mistress; is she yet a prisoner?"

"Si, senor, y tambien la Senorita Linda."

"Where are they confined?"

"They have been removed to the house of Bonito at the carcel, in the room of the Senorita Linda."

"Are they in danger?"

"So says my master, who is in hiding to avoid arrest, and that is why I am here. An attack by your men on the jail early in the morning may save them. There is talk of shooting them at the last moment if the Texans gain the city."

"My presentiment, Manuel," said Guy, rising from the parapet excitedly.

"It was the wave of sympathy flowing between congenial souls."

"Let's descend and admit Miguel. By heaven, something must be done and tonight. Miguel! Await us. Ruiz and I will let you in."

Guy was the first down and soon had the faithful Miguel in consultation.

"Miguel," he said earnestly, "tell me of Beatrice."

"The senorita knows her danger, senor."

"Why did you seek us?"

"To aid me in her rescue."

"Have you a plan?"

"None, senor. Time flies too swiftly to plan."

"We'll plan as we go, Miguel, and rely on our manhood to achieve success."

"Your's is to lead, senor; Miguel will follow, faithful and strong."

"Here is Ruiz, and excited. What is it, Manuel?"

"Jose is without, with a message from the padre."

"Father Ignacio?"

"The worst is to be feared. Our success has enraged the officers of the garrison and there is no time to lose. The cowards would wreak vengeance upon those who sympathize with us, even upon women."

"This from Father Ignacio!" said Guy, half aside.

"Then—then—Beatrice! Oh, Beatrice! Manuel, will you throw your valor in the scale against this intended wrong? A few brave hearts may rescue from their very nest the virtuous prey upon which these carrion crows have fastened."

"Senor, I am with you to the death. Let us find Karnes and decide our course. There will be no lack of volunteers."

"Come, Miguel," said Guy, following Ruiz out. "Come, your mistress and Linda shall pass sentence on their judges."

CHAPTER LV.

"M-a-la--for-tuna! Little peace has there been for Bonito in the last few days. Ruined by robbery, harassed by suspicion; I was miserable enough before my child was charged with crime. Linda a prisoner! The fact seems more like a horrible dream than the truth it is. I left her in tears, but they were shed for me. She bears bravely up, like her friend, the wonderful Beatrice. Both are heroines. Here comes the priest. He, too, will say, like Linda, that my bad luck all comes from my neglect of church duties. 'Tis true, the monte pio has no bad luck and is often at confession."

Here Father Ignacio entered, interrupting the soliloquy of the jailer, who had been slowly walking to and fro in the court of the carcel under the light which showed dimly from above his doorway.

"Ha! Bonito; all alone and troubled?"

"Until you came, mi padre, yet not alone, for hard thoughts were my companions. Troubled? Yes, I have seen no peace for days."

"Cheer up, hijo, troubles go with time, and time is swift of wing."

"But I am growing old, and the same swift wings are bearing me to the grave."

"For which you should be in readiness. It is long since you confessed, hijo, and confession is fruitful of grace, and grace brings strength to bear ills and inclination to turn troubles to benefits. Who suffers here with a proper spirit will lessen the term of probation in purgatory."

"What mortal not a priest or a holy nun suffers with this spirit?"

"Among the women, many; there are a few among the men."

"The monte pio, for instance."

"Yes, the monte pio. He is often at his duties."

"His conscience spurs him. He must go often to escape forgetting the number of his exactions."

"You are envious, hijo."

"Only of his luck. No one robes the monte pio, altho' he robs the public."

"That is his affair and the public's. Have you heard the latest news?"

"News?"

"About the prisoners."

"Linda?"

"And Beatrice."

"I am from them but a moment since; their bravery is remarkable."

"They will need it all, for they have been condemned."

"Condemned?"

"By the thing they call a military court."

"Their sentence?"

"To be shot."

"Women?"

"The decision was that for treason in the presence of the enemy the law knows no extenuation on account of sex."

"Oh, Linda! Nina! It cannot be, mi padre. Let them shoot

Bonito—" then bethinking himself of the vault and its precious contents, he said aside: "No, if I am killed I lose those bags of gold, and the secret will die with me. No, Bonito must live; live to guard and still better hide the treasure."

"Poor fellow, he loves his daughter, and the prospect of her fate sorely affects him," were Father Ignacio's half uttered words.

"Remember, hijo, that there are yet hopes that these jewels may be saved."

"Jewels!" said Bonito, suddenly recalled to the other's presence. There's not a jewel in the bags."

"Jewels to their parents," continued the priest, not perceiving the jailer's mistake. "Don Juan worships his daughter."

"Oh, Linda!—the prisoners mean you?"

"Who else? Of these we were speaking. Bonito, your mind wanders. Bear up, hijo. Perhaps succor may come from these daring Texans who are now not many varas away. Miguel, the faithful mozo, and Jose have gone with a message to Ruiz and Senor Raymond, who——"

"El pajarro, the cause of all my late troubles!" interrupted Bonito.

"A brave youth and full of resources," argued the priest.

"True, and a friend of the spirits, who have given him the secret of passing through a hole that would stop a mouse."

"That is nonsense, hijo; but he is fearless and loves Beatrice and admires Linda——"

"Both are crazy for him."

"And when he learns their danger I am sure his chivalrous nature will plan a rescue. Already the Texans have gained the northwestern side of the plaza, and a bold sortie might be made before the morrow. The sentence of the court has been ordered to be carried out tonight, lest the victims escape through the triumph of the enemy. I hate to confess it, hijo, but the cruelty and indecency of our military almost places me on the side of the rebels."

"It is all one to Bonito; the government plunders through prestimos, and the rebels will ransack you for pesos."

"Go in, hijo, and tell the ladies that I will see them to give them comfort in this sad hour."

"You may enter; a priest's cassock is his pass. The sentinel is in the hall."

Father Ignacio entered the hall.

"He goes to console them. Little use, if they are to be shot. Who pities Bonito for his loss? Who will cry if by chance the new hiding place be discovered and he loses all? It is better to be dead than to live without money; and to live in dread of its loss is harder to bear than poverty."

Father Ignacio found the prisoners in Linda's room.

They little dreamed of the dreadful order which had emanated from their judges who had tried them without their presence or a word in their defense through even a pretended representation. On suspicion with complicity with Ruiz in the late raid, and of their aid in the escape of the American spy, the two fairest daughters of Bexar were to be cruelly executed. The threatened capture of the town within the next few hours gave rise to the determination to have the sentence carried out at once. The good father did not enlighten them as to their intended fate, but chose rather to enliven their spirits by his conversation, hoping that the coming moments might develop something to bar the dreaded eventuality.

"How are you getting along, my children?"

"Quite well, father," replied Beatrice. "Linda has dried her tears. My eyes have yet to be moistened, while my heart is brave and my confidence supreme. We are so glad to see you."

"These are terrible times. The rebels are in the heart of the town, and the garrison is powerless to oust them. Has the firing alarmed you."

"It has made me nervous," said Linda.

"It frets me to think how powerless I am to help whip the cowards who war upon women," said Beatrice.

"I can hardly blame you, hija, for the army seems to have developed into a body of barbarians. They have become brutalized by revolutions."

"They have fallen from the plane of civilization through miscegnation. A mongrel race have few, if any, of the instincts of honor," said Beatrice, through whose veins coursed the pure blood of Castile.

"I cannot quite agree with you, hija. The causes of race deterioration are complex. The governing causes are radical. With Mexicans it is not a question of retrogression, but rather one of advancement. The infusion of Spanish blood was not a benefit to the Aztec without a guarantee of an individualism, which alone can develop character, intelligence and worthy citizenship. Mexico is a country of classes created by unjust though legalized social adjustments, tending to foster arrogance on the one hand and widespread ignorance on the other. It is a mock republic which breeds a few land owners and millions of peons. Land nationalization must be the remedy for the absence of healthy individualism, while a liberal system of education under the auspices of our Holy church will secure a high standard of morality and enlightenment."

"You agree with Senor Raymond in regard to your first remedy. He regards the private ownership of land as immoral, believing that it belongs to the people for use, and that the great value which some locations attain through the presence of population should benefit society, and not be gobbled up by speculators. His ideas about education differ from yours. He believes that religious supervision should not be tolerated."

"Senor Raymond is very bright, but he is young yet," said the priest.

A noise at the outer door here interrupted the conversation. Its opening was followed by the entrance of an officer in full uniform; then three others filed in and took places slightly in the rear of the first. Father Ignacio rose, but the ladies kept their seats. Linda's nervous glance soon fell to the floor, while Beatrice gave the intruders a look which blended defiance with contempt.

The officer who first entered spoke:

"These are the prisoners, Beatrice Navarro and Linda, the daughter of the jailer, are they not?"

"These are the ladies you have named," said Father Ignacio.

"The prisoners will stand and hear the sentence of the court," said the officer.

"Sentence of the court!" exclaimed Beatrice. "A sentence without a trial?"

"The trial has been held and you have been convicted of high crimes."

"A sample of Mexican military justice, and worthy of the barbarism which you represent," said Beatrice, excitedly.

"Stand up, senoritas, and take your medicine. A pretty pair to be sacrificed, I must say, but the law must be executed. Stand up."

"I recognize only the authority of force, and defy that when represented by the minions of tyranny," replied the courageous girl.

"Let them remain seated, captain, and hear the sentence," said one of the other officers.

"Listen to the decree of the court," said the captain.

"Be it known that the court appointed by his excellency, General ————, for the purpose of trying the prisoners Beatrice Navarro and Linda, the daughter of the jailer, charged with having given aid to the rebels and with having assisted in the escape of one Guy Raymond from the carcel of Bexar, have, upon ample and indisputable testimony, found the said prisoners guilty of the charges as stated.

The court, therefore, decrees that the said prisoners shall suffer the full penalty of the law provided for the punishment of the offenses named. It is, therefore, ordered that the said Beatrice Navarro and the said Linda be instantly executed by shooting, and for this purpose they shall be immediately turned over to the provost guard."

Linda fainted before the conclusion of the reading, while Beatrice, still defiant, went to her assistance. While efforts were being made to resuscitate the insensible girl, a guard was waiting outside to convey her and her sympathizing companion to the place of execution on the plaza.

In order to gain time, Father Ignacio claimed that an opportunity be given the condemned to utilize his priestly offices.

For this purpose twenty minutes was grudgingly accorded, and all withdrew save the priest and the prisoners. The former lost no time in communicating his hopes that a rescue would be attempted, and from the great peril that threatened them, he assured the ladies that Guy and Manuel would make success assured by a little less than superhuman effort and the full display of their irresistable courage. The words of the father had a happier effect than could have been produced by spiritual advice, and even Linda smiled as Beatrice, in her ardor, compared the gallantry of her lover with the pusillaminity of the average officer of the garrison.

The moments glided by. A rap at the door, followed by a voice, warned the priest that the time had nearly expired, and that the condemned must be ready.

It was a desperate moment.

Father Ignacio rose to his feet, and after calling to the guard to announce that they would be ready in five minutes, he motioned to the ladies to follow him. They made their way to the hall. Here the sentinel would have been an obstacle, but the quick witted priest went boldly up to him, and in a tone of superiority, said:

"The officer in front orders you to step outside the door into the court until I hear the confessions of these poor condemned prisoners. Let no one in to disturb us."

The soldier had a natural respect for the ghostly office of the father, and the solemnity of the occasion, when two souls were to be shriven in order to enter into the presence of their Maker, caused him to have no doubt of the truth of the message from his superior. He therefore did as he was ordered without hesitation.

Simultaneously with the exit of the sentinel, Bonito's head arose from the opening to the vault, which had not been rearranged for concealment since Miguel forcibly opened it. The jailer felt that his hoard was secure and would be, perhaps, more so if he was thought to be indifferent about the knowledge of the vault's existence.

"Oh, mi padre! They would kill me! Already they are waiting to lead us out to be shot," cried Linda, at the sight of her father.

"Por Dios! No. It must not be. Eh, mi padre! Down with you in the vault; but the sentinel—I forgot—no—he is not in the hall. Then down with you."

As he said this Bonito motioned violently for them to descend. The priest joined in the advice and assisted them down. A noise in the court and an imprecation hastened their movements, and the lounge was arranged by the deft hands of Bonito so as to hide the opening. The noise without merged into an apparent scuffle. An instant later it ceased; the door opened and Guy, fully armed, sprang through it, followed by a dozen men. Quickly and in as few words as possible, the priest informed him of the situation. Guy put his hand to his brow for a second, then decided.

It was an ordeal, but it must be met.

"Go," he said to Father Ignacio. "Go tell them that Bonito and some friends snatched the prisoners from you and bore them to the court."

"But, senor, if this is told them Bonito's life will answer for it."

"Hush, craven! Down you, too, into the vault with the women, where you belong.'

Bonito obeyed.

As the priest left on his errand, Guy sprang back to the court and reappeared a moment later.

"Hamilton, you and Perry watch me and strike when I strike. Let the other men be ready, and if the ball opens, they know what they came for. Miguel, open that trap. Descend and reassure the ladies. When I give the signal, bring them up."

The giant disappeared below with a grunt of satisfaction.

A howl of rage from the garden rent the air at this moment. This, with the succeeding tramp of men in Linda's room, indicated that the priest had told his story.

The door opened and the captain who had read the sentence of the court, appeared.

He was caught in the strong grasp of Hamilton, while Guy deprived him of of his sabre. Perry slammed the door as the Mississippian thrust his prisoner into Bonito's room and placed a guard over it. The capture was made so quickly that the enemy in the room supposed the door had been shut by their man, so when the next entered, he was treated to the same tactics. This continued until five captures had been effected. The sixth attempt miscarried and the retreating soldier fired a shot into the door. Hamilton was about to spring into the room when Guy held him back, saying:

"Not yet, Hamilton; that shot of the enemy is the signal for Ruiz and Karnes to act. If I mistake not, we will bag a room full of the cowards. Stand from the door, for the bullets will be coming."

The warning was none too soon. A volley was poured into the oaken boards, splintering them well on the outside. Others followed, but not a man was injured. According to programme, a general fire was opened upon the garrison from the Texan positions. This firing with the response from the Mexican artillery and small arms was expected to drown the noise of the raid on the carcel. The crack of the Texan rifles and reports of muskets filled the air, when Guy ordered his men to follow him into the room immediately after a strong volley had been poured into the door. With a yell sufficient to appall a not over courageous foe, the men rushed into the room, now containing about a score of the enemy. Guy brandished the cutlass, which had done so much execution the night of his escape, while his men discharged their pieces at the bewildered enemy. Ruiz's voice and Nathan's war whoop in the garden, as Guy's supporting force dropped from the parapet and drove the Mexicans into the building, called forth an answering cheer from those within, succeeded by a combined outburst of enthusiasm as the terrified enemy begged for quarter.

Guy hastened to the opening to the vault and gave a loud whistle. In less than half a minute Beatrice was in his arms. Linda had scarcely reached the level when Ruiz grasped her hand, and before she realized it, he pressed his lips passionately to her cheek. Miguel stooped over and pulled up Bonito, who was climbing the steps as fast as a fat corporosity would permit.

"Es el pajarro! Pajarro fuerte y bravo," said Bonito between the short breaths induced by his exertion.

"Ruiz, put the men in motion—the same route we came. I will take Hamilton, Perry, Roach and Miguel with the ladies. Jose will guide the advance under Karnes, while you bring up the rear. The general fire will save us from observation."

"And the prisoners?"

"Lock the ragtag and bobtail in the cells. Here, Bonito, stir around and do your duty; open the cells. The five in that room we will take with us."

The prisoners locked in, the retreat began. At the exit to Carcel street Jose was found walking his post. He had been placed here by the raiders, who had captured the Mexican guard, with orders to personate the regular sentinel and protect the rear of the party. He was now relieved and commissioned to guide the retreat. The advance was in charge of Karnes. In the centre of the column walked Guy with one of the rescued ladies on each arm and circled by the chosen body guard. Ruiz brought up the rear, driving before him the five prisoners who had been captured in such a novel manner in the hall. The route lay along the south side of the main plaza and necessitated a close brush by the door of Father Ignacio.. The latter had hastened home after witnessing the triumph of his friends in order to pray for their safe exit from further peril. He opened his shutter as the tramp of feet was heard below, and giving the sign of the benediction, he said so all could hear him:

"Pax Domini sit semper vobiscum."

Guy gratefully repeated the response which he had heard iterated by the choir on the Sunday he first attended at mass in San Fernando:

"Et cum spiritu tuo."

"That sounds quite orthodox for an unbeliever," said Beatrice, looking up into her lover's face.

"I remember the benediction as well as the response from my first visit to the Cathedral," replied Guy.

"It must have impressed you."

"Yes; it did, but not nearly as much as something I saw on that occasion for the first time."

"And what was that?"

"Your dear features."

In reply Guy felt a tighter pressure of the fair hand upon his arm.

"The witches are sidin' with us, Perry," said Nathan, in a whisper to the boy.

"How you know?" asked Perry.

"Didn't yer hear the croakin' from that dark winder, and this feller Raymon' answerin' of 'em?" said the backwoodsman, in a solemn tone.

"Was it, Mr. Hamilton?" asked Perry, in a doubting way.

"Was it what?" asked Hamilton.

"A witch that Mr. Raymond was talking to?"

"I might answer like an oracle, my boy, for he was talking just now to one who has bewitched him—ergo she must be a witch—the one on his right arm."

"No, not her; Mr. Roach meant that witch in the window that Mr. Raymond spoke to in some sort of talk. Was that a witch?"

"Perry, witch is feminine, a female. Now, the voice you allude to was not that of a female—ergo, if it belonged to the species witch it must have been the voice of a wizard."

"Yer gettin' into worse mess, Perry, by askin' information from him," suggested Nathan.

"What is a species witch, Mr. Hamilton."

"By species I mean what you and Mr. Roach would term birds of a feather—a disquisition on species would involve an explanation of the term genus, which would necessitate the employment of terminologies that would involve you in a mental darkness blacker than that which is at this moment so apparent to our physical sense."

"What'd I tell yer, Perry," said Roach, disgusted.

"Yer can't git nothin' from an ass but a bray."

"But what was the voice from the window, Mr. Hamilton, in plain words?" asked Perry, still persistent.

"It was that priest we found at the jail. He was saying to somebody—these ladies, I suppose—'God's peace be with them.'"

The strange procession now moved along in silence save the easy tramp of caution or whispered words as comrades exchanged remarks suggested by their raid. The darkness was propitious; the route so well selected that the Texan flank was doubled without adventure, and the gallant actors in the rescue found themselves safe within the patriot lines.

CHAPTER LVI.

The morning after the rescue of Beatrice and Linda from the impending danger of a barbarous execution, the military situation in the city had reached a degree in the solution of the problem of its capture which left no doubt in the minds of the aggressive forces of the speedy success of their attack. The steady advance of the Texan line under cover of the heavy walls of the stone buildings and the increasing casualities resulting from the accurate aim of their rifles had already disheartened the Mexican troops when the daring descent upon the jail very nearly produced a feeling of demoralization.

It was, therefore, no great surprise to the parties on either side when a vigorous fire from the Texans, in which the enemy's artillery on the plaza was silenced, was succeeded by a flag of truce from the Mexican commander offering to capitulate. The succeeding surrender with its terms belongs to the history of Texas. The Mexican forces were paroled, their officers being accorded the honors of war. So the Texans, after long waiting and with vastly reduced forces, made themselves masters of the city of the Alamo. The prize demanded a sacrifice, and with the victims perished a heroic few, among whom was the gallant Milam, the spirit and the leader of the assault. The fall of San Antonio, while it drove the enemy from his last important hold north of the Rio Bravo, was not regarded by the population of the west as secure from a speedy recapture by the forces under the soldier president, Santa Anna. The latter had been long preparing to invade the State, and had already assembled a considerable force on the border, when he received the news of the disaster to the Mexican arms.

Among the citizens of Bexar who knew what to expect from the vengeance of the Mexican tyrant was Don Juan Navarro. He smiled when told of the liberal terms granted to the captured garrison, for he knew what Texans might expect when they chanced to come into the power of the despot. That his views and statements were prophetic, the subsequent massacres which stained the soil of Texas with noble blood will tell, and these, the bloody climaxes of her struggle for independence, will ever mar the record in glaring contrast with the magnanimity of her veterans when, in the flush of victory at San Jacinto, they declined to wreak a just vengenace upon their author.

Don Juan was a marked man. There was no excuse for colonists to rebel; there was still less reason why Mexicans should give to rebels aid and comfort. His daughter had only escaped execution. He, therefore, reasoned that a recapture of Bexar meant death to himself and child if they should remain to become the prey of the barbarous instincts of the dictator.

The afternoon of the surrender, Don Juan was sitting in his room ruminating upon the future, the subject just mentioned uppermost in his mind, when Beatrice joined him.

"I was just thinking of you, my child."

"I hope I am often in your thoughts, father."

"You are ever there, but this time you are connected with a serious question that has arisen and will give me no peace until I dispose of it satisfactorily."

"What can it be?" said Beatrice, flushing. "You said it is serious?"

"Serious."

"What caused it to arise?"

"Today's surrender."

"Well—is that all?"

"No. The town's recapture."

"I see—a recapture would mean renewed danger for us."

"Renewed danger! Yes—death."

"But the Texans whipped them out of strong walls; can they not better keep them out?"

"It looks plausible, but these men are few; not organized; have scarcely a government, and are so confident that they are sure to become careless; they will thereby become ripe for plucking and Santa Anna will pluck them."

"Why not go to their councils, father, and give your views? If you will not, then post some one of them so as to avert this danger. You will find some of them as intelligent and wise as they are brave and chivalrous."

"Senor Raymond, for instance."

Beatrice colored deeply.

"I confess that he was my ideal as I spoke. It was natural that my twofold deliverer should fill the role, as I have found him to be intelligent and wise."

"This is a digression, my child. The danger must be first planned against. Then, if by wise counsels the young government should be equal to the emergencies that war produces, all the better. I have decided that you must go to New Orleans until the dangers of invasion are past."

"To New Orleans!"

"The best asylum I can think of."

"And sister?"

"She has a husband."

"And——" Beatrice hesitated.

"And you have a lover, I suppose you were about to say."

"Oh, father!"

The daughter left the room.

In the notary's office the joy, produced by the news of the surrender of the garrison, was mixed with the bitter of the final leavetaking which death exacts from those whose lives have been intertwined through the congenialities which mark character, or the interests which become developed by intercourse. The faces of those who were grouped around the pallet of Mr. Trigg wore the sad expression which comes unbidden in the presence of dissolution. Guy sat near his pillow, holding his hand, while Perry, full of sorrow, sat opposite. Jones, the other wounded messmate, had passed away during the night, and Karnes was absent on duty. Hamilton stood near the window, giving a view of the section of the river, out of which he gazed with an aimless stare. Nathan had stretched himself upon the notary's chest, his expression more stoical than sad.

"How long is it since the message was sent to Father Ignacio?" asked Guy.

"About ten minutes," replied Perry.

"It seemed to me much longer."

"He won't rally again, so the priest need not come" said Hamilton, turning from the window.

"He might," suggested Guy, "and as he asked for a priest, I am anxious that he be gratified, if he again becomes conscious."

"I want no priest around me when I shuffle off this mortal coil," said Hamilton.

"If you believed as Mr. Trigg, however, you would give much for the presence of a priest. While I would not desire one, I have full respect for the views of the religious. To gratify them is one of the duties we owe to the dying. I would not object to have Father Ignacio with me if I were about to cross the dark river, not, however, on account of his priestly office, but on the score of his purity and benevolence. The presence of such men doubtless detracts from the terrors supposed to be marshalled by the approach of death."

"Here he is now," said Perry.

Father Ignacio entered the apartment. He greeted the persons present in his usual genial manner, and on a motion from Guy, took the latter's seat by the side of the dying.

He felt the sufferer's pulse, then gave a inquiring glance at his young friend.

"You know what to do, father, so go ahead and do it. This is my old friend you met at the mission after the fight."

"The same?"

"The same. If you want anything of us, you have only to command."

"The priest took out his book and turned to the prayers for the dying.

Guy stood at a respectful distance; Hamilton looked indifferent; Nathan was agape with curiosity, while Perry appeared rather awed by the devout look which earnest prayers lent to the features of the ghostly pleader.

The tableau remained unchanged until, with a deep drawn sigh, Mr. Trigg elevated his knees and opened his eyes. His look had the expresson which mutely owns that hope has fled and seems to plead; for what, we will never know until our own sands of life are all but spent. He tried to speak, but failed. He tried again and a few words escaped his lips, but half articulated. Guy went to his assistance, and putting his arm under the pillow, elevated his head.

The change was fortunate.

"This is the praste I saw at the mission?" he asked slowly of Guy.

"It is he. I sent for him."

"But never a word can I understand that he will be saying."

"I am here to interpret for you."

"But it is to confess, I want. Oh, for a little Irish praste, me boy! It's dying I am."

Guy told Father Ignacio what Mr. Trigg's trouble was.

Tell him to say the Confiteor and to confess mentally and I will give him absolution."

Guy interpreted.

"I don't like to, but a praste is a praste the world over, and if it's right, it's right."

Mr. Trigg having consented to the mode of confession, Father Ignacio motioned all to retire to the other side of the room.

In a few moments Mr. Trigg called for Guy.

"Me boy, I feel I'm sinking fast and I want to leave things in ship-shape. Get my wallet, Perry; you know it; it's in the pocket—there—that's it. Me dear boy, I wanted to live to see you enjoy it, but its God's will I shouldn't. The will is in there. It leaves all to you and the sister. The thing that's a troubling of me is the paper that was stole in the camp below. It might be a fortune, for the old man set a great store on it. It was a drawin' of an island and a ship and marks like rings and a bayou. It was a riddle like and had to be made out by another paper that a Portuguese man in this town was supposed to have and didn't know the value of it. The name was there; it's a long one the last was, and the first was Manoel."

Guys' interest arose as Mr. Trigg progressed, and when he had finished, he said:

"Do not worry yourself at this sad time, my dear friend, with any concern in my regard. Your faith teaches you that these moments are sacred to religion, and your heart must feel that they are precious to friendship stripped of all sordid motives, all ideas of gain and gold. Besides, be content about this riddle, for I have both papers; if not the originals, they are certainly copies."

"I am proud to hear it. The will to tell you kept me up, and now —I—feel I'm sinking. Is the father praying for me?"

"He is. Be brave, my dear old friend; Stella and I will ever keep you green in our memories as our dear foster father."

"The dear child. The last bit of a present I sent her was the medal of the Blessed Virgin with the beautiful beadwork, that must have come from the Indians. Tell her, me boy, to wear it and our Good Mother will be good to her."

"A medal with a beautiful beadwork!" said Guy, aside. "It makes me think of one I lost; the gift of Laoni; dear, brave Laoni."

"Tell her I took the medal from a Mexican I captured.

"It's going—I—am—ask him if he has given me absolution—and if he has—God bless him. Tell him its Extreme Unction I want. In my will is a gift to any church of our Holy religion. It will rest with ye to bestow it; and for this praste's kindness be liberal with him."

"Do not worry, my friend; Father Ignacio is here for love of doing good. I will see that your wishes are carried out."

"You're a fine boy, ye are. How dark it is! Perry, is that you? I can just see you. You have done your duty always. Be good to Perry, me boy. He's young to be in the army. It is—so—dark. The riddle is in the pouch—two papers—the gunner told me—there's Lafitte—and—the—rest—show—the—Spanish colors."

The dying man's mind wandered on, his words becoming unintelligible until at last there remained only the long, heavy respiration that precedes the end.

The watchers remained until the last gasp signalled the flight of the spirit.

CHAPTER LVII.

"Are you well acquainted with the island?"

"I know it as well as any lad knows the lanes and by-paths of his native village."

"You have lived here long, then?"

"I came with Lafitte. Here I served under him and am one of the useless things he left behind when he set sail from this bay for the last time."

"Not altogether useless, for you can serve me by your information and earn a doubloon for your pains."

"I never object to pay—if it be for honest work."

"Honest work? Then you have reformed since you quit the life of a rover."

"A rover may be honest. I worked for wages; and then Lafitte preyed only upon the thieving Spaniards."

"After all, it is but a matter of conscience, eh, Josefa?"

This conversation occurred in a curious looking apartment which had much the appearance of a ship's cabin, and evidently had been constructed of a portion of one, with additions of material to make up a land habitation with its conveniences for lights, ingress and egress, etc. The parties participant were two men, one tall and slender with very dark complexion, the other heavy set, of medium height and grizzled with an age that must have attained the vicinage of three score. The last party addressed was a woman, a description of whom would have apprised the reader that she was the Senorita de la Torre, if the dark man, who was no other than Ducio Halfen, had not called her Josefa. The admission of the other party disclosed his character as well as his ideas of the morality of piracy when confined to certain victims. Josefa did not deign a reply to Ducio's inquiry, but sat immobile and upright on the opposite side of a table occupied by the latter and his male companion, and upon which were a few papers lying near an inkstand holding a goose-quill pen.

"Well, to business! Your name is——'

"George."

"George?"

"George—'the pirate'—is my name among the all sorts of Galveston."

"Well, Mr. George, I sent for you to make some inquiries. There is a bayou just out of town—towards the gulf—that makes a bend so as to require two crossings to reach the beach?"

"Unless you go clean around the bend."

"But in a straight course?"

"Then you'd have to cross twice."

"It enters the gulf, finally, between some sand hills."

"Its bound to if it enters it at all, as there's sand hills plum to west end."

"Is this bayou deep?"

"It is shallow. A few holes may be over a man's head, but aside from them, it varies from one to four feet deep."

"What crossings, if any, are over this bayou?"

"Two rough bridges straight out from this wharf."

"You seem to be pretty well posted. Do you go often out that way?"

"Almost every day—a fishing."

"I am glad to hear that, for we expect to be here a few days, and our object in asking you about these things is to find out a good place for a little sport in fishing."

"You needn't pay a doubloon for that, for two months' seining would not get your money back."

"We do not care for the money, as fortune has blessed us with a plenty. Here is your fee, and if you allow us to go with you tomorrow we will explore this bayou and try our luck at fishing."

"I will be at your service, sir."

"Well, then, in the morning as soon as you like we will await your coming."

"There is something more serious than fishing in his looks and questions," said George, as he passed out the door and left his strange patrons to themselves.

"Why not go alone in this business, Ducio? Why engage a witness to spy at every movement we make?"

"We will make merely a casual survey tomorrow morning; then, by ourselves, we can follow the directions of the paper minutely, with no eye to watch us."

"But mere suspicion often leads to dire results. Discovery of the deepest laid plans is often predicated upon an apparently unimportant circumstance."

"This fellow will think we are wealthy people who merely wish a few hours sport."

"But the direction of the bayou and its bends and crossings have little bearing on a chance desire to fish for sport. Then your earnest question about the sand hills told of a reserve interest of deeper import than a fishing tramp."

"Josefa, you have a philosophic bent that I could admire if it were not so infernally pessimistic. This is a season for the bright side of things. We are on the eve of fortune. We are going to find:

"'An iron pot with an iron lid
Beneath the cross securely hid!

It

"'Holds the treasure and the gold
Captured by a seaman bold
From the Spaniards' ample store
And buried here on Galvez shore.'"

"It sounds nice enough," said Josefa, with a yawn.

When Ducio left San Antonio in company with Josefa they travelled with General Almonte and his escort. The general had left just in time to escape capture by Ruiz on the night Guy Raymond was liberated by the raiders. Ducio was afraid to make his way through the country, in a direct course to the island, lest he should be captured and detained for his actions in Bexar. He therefore kept with Almonte's party until he reached the city of Matamoras. Here he found an American schooner bound for Galveston, and took passage for himself and Josefa, arriving in the latter place the day he was introduced, at the beginning of this chapter, in consultation with the pirate, George.

Early the next morning the latter made his appearance with poles and tackle, ready for the fishing tramp. He found his patrons prepared to go, and the trio were soon on their way towards the gulf.

"You haven't heard the news, have you, sir?" said George, looking around at Ducio, who was following arm in arm with Josefa.

"No. What may it be?" asked Ducio.

"The boys have taken San Antonio," replied their guide.

"The boys?"

"The Texans—the colonists—the——"

"They have?"

"That's what."

"What day was it captured?"

"On the seventh."

"And this is the twelfth—five days ago. Glad we were away, eh, Josefa?"

"No difference to me," she replied. "I am growing indifferent to everything."

"To me?"

"I said everything."

"True—I am a person."

"Dogmatically—so is the devil," thought Josefa.

"This sand is terrible to walk in," she complained, as the white, yielding substance nearly covered her instep.

They reached the first bridge. Ducio surreptitiously drew forth a paper from his pocket, and consulted it.

"There is the bend turning towards the gulf," he said in an undertone to his companion.

The bayou stretched away towards the northeast for a quarter of a mile, widening into quite an expanse of shallow water, then gradually narrowing to the eastward and southeastward it doubled on its course, and again confronted the party, about four hundred yards distant, where the second bridge led to the sand hills, from over whose tops the steady roar of the surf was borne inland upon the morning breeze.

"Here is deep sand for you," said Ducio, giving Josefa a helping hand.

At Ducio's suggestion the guide arranged their fishing tackle, each of the party taking a pole. The latter remained on the left bank, while the couple kept the right, next the gulf, and throwing their lines in the stream occasionally, they gradually made their way to where its waters divided the sand hills and joined the ebb and flow of the breakers. On the opposite bank, but two hundred yards away, the more deliberate George was using a deal of patience, and had been rewarded by catching several fine redfish. From under his broad-brimmed hat, he had noticed the movements of the strangers and mentally concluded that fishing was farthest from their thoughts.

"See here, Josefa," said Ducio, as he stood on the highest mound of sand near him. "Here are the hills of sand—five of them. Could anything be plainer? One, two, three—one and two."

"It does seem to correspond with that paper, but I cannot make myself believe that there is anything in it."

"I will test it at all events—once we come here alone."

"Don't say we—for I hate this sand too badly to come again."

"Everything else is pleasant, but the walking. What a splendid day, and what a grand sight is that roaring gulf, with its blue expanse, as it sends those foam-crested lines of curling water in untiring succession upon that lovely strand!"

"You—sentimental!"

"I had a fellow named Hamilton in my mind's eye when I said that. He was full of pedantic fanfaronade. No, not I—sentiment is for fools and women."

"And rascality for dark-skinned male bipeds—like you. If you are convinced that women deserve to be classed with fools, I warn you that disaster may follow the conviction."

"I accept notice, Josefa, and except you from my sweeping assertion."

"Come, Ducio, that fellow is near, and seems to be watching us. If you are satisfied with the appearance of things here, let us go back and not spend any more time flourishing these stupid poles."

"Agreed; but we will walk the beach until we get opposite the road to town. Let us inform Mr. George that we will dispense with his services for the present."

The guide was accordingly dismissed, with an intimation that he would be apprised, should his services be needed again, and the pair walked with slow pace the faultless level of the beach, alternately commenting upon its singular beauty, and debating the best method of disposing of the treasure which they expected to find hidden in the hills on their left.

When evening came Ducio consoled himself that he had perfected every arrangement for the successful removal of the treasure, should he find it. Unknown to even Josefa, he had repaired to the locality in the afternoon, and having run the lines indicated from hill to hill, he had carefully marked the intersection so that he could find, by the light of the moon, the spot he wished to examine. So great was his curiosity, and his desire to possess it, he could scarcely refrain from running the risk of discovery, by at once commencing to dig for the contents of the pot.

But one light wagon could be procured in the little town, and this Ducio secured with difficulty, under the pretense of taking a moonlight drive upon the beach.

When the tardy moon peeped from below the waters of the gulf and had cast a line of flashing silver upon its bosom, Ducio, with his nervy friend, Josefa, seated in the vehicle, was urging his only half willing horse through deep sand beyond the second bridge.

"I came near forgetting it," said Ducio, stopping the animal and jumping lightly out.

He ran back to the bridge and inserting his hand under the first planks he drew out a short spade, and brought it to the wagon.

"You see, I thought of everything," he said.

"A villain is never lost for resources."

"Thank you, Josefa. As you are to profit by this villainy, you are therefore particeps criminis."

At last the wagon stopped, and Ducio leaping out, bade Josefa remain seated until he hunted for his mark. He disappeared over the first sandhill, and after several minutes returned to find Josefa alarmed at an apparition.

"What was it?" he demanded.

"It looked like a human figure crawling on all fours. It went over the sandhill next to the one you crossed."

"It must be an illusion."

Ducio, discovering nothing that would answer Josefa's description of the creeping form, returned to the wagon, helped out his companion, secured his spade and went to work.

He toiled for an hour before he could get a hole of any considerable size to remain open. The dry sand would yield to the universal claim of gravitation, and fill up almost as fast as he could excavate. At last, learning the secret of correct procedure, he cleared away several feet of the dry sand around the center of the objective point. The damp layer underneath allowed a narrower hole to be dug and the sweating operator began to realize that he was making some progress. Frequent rests had to be taken to recover from the unusual .exertion. Josefa grew impatient as the time began to grow into hours, and was about to express her conviction for the third or fourth time of the quixotic aspect of their expedition, when the spade struck a hard substance that caused a ring, as if from colliding metals. The digger could not restrain an ejaculation of delight that rang strangely out upon the night air in almost the key of a shout. He dug more vigorously than ever, and springing into the hole, he rapidly cleared away the sand with his fingers. On he toiled, stimulated by intense excitement, with Josefa watching from above, less demonstrative, but sharing with her companion the strange emotions engendered by the occasion, which seemed to promise a realization of a long fostered hope. Having at length cleared the compact sand from around the pot, he raised the lid and, inserting his hand, found a covering which felt like oilcloth. This he tore away impatiently, when his fingers came in contact with the contents which gave unmistakable evidence of being cold, damp coins. A chuckle came to the lips of Ducio, at the same moment that a gruff, but earnest voice addressed Josefa.

"I was passing on the beach and thought I heard a cry of distress a few moments ago, and came to see what it meant."

Josefa gave a slight scream as her eyes caught sight of a heavy form standing almost over her, and her first idea connected the new comer with the creeping figure of two or three hours before.

Ducio sprang from the hole and confronted the man, while he secretly damned himself for the indiscreet shout when the clink of iron against steel gave evidence of treasure trove.

CHAPTER LVIII.

In a cozy apartment overlooking from a second story elevation a narrow street of a city, from which arose the din of rolling wheels and the hum of metropolitan life, were two females. One, a lady, attired in a morning wrapper, was before a mirror, passing a comb through her hair, which fell in abundant tresses far below her shoulders. The other, a girl in her teens, her development suggesting a budding womanhood, stood at the casement overlooking the world below. Through the slightly open sash floated in vagrant shreds of vapor from the mass of fog whose isothermal veil enveloped the city. Across the street the brick walls and iron-railed verandas of the buildings met the view, extending to a corner, where a broad avenue crossed at right angles. Over a door of the corner building, in distinct letters to indicate the name of the thoroughfare, were the words "Rue Royale." If one had peeped around the corner by the same character of sign he would have been apprised of the fact that the broad avenue was Canal street.

The two occupants of the cozy room had been silent for many minutes, the lady proceeding with her toilet in the most careful manner, the girl watching with apparent interest, what could be seen in the street, when the former suddenly remarked:

"Stella, I would not remain under that open sash. If you intend to keep that position long you had better lower it. If you would profit by your short holiday you should be careful not to take cold. I declare! How dark it is getting! I certainly will have to light the gas if it grows much darker. Whenever I've come to New Orleans it has always been in a fog, but it is a dear old town, for all that, and I am willing to forgive its damp and darkness and fog and all other objectionable features, for its gaieties and pleasures. When we got in last night it was raining torrents. I do hope it will clear up now for a while. Dear me! I'll light the gas. Now, I can see myself. I suppose the Mother Superior was half inclined to refuse to let you come out. She was cross as could be the last time. I don't blame the poor things, though, for I should be cross all the time if I had to be shut up in a nunnery, with death only as a prospect for release. My hair is absolutely rebellious this morning. By the way, Stella, when did you hear from Guy?"

"Only once since I last wrote to you."

"Has he fully recovered from the wound he received at the battle of San Jacinto?"

"He has; but it's healing was very slow. For months it was painful and obstinate, and yielded only to an Indian remedy which he had seen the Lipans use while he was a prisoner."

"When does the young gentleman propose to pay you a visit? I think he must have lost his love for us. It would do him good to catch one more glimpse of civilization."

"Auntie, Guy has had his hands full. All of his interests demanded that he should assist in gaining the independence of Texas, and since the Mexicans have been driven out, his wound first, then other matters, kept him from the undoubted pleasure of a visit to us."

"I cannot see what you could name under the head of other matters."

"You forget, Aunty, that our parents' bodies had to be removed to a more appropriate burial place, and the remains of Mr. Trigg, our second father, he had placed beside them. In a country like Texas this alone was a tedious undertaking."

"You are doubtless right, my child. It is a country of barbarous Mexicans and savage Indians, and will never amount to much until they are exterminated. By the way, you remember the Indian girl that your uncle brought from Texas after the fight of the San Saba,

I believe he called it? Well, he left her with a family in Grand Coteau, with means to pay for her schooling in the convent of that place. She was placed in the convent, as you have doubtless heard, and made wonderful progress, developing the greatest aptness in every study. Of course, when your poor uncle died so suddenly there was no provision made for her continuance at the convent, and she was taken out by her guardian. The family, instead of treating her as an equal, made her a servant, piling up menial duties for her performance, until the girl left them, going they know not where. When I first heard of her quitting the convent, I had a notion to send for her, and make her a companion, just for the novelty of the thing. It would have been a decided *nouveaute*."

"I do not think I can ever bear the sight of an Indian again. The very name brings up the only horrible picture of my past," said Stella, with a shudder, as the scene on the banks of the Salado rose in her mind.

"But this girl, it seems, has proven to be above the standard. I am so sorry I did not write for her before she disappeared. See, child, if my petticoat hangs. Now, pin my collar behind and we will go down to the parlor. I am expecting a caller at ten and have an appointment with my commission merchant at eleven. Oh, me! What a time a woman has with agents and merchants. Widowhood imposes a burden, my child; yet there is a charm about it which maidens may never experience."

Not many blocks away from the Rue Royale, and towards the levee, a low frame building, occupying one corner of two intersecting streets, bore a sign upon its front which could be seen plainly from the levee, and read:

"Sailors' Saloon and Cafe."

The place had a sort of inviting look for the characters who frequented it. Under the wide awning which spanned the sidewalk were armchairs and benches, upon which the off duty sailors and workers of the levee could comfortably pose while they would spin yarns or gossip about questions local or foreign. It was not a place having claims to any great degree of respectability, nor was it yet of the character of the lower dives of the Crescent City. The present owner had run the establishment for several months, during which time there was no lack of custom, and many a time the gossips of the chairs and benches had discanted on the probable savings of George, the proprietor. His other name was not known to the frequenters, and hence the saloon was designated by them as "George's."

George was an easy-going fellow, heavy-set and grizzly, and judging from his dialect and manner, had followed the sea in former years. He never would say much about his past life, except on certain occasions when, half seas over, he would make reference to his sailor's life and brag about being a subaltern under the noted pirate of the gulf. These allusions, uttered rather incoherently, were treated as the vaporings of a rum-befuddled brain, with perhaps some possible tincture of truth for a groundwork. He might have been a follower of Lafitte, and this was believed by some who knew that George had paid a handsome sum in gold to get possession of his present premises.

The afternoon of the day that Mrs. Raymond told Stella she had an appointment with her merchant at eleven o'clock, the front of George's cafe had a good complement of loungers, the weather having faired and the temperature more suitable for the season of early fall than the month of December. Gossip, for the nonce, appeared to have been ignored, and a species of indolence prevailed to make more impressive the puffs of curling smoke emitted from the lips of the smokers.

The quiet of the cafe was destined to be disturbed from an unexpected source. The attention of the corner was attracted by the furious approach of a pair of powerful horses attached to an open carriage, while the driver was making strenuous efforts to hold them in. Beside him sat a lady, who was vainly attempting to assist her companion, but all to no purpose. On thundered the mad team, until it neared the corner. Along the street all eyes had been fixed upon the carriage, but none dared to attempt to arrest the runaways.

Seated at the cafe was an individual of an appearance very dissimilar from the rest of the assemblage, and who was evidently unknown to them, as he had been the target for many a curious look since he had taken a seat. He was long and lean and awkward, and though clothed in decent enough apparel, it had either the demerit of a bad fit, or the misfortune to cover a form of ungainly proportions and sharp angles.

When the flying horses were almost upon them, and the crowd stood with bated breath, as if waiting the tragical end, the awkward stranger sprang to the center of the street, and as the mad animals came near abreast, by a bold and dexterous dash he seized the nearer one by the head gear with both hands, and swinging with their great momentum be fastened himself upon its neck with the tenacity of a tiger. To rein their heads sharply together was the work of the next moment, and within two hundred feet from where he first seized them, the panting animals came to a stand with their fearless captor at their heads.

The man alighted from the vehicle, and helping out his companion, he accosted his rescuer:

"I owe you much, sir, for this, and am willing to reward you by any amount in reason."

The individual thus addressed replied with a tone akin to contempt:

"You don't owe me a cent, sir, 'cept it a ben yer thanks, which yer didn't give and which I don't want."

"Excuse me; I should have added thanks—but in my excitement——"

"No use a mouthin' 'bout it now. Yer look mighty like a French feller I saw in Texas, and if yer is as mean as him, yer wouldn't pay no more than yer'd thank. I'm glad I saved the lady."

So saying the gallant fellow elbowed his way through the crowd which now thronged the street, and made his way back to George's. Here he was quite a hero and was compelled to enter the cafe in order to escape the praises of the populace.

The fancied asylum soon proved no barrier to the public demonstration. George, with an eye to business, encouraged the entrance of the crowd, and led off, himself, in a general treat, in honor of the hero of the hour. The latter's remonstrances against the magnification of a simple act into a heroic deed, were lost upon the mob, if they were indeed audible, further than a phrase or two, above the din and disorder of the cafe.

"You're a hero in spite of yourself, man. It's no use—you'll have to give in and treat the boys in turn," said George.

"Them that's makin' such a hurrah over nothin' is the fellers to treat if they wants treatin.' I ain't got the money 'twould take to satisfy this 'ere crowd."

"You won't lack the money, man, if you will draw on the fellow whose life you've saved. They're a rich couple—Halfen and his wife," said George.

"Halfen! Tho't I knowed him; tho' he don't 'pear as sneakin' as he did in San Antone."

"Come, man, if you know him, all the better. Set 'em up," urged the proprietor, "and I will take your order on Halfen in payment. I'll get the money."

"Stranger!" exclaimed the other emphatically. "Ef you don't want to rile me, jes' stop yer clatter on treatin.' Ye'll git no orders from me on nobody, and leastways on a feller that didn't thank me fer savin' his wife's neck."

With this admonition, Nathan—for it was he—turned abruptly from the counter and left the cafe.

He had only arrived in the city that morning, en route to his home on the Arkansas, and his intention was to spend a few days in the Southern metropolis, in the enjoyment of its sights, as a kind of antithesis to the experiences of his arduous Texan campaign. Nathan's steps led him along until without a consciousness of the particular locality he found himself on the broad flags of Canal street. The afternoon was pleasant, and the avenue was filled with gaily dressed women, entering and leaving the shops and stores—now crowded with stocks of holiday goods. Nathan's awkward figure passed in and out of throngs of grace and beauty, and evoked many a smiling look as wonder and curiosity asserted themselves in a countenance on which the surroundings had implanted an exaggerated verdancy.

He paused before a large show window and gazed intently upon its artistically arranged contents. Stuffed representations of birds and a few of the smaller wild animals were placed upon perches, around the central figure, which was that of an Indian chief, in feathers and war-paint. Nathan's eyes became rivited upon the Indian. He studied the outlines and toggery with the eye of a connoisseur, for if he was familiar with anything it was with Indian character and dress. His first idea upon beholding the mute figure was that a real chief was posing inside the glass, and he instinctively gave the gutteral ejaculation of the Lipans, indicative of surprise:

"Hish-to-wa!"

To his astonishment a soft voice at his elbow, in the same dialect, replied:

"An Indian—but not a Lipan."

On looking around, Nathan beheld a young woman, plainly dressed, also contemplating the figure in the window. Her complexion was dark almost as the average Indian. Her features were delicate and regular and wore a placid, almost sad, expression. As the backwoodsman turned, their eyes met, and his first words were:

"You—a Lipan?"

"A Lipan? Yes. How did you learn their words?"

"I have fit them on the Trinity, and they had me a pris'ner for nigh a year. What yer doin' in Orleans?"

"I am a prisoner. I was captured when our village was burned and have been in the Convent at Grand Coteau. The sisters treated me like their child, and taught me from the books of the white people. The friend, who put me in the school, died and I had to become a nun or leave. I chose to leave, and now I find myself in this big city without friends, and my only hope is to find a place where I can earn my bread."

"Yer'll never do it. An Injun must hear the owl hoot and the birds sing. I'm too much like yer sort, myself, to live in this here town. There ain't no elbow room, and a feller is cooped up and lost 'mongst thousands. No, yer'll never do it, my girl."

"I may never be happy, but I must do something. On the prairies, if there was no one else to call upon, I could bring down a deer or an antelope. Here if one has not silver or gold she must work for others to keep up life."

"I hain't much money, but I could spare you a trifle," said Nathan generously.

"Thank you, sir. I am not begging, and will be able to do without assistance, I hope, until I find employment. I was told that there was an intelligence office near, where one could find out the people who want help."

"Mebbe so," said Nathan abstractedly, as he continued to gaze in the window.

The woman eyed him curiously for a moment. He had fought her people, he had said. His air was more natural than that possessed by the hurrying crowd, bent on some fixed purpose, who looked neither to the right or left, heedless of her presence, and ignorant of the emotions which swelled her bosom. He had been upon the Trinity and probably in the valley of the Colorado. Possibly he might know. She would find out. Nathan was about to turn away when she asked:

"You have been upon the Trinity?"

"I have, for a fact."

"And in the valley of the Colorado?"

"There too."

"Did you know a youth—just grown, fair as a lily, unless where the sun had browned his white skin, and——"

"Mebbe so," answered Nathan.

"His height about equalled yours, and when he walked, there was a nobleness in his movements which suited well the bravery of his heart."

"A fine feller that!? His height was like mine, and you say he walked like me?" said Nathan, straightening up and taking a step or two.

"He was a prisoner to our tribe, and I—I saved his life when they would have burned him. Oh, sir! Have you heard of such a youth?"

"Didn't the chap have any name?"

"With us he was El Bravo; with his own people his name was Guy."

"He got away from you?"

"He escaped with my assistance."

"There is a lot of the boys comin' over from the war, and if I find out where yer youth is, I'll let yer know. I'll come to this place Monday 'bout this time, ef yer kin meet me then."

"I will come. Your name is?"

"Nathan Roach. And yours?"

"Laoni."

CHAPTER LIX.

When Beatrice's father determined to send her to New Orleans to remain, pending the existence of danger from Mexican invasion and the consequent capture of San Antonio, Guy felt keenly the pain of prospective separation. He very sensibly concluded, however, that it was a judicious resolve of Don Juan's, and when he bade good-bye to his lady love he placed in her hands a letter to Stella, in which he urged his sister to become well acquainted and friendly to one who was destined to be his wife. Beatrice had promptly presented this letter on her arrival in the Crescent City, and became a frequent visitor to the convent where Stella was prosecuting her studies. Occasionally the latter would spend the greater part of a holiday with her future sister-in-law, so that in due time they became intimate friends and very nearly confidants.

The morning after Mrs. Raymond had put in execution her intention to call upon her agent, Stella was in her aunt's apartment on Rue Royale, awaiting a promised call from Beatrice. Mrs. Raymond had gotten through her toilet with less difficulty than usual and, radiant in jewels and powder, had gone to call upon a lady boarder in the same house in which she was stopping.

Stella was engaged in the inspection of a lot of ribbons and lace, a contribution to her box from the castaway portion of her aunt's finery. These she sorted and wrapped carefully in tissue paper, placing them in the pretty box on the table with a care and exactitude that suggested her employment might be more to kill time than adopted *ex necesitate rei*.

Beatrice's knock, and inquiry if she could enter, cut short her further care of her ribbons, and the two were soon chatting in their usual confidential manner.

"Guy writes that we may expect him any day from now until New Year," said Beatrice, the pleasure of the announcement beaming from her eyes.

"Why could he not have been more definite? It is just awful not to know on what day to look for him," said Stella half petulantly.

"The schooners leave irregularly, and that may be half the reason."

"You are too ready to excuse him, Beatrice. Just think how long it has been since I've seen him."

"Oh, Stella! I have engaged the services of a maid, and she is to report for duty tomorrow, if not this afternoon. You should see her. She is, I believe, a pure Indian, but much brighter than those I have seen."

"Gracious! A pure Indian?"

"Oh! But she is nice and real pretty. Her features are perfect, and she is as lady-like in her manner and tone as a society belle."

"You can make her a companion then. How did you find her?"

"At the intelligence office. She has just come from a convent. Her patron who was educating her ceased to send her tuition, I think she said, and she left the convent to seek employment. I did not ask of her a full explanation. I am delighted with her."

"I congratulate you; but I hope brother won't fall in love with the pretty maid."

"Why, Stella!"

"But she is such a paragon."

"Well—if he so elects. I would not marry him without his preference above all the world."

Beatrice grew a trifle serious as she said this, and turned her gaze out the window. A tremor passed through her, with a nameless emotion that could have arisen from the recall of a memory, shadowed by sadness, or a prescience whose intuition weaved about the future the mists of dread. Could the morning's contact with Laoni have charged her being with the magnetism of a common sympathy, to be awakened into activity by Stella's chance remark? Perhaps—for in the human organism, who would prescribe the bounds of its sentient dualism?

The entrance of Mrs. Raymond awakened Beatrice from her dream-like mood, as well as avoided a return to the topic which had caused it. She had met Guy's fiancee shortly after the latter's arrival in New Orleans, the year previous, and on the several occasions of her subsequent trips to the city. Her future niece had inspired her with her beauty, but she secretly informed Stella that she could not comprehend why her brother should choose a Mexican wife. Mrs. Raymond's ideas of love and marriage were peculiar. With her, wedded life was a woman's refuge after she became sated with what she termed the pleasures of single life. Love but typified a sexual instinct and, with well-balanced minds, always accommodated itself to the environments of convenience and policy. As to Guy's particular case, the aunt had informed Stella that she had contemplated with much pleasure the selection of a mate for her handsome brother. It was an assumed duty, but one that half way devolved upon her when their parents were taken from them.

Whatever prevailed in Beatrice's manner or disposition to mark a departure from conventional American characteristics appeared to be a charm, in Stella's judgment, and she therefore defended her brother's choice, whenever her aunt hinted at a mesalliance on the score of Beatrice's nationality.

Mrs. Raymond's greeting was marked by an outward show of affection, the caution with which she received Beatrice's kiss arising simply from her concern lest the contact of the latter's lips should spoil the artistic smoothness of her powder.

"Tell aunt Ida about your new maid, Beatrice," said Stella, after the first flow of words from Mrs. Raymond had somewhat abated.

"A new maid!"

"Or a companion," suggested Beatrice.

"She is an Indian," said Stella.

"You are having fun at my expense. You have been discussing what I said yesterday about my poor brother's protege. I was in earnest, however, and if I could find this Indian girl I should certainly take her for a companion or maid, just as she would fit the one or the other position."

"To tell the truth, my dear aunt, I did not for once recall our conversation, and I wonder that I did not, since Beatrice has discovered just such a girl, and from a convent."

"An Indian?"

"An Indian," said Beatrice, towards whom Mrs. Raymond had looked for a reply.

"Where did you see her?"

"At an intelligence office on Conti street."

"And she is now——?"

"I left her there, she having promised to report for duty this afternoon or tomorrow."

"I must see this girl," said Mrs. Raymond, "and if she is my brother's protege from the convent of Grand Coteau, you will have to relinquish your claim to her, Beatrice, for I had decided to make a search for this girl and add her to my train."

"But my contract with her?"

"Is null and void—if she is the girl I mean."

"Verily, an arbitrary decision," said Beatrice half laughing, yet half vexed.

"No; a principle of usage."

"Was there ever such a precedent, Aunt Ida?" queried Stella.

"I will not submit to interrogation. The decision is made and I am going to see this girl instanter," said Mrs. Raymond, putting on her bonnet. After a few glances in the mirror, she left the room for the street.

"She is an imperious woman, Stella, this aunt of yours. She combines within her the three great functions of government."

"As Guy would say, the principle of *'imperium in imperio'* underlies all of Aunt Ida's rulings."

* * * *

Nathan's mind was divided all the afternoon between the adventure with the runaway team and his chance meeting with the Indian girl at the show window. He had no use for the Indians, and his first act on meeting one in the wilds of the west would be to bring his rifle to his shoulder. Yet the squaw, as he mentally termed Laoni, had excited his sympathy. She seemed to him out of place in the busy city, with the tones of the Lipan dialect sounding strangely among the brick and mortar of civilization. He had scalped more than one squaw, but here was one arousing his sympathy and interest. After all, he thought, was not this Lipan girl ahead of the people to be seen around him?

She was natural, communicative and truthful. They were filled with artifice, designing and hypocritical. Look at Halfen—in Texas a sneak and a spy; here an ungrateful villain who had not thanked him. Reported rich, he had doubtless fleeced some one, or many, and was revelling in stolen wealth. In a crude way Nathan pronounced city civilization an iniquity. It occurred to him that it consisted of a class war on the individual who, multiplied, made up the multitude. It was soulless and selfish and in conflict with natural laws. The backwoodsman's mind was full of these reflections when he encountered Ducio, in the convivial company of two or three well dressed men.

The two at once recognized each other.

"You are the person who did me such a valuable service this morning?"

"I'm Nathan Roach, and you orto know that, fur we messed t'gether long enough."

"Gentlemen," said Ducio, "this man—Mr. Roach—is an oddity. He actually saved my neck and prevented serious damage to my horses and carriage today; and he will not take a cent in payment."

"See here, Mr. Halfen, yer said 'bout enough 'bout that. Ef I want pay I kin ask it, an' I don't want yer money, fur I don't know how yer made it. Ef yer want to pay me fur just stoppin' yer team, I'll tell yer how yer kin do it."

"How, Mr. Roach?" asked Ducio with mock gravity.

"This way," said Nathan, beckoning him aside. There's an Injun gal, a nice un, speaks 'Merican, ben ter school and wants a place."

"Well?"

"They say y'ere rich—jest take the gal—fur to help yer wife and yer do a kind deed, and pay me fur the trifle yer talk about."

"But where is the girl?"

"'Telligence Office—she's jest gone thar."

"Well, my friend, you can depend upon my seeing this girl and providing for her," said Ducio starting to rejoin his friends.

"See here!" said Nathan, calling after him. "It's me that'll be the cause of yer gettin' her, and see that yer be just to her."

"All right! All right!" said Ducio with a grin.

"A peculiar fellow," he said as he turned to his companions.

"Very peculiar."

"A hard-looking case."

"A devil in a fight," added Ducio, who thought of Concepcion.

Ducio caroused so late with his boon companions that he did not visit the intelligence office on the afternoon he made the promise to Nathan. The next day, however, so soon as he had recovered from the effects of his dissipation, he ordered his carriage and drove to several intelligence offices before he found the right one. The proprietor informed him that an Indian girl was within, but he feared he was too late to secure her, as a lady had engaged her that morning. Ducio, however, said he would speak with her, having promised to interest himself in her behalf, and alighting from the vehicle he entered the place.

He was ushered into a small sitting room intended as the place of interview between help and employers, before making a contract for service. He waited here only a very short time, naturally speculating on the probable appearance which the Indian girl would make. A vision of a blanketed form with coarse black hair and scrawny figure floated through his mind as he remembered the glimpses he had caught of a procession of braves and squaws of some domesticated tribe. He had little idea of what she should do in his employment, if employ her he did at all. Ducio was not therefore prepared for the entrance of the girl-like figure, full of ease and grace, that stood hesitating as if to address him. He found himself only in half voice as he inquired if she were the person about whom Nathan had spoken to him.

"I am Laoni," she said in well articulated English.

"He did not tell your name. Are you Indian?"

"Lipan."

"You have been long away from your people?"

"Long? Yes, long, when I look at it in one way. If I should count it in the months before I became a prisoner the time would seem to have had the wings of the eagle."

"The time which had elapsed since the destruction of the village about equalled the period of Guy's stay among the Indians, and this comparison presented itself to the girl's mind as she reverted to the months preceding her capture.

Ducio watched her every motion and noted the workings of her handsome, expressive features in mute surprise. There was a delicious softness in her tones that delighted, while only a pleasant accent suggested the fact that the language was not her mother-tongue.

"He said you were without friends, and wished me to call here and offer you my aid."

"It was good of him."

"What can I do for you?"

"I was looking for a place in which to earn my living, and by a good fortune a lady—she said she was a Mexican—came this morning and agreed to try me."

"A Mexican?"

"Yes, sir."

"Tall and slender?"

"Yes, sir."

"A brunette?"

"A brunette?" she asked, as if not comprehending.

"Dark complexion."

"Oh, No! All are fair in the eyes of Laoni."

"My wife said she intended to look for a girl, and I thought she might have gotten here before me and engaged you."

"She did not say she was a wife."

"Perhaps she did not," said Ducio, showing some nervousness. "Ladies looking for help are usually married ladies. If you will await my return, I will now go and find out if my wife has been here. If she has engaged you, I will return and take you home in my carriage."

Laoni having assented, he left the room.

Ducio's mind was in a state of perturbation not usual with him. Laoni had made an impression upon him that caused a thousand thoughts and plans to come and go. Thoughts and plans that boded no good to their subject and which were the fit and natural outcome of depraved and lecherous habits. Who could the Mexican lady be? He remembered that his wife could not have had time to visit the place since he left home. If he had gone the previous afternoon the girl could have been secured. He drove aimlessly around the streets, thinking of the handsome Indian and his purpose to claim her for himself.

A thought struck him.

He turned down Royale to Custom House street, drove several blocks, then stopped before a handsome house with iron steps winding from the banquette to the second story. These he ascended and used the knocker of the door. A portly woman received him, and they retired to the parlor. Within an hour from the time Ducio left the intelligence office, he was back again, and called for Laoni.

"It was as I expected," he said. "It was for my wife you were engaged, and now I am here to take you home."

"Then she was a wife. She looked so young."

"No; the lady was a friend of my wife, who is an invalid," replied Ducio, with a ready lie.

"A little bag holds all I have, and I will be with you in a moment," said Laoni.

As Ducio took a seat beside her in his equipage, he chuckled at the success of his ruse.

A few minutes and the smoking team drew up at the house on Custom House street. The winding stairs were mounted, the same portly woman answered the summons, and Ducio, after placing Laoni in her charge, descended to the street and drove away.

CHAPTER LX.

Mrs. Raymond, having fallen into the congenial company of several lady shoppers, passed in consequence such a pleasant time that she was startled to find out how very late it was when she parted with them, and that she yet had to visit the intelligence office to see her Indian maid. She was so impressed with the belief that it was her late brother's protege whom Beatrice had engaged, she did not experience the shadow of a doubt that she would return home in triumph with her nouveaute.

The intelligence office was about to close for the day, when she presented herself and stated her mission.

"My dear madam, the girl was engaged this morning, and this afternoon, during my absence for a time, the lady sent a carriage for her."

The lady's disappointment was extreme. She could glean no further information—no description of carriage or of driver—no intimation of the direction taken by the vehicle. She turned towards home with a heavy heart. It had beat high on going in anticipation of the pleasure in prospect of introducing a new feature in fashionable life. Added to this was strong curiosity to behold the girl on whom her brother had lavished praises, and who had made prodigious progress in the convent. Could Beatrice have so far defied her as to send for this girl after her positive announcement of her purpose in regard to the matter? Sent for her in a carriage! That was done to hurry the girl away and avoid encountering her in the street. This was Mexican impudence personified. Guy would rue the day he took such an artful piece to his bosom. It was perhaps fortunate that Beatrice had taken her departure from the Rue Royale before the return of Mrs. Raymond from her fruitless visit to the intelligence office. It provided time in which to compare notes and reach conclusions before wrong impressions could precipitate a collision. Stella was watching for her aunt as she came in.

"Aunt Ida, did you see Beatrice's Indian maid?"

"I presume they are in company now. There is but a step from Mexican to Indian," replied her aunt tartly.

"In company? Why, Aunty, Beatrice has just left here. She supposed that you would return with the protege, and she remained late that she might behold the new portion of your train."

"It is well she left, for I am in no humor to listen to her badinage."

"What has Beatrice done?"

"Enough. She has sent a carriage and taken off this girl to outgeneral me."

"There is evidently some mistake, for she could not have done it without my knowledge. We were together every moment since you left, until just before you returned."

Mrs. Raymond cut the matter short by declining to hear any more on the subject. Stella retired to her aunt's room, and drawing a chair near the grate, whose cheery glow made her conscious of the chill of the veranda, soon had her attention engrossed in a book. Her aunt made her toilet for the evening, and repaired to the parlor, all traces of the afternoon's annoyance banished from her features.

The home of Beatrice during her residence in the Crescent City had been with a friend and distant relative of her father, who was a prosperous wine merchant. His abode was a modest structure in one of the most respectable portions of Esplanade street, an aristocratic avenue, upon which some of the first Creole families of the city lived in luxurious style. These formed a circle within which few outsiders were permitted, and these had to possess the merit of true worth and honorable calling to obtain recognition. Senor Rivas, the distant relative who had received Beatrice, was among this favored few. In fact, his wife was a Creole of the purest blood, and his long life in the Creole city had eradicated whatever of the Mexican had been in his disposition and manners. Beatrice had visited the Rivas home on her return from school in Baltimore, and was therefore not quite a stranger in the circle which radiated from the Esplanade street center. To this home she bent her steps when she left Stella awaiting her aunt's return from the intelligence office. The latter's protracted stay had puzzled her. The Indian girl must have refused to break her engagement. At all events, she determined to ascertain on the following morning if an Indian's promise was as little to be depended upon as an Indian's gift. She did not really care for the services of a maid, but the custom of the city made it necessary to have one, and her latest appendage in that line had transferred her allegiance to a husband. Mrs. Rivas was somewhat startled to learn of Beatrice's selection, and very much doubted if an Indian girl could supply the place of her late maid.

It was not a restful pillow upon which Beatrice laid her head when she retired for the night. The dusky maiden filled her thoughts so completely that sleep was banished until the cocks crowed lustily in the vicinity. Then a feverish sleep succeeded, filled with fanciful visions and stranger dreams.

After a late breakfast she was on her way to Conti street. The office was soon reached and there, on opposite benches, were candidates for employment. A rapid glance informed her that her promised maid was not present. She, however, was absent for the reason that she had promised to enter her service, so Beatrice concluded, until the polite proprietor enlightened her.

"The Indian girl!" he exclaimed. "Why, mademoiselle, she is creating quite a stir. So many inquiries! You would not believe, mademoiselle."

"But I engaged her."

"So I believe, mademoiselle. You were the first."

"I was. Did anyone else come for her?"

"Anyone else! First, after you, came a gentleman with a carriage, and he tells the girl he is your husband, and you sent him for her. She went with him at two o'clock. At five, came a lady of middle age and she says she wants the Indian girl. When she is informed of the facts, she was quite serious, mademoiselle, and if it were not wrong to say of a lady, I would say that *elle etait en colere,* mademoiselle."

"Then the girl has been taken away," said Beatrice, in a disappointed tone.

"By the monsieur who said he was your husband."

"He was an impostor."

"Quite probable, mademoiselle."

"No traces as to who he is or where he lives?"

"Not a clue. It was a misfortune that I was not here when it happened."

"I hope no harm will come to her," said Beatrice, half to herself.

The man shrugged his shoulders until they nearly reached his ears to indicate his profound ignorance of what danger the girl might be in.

Beatrice, realizing the uselessness of further inquiry and perplexed to find this second obstacle thrown in the way of her design to secure the services of the pretty Indian, turned her steps homeward. The feeling which possessed her was akin to alarm when she speculated upon the possibility that she had been spirited away by unfriendly hands. She tried to reason that whatever experience awaited her, it would be the result of her own folly; but still there remained a feeling of disappointment akin to the regret ensuing from the severance of the tie existing between sympathetic personalities. She tried to shake off the depression, but it possessed her until she reached the apartments of Mrs. Raymond. The latter had slept upon her own feelings in regard to Laoni's disappearance, and had become convinced, from Stella's statements, that Beatrice had not been instrumental in her abduction, if abducted she had been. She therefore received her nephew's fiancee in a far more docile mood than would have characterized a similar reception the evening before. As it was, their moods were in accord for mutual condolences, and their intentions directed to a common purpose for the unravelling of a perplexing mystery.

Mrs. Raymond was actuated by a will which would not brook the interposition of any obstacle. Beatrice had been captivated by a novel personality which combined the naivete of the natural and artless with the grace and demeanor of gentle training. These were sufficient to interest the betrothed of Guy Raymond, in the girl who had saved him from the stake, to say nothing of the mystic influence which bent them to the common channel through which flowed their all absorbing loves.

Beatrice paused with the sympathy of Stella and Mrs. Rivas. The aunt having slept a second night upon her temporary defeat, found herself in a mood to prosecute a vigorous search for the missing girl. Without communicating her purpose, she told Stella to get ready to go out with her, and soon the two were directing their steps to Canal street. They turned down the latter avenue, when the aunt called a carriage. As the driver shut them inside, to his inquiring glance, Mrs. Raymond replied:

"Place D'Armes."

They whirled away down Chartres and in due course arrived in front of the Cathedral, with Place D'Armes on their right, and the vehicle stopped beside the curb of the latter's sidewalk.

"Remain here, my dear, in the carriage. I will not be gone very long. I have a little business to transact across the street," said Mrs. Raymond.

Having given instructions to her driver, the lady crossed the way and, proceding past the church, entered a front office on the first floor of the next building.

"I wish to see the chief of police," she said to a little man, with a large goose-quill behind his ear, and who arose from his seat at a desk when the lady entered. He replied with a polite inclination

"The chief is engaged with a gentleman in the private office. If madame will wait a moment he will be at leisure."

"Tell him at once that a lady is here on important business and he must give her an immediate audience," she answered in a tone of determination.

"I will report your message, madam," replied the scribe, opening and disappearing through a door, which presumably led into a private office.

In the next minute he reappeared, and announced:

"The chief will see madam at once."

The smile of satisfaction had hardly disappeared from the face of the waiting lady before the same door opened and two men appeared. One, tall and dark, passed on out into the street; the other approached and greeted Mrs. Raymond. The first was Ducio Halfen, the latter the chief of police.

"Madame has important business?"

"Important to myself and another directly—indirectly to the public who suffer from every character of wrong."

"Will madame come to the point? I will be all attention."

Mrs. Raymond detailed her business, which, of course, was the disappearance of Laoni, and an offer of a reward, provided she could be located.

"No clue, except that she went with a man in a carriage drawn by two horses," repeated the chief. "No proof that she went against her will?" he continued.

"But false pretenses were used to get her consent to go."

"Then she is held against her will, if she has become aware that those pretenses were false."

"Quite correct."

"You have no claims on this Indian girl?"

"Well—she was the protege of my brother, who is now dead, and I am therefore her best friend."

"That amounts to something; but if a crime has been committed, that is sufficient for the police to know. The reward, of course, will quicken matters."

After some additional consultation touching possible theories as to the missing girl's whereabouts and the course of procedure to be pursued, the lady took her departure and joined Stella at the carriage.

"Oh, Aunt Ida! A most impertinent looking man almost stopped as he passed the carriage, a short time after you entered that place, and stared so impudently into my face that he fairly frightened me. I will never forget his look. He was tall and dark, with jet black hair and mustache, and such piercing eyes."

"The description of a fellow whom I found closeted with the chief of police," said her aunt. "He looked like impudence personified."

CHAPTER LXI.

Nathan was mindful of his promise made to Laoni that he would return to the place where he had met her, and impart what news he might be able to learn, from returning volunteers, of the youth in whom she was so much interested. He watched for the arrival of the expected vessel, and was present when she landed two days later with a number of the ex-soldiers of Texas. It was with a feeling of disappointment that his eye ran from face to face among those who crowded the schooner's deck, without recognizing an acquaintance. He was about to make an inquiry of one of the men as to when the next vessel would sail from Galveston for New Orleans, when a familiar voice hailed him.

"Hello, Roach! What are you doing here?"

"If it ain't Hamilton! I'm powerful glad to see yer."

"And I to see you, Nathan. Thought you were home in Rakensack before this time."

"I ain't quite broke, and I concluded to see some of the sights in Orleans. Who's with yer that I know?"

"I'm alone. There is none of our crowd."

"Where's Perry?"

"Home—somewhere on the Brazos. I left Ruiz and Guy Raymond on the island. They both had to go to San Antonio on business."

"Guy Raymond—Guy Raymond," repeated Nathan. "She said Guy, and that's the pretty feller she spoke about. Was he oncet a prisoner with the Injuns?"

"Guy Raymond? Yes—for a year or two."

"That's him, then," said Nathan aside. "This Injun gal must 'a' ben his squaw. He's sum 'mong the women. He buckled onto two that night in San Antone where we saved his bacon."

"When is Guy Raymond a-comin' over?" he asked of Hamilton.

"When he gets through his business in Bexar. You remember the jailer Bonito, and his pretty daughter?"

"That's what I do."

"Well. Bonito turned up missing, it seems, and they found him in a kind of a vault under the jail, dead as a mackerel. No one knew anything about the vault except himself and two or three others, and he was dead a day or two before they found him. All sorts of stories got out about bags of gold which the old fellow had hid away down there, and a lot of men explored it and searched the place from end to end, but found nothing. Ruiz received the news of all this by letter, and as he is engaged to the daughter, he left at once for San Antonio, and Guy Raymond went with him."

"But what kept you on the island so long?"

"What I stayed there for was a secret, but I can tell you now. It must, however, go no further. Old man Trigg had some treasure buried on the island, and I, at Guy Raymond's request, stayed with him to hunt it up. We had the description of the spot, and after a day or two's prospecting we hit it. The pot which held the stuff was there, but that was all, except a few coins left through carelessness or haste. There was a paper found, dropped by the fellow who got away with the prize. This paper is safe and will be forthcoming at the proper time."

"Was the old jailer murdered?"

"No sign of violence; so it was put up that he had a fit, or heart disease. Where are you stopping, Nathan?"

"Promiscu'us like. I stop all over, with headquarters at George's place."

"George's?" exclaimed Hamilton. "George is the name of the fellow who disappeared about the same time that the stranger who dropped that passport was on the island," continued Hamilton, aside.

"What kind of a looking fellow is this George, Nathan?"

"He's heavy built, chunky, grizzly, and stoops."

"The very description," thought Hamilton.

"Let us go to George's, Nathan; I'm curious to see this man."

"S'pose yer git settled fust. Yer ain't hardly touched Orleans dirt yet, and I s'pose it'll be a few days afore yer'll leave. Besides, I've got to meet a friend, and it's nigh the time. George's isn't far, and as we pass the second street I'll pint yer to it."

Nathan left Hamilton to join Laoni at the show window, according to promise. He went with more satisfaction since the news through the former would enable him to name the whereabouts of the youth in whom she seemed so much interested.

He found her waiting, but not aware of his approach until he almost touched her.

"This is good of you," she said.

"It war a promise," he replied.

"Some are careless of promises."

"Right's right, with Nathan Roach."

"Have you anything—is there any word from El Bravo?"

"That's his Injun name. What war his Christian name?"

"His people called him Guy."

"I knowed a feller, as purty as a pink and brave as a war chief, with an eye like you said, who was a pris'ner a year or two, and fit the greasers long side o' me from San Antone down, and his name was Guy."

"Oh, it was he—it must have been El Bravo. Was his voice soft and mellow when he spoke words of peace and friendship, and firm and strong when he pushed back a foe? El Bravo had the courage of the war chief, with the tenderness of a maiden. I loved him with all the abandon of a perfect confidence; yet when my heartstrings were torn at parting, no embrace could have been purer than his; no kiss holier than that which he pressed upon my lips."

"Yer thought sights of the feller. How about him?"

"He loved me—but in his love El Bravo's self was lost. It was a love that would lift me from the home of the Lipan, from the dream of a life, content with simple wants and rude customs of my people, and teach me what he conceived to be the better principles of the white men. But tell me of him you knew. His name was Guy?"

"Guy Raymond."

"It is he."

"He'll be here in a week's time."

"You will bring him to me?"

"Ef' I'm here. Tell the truth, I'm gittin' short o' money—but lemme see—I'll stay fur yer, ef I have to roll cotton."

"Good friend—he will repay you."

"Where yer stoppin'? Got a place?"

"I have a place—but it is so strange. A place with nothing to do. A home with the mistress gone. Everything I want is furnished me. I cannot make a move outside the room I have, unless an eye is on me. I was told the gentleman who hired me ordered that I should not go out on the street. I remembered your promise to meet me here, and I slipped out without the housekeeper seeing me. I do not know how they will receive me when I go back."

"Is the place fur off?"

"The third street down from this."

"I've another 'pintment, miss. Say six days from now, 'bout this time I'll be here agin, and ef yer El Bravo is in Orleans he'll be alongside o' me."

"Good friend, how can I thank you? Depend upon it, if alive and free, Laoni will be here."

Nathan strode away, wondering to himself how, despite all his past antipathy for the race, he found himself all but in love with an Indian girl.

Laoni hurried back to the house, which seemed to her little less than a prison, since she knew that she was watched, and that her exit to the street was forbidden. It appeared to her, on reflection, that it was better than wandering around the city. She could not complain, since her wants were supplied without having, thus far, done anything to deserve compensation. She had been told that her occupation would be light or nominal until the return of the mistress of the house, and that she must make herself at home in the meantime. Considering her almost unbroken leisure, she could not account for the restriction which confined her to the house, or the motive that instigated the surveillance. Her absence had doubtless been discovered, and she anticipated the question of the woman who was denominated housekeeper, when that person should note her return. Laoni was the soul of truth, not having yet been contaminated by that essential of civilization, a propensity to lie. When the housekeeper demanded why she had disobeyed a positive order, she replied that it was her intention to get permission to go, but that on seeing no one about, and the time of her tryst with Nathan almost at hand, she made haste to reach the place of meeting.

"It is a fine character you will have, meeting men that way. I suppose he is a lover."

"No, madam. It was on business."

"No love in it, then?"

"No—yes—it was about one I love I wished to hear."

'Caught you in a story. You tried to deny it."

'No—not deny that I love. I denied loving the man I met. With him I had an appointment to learn what he knew of one whom I do love."

"Well, miss, if you want to please the gentleman who's paying you, and keep his good will, you will stop meeting men on the street for any purpose. Please him, and he will lavish money and everything you like on you."

"He can only pay me my wages—what I earn. More than that I have no right to ask."

"You can make the right to ask him everything. He is rich, and a fine girl like you could make him her slave."

"I have nothing to do with the master. The mistress' maid is shielded by the mistress' presence. If she is good I will prove her worthy maid and gain her favor."

"The mistress has been long away. Suppose the news of her death should come, which could happen, seeing she was in wretched health, and the master's love should fall upon the maid? Stranger things have happened. You could not well refuse his money and his heart; you who depend upon a slender pay in this hard world."

"'He would be a false husband who would love again so soon, and she a foolish maid who would trust to his false words.'"

The woman was called away and Laoni retired to her room. The latter apartment was one of the best in the house, being well furnished with the comforts of sitting room and sleeping chamber. This fact alone would have raised a suspicion in a less artless nature, that her position was a pretense, and underlying it a scheme. The man who brought her there had left her to herself, and, through his alleged housekeeper, had held out the idea that the arrival of the mistress of the house was to occur shortly.

The drift given to the conversation by the woman, on her return from meeting Nathan, was doubtless dictated by him to bridge the way to an interview. At any rate, the same afternoon the housekeeper informed her that the master would be there, and she had better put on her best looks. Laoni, filled with her own innocence, and occupied by the joyful expectation of soon beholding El Bravo, little cared if the master came or went, or if the mistress returned, or still lingered wherever she then sojourned as an invalid.

It was evening before Ducio made his appearance.

For many minutes he remained closeted with the housekeeper. When their consultation was over he repaired to the next apartment, which served as a sitting room, and sent for Laoni.

The latter made her appearance immediately.

"You wished to see me, sir?"

"I sent for you to give you sad news," he said, slowly and sadly.

Laoni looked startled; she thought at once of Guy.

"Sad news to me," he continued. "My poor wife, for whom I wanted you as a companion, is dead. Her disease was too much for her, and all remedies failed. While her death saddens me, I feel relieved that her sufferings are ended."

"Then you will not want a maid," she said.

"No—not for her—but do not trouble yourself, my dear girl. Remain here and make yourself comfortable until I see what I will do. I may have use for your services, but if I do not, this will be your home as long as you desire it, or until I can get you a place. I am too sad to talk much, so you will please excuse me. The housekeeper has been told to supply all your wants."

"I am very sorry for your loss, sir, and thankful for your kindness," said Laoni, in a tone of mingled sorrow and gratitude.

As Ducio left the sitting room he met the housekeeper, and gave her a sign to follow him.

"I've gained an important point," he said. "I have won her sympathy. With a woman that is the first step to gain her for yourself. Be cautious how you talk to her, and say nothing that will arouse a suspicion of the truth. Give her everything she wants, and leave the wooing to me."

The woman watched the retreating form of the villain as he left the hall for the street, then turned away muttering:

"He is a precious scoundrel. It was this way I was betrayed. First my sympathy—then my confidence—and then—ah! then——'

CHAPTER LXII.

In that portion of New Orleans below the Place D'Armes, and which stretched away to its lower outskirts, where the narrow streets were paved with cobblestones and the roofs of the old-fashioned buildings were made picturesque by their coverings of red-hued pottery, lived the poorer class of its population. Here dwelt the mixed element, whose composite pedigrees, dating back many generations, had been lost in the weld of indiscriminate admixture and ultimate homogeneity. This caste however, presented the usual gradations of social distinction. The more favored of fortune held aloof from the plodding mass and aped the manners of the purer blooded aristocracy of wealth. A middle class, composing the more numerous set, and among whom were counted some few families of undoubted respectability and pure lineage, but forced to a lower plane by the weight of poverty, formed the next social strata. The lower extreme, defining no certain boundary in its ascending tendency, extended to the wall where slavery began.

From the darker side of this wall Halfen did not owe his origin, because his mother had been a freed woman before his birth. His father, a man of influence, and at one time wealthy, had sent him to an institution of learning, where he was admitted as a Creole of respectable parentage. When Ducio returned from Texas he was drawn to the location where his changed fortunes would be best adapted to excite the envy or command the admiration of his own element. He purchased a home not remote from the cottage where he was born and where lived his mother, until her death. To this home he brought Josefa, and here they passed the succeeding months in that harmony of intercourse which can be depicted as characteristic of willful yet discordant natures. Josefa had paid the penalty of attaching her fortunes to the career of an unprincipled adventurer. On the day of the runaway, when Nathan Roach exhibited his daring feat, she was out for the first time in many days seeking a respite from an ever encroaching ailment which seemed to be draining the fountain of her vitality. She discovered, when too late, the true character of the step she had taken, and realizing the impossibility of a retracement that could reunite broken ties or obliterate the lapses from propriety, she determined to meet the future with the stoicism of her peculiar disposition. She therefore settled down to the condition imposed by the inevitable, just tolerating the man who had ruined her and, who was not further lowered in her estimation by the knowledge of the stain which rested upon his birth.

Her health was failing.

This she realized without even a self inquiry if it were to be attributed to physical or mental causes, or to a combination of both.

The discovery of the treasure had enriched them beyond the fear of ever wanting for the luxuries of life, but the fortune had failed to bring happiness. Ducio was wild and dissipated and she saw but little of him.

The next morning after Ducio's interview with Laoni he was seated in his private room at home, apparently in a deep study over some issue which he had been debating in his own mind. He arose and paced the room a few moments, then going to an old-fashioned press which stood in a recess to the left of the mantel, he produced a vial, which he held up for inspection a moment, then shook it while he reached for a goblet on a table. Into this he poured a small quantity of the liquid from the vial, and afterwards diluted it with water from a pitcher. He regarded the decoction for a while as if to decide upon the proportion of its composites, then, as if to assure himself, said aloud:

"That is larger than the addition I should have made, but the prescription seems too slow to me. She's got a constitution like a mule. It is a wonder she don't suspect me, but that's where I am a successful villain. I am all tenderness when I am with her, and have never done a thing to make her think that I am tired of her. True, I am much away, but she has become used to that. I will now go and give her this medicine, and trust its effect will be all that is desired—*by me.*"

Leaving the room he crossed the hall and entered a door, which he closed behind him. The atmosphere of the apartment seemed purer with the rascal's exit—the tick of the mantel clock came clearer and lighter. Through the half open door of the press the vial from which the potion was dropped into the goblet showed itself nearly filled with its pinkish contents, while the broad-mouthed pitcher stood stately and white upon the enameled waiter overlooking the down-turned goblets by its side.

Several minutes passed before Ducio returned.

"Another week will settle it," he said, as he rinsed the now empty glass, and threw the water into the fireplace. "'Another week—and I can bring this strangely bewitching Indian here, if I manage to keep down all suspicion of the part I am playing. Laoni! A pretty name. If I am not sentimental I am drifting that way. Strange, too—and about a squaw! Come, Ducio! For shame!"

"Now to George's," he continued, taking his hat. "The rascal sent for me, and I suppose, as usual, to bleed me."

* * * *

Hamilton and Nathan kept their appointment to meet at George's. The Mississippian was much amused at his companion's story of the interesting Indian and the details of their two interviews at the show window. Nathan however suppressed that part of the conversation with Laoni which referred to Guy Raymond, as he was rather tickled by an intimation from Hamilton that the pretty squaw must be in love with him. At George's they entered, and Hamilton called for a luncheon with coffee. The proprietor, who was not present at first, soon entered. He was keenly eyed by Hamilton, who mentally compared him with the description he possessed.

"Roach, that's the man."

"What man?"

"The man who knows something about the missing pot of money that belonged to Guy Raymond."

"Whew! You don't say so."

"A little lower tone, Roach."

"Kin yer make him tell—think?"

"That's to be seen. I've spotted him—and that's one step."

"Yes—but they say he's a slick un."

"Things naturally develop, Mr. Roach. Evolution does not stop with material things; facts are evolved from theories; we assimilate facts and make deductions. Now, by this process——"

"Look here, Hamilton, that's 'bout 'nuff o' that. What in thunder yer talkin' 'bout? I sorter thought yer got cured of yer old distemper."

"Roach, I'm dumb."

"No, man; talk sense. Yer knows how ef yer want to."

"We, Nathan—we'll keep him spotted 'til Guy Raymond comes."

"That's what we kin do. I've promised to stay a few days ef I have to roll cotton."

"No use of that, Roach. Draw on me. By the way, I have a tip-top place, old boy. Come, I'll show it to you."

The two went out together.

Ducio called at George's in response to the latter's message, and was received, as he usually was, in the room in rear of the saloon.

"What's the matter?" he asked of the ex-pirate.

"Nothing serious; but I wish to say that yesterday a lot of fellows landed here from Texas, and one of them named Hamilton came here with the man who stopped your team. He eyed me so sharply and strangely that I concluded he knew something of my past, and possibly he might have got wind of that operation of ours in the sandhills."

"Hamilton! There was such a man in a mess I was with in the army. Describe him."

"Large, tall and handsome, hair brown and wavy, nose a little raised in the middle."

"That's him."

"Any danger?"

"Think not; he knows the papers were stolen; but no one knows who stole them."

"So you believe."

"So I know."

"Maybe so."

"Well, watch him, George, if he returns; and if you find a chance, sound him."

"Your commands will be obeyed; but see here, Halfen; this is work—work for your benefit. I've done up two or three things for you that have been thanky jobs."

"But, George, in this you would be implicated. If this fellow has a clue, and his suspicions are excited by your presence, who is interested and who is it that is giving the thing away? See?"

"That is true; but what have I to lose in comparison to you? The way things have been working lately I'd not be loser if you were flat broke. See?"

"You say the fellow who stopped my horses was with him?"

"He was."

"Better win him over—you know how to work it. If anything turns up, send me word at once. I have something very important to attend to and must be off. Au revoir."

Mrs. Raymond slept late the morning after her visit to the chief of police. Her head had been set on finding the Indian girl more from a determination to not be outwitted than from any personal consideration for the missing one. It was therefore among the small hours when she and Stella passed from consciousness and discussion into dreamland. Stella, who was first up in the morning, made a startling discovery. Burglars had evidently been in their apartment, as the blinds on the veranda had been forced and the sash was up. She arose and closed the blind, and took a glance around to see if she could detect any evidences of their work. Her aunt was sleeping soundly and she refrained from disturbing her until the desire to communicate the probable robbery overcame her.

"Aunt Ida! Aunt Ida! Robbers have been in our room."

Mrs. Raymond sprang from her bed, having quickly comprehended what the words of her niece implied, for they placed in jeopardy her valuable jewelry, laid away nightly in her wardrobe.

"Gracious, child! How do you know?"

"See, Aunt Ida—the blinds—three slats cut out and a piece of glass from the sash."

"My God! My diamonds!"

She sprang to her wardrobe. The case was there—the diamonds gone. The lady sank to a chair, put her head in her palms, and the tears trickled through her fingers.

"What is missing, Aunty?"

"Oh, child! All gone."

"You'll get them again, Aunty. Don't distress yourself."

"See if you have lost anything, my child."

"I, Aunty? I have so little to lose. There's my box with my ribbons, and that medal Mr. Trigg sent to me, and a pin and bracelet," said Stella, taking her box from a shelf and opening it.

She paled a little as she raised her eyes from the open box and caught her aunt's look of inquiry.

"Aunty, they have robbed poor me, too. Pin and bracelet are gone—and—the—medal."

"The villains!" exclaimed her aunt.

"I wouldn't mind my loss, Aunty, if your diamonds had not been taken. Still, I felt so much attached to that pretty medal with its snowy beadwork."

"A fine police force they must have here! The chief himself looks brimful of stupidity. I suppose this will necessitate another trip to Place D'Armes."

When Ducio left George's he drove rapidly for several blocks and halted his team in front of a shop which displayed the three golden balls. He entered the place and greeted the sole occupant with familiarity.

"Jacques, I'm in a quandary. I want to make a holiday present to a girl—a young woman—a friend of mine, and I don't know what in the world to select. Maybe you can help me out."

"Well, monsieur, if you will tell me something about the tastes of mademoiselle, I may be capable to decide for you."

"Tastes! I don't know much of her taste, but I will say this, that she's an Indian—but a devilish fine Indian—a real lady and pretty as a pink."

"But a dark pink, I believe, monsieur, if she is an Indian."

"Only a figure of speech, Jacques. I might have said pretty as a lily and it would have been as applicable."

"Well, monsieur, I think I have the very article you should have for the Indian lady. It is a medal, monsieur, and only brought in this morning. I paid more than I should as it was so odd—so unique."

The man held up the article he was praising, and it was a remarkably showy trinket of Indian manufacture, attached to a silver medal.

"This might serve my purpose if the girl is a Catholic, and of this I am ignorant."

"It is pretty enough for a Protestant, monsieur, and plenty cheap to make you decide to buy it."

"'How much?"

"Three dollars, monsieur."

"A bargain, Jacques; I believe it is just the thing."

"The price is an argument, monsieur, that often decides if a present shall be suitable.'

"With some, I grant you, mon ami; but with your humble servant price would not be a bar to getting what I thought would serve my purpose, in this instance, especially."

"Is there nothing else—nothing to suit madame? She was here with you some months ago, and much admired these diamonds."

"There is something else," replied Ducio, as if noticing only the first part of the other's inquiry. "Here, Jacques, this pretty box, with the enameled top; it will do to hold the medal. Lay it in so that the beadwork will cover the bottom with the medal displayed in the centre."

Ducio superintended the arrangement of the medal in the box, and when the whole had been neatly wrapped and secured with cord he took the package and re-entered his vehicle.

Hamilton and Nathan Roach, in order to carry out their purpose to discover the character of the connecting link between Ducio and George, passed much of their time at the cafe kept by the latter. George, in pursuit of Ducio's aim to learn what Hamilton might know or suspect of his connection with the abstraction of the treasure from the sandhills, made himself very agreeable to both the latter and his backwoods friend. To Nathan he extended illimitable hospitality under cover of admiration for his proven daring in the arrest of the runaway team. To Hamilton he was attentive and courteously polite. Nathan, honest and unsuspecting, received his advances with good will, but insisted on paying for whatever he ordered in the establishment. He refused also to be pumped, when the host so far trenched upon the borders of the secret, confided by Hamilton, as to make the step easy and natural that would pass the bounds that guarded it. The oft repeated approach which the conversation made in this direction when, and only when, the participants were confined to himself and the gracious host of the cafe, finally aroused the usually dormant suspicions of the Arkansan, and he communicated to Hamilton this peculiarity in George's intercourse with himself. Hamilton, with sharper wits than his friend, and less conscientious about making an account with the proprietor, already was conscious of a score against him on the slate of the cafe. He resolved to lead George on, step by step, to a tacit acknowledgment of Ducio's perpetration of the robbery of the sandhills and, to succeed, he felt the necessity of the ex-pirate's induction into more or less drunks of a degree to induce loquacity and confidence. George, on his part, had become convinced that Nathan's simplicity was assumed, and that his abstemiousness was the guarded role of the detective. Hamiltons' looseness and convivial disposition deceived him completely, and he soon began to feel perfectly at home with the Mississippian.

While this state of affairs was in existence at George's, other events pertinent to this story were transpiring in the city. Mrs. Raymond had, as a matter of course, informed the police of the loss of her diamonds and of the little trinkets of her niece. The wise eyes of the detectives had inspected her rooms and viewed the cut blinds and broken sash, and minute descriptions of the jewels and articles taken had been noted. The disconsolate lady had offered an appropriate reward, the detectives bowed and departed, and there, for the time, the matter rested.

Beatrice was over to offer her sympathy as a solace for the distress occasioned by the losses of her friends. For the nonce the robbery nearly, if not quite, obliterated the interest which, for the day or two previous, had grown to large proportions, in the case of the Indian girl. The aunt was as one bereaved for two or three days, and refused to obey the recurring inclination to promenade Canal street, or even to appear in evening dress, with powdered face and artistically tinged cheeks, in the drawing rooms of the hotel. Stella regretted her loss, but grieved for her aunt's perplexity.

How was it with Laoni? One—two—three days passed since Ducio elicited her sympathy by the relation of his wife's demise, and evoked her gratitude by the offer of his friendship and patronage. She experienced a quiet, happy calm, in which was contemplated a satisfactory solution of her difficulties. In this future Ducio assumed a fraternal role, which placed him high upon the plane of disinterested humanity and softened to her Indian mind the harshness which white civilization seemed to emit from beneath its cover of selfishness and greed. In the glamour of the picture, born of suspicion of right and truth in her environment, Laoni beheld the recreant Ducio, hand in hand with El Bravo, the lost love of the San Saba, pouring out his heart's thanks for the care bestowed upon the daughter of Walumpta. The day thoughts merged into night visions—the reverie blended into the dream.

For the first time since El Bravo left her upon the mountain side Laoni approached near the goal of a remembered happiness, almost to the brink of a treasured joy. Around her were friendship and favor—almost in reach the dearest of hopes. In this mood of perfect content did Laoni remain until the return of him to whom was due the charm of the lagging hours. She stood at the casement surveying the metropolitan scene over which the partial season had spread the mellowness of a balmy atmosphere. The genial temperature had nearly depopulated the dwellings, and brought to the streets the populace, gay in manner and costumes. From the pavements her eyes turned away across the piles of masonry, little heeding the picture of turrets and towers, of chimneys and corners, of walls and angles, in her deeper reflection upon the oddities of this white civilization. There was so little of freedom in this pent-up life, devoted to money getting, with so little of the natural in the aims and aspirations of a purely artificial existence. Away out on the far away San Saba her thoughts took refuge as if to rest from the contemplation of the babel before her. The serene hills, the grand mountains, the stretching plains, the green mottes and blue lines of timber of her native place rose before her, and her heart yearned for the home of her tribe. Was not its freedom and quiet superior to the restraint and friction of the huddled masses of this great city? Beneath her eyes a carnival of noise and acting was in progress in honor of the nativity of the God of the white people. Among the passers were men, reeling from the effects of liquor, whose shouts added to the din of the explosion of small arms, torpedoes and firecrackers, while small boys jeered and stoned the inebriates. Laoni thought of the first lessons she received from Guy upon the subject of the Christian faith, suggested by the display of her medal. She remembered how strange and incongruous sounded to her ears the story of the incarnation and the redemption, and how El Bravo doubted the supernatural origin of Jesus. Since then she had come in contact with the saintly sisters of the convent at Grande Coteau, and had been taught the faith by its ablest advocates. She loved her teachers and respected their pious zeal, but her first impressions refused to give place to an unseeing faith. She demanded reason in the religion of her acceptance—as her ideal of the Supreme Being was the essence of reason as he was the spirit of truth and justice. Her contact with Christian civilization had not been calculated to excite her enthusiasm for its practical workings. She could not acknowledge the claims of a system that confined its excellencies to rules, rubrics and theories. To her mind Christianity, despite the unreason of its claims to a divine origin, could be a useful factor in the upbuilding of humanity only by its strict, practical application, whereas, from her standpoint, it was an enthroned myth, for consideration, mostly by females, one day in seven, and to become wholly neglected and ignored the other six days. These might be the conclusions of her rude Lipan intellect, but they were irresistible, and refused to be laid aside.

Since Ducio's noble offer of his friendship, her heart had somewhat softened, and she thought if Christians generally could be actuated by their religion to carry out the spirit of the golden rule as he had done, they could make many converts who would be rather affected by the results of the faith. than by the justice of its claims to have been organized above the clouds.

While Laoni was thus mentally constituting Ducio an ideal Christian, she caught sight of that worthy crossing the street. Their eyes met as she drew back, and he waved his hand pleasantly just before he disappeared beneath the projecting veranda. She judged that he was about to enter the house, and a presentiment warned her that he would call for her.

Her impression was correct. The housekeeper some minutes later appeared and stated that the master desired to see her and, if she did not object, would see her in her room.

"It's a half sitting room anyhow," said the housekeeper, "and you are such a tidy creature your room is always in order."

Laoni, seeing no impropriety in admitting her new friend to her room, assented; and having no face powder or hair to arrange, or curiosity to gratify by glancing in the mirror, assented at once.

She was more at ease when Ducio entered than was the villain himself, for in her artlessness she was purely optimistic, and in her innocence suspected nothing but kindness from her avowed protector.

The talk began about the usual way, and on the one side about everything but what was uppermost in his mind.

"You have not made up your mind what I shall do yet?" she asked, after a pause in the conversation.

"Not exactly," he replied. "I've had you a great deal in my thoughts, because I knew you would be lonesome up here with only the housekeeper to see. I have kept in seclusion since my sad luck, but as tomorrow will be Christmas, I thought it would be best to shake off sadness and share in the current of joy that should only be felt in this time when Christ proclaimed peace on earth and good will to men. Besides it is not manly to grieve. Your warriors are fine examples of the manly spirit. They look upon death with a cool and calm philosophy which puts religion to the blush."

"Yet you are a Christian."

"I try to be."

"It seems that all try and few ever succeed."

"Pretty true. Did the convent convert you?"

"As a respecter for the institution—yes. Some of the nuns are pure and holy women. As to religion—I am a Lipan still at least, in my unbelief."

"I have often wished that I were an Indian," said Ducio with a sigh. "I am tired of this thing they call civilization. It is hypocrisy from beginning to end."

"Are you in earnest?" asked Laoni.

"In earnest? If I could fly from here tomorrow I would not stop until I reached the lodges of a natural people, lifted above the contamination which comes of chasing after money. If I could find a tribe who would receive me and treat me like a brother, I would pledge my life to its service."

"Oh!" thought Laoni. "If El Bravo had been of this mind."

"You will change," she said to him. "You are now affected by the loss of your wife. A little time will bring back the contentment you had before. You will stay with your own people."

"To tell you the honest truth, Laoni, I was never happy with my wife—in fact, we were never congenial. For the sake of appearances we kept up a semblance of harmony, and if I speak truthfully, I will say that I am relieved that death has cut the tie which the policy of the church made it decline to sever. Laoni, I have never loved but once, and then it was not my wife who roused the feeling."

"My poor friend, I am sorry for you. But the one you did love? She never knew it, as you could not tell her while the wife was living."

"Your are right. It has not been many days since I met this love. I could not tell it to her—for the woman who called me husband still lingered. I crushed down the feeling until my heart fairly bled in the throes of my struggle to keep from speaking—to keep from throwing myself at her feet and confessing all."

"Poor man," said Laoni; and then, putting her hand to her brow as if to help her thoughts, she said aside: "This wild, true love! How like the passion that fills my heart. Oh! El Bravo!"

"Laoni, you pity me. If I should tell you of this woman—if I should own the truth—trusting to your generous sympathy to not hate me for the confession—would you still pity me—would you still call me friend, and try to soothe my wounded heart?"

"Love is a holy feeling," she said. "Why should I hate you for this confession? You come to me as a friend to ease your bosom of a secret that weighs upon you. You have my sympathy. Why not go to this woman, and if your love is honorable—tell it in her ear. Perhaps she will learn to love you if her heart is not another's."

"Your words are comforting. I have known her only since the day I met you, Laoni. The hour I spoke to her was the hour you first heard my voice. The woman I love is an Indian—the mother who bore her was the mother of Laoni—and Laoni had never a sister."

"Is this the truth?"

"Aye, the truth," said Ducio, throwing himself beside her. "Laoni, accept my love. It is the most costly gift I can offer you—you who are in the midst of an unsympathizing race of strangers—without other protection than mine. Think of it, Laoni—think before you answer."

"Think of it? Think of my answer? It would be useless thought. My friend, if I were to think from now until the weight of years will have brought me to the grave, what would be my answer—if in my troubled sleep every dream should be filled with this scene and the memory of your words, thoughts and dreams alike would conjure the presence of one to whom my heart has long been given—and the answer would be the same as it must be now. My sympathy and my friendship you have won—without asking. I have no love to give."

"Then there is no hope for me?" said Ducio, rising and walking the floor.

"You have had my answer."

"Does he love you?"

"You have no right to ask. It would be the same if he did not love me. If he loves another and is happy, I will try to purge the selfish from my love and be content. I would not boast of love which would refuse to make sacrifice for the loved one."

"Laoni, I cannot be content with your answer, but will return another time and press my suit. If you still decide that we cannot be more than friends, then I will yield. In the meantime, let me be your protector, and prove that I, too, can tear the selfish from my love. I brought you this little token for a Christmas present. I knew not of your views on religion, but as I brought it, I will leave it, and trust you will find in it a pretty relic—besides being partly the handiwork of the Indians."

She took the box from him, thanked him, and placed it upon the table.

Ducio took his departure with a look of disappointment, while a sinister expression flashed from his dark eyes.

As soon as she was alone Laoni opened the pretty box containing the gift. She raised the fine pink packing, and uttered a low cry as she recognized the medal which had once rested upon her bosom. She did not faint nor did she sink into a chair. Her eye glowed with a fire that was kindled by the emotions of wonder, doubt and conjecture.

The gift she had made to El Bravo! Could he have arrived in the city, and if so, how came he to part with the medal? Murdered and robbed, or simply robbed, and by whom? By this alleged friend and protector? Perhaps—perhaps not. A mystery? He was doubtless yet in the house. She would go and demand an explanation. To this end she left her apartment in pursuit of Ducio.

He was not in the sitting room. The housekeeper's room was empty, but Laoni heard voices on the back gallery immediately under the latter apartment. This alone would not have made her pause. The tone and the words which caught her ear caused her to approach still closer the window and listen. Ducio was talking.

"She is a sentimental fool. Imagine a squaw with sentiment!"

"Not much of a fool," said the housekeeper.

"True enough. I went in bold, but her manner made a coward of me, and my tactics were changed to real love making. You should have heard the stuff I spit out, and which she swallowed."

"But didn't digest."

"Not much. But I will bring this girl to her senses if I have to drug her into it."

"She ain't worth it, Ducio."

"Maybe not; but my dander is up and I mean to win. I will come tomorrow and give her a last chance. Then she will be my prisoner and my slave. She is unsuspecting now, and needs no watching. I left her a bauble which I bought of Jacques, and which will amuse her until I return."

Laoni was much surprised as well as alarmed by what she heard fall from the lips of her supposed friend and protector. Her natural step was to conceal the fact of her having overheard the conversation just narrated, and she therefore hastened back to her room. Here she considered the situation. A continued stay in the house which in the earlier hours of the day had appeared to her so pleasant, and had induced her to recant many of her mental strictures on the worthiness of the Christian civilization, was now out of the question. She stood aghast at the hypocrisy that could assume the role of sentiment and earnestness, as did Ducio. She did not dream that the worst features of social depravity could so successfully masquerade under the form of lofty sentiment.

She comprehended her danger well, and in the thought of it she ceased to speculate upon the presence of the medal. The latter she placed upon her bosom; the handsome box was unceremoniously pitched into the closet in the corner. Laoni had no definite plan of escape, but calmly awaited night and a quiet house. She did not dare to wait too late for fear of walking the dark streets alone. Her little bag was packed, and nine o'clock found her under the gas light of the nearest corner. Here she hesitated. Where should she turn her steps to avoid the encounter of the roughs of civilization? In all the wide world there were but two places in which an undoubted welcome would be hers—the village where she was born—the convent at Grande Coteau. The realization that the danger she had escaped was greater far than any she had to dread in the streets nerved her to proceed. She moved aimlessly on. At length a thought suggested itself. Why not find the Convent of the Sacred Heart in the city and appeal for protection? She would ask direction from passers by. These she met, but they hurried on, and were gone before the words could fall from her lips. One or two, in less haste, presented appearances so forbidding that she feared to confide to them her ignorance. At the next corner she met a policeman. She knew him by his badge, and felt no hesitation in accosting him and requesting to be directed to the Convent of the Sacred Heart.

"It is far from this, madam. Are you acquainted with the city?"

"No, sir, and I would like your advice and protection?"

"That you shall have, madam, as long as you are in my beat, but that will not find you the convent."

"Could you not show me the way I must go, and then I could get other policemen to show me further on."

The officer was about to proffer some sort of advice, but suddenly stopped and requested Laoni to come nearer to the light. She complied at once.

"I just wanted to see your face well, madam, for I did not know but what I had seen you before. Come along with me and I will show you the way and see that no harm comes to you."

Laoni was grateful for the offer, and expressing her thanks, walked on by the side of the city's guardian.

CHAPTER LXIII.

The hospitalities of the cafe, showered as they were upon the susceptible Mississippian, had the effect of neutralizing his purpose to bring out the criminal connection existing between the proprietor and the guilty Ducio. Even Nathan in his simplicity saw the tendency of matters, and in his quaint way urged upon his friend the necessity for more prudence and less indulgence in the convivialities of the place. Hamilton would argue that success depended upon unrestrained intercourse and the consequent confidence it would create in the mind of George that they were ordinary visitors and patrons. Notwithstanding the quantum of truth contained in the latter argument, Hamilton's actions and the gusto with which he seemed to enjoy the hours passed in the resort in question indicated that the beam was tipped by the weight of Nathan's assertion.

The night on which Laoni escaped from the house on Custom House street, Hamilton and Nathan were as usual passing away the evening at the cafe. The two were engaged at cards, each having chosen a partner from among the habitues of the resort. There were few others present besides their party, the proprietor and three or four loungers. George had been busy behind his bar and was for the moment leaning forward on his elbows regarding, in a rather abstracted manner, the four-handed game of euchre. His attention was suddenly attracted by the entrance of a slight individual, who came to a halt at the screen and beckoned to him. George, having replied by a nod, leisurely passed from behind the bar, and making a jocular remark to the card party; passed on out to the front, where the newcomer awaited him.

"Well, what is it?" queried George.

"The beeks are after me, and I've skipped them, but they know my dives and I'm at my wit's end."

"What have you forked last, that they're so hot on your trail?"

"Didn't they tell ye?"

"Not a word."

"We trapped the diamonds, but we feared to sell them or to keep them."

"Oh! You were with Jem."

"That's it."

"Have you any of the boodle on you?"

"No more'n the ring."

"I've rigged a play on one of the fellers at the table within. Do as I bid you and it will lay the hounds off the scent. Look—see that coat upon the peg. Fool around there a bit and drop the ring in the pocket."

"But it's worth a pile."

"So's your liberty; now choose between it and the ring; to be caught costs you both."

"Boss, you're right; here goes."

The fellow entered the room and a few moments later had dexterously deposited something in the pocket of a coat hanging upon a peg not far from the table where sat the card players. This accomplished the fellow returned to the front where George awaited him, with a paper in his hand, upon which he had hastily written while the other was in the room.

"It's in the pocket—what now?"

"Here," said George, handing him the paper, "take this to the station and see that some of the police get hold of it; but take care that they don't find out you brought it."

"Trust me for that," said the fellow.

"Be off now, and don't blunder."

Perhaps an hour might have passed after George's messenger had left, before any other arrival occurred at the cafe. The card playing still continued, interrupted only by a call for cigars or something to drink, as one or the other side was declared loser. The arrival alluded to was a man of medium stature and ordinarily dressed. He entered with an easy air and seated himself near the front screen. A few moments later a second individual appeared in the door, glanced around the place, accosted the first arrival, and seating himself by his side, began a conversation in a low tone.

The time was within an hour of midnight when the card party broke up and the players were about to disperse.

"Come, Hamilton, it's 'bout time we was goin'," said Nathan, who thought he saw indications in his friend's manner suggesting an inclination to linger yet longer.

As Nathan spoke he took down the coat from the peg and leisurely put it on.

"I'm ready, Nathe," said Hamilton. "Good night, George. We'll give my friend from Arkansas and his partner a chance to revenge themselves tomorrow night."

"Hold, gentlemen!" said one of the two men who had last arrived, and who maintained their positions near the door.

"We are officers of the police," he continued, "and have the best of reasons to suspect that some stolen property is concealed upon one of this party. As you are doubtless all honest men, and are not conscious of having any such articles on your persons, you will not object to being searched."

"What kind of articles do you suspect us of having?" asked Hamilton.

"Diamonds," replied the policeman. "Have you any such things about you?"

"That's rich, eh Nathe? To suspect us of having diamonds! Search away, Mr. Policeman, and welcome," said Hamilton.

"I never seen one in my life," said Nathan, "though I hear'n tell of 'em."

"I'll go through you first, then," said the officer. So saying he ran his hand in one pocket, then in another, and drew forth a ring.

"Here is something," he said, and holding it up, the jewels showed their value by their sparkling brilliancy.

"This answers the description, my friend, of what we are after. You will have to go to the station and account for the possession of this ring."

"How'n thunder did that git in my pocket?" exclaimed Nathan, much astonished.

The officer smiled.

"There must be some mistake," said George, "for this man is honest, I am certain."

"I'd like to see the feller what 'ud say the contrairy," said Nathan.

"You will have to go with us to the station. Come along quietly and if you can explain things it will be all right. The looks of things are against you now, and we hope you will get out of it."

"Would yer go, Hamilton?"

"You will have to, Nathe."

"Have to! And me innercent? I've fit greater odds than two."

"I will go with you, Nathan. Resistance would only get you into further trouble."

"Well, boss, I'll go; but see that yer don't run this thing in the ground. Ef yer put that ring in my pocket, as I s'pects yer did, fur to git me inter trouble, I'll live on yer trail until I git both yer scalps."

The party filed out the door and proceeded down the street, the prisoner between the two officers and Hamilton in the rear.

George looked after them and chuckled as he turned into his den.

"If he was on my trail, I turned the tables on him. It was a jolly thought of mine and he will have a hard time accounting for the way that ring came to be in his pocket."

Nathan occupied the attention of his escort, while en route to the police headquarters, with protestations of his innocence, interlarded with hints as to the danger which might accrue to any one affecting belief in his guilt.

"It's a put up job," he stated, and intimated that he would get out of it if he had to fight out. Hamilton's frequent suggestions that he had better reserve his remarks for utterance before the proper tribunal, and not waste them upon his heedless captors, had the effect of stimulating the prisoner's loquacity.

The next morning, before the opening of the police court, the chief had ordered that the two prisoners who had been taken with the articles stolen from the apartments of Mrs. Raymond be brought, separately, to his private room to be interrogated. Laoni was first introduced in obedience to the chief's order. Her face wore a slightly troubled expression as she entered and turned her eyes from the hard stare of the officer around the room, in half inquiry as to why she had been brought there. The chief, after a few whispered words to a lawyer-like looking personage at his side, addressed her:

"Young woman, how long have you been in the city?"

"Seven days," she replied.

"You are an Indian?"

"A Lipan."

"You have seen this before," he asked, holding up the medal taken from her by the policeman, who, under the pretense of escorting her in the direction of the convent, had taken her to the station as his prisoner.

"It is mine."

"By what claim?"

"My father's gift."

"You brought it with you to the city?"

"No."

"Has your father been in the city since you came to it?"

"No."

"You will have to explain to make me understand you."

"It was a gift to me years ago. I gave it to one who was dearer to me than myself. It can only be his or mine. How he parted with it I know not. The person who put it in my hands in this city can perhaps explain where he got it. I do not claim it through this person. The medal is mine, or it is his to whom I gave it."

"You refuse to tell where this person got it who, as you say, put it into your hands in the last day or two?"

"I could not tell you because I do not know"

"Are you acquainted with a man by the name of Roach—Nathan Roach?"

"Yes; I have met him twice."

"Where?"

"At the show window."

"What show window?"

"Where there is a figure of an Indian."

"On Canal street?"

Laoni shook her head.

"Didn't Nathan Roach give you this medal?"

"No."

"Who did, then?"

"The master—he who employed me."

"His name?"

"I heard it, but it was so short—the time I was there—that I cannot remember it."

"Why did you leave?"

"He was a bad, false man, and I could not stay."

"But you took his present."

"Because it was mine—mine or El Bravo's."

"Yours or whose?"

"His to whom I entrusted it."

"All this is a very likely story," said the chief, giving a side look and a meaning smile to his companion. "Young woman," he continued, "this medal is the property of a young lady of this city, and was stolen only night before last from her sleeping room. You will have to be kept a prisoner and answer before the police court, which will commit you for theft unless you produce better evidence of your innocence."

At a motion from the chief Laoni was conducted out by the officer who had brought her to the room. The lawyer-like individual looked over his glasses at the girl's retreating figure, and when she was out of sight he turned towards the chief and remarked in measured tones:

"A remarkable looking girl. A half-breed, evidently. Some of these half-breeds are regular gypsies, and for them to steal is second nature."

In a few moments the same officer reappeared with Nathan Roach.

The latter strode in awkwardly, in advance, and after a step or two, hesitated and turned inquiringly towards his conductor. The officer motioned him to proceed, and he took a position in front of the chief and his companion.

While the chief wrote rapidly for a minute, the other eyed Nathan through his glasses; then, as if not satisfied with the inspection, he ducked his chin and contemplated the backwoodsman over their rims.

Nathan returned the inspection with a stolid indifference.

The chief put down his pen and turned the writing over to the other, with the remark in an undertone:

"That is about the substance of what she said."

Then, giving the newcomer his attention, he asked:

"Your name?"

" 'Pears to me yer all orto know it by now, fur ef I've told it oncet, I've told it a dozen times."

"You will have to answer, sir."

"Well—see here, mister; I'd like to know who yer is. I'm 'rested fur nuthin,' and pulled 'round from piller to post, and it's my right to know before who I'm brought and questioned."

"I am the chief of police, and as you have been arrested for having stolen property in your possession, it is my duty to question you as to how you came by it, so that if you are not the thief, you may be able to give information that will lead us to find the really guilty one."

"That's more sensible like. I ain't guilty of nuthin,' and ef I knowed who put that ring in my pocket I'd not only let yer into the secret, but I'd thrash the stuffin' outen him to boot, or my name ain't Nathan Roach."

The chief wrote down his name.

"What did you do with the medal you had?"

"Never had none."

"Never saw this before?"

"Never did—as I knows on."

"Do you know an Indian girl or woman named—named—let me see that paper, captain—named Laoni?"

"I struck up with one of that name the other day."
"How often have you met her?"
"Twicet."
"Where?"
"Canal street."
"What part of the street?"
'Blamed ef I know. It was by a store with a big winder that had a Injun in it, and that's how we got acquainted. I was lookin' and she was lookin' and I said somethin' in the Lipan talk to myself when I spied the Injun in the winder, and the gal, she's a Lipan, and she took me up right straight and, sir, we was a-talkin' Lipan for an hour. She had a sweetheart in Texis, and I promised to git news of him. We met oncet more after that, and was to meet agin in six days."

"Did you not give this medal to the girl at your last meeting by the show window?"

"Didnt't I tell yer I never seed it before?"

"Answer my question."

"Ef I never seed it before how'n thunder could I give it to anybody? Peers to me yer simple minded to ask such questions."

The chief smiled.

"This girl said you gave her the medal."

"I'll never believe she said it."

"Have you any friends or acquaintances in the city who could vouch for you?"

"Only Tip Hamilton, and he has only been here five days and I've been here seven."

The chief whispered to the captain to notice how well the prisoners had made up their story as to their arrival in the city, times of meeting, and so forth.

"But this goes against them," said the captain.

"So it does, but they have an object."

"They are part of a gypsy band, no doubt—great thieves—great thieves!" said the captain.

"So you know no one in the city?"

"There's the feller and his wife I kept from breakin' their necks by stoppin' their hosses. But they don't know nuthin' 'bout me, and ef the truth was known, care less, even ef I done 'em a favor."

"Give the name, anyway," said the chief. "He may return the favor by going on your bond."

"Halfen—Ducio Halfen is the feller's name, and George—the one that keeps the coffee house and saloon—is another name yer mought put down, although he ain't much of my stripe no more'n t'other."

"Halfen's endorsement will not have much weight in the scale of honesty," said the captain, dryly.

"But his money will in the scale of justice," said the chief.

CHAPTER LXIV.

"Stella, I have to go to that hateful police court, and so have you. Be ready, child; the summons said ten o'clock. I wish it had been the bracelet or pin instead of the ring that they found. The very cheapest thing was the first to come to light—I mean your medal. The girl must have been a fool to wear it openly. This dress is good enough for a dirty court room. Beatrice sent word that she would not be here this morning. That means she did not care to go with us. Beatrice will never suit Guy. She is too changeable. There's that hateful agent of mine crossing the street; coming here, I'll bet. Watch the hall door, child, and if the servant comes for me, say I'm out. If anything will make me marry again, it would be to get rid of agents."

Mrs. Raymond and Stella were on time at court, and were compelled to wait a few minutes before the entrance of Nathan Roach as a prisoner. His case was set to open the proceedings. The captain, with spectacles, was present and represented the State. The two policemen who made the arrest swore to the fact and stated that the ring shown in court was found in the coat pocket of the defendant. George swore that he saw Nathan hang his coat on a hook about an hour before his arrest and that no one had been in that part of the saloon between the time of hanging it there and its being taken down by the defendant. Mrs. Raymond identified the ring as one of several pieces of jewelry stolen from her rooms by burglars two nights before.

Halfen had been summoned as a witness, but not having made his appearance, the court was about to decide that it could not wait for him, when he entered the hall. He was placed upon the stand and duly sworn.

"Do you know the defendant?"

"I do."

"Have you ever seen this ring before?"

"I think not."

"Never knew of the defendant having it in his possession?"

"No, sir."

"Did he ever offer you any jewelry for sale?"

"No jewelry.
"Any other articles?"
"A medal."
"Describe it."
"A silver medal attached to bead work."
"Would you recognize the medal if it were produced here?"
"I would."
"Is this it?" asked the attorney.
'That is the medal.'

Hamilton, who was sitting by Nathan as his counsellor, had to use all of his strength to keep Nathan from springing over the short space between him and the perjurer. As it was, he gained his feet and simultaneously the word liar hissed through his teeth, while his outstretched arm and extended claw-like fingers indicated what the result would be if he could reach his traducer.

Hamilton was the sole witness for Nathan. He took the stand and outlined his acquaintance with the accused, his constant companionship with him since his arrival in the city; and even if he did not possess the honorable character with which his evidence clothed him; even if he were the criminal which circumstances and the direct evidence of Halfen seemed to make him, it was nearly impossible for him to have committed the crime of burglary without the knowledge of his constant companion.

The speech of the prosecutor was short and pointed. The case was so plain that it would be presumption to make an extended argument before the court. The web of circumstances was woven without a break in its perfection, and was made clear and definite by the testimony of a direct witness as to the possession of other property stolen on the same occasion when the missing jewelry was taken, a portion of which was discovered in a pocket of the defendant.

At the conclusion of the attorney's remarks, Hamilton requested the court's permission to represent the defendant, who was unable to employ counsel. He (the speaker) could produce the evidences of his right to plead a case in his own State, but they being inaccessible, he would have to rely upon the indulgence of the court of a sister commonwealth to take his word for it. After a few pertinent questions, the court acceded to his desire, and the Mississippian began:

"Your Honor, I have watched the progress of this case with much interest, because from its very inception—from the moment when those two well meaning policemen laid their official hands upon this defendant up to the conclusion of the testimony, I have sniffed the strong odor of a deep laid conspiracy to bring to ruin the character of their victim, and by encircling him with the meshes of the law to take away his liberty. If this be true, there is a deep set purpose, and if this purpose be not confined to narrow limits, there may be other victims to sate the appetite and cram the voracious maw of this plotting monster. It is true that the evidence is in and the argument has opened, but with the words of the prosecutor, there flashed upon my mind an incident or two which the furtherance of justice and a desire to shield the innocent demand to be looked into. I ask the consent of the court under the plea of newly discovered evidence to allow the recall of one or more witnesses to reply to questions purely germane to their direct testimony. I believe your Honor will view this request in its equitable bearings, and that the State will not interpose objections."

The court having assented, Hamilton called for the first witness.

A policeman took the stand.

"You arrested the defendant?"

"I did."

"On what species of information?"

"A paper saying that in George's saloon was a coat hanging which belonged to one of four men playing at cards. In a pocket of the coat was a piece of the jewelry which had been stolen from a house on Royal street."

"What followed?"

"I got a chum and went to the place, saw the coat and waited for a man to claim it. The one who claimed it was the defendant here. We arrested him, and on searching the pockets of the garment, found the ring now in court."

"Have you this paper?"

"Here it is," handing the paper.

"Whose writing is it?"

"That I don't know."

"Are you an expert in handwriting?"

"How?"

"In telling the same hand on different papers."

"I'm pretty good that way."

"Examine this and say what resemblance there is between it and the note you received."

"I should say the same person wrote it."

"Call the saloon-keeper—Mr. George," said Hamilton.

George, who was in hearing, came forward.

Hamilton interrogated him:

"George, who wrote that?"

"I did," was the reply.

"What is that paper?"

"It is a receipt I gave you."

"Now tell this court who wrote that."

George took the note which the policeman swore he had received as information against Nathan. His hands trembled as he regarded it and in a hesitating manner, he replied, as Hamilton confronted him sternly:

"I couldn't say, sir."

"Did you not write that and give it to a fellow who was in your saloon for a few minutes on the night of the arrest, to take to the station?"

"If I did I don't remember."

"Did you not have a talk with Halfen about that note?"

"I don't remember."

"Have you not talked with Halfen about crushing this defendant and some one else who was supposed to know a good deal about your's and his operations somewhere—on a certain island, for instance?"

The witness half rose, reddened and resumed his seat in an agitated manner.

"Answer my question."

"I don't know what you are talking about."

At this point of the proceedings Halfen rose to leave, when Hamilton asked the court to detain him as he wished to call him to the stand.

The court requested Halfen to remain.

"What does he wish with me?" asked Halfen.

"You both will know before I get through with you."

"Now, Mr. George, I wish to know if you did not see a sneaking-looking fellow at the door while we were playing cards?"

"Think I did."

"Didn't he beckon to you?"

"Perhaps he did."

"Did you not go to him?"

"I walked to the screen."

"Did not this fellow walk into the saloon after you went to the screen?"

"He might."

"Don't you know he did?"

"If he did I don't remember."

"You can stand aside. Call Mr. Halfen."

Ducio came forward.

"In your direct examination you stated that Mr. Roach, the defendant here, offered to sell you this medal?"

'I did."

"What time was that?"

"Day before yesterday, I think."

"What place?"

"On Conti street, somewhere."

"About what hour?"

"Between ten and eleven."

"Was any other person present?"

"No one."

"You may stand aside. Will the court please swear me?"

The oath was administered.

"I wish to make a statement to impeach the testimony of the witness Halfen. On the day he stated that the defendant offered him the medal for sale, on that day between the hours of ten and eleven and many blocks away from the street he names as the place where the offer was made, this dfendant and myself were in company in my quarters where I was engaged the whole morning mostly in writing letters for myself and one for the defendant. Furthermore, I will state that during the entire day, froin the hours mentioned until late bedtime, I was in company with Nathan Roach, this defendant here, and that we slept in the same room that night. I will also state that on the night of the robbery we occupied the same room, and on going to bed, there was but one vacant chair. On this the defendant spread his clothing first. I retired a little later and placed a portion of my own clothing over his. The next morning I arose first and will swear that from all appearances not an article on the chair had been disturbed."

After Hamilton concluded his testimony, he resumed his argument.

"I do not think, your Honor, that the finely woven web of the State appears so intact as it did a while ago. The alleged clearness which the direct and positive testimony imparted to its structural beauty has assumed, to the eye of reason, a decidedly muddy hue, covering with the mephistic odors of perjury the rotten structure erected by a mean conspiracy. Your Honor must have noted how the witness, George, squirmed when I questioned him as to who wrote the receipt and who wrote the note. How he swore in his direct testimony that no one had been near the hanging coat, or even into the saloon, and when cross-examined he could remember nothing. If he wrote the note he could not remember. His memory was decidedly bad concerning this villainy, but when I stirred the depths of his self-accusing conscience by allusion to another villainy committed in a distant place and wherein another witness in this case was particeps criminis, how it fell upon him like a thunder bolt of Jove and raised him nearly out of his seat; how the tell-tale color fired his cheek and his nerves became unstrung in conscious guilt. The conspiracy is plain—the ring placed in the coat by the stranger who beckoned to George; the note sent through him by George to apprise the police. The identity of the two handwritings, which must. be apparent to this court and to anyone who will give the papers but a hasty inspection, is enough to crush their scheme. It takes an expert, your Honor, to avoid the characteristics of handwriting. The uneducated and the clumsy pensman, as is this man, cannot do away, if they try, with the tell-tale peculiarities of writing. Then, to crown the pyramid of infamy erected by these unhandy plotters, comes the perjury of this wretch in human shape; this blot upon created things; this so-called man to whose name, in the eternal fitness of things, was denied the ordinary euphonies which sometimes detract from the ungainliness of personality. It is in evidence that his story here was pure fiction. I laid the predicate to catch him and he sits there impeached before a court of his country and we defy him to clear his skirts. But he has learned so many lessons in infamy that the role he played here has become the second nature to which his whole character is bent, and he has reached that depth in the abyss of moral turpitude that precludes every further movement that does not tend to the lowest deep. Your Honor, I have done with this case. I thank you for the privilege granted me to defend this man, and I believe that without one word from my lips after the cross examination of the witnesses and my own testimony, your decision would have been the same as it will be now."

The court rendered its decision at once. The defendant was admitted to bail in a nominal sum and in the meantime remanded to the custody of the sheriff with an injunction for good treatment until the same should be furnished.

Hamilton explained to Nathan the nature of the court's action and assured him that it was equivalent to an acquittal.

The backwoodsman grasped his friend's hand and thanked him for his assistance.

"Yer is a trump, Hamilton, and I shall never forgit yer talk; but Lordy, man, yer flew off inter that lingo that a feller couldn't make out the head or tail of it, but I low'd yer was givin' of 'em fits."

Nathan's first impulse when he thought himself free, was to go for the false swearing Ducio, the ingrate, who could so soon forget the service he had done him in the instance of the runaway team.

But Hamilton told him to keep cool and to leave Ducio to him and he would afford him ample opportunity for revenge. Meantime, he would get him a surety on his bond.

The case against Laoni was next called, and Nathan, who was still in court, was dumfounded to find the defendant who appeared was his Indian friend His demonstration to give her a warm salutation was checked by the officer who had her in charge. So soon as she was arraigned the State's attorney asked for a postponement of the case until the afternoon. Mrs. Raymond for the first time learned the nationality of the accused and was struck with the idea that she must be her Indian, and if that were the case she must be innocent. She requested the court to allow her to interview the prisoner, to which a gracious consent was given. The lady introduced herself as being the person who had lost the jewelry, and told Laoni that she would like to hear what statement she had to make. A long interview followed, in which Mrs. Raymond became acquainted with much of Laoni's story and recognized her as the protege of her late brother. The information that the medal was claimed as the property of the lady's niece had a depressing influence on the satisfaction which Mrs. Raymond's announced relationship to her late protector should have produced in Laoni's mind. She wondered how it could be, never suspecting that El Bravo would have willingly parted with her gift. It caused her to look with suspicion on this newly proffered friendship which might eventuate in duplicity like the hollow protestations of Ducio. It was something to have her story believed in regard to her innocence of the crime, and comforting to be assured that influence would be brought to bear to arrest further prosecution. Mrs. Raymond thought the girl was mistaken about the medal, but regarded the matter as too trivial for much consideration. Stella could well afford to relinquish the bauble which had no importance as a relic and little intrinsic value. She remained until the court reconvened, when she prevailed upon the attorney to nol pros the case. The triumphant lady took her new charge in the carriage with herself and Stella with the view of domesticating her at once at her hotel, but at the earnest request of Laoni, she left her at the gate of the Convent of the Sacred Heart.

The sounds of the carriage wheels had not died away when the door swung open to admit the girl to the holy precincts of the institution. Within such she had seen and learned all that redeemed the white man's civilization from the basest selfishness and greed, and the familiar forms, the charming quiet, the orderly appearance, the frank welcome vitalized her drooping spirits and settled upon her a feeling of content, of asylum from the pitfalls and menaces of the Christian world. Her credentials were ample to admit her to the hearts and care of the ladies of the order, whose house could be hers until she would be able to better define her future.

The next morning Laoni found herself more content. It was the day on which she was to again meet Nathan. She had little idea of seeing with him the form which most filled her mind, but the light of hope kindled by the words of her rude friend had never paled, and she felt assured that she would sometime soon see El Bravo.

On leaving the Convent gate to keep her appointment, she encountered Beatrice, who was about to enter. An immediate mutual recognition followed.

"Are you staying here?" asked Beatrice.

"For a time," replied Laoni, "and until I get a place."

"You broke your engagement with me and hired to another. Why have you quit your place so soon?"

"I was fooled. They made me believe that I was going to you when I got in the carriage."

Beatrice's interest became so aroused that she walked along by the side of Laoni while the latter gave in brief the details of her experience.

"Now that you are free from it all, will you come and stay with me as you intended?"

"You may come tomorrow morning at the Convent and I will answer."

"And now you are going to———"

"I must meet a friend. On what he tells me or on what I see and hear at the meeting will depend my coming to you."

"A lover, perhaps," thought Beatrice.

"Do not let anyone persuade you into more scrapes, Laoni. Can you depend on this friend?"

"On him! Yes, and better on one who may be with him. To meet or hear of this one is why I have to meet a friend."

"Be careful that both do not prove false. It would be a blow to find, between the two, a friend and lover, both untrue. Is one an Indian?"

"No. Both are white, but so different; both are honorable. But one is rough as the stone just from the mountain side; the other as smooth and shapely as its mate after it has left the hands of the skillful workman."

Beatrice wondered much at Laoni's words, and thought that the Ursulines had not curtailed her opportunities for acquaintance with men, nor had a Convent life dulled her manifestly acute perceptions of the rough and the polish in masculine character.

"Yet you regard both alike?"

"Both alike? Oh, no! The one I long to meet is before the world, before Walumpta, my father. Without him the light would dim to darkness; there would be no aim to live unless my life means a journey to the death which will unite us."

"He loves you?"

"He did love me; not wildly as I loved him, but yet with a love on which angels could smile. But it matters little how well I am loved, Laoni's heart can only be El Bravo's."

"El Bravo's!" thought Beatrice. "Did not I hear that before somewhere?"

"Well, Laoni," she said, "I will leave you here. I hope you will meet your—your friend; and whether you do or not, I trust you will be ready to go home with me in the morning."

Laoni's grave face did not respond to the other's smile, but, uttering a mechanical good-bye, she turned away to Canal street.

She found Nathan awaiting her, apparently in patience, as he was regarding things around him with an air of curiosity, which was none the less emphasized by a partly open mouth and hands crossed behind him under the tail of his coat.

She placed her hand lightly on his arm before he saw her.

"Thought yer'd give it up," he said.

"I am a little late. I was talking to a lady part of the way, and we walked slow."

"Well, he ain't come," was his abrupt announcement.

"No? You could not help that."

"Wish'd I could; he'd a come."

"No news?"

'Not a word. Say, did that feller Halfen do yer any dirt?"

"Any dirt?"

"Treat yer bad and——"

"He would have done so, but I escaped."

"The liar! Said I'd steal! He'll feel me yit. Yer know somethin'? We're goin' to raise him out'en his boots."

"Out of his boots?"

"Goin' to clean him up—walk through him—squelch him."

Laoni did not exactly understand the phraseology employed by her friend and remained silent and thoughtful.

Nathan continued:

"Hamilton says he's got to regorge or degorge or disgorge or sumthin' like that. He means that he's got to give up some stole money and property and so on. He's been stealin' like thunder;

and see here, miss! what he's been stealin' b'longs by rights to this young feller yer want to see so bad. Ef he thinks a lot of yer, or half as much as yer do of him, ye're certain of a pile when we git through with Halfen."

"I do not care for his money. Money seems to be the real god which is worshipped by the white people. The God of their religion condemns the worship, yet they go on setting up gold and silver above Him, while they claim to believe it to be wrong. In this the white people are two-faced."

"Ye're like me, miss; yer will spit out the truth. I tell 'em this here city life is a pore excuse. Give me a rifle, a scalpin' knife and freedom everytime."

Laoni's disappointment, though great, was borne with a natural stoicism that concealed it effectually. She gave Nathan her address, stating that if she was not at the Convent, the nuns would know where she could be found. He promised to apprise her of the arrival of Guy or of any news affecting him, which he might hear. After the good-byes the backwoodsman turned again and again to take a look at the retreating form of the girl, until she turned a corner.

"Ef ever I'd thought I'd keer that much fur a squaw! Thar's sumthin' 'bout her that makes a feller feel all-overish. Blamed ef I don't wish she didn't like that feller in Texis so powerful much. Any how, ef he ain't stuck on that gal we rescued that night, I'm the worst fooled sucker in Orleans."

Nathan heaved a little sigh, but soon forgot his sentimental strain after he caught sight of Hamilton, who was approaching from the levee.

"I can give you the news you wanted this morning, Nathan," he said.

"What news?"

"Guy Raymond will be here tomorrow or the **nex**t day."

"The dickens yer say!"

"He, Manuel Ruiz, Perry and that old jailer's daughter. I got a letter from Perry. They would have left by the schooner which brought the letter, but it had no accommodations for passengers, and on account of the lady, they waited two days for another vessel."

"We'll make Halfen howl then, fur all the triggers is fixed."

"Let's take something on the strength of it, Nathan."

"Ye're never hard up fur 'scuses to take a drink; it's yer failin'."

"But consider the occasion. Where'll we go—to George's?"

"To George's."

CHAPTER LXV.

"She is a singular girl," thought Beatrice, when she parted with Laoni. The latter's frankness impressed her favorably. Her strength of mind was apparent from her perfect self reliance. The qualities were the concomitants of character in a natural person, one untainted by the artificialism demanded by the customs of the society of civilization. The seeds of moral training, sown by the Convent teachers had fallen upon good soil. The precepts of the Christian nuns had been turned to practical use by this child of nature, and the result was a character for imitation, an embodiment whose exterior was a reflection of an interior of sincerity and truth. Laoni was a natural person. She was not more virtuous than when she clung to youthful Guy in her native village; her character was merely remodeled in the mould of a civilization which had failed to leave the impress of its blemishes. Hence she could not fail to excite the admiration of those who would behold, in practical life, the reflection of theoretical good. The gawky Nathan, the villainous Ducio, the fashionable Mrs. Raymond, the refined and beautiful Beatrice—all beheld the traits which distinguished the Indian girl; traits, however, which affected them dissimilarly. With Beatrice, the interest was heightened by something more than mere admiration—by a feeling she could not shake off, and which was akin to fascination. The ensuing morning she was impatient until she found herself out of the house and on her way to the Convent. Laoni was expecting her.

"I will not be long," she said, as she turned to go for her satchel and take leave of the sisters.

"He did not come, then?" said Beatrice, half inquiringly.

"I will tell you when we are going," replied Laoni, as she left the reception room.

She had hardly disappeared before the front door opened and Stella entered from the street.

"What! Stella?" exclaimed Beatrice.

"It is no one else. Good morning, Beatrice; you've been here since mass?"

"I've just come, and have not been to mass. Does this mean that your holiday is over?"

"Yes. Studies begin today and I would not miss them for a pretty. But what brings you to the Convent?"

"I'll tell you another time."

"I can guess."

"Guess."

"That girl."

"That is very indefinite," said Beatrice, smiling.

"You and aunt will have it."

"I can stand it."

"Have you seen her?"

"I have."

"And secured her?"

"I have."

"I find her a strange person, don't you, Beatrice?"

"Strange? Yes. To say the truth, she is an oddity. So plain and natural; so much at ease, with an expression upon her shapely features that invests her with a real beauty in contrast with her brown complexion and her Indian birth. There is a something which seems to impress me while in her presence that I have had some intercourse with her in the past, yet I know that it must be only an impression."

"It is strange about my medal. She claims it."

"It might have once been hers."

"In the Indian country?"

"Possibly. I'd give it up to her, poor thing. You set little value upon it, seeing you are no Catholic."

"But Mr. Trigg——"

"Oh! He is dead and gone and——"

Beatrice was interrupted by the entrance of Laoni, ready to go with her. Laoni regarded Stella for an instant.

"You are the young girl who was in the carriage?"

"Yes; with my aunt. Good morning."

"The medal was stolen from you?"

"It was."

"And you—you got it—from——"

"From a friend in Texas."

"I am ready to go," said Laoni, turning to Beatrice.

"Good-bye, Stella," said the latter. "Somebody will be here in a day or two, when I am fearful your studies will be interrupted."

"For a day, perhaps, for of course you will monopolize him. If you see him first, bring him right here."

The two girls, the Mexican and the Indian, walked for a time in silence, each occupied by their thoughts; how nearly similar, in regard to their object, will be left to the reader to infer. There were only a few persons in the street. A block or two ahead a crowd of boys and men were around an organ-grinder who was amusing them by the antics of a monkey.

Beatrice broke the silence:

"How about the friend you went to see on yesterday?"

"I found him waiting."

"And alone?"

"Alone."

"Did his words give you any comfort?"

"Yes. In his rough way, he fed the hope that led me to the meeting. I will not trouble him more. If he hears of anything he will know how to find me."

"If he hears of this dearer friend?"

"Of El Bravo—yes."

"Had he no other name?"

"To me he will always be El Bravo. 'Twas so I used to call him in those sweet, peaceful days when the beauty of his smile made the hills seem greener, the mountains grander as we walked in the mellow light of sunset, where the waters of our river poured over the rocky fall with a roar that could be heard beyond the village. His other name——"

"A scream from Beatrice interrupted her. They had reached the corner where the organ-grinder had installed himself in the street, and as they were about to pass, the monkey, at a sign from his master, dashed up to Beatrice, hat in hand, to beg for money. His appearance was so sudden and contact so close that she screamed from absolute fright. Laoni, seeing in the cause of her alarm a hideous but unknown form, at once interposed and dealt the animal a severe slap. The monkey recovered himself and springing at his assailant, bit her on the finger. The organ-grinder dragged his pet away by the rope just in time to save it from a crushing blow aimed at it by a queerly dressed individual, who had a little before been endeavoring to drive a trade with the monkey's master. With the failure of the blow to settle the monkey, the disappointment of the individual found vent in his peculiar language.

"I'll be dad seized ef I didn't like to wind up his persimmons. Madam is yer hurt much? Well, if it ain't you!" he exclaimed, as he met Laoni's look.

"My finger is bleeding from the bite of that ugly thing," she said.

"The pestifferous wretch! The master ain't a bit better'n the monkey, and I've a notion to jess clean him up fur paradin' a dangerons brute."

"He is not to blame," said Beatrice. "I suppose I was foolish for screaming. We are much obliged to you, sir, for coming to our rescue."

"Nary a thank, mum. I was a little hot with that ar I-talien afore yer cum up, seein' he wouldn't offer me but a picayune for this monkey jacket that I fetched all the way from Texis to sell to his perfession. It is oncommon suitabul for a monkey, and the little Mexican offiser who I took it off of looked like he mought be first cousin to one."

As Nathan said this, he drew from beneath his coat the jacket in question, still glittering with its wealth of lace and buttons.

"You would find a better market for your jacket at the pawn shops," suggested Beatrice, smiling.

"But my heart was set on seein' the monkey wear it," said Nathan, whose attention was suddenly attracted by the departure of the Italian and his monkey.

When the backswoodsman looked around again for Laoni and her companion, they had disappeared.

"Blamed ef I didn't furgit to tell her 'bout the news Hamilton got in that letter," he muttered, as he tucked the jacket under his coat and struck out down the street.

Laoni was assigned to her apartment at the Rivas home, which was adjoining the one occupied by Beatrice. The latter informed her new maid and companion that her duties would be light and that she need not concern herself about them for the day. Her necessary wants and requirements would be inquired into by her friend, and all that would be needed would be supplied. The room was neat and tidy, well, though simply, furnished and calculated, with the assurance of her new friend's protection, to make her feel as contented as circumstances would permit. As she glanced out of the window from this cozy asylum to take a survey of the vicinage she thought that here she would remain until the coming of El Bravo.

When Beatrice was alone in her room that afternoon she unlocked her little writing case and drew out a letter which had been opened. She took it from the envelope and reread it.

It was from Guy Raymond.

She looked out of the casement in a dreamy, abstracted manner, and gave full play to her thoughts.

"He will be here tomorrow, perhaps. Wonder what he will think of my Indian maid?"

Twenty-four hours' stay within the walls of the Rivas mansion had made Laoni feel that she was in the midst of a family whose characteristics filled somewhat the measure of the ideal she had formed of the people to whom Guy Raymond belonged. She began to realize that there could exist an approach to the standard of the theoretical morality of civilization in practical life. She was ready to be convinced of this at all events with further experience. These reflections possessed her mind the next day after her arrival in her new home when left alone by the absence of Beatrice on a shopping tour for her benefit, to procure those necessities deemed essential to a wardrobe becoming her newly assumed position. The day was cloudy as she entered her own apartment from that of Beatrice, and to admit more light she drew aside the curtains and threw open the front blinds. Naturally she glanced out upon the street as she lowered the sash again, and became almost transfixed at something that caught her vision. A figure so familiar, a portion of a face from under the hat brim and the owner of both passed under the veranda as he crossed directly towards the house. The powers incident to her extraction, for the moment, deserted her and she trembled with emotions of ecstacy, of doubt, as to the realism of her vision. The door to the hall was open. She stood rooted to the spot until the tinkling of the doorbell noted the presence of a caller. She stole quietly to the railing guarding the space down which extended the flight of steps and listened. The servant had already answered the bell and the words greeted her ear.

"This is the right place. I will go up and tell her that you wish to see her. Your name——"

"Just say it is one whom she is expecting. She will know."

The voice was Guy Raymond's. Laoni recognized it. She heard him say that she was expecting him. Nathan had furnished him with her address, procured at the convent. It was all so plain to her. He had just arrived and had hastened to discover her whereabouts. Was this not evidence that he loved her the same as when he sat beside her on the rock above the fall? All these thoughts required but an instant to flash through her mind, and without waiting for the servant to notify her, she hastily descended to the drawing room.

Guy, who had arrived that morning, needed no pilot to guide him to the number on Esplanade street, where dwelt Beatrice, she having fully posted him of the locality. So, after brushing up for the occasion, he very soon found himself in the Rivas' drawing room. Not anticipating a very prompt descent of his ladylove from the regions above, he did not seat himself, but stood with his back to the door by which he entered, looking at a fine oil painting over the mantel. The room was so dark that he was on the eve of deciding that it would require more light to determine its character and degree of excellence, when he heard the rustle of skirts, and turning caught in his arms the form of a woman.

"Darling!" he said. "Darling—did you know who it was?"

"You wrote you would come."

"True—but some one else might have called this morning, and this room is so dark."

"Who would call for me but you? Besides I heard your voice in the hall, and I would know that voice anywhere."

"I would never have recognized yours, my darling. It has so changed."

"Because you never heard me speak your language before."

"You forget. We often spoke it in Texas."

"Why trifle so? Or have you forgotten, in this short time, that my tongue never uttered the words of your people and that all I know of your past you told me in a language which you learned from these lips."

"What a strange delusion! Look up, Beatrice, and tell me you it is who are trifling."

"Beatrice! Beatrice—did you say?" said Laoni, drawing away from him. "Oh—El Bravo!"

"El Bravo! El Bravo? Is this a real, waking interview?" said Guy, rubbing his eyes. "That name! Her voice! English as pure as any! And in this place! This house! Expected me by letter!"

"Who are you?" he asked earnestly.

"Your darling but a moment ago," said Laoni. "Who is then your darling, since I am not? Who did you expect to meet here having a better claim to be your darling?" said Laoni passionately. Using the Lipan dialect, she continued: "I see it all now. Laoni is forgotten. El Bravo of the San Saba is lost in the person of Guy Raymond surrounded by the pretenses of civilization."

"Laoni, is it indeed you?" said Guy, drawing back the heavy curtains. "Laoni of the San Saba is as dear to me as the sister of my own blood, but your presence here, speaking my own language with an ease and culture so remarkable, has made me doubt my own senses. How came you here thus changed?"

"Are you not changed? Changes do not always appear on one side. Laoni can change as well, but she has never forgotten El Bravo. The slightest thing he gave her she has saved—some trifles he merely touched were kept as treasures. Prove to me that you have kept me in your memory if not in your heart by some slight token, if it be only to show me the medal which I gave you, and I will be content."

"The medal! It was lost or stolen, at a camp before I ever reached Bexar."

"Who did you expect to meet here in this house?"

"Miss Navarro—a lady friend of San Antonio," replied Guy, rather hesitatingly.

"A friend? A darling friend," said Laoni.

"You are my darling friend," said Guy, approaching her and putting his arm around her.

"Laoni, is Miss Navarro in the house?"

"She is not, but she will be here shortly. I had better go before she comes, as my presence may confuse you both."

"No, darling, do not go, but tell me in a few words how came you here and who has taught you our language."

"You will know soon enough. Take away your arm and I will go to find her whom you came to see."

Guy stooped over and kissed her cheek, and when he raised his head, Beatrice in street dress stood in the door, looking at them.

"This is Mr. Raymond," she said, looking sharply at Guy. "I hardly recognized you under the circumstances."

"How do you do, Beatrice? In Laoni here I found an old friend, whom I did not expect to see. It was a mutual surprise."

"I am sorry I interrupted your warm greetings, but this is my parlor and the servant stated that a gentleman was here to see me. This girl is my maid. Does Mr. Raymond still desire to see me?"

"That was the object of my coming, and there has occurred nothing to change my desire to see you.'

"Indeed!"

Laoni felt the embarrassment of her position, and without any attempt at explanation, passed out and up to her room.

"Beatrice," said Guy, "I hope you are not offended. This girl saved me from the stake."

She stood motionless regarding him.

"Go up and take off your bonnet and return to me. I have much to tell you."

"Indeed!" she said, and turning away, slowly ascended to the second story.

How long Guy waited he knew not, before a servant appeared and stated that Miss Navarro would like to be excused from seeing him that day.

CHAPTER LXVI.

Conveniently situated to the convent of the Sacred Heart was another religious institution, composed of women who had renounced the world, as constituted by the tyranny of custom, with its checkered experiences, and who devoted their time and energies to the alleviation of the ills with which a false civilization has honeycombed the social fabric. As at the convent, the members of this order of mercy were of the Roman Catholic faith. Their religious belief was, however, not obligatory from any clause in the organic law, but rather a natural resultant of the encouragement thrown out by the Catholic hierarchy for the formation of charitable institutions. In the convents, whether cloistered or not, adhesion to the Catholic doctrine was a sine qua non for admission even to novitiates. The Little Sisters of the Poor—for that was the name of the charitable order in question—were beloved and respected by the citizens, who showed them every mark of courtesy whenever their well-known habits told of their presence on the streets, on their way to the hospitals or bent upon some mission of mercy.

The morning after the incidents which closed the preceding chapter of this story, the doorbell of the house of the Little Sisters announced an early caller. The doorkeeper admitted a woman closely veiled who wished to speak with the principal. The latter soon responded, when the visitor handed her a note, which she at once read, after motioning the other to a seat.

"You think you could stand the life?" she asked of her visitor.

"Stand it! Great endurance is a part of my nature. The mother superior wrote, in that note, that I am an Indian."

"True—but I should think because of that very blood you would grow restive under restraint."

"If I grew restive you would never know it. Your faith encourages you to persevere in good deeds in spite of difficulties and privations. With me it would be a patient philosophy."

"It is true, as the superior states in her note, that we have no expressed rule that fixes our religion, and it is only by implication that we must be Catholics. We could not admit you to full membership, in the absence of all precedent, without having a consultation, and seeking the advice of the bishop. However, you are welcome, and we shall find you plenty to do as a volunteer; but to co-operate with us you will have to assume our dress."

"I thank you very much, good lady."

"Sister Agnes, you may call me. Come with me and I will provide you a dress."

"You have them ready made?"

"Oh, yes! And easy to suit. We are not so particular as to the cut and fit of our dress. We leave that to the world; service is the only consideration here."

Laoni followed Sister Agnes from the apartment, to enter upon a role which she little anticipated a few hours before.

When she regained her room after she left Guy in the parlor she began to deliberate on what appeared to be the situation of affairs between El Bravo and the young lady who had taken such an interest in her. The morning's incidents had made to her a revelation that she might have anticipated had she not been, as she was, a genuine child of nature, pure in motives, and untainted by the shadow of selfishness in her love for the boy hero who had come to her mountain home to change the whole bent of her existence. El Bravo loved her; but did his love for her stand as a bulwark to withstand the inclinations of his heart to break away and welcome attachments which his attractions must induce from the women of his own race?

Her philosophy raised the point—her good sense recognized its potency.

Beatrice's steps along the hall to her own room attracted her attention. She approached the closed door of communication and listened. Sobs came first—then words:

"Oh, that I ever loved such a man! Here, under this roof, with his paramour—and she an Indian! The impudence to go to this parlor—unasked for—and to be found in his embrace. He may take his Indian and go—and I wish him the joy that must come from such congenial company."

Laoni entered Beatrice's room.

"Lady, your words are full of injustice. If the Indian girl is of an inferior race she is the more proud that she can rise above the selfishness of the white girl. You cannot love this man more strongly that she you call his paramour. You cannot respect him so well or you would not attack his virtue from chance appearance. If I love him it is for his bravery and for a gentle modesty which the pure alone can know. Our meeting was one of the accidents of life, and if I saved him from the flames it was for himself, not for Laoni—for himself to work out a destiny, in the enjoyment of the friendships which his nobleness must attract—in the light of a love fit for virtuous manhood. If this lovelight come from your eyes and burn in your bosom. Laoni's act is as unregretted as her aim was unselfish when she scattered the fagots that would have destroyed him."

"If you are so unselfish, why did you rush to his arms when he came to see me?"

"You judge me wrong. I was told that he would seek me here."

'Who was your informant?"

"Do you remember the fellow who aimed the blow at the monkey?"

"That ragamuffin?"

'He is a noble fellow, but ignorant."

"A fit go-between. Leave me, if you please. I am sick of this talk—sick of him—and sick—of you."

"While I am sorry for your displeasure, I pity your weakness. When selfishness so narrows the mind that justice and charity are forced to retire—then there is nothing left but pity for the unfortunate."

"I scorn your pity, and insist that you take yourself away."

"It was a part of my object in entering your room to tell you that I am about to leave. What should have been a bond between us has made separation necessary."

Laoni closed her door behind her. She heard the message sent below through the servant and waited to hear the exit of Guy Raymond. She went to the veranda and watched him move slowly and dejectedly away. Her look followed him as long as it was possible to see him, and then a tear glistened in her eye as she drew down the sash and made preparations to depart. Her first destination was the Convent. Here she advised with the good Mother Superior, resulting in her determination to seek refuge with the "Little Sisters of the Poor."

Before Nathan had had an opportunity to apprise Guy Raymond that a dusky maiden was desirous to see him so soon as he arrived in the city, the latter made his unfortunate call at the Rivas home. When on the next morning he stated Laoni's wishes, Guy merely said that the interview had taken place. Disconcerted at what had happened, he thought it a good idea to utilize Nathan in discovering some inkling of the effect of the denouement of the day before. He informed him of his desire to learn if Laoni was still at the house on Esplanade street, and if not, to ascertain her present whereabouts.

"Yer goin'ter write it down?" queried Nathan.

"Oh, no!" said Guy. "You just call as if to see her as a friend, and if she is there ask her privately if she is going to remain, and if not where she is going to and that I wish to see her.'

"I see; yer wants to talk 'bout ole times. Yer mite a said as much when yer seed her."

"I saw her only for a moment and had not time to speak of it."

"Well, its nun of my bizness and I'll jess do as yer say."

Nathan started out on the trail, as be mentally expressed his mission, to find his squaw friend. He proceeded some distance in a kind of abstracted manner when he discovered that the Rivas address had entirely escaped his memory. He hesitated a moment when he realized this fact, then struck out at a rapid pace until he reached the Convent of the Sacred Heart.

Here he learned from the nuns the new address of his friend. With some inquiry he found the house of the Little Sisters, from which he saw two figures, dressed in the garb of the order, emerge and proceed down the street. He deliberated a moment as to whether he would accost these for information or enter the place at once. He concluded to pursue the latter course.

Not noticing a bell, a sister responded to his loud raps.

"Is there an Injun woman here named—named Laoni?"

"Laoni? Not that I know of, sir."

"She was here; so the lady said over at the Convent."

"Wait a moment and I will see."

The sister was soon back and announced:

"The person you inquired for just went out as you came in. She was with another sister."

"Both of 'em had on them ar dresses?"

"Yes; both dressed alike."

"She's jined, then," Nathan said half aside.

The sister was amused.

"If you go quickly you will overtake them."

Nathan took the hint and soon his long strides were conveying him at a rapid pace.

"Whew!" he said to himself. "Jined them ar folks! He's seen her an' had a row—bet a quarter. Now she's ben an' gone an' done it."

Before long his rapid gait brought him in the sight of the two forms who had left the house of the Little Sisters.

Another dilemma confronted Nathan.

Which was which? was his mental query. Both the same height and both muffled up so that their faces could not be distinguished. He followed on at a respectful distance, trying to formulate a course of procedure, when one of the two objects of his interest glided into the door of a building, while the other proceeded on.

Now, Nathan thought, he had only one to confront and he trusted that luck would make that one Laoni.

Striding along up to her side, he touched the sister on the shoulder.

"Scuse me, mum. Is you Miss Laoni?"

The startled woman gave a slight scream, and seizing each side of her projecting hood, gazed, frightened, at her accostor from between her hands.

"Scuse me, I said. Didn't mean to skeer yer."

"What do you wish, sir?"

"I see you ain't her. Kin yer tell ef the other was?"

"What other? Was who?"

"Fact—I didn't say who—Laoni, the one that jined yer today. Was that her that slipped into that door?"

"It was her; but you must wait until she comes out, as she has gone in there to see a sick person."

Nathan was rather crestfallen at this announcement. He sat down on the curb to think. It did not take many minutes to exhaust his patience.

He determined to not return from a trail so fresh as the one he was on, and vowed that he would get the information Guy wanted if he had to invade the sick chamber.

He cautiously opened the door through which he had seen the sister disappear from the street. Inside was a hall with a flight of steps on one side and two doors on the other. He tread lightly as he advanced with the cat-like movement he learned in his Indian scouts. The house was so still that it seemed to invite caution without any apparent reason for it. There was not a soul in the two lower rooms. Nathan noiselessly ascended the steps and gained the upper hall. Here he heard the soft murmur of voices, and finally located the sounds as coming from a room on his left. He listened.

"Sister this is good of you, but what you can do for me will be of no use. Nursing, anyone can do; and your time is so in demand that I feel it will be wasted on me. As for religion, I have none, although all my people are Catholics, and my uncle is a worthy priest."

"I assure you, religion does not bring me here, unless it is the religion of humanity. I myself have no faith—no Christian belief—but my heart goes out to all my fellow-creatures, especially if the hand of adversity be upon them."

"Your words are strange, sister, considering your calling, but they find an echo in my heart. The hypocrisy in religion; the gulf that separates its theory and practice, digusted me and made me worse than I would have been if I had only learned the morals which spring from the lessons of duty."

"You said that your sickness is unnatural."

"It comes from slow poison."

"Slow poison?"

"Yes. The wretch who ruined me, who owns this house has administered it under the name of tonic."

"Have you taken it lately?"

"Only yesterday I discovered it. I had a chemist to analyze it without his knowledge."

"He should suffer for it—the——"

Nathan heard the conversation up to this point, when he became aware, as well as alarmed, at the approach of steps from below. His attitude had a rather compromising appearance, although his mission was one of conscience, and without reflection, he darted into the opposite door. The apartment in which he found himself had the appearance of a private chamber of a gentleman—half study, half sitting-room. Easy chairs, a table with pitcher and glasses, shelves with books, before which curtains were partially drawn, and a lounge composed the principal objects of its furniture. A closet to the left of the mantel showed through a half open shutter a number of vials and a bottle or two. In one of the latter a pinkish fluid covered an inch from its bottom. Nathan was now apprehensive that the person might enter this room, and to prevent discovery, glided behind the curtains which veiled the book shelves. He had no sooner gained his position when from behind the curtains he saw Ducio Halfen enter. The villain drew off his coat and, taking from his pocket a large wallet, he advanced to the right side of the fireplace, and touching a spot in a panel of the sealed wall, a small door sprang open, disclosing what appeared to be an iron safe. This he opened with a key, and depositing the wallet in an inner drawer, he reclosed the hole.

"Fifty thousand dollars in bills and securities!" he said slowly. "That makes about one hundred and fifty altogether, and in good shape to get away with. I'll show Raymond, Hamilton and company that they will have nothing to get hold of; neither Halfen nor money."

Nathan grit his teeth and almost whispered:

"He means comp'ny is me."

Ducio went to the closet and took the same bottle he poured from on a former occasion, and putting a portion of the pink stuff in a glass, added water. He held it up, saying:

"If she suspected what this 'tonic' is!"

"Now to her room."

As he passed out Nathan gave a sigh of relief and when he heard him shut the door of the sick room, he strode from his position, and seizing the bottle of tonic, held it up, saying:

"Pizen, I reckon."

His next act was to put the bottle in his pocket.

Proceeding to the place where Ducio had opened the little door, he was much astonished to find no trace of one. He touched the panels in many places affecting the manner of Ducio, but no response came to his manipulations.

"I'm blamed ef he ain't a shore nuff rascal! I'll git behint the curtain and mebbe he'll do it agin, and I'll watch closer."

The Arkansian examined everything in the room, and found articles, the use of which he could not guess. The amusement served to make the time pass rapidly during Ducio's absence, which stretched out to many minutes before the noise of the opening of the opposite door indicated his return. Nathan lost no time in seeking his hiding place. The first thing which seemed to strike Ducio was the missing bottle. He looked for it in the closet. He felt certain that he had left it on the table.

"The devil!" he exclaimed. "I must find it and throw away the contents, for I believe, from her manner, she suspects that it is poison. Could I have been so absent-minded that I locked it up in the safe?"

So saying he went through the same movements to open the shutter and the safe. The bottle was not there.

"God! Could I have taken it in her room and left it there?"

Evidently frightened at this surmise, he left his safe open and hurried to Josefa's room.

Nathan, observing his opportunity, sprang to the open safe and, pulling open the drawer, he took the wallet and the other contents out and shoved them into his capacious pocket. Replacing the drawer, he was back in hiding just as Ducio reappeared.

"The d—n house is haunted, or she has got that bottle; but I will swear that I left it on this table. Hell and furies! I left the safe open."

He quickly banged the door of the safe, locked it, and then closed the wooden panel with an air of relief.

"Suppose I had gone out and left it open?" he mused aloud. "Now, I must go and make my arrangements. Financially, I am all right. The next thing is to bluff Raymond, Hamilton and company in their designs on myself. But d—n me, if I can undertsand about that bottle."

It was not until Ducio slammed the front door that Nathan issued from behind the curtain.

"He sed I was the comp'ny; wasn't wuth namin', but peers to me comp'ny is somethin' in this 'ere game."

While he spoke he drew out the late contents of the drawer, and seating himself at the table, he gave the packages a partial inspection. The wallet was the first looked over, then several envelopes were peeped into. A packet tied neatly with red tape offered so much resistance to his clumsy fingers that he concluded not to open it. What he saw proved an enigma, for Nathan never heard of bills of exchange, certificates of deposit and the like. All were replaced in his pocket and he descended to the street without having been discovered. His intention was to make his presence known and call for Laoni, but he was saved the trouble by the appearance of the new sister in the street door.

"Howdy," he said.

"Do you know me in this dress?"

"In that rig; but mebbe I'd a had to look twiet ef they hadn't tole me."

"The sisters?"

"The one that come with yer."

"You have been waiting all this time?"

"He tole me to see yer and find out whar yer staid."

"El Bravo?"

"Yes; him."

"Poor El Bravo!"

"Not so pore when I gits thru with him, ef I ain't mor'n comp'ny."

"Is he happy?"

"Ef he ain't he orto be; rich and all the gals pityin' him."

"If he wishes to see me he can find me out by asking at the Little Sisters' house on ——— street."

"I'm cocked and primed on that ar. Done ben thar. And so you jined! But see here, miss; it ain't no proper callin' for a Injun woman and a likely one like ye are. Yer will shorely pine away in this here town. It ain't wuth shucks."

The couple moved on up the street as they conversed, attracting the attention frequently of the populace. The lean, angular form of the man towering above the sombre figure of the sister, who raised her face to his to address him or to catch a fuller meaning for his odd expressions. Nathan was well satisfied with himself and this complacency was not lessened by the knowledge that in his homely coat he bore the vouchers to a fortune. The fact lent a zest to his inclination to advise his Indian friend on the plans for her future.

CHAPTER LXVII.

Beatrice's feelings in regard to the apparent unfaithfulness of her lover were not at all softened by the calm utterances of Laoni in reply to her charges and inuendoes. Her passionate nature had budded and bloomed in a Spanish atmosphere and inherited the fire of the Castillian blood. The love she bore for Guy Raymond was passion or nothing. The accidents of intercourse could not modify its volume nor change its bent. Her's was not a disposition to crush the selfishness from love and view, with unabated interest, the loved one through an altruistic lens. With Laoni, Guy's affection for another mattered little if its bestowal contributed to his happiness. The altruistic character of her regard for the youth who had awakened the dormant nobility of her simple nature, elevated her above the pitfalls which beset the course of love springing from mere sexual attraction.

Beatrice awoke on the morning following her dismissal of Guy unrefreshed and feverish from a restless night. An analysis of her mental state would have discovered a prevailing resentment whose force had a dual direction. Her first decision was that Guy should feel the share harbored for him, and under this impulse she dashed off a communication, full of cutting phrases, yet coolly and definitely expressing her determination to see him no more. The note was read over, then folded and laid upon her writing desk. She had not seen her maid since she had dismissed her in anger, but it was not long before she discovered that Laoni had not occupied her room, and that she must have left the premises the evening before. As the day wore on, Beatrice felt her heart soften towards him whose arrival she had so longed for for months, and she began to find herself forming more than one excuse for the convicting appearances which had so nettled her bosom.

She concluded to write another note.

The tenor of this later communication was radically different from the one written in the early morning. It was really apologetic for having so far misjudged him as to call forth her abrupt message through a servant. She owned to a soreness, caused from conclusions suggested by appearances that were at first glance manifestly compromising to himself, but hinted that explanations would be in order to set himself right, if he still cherished the love which he once professed.

This note she folded and laid beside the other, but taking up the first she reread it, half smiling at its stinging phrases, then opening the desk she dropped it in, mentally resolving to preserve it as a curiosity. While she was thus engaged, the house maid came in to straighten the apartment and its mistress temporarily vacated it.

Housemaids, like other women, have their quota of curiosity, but the world's experience proves that those who follow the laudable avocation of housemaid have absorbed an undue proportion of this distinguishing trait in feminine character. The maid had an inkling of the trouble that had sent the young lady to the seclusion of her chamber, dismissed the gentleman, caller, and made a vacancy in the position of lady's maid. She took in the note reading, the expression of the reader, the deposit in the desk, and the folded communication lying on its top. It was a golden opportunity. Beatrice gone, the note in reach. The maid spelled through its contents, while she pricked her ears to detect any approach. Only half satisfied, she went to the door, listened, then returning to the desk, she raised its lid and drew forth the note deposited there by Beatrice a few moments before. The girl's eyes brightened as she gleaned the import of its cutting sentences. She had not completed the reading before the sounds of footsteps alarmed her. Hastily folding the notes she raised the desk lid and dropped in the last written note. The one she had taken out of the desk she placed in full view upon its top. Satisfied that she had placed everything exactly as found, she began to ply her broom to the cadence of a low air, which it was her habit to hum.

That morning Beatrice dispatched a note to Guy Raymond. The note sent was taken from the top of the desk where she had placed it about an hour before. Her heart felt lighter as she speculated on the probable effect of her missive and she congratulated herself that the first one written was safe inside her escritoire.

Guy's reception by the woman he loved had half dazed him. He secluded himself for the next day, and when he issued from his retreat it was only to visit his sister and aunt. His steps were first directed to the Sacred Heart, where he called for Stella. With the latter he proceeded to the Rue Royale. Mrs. Raymond was never a favorite with her nephew. She so differed from his dead mother; the latter being the standard by which he gauged womanly character. It was during this call upon his aunt that he received the note from Beatrice, directed to Mrs. Raymond's lodgings. The taciturnity of the nephew had been noted by the woman of the world and her sharp-witted mind detected the change produced in Guy's manner, as he obviously recognized the handwriting of the superscription. If it were not for respect for his aunt's presence, it was doubtless from a desire for greater privacy that he consigned the note to his pocket unread.

A hope stirred within him that the mute messenger would give him consolation.

He became more communicative and his conversation drew elasticity from a lighter frame of mind.

When he was on his way back to the Convent with Stella, she suddenly asked:

"Who was your note from, brother?"

"Why?"

"Was it not from Beatrice?"

"Yes."

"And you have not read it?"

"You know I have not."

"What's the matter, brother? You have barely mentioned her."

"Let us talk of something else."

"O, Guy!"

As Stella made the latter exclamation, a sister of charity turned the corner and brushed by them. She wore the habit of the Little Sisters, and from under her long bonnet she gave the pair a searching glance.

It was Laoni, who had just quitted Nathan's escort to return to her new home. She would have accosted her friend, but the circumstance of his being in such apparently intimate relations with Stella startled even her Indian nature and produced sensations which for the moment precluded utterance of words. Guy's company was the girl who claimed the medal which he said he had lost. Was Guy Raymond untruthful? Impossible! Yet this girl was hanging upon his arm and owned the medal which she had given him.

"Was that one of the nuns?" he asked of Stella.

"Oh, no!" she replied. "They have a different dress. You saw their habit at the Convent."

"Yes; but I took little notice of it."

"She who just passed is one of the Little Sisters of the Poor. A pure Indian girl joined them this week; the same that Aunt Ida mentioned in connection with her robbery. She was found in possession of my medal. Oh! I must show you my medal; the one Mr. Trigg sent me."

"A medal? The old man mentioned it on his death bed and his words impressed me, as I was still deploring the loss of a medal of singular workmanship, which had been given to me by a very dear friend."

The two had reached the Convent gate at this point of their conversation, when Guy, whose mind was on the unopened communication from Beatrice in his pocket, excused himself to his sister, promising to call for her the next morning. He took a brisk gait down the street and, when he had turned a corner, his hand sought the note in his pocket.

Moving slowly he tore it open, then halting, he leaned against a post of an awning and in a few moments knew its contents. As he read, the warm blood colored his cheek; his hand trembled so that the paper shook like a leaf, then his arm fell listless, while the fingers crushed the missive in a clenched embrace.

His first words were uttered in a faltering voice:

"Was it love, or infatuation? Can she be worthy who could write this stinging note, even with provocation?"

He summoned to his support his calm philosophy.

Beatrice had manifested noble traits which had commanded his admiration and inspired his love. He imagined she owned a force of character which fortified her against hasty judgments. But here, in his hand, was evidence of a morbid sensibility capable of multiplying the woes of life from the mere appearances of wrong. Yet, could there be love without more or less selfishness permeating its sensuous labyrinths? Any other love must be purely altruistic, and had this latter love any existence? His mental inquiry was answered by a mental picture. There were the outlines of a mountain, upon whose side a female figure waved her hand to a receding horseman. A little sigh escaped Guy's lips as his heart, sore with disappointment, was touched with a tender memory of one true devotion which, although never requited, yet burned with steady and undiminished flame. Lost in his reflections, he passed the portals of the institution of the Little Sisters. One of the inmates lingered upon the porch, watching him with interest. As he passed, she followed him with her eyes, while in low, familiar tones, she said:

"Oh, El Bravo! You, too, are sad."

The night following Guy's receipt of Beatrice's note, George's cafe had its accustomed quota of frequenters, who had gathered at early lamplight to spend their small change in drinking or amusement, or to lounge in the front, entertained by some news peddler from among the denizens of the city, or listening to a yarn spun by a loquacious sailor, or longshoreman.

Within the bar, George was just resting from an active dispensation of drinkables, when a young man entered from an inner side door and approaching him, said, in an undertone:

"They want you in there;" at the same time motioning with his head in the direction of the door which had admitted him.

George made no reply, but followed the messenger. They both disappeared through the side door. The room they entered was a private apartment, maintained for purposes which would not admit of the general presence of the public.

Around a table were several familiar faces. Guy sat facing the door; on his right Hamilton posed, with an elbow on the table, while his fingers combed the wavy locks about his brow. On the left Manuel Ruiz sat upright, with an easy grace, in contrast with the ungainly make-up of Nathan Roach, who bestrode a chair, while his elbows rested upon its back to support the bony chin enclosed within his palms. Perry came in with the ex-pirate.

Hamilton spoke:

"Mr. George, is Halfen in the city?"

"I don't think he has left."

"Where can he be found?"

"He has several hiding places, but I think he is generally at No.—— Custom House street.'

"That's the place I spoke to you about," said Hamilton, addressing Guy.

"He comes here often, does he not?" continued the Mississippian, with the intonation of a cross-examiner of a witness.

"Not often now, but I expect him tonight."

Hamilton leaned over to Nathan and whispered something.

A gleam of intelligence illumined for an instant the features of the latter, as he arose and spoke aside to George in a tone that did not reach the ears of the others.

In another moment he resumed his seat, giving a nod to Hamilton.

The latter again interrogated the witness:

"You are ready to carry out all you promised in this matter we have against Ducio Halfen?"

"I am, with the understanding that you gentlemen are to protect me as you promised."

"We are pledged," replied Hamilton.

"That's what we are," exclaimed Nathan, stretching his legs and clasping his hands behind his head. "We ain't arter yer scalp."

George was here dismissed.

"Now, Mr. Roach," said Guy, "what is it that you have to show?"

Nathan cleared his throat and, rising, ran his hand into his deep pocket, from which he drew the prizes he captured in Ducio's room.

"What's in the bottle?" asked Ruiz, smiling at Nathan's manner.

"Pizen, I reckon. It's what he's feedin' his wife on."

Guy and Hamilton began to inspect the contents of the packages and envelopes, and as they progressed they would hold up their discoveries and pass remarks upon the evidence which each mutely proffered of Ducio's villainy, or of his preparations to depart.

"This is a haul you've made, Mr. Roach, and no mistake," said Guy.

"Who would have guessed such shrewdness lurked beneath an exterior so verdant!" exclaimed Hamilton.

"Yes," responded Nathan; "comp'ny done it all. Peers to me comp'ny is the biggest part of the bizness."

"What about the key of that safe, Mr. Roach?" asked Hamilton, gravely imitating Guy in mistering the backwoodsman.

"Yer seen me talk to him when yer give me the sign. Well, he sed he'll shore git it tonight ef Halfen comes."

Ruiz wondered how he would manage that.

"Steal it; steal it," suggested Nathan. "Thief to ketch a thief."

"Well, what is to be the program?" asked Hamilton.

"As you are a lawyer," said Guy, "let us hear from you. You are leading counsel in the case."

"Well, let us see. We must find the will. I will name the proceedings in their order:

"A search warrant; arrest, if he can be found; examination of his house; examination of his safe, if the key is to be had; dying declaration of his wife or companion.

"If we progress this far, other steps will suggest themselves as the case will unfold. An inventory of these papers and documents should be made and deposited for safe keeping, and then we can adjourn this meeting until some hour tomorrow, when we will be in possession of the search warrant and, possibly, the key, which George has agreed to produce."

An hour later the friends separated for their lodgings.

CHAPTER LXVIII.

Josefa still lingered in her sick room. The Little Sisters had supplied her with the necessary attendance, which Ducio had failed to provide. Laoni was the most frequent watcher by her side. The day after she had encountered Guy and Stella arm in arm, she found her patient much worse, and became convinced that the end was near.

There were times, lasting for minutes, in which her mind was clear and her pain would subside. In one of these intervals she requested her attendant to summon the druggist who had been preparing the tonic which she had been taking.

The errand was soon performed and the druggist of the vicinage stood by her bedside.

"You have prepared the tonic which Mr. Halfen has been getting for me?" Josefa asked.

"I have, madame."

"What is the dose?'

"Ten drops."

"Could more be taken?"

"It could be increased gradually."

"What would be the effect of the tonic if administered from the beginning in doses of a tablespoonfull, more or less, three times a day?"

"It would act like a slow poison."

"If one should so take it for two months?"

"It would be a powerful constitution that could withstand it so long."

"Then I must have a powerful constitution, for I have taken it in such doses for sixty days."

"The directions were plainly given."

"And he understood them. Oh, that villain!"

Josefa here passed into a semi-conscious state, muttering words incoherent or unintelligible.

"Sister," said the druggist, "this Madame Halfen, where does she come from?"

"She says that she is a Mexican, and came here from San Antonio, in Texas "

"Her maiden name was———?"

"I do not know it—more than Josefa; that is what he calls her."

"Josefa de la Torre! It must be the same. She is wasted, but the voice I cannot forget. Poor Josefa! Sister, I was once her father's secretary, and knew her when———"

Confused sounds in the hall interrupted any further homily on the part of the druggist, and Laoni, on opening the door, was confronted by Nathan and a stranger.

"You here?" exclaimed Nathan.

"Yes; it is my watch," she replied.

"Still stickin' to 'em."

"What do you mean?"

"Thort yer'd a tired of 'em and that audacious riggin' afore now."

"Who is with you, and what is wanted?"

"This feller is a offisser and has a serch warrant to 'low us to ransack that room or any other place in this here house."

Laoni saw Guy Raymond among the others in the hall, and immediately turned towards the sick bed to avoid being recognized.

The party took possession of Ducio's sanctum; the druggist took his departure and the volunteer sister was left alone with her charge.

Josefa again rallied, and fixing her clear, dark eyes upon her attendant, inquired for the druggist.

"He has gone," said Laoni.

"I never saw him before, yet his voice is so familiar."

"Laoni," she continued, "I wish to make a dying declaration. I am nearly gone and I want to leave behind me evidence that will avenge me upon my destroyer."

"You are too weak now. Don't think of it."

"But I will be no stronger; this gradual sinking makes me weaker with time."

"I will tell your wish to parties now in the house, who are searching for something in his room."

Has it gone that far? I expected it. Ducio's career of crime will not last much longer than the life he has wrecked."

* * * *

A week has passed. In that short space much has transpired affecting the actors in this now closing narrative.

Josefa died the second day after the execution of the search warrant, in the full possession of her mind. She was surrounded by kind and pitying faces, among whom were Linda and her husband, Manual Ruiz. Nathan also was in the room, visibly affected. Beside her was a priest of the Roman church. His benevolent features seemed better fitted for the smile which one could not fail to observe must often deepen the dimples of his cheek, than for the troubled, anxious expression which clouded them. The reverend attendant was Father Ignacio. His hope, when he received the summons to come to his sister's wayward child, was to reclaim her soul at the last moment. But Josefa died as she had lived—a skeptic, refusing the last holy rites at the hands of her uncle. Laoni looked on mutely at the efforts to overcome the unbelief of the niece, the good Father little suspecting that the sisters' garb draped a personality animated by a mind equally skeptical. Indeed, he frequently called the sister to his aid when he wished to impress upon Josefa the necessity of faith and repentance. But Laoni, silent, merely bent her head, sorrier for the anxious uncle than for the dying niece, who, she believed, had suffered enough to more than balance the pains of the alleged purgatory.

Guy and Hamilton were not present, but armed with the last declaration of Josefa, they were working to prevent the escape of Ducio from the city. The search warrant had placed Guy in possession of Mr. Trigg's will, which was found in the safe from which Nathan had abstracted the papers. But the wily Ducio had eluded their traps and, rumor stated that he had fled to Texas.

Mrs. Raymond took exceptions to Guy's neglectful treatment, as she termed it, of herself, he having called upon her but once, and whisked off to her plantation. She did not forgive Beatrice for daring to employ the Indian girl, and when she went to say good-bye to Stella, she remarked that her brother and the Mexican girl were about on a par and well matched.

But Beatrice! What of Beatrice!

For days after sending her note to Guy she had waited his expected coming to effect the reconciliation, which her communication was intended to make more than probable. But her lover came not, and she became convinced that he had never truly loved her, if the memory of the unfortunate episode at their meeting could not be effaced by the conciliatory and almost apologetic tone of her writing. Keen disappointment was followed by depressing, relentless, heartache as the dragging hours multiplied and yet he stayed. Wretchedness and humiliation succeeded, and would have leveled her to the dust had not pride come to relieve with its bouyant, if not remedial results. In a frame of mind that may be depicted from her woful experience, Beatrice came face to face with the priest of San Fernando.

"Beatrice! Hija mia," were his first words.

"Father! you here?" was her reply as she placed her hand in that of the priest.

"You have not heard? Josefa is dead. I came in time to see her pass away."

"I knew she was in the city, but her false step was a bar to our intercourse. Of course I could not recognize her."

"We are all sinners in our own peculiar way, my child. Josefa made a mistake—a great mistake—in fact, her whole life was a mistake; but she had some good traits," pleaded Father Ignacio.

"Mistake—mistake—" repeated Beatrice, absent-mindedly. "Yes, I made a mistake."

"You? You have made one? What mistake, hija?"

"True! We were speaking of Josefa," said Beatrice, recovering from her abstraction. "With the loss of virtue, what is woman?"

"Yet," said the priest, "the Master never uttered a more fitting rebuke than when he spoke the words 'Let him who hath no sin cast the first stone at her.'"

"No one is perfect," said Beatrice, only half addressing the father. "Not even he."

"Halfen perfect! The question should be, has he a redeeming trait?"

Beatrice blushed as she comprehended Father Ignacio's misinterpretation of her allusion to Guy.

"Tell me, father, when do you return to Texas?"

"The day after tomorrow, if nothing happens to prevent."

"I will go with you."

"You?"

"Yes—I must—I will."

"But, hija, I go by Red river; a long and tedious way."

"It matters not. I must go, and I prefer your company."

"Well, hija, if you will; but let us walk; I am going to the Convent, and you?"

"To the same place."

As the priest and lady turned to move away, the eyes of a couple across the street followed them, as if they were recognized. The couple were not observed by Beatrice nor her escort, or the former would have recognized the man to be her deliverer from the monkey's assault, and the woman as her late maid and probable rival.

"Ef that aint' the Saint Antone priest!" exclaimed Nathan.

"The other is Miss Navarro," said Laoni.

"Yer don't know the preacher, then?"

"He is a priest, from his dress."

"Yaas, that's so; his name's Father Nash-sho, and he's sho' a fren' to Guy Raymond."

"Is the name Ignacio?"

"That's what I sed."

"He took my part today."

"How?"

"You see I no longer wear the Sisters' dress."

"Yaas, I was a-goin' to ask yer. Yer've quit 'em?"

"The bishop told the sisters that he could not allow me to be one of them—even in name."

"Not 'low yer? He's got the say-so?"

"He was shocked at my lack of religion."

"So yer ain't got nun?"

"I have plenty of religion, but I have not, it seems, the faith in all their mysteries and miracles which they consider necessary for a person to have, to escape punishment in eternal fire."

"It's a hot place, they say," said Nathan seriously.

"So the bishop, who is probably a good man in spite of his bigotry, insisted I must put off the dress and be not allowed to assist them in their good work."

"Well, it's better fur ye," said Nathan consolingly.

"And it seems," continued Laoni, "that this Father Ignacio, who heard the bishop's order, interceded for me."

"Jes' like him—jes' like him; he almos' fit the night we took out Mr. Raymond. An' the bishop wouldn't lissen?"

"No, he feared I might do harm."

"Well, yer better off. Yer shan't want a frien's long as Nathan Roach's got the wherewith. Go back to Texis with me. I'm goin' to stay home a day in Arkinsaw, an' then I pitches out fur Texis and liberty. I'll interdoose yer to my ole mother. I've got hosses and saddles, and Mister Raymond's ben liberal fur what I've done, an' I ain't pore by a jugfull. So, Miss Laoni, come, an' I'll fight fur ye an' die fur ye, ef it comes to the scratch; an' there ain't a man that kin stan' an' charge Nathan Roach with cowardice an' not stickin' to a promiss."

"Thanks—many thanks, my friend. I will think it over. I am going to say good-bye to the Sisters, and I did hope to see another one who is dear to me—but it may be better that I do not."

Laoni's face looked graver.

"Is it him—El Bravo?"

"Oh! *You* remember."

"Yaas; yer talked 'bout him so purty befo' he come over."

"I will speak well of him still. If I loved him, it was not on condition that he should think well of me. I loved him for his beauty, for his bravery, for the noble words that flowed from his lips and sounded more musical than the leaping, laughing waters of our village fall."

"Has yer seen him?"

"Once; for some minutes."

"And ben here so long?"

"But so busy."

"'Scusin' of him?"

"But it is a fact."

"I'll see him."

"Not a word, Nathan—or I will answer you now about the trip to Texas."

"An' say?"
"No."
"Then I'm dumb."

The two had been walking during this dialogue, and having now arrived opposite the house of the Little Sisters, Laoni bid her friend good-bye, for the present, and entered the place.

* *

Nathan's destination was the lodgings of his friend and benefactor to whom he had alluded as having been so liberal. As his call was by appointment, Guy was expecting him, and while waiting for Nathan's appearance had been discussing with Manuel Ruiz and Linda the future movements of the party. Guy's heart was heavy from the result of his meeting with Beatrice, but it made him all the more assiduous in the duties which applied to his business affairs, as increased activity in any direction would tend to lessen the heavy weight of disappointment which his sweetheart's reception had created, and which her subsequent communication intensified.

He had been urging the bridal couple to accompany him to New York, where his purpose was to inaugurate an emigration movement to the young nation whose star of existence had just risen above the horizon of revolution. Manuel hinted that his friend should make the trip his own bridal tour, in which event he would not suffer from the selfishness of his and Linda's cooing. But Guy, without divulging his trouble, gave him to understand that obstacles, more or less serious, prevented such a consummation.

"We called twice, but failed to see her," said Manuel, alluding to Beatrice.

Guy avoided the subject, and was relieved by the announcement that Nathan was below.

He remained for quite a time in conference with his caller, and, before finally dismissing him, walked by his side for a short distance on the banquette. Nathan seemed to be very grateful, for he said:

"I'm more'n thankful fur this. I never calkerlated on so much."

"You have paid me in services; it is your due," said Guy, earnestly.

"An' Mr. Hamilton—is yer settled with him?"

"No; he left last night for his home in Mississippi, having received a hasty summons. I will take care of his interests though, and notify him by letter."

"Oh! I knowed yer would. I was jes' thinkin' what a pile he

must 'a' got, seein' how fine yer done with me. Perry's gone, too."

"I have half way adopted Perry. He was such a favorite of Mr. Trigg. I sent him to Texas on business."

"All a-goin," said Nathan, with a sigh.

'And you, Nathan—will you leave shortly?"

"Shortly? I'll make a straight streak from here tomorrer; and who do yer think is goin' with me?"

"I am at a loss to answer."

"Somebody that thinks a powerful sight of you."

"Of me?"

"Yaas," said Nathan, with a grin, and watching Guy's face.

"It cannot be Beatrice," thought Guy, rather worried. "I will have to give up," he said, finally.

"Why, Laoni."

"Laoni!" exclaimed Guy, stopping short. "Has she not joined the Sisters of Charity?"

"Yaas," replied the other, "but the bishop put her out 'cause why she couldn't swaller their mirrowcles—an'—lemme see—an' didn't have no faith—that's what she sed."

"Faithful to her first impressions," thought Guy. "My first lessons are bearing fruit that may make her lot a hard one."

"She is going with you—where?" he asked of Nathan.

"To Arkinsaw; then, after a day or so, to Texis."

"Well, Nathan, I can trust you," said Guy, pulling out his pocketbook. "Here is a check on the bank, intended for Laoni. Draw the money and use it for her benefit as long as she is with you. Should you part, then give to her what remains unspent. Guard her as the apple of your eye and never leave her until she is with friends. Whatever of expense you may suffer, or trouble you may experience in her cause, I will repay and reward you for. To her I owe my life."

Guy paused, then said aside:

"To her I owe the loss of—Beatrice."

"Mister Raymond, yer kin trust Nathan Roach. He ain't skeered of a Injun or a white, that walks the yearth. I'd give a purty ef Laoni thort as much of me as she does of El Bravo—as she calls yer."

Guy started—at the old name. It brought up so many thoughts connected with that brave, true child of nature—faultless and loving Laoni.

Giving the backwoodsman some instructions about the check and the amount, Guy bade him good-bye and turned back to his lodgings, sadder than when he left them.

CHAPTER LXIX.

Reader, if it has been your fortune to breathe the atmosphere of the isothermal belt which traverses the rolling uplands of Texas and winds in and out the lesser ranges of the mountains, during that enchanting period that intervenes between the first chilling winds of the ides of October and the more defined norther which ushers in the last month of the year, you doubtless will recall the balmy air, laden with a bracing odor, that mingles its viewless fragrance with the waves of heat ascending from the cooling earth. The smoky line, bounding the view, lends density to the shadows, which a low descending sun causes wood or mountain to form along its eastern base. There is barely a touch of autumn in this southern picture. Verdure still lingers with scarce a paling leaf to indicate the season. Yet he to the manor born, though waking from a Rip Van Winkle slumber, would take in the familiar view as the product of a Texas Indian summer.

It was such an afternoon as this, about ten months succeeding the incidents related in the preceding chapter, when the blue hills and the head waters of the San Saba overlooked a more than ever charming view of tableland and prairie, with mottes of timber nestling in a bed of mist to the westward, while in the east they here and there stood inverted by the mirage. The valley of the village where Walumpta ruled was just the same, except a noticeable change in the reconstruction of the huts and dwellings which succeeded their destruction by the Rangers at the time they raided the Indians' nest and captured Laoni. The grand mountain stood sentry, still as familiar to the view as when Guy Raymond looked back to catch the last parting signals from the faithful girl.

On the eastern hills which girded the valley the zig-zag path crossed to the outer plain, still impeded by rock or tree trunk. Here, on this afternoon, near the very spot where Guy and Pedro replaced the fallen deer upon the latter's pony, the self-same Pedro and Chicha, his spouse, were in conversation. The former was squatting prone upon the ground, rolling a cigareta, while the squaw lay full length, with her head resting upon a hand supported by her elbow. Between them was a pile of meat, whose character was indicated by a fresh buffalo calf skin that was all of a heap near Chicha's feet.

"You are a lazy squaw, Chicha. This is the third time you have rested in a mile, and that skin does not weigh a quarter as much as these cuts of meat," said Pedro, between the puffs from his freshly lighted cigareta.

"But you are stronger, and don't tire so quick," remonstrated Chicha.

"Strange talk, for a squaw!" replied her lord. "I have spoiled you, Chicha. If I had been a pure Indian you would be my drudge and would have both skin and meat to pack. Your braves don't work. My Mexican raising has left a soft spot for women, and therefore you are rotten spoiled."

"But you are always mad if your tortillas are not hot, and an Indian would not care," retorted Chicha.

"Very well. I'll take cold tortillas, then, without a grumble, but you must pack brushwood and water and carry this meat. From now on I'm an Indian husband."

"I'll tell Laoni of this," she replied, "and she will not brag on you so much."

"Laoni! She is no longer Indian nor anything but American. Even Walumpta is almost heartbroken at the change. And then she has no talk any more for El Bravo, but shakes her head and casts down her eyes, as if for shame that she has forgotten him, when one speaks his name."

"That's where you are a fool. To have few words shows that she has a heart for him, and her eyes go down in sorrow that he is away."

"A woman is so wise—in her own mind. Can't you see she loves that ugly fellow who came back with her? He went yesterday out on some sort of a scout, and she is now at the foot of the hills watching for his return. She must love him—but truly, not for his beauty."

"Maybe it's the scout he's on that makes her watch, to hear his report," suggested Chicha.

"Your wisdom will kill you yet, if laziness don't get ahead of it. Come; shoulder the hide. The sun is nearly gone."

"And the meat—must I pack it, too?"

"No; but remember my tortillas—they must be hot. Wait, Chicha, here comes Laoni. Let her pass—but not a word to her about the water and brushwood."

Laoni was really at hand. She approached mounted upon a spirited pony, with side-saddle and ornamented bridle, which looked remarkably un-Indian. Her dress was a mixture. The corsage and skirt were American, the latter short, however, revealing the fine texture of her mocassin, while her dainty Indian cap surmounted the black tresses which fell in a plait down her back. Her face wore an anxious, thoughtful expression, while she turned more than once to glance across the country or to address a word to an Indian youth who, also mounted, followed in the rear. Pedro greeted her.

"What, Pedro! Overloaded? You and Chicha both look tired. Wallah will take the hide from Chicha, and then the meat divided will be light for each."

Wallah, the Indian youth, reached for the hide with just an audible grunt that might have meant a deal interpreted, while Chicha indexed her satisfaction in her features.

"I know Pedro is good, and will not overburden you," Laoni continued, addressing the squaw. Then turning to Pedro, she said:

"Hasten to the village, good Pedro. I have something for you to do, and the sun is now behind the western hills."

"Did you see him coming?" asked Pedro.

"Nathan? No; he had to cross the mountains, and will come by the canon. He sent Wallah here to say as much."

Pedro's look indicated that he was puzzled as Laoni left them at a sharp canter. He knew that something was troubling the daughter of the chief, and that the ungainly Nathan had been dispatched on some mission. Something must have happened while he was on the hunt, and he was keen to meet his appointment with Laoni to satisfy his curiosity. He questioned Wallah, but he would not admit that he knew more than what had just been revealed. He had ridden with Nathan blindly and had returned with the news of his having crossed the mountains and by what way he would return.

* * * *

In order to explain Laoni's anxiety and the character of the mission on which she had dispatched Nathan Roach, it will be necessary to revert to the incidents of the day before and to indulge in a glimpse of retrospection.

The visit to Arkansas had been performed and Nathan, true to his program, remained a very short time in his backwoods home. In company with Laoni he made his way to Alexandria where, through the munificence of Guy Raymond, he was enabled to procure a complete outfit of light wagon and team, two saddle horses and supplies for their subsistence. Laoni added some substantial presents for her father and some of his friends, besides many trinkets calculated to please the squaws of the village. Thus equipped they set out for their destination, where they arrived after many days, which were not devoid of the perils incident to travel through a wild territory. Nathan was in his element however, and Laoni had not lost her Indian constitution amid the seductive elements of white civilization. They therefore enjoyed a trip through haunts where nature ruled unrestrained by human artifice, and when the village was reached, regret was only on the side of Nathan, who thought he would like it to last forever. Walumpta was overjoyed to see his child alive and well, but was jealous of an obvious change in manner, heightened by the metamorphosis in her costume. The effect of the presents which she brought somewhat counteracted this feeling in the chief and certain Indians, while the trinkets for the squaws gave them a day of unalloyed happiness. Nathan was depicted as a white brave commissioned by El Bravo to protect and escort her to her friends, and to be indefinitely subject to her commands. The first part of Guy's injunction was generally commended, but the Indians considered Nathan's mission ended with her safe return. The months which followed gave to the one a perpetual round of the pleasures of frontier life, while Laoni, not free from brooding over the past, and apprehensive for her future, employed her time in studying the interests of her tribe and trying to impress her father with the importance of those economies calculated to secure a more general prosperity to his people. Nathan's simple nature was easily satisfied with his surroundings, and but one thing troubled him.

He loved Laoni.

She had given him kindness—friendship—but there had never been a look of love.

He had never broached his passion save by simple acts and a devotion which she fully prized.

The day she sent him on a mission his reserve broke down, and Nathan departed a confessed lover.

That day Laoni was in her lodge, resting from an early ramble on the mountain, when Wallah, an Indian youth faithful to her interests, tipped softly into her presence.

She looked up with a question on her features.

"There is trouble in the village," he said, softly.

"Trouble?" repeated Laoni. "Explain."

"A scout came in when the morning broke and brought a letter, which he kept hid, but which I chanced to see. I heard your name, then several of the leaders led him to the council room. I followed, and creeping through the opening just behind the screen, I listened to their words. The braves were troubled. It seems the scout was out two days from Bexar and came upon a camp of white men, which he boldly entered. He was surprised to find one who could speak the words of our tribe, and found him to be El Bravo, whose life you saved. All went well and El Bravo gave him presents, and feasted him and gave him a letter to fetch to you."

"El Bravo sent me a letter!"

"Hold; a word more. The scout promised to put it in your hands, but that night, when he was prepared to leave, two Mexicans—teamsters, for there are some wagons—while talking by their camp fire, spoke of this valley and the mine, and he found that here they are coming with tools to go upon our mountain and work the mine—that I, a Lipan, am forbid to see. The scout, alarmed, slipped from their camp and hastened here, and now they have your letter and the news, which means death to the coming white men."

"Who has my letter?" exclaimed Laoni, rising.

"Be quiet, Laoni; it will be worse if they know you have the secret. For then a warning to the strangers may go too late."

"Wise Wallah! Your words are true. Oh! If I could see his letter—El Bravo's letter—to Laoni. He coming! Shall I warn him? If I do he will turn back—and I not see him. If I do not warn him—Oh! Then—there will be a battle—and he may be killed —dead to Laoni—but also dead—to her. If he could be taken prisoner and brought here—I could save him. But would he stay—stay here with Laoni—away from her? Oh—that I had a friend to advise me! Wallah! Where is Nathan?"

"Just back from a hunt. He has killed enough game for the whole village."

"Tell him Laoni wants him; be quick, Wallah; tell him to come at once.'

"A message that will give him light heels," Wallah said as he hastened out.

"Poor, simple Nathan!" mused Laoni. "He loves me, and has been faithful to his promise to El Bravo; but the same cruel fate which builds the wall between El Bravo and myself has raised the barrier that parts me from this faithful heart. Here he comes."

Nathan entered with a look of inquiry.

"You sent for me?" he said, in Lipan.

"Speak English, Nathan; what we say the walls must not understand."

"Well, what is it?"

Laoni related to him rapidly the intelligence brought by the scout; the fact that the council had it under consideration; the danger such an expedition must incur, when the sworn policy of the tribe was to suppress the knowledge of the existence of the mine; the certain fate which must await Guy Raymond in the event of his capture, should he have divulged the secret. Everything was discussed until Nathan was fully posted on the situation.

He stood mutely pondering its gravity.

"Have you no words for me?" she asked.

"A few," he replied.

"Well?"

"Turn 'em back, ef they'll go; or ef not, warn 'em of the risk, and ef they come anyhow, let it be with permission or a fight."

"Will you go to him, Nathan?"

"I'll go to the crowd."

"To these men?"

"Yaas."

"Now?"

"Right off."

"How will I ever repay you, dear, good Nathan?"

"Pay me?"

"Reward you for your kindness."

"Laoni, I promised to perteet yer, and outside er that, I'd do it anyhow, fur you have put a spell on me that I can't break. The only pay that would hit the mark is to tell me that, when I git worthy, yer will give me yerself and let me perteet yer till death. I'd have a better right then to keer fur yer."

"It would be poor pay, Nathan."

"Why, if it suits me? Yer love Guy Raymond; what good will it do yer when he marries that gal in San Antone?"

"Nathan, dear Nathan; save him for my sake. I do love him, but if he marries—Nathan—then—if you still love this poor girl, and have still a wish to make me your wife I will not say no. Laoni should not live in vain, and will not if by her sacrifice she makes one heart happy."

"Dear Laoni!" exclaimed Nathan, advancing a step.

"Let us be moving," she said, raising her hand deprecatingly. "Go, Nathan; ride my Eagle, and do not spare him. Find these men and tell them of their danger. Tell El Bravo if he comes to come alone and no harm will befall him; but to come in force, even with no intention to touch the mine, will now be dangerous. Take Wallah with you, for you may have need of a messenger."

"Yer purty good on a plan, Laoni, but when it comes to foolin' injuns, then Nathan's some hisself. Trust me with the warnin' of 'em. But ef tomorrow night, at furthest, a crowd goes out, it's to meet these fellers, and they'll go on news from scouts, fur I'll lay a dozen of 'em has been put on the trail of El Bravo and his layout.

Ef Wallah goes, who will yer git to spy?"

"There is Pedro."

"Yaas, Pedro, but he's stupid"

"But willing."

"Well, I'm off. Good-bye, my gal," and Nathan's leave taking would have been more affectionate, but Laoni's hand went up again, and he satisfied himself by throwing his sentiment into a lingering glance as he backed out of her presence.

It was late when Pedro presented himself at Laoni's lodge to keep his appointment, made that afternoon while she was returning from a survey of the prairie in the hope of catching a glimpse of Nathan returning from his mission.

Pedro had been her first medium through whom she had communicated with Guy when he came a prisoner to the village, and this fact formed a major portion of the sentiment which made him a favorite. Her preference won his fidelity to her interests. She therefore, had no difficulty in enlisting him in any service.

"Why did you not come earlier?" inquired Laoni

"For good reasons," replied Pedro.

"Let me hear them, good Pedro."

"Your lodge was watched, and I waited until the young moon went down."

"My lodge watched?"

"A report is in the village that you are sending news to the white men, and that a letter is here from them to you. The council has been together all day, and they would give a hundred buffalo skins to know what the writing means."

"If they will bring it to me I will tell them every word. The letter is from El Bravo."

"El Bravo?"

"El Bravo."

"But there are others with him; and, Laoni, they say he has told them the secret of the mountain."

"Go, Pedro, and learn if the council is still together. Spy into what they say and do and when you are satisfied on what they have decided, come at once and tell me. They will not suspect that your stupid look hides a world of cunning."

Pedro leisurely left the lodge.

"His movements would not surely cause one to think well of his cunning," said Laoni, turning from a lingering look at the receding form of the Mexican.

"Watching me!" she continued. "Watching the daughter of Walumpta! This secret of the mine has come to be a deep-seated superstition, when it might be used to benefit the tribe. Here comes Wallah. Perhaps he has news for me."

The young Indian made his entrance in a quick, nervous manner.

"You have news, Wallah?"

"News, and strange news."

"Strange?"

"The council is closed, and a message is to be sent to El Bravo and his friends to come to this village and be the guests of the Lipans."

"Is there no treachery behind this strange invitation, when it is believed that they come to work the mine?"

"That is with the council," replied Wallah. "The braves are not called together, and only four spies have left the village."

"And El Bravo's letter to Laoni?"

Wallah shrugged his shoulders.

"And why watch this lodge?"

Wallah looked surprised.

"Pedro said it," asserted Laoni, in reply to his look.

"To see who belongs to your council," suggested Wallah, with a half humorous grunt.

Laoni walked excitedly to and fro for a moment, then said:

"Go, Wallah! Tell Walumpta, my father, to come to Laoni. If El Bravo is in danger I will know it, and I will know if the daughter of the chief cannot be trusted to receive a letter from one who is dearer to her than life."

CHAPTER LXX.

The rugged sides of a canon overhung a spring, which bubbled from beneath a boulder, and sent a current of limpid water through torturous turns until it expanded into a pebbled basin, then distributed itself into the shining quicksands, some yards further on, at the mouth of the gorge. Here a flood of golden sunbeams came across the unbroken prairie lighting the hillsides, in contrast with the deep shadows cast, by the western acclivity around the precincts of the spring and toning down the snow-white canvas that surmounted the wagons of some campers, whose animals were drinking at the basin or browsing near at hand. There must have been a dozen or more of individuals belonging to the party which had selected the well known place as a proper camp in which to rest after the fatigue incident to an all day travel over a country whose roads were no more than horse trails. The faces of the groups were decidedly American, save two or three whose owners were busy attending to the teams, and who spoke the musical words of the Mexican dialect. A group near the spring was composed of several who, appearing to have no special duties to perform, were conversing on some subject that elicited occasional sounds of merriment. One of these, a large, fine looking fellow, with wavy locks and rather flashy dress for the frontier, sat upon a camp stool and held in his hand a flask of liquor, while he was entertaining his auditors with the rehearsal of something which occasioned the laughter.

"But Hamilton," remarked another of the party; "you must acknowledge that Nathan is a rough diamond."

"I'll grant it, Guy," replied Hamilton. "A rough diamond of the purest water, and I'd like to see the fellow very much."

"I think he's in the Indian country, and you may be gratified," replied Guy.

"Do you know that I thought he was in love with that remarkable Indian girl of yours. He could talk of no one else, at times, while we were in Orleans. We have been running on so much that we have forgotten our whiskey. There, Guy, take some, just to counteract the effects of a change of water, you know."

"Just a little, Hamilton, as a stimulant; but I do not believe that Laoni could ever care for Nathan more than she could for a faithful friend," said Guy, Hamilton's digression not removing the effect of the allusion to the backwoodsman's love.

"You think she is too much absorbed in her hero," said Hamilton, laughing.

"No," said Guy, slightly coloring; "but Laoni is a remarkable girl, as you said, and is far above the average woman of civilization. Nathan could hardly fill the void in such a woman's heart."

"You are in love with this paragon, I do believe. You will have a chance to pay homage to her virtues in a short time."

"I do believe there comes Ruiz! He said he would join us here. Yes; it is he," said Guy, waving his hat at an approaching party of two horsemen.

A return salute confirmed him in his opinion.

A few minutes more and Manuel Ruiz dismounted near them and threw his reins to his mozo.

"Welcome, amigo mio."

"Glad to see you, Manuel."

"Any news?"

"I've brought some mail for you fellows and it is in my saddle bags; and news, yes, news you would never guess."

"Anybody married?"

"Anybody dead?"

"Old Santy fixing up an invasion?" asked Karnes, who had come up in time to greet Manuel.

"One guessed. Some one is dead. But don't begin to look sorry, for none here will regret it."

"Who can it be?" asked one.

'And we won't regret it?" from another.

"You have not heard from Ducio?" said Hamilton.

"Ducio is the man. He is as dead as Hector."

"How?"

"Where?"

"When?"

"Be patient and I'll tell. Bonito, my wife's eccentric father, always believed that Ducio robbed him of some of that gold in the vault, and from the manner of his death I am convinced the old fellow was correct. You know the quarters at the carcel have not been occupied for a time, and any bold man could get into the place. Well, one of the prisoners in your old cell, Guy, stated that he had heard a noise under ground for two days like some one picking at the foundations, when it suddenly stopped. Father Ignacio, thinking that something supernatural had happened in that vault, took a notion to investigate the cause of the noises heard by the prisoner. Well, he sent for me and, together, we made the exploration and found a quantity of debris scattered in every direction over the vault floor, and one very large stone had fallen, together with a portion of the arch, crushing the body of a man, portions of which showed from under the mass. On clearing away the stones we recognized the body as that of Ducio. He thought the treasure was still secreted there, and lost his life in searching for it."

"Requiescat in pace," from Hamilton.

"Poor devil!" said Guy.

"D——d villain!" concluded Manuel.

"Let us have the letters, Manuel; I presume there is one or more for each of us. I am dying to hear from Mississippi," said Hamilton.

"Here they are," and Manuel produced a package from his bags.

"One for Hamilton, three for Guy and one for Karnes. And here, Sir Raymond, is one handed to me to deliver to you. The writing is no doubt familiar."

As Guy took the last, a more serious expression came over his features, and with no more than a glance, he transferred it to his pocket.

He gave his attention to the other three, while Hamilton and Karnes broke the seals of their communications. Hamilton appeared tickled at the contents of his letter, and once or twice laughed outright.

"What amused you so in your letter, Hamilton?" asked Karnes, as he folded his own and put it away.

"Something that Guy will be interested in," he replied.

"Well, let us have it. I am about through with my reading," replied Guy.

"How about the one in your pocket?" queried Manuel.

"I'll read that at my leisure," he remarked, developing a slight appearance of annoyance.

"Well, Guy, your Aunt Ida has went and gone and done it."

"What does that mean, Hamilton?" asked Guy.

"She has married a youth, young enough to be her third son."

"The deuce!"

"And actually looked no more than twenty in her bridal robes."

"I thought she would go off in that way some day. One of my three letters is from Perry. The boy is studying hard, and I am confident that the money I will spend on his education will be well invested."

Another of Guy's letters was from Stella. She had not heard of her aunt's marriage. She mentioned the receipt of a letter from Perry, and also alluded to his having called on her at the Convent, while passing through the city en route to college. Guy thought he discovered between the lines of her writing a sentimental partiality for Perry, which brought a smile to his face.

The third letter was from Father Ignacio, a friendly epistle urging him to take care of himself and commending him to the care of the Virgin, whose medal he had in his possession. It was the medal restored to him by Stella, on the discovery that it was the one which Laoni had given him.

"And the fourth letter? The one in his pocket—unopened and unread. He wandered away to himself and had time to glean its contents before the fading twilight merged into the feebler light of the young moon.

It was from Beatrice.

From the unhappy day when she had dismissed her lover in anger, she had suffered. Suffered first from suspicion, then from jealousy, and at last from doubt as to what to attribute Guy's unyielding displeasure. Since the supposed dispatch of her note, written in a spirit of contrition and appealing for a reconciliation, she concluded that no reparation on her part could appease the displeasure which her hasty judgment had aroused. So the time wore on, and the beautiful face grew pallid and serious, while she became a recluse to the world. She learned of Guy's return from the States, and then that he had departed on an expedition to the Indian country. The very day of his departure she was overhauling and destroying some of the letters and papers in her escritoire, when she came across the note which she supposed Guy had received from her. In a moment the situation became plain to her. Two notes had been written; one severe and uncompromising, the other just the reverse. The latter was still in her possession, therefore, the former had been sent through mistake. She could not account for the substitution. From Linda she learned that Manuel would follow the expedition in a day or two, to overtake it at some designated point. She would write to Guy in explanation and enclose him the note he should have received in New Orleans.

When her resolution had taken definite shape, she wrote as follows:

"Oh, Guy! I have discovered why I have not looked into your dear face since that miserable day when you called and I acted so hastily. I wrote you a note under the influence of passion, generated by suspicion. When I read it over, I laid it aside and wrote the one I enclose in this. Through a misfortune which I shall regret throughout my life, I, by some means, sent you the first note, believing I was sending the second. In looking over some old letters in my escritoire today, I discovered the second note (the one inclosed) and in a moment the truth burst upon me, revealing the justice of your course all this time—under the impression that I meant all the other cruel note contained. You have my explanation. Can you forgive? Can you forget? Can you return to the old love, take up and reunite the severed thread of our happiness, forgetting in a more perfect union the rupture which, while it has been like a thorn in my heart, must have been painful to a noble nature like yours? Manuel will hand you this. Your answer will constitute my earthly happiness, or be my living death.

Beatrice."

Guy's musings over the contents of the letter were interrupted by quite a commotion among the party he had recently quitted, and, by the blaze of a newly-lighted fire, he descried the form of a stranger. The latter's words, however, at once gave him away, and Guy hastened to greet the new comer. Nathan had discovered their camp and the more difficult part of his mission from Laoni had been performed. He reserved the true statement of his errand until he could detail it to the one in whom she was interested. Guy anticipated trouble if the Indians imagined that they were bent on exploring the mine, with or without permission, but supposed that his and Laoni's joint influence would deter them from open hostility if the expedition could be shown to be entirely pacific.

Nathan's report, however, gave a serious aspect to any further progress, or even a failure to retrace the steps already taken. The word was passed at once to the men to look to their arms and have them ready for service. A council of war was held, and by Nathan's advice, a clump of timber and undergrowth situated an hour's travel further on, was selected as a spot to be occupied the next morning, where to await developments from the Lipans. Nathan was sure they would not be along before the next day, and that the party would have ample time to fix themselves snugly in their concealed position. He and Karnes had fought Indians until to be so engaged appeared like second nature. The disposition of the whole force was, therefore, left to these two frontiersmen, and under their direction, an early hour of the ensuing morning found the party concealed in the motte of timber selected, the undergrowth completely hiding men, animals and wagons from exterior eyes. The two directors then left to scout the country in advance in order to detect any approach of Indians. To this end they stopped in a point of timber whch extended like a bold promontory into a boundless sea of prairie, about six miles from the position of the main body.

Both men had been over the ground before.

"Golly! This here's the place, Karnes."

"You're right, Nathe, and it's the last."

"That's what; but Lordy! couldn't we see 'em ef they was a comin'? It's a ten mile stretch to them ar hills."

"And it wouldn't hurt, Nathe, if we were a bit closer to them same hills."

"Yaas, but don't yer see, Karnes, when they gits opposite this motty country they is goin' to make straight fur this pint, fur they can't see no more like they could where there ain't no mottes."

"You are right again, but we could fix our stand two miles closer in that motte yonder."

"Yaas, honey! And ef yer'd want to run? The Injun no more'n knee high wouldn't want a spy glass to see yer. Now, in this here pint, when we see 'em, we kin take plenty time, and move slow back on camp. They're bound to beat down through here to find us, and not knowin' we're up to snuff, they'll jess drap right on to the end of our rifles. Tell the truth, Karnes, I don't like to open on them Lipans; blamed ef they haven't done me right."

"Well, if they won't fight, we won't."

"Thar! By jingo!" exclaimed Nathan.

"What; see 'em?"

"Ef I know a Injun."

"I don't see a sign."

"Not on the hills, man; here, not two miles—one—two—three—four—five—six."

"Now I see; they are coming."

"Six! They shore don't mean fight; us two could wallop that crowd."

"Let's move back, Nathe. We've at least two miles of open prairie to cross ahead of 'em and we'd better be going. There may be more than six, for you remember they used to divide up and meet; divide up and meet as they went in the Trinity country."

"You don't 'spose I don't recoleck. They teached me them tietacks when I got this here arrer mark in my cheek. I was watchin' in front—watchin' in front—when zip! came one er them ar fernal arrers from behint and stuck right here. Mebbe I didn't git the devil's scalp that done it."

The scouts cleared the open prairie in time to be unobserved and took a new position for observation.

"Nathe, there is only four now," said Karnes. pointing to four little dark spots that would not have been noticed by an unpracticed eye.

Nathan looked steadily for a moment in the direction indicated, then said deliberately:

"Four nothin'!"

"What do you mean, Nathe?"

"Them's four more, ole fel'. Them six what we seed'll come out of that pint or I don't know Injun ways. Don't yer see; they's bent on meeting' right here; they'd be fools else."

The correctness of Nathan's prediction having been confirmed by the appearance of six mounted figures on the edge of the timber they had left a short time before, the two friends watched them with interest.

"See, Nathe, the rascals are looking at our tracks."

"Didn't I know they'd do it! Tell me 'bout Injuns!"

"They are making signals to the four," remarked Karnes.

"To tell 'em 'bout them tracks, I reckon."

"What'll they think, Nathe?"

"Know we're scouts."

"Why?"

"Tracks fresh, comin' and goin'."

"Then they'll know——"

"That we've saw 'em."

"Let's move."

"I'm with yer.'
"How'll them new fellows take it?"
"Speck some er their hair'll stand."
"Hamilton's all grit."
"And Guy Raymond?"
"Oh, that's a sure thing. He's as good an Indian as you, and brave."
"He kin shoot. Recoleck that night in town when he tumbled the greaser from the bridge by the light er his torch?"
"Let's spur up, Nathe; we must get to our folks quick. Even ten Indians must be prepared for."

In the camp every disposition had been made of the men, wagons and animals according to Karnes' suggestions, under the direction of Guy, and the return of the scouts was impatiently awaited. He found good use for the picks and shovels in baring the ground several feet in width around the edge of the motte on the south and eastern faces, completely clearing away the tall grass and dry combustible debris. Hamilton's curiosity was excited by this seemingly unnecessary act and he asked Guy if he intended to dig a ditch and throw up fortifications. Guy put some of the men to work cutting green branches to interweave with the more scanty growth and more thoroughly concealed their position. The day wore on, however, until the sun had sunk low enough to cast the shadow of the motte far out into the opening to the east, and still no Indians had appeared. The discovery of the tracks of the scouts' horses must have decided the Indians to a more prudential advance. Nathan was sure they had a plot, and suspected they had a notion that the motte concealed the party, for its occupation was Indian tactics.

"They is bent on takin' night fur it," he remarked.
"Or waiting for reinforcements," suggested Guy.
"Mebbe so."

Night fell. The stars came out one by one, then the constellations flashed and sparkled in the firmament. The camp was still and fireless, and should the Indians come, they would have heard no sounds to indicate the presence of the white men, unless they should venture within a few yards of the motte and catch the sneezing of a horse or the tones of low conversation.

Four sentinels were placed without the edge of the timber, well concealed, in a recumbent position, in order to detect the form of a crawling enemy. Nathan volunteered in this latter service for the night, as he insisted that a greenhorn would never detect the snakelike movements of a Lipan warrior. Guy and Karnes took places at other points, determined to sit the night out in watching for the expectant foe. The former found a convenient log for a seat, from which he could survey a quarter of the outside approach for a distance that embraced quite a sweep, as his eyes became accustomed to the uncertain starlight. By his side lay a dog, whose head he occasionally stroked, half mechanically, half caressingly, as he peered out into the darkness, or spoke to him in a low tone.

"Would you know her, Rolla? She was so kind to you. Do you remember how she would pat your head when you would put an ugly paw on each of her shoulders? I was a long time away from you, Rolla, but with all Father Ignacio's good treatment, you knew your master and left him for me. Good Rolla, you would know Laoni, too."

Rolla gave a low whine, then suddenly sniffing the air, he growled fiercely.

"That means a good deal," said Karnes, coming over to Guy. "Do you see anything?"

"Nothing."

A shot from Nathan's rifle immediately followed Guy's reply.

The report of the piece bringing the men together in a huddle, Karnes ordered all back to their posts. Nathan slided in on his belly to reload and report what he had seen.

"A head bobbed up when the dog growled," he said, "and I blazed away. They knows we're here; they smelt us out. I don't know ef I got the imp or not; it's purty dark to aim."

A whiz of arrows and the crack of several rifles cut short Nathan's report and he hastened to his post.

A yell as if from fifty throats followed the discharge.

"Waste no ammunition, men. Fire only when you see something to shoot," shouted Guy.

Another discharge of rifles was answered by shots from the pieces of Karnes and Nathan, who aimed at the places where they beheld the flashes of two hostile guns.

Another yell and all was quiet during the next half hour.

Out upon the prairie a flame suddenly flashed up, then another, and another, until a chain of fire encompassed two sides of the motte.

"I thought it would come," said Nathan

"The cowards!" said Karnes.

"Now, Hamilton, you see why I cut the grass away, and made a bare streak on three sides. I have lived with the Indians and know their tricks."

"I see; I see," said Hamilton. "I'll make a note of that for my literary work."

"You will have plenty notes before this expedition ends," said Guy.

"I don't know, Sir Guy. It looks like these redskins were about to put a stopper on all my future acts, and they include your biography."

"A pity, Sir Tipton; but it will be a greater pity to be cheated out of your forthcoming 'Jones in India.'"

"Poor Jones; I'd almost given that up. You missed it by not knowing the living man. I'm afraid his heirs and executors and administrators would pounce on me for damages, in an action for libel and defamation, if I should write half he told."

The roar of the fire, which now leaped high up, licking the air with forked tongues, came down upon the wings of the wind, which seemed to increase in velocity before the heat of the devouring element. In a few minutes it had reached the motte. The majority of the men were placed on either flank, to draw down upon any of the enemy who might have approached those points to cut off the anticipated fugitives from the timber. The long tongues of flame reached across the bare space and singed and twisted the leaves and twigs; caused the animals to snort and tremble with fright; then suddenly they failed for want of material, a flicker here and there indicated a burning tuft, and the danger was over. On either hand the fire swept by, and during the remainder of the night a bright line told of its progress westward.

The failure of the attempt brought a yell of disappointment from the Indians. Guy longed for daylight, feeling confidnt that he could negotiate a peace treaty with the enemy. The danger of another attack was, in the opinion of the leaders, over for the night, as the cleanly burned ground afforded no hiding places for the creeping foe. So all but two watches laid down to rest.

Guy and Rolla remained awake. The dog's uneasiness manifested that he pretty well comprehended the situation. He lay at the feet of his master with ears pricked and almost motionless. The strong wind had abated its force and was reduced to a steady breeze, bearing the fumes of the burnt prairie.

Suddenly the dog rose to his feet, and with nose upturned, rapidly sniffed the air; then, whining as if for joy, he placed a foot upon Guy's arm and licked his hand.

"I don't quite understand you, Rolla. What is the matter now?"

Rolla put up his other paw; took a sitting posture to more squarely look into his master's face, whined and wagged his tail.

"You are certainly in a good humor, my dog. Has the enemy left?"

Rolla gave a low bark, rose and frisked about, then, sniffing the air again, sprang through the wall of undergrowth and disappeared.

"Is the dog crazy?" muttered Guy, as he sprang up, as if to recall him.

For once Rolla's manifestations mystified his master. Before, he had scented the Indians and growled his displeasure; this time the scent of something had made him decidedly happy and he appeared to have deserted to the enemy. He called to Nathan for a solution of this piece of canine acting, but for once that worthy was not in a communicative humor. While still perplexed over his problem, Guy's ear caught a familiar sound. Dwarfed by the distance, the notes of a refrain confined to the monotones of Indian melody floated in upon the breeze, bringing to his frame a strange sensation and to his mind a dream-like consciousness of a portion of his experience, wherein he recalled the stern barbarism and the weird customs of the Lipans. The voice of the singer grew more distinct and the words of the dialect partially clear to the now eager listener. The chant was now remembered and the voice so unmistakable that Guy mechanically parted the bushes in his front and exclaimed:

"Nathan! Nathan! The problem is solved. Rolla left me to go to Laoni. 'Tis she who is singing, and she sings to let me hear it that I may know of her presence. Rolla found her out first and went to her. I'll warrant he is with her now."

"That thar is the peace chant she's singin'—ef it's her—and long as it's her I reckon they means it."

"I will answer it," said Guy.

"Blaze away, then."

Guy waited a moment, then, in the rich, clear tones of his fine voice, he took up the chant, and for the few moments he sang he was surprised to find how readily the long unthought of words returned to him. A clear bark from Rolla indicated that the dog was making himself at home in his new company.

Finally, and against Nathan's advice, Guy determined to follow the dog's example and find her whose voice had betrayed to him her presence. Taking his rifle, he stepped lightly into the open prairie, and in another moment the darkness shut him out from Nathan's view. Let the same mantle fall upon the interview, if one he had with her, who loved him better than life, and who, if she were at hand, was present to save him from threatening danger.

The changed conditions were soon known through the camp, and the gray dawn found the men astir and curious to know many things.

What had wrought the change? Had there been any casualties?

Had any terms been made as the basis of a truce?

Hamilton, having slept soundly after the fire had swept by, was completely in the dark, and endeavored to draw some light from Nathan. But Nathan, from some late cause, was dogged and did not care to be communicative.

"How did Guy know that they wanted a truce in good faith?" was the last of fifty questions he had propounded to the rough diamond.

"Oh, he heerd the gal sing, and knowed her voice," replied Nathan, peevishly.

"Sing?"

"Don't yer know what singin' means?"

"But what made her sing?"

"Nobody. Ain't she her own boss? You is powerful ignerent fur a feller what's ben to collige."

"I will have to surrender," said Hamilton, with a sigh.

"They ain't to be no s'renderin' on our side. Nathan Roach don't s'render to Injuns."

"Good-bye, Nathe, I make profound obeisance to the unfathomable depths of your innate stupidity."

"That's some of yer hog lattin, I reckon," was the rejoinder that Nathan sent after Hamilton's retreating form.

CHAPTER LXXI.

Laoni was correct. The interview with her father, who responded to her summons through Wallah, was a stormy one. The chief owned to her that the contemplated invitation was a treacherous move to get the parties in question into the power of the tribe.

Laoni's indignation knew no bounds. She hurled invective at the infamous council, which she portrayed in the vilest colors, and discanted on the probable prospects of her people with the drag of such a contemptible body to make rules for them. She declared that the deception should not be practiced nor an attack made upon the white men who were coming. If her father had become too timid to govern his tribe, she would take the authority out of his hands. The council should be dissolved, for they were unfit to advise the chief, and would render more valuable service by helping the squaws to pack wood and water. She gave notice that if the life of El Bravo was taken, or if he received bodily harm, the council should answer for it with their worthless lives.

Walumpta was amazed at his daughter's words, but her manner fairly awed him and deprived him of language for reply.

He found words for expostulation, however, when .Laoni summoned Wallah, and directed him to call together the younger warriors of the tribe, who would not see the chief's daughter insulted by a set of cowardly old squaw men. She wanted the young men, the braves of the Lipans, to come to Laoni's lodge before the sun. Walumpta knew his daughter's popularity and he knew that if she raised the standard of revolt the flower of his people would flock to it. He withdrew to warn the council and to advise a reconsideration of the treacherous program.

Before the dawn Laoni was making her preparations. A black mare, the favorite of her two horses, was caparisoned ready for her to mount, and the morning twilight disclosed a goodly number of the young Lipans assembled in front of her lodge. By the time the sun appeared their strength was nearly a hundred. The bow and arrow was their almost universal weapon, a rifle here and there showing itself. Quite as many braves, mostly older men, had been dispatched against the white expedition, and the present response to Laoni's call had left the lodges of the village nearly bare of active males. With their adherence, she was mistress of the situation, and she determined that the council should see it.

Laoni's hold upon the hearts of the Lipans was of the character that springs from personal magnetism. Those qualities of mind and heart, which elevated her above her environment, had their effect, without especial limit, and variously affected the elements that reflected her peculiar distinction. A majority of the council could not conceal their dislike for the chief's daughter, an ingrained jealousy of innovation and a prejudice against any covenant with the whites, causing them to view with impatience the popularity of Laoni. Other of the older braves grounded their opposition in their aversion to squaw rule. But the young warriors bowed to her influence, and had only admiration and love for this princess of their tribe. Her fine personality had much to do with the spell she had woven. The summons of the flower of the Lipan youth, by her messengers, meant an extraordinary occasion and prepared them to make demonstrations of fealty to her interests not in line with the usual stolidity of the Indian.

As she appeared, dressed in a handsome costume and adorned with the significant plumes and paint of the war, the young braves greeted her with grunts of approval. She mounted her mare with ease and grace, and riding to the right and left through the crowd, she surveyed them with an air of pride and satisfaction.

All eyes were centered on her in mixed admiration and inquiry, and at length when she began to speak, her musical voice attracted the closest attention. Her exordium was a statement of her present grievance, and the wantonness of the council in attempting to perpetrate a useless massacre. Her argument was an ingenious effort. Drawing gradually away from the Indian view of duty, she led her auditors through byways, made fascinating by her subtile powers, until they found themselves willing followers along the highway of her own exalted altruism. She condemned her father's weakness, but scored the council. Her peroration was an eloquent appeal, not for herself, but for her people, for El Bravo, the adopted of the tribe, whose blood had been shed in their defense, for a pacific policy towards a people whose numbers were like the blades of grass in the prairies. She had been among this people, in whom she had much to admire, and much to condemn. She spoke of the secret of the mine and showed how it could be utilized, for the benefit of the tribe, by allowing it to be worked for a stipulated rental. She announced her intention to go forth to the relief of the coming expedition alone, if need be.

At the conclusion of her speech there were signs of approval on every hand, and when she directed all in sympathy to follow her as she rode away, there was not one warrior who hesitated. The party filed through the avenues of the village, subjected to jeers from some of the old men and squaws who were in sympathy with the council. On the other hand, there were not wanting expressions of approval and, among those who gave vent to them, none were more demonstrative than Chicha and the Muja, as Pedro passed in the line. When Laoni concluded that her demonstration had produced the effect she desired, she gave the command to follow the trail of the band which had left the night before in quest of the white men. Two of the more experienced trailers were selected for guides, and the party set out at a gallop with Laoni in the lead. It was a long ride before them, and night had veiled the landscape before they had any token of the vicinity of the band they were trailing or of the whites to whose rescue they were hastening. It might have been three hours to midnight when they saw a fire some miles to the southeast. The party halted; then, as the flames became larger, they took the direction of the burning grass, and the fleet ponies went flying over the prairie.

To the Indian girl's quick perception there were chances that the prairie fire had connection with her mission. The distant, glowing point no sooner became their destination than her whole being was nerved with the hope that she would not be too late to prevent a collision. Her eyes were strained across the dark expanse, prompted by yearnings of the soul within, to leap forth and skim the visual line. Her mood seemed to be communicated to her flying animal, for she had distanced her followers, whose yells from the rear, as they urged on their ponies, came unnoted to her ears.

The fire had become a long, bright line as Laoni approached, and disclosed the motte of timber in its foreground encircled by the fuming debris with here and there little spurts of flame, as greener patches were succumbing to the devouring element.

A moment more, and her mare bounded aside to avoid a growth of scrubby prairie oak, and against the bright background she discried the heads and shoulders of several Indians. At the instant of this discovery she received a challenge, reined up her mare, and for the first time realized that she had left her force behind.

Before she could reply to the challenge, her bridle rein was seized and several forms surrounded her.

"Who among the Lipans dares to seize my reins after he has seen that I am Laoni?"

"If Laoni comes to undo the work of the council, then she will find Ponseca has his orders."

"Ha! Fonseca! So, you would hold me prisoner if I say that here, I command, and that what the council has done shall be undone, as the work of traitors to their tribe and rebels to their chief"

"You command! A squaw-chief!"

"Ponseca will find out who will command. Ponseca need not put his ear to the ground to hear the noise of four hundred hoofs. I have outridden a hundred of the young warriors of our tribe who will obey Laoni for Walumpta's sake, and for the glory of the Lipans."

"Is it glory to set brother against brother?"

"The folly of the council has done it. They have taken away Walumpta's power. The bold lion has been caged and a pack of cowardly wolves have full sway."

"You have come to help these white men who have already shed the blood of two of our warriors?" asked Ponseca, still defiant.

"I will not waste words, Ponseca. If you all had met death in this cowardly work, who could be blamed but the council for sending you; or yourselves, for coming?"

At this moment the followers of Laoni came up, arriving by squads, and she was soon surrounded by them and their panting ponies. Ponseca still manifesting obstinacy, Laoni directed that he be disarmed and guarded and, if he became violent, to be tied. She gave orders that the band, operating against the white men, should be at once assembled, and if any disputed her authority that they be arrested and guarded. Those around her gave in their allegiance, and from them she gleaned the operations of the day and night. The two casualties on the Indian side amounted to no more than wounds. She could not learn of any on the part of the occupants of the motte. Knowing that it would be dangerous to approach the latter before morning, she directed the Indians to seek repose, while she, Wallah and Pedro would watch over their slumbers. (

Ponseca and a few other malcontents were separately located and guarded, the irate ex-commander giving vent to his spleen by taunting Laoni with love for the whites, and insinuating that she intended to spend the night in the motte.

When everything was arranged to her satisfaction, she bade Wallah and Pedro to accompany her on a tour of inspection. No light now, but that of the stars. In the distance the prairie was still burning, but a look at its paling blazes only rendered more indistinct the contemplation of adjacent objects.

The trio reached a point opposite the position in the motte where Guy and Nathan were placed and, finding the felled trunk of a lone tree which had been uprooted in some storm, the girl seated herself and bade her companions to follow her example, to take a rest, and use their ears for any sounds that might come from where El Bravo and his comrades lay in expectancy of attack.

"The breeze is wrong for that," said Pedro. "It is blowing from us to them."

"It is so close, though," said Wallah.

"About rifle shot," said Pedro.

"If you talk too loud," cautioned Laoni, "the breeze will take your words to their ears. I wish to hear first from them, without letting them know that we are here. Listen! A dog's bark! Pedro, that sounded like Rolla."

"It may be, but I can't tell one dog from another by his bark."

"But I loved Rolla so."

"Because of El Bravo."

'Well, have it so. He was El Bravo's faithful friend."

"What is this?" exclaimed Pedro, as something rushed by him.

Laoni's words, uttered immediately after, answered his inquiry:

"Oh! Rolla, it was you. The breeze took my scent to you, and you have come to see Laoni. Oh! Rolla! Is El Bravo well? Is he hurt? Good Rolla! To come to Laoni."

The dog whined his replies and nestled his head in her lap. She caressed him for a while, musing on her proximity to one she so loved, when an idea struck her.

"Pedro," she said. "I will sing the peace song which El Bravo often made me sing for him when we would sit above the falls in the evening. He will hear me, and know that if I am here, they will not be attacked again."

"Sing it then," said Pedro, emphatically, and added: "You might go where he is tonight if you would go singing that."

"But I would not do that. Did you hear what that vile Ponseca said?"

"Oh! Ponseca! Ponseca! I would not mind him. Ponseca is an old fool."

Not heeding what Pedro said Laoni began to sing. Her voice, a little low at first, rose as she proceeded, and sounded strange in the stillness and darkness of the prairie. Rolla whined his approval, as the song doubtless recalled the olden time when he chased the rabbits and how, after his fruitless run, the still familiar voice had guided him back to the spot where sat his master and the singer.

Suddenly she ceased to sing. Was it the echo of her words which came back? No; the voice was rich and manly. El Bravo had not forgotten. The words—the air—just as he sang them before the day when that fatal raid determined their separation. Her head bent forward over the dog which she caressed tenderly, as these thoughts filled her mind. The stoical side of her nature gave way, and tears fell upon Rolla's upturned face. The girl lapsed into a kind of ecstacy as she bent over El Bravo's faithful friend. The thrill which coursed her being culminated when a gentle touch upon her bowed head made her realize that Pedro had called her name. When she looked up a smile was upon her face, for, by a mysterious prescience she knew that El Bravo stood before her.

"El Bravo, my life!" she said, in the Lipan dialect.

"Laoni! Twice my savior!" he replied, in the same tongue.

He seated himself beside her and drew her head to his shoulder; then, taking from his pocket a medal, he suspended it around her neck. She took hold of it to see what it was and, by the feeling, knew that it was her parting gift to him on the mountain side.

Again let the curtain fall upon this pair who represented, in their fullness, the purity and goodness of antipodal states of human life.

It was a gala day in the Indian village when Laoni made her entry with her little army, escorting the captured white men; captured by the arts of peace and friendship. They arrived on the second day after the rescue, but the wagons of the expedition had to be left across the hills, as the valley was inaccessible to vehicles.

Couriers had returned in advance of the main body and announce the success of Laoni in gaining over nearly the entire fighting force of the village. Her courage and address were commented on, and not a few, who violently opposed her the day before, were now ready to welcome her. Walumpta, who had been the puppet of the council felt relieved by their downfall, but was not a little chagrined that he had not forestalled his daughter's act. Laoni's first move, when she brushed off the dust of her short campaign, was to call a meeting of her adherents and announce the permanent dissolution of the old council, and to appoint a new one, half of whom were selected from the young men of the village and the other half from the middle-aged and more experienced. Old men were entirely excluded. The chief' power was declared to be supreme in all matters not purely civil.

When Guy was preparing his outfit, to meet the demands of the expedition, he laid in a large supply of presents for the Indians. These were brought in from the wagons on pack animals or by hand, and distributed. This proof of his pacific intentions made him a greater favorite and furnished a strong excuse for Laoni's revolutionary act. The presents even won over members of the old council. But a few rejected the new order of things, and disdained to touch the presents offered to them. Among the more pronounced of these was Ponseca. He was released by order of Laoni, with an admonition to reconcile himself to what had happened. But Ponseca sulked. He took himself to the hills and brooded over his disgrace. Guy's quick eye noted this, and after failing to win him from his mood, he warned Laoni that mischief was in the Indian's heart. Under the new regime the injunction to keep away from the mountain became dissolved by edict of the chief, ratified by the council and negotiations were entered upon between Walumpta and the members of the expedition, looking to the reopening of the mine at a future day, and the payment for the privilege an annual rental, to be determined by the value of the yield, the rent to be appropriate to the use of the tribe.

Within the week the objects of the expedition had been attained and most of its members, freed for the present from further cares in the matter, joined the Indians in hunts, or went about exploring the wild country.

Guy passed his time visiting old haunts and, in the evenings, he would go with Laoni to the falls and sit upon the rock where he took his first lessons from her in Lipan lore and language. They enjoyed these occasions; Laoni drinking deeper, perhaps, from the cup of their happiness. Yet with the sweet draught there was a bitter that manifested itself in a melancholy alternating between the trustful looks and bright smiles which she bestowed upon El Bravo.

One evening, when they had repaired to this favorite spot, Guy mentioned the nearness of the time when he would return to San Antonio and other points where his interests called him. On hearing this Laoni remained silent for some moments, then asked:

"Will El Bravo stay long in San Antonio?"

"I cannot say," he replied, "as it will depend on some things which may happen and which I cannot foresee."

"The humor—of Beatrice—for one," she said, without looking up.

"That may be one thing."

Guy uttered this half reluctantly.

"Laoni hopes—that she will make a good mate for El Bravo."

"Have you the medal?" asked Guy, anxious to change the subject.

"Oh, yes," she said, abstractedly. "Laoni will wear it until El Bravo goes, and then—then he will take it. How I wronged my Bravo when the medal came to me in that far away city, and a pretty little girl claimed it. If I had known that it was your sister it would have saved me so many thoughts. Strange—that the medal found the way to her after it got lost."

"Strange, indeed! But it was all the result of superstition. The Mexican, captured by Stella's guardian, bought it from the monte pio to protect him on his trip, and poor Mr. Trigg wanted Stella to wear it so that the Virgin Mary would favor her."

Laoni heard, but her thoughts were not on the subject of the medal or of the Virgin. She turned her eyes up to his and gave him a long, earnest look; then translated it into language.

"El Bravo, when you go from this village you have seen Laoni for the last time."

"Why so, dear Laoni?" he asked, taking up the hand which, in the earnestness of her feelings, she had placed upon his knee. "You have but to consent and you can go with me. I am able to take care of you all your life."

She shook her head slowly, her sad expression yielding not an iota at the generous offer.

"This is not a fit place for you," he continued. "Why not come with me?"

"You say—this—and still remember our meeting—when you called to see her—instead of—of me?"

"But our relations will be better understood."

"Even if this would be true—in her—her case—what about the crowd! What would your society world say? I would be scorned and you would be scandalized in that civilization where virtue is so rare that few will believe it has any existence. A liar thinks that no one tells the truth. A thief believes everybody will steal."

Her companion took a long breath, but did not reply.

"El Bravo is mistaken. This is a fit place for Laoni. In your civilization I would not be respected, without wealth, if my face was fair like the face of your Beatrice, but as it is, my Lipan blood would shut me out from your friends, the same as it deprives me of the love I would die for."

"But Laoni has my love. Loving another does not raise the mountain between us that your imagination has piled up. If I love Beatrice, it does not take from my love for Stella—it does not lessen my deep love for Laoni."

"Yet it tears you from me. What to Laoni is this village—these mountains—this pretty fall, when you are gone—gone from her forever? This rock is no more than the one further down the ledge— only that here you have rested by her side and made the evenings happy. Since you walked out from the flames and the claws of the council you have been the mainspring of my life. Every move— every hope—every resolve has been inspired by you. The nerve to begin and carry to a successful end the fight with the old council was rooted in my love. Failure would have cost me my life—but that was little thought of when yours was at stake. Success has silenced my enemies, but it has not wiped out the revenge which yet lurks in some of their hearts. Ponseca will never——"

Laoni's words were cut short by the report of a rifle. Immediately succeeding the shot she placed her hand to her side, and falling towards Guy he caught her in his arms.

CHAPTER LXXII.

Of course Nathan's diversion, after things had quieted down in the village, was hunting—and hunting by himself. He did not believe in having company on such occasions. He wanted elbow room always, and that was the reason he left Arkansas. He believed a true frontiersman ought to emigrate when settlers got to crowding up within five or six miles of him. The day that Guy and Laoni were having their affecting interview at the falls, Nathan went out to kill a buffalo. An all day tramp around their watering places was fruitless in results, and Nathan was not in the best of humors when he crossed the hills, contiguous to the mine, to enter the valley from the northwest. Nathan's bad luck nettled him considerably, but he finally dismissed the subject and got to ruminating on a diversity of things. Finally Laoni's half-way promise to consider his pretensions, at some future time, occupied his mind. He knew how she loved Guy, but hoped, with Guy's departure, she would look favorably on his suit. He made quite a detour to enter the valley near the mountain, for that route would bring him by the falls and he knew she would be there talking to Guy. Nathan was quite philosophical in his reflections about her attachment to another, and resolved to await events. He trudged along, his crude thoughts keeping no certain channel, but swayed from the purpose of his route by any and all objects that met his quick eye. He had passed the summit of the divide which separated him from the valley and reached the head of a gorge running a zig-zag course down the hills, terminating just below the bold, deep spring, whose waters rushed foaming to the falls a few hundred yards below. He stopped for a moment to decide whether to take the gorge itself or follow its margin, to secure the better route to the edge of the stream. While still undetermined he noticed, way down the hollow, the form of an Indian. He carried a rifle and was following the bed of the gorge.

What's good fur a Injun is good fur me," he thought, and at once descended to the rocky bottom. His movement caused him to lose sight of the Indian, but a moment later a turn brought him into view. He had mounted to a high point on the bank nearer the village and, half stooping, was peering over the tops of the young growth that lined the hillside. Suddenly he crouched down and in this position left the high bank, then bringing himself erect, he walked on towards the spring, disappearing in one of the abrupt turns.

"That's that ar scoundrel, Ponseca," said Nathan, "and he's arter no good."

With Nathan's expressed conclusion, he mentally decided to watch the bad Indian and determine if it was a correct one.

Oh! Nathan Roach, if you would have only put certain facts together—facts that you knew—and thought of the locality in which this villain, of your own dubbing, was performing in this stealthy manner, and then asked yourself why you had taken pains to cross the hills near the falls, you would have guessed the crime he was bent upon.

When Nathan next saw the Indian, whom he had recognized as Ponseca, he had gained another high point much closer to the falls, and was in the act of firing his rifle. The discharge of the gun occurred in the same second, and Ponseca fled across the gorge and towards the mountain.

"That devil's shot sum 'un," said Nathan, "and I'll foller his trail fur luck, ef I is tired."

He pushed on rapidly now and took the fugitive's trial where he left the gorge. Here he found a dim path which he must necessarily take on account of the almost impenetrable character of the growth on either side. The trailing was easy here, and Nathan pushed on swiftly for a half mile, when he found himself out of breath and almost out of the thicket. The latter ended a few yards further, and the backwoodsman was shrewd enough to not leave it before reconnoitering the open space beyond. He accordingly took to the bushes and, on all fours, crept along until he secured a position where, unobserved, he could sweep the opening with his eyes. He was rewarded beyond his expectations. Ponseca had halted in a little clump of mountain oaks near the rocky wall which shut in the approach to the mine on the eastern side. He was in the act of reloading his gun, which he went about the more leisurely as he looked from time to time earnestly in the direction of the village.

"The stinkin' villain!" said Nathan, between his teeth. "My Gawd!" he cried out, as a thought struck him. "Gawd a-mighty! Ef he has done that! But I won't kill him. I'll jess break his right arm, so he can't load, and then he's my meat. Ef he's done that—whew!"

Nathan drew a bead on his victim. The crack of his rifle followed, and Ponseca's right arm fell; the ramrod with which he was about to drive the bullet home dropping to the ground. Nathan reloaded rapidly, and by the time the Indian had recovered somewhat from his astonishment and was endeavoring to get his gun and rammer together, he was out of the bushes and in a full run to follow up the advantage he had gained by making a prisoner. Ponseca clubbed his piece with his solitary hand; then, bethinking himself of his knife, he threw away the empty gun and furiously flourished the other weapon.

Nathan could not help smiling when he thought how soon his adversary would have to surrender his long knife.

"Ole Pawnsake," he drawled out in the vernacular, "that ain't-a-gwine to work."

Then in Lipan he ordered him to surrender or he would break his other arm.

The threat had no effect. On the contrary, Ponseca redoubled his demonstrations and replied defiantly.

Nathan, seeing no alternative, shot the knife from his hand, disabling that member also, then, springing on him, he felled him with his clubbed rifle.

To tie the discomfited Indian was the work of the next few minutes. This was done in the most artistic, frontier fashion, with some buckskin strips, a supply of which Nathan always carried with him. Knowing that he would have to drag or pack his prisoner, Nathan concluded to leave him on the spot until he could learn the extent of the mischief which had been done by Ponseca's shot.

Prophetic words! "Ponseca will never——" He will never forget. He did not forget.

Guy at first could not realize the situation. Laoni's subject and its sadness had induced a reverie to which he had so far succumbed as to only half digest her meaning. The fullness of his mind, trying to devise some method to dissipate the cloud over hers, made him nearly oblivious to his surroundings. The shot did not sufficiently awaken him to connect the discharge with his companion's movement. He gazed anxiously into her face. A look of pain—then a faint smile suffused her countenance. To his rapid inquiries she held up a hand stained with blood.

"Ponseca—did not forget," she murmured slowly.

Guy's first idea was to stop the flow of blood until he could get assistance. Before help was at hand he had done all in his power to close the wound. A robe was made into a stretcher and stalwart arms bore the wounded girl to her lodge. The news flew like wildfire and many were the young, fleet-footed braves who were soon scouring the hills, seeking the assassin. Some of these met Nathan just crossing the gorge on his return from where he had left his bound prisoner. Directing them where to find him, he hastened with greater speed, now that he knew the enormity of Ponseca's crime.

His victim lingered for a day, declining to take the opiates designed to relieve her of pain, for the reason that she did not wish to lose consciousness. Her last words were addressed to Guy:

"It is better that it should be so. Laoni's life would be a bother to El Bravo, but her memory will be easy to love."

Nathan, to whom she spoke several kind words of farewell, wept like a child, and was compelled to leave the lodge to suppress his emotions. Karnes, Hamilton and Ruiz stood in the background, their moistened eyes showing that their sympathies were touched. Walumpta, weighted with grief, had thrown himself prone upon the floor. Pedro and Wallah and others who loved the dying girl stood without, dejected and silent.

And Rolla—sage dog! He knew that some climax was at hand. He had crept in while Nathan was lamenting and, with a whine, had placed one paw upon the couch, while he looked from one tearful face to another.

The last act was nearly played, and the curtain slowly dropping whose fall would end the role of its most interesting character. It descended slowly—slowly—in cadence with the failing pulse of the sufferer—and when it touched the boards: Laoni was dead!

CHAPTER LXXIII.

It was an evening in October. The old Mexican town of San Antonio was dull and still. The darkening dusk had not been pierced by a ray of light from door or widow, save from the monte pio's on the plaza and the Candelario's on Carcel street. In the latter resort, the proprietress was still dealing out chile con carne and other Mexican dishes to the lovers of good eating, and on this evening she was serving two of her most appreciative patrons.

One was the monte pio.

The other was Jose, the major domo. They sat vis-a-vis, watching the movements of the hostess as she placed their steaming dishes upon the table.

Their conversation had evidently been interrupted by the appearance of the dishes, for the monte pio resumed:

"You say Monday of next week?"

"Yes, amigo, on Monday; and it makes me sad to leave Bexar."

"But you are not obliged to go. Let el padre take care of himself."

"Impossible, amigo. I belong to el padre, Ignacio. Where he goes, I must."

"I was told that he was going to Mexico a month ago."

"So he was," replied Jose, "but you see, he loves the Senorita Beatrice like his own child, and Senor Raymond like his own son, and these two would have no one but el padre, Ignacio, to make them husband and wife. To please them, he has waited over to do them up."

"Is the bridegroom here?"

"He came today."

"They have been engaged for a long time. I wonder they did not marry before this," said the monte pio, by way of gossip.

"There is a pretty little story about it," said Jose. "I heard it from el padre, Ignacio. In fact, I listened at the door when he and Senor Raymond were talking."

"Let's have it, Jose. I'm interested."

"You see," said the other, leaning over the table, "about a year ago Senor Raymond's Indian sweetheart got killed, up in the Lipan country. You remember, amigo, the time I sold you his pony and outfit; well that was the time he came first from the Lipans, where he had been a prisoner and had fallen in love with the chief's daughter. Well, she died a year ago, it is said, in Senor Raymond's arms, and he promised, or vowed, or something, that he would not marry for a year and a day."

"What is the day for?" interrupted his auditor.

"Quien sabe. Maybe some heretic superstition. You know the senor is not a Catholic."

"Well, go on."

"Where was I? Oh, yes. It has been a year and a day since she died—the Lipan girl—and Senor Raymond is here prompt enough, ready to take the beauty of the Navarro family."

"And he marries?"

"The day after tomorrow."

"And will live at the Navarro's?"

"Not he. The senor is rich. El padre says he got a whole big pot full of gold that some pirate told him how to find, and then he owns half of Texas, I believe—anyway he has leagues and leagues of land."

"What has his pot of gold, or land, to do with his not living with his father-in-law?"

"But he is going to the big gringo city, New York, for a time, and is going to send out people to buy his land and to work some mines he has found out."

"Ruiz has the mine," said the monte pio.

"Senor Raymond has nothing to do with that mine. There is where he lost his Lipan sweetheart that he loved so well, and he won't go back there."

"Ruiz will sink all Bonito's gold in that old Spanish mine," said the monte pio.

"No; he is making it pay. When he came here a month ago, after supplies, I asked that pretty gringo—Nathan, they call him—how it was doing, and he told me they had struck a rich vein."

"Nathan?" said the monte pio. "I remember; I sold him a new rifle to take back."

"Yes; he does all the hunting and scouting for the mine workers."

At this moment, to the surprise of the two, Guy Raymond entered.

"Good evening," he said, pleasantly.

"I was just giving the monte pio a little history about you," said Jose.

"Ah!" said Guy. "I hope you put my best side forward."

"About your escape from the Lipans, when you sold your stuff to our amigo here and had a balance to your credit."

"The senor has a good one there now—between us."

"And that is what I want to see you about," said Guy.

"You can have it, senor, in ten minutes."

"That's not it. In fact, I am going to let you keep it for a while."

"How, senor?"

"Well, tomorrow morning I will call and fix up matters with you. I want to leave a certain amount in your hands for Locaria Landina. She used to live at Concepcion. She was kin' to my old guardian, and nursed him after the fight there. She is poor and needy and I want to have a house built for her and the rest of the money kept at interest for her, but in the morning I will have everything in shape."

"You are a good man, senor," said Jose.

"Only trying to be just and grateful, Jose."

"You will be leaving soon, senor?"

"Yes, for the Northern States, on business and pleasure."

"Is Perry in those states?" asked Jose.

"At college there. I will see him when I go on. He will finish in seven months and be with you here in Bexar."

"Will you pass through New Orleans, senor?" asked the monte pio. "If you will, I would like you to take a small package to a friend."

"With pleasure. I have to go there to get my sister, who will go with us to the North."

"Jose," continued Guy, "you remember Hamilton?"

"That fine, big fellow?"

"Yes."

"I never could forget him."

"I saw him in New Orleans the other day. He is writing an account of my adventures. He has made a fine character out of his recollection of you."

"I always thought I would be famous," said Jose. "And he is going to put it into a book?"

"Have it printed."

"Santa Maria!"

"There is one thing I wish to ask you, Jose; has Karnes been here lately?"

"Have you not heard, senor? He never got well, and died on the Brazos about a month ago."

"He was a gallant fellow. Poor Karnes."

Two days later an ambulance with four mules attached stood in front of San Fernando. Early mass had just concluded and the congregation had dispersed, save a small knot of persons who stood within the grand portal. They were taking leave of a couple who had been pronounced husband and wife by Father Ignacio. The pair were escorted to the ambulance, into which the gentleman assisted the lady and then followed himself. The driver and a mozo took the outside seat. The bride looked out as the vehicle moved away and said:

"Now Linda, the next time Manuel comes in from that old mine, keep him here with you until we return. Guy says we will be back in three months."

THE END.

CPSIA information can be obtained at www.ICGtesting.com
Printed in the USA
LVOW04s0326151015

458220LV00012BA/140/P